"*The Trumpets of Jericho* is a long journey of a book, but Dolan deftly uses narrative, dialogue, and the setting of the Nazi death camp Auschwitz in all its horrific detail to hasten the reader to its unexpectedly upbeat conclusion. Powerful... inspiring... painstakingly researched. An emotional roller coaster of a novel... Strongly recommended for those seeking to understand the extremes of good and evil mankind is heir to."

- Blue Ink Review

"Imagine the Marquis de Sade writing in collaboration with Leon Uris and you have *The Trumpets of Jericho*. Nightmarish yet moving, it makes the heart weep and sing all at once."

- Bonnie Abrams, Rochester (NY) Center for the Holocaust

"Complex... compelling... chilling. Though a sweeping epic of a novel told in multiple points of view, it never stumbles when it comes to juggling the diverse thoughts and actions of its many characters. *Trumpets* is a significant book in that... it is the first to make pertinent a little-known but crucial act of rebellion at Auschwitz. For that alone, it is a valuable contribution to not only the literature of the Holocaust but historical fiction in general."

- Foreword Clarion Reviews

"An emotional and historical tsunami of a novel seamlessly written by a brilliant author devoted to giving forgotten heroes a voice. Make no mistake: Dolan is the next Uris!"

- Rajah-Rao Literary Endowment

"The author's attention to detail, diligence of research, and powerful character portrayals make this first-ever book on the defiant 1944 Jewish uprising at Auschwitz a riveting read for not only experts on the Holocaust but those new to it."

- Rebecca Hoag, Education Committee, San Antonio Holocaust Museum

The Trumpets of
JERICHO

The Trumpets of
JERICHO

a novel

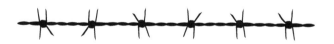

J. Michael Dolan

The Trumpets of Jericho: A Novel
J. Michael Dolan
www.jmichaeldolan.net

Originally Published 2017 by
Monochrome Books

Republished 2019 by
Helium Books
1911 County Road 306
Lexington, Texas 78947

Updated Second Edition
Paperback ISBN: 978-0-9987008-7-8
eBook ISBN: 978-0-9987008-2-3
Library of Congress Control Number: 2017909834

Cover and interior designs by Austin Texas Print, Inc.
Certain stock imagery by Thinkstock ©

Printed in the United States of America

*To my mother Louise, who helped with the
typing of the book and read it twice—
To my son Patrick and his wife Lisa, who endured
uncounted hours listening to me ramble on about it—
To my grandchildren Sebastian, Jolie, Alyssa, and
Julian, who I ended up writing it for—
And finally to the heroic dead, who stood at my shoulder
throughout the process to make sure I got it right.*

Author's Note

I consider Trumpets to be a work of history as much as one of fiction and have striven to ensure its content adheres to fact. Of the dozens of people who inhabit its pages, only a very few are imagined: the Poles Pippel, Wojowiecz, Witek, Bronski, and Menachem, the Hungarians Lazar and Svoboda, the Russian POW Ustinov, the German generals Steiner and Ehler. All other named characters are real. Please note, too, that my research wasn't confined to the eighteen works in the bibliography located in the Addendum at the back of the book; I also made use of the internet and even a few movies.

That being said, I did find it necessary on occasion to diverge from the historical record, mainly but not restricted to the timing of certain details. I did this not only in the interest of plot but to address the contradictions and bridge the gaps that exist in that record. Seldom, however, did I feel called upon to improvise—you as the reader can rest assured that the adventure you are about to embark on is as truthful to events as the novelist's pen can set down and him remain a novelist.

Auschwitz, the main camp

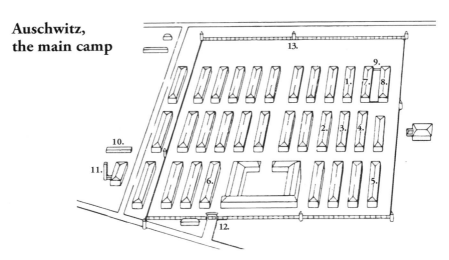

1-5. Ka-Be, the hospital complex   6. Block 24, registry and records
7. Block10, medical experimentation   8. Block 11, punishment   9. The Black Wall
10. Block 35, Gestapo HQ   11. Crematorium I   12. Camp gate   13. Watchtower

Birkenau, the extermination camp

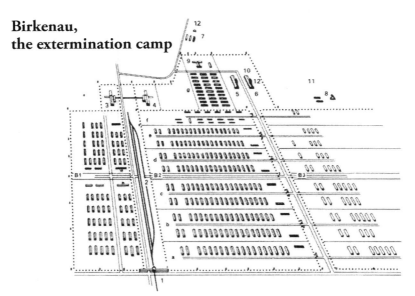

1. Main gate   2. Ramp   3. Crematorium II   4. Crematorium III   5. Crematorium IV
6. Crematorium V   7. Bunker 2 (later Bunker 5), with three changing rooms
8. Bunker 1, first gas chamber in Birkenau, with two changing rooms   9. Sauna
10. Site of cremation pits near Crematorium V   11. Site where in 1941 thousands of corpses
were buried   12. Site of cremation pits near Bunker 5 in 1944;
B1, Women's camp;   B2a, Quarantine camp;   B2b, Czech Family camp;
B2c, Women's camp;   B2d, Men's camp;   B2e, Gypsy camp;   B2g, Canada;
B3, Mexico camp, partly completed

Military Ranks

SS	U.S. Army Equivalent
Reichsführer	General of the Army
Oberstgruppenführer	General
Obergruppenführer	Lieutenant General
Gruppenführer	Major General
Brigadeführer	Brigadier General
Standartenführer	Colonel
Obersturmbannführer	Lieutenant Colonel
Sturmbannführer	Major
Hauptsturmführer	Captain
Obersturmführer	First Lieutenant
Untersturmführer	Second Lieutenant
Sturmscharführer	Sergeant Major
Hauptscharführer	Master Sergeant
Oberscharführer	Technical Sergeant
Scharführer	Staff Sergeant
Unterscharführer	Sergeant
Sturmmänn	Lance Corporal
Rottenführer	Corporal
Oberschütze	Private First Class
Schütze	Private

Roza Robota
c. 1942 Ciechanow

"...not the most beautiful face in the world, or at least not as quintessentially feminine as the rest of her, but one was drawn to it nonetheless. Her nose was a little aggressive, the jaw a bit square, but the mouth was sumptuous and quick to smile, her eyes intelligent. Noah couldn't recall coming across eyes like those before. So brown they shone black, penetrating yet kind, they didn't stop at your exterior so much as peer inside you...

"No, he'd never seen eyes quite like those. They helped make her that breed of woman who only got prettier the longer one looked at her."

Someday I will understand Auschwitz. This was a brave statement but innocently absurd. No one will ever understand Auschwitz. What I might have set down with more accuracy would have been: *Someday I will write about Sophie's life and death, and thereby help demonstrate how absolute evil is never extinguished from the world.* Auschwitz itself remains inexplicable. The most profound statement yet made about Auschwitz was not a statement at all, but a response.

The query: "At Auschwitz, tell me, where was God?"
And the answer: "Where was man?"

Sophie's Choice, William Styron

Why then do you say now: Let us persecute him, and let us find occasion of word against him? Flee then from the face of the sword, for the sword is the revenger of iniquities: and know ye there is a judgment.

The Book of Job, 19:28-29

1942

Autumn

For the first time in his life, Noah Zabludowicz felt like a caged animal.

The train sped through the Polish night, its gentle rocking belying the fear and uncertainty gripping its occupants. That the cage was a moving one did nothing to lessen Noah's feeling of entrapment. On the contrary, the analogy was as inescapable as it was ominous: there was little difference between the cattle this car was intended for and the hundred-plus Jews from the town of Ciechanow herded into it days ago.

That it had been used to transport livestock was evident from the dirty, gray straw littering the floor. This was the sole "amenity" provided them by the Germans, so that by this, their third night aboard, the people packed inside weren't faring well at all. Along with the discordant chorus of coughs, snores, sneezes, and less polite emanations one might expect in such close quarters came the spasmodic, muted rippling of tears.

Noah bent down to where his parents knelt, or where he figured they were. Though a few candles fought the blackness, he could barely see his hand in front of him.

"Papa?" he said softly, should his father have fallen asleep. "Papa, you awake?"

"Yes, son, right here." Never had the familiar voice sounded so tired.

"How is Mendel doing, papa? Has he gotten any better?"

Little Mendel was only eight, the youngest of Noah's one sister and eight brothers. Next was Hanan at twenty-one. Their parents had been embarrassed at such a late-in-life pregnancy, but the family had applauded the middle-aged couple's continuing passion. As the fruit of this passion, Mendel's siblings doted on him. It was a wonder he wasn't spoiled rotten, had in fact grown into a sweet child, well-behaved, undemanding.

He'd fallen ill a week ago. Nothing serious, not in normal times: a fever, some nausea, next to no appetite. In normal times, before the war, before the SS, before the ghetto, there would have been little cause for concern. A stomach virus perhaps, easily treatable with a few days rest and his mother's warm chicken broth.

That was then, though, this was now, and those close to him were worried. After three years in the ghetto, three years of meager food and a raft of other wants, everyone's resistance was low, none more than the children's. People had learned to their horror that a small infirmity often flared into something lethal.

"He's sleeping now, finally," their father replied, "but he's still got that fever. You heard him begging for water. If only we had a little water…" The words trailed off wearily.

The Nazis had issued their *diktat* the evening of November 1st: by early morning of the 4th, all residents of the ghetto must be ready to vacate it, bringing only what they could carry. They were being resettled, they were told, somewhere to the east.

The news couldn't have been worse. Everyone was in a daze. Since moving to the ghetto, they'd been living under the threat of deportation, but after so long most were confident it would never come. Now here it was, staring them in the face, with little more than two days to prepare.

As in anguish as people were, this left them no time to sit around wringing their hands. What perishable food they had was cooked, essentials packed, valuables taken from permanent hiding places and made fast in portable ones, but no one thought to bring water, assuming their handlers would provide it. Yet they'd been given none at the station, nor did it appear they were going to get any. The train had stopped for water once to fill the boiler, but their guards had ignored the pleas coming from the cars.

Noah found his dad's hand in the dark. "It's going to be all right, papa, you'll see. Something tells me this is almost over. I bet by tomorrow we'll be settled in our new home."

From out of the blackness a voice, smirking, sarcastic. "Uh-huh, and where will that be, this new home of ours? At the bottom of a pit, covered over with dirt?"

"You be quiet, Pinchas!" Noah saw no need to further upset his poor father. "This isn't the place for that. You may be my older brother, but I'm telling you, not now."

"Yes, I am your older—"

"Noah, Pinchas!" Their mother's words were an angry whisper. "Shut up, the both of you! Aren't things bad enough without us fighting among ourselves? Besides, if you should wake this little boy..."

She waited a moment before continuing, her voice suddenly awkward. "Noah, help your mother up. I—I have to—Just help me, dear."

She had no need to spell it out. He'd escorted her to the latrine before, and it hadn't been pleasant. Not so much from the effort involved in getting her there, or even the squalidness of the facilities, but from the guilt at having to be a party to her humiliation—both the guilt and the shame at being powerless to prevent this assault on his own mother's privacy, her dignity.

He lit their candle, and with him in the lead they plunged into the wall of bodies. "I'm so sorry," she said, as uncomfortable with the situation as he. "I'd have asked your father, but at night..."

"Mama, please." He squeezed her hand. "Don't say another word. I'd carry you there if I had to, you're my mother. I love you."

Actually, he'd had to carry Mendel half a dozen times, no easy feat. Fifty adults in a freight car, with baggage, would have been a torment; a hundred was a hell hard to fathom. Even after arranging their possessions so as to stand on the stuff, the deportees were crushed together in a solid mass. There was no room to sit, much less lie down. People had to take turns getting off their feet, and even then the best one could do was kneel, or if one absolutely had to sit, curl into a muscle-cramping ball.

Breathable air was in short supply, most of what there was having been exhaled many thousands of times. Those with respiratory problems, and the elderly and very young, had the hardest go of it. People panted like dogs, passed out, panicked, fought. The most coveted spots were a tiny, barbed-wire window next to the ceiling, and the occasional place along the walls where the odd crack in the wood let in some oxygen.

Those who'd lost the battles for these were in no mood to be accommodating, and the space the Zabludowiczes occupied was the length of the car from the latrine. At best they faced a long, slow slog, at worst a potentially dangerous one. It wasn't easy for even those standing to make room, while all but impossible for Noah and his mother, in the dark, balancing on bundles, to avoid stepping on those struggling to sleep. As they followed the precarious light of their candle, curses, even threats, rose up around them.

One look at Noah, however, and even the surliest backed down, and not because he had an especially pugnacious appearance. His were the gently masculine, come-hither features of the romantic matinée idol, classically handsome in a non-rugged sort of way… drawing-room, tuxedo handsome.

His nose was finely chiseled, the eyes dark and a touch lazy, the lips in their fullness as close to feminine as they could get and remain a man's lips. Six feet tall, he was muscular, but not so heavily that it showed beneath his clothing. His hair was a light, wavy brown just starting to thin at the forehead. He'd never worn a beard. His hands and feet were on the small side. He had a weakness for sentimental love songs. Hated losing his temper.

Yet there was something about Noah that made one reluctant to cross him, the serene self-assurance of a man who knew how to handle himself in a fight. The stub of a candle he was holding may not have been much, but did light up his face, and on it was written this: "I have to get through, I have no choice. Please let me by or I promise you'll be sorry." People grumbled and were slow to move, but without exception gave ground.

Despite having been born in Ciechanow and living all of his twenty-six years there, he knew none of these individuals he was forging a path through. There were the Vlasics, and the Tabakmans from Silewski Street, but both families stood with his at the back wall. Everyone else from their dress looked to be rural Jews, collected from the outlying *shtetls*. Ciechanow was the biggest town for miles, a terminus for the entire region's Jews. Its Hebrew population before the war was six thousand; the few square blocks allotted the ghetto ended up housing double that.

Just because he didn't know these people didn't make it less distasteful for Noah to have to shove his way through them, no matter that he was all apologies. But as bad as he felt about adding to their discomfort, it couldn't be helped. His mother could never have made it to the latrine alone.

At last their objective loomed in front of them, a couple of bed sheets tacked across a corner of the car. Since the Germans hadn't given them so much as a bucket for this purpose, the deportees had been forced to improvise. The call had gone out for linens, towels, and cooking pots, the bigger those, the more welcome.

The smell was impossible. Bad as it was elsewhere, here at its source it was more than mere smell; Noah, if it were daylight, could imagine it browning the air. When he'd brought Mendel this morning, two of the pots were overflowing. What must it be now? He handed his mother the candle and watched her duck behind the curtain. Her exclamations of disgust made his ears burn.

Later, the Zabludowicz siblings huddled awake. Not counting Mendel, there were four of them. The two eldest brothers had emigrated to Palestine years before the war; the twins Ezra and Ehud were trapped in the Warsaw ghetto; and on his twenty-third birthday, Joseph and a few hundred others were plucked off the street by the Gestapo and put on a train. Their mother still had the scarf she'd knitted him as a present, still wrapped in gay paper.

The night was at its blackest, dawn close by. Having put out their candles, everyone was trying to sleep as best he could. But for the snoring of the adults and the whimpering of a few thirsty children, the only sound was the clickety-clack of the wheels on the tracks. The cattle car was less like a prison than a tomb.

"Pinchas, I'm sorry about earlier," Noah said. "I didn't intend to disrespect you."

His brother shrugged unseen in the dark. "Forget it, you were right. It's neither the time nor the—"

"Not the time?" It was their older sister Deborah. Though just turned thirty, she was years a widow, with no children to show for the marriage. "If *this* isn't the time, when is?" she said, less interested in her brothers' rapprochement than in what awaited them at journey's end. "And I agree with Pinchas. I've always agr—"

"Oh, swell!" Too loud. Noah took it down a notch. "This conversation again? How many times, if you don't mind my asking, are we going to have it?"

She ignored him. "I've always agreed with Pinchas. Resettlement in the east… just what does that mean? Can anyone trust the SS? Is that still possible?"

Noah didn't trust the buggers, either. Only a chump or a simpleton could. He did, however, find it difficult to accept some of the more outlandish rumors circulating of late, the slaughter of entire communities, deaths in the thousands.

"I'll say it again, Deborah, and you, too, Pinchas. It would make no sense for the Germans to kill us. Things aren't going well for them in Russia. The *Shomeir* have a radio, I heard the news myself: the Wehrmacht is bogged down, some place called Stalingrad."

"Your point?" Pinchas asked, as if he hadn't heard it before.

"The Nazis are going to need us. Victory is looking more elusive for them, the war a longer, more difficult prospect; maybe, as in the last one, a stalemate. Believe me, the Germans will be hurting for slave labor. Already are. Didn't their officers tell our Council we were being sent to work in some factory somewhere, to assist in the war effort?"

"And you bought that?" His sister's eyes were arched with brows as thick and black as her hair; he could picture them now bunched together in exasperation. "The SS would say anything, are capable of anything. You haven't, brother Noah, figured that out yet?"

This was hard to dispute. The Germans had behaved abominably since their defeat of the Poles, Ciechanow being but one example. Life had been cheap in the ghetto. Aside from those fatalities brought on by SS indifference—disease from too many people living in too small an area, lack of medicine, lack of food, the shortage of coal and other fuels—setting foot outside its boundaries without a work pass had meant death. The same for any Jew seen outdoors after sundown.

Nor was disease or the unauthorized leaving of it the only way the ghetto had killed. The Nazis had drawn up a hundred infractions punishable by death. Permanent gallows were erected in the plaza fronting the synagogue, long since shut down, and hardly a week had passed that hadn't seen hangings.

Homicide had taken other forms, too, much of it random and without provocation, on the whim of the Gestapo or SS man in the street. Boredom, drunkenness, or both were often at the root of these tragedies. Add to this the periodic roundups like that which had snared their brother Joseph, and by November the ghetto's numbers had been reduced by almost half.

"Capable of anything?" Noah said. "That I *don't* buy. Bad as the SS are, do you really think them, these Germans of yours—as a government, a people, a civilized European nation—up to mass extermination? The murder of children, whole populations?"

"What of Pippel then?" Pinchas countered. "Explain Pippel to me."

Noah's laugh was dismissive. "Ah, yes, the famous Pippel. Which Pippel, the mad? Or Pippel the fool. Or maybe Pippel the hopeless sot, the butt of a thousand jokes since even before the war."

For as long as anyone could remember, Pippel (last name unknown) had been one of the more colorful members of the Jewish community. Most thought him demented in a harmless way, and the opinion had weight. He was a beggar by trade and a drunkard by inclination, though with the establishment of the ghetto, wine had grown scarce. But even sober, Pippel would suffer the occasional lapse into daftness. These might consist of animated conversations with himself, walking backward wherever he went, mild disturbances of the peace, and so on.

During the warmer months, he slept in alleyways or on the stoops of the sympathetic. In winter, no one was sure where he holed up, but he was always on the streets early to beg.

Then one day the Gestapo nabbed him and threw him on a train. Everyone figured that was that until surprisingly, a week later, he showed up back in town with a bandage on his head and a wild story to tell.

According to him, half an hour after leaving the Ciechanow station, the small train carrying him and two hundred others turned onto a spur, eventually stopping at the edge of a forest where everyone was ordered out. Awaiting them was a platoon of SS and a pair of trucks. Shovels were passed out, and the people led at gunpoint to a clearing in the woods. Here they were told to dig a ditch, then lined up by tens at the rim of it and shot.

Pippel claimed to have been only grazed by a bullet and left for dead. When he regained consciousness, he clawed his way out of what should have been his grave to find the Germans gone—and silence, a deathly silence that spoke volumes. A friendly farmer later tended to his head and gave him food, and traveling at night, well away from any roads, he made it to Ciechanow and slipped back into the ghetto.

That was his tale, though few gave it much credibility, bandaged head or no. If it had been anyone else, maybe, but Pippel the *meshugga?* Persistent as he was impassioned about his alleged ordeal, he would grab passersby on the street and pressure, cajole, beg them, not for alms but simply to hear his story. He'd been saved, he said, to warn them of the danger they and their families were in. Maybe then some might escape.

But people didn't want to be warned, certainly not by the likes of him. The whole thing was preposterous. If what he said was true, everyone taken from the ghetto so far—every man, woman, and child—was dead. That was inconceivable. That just couldn't be. His were the delusional rantings of a lunatic.

Spurned, Pippel grew morose and started keeping to himself, and in the year that followed, the episode was forgotten. But not by everybody. Some remained suspicious.

"Madman, perhaps," Pinchas conceded. "Fool, undoubtedly. Butt of countless jokes, yes, but what if this once what he was saying was true? I heard him myself, and I can promise he's never been as lucid. Nor as deadly serious. So it was a crazy story—it's been a crazy three years. What could be crazier than hanging men and women in the very shadow of the synagogue?"

Noah threw up his hands, but in the dark no one noticed. "You go ahead then and believe the addle-brained old drunk. I personally think he made it up to try and get sympathy, and the handouts that go with it. Did any of you actually see him put on a train?"

"Oh, come on, Noah," Deborah said. "That isn't fair. How are we supposed to—"

"Not fair? I'll tell you what's not fair: that this argument is always two to one, you and Pinchas against me. Well, guess what, tonight is different. Tonight a fourth party is present, someone who used to leave the room whenever we talked about this, but who can hardly leave now. Hanan, what about it? What in your opinion do the Germans have planned for us?"

Their brother Hanan had been a studious child, more apt to stay indoors with his books than go outside to play. This served him well in school. His parents, everyone, had held high hopes for him; when the Wehrmacht invaded in 1939, he was a week from the University of Krakow. He'd wanted to study philosophy, then teach.

In keeping with his solitary nature, the boy wasn't much for confrontation, either. But he had been listening.

"The Germans?" At the sound of his name his head popped up, almost losing him his glasses. "I—I'm not sure. It's hard—hard to say exactly. Except..."

As if someone pressed a button, he shifted from startled to authoritative, to the professor he still dreamed of becoming. "Except if thousands *were* dying, even death camps as some say, how could the SS keep those a secret? Escaped prisoners, nearby villages, the partisans in the area... the world would have to know, which would mean we would, too."

His next sentence took all three of them aback.

"As for Pippel and his story, if anything I'd call it encouraging. If he was telling the truth, our chances are good. He said the death train halted thirty minutes out of Ciechanow. But we've been going for three days now, and who knows how much longer? I'd say we were out of immediate danger, and then ask this: why would the Nazis go to the trouble of transporting us this far only to kill us when we got off the train? I have to agree with Noah. They must need us for something."

Again, invisibly, Hanan slid his glasses up. "And if Pippel was lying, even better. Not only would it support the case for the resettlement being genuine but undermine all those other horrible rumors. Let's pray he was lying, but if not, so be it. Whatever the truth, there's no reason to panic.

"Anyway, that's—that's how I see it." Another button, and the professor vanished. "Please don't be sore, Pinchas. Or you, Deborah, please. The last thing I want is to make anyone mad."

Nor had he. In spite of themselves, both found his logic comforting; not enough to dispel their fears altogether, but some. By what Pippel had said, they should already be dead. Could Noah be right after all? Even if the beggar's tale was true, his allegation of murder had occurred more than a year ago, with the German Army riding the wind. It was a different war now. Perhaps the swine did need slaves.

And with that, the argument was over. Everyone was too tired to talk anymore, their tongues too thick from thirst. It was a good time to stop, too, on a positive note. Even Noah, who'd been trying to convince himself as much as anyone of their safety, even he felt better after hearing the boy speak.

He searched him out in the dark and embraced him. "Thanks for coming through, Hanan. I know you're not much for bickering, but trust me when I say you'd make a hell of a lawyer."

He'd always admired his kid brother's erudition. As sharp as anyone, school hadn't agreed with him. He wasn't the academic type, enjoyed working with his hands more than his head. He did think highly, however, of those who could boast the latter, envying their talent for living by their wits.

Pinchas was bright, too, but lacked Hanan's education. An electrician by trade, he played a prodigious game of chess. Noah had left school as soon as he could to drive trucks, ended up working for the Silvers, who owned a fleet of them. The Silver and Zabludowicz families were close, had been for years, but it wasn't until he started driving for them that he got to know, really know, their only male child Godel.

Though three years Noah's junior, Godel Silver and he became the best of friends. People puzzled at the attraction; the two weren't at all compatible. Careful—having chosen the roughneck life of a trucker—to keep his softer side private, Noah succeeded in projecting himself as a man's man, all action and physicality, hard-nosed practicality. By no means a ruffian, he found himself skilled with his fists, and when called for, didn't hesitate to use them. Godel by contrast was a self-styled lover, not a fighter, a dreamer not a doer, a skinny kid who wrote poetry to try to impress the girls, hoped to be a real writer one day. He wasn't a pushover, but though he would if provoked, wasn't much for pushing, either.

Yet the pair had hit it off. The connection was a mystery to everyone.

Noah, too, couldn't figure out the dynamic in play, until the day it struck him that Godel was cut from the same cloth as Hanan. Both loved words and reading, relied on brains rather than brawn, were complaisant but not cowardly, had integrity to spare. To Noah, the esteem in which he held his friend was but a reflection of the even greater one he had for his brother.

But there was another reason, too, an admittedly darker one, and though he would never have confessed it to anyone—had trouble acknowledging it himself—did allow it was a factor. It had nothing to do with he and Godel being pals. That had arisen six years ago, this in the past three only. But he couldn't deny that during those three years it had him seeking out Godel's company more than he might have. This "it" had a name—

And that name was Roza.

With the morbid talk at an end and the Zabludowicz's little patch of the cattle car quiet again, Noah was free to let his thoughts drift toward something more pleasant, to the remarkable creature that was Roza Robota.

He'd watched her grow up without being much conscious of her. He might see her on the street every so often, or in her father's hardware store when he came by with a delivery, but five years her senior he hadn't paid her much mind. For a brief period they'd been fellow scouts in the *H'Shomeir H'Tzair*. Roza had joined the Shomeir when she was twelve, the first year she was eligible, but by then almost eighteen, Noah was on his way out.

The H'Shomeir H'Tzair, Hebrew for Young Guard, was a Zionist youth group that on the surface promoted camping, sports, and other activities, but in reality had a more serious agenda. Simply stated, the Zionists saw no future for the Jew in Europe. The attempt at assimilation had failed. It was time to get out, start over somewhere else.

This had nothing to do with Hitler and the ascendance of Nazism; by the turn of the century, Zionism was going strong. Though traditionalist Jews rejected it, believing that suffering should be endured passively and in submission to God's will, the movement had flourished. After a thousand years and more of discrimination, persecution, and not a few bloody pogroms at the hands of the Germans, Russians, and Poles, the Zionists argued that to be truly secure the Chosen People needed a country they could call their own.

Several geographic areas were considered, but in the end none was deemed preferable to their ancestral homeland: Palestine as it was known to the rest of the world, *Eretz Israel*, the land of Israel, to those Jews longing to return.

Enter the Shomeir, whose real purpose was to encourage *aliyah bet*, emigration to the Holy Land. Like any scouting organization set up for children, its main inducement was fun. There were lots of crafts and competitions—track and field, soccer, swimming—overnight stays in the woods, horseback riding, sing alongs. Accompanying this, however, were instructions in Hebrew, Jewish history, and training in the fundamentals of farming and construction.

On Lag B'Omer, the feast day commemorating the miracle of the manna from heaven, the troops of the Shomeir, flags flying and trumpets blaring, would march to the plaza next to the synagogue. There they would cheer speeches extolling the virtues of Eretz Israel and the freedom and opportunity awaiting there. A celebrated rabbi might speak, or a former resident of Ciechanow who'd made aliyah, back from Palestine with a firsthand account of life in the land of milk and honey. Afterward, there would be singing and dancing into the night.

Even after he left the Shomeir, Noah remained an ardent Zionist. For him emigration was the only acceptable course. The Poles of Ciechanow had never hid their dislike of their Jews, an animosity that became evident as soon as one ventured outside the Jewish parts of the city. The refusal of some restaurants and other businesses to serve them, the stony stares in the streets, the literal stones sometimes thrown at them should they happen to wander into the wrong neighborhood—the list was as long as it was insulting, and though he'd gotten used to it, Noah never ceased battling it.

It was on Gentile turf that he'd learned how to fight, and over the years made many a *goy* regret his bad manners. He was all set to follow his oldest brothers to Palestine when the German Army intervened, and would have attempted the trip regardless if it hadn't meant deserting his family.

Then came the SS, and with them the ghetto, and neither he nor anyone was going anywhere. Not that he was the kind to give in without a struggle. Word reached him that the leaders of the Shomeir and some of the older scouts were fighting back after a fashion, sneaking out of the ghetto at night to steal food and medicine from the Nazis and sabotage what equipment they could. They also had a radio capable of picking up the BBC in England, and were printing the information acquired there in an underground newspaper.

Godel Silver told him this. He'd been helping to write the paper, even joining the Shomeir on their midnight forays. Never a scout himself, he had a new girlfriend who was, she having persuaded him to throw in with them.

Noah was impressed, wanted to help, too. He asked to meet Godel's girl, and agreed to do so the next day over some ersatz coffee at the Yellow Rose Café.

The Yellow Rose had once been hopping, the preferred eatery of the town's Jews, but though its menu was a ghost of its old self, it still offered some things. Simple baked goods for the most part, meatless soups and stews. That was on a good day; usually there was nothing but matzos and ghetto tea. A corner of the ceiling had caved in from dampness, the tables and chairs grown wobbly, the cutlery sparse. But to the great satisfaction of its customers, who looked on it as a link to the past and counted its survival a moral victory, it remained open.

Come morning, Noah was the first to arrive. He sat facing the entrance, ordered some "coffee." When the couple showed up, she wasn't at all what he'd expected. The only girls he'd seen Godel with had been on the petite side, and quiet if not plain shy. This one was almost as tall as her partner, by no definition fat but not skinny, either. She didn't wait to be introduced. Noah shook the proffered hand.

"Hello, I'm Roza." The voice was husky, deep for a female but the more alluring for it. There was a throatiness to it that spoke of vigorous passions. "Hope you weren't sitting here long."

The name meant nothing to him, nor did he recognize the face, but could tell this right off: the girl had an earnestness about her, an intensity, inconsistent with her age. As soon as she sat down, her gaze locked onto his.

"You don't remember me, do you? You used to make deliveries to my father."

Noah went blank. He couldn't for the life of him...

"Roza Robota," she said. "Isaiah Robota's daughter."

He smacked his forehead in recognition, nor was the gesture an exaggeration. It was both her, and not. The last time he'd seen this Roza, or could remember seeing her, she'd been all knobby knees and dental braces, her body as angular and spare as a box.

Now here she sat in a flower-splashed summer dress, buxom, curvaceous, thick black hair to her shoulders, not the most beautiful face in the world, or at least not as feminine as the rest of her, but one was drawn to it nonetheless. Her nose was a little aggressive, the jaw a bit square, but the mouth was sumptuous and quick to smile, her eyes intelligent. Noah couldn't recall coming across eyes like those before. So brown they shone black, penetrating yet kind, they didn't stop at your exterior so much as peer inside you.

But despite the impression that they'd already sized him up, taken the measure of him as not only a man but a person, not for one second did he feel judged. His innards exposed maybe, the core of him examined, but with a forgiving lens.

No, he'd never seen eyes quite like those. They helped make her that breed of woman who only got prettier the longer one looked at her.

In age, however, she was as much girl still as woman. He wasn't expecting a lot from an eighteen-year-old. Then she began talking, small talk at first, but after served her coffee came to the point of their rendezvous.

The Germans were evil, she said through bared teeth, and the evil was just beginning, worse was yet to come. Their people were in peril as never before. The SS weren't just killing indiscriminately, women and children and the old, but the casual way they went about it, as if squashing insects. Their savagery had no anger to it, little emotion at all, and that was what had not only her but others worried. If a cataclysm were to be prevented, the Jews would have to start resisting.

"We already have," she said, leaning across the table toward Noah, "but we've got to do more. And we're going to need men like you to help us. You're a fighter, Godel tells me, the terror of the *goyim* street toughs. He said he's watched you take on two at a time and whip them."

"Three," Godel said. "You should see him, he's murder."

Roza leaned closer. "Here's your shot then to go up against the biggest bully of all. How'd you like to mix it up with the son-of-a-bitching Nazis?"

Before he could answer, she beat him to it. "I can tell you're interested. It's written all over you. Am I mistaken, my love, that your friend here is just itching in his pants to join us?"

"Far be it from me," Godel said, "to disagree with so persuasive, and I might add, beautiful a girl. Noah?"

"Uh... I don't see as I have a choice," he grinned in mock resignation.

"Good, it's settled then." Roza reached for her cup. "Now I get to shut up awhile, about business anyway, and drink, or try to drink, this ditch water they call coffee."

That was how she talked, with a moxie beyond her years, a sassy exuberance that won one over instantly. Noah was interested all right, and in more than just her offer. After listening to her for only a few minutes, this much he knew: she might have worn a dress, but was as scrappy as he; might have had long, lush hair and soft, womanly skin, but was as full of fight as any man—might have possessed a body designed to give birth and suckle, but inside it beat the heart of a warrior, a lion. One look into those black eyes ensured him that if it ever came down to it, the only way the Germans were going to stop her was to kill her.

It was right then and there, not thirty minutes after meeting her, that he began falling in love with his best buddy's girl.

As clear as this was in retrospect, at the time he didn't see it. His mind was elsewhere. Suddenly, a sword had been thrust into his hands, a chance to be a man again. Not that the call to action turned out as warlike as he'd wanted. He soon found that his new comrades-in-arms didn't do any actual fighting. Unguarded trucks and small storehouses were what the Shomeir raiders were after, and anything else the Nazis happened to leave unattended.

But even without guns and pitched battles, playing hide-and-seek with the SS was as dangerous as it was exhilarating. Only doable when there was no moon, even then it bordered on the suicidal. To be seen was to be fired upon, executed on the spot if captured, a price some of them did wind up paying. But aside from the good their plunder did their downtrodden people, for every one of those bravehearts who dared defy the curfew it was worth risking their lives to harass the detested Germans.

No one was more fearless, or effective, than Roza. It was her idea to lure the guards from their posts by disturbing the night stillness a street or two distant. Sometimes a soldier would stay behind while the others ran off to investigate, sometimes one wouldn't. If this last, the Shomeir hidden in the shadows would swoop in and grab what they could. Roza insisted on playing the role of decoy, and had more than a few close calls eluding her pursuers.

As the weeks wore on, she argued for hitting the SS harder. The Shomeir in their thievery had acquired some munitions: a handful of guns, a supply of ammo, even a crate of hand grenades. Roza wanted to turn the Nazis' weapons against them, and whatever others could be improvised. She was tired, she said, of seeing only Jewish blood spilled.

Upon her petitioning them, the elders of the ghetto discussed her suggestion, but in the end voted it down. For one, they said, it would be self-defeating. The SS had a standing order that for every German soldier killed at the hands of partisans, a hundred civilians would be rounded up and shot. For another, if the Nazis suspected it was Jews gunning them down, who knew what they'd do? They might massacre the entire ghetto.

Acceding to the logic of this, Roza backed off, but continued to stew. Her hatred for her race's enemies was equaled by her frustration at being unable to stop them. She raged at not only the Germans but her own powerlessness, as if she was partially to blame for the crimes that kept accumulating.

It particularly ate at her that she couldn't even protect her own family. Her parents lost their savings, confiscated by the Nazis. Her brother Israel, two years younger than she, had always been sickly, and life in the ghetto hadn't helped. The cough he'd developed lately wasn't going away.

It was what she had to watch her older sister sustain, though, that galled her the most. She and Shoshonna worked together on a forced-labor squad outside the ghetto, helping demolish Jewish homes to be rebuilt for the German colonists streaming into the area. This was degrading enough, as if the Semitic taint was too dirty and deep to be scrubbed out or painted over. But to see the delicate Shoshonna, the beauty of the family, bending beneath her load of bricks, her dress dark with sweat, their guards leering and even pawing at her—this was too much for Roza. She was hard put to restrain herself, but if she had stepped in, it probably would have been the death of both of them.

No one felt sorrier for her than Noah. His admiration, his love for her had quickly taken root and blossomed. She was the woman he'd always dreamed of but never thought he'd find, had given up hoping for out of doubt she even existed. A glorious anomaly, she was feminine in all of the appropriate ways—nurturing, compassionate, physically voluptuous—but refusing to confine herself to the limitations society placed on her sex, also outspoken, uncompromising, indomitable.

She was, in short, the perfect match for him, only now that he had by luck alone found her, she was someone else's. And not just any someone; he and his unwitting rival had been friends since their teens.

That the pair knew nothing was no accident. Noah was committed to keeping his affections a secret. To do otherwise would have been not only unseemly but unprincipled, as well as doomed to failure. The two were quite hopelessly in love, as happy a couple as any he knew. Far be it from him to intrude on their idyll.

Despite the pain bred of his thwarted desire, he was genuinely glad for the both of them, never even contemplated breathing a word of the ache in his heart. To bask in the sun of Roza's presence, to be rewarded with a smile, the occasional sisterly hug, was the only satisfaction he allowed himself. They were crumbs, but he was a starveling and would take what he could get.

He did jump, however, at every opportunity to be near her, and not just out of love. As plenty of others could affirm, to be in Roza's presence was to feed off her strength. Her courage made them braver, her tenacity them more determined. Confidence wafted from her like some medicinal vapor. When she spoke, one's doubts and fears melted into the air. Noah especially enjoyed hearing her belittle the strutting SS.

"They aren't supermen," she would say. "Hell, they aren't even men. You want men? Go to the Wehrmacht, the regular German Army, doing battle with the Soviets on the Russian front. And who are the big-talking SS waging war on? The unarmed civilians, the women and children of the ghettos.

"They're not soldiers, they're murderers, shameless cowards all, and one day as sure as the sun rises they're going to pay for their crimes."

Noah's contempt for their masters mirrored hers. On only one point did they differ, their respective attitudes toward what the Germans ultimately had in mind for their people. Roza was fatalistic, subscribing to much of the more sensational talk, while he continued to have difficulty believing such things possible. But whatever future the Nazis envisioned for them, both had no problem agreeing it wasn't going to be pretty.

Look at them now, he mused, surveying the packed cattle car. They may not have been on their way to their deaths, but were being freighted like so many animals to a destination unknown, without the least regard to their comfort. If this was how the SS saw fit to treat them en route, what could they expect at the end of the line? Forget comfort—were they to be deprived of the barest necessities while being worked half to death? Perhaps one day they would remember the ghetto with fondness.

Dawn was breaking at last. Noah could see the first feeble gray of it through the cracks in the walls. He noticed, too, that the train was slowing. Before long, brakes squealing, it lurched to a halt, bringing everyone to their feet.

Excitement filled the wagon. They'd only stopped three times, once to take on water for the engine, once to change guards, and again for a tense half a day outside of Wroclaw. Was this it, the end of their journey? Those at the ceiling window reported a barren landscape of yellowish earth, isolated clumps of trees.

The mysterious smell that had been nagging at them did seem more pronounced here, had been getting stronger with each mile. It stank like something burning, something oily. One could almost feel the grease in the air, as if someone was incinerating animal fat, an ungodly amount of it. But who would do such a thing and why? No one knew what to make of it.

A few minutes and the train was moving again, if at a crawl. Leaving the main track, it veered to the right, bringing from the window less than helpful word of a thick woods. But the other side of the car was soon urgent with news. Through the cracks, people had spotted something, and it had them buzzing. One of the shtetl Jews turned and said something to Pinchas.

"What is it?" Noah asked his brother. "What's going on?"

"A station. We just passed a station house, a good-sized one, too. Which means a good-sized town. This could be it."

"What was the name of the station?"

"Auschwitz," Pinchas answered. "The man said it was called Auschwitz. He's never heard of it, no one has, but… Noah, tell me, that stink. What do you think it is?"

He had no idea, couldn't even guess. The farther the train went into the woods, the more invasive it grew, overpowering even the reek of their latrine. He wished Roza was here. Not that she would have known, either, he just wished she was here.

In the confusion at the Ciechanow platform four mornings ago, the Robotas and the Silvers had become separated from Noah's family. He thought he saw them board the same boxcar, but couldn't be sure. If they did, at least Roza and Godel were together. At least they had each other at this uneasy moment.

That would do, would have to. Noah would have felt better if it had been the three of them, but was glad for the two. As the train crept deeper into the forest, into the smell, he tried pretending the girl next to him was Roza, but it didn't work.

*   *   *

Shoshonna Robota clung tight to her sister against the raw November wind. "Roza, where are we?" Her voice was small, her eyes big. "Wh—what kind of place is this?"

Roza didn't answer. She was trying to make sense of the whole thing herself. Beneath their feet spread the unloading ramp, concrete, enormous, so big not even the thousands of them filled it. They were in some sort of line, the women and younger children, inching their way toward a cluster of SS. Their men formed a parallel line some meters off. Roza kept looking for her father, her brother, Godel, Noah, too, but for some reason couldn't find them. They must have ended up farther down, toward the rear.

To her left stretched another, less fragile queue, the wood and iron of the cattle cars they'd just vacated. Despite the torment they'd endured in those dungeons on wheels, she viewed them now almost with longing. Never had she been so menaced by her surroundings, not on her worst day in the ghetto, not on the labor gangs conscripted there and guarded by drunken soldiers, not even on those midnight raids outside the ghetto walls. The people of Ciechanow might as well have been transported to not merely another part of the country but another world.

The air was an uncanny green, the sun unable fully to penetrate the river of smoke filling the sky. Feeding this river was a single boiling black wall taking up half the southern horizon, its origin obscured by forest. The inexplicable, greasy stench that had plagued them for miles was so intense here as to raise one's gorge.

As soon as they'd been shouted off the train, their bundles were ripped from their hands by a swarm of living scarecrows in filthy blue-and-white-striped burlap. Stinking to high heaven, impossibly thin, these loped along with an odd mechanical gait, eyes bright with hunger.

"*Warum?* Why?" Roza had asked one of them in German as he walked away with her suitcase.

"*Verboten*," the creature had croaked, tossing it onto one of many rapidly growing piles.

Corpses lay alongside the train in short, orderly rows, casualties of the trip, some already bloating. A pack of stray children careened by howling like wolves, some scarecrow men in pursuit. Other noises rode the green air, noises to unhinge the nerves: the barking of fierce dogs straining at their leashes, the just as angry snarls of the Germans, the wailing of families freshly torn apart.

It hadn't been easy separating the sexes. Blood had been spilled. In the turmoil, Roza was knocked down and lost sight of her father and the rest of their men.

This she had seen, on the ground a few feet from her: a middle-aged couple in a desperate embrace, their fingers digging into each other's flesh. The man was holding onto the woman's blouse with his teeth, she crying hysterically, her face purple. The two soldiers struggling to disentangle them finally gave up, and cursing, reached for their nightsticks. Several blows to the head later, killing blows from the crunch of them, and the two were dragged off like so many sacks of cement.

What kind of place indeed. When in a voice even smaller Shoshonna again put the question to her, Roza spoke loud enough for them all to hear, her mother, grandmother, her Aunt Sara, the Silver women.

"Don't worry, Shozhka, everything's fine. We're going to be... just fine. It won't be long 'til we're all together again, drinking hot soup."

This was to corroborate what the officer had said, the one who'd earlier strolled imperiously past them. "*Frauen, bitte,*" Roza had heard him croon, "Ladies, please..." Then, everyone's German having improved much the last three years, "Keep moving, please. There is no need to be frightened. Tea and soup are waiting; the sooner we finish here, the sooner you'll be setting up house."

Though she'd loathed his peacock airs and phony goodwill, she was grateful for the effect his words had on the others. Her mother, her aunt, even Shoshonna for the moment were noticeably less ill at ease after his passing.

One thing this strange new world had in common with the one in the ghetto was its pantheon of SS officers swaggering about. In their splendor, their regal self-possession and pomp, they paced the ramp as if detached from its meanness and squalor. Immaculate in full battle dress, brass flashing, boots gleaming, they appeared only reluctantly to condone the brutality shown by the lower ranks, the surliness of the scarecrow men. Borrowing from their Prussian forebears, they radiated a military propriety, a civilized urbaneness that made one want to believe here were men who could be trusted.

Not that Roza did, not for one second. She hadn't trusted the apes for years, nor from what she'd seen of it was this the place to begin. Having dismissed the officer's glib reassurances as soon as she'd heard them, she'd returned to the thing bothering her the most. Such smoke, such a fire, so godawful an odor—what on earth were the Germans burning? Opinion held it to be garbage, or so she kept hearing. It certainly stank like it, but what sort of garbage? She could detect a faint undertaste to the smell now. She hadn't picked up on it before, but here, nearer its source, one couldn't miss it. Or mistake it for what it was, the distinctively acrid, burnt-metal bite of scorched hair.

Suddenly, at the head of the line, a new commotion broke out: wild weeping, shocked protestations, the deep, rumbling cough of big trucks starting up.

Until that moment, Roza hadn't noticed the trucks. She had, though, been watching what seemed a selection taking place, up where the gathering of SS men stood. One of them, an officer—and presumably a doctor, wearing as he was a white armband emblazoned with a blue caduceus—was directing part of the women to a group on the right, the rest to a much larger one on the left. Now these latter, to their and their families' despair, were being loaded onto open trucks.

A groan went up from the line of women. Shoshonna would have crumpled to the ground had not Roza caught her. Their Aunt Sara was beside herself. "They're doing it again!" she shouted. "Splitting us up! I won't let them—I won't. I'm not leaving my children!"

Roza didn't know what to say, not this time. The last thing they needed was to lose their composure, yet how to explain what was happening, and in plain sight? To her relief, her mother Faige rose to the occasion.

"Sara, calm down!" she cried. "And for heaven's sake, open your eyes! Look there, up ahead, and tell me what you see."

"What do I see? People bawling and tearing at their hair as their loved ones are trucked away, where to is anyone's guess! I'll say it again, I'm not—"

"Now, tell me who it is they're putting on those trucks. Go on—look! Children and their mothers, and the obviously sick and crippled, and of the others not a one under forty. While those staying behind are all young, the healthiest and strongest. What does that suggest?"

At the words "children and their mothers," a squinting Sara could see it was true, no child below sixteen had been separated from its mother. She brightened on the instant, her two sons falling well under that demographic.

Still, she hadn't a clue what her sister was driving at, and this annoyed her. "Tell us, Faige. What *does* it suggest?"

"That the Germans are dividing us according to our capacity for work. Would you expect anything less of them, less efficient, I mean? To us middle-aged, in addition to other, lighter duties, will fall the care of the ill and handicapped, the young and very old. This will free up the rest for the heaviest labor."

She laid a hand on each daughter's shoulder. "I'm sorry, Roza, Shoshonna—and you, Mrs. Silver, for your Godel and Marsha—but you might be marching off to work this very day, with the rest of us riding those trucks to our new homes. We were all hoping to get a respite after our miserable journey, but it's not to be helped. We remain in cruel hands.

"But don't worry, children, when you get back tonight we'll make you as comfortable as possible. By then, as the young officer said, we'll have gone far toward setting up house."

Eager as all were for such an explanation, her words fell on receptive ears. "But why trucks?" Shoshonna asked. "How far away could these new homes of ours be?"

"Who's to say?" replied her mother. "It could be a few miles. Again, German efficiency. Would you expect Gemmy here, or that woman there, or that one on crutches, to be able to walk even a mile, especially over broken ground?"

Gemmy was what everyone called Roza's and Shoshonna's maternal grandmother, and had for so long neither was sure of her real name. She'd done poorly on the train; her lungs as brittle as the rest of her, she'd passed out more than once from lack of air. She was doing better outdoors, however. With Faige's and Sara's help she was walking, each taking turns lending her an arm to lean on.

"But I don't want to leave you, mama." Shoshonna sounded more like twelve than twenty-three. "I'm scared, and not just for myself but all of us."

"Don't be silly, dear," she said, embracing first her and then Roza. "There's no need to be afraid. Tonight when I see you again, I'll give you each two hugs."

Roza's admiration for her mother was as great as her love for her. It wasn't solely at the auspices of the H'Shomeir H'Tzair that she'd learned to take pride in her Jewishness. As a young woman, Faige Robota had been a pioneering Zionist, one of the movement's early adherents, and even after starting a family had remained active in the cause. As they got older, she would regale her children with not only stories of those days but tales from the Bible of fierce prophets and proud kings.

It was she more than their father who'd steered them in the direction of the Shomeir. Intelligent, courageous, and to many a beauty still, her mother was everything Roza had grown up wanting to be. But though she would have liked without reservation to buy what the woman had said—and a part of her did, there was no faulting Faige's reasoning—a voice inside her kept whispering the Germans were up to no good.

With the racket of the trucks and the lamentations of those families being divided, conversation became a chore, prompting the women to walk in silence the rest of the way. Not that by then they had far to go. The closer they came to the SS doctor the faster the line moved, until all of a sudden it was they standing in front of him.

His boyish looks surprised Roza; he didn't seem much older than her Godel. Even so, he bore himself with the same kingly mien as the other officers.

He also, to her uneasiness, was enjoying himself. Why this should have bothered her, she didn't know. His hat rested at a rakish angle, his arms jauntily akimbo. A smile curved his lips, but it was cold as a crocodile's, and smug, as if he knew something they didn't, was in on some joke about to be enacted at their expense.

Sara and her sons were first. He took the three of them in at a glance. "And how old are *you?*" he asked the children, his voice not unkind. "Eleven" and "Thirteen" came the answers, whereupon he nodded as if to say "Good boys" and pointed them with their mother to the left. Wordlessly, he waved Faige and Gemmy the same direction, Roza and Shoshonna to the right.

Thirty seconds and it was over. Shoshonna was crying now, refusing to budge until her sister took her by the arm and gently forced her along. She, too, would have liked to cry—it was her mother, too—but someone had to be hard or they weren't going to get through this.

The women kept in eye contact across the gulf separating them. Roza was all sunshine and thumbs-up, but a cacophony of alarm bells was going off in her head. The Germans might be pretending as if they cared for their well-being, but their actions told a different story. The purgatory of the train ride; the older couple's casual murder on the ramp; the plundering of their possessions, which even now the scarecrow men were ransacking; the strange, fetid smoke with its tincture of burnt hair; the dogs, the machine guns, the breaking up of families, the enigmatic malice behind the SS doctor's smile—all of it made her skin shrink that her mother was about to climb onto one of those trucks.

Could her imagination be getting the better of her? Maybe that couple earlier had been beaten merely unconscious, not killed. Maybe it was only garbage burning (what else could it be?). Maybe her mother was right, and they were being admitted to this place separately, and at the end of the day would be reunited. A reasonable argument could be advanced opposing each of Roza's misgivings. Was it possible she was being premature? Paranoid? Both?

Her questions were soon answered. It was Shoshonna who noticed the woman first.

"Roza, isn't that Mrs. Wojowiecz?" she said through her tears. "What is she doing?"

A young woman was hurrying toward them from the group on the left. She walked head down, arms swinging at her sides. They knew her from their father's store; she used to come there with her plumber husband. They had a daughter, an angel of a child, three, maybe four, with pudgy red cheeks and curly blond hair—the same little cherub toddling after her now but unable to keep up.

"Wait, mama, wait!" she cried, reaching out her tiny arms.

"Take care of your child, woman!" one of the scarecrow men shouted.

"It's not mine, sir!" She covered her face with her hands. "Not mine, I swear!" She began walking faster, desperate to reach those pointed to the right, to reach and lose herself among those not going on the trucks. But the girl kept running after her, sobbing now, frantic. "Don't leave, mama! Please, mama, stop!"

The woman, without slowing, clapped her hands over her ears. "It's not mine, I tell you! Oh, God help me, it's not!"

Head still down, she didn't see the blow coming. An SS-*Schütze* intercepted her and with a sickening thud knocked her out cold with the butt of his rifle. Two of the scarecrow men scooped her up and rushed her out of sight. Another followed with her daughter, screaming now at the top of her lungs.

The two sisters gaped at each other in disbelief. Whether Shoshonna understood the implications of what they'd witnessed, Roza didn't know, but wasn't about to share them with her. That Mrs. Wojowiecz would have gone to any length to escape the trucks was clear, but why? She'd obviously figured out she'd been marked for them because of her daughter, but to abandon her like that, her own flesh and blood... What could have driven a mother to that?

It could only be one thing: fear, the icy breath of mortal fear on her cheek. The question remaining was what had convinced her she was in peril, and Roza, in a quick calculus, again could think of but one answer.

Somebody, one of the scarecrow men, must have told her something, scaring the motherliness right out of her. She was young, she was pretty, wanted so much to live, had panicked and as impulsive, as ignoble as it may have been, the instinct of self-preservation had triumphed over the maternal one. Nor was it likely the mere suggestion of danger could have made her or any parent desert their little one. No, she'd learned for a fact what being sent to the left meant, that those getting on the trucks weren't coming back, ever.

It had to be that, couldn't be anything else, and if so then everything from the nauseating black smoke to the excesses on the ramp suddenly made sense. The suspicions deviling Roza since exiting the train had in a flash become hideously real. It wasn't resettlement, it was mass murder. The German people had gone insane. The awful stories that had arisen the past year were true after all.

She'd once given shrift to these, warning of catastrophe if the Jews failed to resist. The more she'd pondered them, though, the more far-fetched they'd seemed, if for no reason than from an operational standpoint. Supposing even Nazi bloodthirstiness capable of rising to such heights, did the Germans, or for that matter any nation, possess the means, the imagination required to wipe out an entire branch of the human tree?

She hadn't thought so, but just like that here it was, right in front of her. The possibility of it anyway. Yet what could she do? To motion her mother over to what must be presumed was the side of the living would be to watch her clubbed down as Mrs. Wojowiecz had been. Roza could only look on in impotent anguish as she and her grandmother, her aunt and her cousins climbed aboard one of the trucks and were hurried off.

She might have broken down then and there, Shoshonna or no, had not a pair of emotions come to the fore to sustain her. The first was born of a natural response to the vile secret she'd just deduced, and consisted of the hope that maybe, just maybe, she was wrong. Her gut told her differently, but there was always the chance the poor, pitiful plumber's wife had acted on a hunch only. This was doubtful, but optimism died hard, even on the threshold of hell.

Though she didn't know it yet—couldn't even say, really, where they were—it wasn't just on the threshold but inside the living hell that was Birkenau, the *Vernichtungslager*, the extermination camp, that the second emotion helping now to steel her was going to come in handy. In this, she was ahead of most on the ramp, for while hope still puttered lamely at the periphery of her consciousness, hate overran it, consuming her like a fire devouring dry tinder.

At that moment, she began to hate the SS as never before, their haughtiness, their lies, their despicable black hearts, and it was this hate, more than some fool's paradise, that not only kept her from falling in a despairing heap to the ground but would see her through the long months of her nightmarish new life.

An hour later and the morning's business was done, the last truck bouncing springily into the forest. Or rather, the last truck intended for people. There was other cargo to cart away, and the scarecrow men were hard at it. Roza saw them pile one suitcase and footlocker after another onto the beds of more trucks, stuffing their mouths with whatever food they could find.

The only deportees on the ramp now were those who'd be walking, and in short order they were, beginning with the men. These, who had for some reason undergone a second selection, were being led off in a formation five abreast, with the exception of forty or fifty kept back. She stood on tiptoe and scanned both parties for signs of the men of her family, but again met with no success. The attempt wasn't lost on her sister.

"I don't see papa or Izzy, either," Shoshonna said. "What could have happened to them?"

"Nothing." Roza struggled to sound nonchalant. "They're either among those there," she said, nodding toward the two batches of men, "or went on the trucks. You heard what mama said, Shozhka, we'll be seeing them soon. How about we just worry about ourselves for now, okay?"

Then it came their turn to be marched away, also in a column of fives, escorted by soldiers with faces as hard as their helmets. A limestone road took them from the unloading ramp into a treeless field. Twenty minutes more and it skirted a small rise to reveal a barbed-wire fence running a good half a mile. White ceramic conductors dotted the length of it, meaning it was electrified.

Outside it, a parallel line of crude watchtowers receded into the distance, each manned by a soldier on a machine gun, while behind it squatted row after row of flat, rectangular gray huts nestled in a pestilential sea of churned mud. Roza scanned these anxiously, searching for signs of life.

She would have been better occupied paying closer attention to her feet. If she had, she could have quit deceiving herself with even the illusion of hope, and unencumbered by same sought a greater degree of both solace and resolve in the purgative furnace of her hate. For scattered among the pebbles and crushed limestone on which she walked were bits of bone, tiny, semi-pulverized, but unmistakably human.

*   *   *

Zalman Leventhal lay in his bunk smoking a cigarette, sluggish with schnapps. It hadn't taken many swigs of it to get him there, either. Despite a full head of reddish hair, unusual for a Jew—it earning him the nickname "Irish" growing up—he'd never been much of a drinker, certainly not to the extent the real Irish were said to be.

Through a window he watched a light snow flutter down. The weather had taken a sharp turn for the colder since his arrival at the unloading ramp four days ago. Two coal-burning stoves kept the room warm.

Their snug accommodations had him at a loss. Clean, spacious, well-appointed, a platoon of SS would have been happy to call the place home. The floor was dark linoleum, the walls a white stucco, at one end of the room a large, oaken slab of a table at which to eat. Each man had his own bunk complete with pillows and fresh linen. From the ceiling, fluorescent lights dispensed a uniform white glow, while at the other end of the barracks, partitioned off for privacy, shone a three-toilet, enameled beauty of a bathroom. Leventhal wasn't the only man wondering what the Germans were up to.

There were fifty of them, all from the Ciechanow transport, all in their twenties or late-teens. They'd been selected, they were told, on the basis of their ages and physiques for a permanent work detail—the *Sonderkommando*, or Special Squad—their keepers assuring them they'd be cared for.

Nor for a change were the Krauts lying. Not only had they wound up in this three-star hotel of a hut but been issued fine coats, boots, and other civilian clothing. The food was the best and most abundant Leventhal had seen in years: cured meats, bread and jams, pickled vegetables, various cheeses.

After the privations of the ghetto and then the cattle car, it was all very mysterious. They were even, in addition to cigarettes, provided liquor of all things, and though he'd hesitated at first to partake of the stuff, in the end he'd given in, if only to take the edge off his anxiety.

For while he and the others lacked for nothing materially, news of their families was denied them no matter how much they begged. The SS, in fact, weren't telling them much of anything, not even what was so special about the Special Squad. Just about all they did know was they were in a concentration camp, and could only guess what their loved ones were going through. Leventhal's two sisters had seven children between them, and his mother a bad heart. To conceive of them in this place of punishment was beyond bearing. Children in a concentration camp! It defied all that was comprehensible.

Then there was the prisoner from Danzig, an enigma indeed. He'd barged in on their evening meal a couple of nights before, all bluster and brass, though how he got past the guard posted day and night at their door no one knew. Unlike the scarecrow men at the ramp, his stripes were starched and creased, the flesh beneath them ample.

"The name's Witek," he'd announced, "and I'm looking for a Noah Zabludowicz. We knew each other from Danzig, though he hails from Ciechanow. Can any of you yahoos tell me if he was on this transport?"

Several said they'd seen Noah marched off with the other men on the ramp. "And how'd you get in here, friend? We've been locked down from day one. Nobody in or out."

Witek reached in a pocket and tossed a pack of cigarettes on the table. "Currency of the realm, my man," he said with a hearty laugh. "The SS are easily bribed, especially the rank and file. Six cigarettes a day is all they're rationed."

"So how did you come by so many?"

"The same way you got yours, and those warm clothes, that tasty smorgasbord there. From the transports, where else? Everything comes from the transports. You'll find that out when you start working."

"And what work is that?" This from more than one.

Witek smiled and shook his head, slipped the cigarettes back in his pocket. "I could tell you, but I wouldn't want to spoil the Germans' surprise. No, definitely not. Now, let me get this straight: you sure you saw Noah leaving the ramp on foot and not on one of those trucks?"

Of course they were sure, and two of his brothers with him. The Zabludowicz family was well-known in the ghetto.

"Good. He's probably still alive then. Being the fine physical specimen he is, I thought he might be in here with you fellows. I'll catch up with him sooner or later."

One of them spoke for them all when he asked, "What do you mean, 'still alive?' What does getting or not getting on the trucks have to do with that?"

Witek's face went blank. "You're joking, right?"

Silence, the seconds slow as snails.

"You're not joking," he said at last. "Good grief, what a bunch of blind yahoos you are! The smoke, that smell... where in blazes do you suppose you are? This is Birkenau, boys, not some Tatry ski resort. What—did you think the SS were throwing some giant cookout for everybody?"

"What are you saying?"

"That anyone taken from the ramp on one of those trucks is a goner. *Alles kaput. Touts finis.* Frizzled away into ashes. Gassed, then cremated in open pits, the lot of them."

They didn't believe him. Refused to believe him. Couldn't imagine why he would say something so bizarre. They made noises as if to argue with him about it, but didn't get very far—having learned what he'd come for, he left with a disgusted look and a sarcastic wave goodbye.

They stayed up half the night arguing instead among themselves over what he had to gain from trying to scare them like that. In the end, they could arrive at one conclusion only: this Witek was a scoundrel who'd taken advantage of their greenness to have a little sadistic fun at their expense.

Leventhal shifted uncomfortably in his bunk, debated whether to follow the cigarette he'd just stubbed out with another. Outside, the snow had stopped, the sky through the window threatening to clear. In spite of the condemnation he'd helped heap on their visitor that night, he wasn't so sure anymore. An evil feeling had been mounting in him since, and no matter how much schnapps he drank it wasn't fading.

Could the man have been telling the truth after all? As impossible as this was, it would explain that malodorous smoke everyone was having trouble rationalizing. And the cocky Witek had been right about one thing: whatever was going on, Birkenau was no playground. The electrified fences, the guard towers, the heavily armed SS... it was a concentration camp all right, regardless of the lenience unaccountably shown them.

Tired of wrestling with it, he decided against the cigarette in favor of a nap. He dreamt it was summer and he was at a lake, swimming. He hadn't been swimming in years but missed it, was good at it, had the body for it: slender but strong, loose-limbed as a seal.

But that wasn't all that had drawn him to it. Even as a child, he'd liked the solitude swimming afforded, just him and the water, alone in a world of water, the way it insulated a person from dry land and its complications. From other people and their demands. In his dream, the lake reflected diamonds in the sun. He was knifing through the water, blue water bright with diamonds. So beautiful, he couldn't remember anything so beautiful...

When loud as a gunshot, the door to the hut slammed. Leventhal snapped bolt upright to see a thirtyish bear of a man, a stranger, plunk two heavy brown bottles on the oak table.

"Okay, lads," he bellowed, "listen to me! The name's Kalniak, and I'm to be your kapo, or foreman. One last schnapps then we're off to do a little work. It's about time you lazy sods were earning your keep."

Without a word, as if awaiting this very order, the men pulled on their coats, and in anticipation of the cold each downed a shot before filing outside. The frosty air seized them by the nose, bit into them. The late-morning sky was a sheet of metal, its overcast sun shedding an aluminum light.

Quickly, they formed a column and headed out, two soldiers on either side of them. They sloshed after their kapo through the muddy snow without speaking. About to learn at last what the Germans had been saving them for, they were too nervous for talk.

Once past the main gate, where they were counted and the number recorded, they took a road toward a growth of trees from which billowed a wall of smoke. It was the same woods they'd seen from the unloading ramp four days ago. A murmur of relief rose from them—they'd been assigned to tend the fires burning the camp's garbage. That wasn't so bad a job. "At least we'll be warm," Leventhal overheard someone say.

The road turned into a snake upon entering the wood, winding this way and that through the trees. After half a mile, it emerged into a clearing occupied by a long, single-story wooden building. An SS lieutenant strode up and called the column to a halt. After conferring with the *Sturmmänn* in charge, he picked five prisoners to accompany him. As these set out for the barracks, Leventhal heard with his spotty German part of his orders to them: "Underwear in one pile, shoes in another, coats and all other garments in a third, *verstanden?*"

Through the hut's open double-doors, he saw clothes hanging from hooks the length of one wall, others strewn on the floor. But where were the people these belonged to? And why out here, in the woods, had they been made to shed them?

The answer to both questions lay down the road. Another clearing, another building, an arrowed sign nailed to a tree: zum Baden, to the baths. That explained it. Upon entering Birkenau, Leventhal had to undergo a shower and delousing himself. With so much flesh crammed into so small an area, pest-induced epidemics must have posed a constant threat.

The bathhouse, like the undressing barracks, was twice as long as it was wide, but instead of wood was built of brick and roofed with red tiles. It had no windows. A large door made of heavy wooden beams stood agape. An older *Scharführer* leaned next to it, his back against the brick, smoking. At their approach, he stood erect, and with a sweep of his arm invited those in front of the column to have a peek inside.

Leventhal was among these, but with the sun having pierced the clouds and the glare off the snow blinding, the doorway was an opaque black square cut in the brick. It took him a few seconds to adjust to the dark interior—and a few more to convince himself what he was seeing was real.

The room was filled with dead bodies from the floor to the ceiling, men, women, and children in a snarled, naked mass. Arms and legs were twined together as intricately as woody vines. From just inside the door, the open eyes of a girl seemed to be staring reproachfully into his, as if to say, "Look, look at me... I'm only *fourteen*."

With a cry, he stumbled backward, his terrified gaze falling on the *Scharführer*, who couldn't have been enjoying the moment more. He was grinning like a wolf, his eyes darting from man to man, feasting on the shock and bewilderment he found. After he'd got his fill, he waved their kapo over.

"You, Kalniak, listen up. I want *this* trash out here," he said, pointing to Leventhal and the others, "to take *that* trash in there around to the back where it belongs. And I want it done fast. Word is we're in for a busy goddamn day."

The next thing he knew, Leventhal was standing among corpses, the air in the death room sodden with the stench of excrement and vomit. He didn't know what to do. WHAT WERE THEY SUPPOSED TO DO? Some of the bodies lay helter-skelter on the floor, but most were piled in knotted heaps taller than he. He took a woman by the arms and pulled, but she remained stuck. He'd never touched a dead person before. The skin was wet, still warm...

When he woke, he was sitting with his back to the wall, the burly Kalniak bending over him.

"You've fainted, boy," the kapo said, "but you've got to get up. C'mon, up!" he repeated, tugging Leventhal to his feet. "They'll kill you if you don't."

The man hustled him to the door, made him take some deep breaths. "Good, that's better. Now let's to it," he said, pulling him back inside. "You've got to keep working or..." He drew a finger across his throat. "Don't look at their faces, it makes it a lot easier. It also helps to start at the top of the pile and work your way down. Got it?"

Leventhal nodded, and swallowing hard, was reaching up for a pair of ankles when he saw the showerheads hanging from the ceiling. Having already noticed the concrete floor dark with water, even puddled in places, he paused in mid-reach. Had these people been run through a shower after all? But why do that and then kill them? It didn't gibe.

"Quick, here comes the *Scharführer!*" Kalniak hissed. "Get to work!"

He grabbed the ankles and yanked the corpse down, its head hitting the floor with a crack. Someone else seized its wrists, and together they lugged it out the door. The Germans were waiting for them with curses and clubs, and off they sprinted in the direction they were driven, their grisly burden bouncing between them.

Leventhal tried not to look at his co-worker or the thing they were carrying, fixating instead on the back of the man running in front of them. His shame at being a participant in murder, even if it was only at gunpoint and after the fact, wasn't something he had any desire to see in another.

A fresh dreadfulness greeted them at the rear of the building. The room from which they'd come was only one of two apparently, for here a different contingent of wretches was dragging corpses out a second door and laying them on their backs. Hundreds stared unseeing into the sun as teams of prisoners moved among them, some cutting the hair off the heads of the females and shoving it into sacks, others using iron bars to pry open mouths. After a quick search, bloody pliers would start ripping out teeth.

Leventhal didn't get it, until told those were gold teeth they were dropping into their tin cans. Harder to watch yet, body cavities were being mined for loot as well, an indecency not even the children were spared.

A narrow metal track bordered the far edge of the yard, atop which stood a line of open trolleys. Still another commando worked this station, filling the lead car with bodies before pushing it into the trees. From behind these gushed the smoke.

He made over twenty trips from the death chamber, running both ways, too tired and stunned to think. But that might have saved him, for to dwell on what one was seeing, what one was doing, was to risk giving up and collapsing in despair into the snow. The path was littered with those who had done just that, their nightmare ended by an SS bullet to the head.

One thought, however, would not be silenced. How in God's name had the Nazi monsters done it, killed so many people, and with no blood? The only blood Leventhal could see on the bodies was the occasional trickle from noses and ears, and that oozing from various scratches and scrapes, as if those so stained had been in a fight. Many also had a peculiar bluish tint to their hands, feet, and faces, though for all he knew, their being naked, this was caused by the cold.

Then with a start, he remembered what their visitor Witek had told them.

Of course, what else could it be? Apart from explaining the absence of lethal wounds, gas—poison gas—was the ideal solution, not only effective and efficient but from where the SS stood, neatly in sync with their ideology. They'd always been loud in vilifying the Jews as parasites, vermin, and how better to get rid of vermin than to fumigate?

He was able to confirm this only after the room had been emptied and he was sent in as part of the crew to "clean it up for the next batch" as the *Scharführer* put it. This involved hosing the blood and excrement off the plaster walls, digging the fingernails out, spraying down the floor, and sweeping the offal out the door and along the path into a drain. Only then did Leventhal notice the blue pellets scattered at opposite ends of the room.

They lay in two patches up against the left and right walls, above each patch a narrow vent cut into the brick and plaster. It was simple to piece together how the deed had been done. The Germans had poured the pellets in through the vents, where they'd reacted with the air to produce the deadly gas. The showerheads were dummy, meant to deceive. As for the wetness he'd encountered before, later he would learn the bodies, too, were hosed down, moisture rendering the granules inert along with any remaining gas.

He was to discover many such things, unspeakable things. Why in their death struggles, for instance, the victims ended up in piles: the gas spread at ground level, then slowly rose. In their terror, their mindless panic, the people climbed atop each other to try and escape it, the strong crushing the weak beneath them. Judging from some of the injuries, the fighting had been fierce.

This and other revelations lay in Leventhal's future, not that at the time he imagined he had much of one. What were the odds of the SS allowing him and the others to go on breathing, they who were in on the Nazis' abominable secret? The only thing that could save them was if the Germans continued to need them, and that was going to require a steady supply of corpses. A ghoulish prospect, nor was this just a figure of speech. It hadn't taken them long to realize their survival, like that of the cannibalistic ghoul of myth, was dependent on the ready availability of dead flesh.

Once both chambers were ready, a squad of *Schützen* marched the men into the woods. Some feared this was it, that they were about to be shot, but their guards merely wanted them in their bloody clothing out of sight until they were needed again. One informed them the last of this transport was even now at the undressing barracks, and they'd better rest while they had the chance.

Leventhal lay on his back and studied the trees towering above him. It felt good to lie down, and not just because he was bone-tired. How easy, how inviting it would be to keep lying there after the order came to get back to work. It was no longer dying that frightened him, but living. Survival as what, a craven accessory to the slaughter of his own people? A future doing what—mopping up the gruesome messes of the blood-crazed SS?

Given what he knew, he was destined to die anyway, if not sooner then later. To do so today would forgo him much, as there could only be more horridness ahead.

That it would be easier, however, didn't make it right. Suicide wasn't an option, and never would be. As tempting as it was, he had an obligation to live, live and bear witness to a crime the Nazis were sure to try and cover up one day.

How he was supposed to accomplish either he had no idea, but of this he was positive, and had been from the moment the dead teen-aged girl's eyes had met his: whatever it took, however long it took, he wasn't about to let these murderers of children get away with it. Somehow, some way, he would tell the world what he'd seen, and the world, whether it wanted to or not, would have to listen.

The sky through the gaps in the treetops was busy with smoke. Leventhal watched it race from east to west like so many souls departing this earth. Before the war, he'd attended a *yeshiva* school in Warsaw. He knew his Bible and recalled it now, and the accursed valley of Gehenna, where during the reigns of the evil kings Azah and Masseneh the children of Israel were sacrificed then immolated on the altars of the pagan god Moloch. Now, incredibly, Gehenna burned again, somewhere out there at the end of the German trolley tracks.

He attempted to picture what such an inferno might look like, but mercifully blanking his brain, shut his eyes and tried not to think of anything at all.

*   *   *

From the top of the rise overlooking it, SS-*Oberscharführer* Otto Möll surveyed the meadow and smiled. It was a clumsy smile, unpracticed, but he was getting better at it; things were going so well for him, there'd been less call for his usual scowl.

Half of the snow-sprinkled meadow looked ablaze, though only three stacks of corpses were burning. Still, those were enough to make the sergeant happy. Möll cut a striking figure as he stood alone on the ridge. An inveterate poseur, he never missed the chance to appear as grandiose as possible. In truth, he felt he had to, seeing how removed he was physically from the Aryan ideal. Short, stocky, heavily freckled, with hair the color of wet sand and thinning rapidly at the age of twenty-eight, he didn't come close to the tall, blonde Viking archetype.

Offsetting this some, one of the beauties of the dashing SS uniform was its ability to make its wearer more imposing than the sum of his parts. Thus his habit of always decking himself out in full dress, every button and bar gleaming, leather buffed to a shine.

He also liked when possible to have his dog Hannibal at his side, a magnificent silver and black German Shepherd of formidable size and exquisite markings. The dog stood on the alert beside him now, the perfect accessory, though today the beast was trumped by an even more impressive embellishment to its master's person.

Formally presented to him just yesterday by none other than the camp commandant, *Obersturmbannführer* Rudolf Höss, Möll reached up and touched it as if to confirm he hadn't dreamed it. It was the *Kriegsverdienstkreuz*, the War Service Cross, one of the most coveted medals the Third Reich could bestow. The *Führer* himself had to authorize it, and only those soldiers who'd done something exceptional were considered. Now here it was for all to see, hanging improbably from a ribbon round the neck of an ex-ditchdigger from the German hinterland.

His gaze abruptly narrowed, the smile disappearing. What the bloody hell! Could those idiot Jews be screwing up again? One of the fire pits scarring the meadow wasn't burning properly, might even be sputtering out. Off he scurried down the hillock, Hannibal trotting ahead. He would show them what's what, the damned cow-headed kikes.

Möll's rise in the SS, if unmeteoric, had been steady. After serving a year and a half in two different concentration camps, first at Gusen, a subcamp in the Mauthausen system, then the larger Sachsenhausen outside of Berlin, he was promoted to *Unterscharführer* and in early 1941 assigned to the expanding Auschwitz complex in Poland. Before Hitler, his parents unable to afford an education for him, he'd had to make a living as a landscaper, hardly a reason for pride at the time but fortunate later as it ended up his ticket to Auschwitz, a posting he'd yearned for since hearing of the place. His foot in this new camp's door was as *Kommandoführer,* or SS supervisor, of its groundkeeping department.

But both his ambition and talents went far beyond that, a fact soon recognized by his superiors, who sought to put him to better use. By summer, he was in charge of the notorious penal commando, a punishment detail in which troublesome prisoners were prescribed half rations, the hardest labor, and the most sadistic kapos. As often as not, it ended up a death sentence.

Möll flourished in the role; here he invented the game of swim-frog. Numerous fishponds studded the area, a prime source of SS food. In swim-frog, prisoners were forced to paddle to the middle of one of these and remain there, treading water, croaking like frogs. Before long, they would tire and head for the shallows, where their guards would repulse them with pistol shots. It was only a matter of time before they started sinking and drowned. The sport, as the Germans saw it, was to keep them croaking to the end.

It wasn't only the inmates who were deathly afraid of Möll. His brother SS, too, particularly those who served under him, did their best to avoid him. He brooked no nonsense from either side; with a temper to match his gingery hair and ruddy complexion, he was a tiger to both. He only had one real eye, the other being glass, leading to the inevitable moniker "the Cyclops."

For almost a year, he was the terror of Block 11, that prison within a prison where the penal commando was quartered. But even this, his superiors realized, wasn't utilizing the man's potential to the fullest. By spring, with the completion of Birkenau, built to be the killing adjunct to Auschwitz, Hitler's Final Solution to Europe's Jewish problem had begun in earnest. Two confiscated Polish farmhouses were converted into provisional gas chambers, together able to snuff out two thousand people within minutes. Assisting them was the main camp's original crematorium, its morgue having been modified into a 700-person gas chamber.

These were as nothing, though, to what was coming, four permanent crematoria, enormous state-of-the-art killing machines capable of "processing" just under eleven thousand at a time. Even now the four were under construction, growing out of the soil of Birkenau like huge, sinister flowers, scheduled to assume full bloom any month now.

It was to be a glorious campaign against the *Rassenfiend*, the devil race, and Möll was determined to be in the thick of it. He'd lost his eye to a Jew, but that wasn't why he hated them. That had resulted from a simple car wreck, an accident, no one's fault really; the roads were iced over, the other driver happening to be Jewish. It would have been petty of Möll to bear his kind any animosity for that.

On the other hand, as everyone from the *Führer* on down knew, for a thousand years the Jew had been the mortal enemy of the German *Volk*. Recent history had confirmed this. The shameful armistice of 1918 to end the Great War; the humiliating Treaty of Versailles that followed; the divisive socialist republic shoved down German throats at Weimar; the runaway hyperinflation that had stolen what little wealth the young Möll's parents did have—all were the doing of the insidious global Jewish conspiracy, and for these and countless other crimes they deserved to be erased from the map of the new Europe.

An SS doctor had explained it to him quite concisely once, using an analogy from his trade. "The Jew," he'd said, "is the gangrenous appendix in the Aryan body politic. Cut out the appendix and the body will be healthy again."

Möll requested and received permission to transfer from Block 11 to the two gas chambers hidden among the groves of birch trees for which Birkenau was named. There he toiled for three months as transport after transport rolled in, until by August's end 110,000 of the Chosen People lay buried nearby.

This, however, came to pose a problem as unforeseen as it was unpalatable. Under the relentless beating of the summer sun, the ground these victims occupied began first to swell, then turn color from dirt-brown to an alarming dark red. A network of widening cracks surfaced, out of which was soon seeping a black evil-smelling sludge that not only stank for miles but threatened to contaminate the local groundwater. Chlorinated lime was spread but had no effect.

The Nazis decided to exhume the corpses and burn them. The first knot in this plan was that no one wanted the repugnant and technically difficult job of supervising such a mess—no one, that is, but a certain barrel-chested, one-eyed, strawberry-blond *Unterscharführer.* Hungry for acclaim, Möll jumped at the chance, and while others scoffed at his foolhardiness assembled a Sonderkommando of a hundred and fifty French Jews and went to work.

Not even the Cyclops was prepared for what awaited them below ground. The shovels hadn't gone a foot down when an odor gushered forth that knocked the Frenchmen to their knees. There most would remain for some minutes gagging loudly, along with many of the SS, who temporarily themselves were in no condition to bully them back to their feet. It was a smell the senses weren't built to withstand, incapacitating both slave and slave driver alike.

When the digging did resume, it didn't take long to reach the appalling stink's source. Another foot into the soil and the bodies began to show, blue-black, disintegrating, crawling with worms, stacked in descending layers how deep no one knew. As much as

Möll despised all inmates, in particular that social virus, that racial parasite the Jew, one glance into those months-old mass graves elicited a sort of sympathy from even him. How did they manage to keep going, he wondered, those down there in the muck, up to their ankles in corpse soup, their clothing, their skin, their faces smeared with it?

That first day, thirty of them were shot for refusing to work, and had to be replaced. Möll, his inchoate sympathy aside, would have liked to make a better example of the thirty than simply shooting them, but time wouldn't permit.

The second part of the operation, too, went far from smoothly at first. His orders were to cremate the corpses on tall, wooden pyres, but this had presented problems. These tended to burn unevenly and too fast, leaving a portion of the dead intact.

His idea, his brainstorm, was to concentrate the fire by partially submerging it in a long, rectangular open pit. After a few days' trial and error, he found that an excavation two meters deep and eight wide burned the hottest and longest. By arranging the bodies in tiers between layers of kindling, and setting the length at forty meters, twelve hundred could be disposed of in less than six hours, including the removal of the ashes.

By the middle of October, to the delight of those who'd given it to him, the job was completed, Möll's final order being the liquidation of the entire Sonderkommando involved. Then came the Kriegsverdienstkreuz and his almost as startling promotion two full grades to the rank of *Oberscharführer.* He was reassigned to the groves of white birch, this time as director of the new open-air incineration program.

Möll could see what was wrong with the fire pit in the meadow before even reaching it. Although the stokers continued to work it with their long, iron pitchforks, those supposed to be ladling the kerosene onto the problem areas of the fire lay sprawled in the snow, scoops at their sides.

"What the Christ are you fucks doing?" he roared. He had not only Hannibal now but several *Schützen* in tow. "Why aren't you feeding that fire?"

Everyone sprang to attention, the stokers dropping their forks. No one dared speak.

"*Answer me!*" Möll screamed, his color approaching that of the coals in the pit.

"*Herr Oberscharführer,*" one said finally, his voice frail, "we ran out of fuel. Kapo Bronski went to get more."

"And when was that?" he demanded, pacing furiously in front of them.

"Half an hour ago, Herr *Oberscharführer.* We—"

"Half an *hour?*" Möll ceased pacing and wheeled on his audience of soldiers. "Find this Bronski," he ordered, "and bring him to me. On the double!"

They were back in minutes, with the kapo and the kerosene. "He was with a woman, sir," one of them reported, "in the shed back of the fuel dump."

"Oh, he was, was he." Möll unexpectedly broke into a smile. He circled the kapo slowly, hands clasped behind him. "Is that true, Kapo Bronski? Were you with a woman?"

"Y-yes, sir," the man answered in competent if quaking German. "But we were just talking, I—I swear. And I lost track of—"

"Just talking, you say. My, how virtuous of you." Möll stood in front of him, not a foot away. "And in the course of this… conversation, you lost track of the time. Quite understandable. It could happen to anybody.

"But what about my fire? It's not faring very well, and as you can see, the sausages aren't done yet. How do you propose we get it going again? What type of combustible would you suggest we use?"

The kapo's eyes bulged with fright. "Why, the kerosene, sir. It's—it's what we always use."

"Ah, yes, the kerosene. The same kerosene that should have been here half an hour ago. I have a better idea, though, an even more fitting way to revive it. And you can help me with that, Bronski." He turned to the guards. "Seize him."

Two of them took hold of the kapo and followed their sergeant to the edge of the fire pit. "*Whew!*" Möll said, shying from the heat. "It's a bit warm over here, isn't it? And about to get warmer—for you anyway, kapo."

He looked at the soldiers and jerked his head toward the fire. Within seconds, they'd pummeled their victim to the ground, grabbed him by the arms and legs, and flung him into the middle of the smoldering pit.

He tried to scramble out, but quickly sank to his waist in the glowing coals and began screaming. Thrashing wildly about, he was soon knocking charred wood and body parts everywhere. With a curse, Möll drew his revolver and put an end to the kapo's agony. He'd wanted it to last longer, but the man was in danger of busting up that whole part of the pyre.

For all of its functionality, the concept of the incineration pit did come with one drawback. With two meters of the fire below ground it restricted the flow of oxygen, a situation exacerbated after it began to settle. Constant stoking helped, but one needed chemicals to keep the thing burning. These worked, but were expensive. With the hostilities in Russia beginning to tax reserves, methanol, kerosene, and especially gasoline weren't only costly but difficult to locate at any price.

Möll had in theory arrived at a possible solution. He'd observed that as the corpses twisted and sizzled in the fire, they exuded a considerable amount of liquid fat. This did nourish the flames some, but too much was lost in the ground to make a difference. Now if this bounty of sufficiently volatile fluid could be harvested before draining away, then *ipso facto* dilemma solved, and less the need for synthetic fuels.

He didn't lack for ideas on how to implement his theory, but realistically speaking, was it worth the trouble at this stage to try and fix things? The four Birkenau crematoria, with their forty-odd ovens, were promised at the latest by January. Why bother perfecting the fire pit with that many cast-iron ovens on the horizon, designed and manufactured specifically for cremation? These would doubtless be able to take care of the bulk of any Jews the SS were likely to get their hands on.

The new *Oberscharführer*, therefore, chose not to vex himself with the problem. The present methodology was good as it was. Instead, he devoted what time he could to basking in not only his recent triumphs but the satisfactions of the job at hand, content in the knowledge he was doing something important with his life. More than important: earthshaking, historic. Something men would remember, would marvel at for centuries.

Jewish lore held that in the days of Moses and the Egyptian captivity, their God unleashed a final plague to break pharaoh's will. This plague swept the land in the form of the merciless Angel of Death, its mission to kill every first-born Egyptian male. The Israelites called this frightful entity *Mal'ach H'Mavet*.

Möll's fantasy, his conceit—or as he would have it, his destiny—was to be a latter-day Mal'ach H'Mavet, except in reverse, with the Jews at not only their fickle Jehovah's mercy but his. Whenever he indulged himself thus, he had to chuckle at the irony of it: he, Otto Möll, an agent of the Hebrew God! On the surface, a notion so cockeyed as to be laughable, yet incongruous enough to seem somehow, if perversely, almost plausible.

The great thing, the truly wonderful thing, the thing that got his adrenaline going whenever he thought about it, was the fact—he'd done the math while still at the bunkers—the fact there were eleven million Jews trapped within the current borders of the Reich.

Apart form his duty as a soldier to protect his country from its enemies, if that wasn't the career opportunity of a lifetime, he didn't know what was.

1943

Winter

There'd been a break in the weather going on three days now. Long enough that people were grateful for it, but at the same time dreading its end. Then again, in January, in this part of the world, even one day with the thermometer struggling past forty—with no ice and no wind, no flying needles of snow—was like a gift from heaven. Noah Zabludowicz scanned that heaven for some hint of change, an opening or other irregularity in the featureless gray overcast.

To his relief there was none. It was as if a great bowl had been inverted and placed atop their little swath of countryside, shielding them from the storms raging on the other side of it.

The closer he and his crew got to Block 16, the more nervous Noah. This was the most dangerous part of the operation. Should the wrong people see them sneaking into the barracks, they'd have some questions to answer—only they didn't have any answers, or none the SS would have found satisfactory. Oddly, one seldom ran across the Germans inside the camp, though it paid to stay vigilant. Overconfidence could get a body killed as quickly as anything.

This evening, the way was clear. Two pairs of men carrying four kettles of soup slung from poles on their shoulders slipped through the back door of #16 and set their load down. Today, as every day, there the four pots would sit until the residents of the hut returned from their day's work. The *Blockälteste*, or barracks elder, and his assistants were bribed.

All but a few of the prisoners quartered here were from Ciechanow, and thanks to Noah's audaciousness had been enjoying double rations for a month now. It was only *lagersuppe* to be sure, mainly turnips and cabbage, the color and consistency of dirty dishwater but food nonetheless, and as such precious beyond price.

Not that his friends and ex-neighbors were the only beneficiaries of Noah's largesse. He was also running a ring that distributed stolen food to the starving. Some of the inmates had taken to calling him the Messiah of Bread.

As resourceful as he was, he'd also been blessed. After three weeks of quarantine, he and his brother Hanan were sent down the road to the *Stammlager*, or main camp (Pinchas was kept in Birkenau, where electricians were needed), and ended up in the Bauhof *Kommando* pouring cement. The work was hard and outdoors, the weather bitter cold, and to make matters worse, their kapo a particularly brutal one.

Most kapos of the regular labor gangs weren't only German and Polish criminals but the most depraved those country's penal systems had to offer. Nor was this by accident. The SS required a daily attrition rate among their slaves of twenty percent more or less, how the kapo went about this was his or her business.

Noah's and Hanan's, an ex-boxer imprisoned for loan sharking, practiced an assortment of methods, but his favorite was to throw someone who'd displeased him to the ground, place the heavy cane he carried across the man's throat, then stand on it and rock back and forth until the neck was a pulpy mess. It was normal for a three-hundred-man squad of the Bauhof to go to work in the morning, and two hundred and fifty return at night bearing the bodies of their dead.

On one of those nights, after lights-out, the men from Noah's block were rousted from their bunks and run through a selection, common during the day but rare after sundown. Fifteen were singled out, including the two brothers, and told not to report to their work details tomorrow. This didn't bode well for them and they knew it. Few were to sleep much afterward, their thoughts unable to stray for long from the all too nearby crematorium.

In the morning, their fears proved unfounded. After the others were marched off to work as usual to the rousing strains of the camp orchestra, the fifteen were taken to Block 25, where the barracks elder informed them they were to be his new *Stubendiensten*, the old ones having been transferred to the subcamp at Jawischowitz.

A Stubendienst was a low-level aide to the elder, responsible for keeping the hut clean, bringing food and supplies, lice control, security, and related duties. Most barracks employed two or three of these at most, as both the place and the prisoners were meant to stay filthy and under-provisioned.

Block 25, however, was one of two that housed the camp *Prominenz*, or prominents, the cooks, doctors, tradesmen, clerks, and other prisoner-functionaries without whom no lager could operate. Theirs was more dormitory than hut, as furnished for comfort as it was scrubbed, with its own bathroom and showers, a wood floor instead of dirt, one person to a bunk rather than the customary several. And what bunks they were! With sheets, pillows, mold-free blankets, real mattresses, not the shapeless sacks of straw most prisoners had to contend with, so thin it was as if one was sleeping on the wooden slats beneath.

It was easy to spot a prominent. He might be wearing the standard striped burlap, but cut to fit and always laundered. He would also have proper shoes, not the ill-fitting, blister-causing clogs issued the ordinary inmate. The men of Block 25 enjoyed many such luxuries, so many it took fifteen Stubendiensten to attend to them.

One chore, though, was never demanded of these, the fetching of the hut's daily ration of soup. The soup wasn't needed. Such was the power and wealth of the Prominenz, they were able to buy their own food, either on the black market or from the SS. Spoils filched from the living and dead, a diamond ring, a gold tooth, could go far in that respect.

Thus were Noah and Hanan delivered from the cement commando and its lethal kapo, but this wasn't to be their only piece of luck. Their second day on the job, one of the prominents came up behind Noah and wrapped him in a bear hug. He, thinking it an attack, broke free.

"What—you don't recognize me?" the man said, laughing. "I'm your pal Witek from Danzig, the same Witek who owes you his life, Noah Zabludowicz. And as long as it's been, I haven't forgot my debt."

As Noah was to learn, luck had nothing to do with getting him and Hanan out of the Bauhof. Witek, having asked around, traced them to Block 16, and paid his block elder to recruit his new Stubendiensten from there. Part of the deal was that the Zabludowicz brothers be on the list.

Noah couldn't believe his good fortune. To find this man of all men in Auschwitz, and a prominent no less! Five years ago their lives had crossed, or was it five hundred? He was in Danzig dropping off a truckload of steel parts for the Silvers. It was a gray March morning, a nasty fog slinking the streets. From the unloading dock, he saw a man entering the near intersection. He only noticed him because the fool was happily walking along with his head buried in a newspaper, oblivious to the garbage truck barreling down on him. Nor because of the fog did the driver appear to see him.

Noah, being Noah, didn't hesitate. Springing from the dock, he dashed in front of the truck, and with a flying leap slammed the man out of harm's way. But the bumper just caught Noah's lower leg, and it was the emergency room for him.

The simplest of fractures, nothing to make a fuss over, but Witek was right there and effusive in his gratitude. He visited his rescuer both days he was in the hospital, paid his medical bills, and after that—every birthday, every Hanukkah for three years—kept paying, sometimes with presents but more often cash, delivered in the mail to his apartment in Ciechanow.

Then one day the gifts stopped, and Noah figured that was that. He was fine with this, too, seeing as he hadn't asked for anything in the first place. Not until Block 25 did he discover why they'd quit coming. In 1940, the Gestapo arrested Witek for dealing in smuggled goods and sentenced him to what was then the brand-new Auschwitz camp, where he not only survived conditions even harsher than today's but prospered. Within a year, he'd finagled his way into the camp kitchen, where he was working as a cook when he tracked the brothers down.

Now to know a *cook* at Auschwitz was an advantage not to be underestimated. To know a cook meant life, though Noah wasn't so crass as to be concerned for himself only. He soon made a deal with Witek for the disposal of "excess" food, and from here his reputation as the Messiah of Bread began.

Every day, he and three others would go to the kitchen and pick up the soup ration for Block 25, but take it instead to the Ciechanow hut. In addition, twice a week he'd make off with a princely quantity of bread, a good half a large cartful. Bread served a dual function at Auschwitz, both as food and the camp's most popular unit of currency. Everything from shoelaces to sex could be purchased with bread.

But Noah wasn't out to enrich himself any more than he was to save just himself. Instead, he and his confederates would speed their windfall from the kitchen to some predetermined hiding place, different each week, from where it was passed to those in direst need of it, that caste of prisoners known in camp jargon as the *Muselmänner*, or Moslems.

They were called this because of their resemblance to the famished beggars of Calcutta, and were the rule in Auschwitz rather than the exception, especially among the Jews. They were those who'd given up, who no longer cared, no longer hoped, no longer thought much if at all, those so debased by overwork and hunger they seemed to substantiate the Nazi belief the Jew wasn't fully human.

A man performing even moderate physical labor required four thousand calories a day; the ration for Jews at Auschwitz-Birkenau was eight or nine hundred, often less. This was the total calculated to keep a prisoner alive and working for three months, which from an economic perspective was quite sufficient for the SS.

The Muselmänn was as painful to scrutinize as contemplate. Open sores broke out all over him. The lack of albumin and other proteins deprived him of all energy; it was an effort for him to walk, even roll out of his bunk. His eyesight and hearing deteriorated, as did his mental faculties; confusion, loss of memory, and a general apathy are symptoms of a shortage of vitamin B. Slow in comprehending orders, he was beaten hard and often for what was mistaken as defiance. The eyes were empty, the face expressionless, the brain fixated on two things: how to avoid further beatings... and food, always food, all he talked about was food and how and where he might find more.

Crawling with lice, unsteady afoot, his body and uniform indescribably filthy, he shambled about like something out of a horror movie, a constant discharge leaking from his nose, the *Durchfall,* or starvation-induced diarrhea, from another aperture. Once he'd reached that point, the game was all but up. Once the Durchfall arrived, the gas chamber wasn't far behind.

Noah, too, had known hunger. Before they could be admitted to either Auschwitz or Birkenau proper, all prisoners had to spend a month or so in quarantine. Also called the visa, this was a sort of boot camp to train them in the grim realities of their new lives. The word visa came from the Latin verb *visere*, to investigate, which was what Q-Camp was for: to determine if the choices the SS doctors had made on the unloading ramp were correct, and those not put on the trucks did have the strength to serve out what life was left them as slaves of the Reich.

There was no work in quarantine, so the rations were poor. The dreaded nettle soup was common, a noisome concoction of milky fluid bubbling in its cauldron. Orange rings of margarine floated on the surface, at the bottom fibrous stalks of chopped nettles and other weeds that not only looked inedible but smelled worse. Nor was the "bread" any better, a crumbly mess fashioned largely of wild chestnuts and sawdust.

Death by malnutrition is one of the more agonizing. Essentially, it comes from the body feeding on itself, first its reserves of fat, then muscle and other tissue. In Q-Camp, Noah had felt this very hunger, not that of a missed meal or even a day or two of meals, but a silent and continuous scream from the body, a tortured cry every waking minute from every slowly dying cell, a demand that never ceased nor gave surcease from pain. It was the hunger that in its terrible, self-predatory alchemy transformed men into obscenities, into something not men.

He still wasn't sure how he and his brothers made it out of the visa alive. They'd entered it that first day after leaving the ramp, their hair on body and head having been clipped to curb lice, issued the repulsive rags and impossible clogs supposed to serve as their only clothing. Around midnight, as they lay part of a comfortless five in their box-like *koje*, or bunk, their cover a single blanket fetid with mold and urine, they were awakened with shouts and blows and driven outside into the freezing yard.

It was their first *Appell*, or roll call, and only in Q-Camp was it done at night. They were out there a full hour, during which their kapo and his assistants, after lining them up in rows, stalked these with jeers and clubs, lashing out at their whim.

They would endure another Appell at dawn, and another at sundown. Sandwiched between was a typical day in quarantine.

Breakfast was a cold half-liter of something optimistically called coffee. Then it was off to the latrine, a few planks thrown across a ditch. Crouched perilously on these, often so jammed together they couldn't help soiling each other, the prisoners had less than a minute to do their business, without so much as a scrap of paper to clean themselves.

After that it was back to the *Appellplatz*, not for counting but drill. Here they were taught how to march with the proper precision, moving as one in tight formation, backs rigid, heads high. Hours were devoted to training them in how to remove their cloth caps in unison, the kapos not satisfied until their arms slapping the shapeless things to their sides produced a single, sharp crack. The inmate slow to learn this, or who had trouble keeping cadence when marching, or maybe the kapo just didn't like the cut of his jib, was beaten. To death, as often as not.

The activity known as *sport* was a staple of the visa. A kapo would pick ten or twenty prisoners, on occasion at random but usually those who'd wound up on his bad side, and run them through a rapid-fire series of exercises, he and his henchmen raining blows on them throughout. "On the ground! Now get up! Run! On the ground again! Crawl forward! Up again, on the double! Jump!"

After ten minutes of this, men would begin dropping from exhaustion, and if unable to continue bludgeoned to death where they'd fallen. Sometimes the kapo would leave one or two of them alive, sometimes he wouldn't.

Another tradition was "the 25," a disciplinary measure considered comparatively light, practiced not just in quarantine but camp-wide. The transgressor was made to drop his pants and lie on his stomach across a bench, baring his buttocks and thighs. Twenty-five blows were then administered using a heavy wooden club sawed in half lengthwise, the recipient forced to count each wallop aloud. If he missed one or confused the count, his assailant had the option of starting over again.

The man punished thus often had trouble walking, much less marching to his kapo's standards. Or the skin having ruptured and become infected, it was off to the gas chamber for him, the cure for just about every malady at Birkenau.

There were a hundred ways to die in both Q-Camp and beyond, but somehow Noah and Hanan—and as far as they knew, Pinchas— were among the living still. Not so their younger brother, poor innocent little Mendel, nor their just as innocent parents, nor any who'd ridden those trucks into the woods that first day. Few had believed it when told their families were dead, but quickly the truth sank in, there could be no denying it, and in short order they came to know not only when and where the killings had occurred but how.

He would discover his sister Deborah was gone, too, a victim of the great Hanukkah selection of December 5th, one of two thousand women from Birkenau's female lagers alone trucked naked to the gas. The Germans tried whenever possible to coincide such actions with the bigger Jewish holidays, a practice born of the same sneering cynicism written in steel atop the main gates into both Auschwitz and Birkenau: "*Arbeit macht frei*, Work will make you free." And so it would—free of this world, of one's body, one's life. Work here, as the Nazis enforced it, was designed to kill.

But with Witek, Noah had been fortunate. Most were who'd made it as long as he had without becoming Muselmänner. Again, though, it was more than about saving himself or, truth be told, anyone else. He wanted, as he always had—in the ghetto, before the ghetto, before the war—to fight back, to punish those who persecuted him and his. He hadn't made his deal with Witek out of philanthropy alone. The stealing (or as he preferred, the redirection) of food was also an act of resistance, a subversion of the bestial *Disziplin* the despotic SS had established in this little kingdom of theirs between the Sola and Vistula Rivers.

Yet he ached to do more, to take his subversion a step further, and to that end began making inquiries to those he thought could be trusted. There was talk, vague, circumspect, and maddeningly bereft of details, of a secret organization within the camp that worked in opposition to the Nazis. No one could tell him the name of a single member of this outfit or how it operated, but the mere suspicion it existed was a boost to the morale of many.

Many, sadly, but not all. Which was why Noah had to be careful whom he approached about it. An informer could be bought for a loaf of bread, or a kapo or other functionary be more than eager to rat a man out if it ingratiated himself with his German masters. Caution, however, was getting him nowhere. Not even the veteran Witek could help him, had warned, in fact, it might be in his best interest not to snoop around.

Then just this evening, after the four clandestine urns of soup had been disposed of, the prisoner Erich Kulka—also from Ciechanow, though Noah knew him only in passing—wandered into Block 25, and after they'd exchanged pleasantries told him a certain Bruno Baum wished to meet with him.

"Tomorrow, 9:00 a.m.," Kulka said, "at *Ka-Be's* Block 20," handing him a pass in case the SS stopped him.

Noah had heard of Bruno Baum. He was an important personage in the camp, a Marxist *and* a Jew, but despite this dual liability, kapo of one of the convalescent wards in the inmate hospital complex, the *Krankenbau*, or Ka-Be.

Baum's fame as a writer and politico under the Weimar Republic had preceded him. Among other distinctions, he'd served in the German *Reichstag* as a member of the Communist delegation. Noah couldn't imagine what he'd done to attract the attention of such a luminary, unless it was Block 16 and the soup scam he was conducting. Had he run afoul of some kind of protocol regarding such things? Was today's delivery to be his last, or almost as bad, its frequency reduced?

He would have something to say about that, but knew, too, if push should come to shove, he was in no position to defy the Prominenz.

A cheerful Kulka met him at the appointed hut the next morning and led him inside. A prisoner he guessed to be in his mid-forties sat at a desk in a small, bare room poring over a stack of papers. Even sitting, one could tell he wasn't a tall man. Every part of him seemed slightly miniaturized, his ears, his nose, his hands, arms slender as a woman's. Like Kulka, he wore the starched stripes of a prominent, nor was his scalp shorn like a sheep's pelt, but shaved fashionably to the skin with a razor. The eyes below it were tired—no, sorrowful was the better word, as if weighted down with grief, with all the woes of the world.

"Noah Zabludowicz, Bruno Baum. Bruno Baum, Noah Zabludowicz," Kulka said, shutting the door on his way out.

Baum rose and shook his hand, offered him a seat. Noah got right to the point. After mulling it over all night, he'd decided the best defense was a good offense.

"Listen, Herr Baum, I'm not sure why you wanted to see me, but I've got an idea it's something to do with the men in Block 16 and the double rations they've been enjoying. Now, I want you to know I wasn't trying to step on any toes. The last thing I'm in the market for is trouble, and if I'm going about it the wrong way—meaning the extra soup—I'd want you to tell me.

"But those are my friends in that hut, my townsmen... my *landsmanschaft* as we say in Yiddish, and it's going to take a lot to convince me to quit doing my damnedest to help them."

Something almost a smile flitted across the older man's face. "I see," he said, picking up a pencil and twirling it slowly between his fingers. What followed wasn't only in a more than serviceable Polish but a deep, velvety bass that belied its speaker's build.

"Fortunately, my dear Zabludowicz, in view of your obvious determination, that is not why you are here. We know all about Block 16, and your bread program, but these are your affairs, not ours. Still, we do find your—how do you say it? Your initiative to be commendable.

"And that *is* why you are here, because we feel you can be of help to us. That and the fact you have been trying hard, and most carelessly I might add, to reach us."

"Us?" asked Noah not a little sheepishly at having jumped to the wrong conclusion.

"The underground, Battle Group-Auschwitz... the international resistance movement here and in Birkenau, working in concert with the *Armia Krajowa*, the Polish Home Army. We are the people you have been searching for, and look forward to you joining us in our fight against the SS butchers."

So it was true, there *was* an underground! And from the sound of it a formidable one. Though this was the last thing he'd seen coming, Noah didn't hesitate. "Sir," he said, sitting higher in his chair, "consider me at your service when and wherever you need me."

Baum nodded once, then got right to business. "I will be your only contact, at least at first. The fewer operatives you know, the better, both for them and you. Do not write down what I tell you, ever—memorize it instead. You will soon be transferred to a commando that goes to Birkenau every day, where your mission will be twofold. Are you aware of what the Germans are building in Birkenau?"

"A new crematorium, or that's the rumor anyway."

"Four new crematoria, each several times larger than the small one here. The SS have... ambitions that curdle the blood. When those factories of death are finished, which will not be long now, you are to establish contact with a kapo of the Sonderkommando and report to us daily on how many transports of Jews are arriving, with how many aboard, and how many of these are being gassed. I will give you the name of the kapo when we are ready for you. Any questions, Zabludowicz?"

Noah shook his head, though it did surprise him that any of the Sonderkommando should be part of the resistance. He'd assumed since learning of them that they were the vilest of collaborators, willing to work hand in murderous hand with the Germans.

"The second part of your assignment," Baum continued. "is more immediate. There is an ammunition manufactory, formerly a subsidiary of Krupp, located not far from here. The Weichsel-Union *Metallwerke* employs slave labor of both sexes. Of interest to us is the room where the gunpowder is stored, apportioned out, and injected into the detonators of the bombs and shells. This room is staffed by female prisoners only.

"As you may have surmised over the years, the Nazis are embarrassingly provincial in their attitude toward women. To them, the so-called gentler sex lacks both the gumption and animal cunning to engage in sabotage or any serious mischief. When they do transgress, it is only because they have been led astray by men. This is why, not counting the German *Meister* in charge of it, the SS allow only women, and precious few of them, anywhere near their gunpowder. And why they are strict about keeping those few segregated from the male population.

"We want that gunpowder, Zabludowicz, we need it—you will be told why later—but we cannot get to the women handling it. Two of our agents have been trying for weeks, but have yet to come close. You, however... You came on a rather large transport, did you not?"

"From Ciechanow, yes."

"Perhaps you know of a woman from that same transport and now in Birkenau who would be willing—and smart enough, and above all, brave enough—to establish a cell in the Union *Pulverraum* and oversee the regular delivery of some of its inventory to us."

Noah almost jumped from his seat. "I do know such a person, yes! The perfect person, if she's still alive. She's an... an old friend, and even if she isn't in a position to help, I can't tell you what it would mean for me to find her. My brother, too, holy God! How much freedom would I have in Birkenau?"

"As much as you require. That can be arranged. But first, I must ask you this." Baum measured him through half-closed eyes, like an artist a model. "Can this person, this woman, this friend of yours be trusted? More than you can imagine is riding on this remaining a secret."

"Trusted? I'd stake my life on it, and those of my brothers. And if I may, Herr Baum, yours, sir, as well. I must get to Birkenau. When can I go to Birkenau?"

Later, Baum requested a meeting for that evening with his superior in the underground, its recognized leader Josef Cyrankiewicz. They scheduled it for the latter's hut, as private a place as any, for he was Blockälteste of the barracks and had his own room at one end of it. Baum knew this room well. A large hardwood table took up a quarter of it, its polished rectangle bordered by six matching high-backed chairs. The only elegant piece of furniture Cyrankiewicz allowed himself, the rest was a hodgepodge of battered pieces. He did have a small kitchen, though, and an even tinier bathroom. Such were the privileges accorded a block elder.

He found his chief sitting at the familiar table, head in hands, lost in thought. A single lamp bathed the room in a dim light. So powerful was the prisoner Cyrankiewicz, and long the reach of his Battle Group-Auschwitz, he also commanded the Home Army, issuing his orders to the partisans outside the wire via those working undercover as civilian laborers inside it. The SS were harboring their most-wanted nemesis in their midst and didn't know it.

"Hello, Bruno," he said, rising to shake his visitor's hand. He was a large man, over six feet tall, with the flattened nose and square, jutting jaw of a prizefighter. Baum's hand in his was a child's. "What was it you wanted to see me about?"

Baum took a seat. "I recruited that Zabludowicz fellow today. Can see him being a good man for us."

"How so?" Cyrankiewicz said. "Would you care for some hot tea?"

"Thank you, sir, no. Well, for one, there is a possibility he could be of use right away. He might have a contact who can help us crack the Union gunpowder room."

"Ah, that again, hard-headed Bruno's beloved gunpowder. I thought we decided last week we weren't going to be needing it after all."

"Pardon me, sir, but nothing was decided. If you recall, I disagreed most strongly with the Steering Committee's recommendation, and the matter was put on hold. And I still disagree. I believe it imperative we have the gunpowder on hand should the situation arise in which it becomes necessary."

"That situation, I suppose, being the general uprising you've been pushing. Followed, correct me if I'm wrong, by a mass escape."

Baum's silence spoke for itself.

Cyrankiewicz got up from his chair and made for the one window, where he himself stood silent for a long half-minute staring into the blackness. No moon shone that night, but every few seconds the white sweep of a searchlight lit his form.

"Are you aware," he said finally, "that just this morning the city of Stalingrad fell to its rightful owners? Field Marshal von Paulus and the entire German Sixth Army are in Soviet hands."

"Great news," Baum said, "but not unexpected. The Sixth Army has been surrounded and cut off for weeks now."

Cyrankiewicz returned to the table, but remained standing. "I suspect this might be a turning point in the war. The Wehrmacht is not only reeling but depleted, perhaps irreparably. Soon it will be the Russians who are on the offensive, and Herr Hitler isn't going to have the men and matériel to stop them. All of which makes your notion of an armed uprising less attractive. Better to wait for liberation than risk a slaughter trying to make a run for it."

"Better for whom?" Baum shot back. "The walking dead of the Sonderkommando? The tens of thousands of Jews here and in Birkenau? Only a fool would see the SS leaving a single one of them alive."

"The Sonder, Bruno, are what—a few hundred men at most? And the Jews, despite their numbers, but a percentage of the inmates. We're responsible, remember, for the safety of *all* the prisoners, and I hardly think an attempt at a mass breakout would be honoring that responsibility. Do you realize how many could die in such a venture, not to mention from the reprisals likely to be leveled against the rest of us?"

"But what of the Möll Plan, commander? Our intelligence has confirmed not only its existence but that the SS have adopted it as official policy."

Cyrankiewicz fell back in his seat with a sigh. "*Oberscharführer* Otto Möll... the man's starting to make quite a name for himself, isn't he? Frankly, I'm puzzled the Germans would sign off on such a plan. How does it read again?"

In response to a request from the camp administration about what to do with the inmates in the event the Red Army ever draw near, First Sergeant Möll had submitted his idea, which to the surprise of him and others was accepted. What won it this honor, aside from its ruthlessness, was the attention to detail he'd put into it: the logistics, the numbers, the coordination and timing, exactly how the thing could be done and by whom.

Both Auschwitz and Birkenau, Baum informed his boss, were to be surrounded by tanks and artillery, and with the help of bombers from above pounded into rubble. The infantry would go in after to dispose of any survivors.

"Really, Bruno, doesn't that strike you as something of a reach? I wonder that you even bring it up; I'd have sworn we resolved that last week as well. Among its other hitches, with the Russians having fought their way this far into the Reich, would the Wehrmacht and *Luftwaffe* have that many tanks, guns, and bombers to spare? I don't see it, and more than one of your brother officers is with me on that."

It was Baum's turn to sigh. "I must admit, it does want logic, but still feel it unwise to discount it entirely. For argument's sake, say we drop it for now, as long as you give me your take on Mexico instead. Please, if you will, explain Mexico to me."

Cyrankiewicz didn't follow. "Mexico?"

Baum had been careful not to bring this up last week, saving it, as the Americans would say, as his ace in the hole.

"That is what the prisoners have taken to calling the tenth and newest lager in Birkenau, still under construction but due to the crowding in the other nine, inhabited all the same. Conditions there are catastrophic. No electricity, no water, a good part of the huts without roofs yet. So regular are the transports becoming, while two-thirds of their cargoes are being sent straight from the ramp to the birch groves, they are being admitted into Birkenau in such numbers as to make its landlords uneasy.

"Forget quarantine—a lot of these new arrivals are going directly to Mexico, where they are living in the open, blankets their only protection against the elements. Hence the name of that tragic place; those condemned to it resemble nothing so much as Mexican Indians bundled in their serapes."

"I'm all too mindful," Cyrankiewicz said, his irritation plain, "of the disaster brewing in the *B3* lager. I've just never heard it called Mexico of all things."

"My point, sir, is this. *B3*, when finished, will be as large as the other nine lagers combined. Even if the transports were to double, that would still be larger than needed. But they are not going to double, they cannot, there are not enough hours in the day to process that many, even with four crematoria."

Baum edged forward in his chair. "For whom then are the Nazis building this huge new annex of hell? And why, as intelligence has also established, have they drawn up the blueprints for four *more* crematoria, which would bring the total to a mind-numbing nine?"

Cyrankiewicz knew of these blueprints, but had believed them no more than empty Nazi hubris. In fact, as derelict as he felt about it now, he'd forgot all about them.

"The answer," Baum said without waiting for one, "is as unavoidable as it is horrifying. Apparently, Hitler has plans beyond the eradication of the Jews. Once they are no more, it will come the turn of others, the Poles, the Czechs, the Russians, maybe the Slavs as a whole, all the 'inferior' peoples polluting his Greater German empire. It is a mad dream, a nightmare, but what is Hitler if not a madman? There are no lengths to which he would not go to secure his Thousand Year Reich.

"Nor should one assume the arrival of the Red Army an inevitability. A total defeat of the Nazis could be seen as unrealistic as total victory for them now. The Wehrmacht, don't kid yourself, is still a power, could easily dig in and hold, the lines stabilize, become static as they did in the last war. Leaving the SS free to enjoy their new and expanded Birkenau, and us with as little, perhaps even less a reasonable chance at escape. What good would our procrastinating have done us then?"

"So what are you proposing?" asked Cyrankiewicz. "That we resign ourselves to the Soviets not coming anytime soon, maybe never, and going through with our plans, unpromising as they are, blow up the cremos and make a mad dash for it?"

"Uh, not *we* exactly, general. Not we at all. I have been thinking more and more of late that a double breakout might not be the way to proceed. Auschwitz is two miles from Birkenau; an uprising in both places would be all but impossible to coordinate, and the Home Army, whose assistance I need not tell you is vital to its success, would be spread so thin as to endanger the entire operation. And what of Auschwitz III, Monowitz, where Siemens Electric, Bayer Pharmaceutical, I.G. Farben and others have factories working twenty thousand slave laborers to death? How would we go about extricating them?"

Suddenly, the staccato pop of gunfire shattered the still of the night, like a string of firecrackers going off. Then another string, then quiet. Baum paused to verify it nothing before picking up where he'd left off.

"I say we target Birkenau alone. This would benefit both the men and women trapped there, *and* us. For one, it would solve the problem of conducting a double- or even triple-pronged engagement. Second, most of its inmates are Jewish, destined to die whether the Russians show or not. An escape would afford at least some of them a shot at survival. And with Auschwitz having kept the peace and stayed out of the fight, SS retaliation would almost surely be limited to Birkenau. Or even to the Sonder alone, when discovered it was they who led the rebellion.

"This we have already agreed on. No demographic in camp is better suited than the Sonderkommando to spearhead an attack. They are not only the healthiest but possessed of the most resources, and as crucial, the motivation: as its victims, none are more aware of German diligence in eliminating them periodically as eyewitnesses to their great crime.

"Yes, I can see the Sonder bearing the brunt of the blame, their guilt compounded by their dynamiting of the crematoria." Baum grew bigger in his chair, his face hardening. "This last, as you just alluded to yourself, remains essential to the plan, and why I recommend the giant's share of the gunpowder be committed to the Special Squad.

Whether they or anyone escapes, the killing machinery will have been put out of action. Nine death houses, Josef... we cannot let that happen."

Cyrankiewicz, chin in hand throughout Baum's disquisition, said nothing for a moment. "Your point is well taken, my friend, several of your points. You and I will raise the question with the Committee again day after tomorrow, but I suggest in the meantime you go ahead with—no, expedite—the penetration of the Union works. Mind you, I'm not guaranteeing an insurrection in Birkenau or anywhere. But as you said, it can't hurt to be prepared."

"Thank you, commander. Day after tomorrow then."

"I am concerned," the Pole added, "about the men of the Sonderkommando. Should it be approved, readying a project like this is going to take both time and patience. I have no idea how much of either remains to this squad, but exactly how desperate are they, the poor devils?"

"The 8ᵗʰ Sonder was liquidated ten days ago, leaving only those skilled in cremation and such. This gives the 9ᵗʰ the four months generally allotted the squad, perhaps more if the transports continue to arrive in the numbers they're starting to.

"But that need not matter, not after we dangle the help of the Home Army in front of them. Once they learn the Armia is on board, prepared to fight alongside them—when the moment is right, of course, meaning when we say it is—you can stop worrying about the Sonder forcing the issue on their own. If indeed that is what you are getting at... sir."

Cyrankiewicz rose to his feet, signifying the meeting was over. "Thank you, Bruno," he said, engulfing Baum's hand in his. "I've always congratulated myself for insisting that you, a Jew, be admitted to the Committee. Your advice, your dedication continue to be indispensable."

As Baum made in the dark for his barracks, the words wouldn't leave him. "You, a Jew," the man had said—why not just a simple *you*? Not that Baum had taken offense, for there'd been none to take. Not one administered on purpose. Most Poles, even the best of them, as suckled on anti-Semitism and from as early an age as the Germans, were incapable of embracing the Jew as an equal.

Still, he had to wonder how many of his people had perished that day, or for that matter since he and Cyrankiewicz had sat down to talk. A faint, rosy glow pulsed above the tree line to the north; the last of the new *Oberscharführer's* fire pits were dying out for the evening. Granted, a little unintended bigotry or the occasional racist slur was something to be expected, and certainly no cause for high dudgeon. But to what extent, one had to ask, had such innocuous behavior led to the slaughter of children and the emergence of creatures such as Otto Möll?

On the brighter side was Noah Zabludowicz, who'd impressed him even before their meeting with what he'd accomplished. Upon sitting down with him, Baum was further taken by the young man's loyalty to his pals, his eagerness to act, his whole demeanor. He detected both a strength and a fire to this Zabludowicz that made him one to be not only relied on but reckoned with. Which was why he had no problem handing him so critical a first assignment, and more in the future.

Along those same lines, he was curious about his new recruit's possible contact in Birkenau. What kind of woman would a man like that be so quick to stake his and others' lives on? She must be something special to have earned such an endorsement. Perhaps this "old friend" of his, as he'd called her (the light shining from his eyes at mention of her spoke of something stronger than friendship), perhaps she, too, would end up proving of value to the Resistance, both now and later.

If, as Zabludowicz had said, she was still alive. And that, Baum told himself, as he had so often about so many others, was a big if.

*　　*　　*

The icy wind tore at Roza Robota like a living thing. It tried to knock her off her feet, possess her, make her its own, driving the snow up the sleeves and down the collar of her tunic in search of the vulnerable flesh underneath.

The storm had been howling for half an hour and showed no sign of letting up. If anything, it was growing stronger. She lowered her pick axe and made for the woman working nearest her.

"It's getting worse, Trina!" she yelled above the wind. "Have you seen the guard lately? Where is the guard?"

"In there!" the woman shouted, pointing to a small barn just visible through the blizzard. "I saw him duck inside a few minutes ago!"

"That does it then! Help me get the others!"

Soon, all five of them huddled behind a fragment of wall. Mercifully out of the wind, they held tight together to try and feed off each other's body heat. Theirs was the misfortune to have landed, as most did after Q-Camp, in an *Aussenkommando*, an outdoors work gang. They were part of a crew assigned to demolish some inconvenient Polish farm buildings for the construction of a new clinic for the SS. It was the same work Roza had been forced to do in the ghetto, but here, on starvation rations and without the protection of a coat, every day hastened her nearer the grave.

"What if he finds us here, the guard?" one of them said. "He'll put us on report, which means a thrashing later."

"Beats turning into five Jewish popsicles," Roza said. "Besides, he's in that barn over there, and not likely to be leaving it. Would you stick your nose out in this if you didn't have to?"

They pressed against each other wordlessly after that. Though it was better behind the wall, Roza's feet were as numb as two rocks. Should the storm last, they were going to be in big trouble. Even if they didn't end up popsicles, it could cost them some toes and a trip to one of the bunkers.

While the gas chamber was never far from most prisoners' thoughts, theirs weren't only somewhere else at the moment but tuned in to the same thing. It was what they started thinking about around this hour every morning, if none was so careless as to think it aloud.

Until to their shocked disapproval, the newest to the commando, a seventeen-year-old from Krakow, did just that. "How much longer before noon, before the soup?" she moaned. "I'm so hungry. So hungry…"

They frowned, but let it go. She was green and didn't know any better. Their silence, however, was as arctic as the weather. Recognizing it for the reprimand it was, the girl, too, went quiet.

But not for long. "Chicken and dumplings," she burst out, half dreamily, half defiant. "My grandmama was famous for them. She'd put a whole chicken in, and the dumplings as big and white as this," she said, scooping up a handful of snow.

With that, none could resist; the game was on. "Potato pancakes," another chimed in, "with onions and lots of flour. Golden-brown at the edges, spoons of applesauce on top."

"Apples, yes, but in a cobbler, fresh from the oven. Bubbling in its pan, all shiny with sugar."

Roast leg of lamb, lemon meringue pie… on and on, there was no end to it, a pathetic litany of favorite recipes, more torment than joy but insuppressible all the same. Only Roza abstained, if unable to keep at bay the image of her mother's pot roast swimming in tomato gravy. For weeks, she'd watched those around her indulge in this little pastime, and to her it was far from harmless. They were obsessing on food because they were starving to death, as if having the words of it in their mouths, pictures of it in their heads, was compensation for the physical absence of it.

Not that the five weren't exhibiting more conspicuous signs of hunger. All but the new girl looked decades older than they were, their faces sunken, the skin gray, noses like beaks, their eyes those of hunted animals, bewildered, afraid. Mysterious, oozing sores pocked their cheeks and foreheads. Their breasts were going fast, their periods gone already, this causing their feet, lower legs, and abdomens to swell.

Their filthy uniforms swallowed them, the bones of their shoulders and hips as sharp beneath the cloth as metal pipes. The flesh was pulled so tight over their wrists, elbows, and knees, it glistened red as if burned, was painful to the touch. If not Muselmänner yet, they weren't long for it.

Though she missed them with an ache that was never going to stop, in a way Roza was glad her father, mother, little brother, and the rest of her family had departed the unloading ramp that first day on the death trucks. The same part of her grateful for this hoped Godel was out of his misery, too, for by now she understood why they'd been brought to this place: to perish, each of them, there was no getting around it. One way or another, the Germans weren't going to rest until they'd done away with them all. Better to go quickly before one had time to suffer, before the pick axe, the cold, the sores, and the lice, the crippling hunger that made each minute, each movement an ordeal.

Shoshonna was dead, too. She hadn't lasted two weeks. Roza had blamed herself for failing to save her, but now if she had it to do over, she'd have let her stay with their mother and be driven away on the trucks.

In retrospect, actually, her sister *had* died that first day. Or rather, had begun to. From the ramp, their guards walked the four hundred women left from the Ciechanow transport into the camp and a hut devoid of furnishings but for two folding metal tables. There they were ordered to stand and remain at attention, and the door bolted from the outside.

Thirsty, exhausted, dirty from their journey, afraid for both their kidnapped loved ones and themselves, they did as commanded, murmuring nervously to each other, waiting for something they were sure was going to be bad. After an hour, most were sitting silently on the cold, concrete floor.

Suddenly, the door crashed open and in swung three large, mannish women, big-boned, square-jawed Czechs, clad in the same stripes as the scarecrow men but wearing jackboots and waving clubs. These screamed the women to their feet and toward the tables, on which they had to leave what possessions they still had, wallets, jewelry, eyeglasses, everything.

This done, they were ordered to strip to the skin and be fast about it, clothing in one pile, shoes and belts in another. Here they hesitated, but the clubs of the three quickly had them tearing at their dresses. Naked, they were chased out into the mud and the chill, and a second hut.

This barracks, too, was bare save for three knee-high stools at one end, around which a dozen young *Schützen* were drinking from bottles of vodka. As the nude women and girls poured through the door, a chorus of jeers and wolf whistles greeted them.

The new internees couldn't know it, but typhus at one time had been the curse of the camp and raged intermittently still, endangering prisoners and SS alike. Since the lice that spread it lived in people's hair, shaving was mandatory for those entering Birkenau and at regular intervals thereafter.

At each stool stood a male prisoner-barber. One of the Czechs led three of the women to the front and had them sit. The barbers scissored as much of the hair off their heads as they could before resorting to electric clippers to buzz it to the scalp.

Following this, they were directed to get up, reach for the ceiling, and the hair under their arms removed. This drew a few sniggers from the soldiers, but not until the women were told to climb atop the stools did the SS men's fun really begin. Unless it was a beating they wanted, the three were made to stand legs apart, thrust their hips forward, and present their genitals to the clippers.

At this, their audience erupted, their guffaws and lewd comments caroming off the walls. A groan went up from the crowd of women. Roza felt her sister, who'd done all right up to this point, sag as from a blow.

"Oh God, no!" Shoshonna gasped. "Roza, I can't. I won't!"

"But you must!" she said. "You can and you will. You've got to or those Czechs—"

One of the latter wheeled on their charges. "Quiet, all of you! Stupid sacks of Jewish shit. You'll be quiet or you'll be sorry, I promise you that!"

"Those damned Czechs," Roza whispered, "aren't playing around. Pull yourself together, big sister! You can do this!"

Shoshonna shook her head with a vengeance. "No, please, there's no way I—"

Roza cupped her sister's face in her hands and held it to hers. "Listen, Shozhka," she said, their noses almost touching. "Listen to me: they'll hurt you if you don't do what they say, hurt you bad. I've seen it today already, earlier this morning on the ramp. You're going to—look at me!—you're going to have to try and distance yourself from it. Just get up on that stool and shut your eyes, close your ears, imagine yourself somewhere else, and it'll be over before you know it. It's not as if they'll be doing you any harm physically up there, but they will if you resist.

"You want me to tell mama and papa you were put in the hospital, or worse, for trying to defend something as meaningless as your modesty?"

Shoshonna said nothing, but the refusal in her eyes had softened some. Despite the impossibility of doing what she was being asked to, it was difficult to argue with what her sister was saying. When it came her turn, she walked to the front without a fuss, but no sooner had she taken a stool than the tears began to flow.

Roza, preceding her, had stared her tormentors down, then held her head high throughout the procedure. This made her not nearly as much sport as her sister, who once standing atop the stool was bawling like a baby. This only goaded the Nazi hooligans on.

When a moment later the barber was finished with her, the drunken boy-soldiers gave her and her *"rosig klein Muschi"* a loud, mocking farewell.

Shoshonna wasn't the same after that. They all looked different, even comical, with their ridiculous shaved heads, but Roza sensed her sister had lost more than just hair. Through the shower, the delousing by powder, the issuing of the musty stripes, she moved as if sleepwalking, indifferent to her surroundings. Upon their reaching Q-Camp mid-afternoon, she still wasn't herself, though Roza had every confidence she would snap out of it.

By the third day, she'd withdrawn even further, especially after learning of the murder of their family. This took the last of the wind out of her sails. Roza had to watch her constantly, to see that she ate, babysit her during drill, and most troubling of all, keep her from sneaking off to the electrified fence. She intercepted her twice heading suspiciously in that direction, but while she denied any bad intent, Roza wasn't sold.

Then one day she was assigned to help carry the soup from the kitchen, forcing her to leave Shoshonna in the care of some friends. When she returned, she had but to look at them to know her sister was dead. They'd tried to restrain her, the women said tearfully, but she'd broken free and run, like a crazy person she'd run, screeching for her mother all the way to the wire.

But for her Godel and Noah, both likely dead or dying by now, too, Shoshonna was her last link to the past. Now with her gone, Roza had nothing left. Everything that could be taken from her . had been, her family, her dignity, the clothes on her back, even her hair. Or so she thought. A week and a half later, she was to find out otherwise when the last thing she possessed was snatched coldly away, something she hadn't figured it possible to steal.

It happened her next to last day in quarantine. After the morning roll call, she and the rest slated for "graduation" were lined up and marched to the camp registry. There they filed past a prisoner-clerk (so clean, so fastidious in his pressed blue-and-whites!), giving him their names, ages, ethnicities, and places of origin, which he typed onto index cards. A strip of cloth was hurriedly sewn onto their tunics, each stenciled with a five-digit number. They then passed a dozen at a time into a smaller room crowded with a table and several chairs.

Seated at the table were a couple of prisoners equipped with what resembled over-large writing pens. Roza was sat down, told to roll up her left sleeve, lay her arm flat, inner forearm up, and on this was tattooed the number on her chest.

It hurt, but was over in a few seconds. Its psychological impact, however, its implications, were dire. Later, their block elders would tell them these numbers were to serve from this day as their only permissible names. They needed to forget their old ones, for like their lives before the camp these no longer existed. Each would be addressed as number such-and-such, and announce herself as same. *That* was to be her name, now and forever.

To Roza, this was the final and most sinister insult. Having lost everything, now even her name was no longer hers! What kind of person had no name? Someone who wasn't a person, less than a person, inferior, subhuman. With this theft of one's identity, the progression from *Mensch* to *Untermensch* was complete and the victim ready to join the general population.

Again, the inescapable analogy of the cattle car: they weren't women anymore, but livestock, so much meat on the hoof, soulless commodities to be herded into pens and treated, or mistreated, as their handlers saw fit.

The tattoo to her was less a means of identification than an augur of impending extinction. But if she *had* been marked to die, if this thing on her arm was but a prelude to that, Roza vowed on the very day she received it that unlike her unhappy sister's, her death would be neither a capitulatory nor solitary one. How she was supposed to pull this off she didn't know, but she'd be damned if she was going to leave without taking someone with her. An SS *Schweinhund* ideally, or failing that a stinking kapo, but someone, anyone, with Jewish blood on his hands.

In the weeks since, this had given her life purpose, sustained her in her despair, kept her from even considering succumbing to the torpor that had killed her sister. It helped get her through not only the terror and backbreaking slavery of the day but what awaited the prisoners back in their lagers at night.

The first of these tortures was the evening roll call, where regardless of the weather, the exhausted inmates had to stand at attention as they and all those who'd died during the day—or been sent to the hospital or punishment block, or transferred to another of the camp's lagers—were counted. And if the numbers didn't tally, recounted until they did.

Next came the latrine, in its way just as awful. In the *Bla* women's lager, one didn't have to be within sight of the latrine hut to smell it. A concrete trough in the floor ran the length of its interior. Above this ditch stretched two parallel lines of wooden beams, against which those using it were expected to lean their backs while squatting. No provisions were made for either privacy or paper. Since there was never more than a trickle of water to keep this sewer flushed, and thousands of women, many with diarrhea, seeking relief at the same time, the floor around the trough was usually slippery with a revolting, brown slush.

Upon entering their barracks, each was handed her supper, seven ounces of grayish bread sometimes smeared with a margarine derived from lignite. Finally out of the wind and snow, they suffered a new discomfort inside. With the deportees arriving in serious numbers now, the huts felt as if they were shrinking, their original capacity of two hundred and fifty become ancient history. The narrow aisles between the vertical tiers of bunks were quick to fill with traffic, the air to thicken with dust from the dirt floor, the reek of unwashed bodies. One didn't have to be claustrophobic to experience difficulty breathing, to feel the walls closing in, the crush of flesh from all sides.

Still, but for a few minutes over soup at lunch, night was the only time they had to socialize—to mingle, talk of home, of the camp, the latest rumors, tend to those casualties of their broken-down clogs, each other's throbbing, bleeding feet. There was always business to conduct, too, in those bustling aisles, the bartering of goods, the exchange of favors, the trade in services, the collecting of debts. Then ready or not it was to bed, the lights blinking once before going off for good five minutes later at nine o'clock.

Far from providing a respite from the afflictions of the day, sleep also had its thorns. The cramped, boxy kojen could barely hold two people, much less the five or six regularly crammed into them. Nor did it help that a prisoner's shoes, food bowl, and other possessions had to be taken to bed with her to prevent their being stolen.

When she did manage unconsciousness, after all the shoving and shifting for position, the fighting over the blanket, then came the dreams, most of them about food. In these, they not only saw whatever delicious dish they'd conjured but held it in their hands, raised it to their lips, smelled the aroma of it, and were just about to bite into it when it was ripped away, or something else intervened to prevent its consumption. It was the Tantalus myth brought to terrible life, and as often as not Roza would wake from it with saliva smearing her chin, tears her cheeks.

They shared other dreams, too, these forgotten women of Birkenau, formless phantasms, as from a fever, of angry orders shrieked, vicious slaps to the face, naked bodies alive and dead, the unending, ice-laden Silesian wind. That their dreams should be mostly nightmares was but a reflection of their violent, nightmarish days. It was as if the camp itself was alive, a malicious entity in its own right working in concert with the SS, the one harrowing its defenseless victims by the light of the sun, the other continuing the abuse at night by poisoning their slumber with its Grand-Guignol dreams.

Looming over it all in the blackness of the barracks, especially those blackest of hours after midnight, was the specter of the reveille bell, its long, electric burst at 4:30 seldom finding many fast asleep. The anxiety arising from its approach and the fresh day of agony it presaged were too disruptive to leave even the deepest repose undisturbed: most prisoners lay half-awake in anticipation of its ringing, able to predict it almost to the minute.

With that came chaos, hundreds tumbling from their bunks, hurrying to make their "beds" to the exact specifications of the Germans, hurrying to exit the barracks ahead of the curses and kicks of the hut-sweepers, running to stand in line for cold coffee, running to stand in line at the latrine, running to stand at attention for an hour or two of freezing roll call.

Then the work squads were formed and the march out of camp begun, passing the bodies of those who'd died during the night. Piles of corpses lurked everywhere in Birkenau; with the air being conveniently refrigerated this time of year, and the stream of transports keeping the fire pits filled, the dead might be allowed to stack up for days.

In addition to the disquieting glimpse into their own futures this gave the prisoners, the situation was made to order for the swarms of rats infesting the camp. The mounds of naked dead crawled with the creatures. So abundant were they, and as a consequence so emboldened by hunger, in the hospital wards they often didn't wait for their prey to breathe their last, feeding on those still alive but too far gone to move.

The Aussenkommandos left by way of the main gate every morning to the lively tunes of the camp orchestra, composed itself of inmates. They played mostly German military tunes, with which those heading out were required to keep in step. By then, the blisters on the womens' feet would have reopened. To march as expected, they had to ignore the electricity shooting up their legs at each footfall and try to subsume themselves in the music, lose themselves in it, letting it fill them to the exclusion of all else.

To the woman once known as Roza Robota, now prisoner 73476, even more excruciating than the pain in her feet was the smug crowd of SS always thronging the gate. A few showed up every morning to gloat over this fascinating thing they'd created, this synchronized mass of gray men and women moving as one against their will to the war songs of the Fatherland. Moving *without* will, without emotion, without thought, the beat of the drums and crash of the cymbals propelling them forward.

More than just slaves, they were an army of mindless automatons thousands strong, subjugated to their cores by a handful of Aryan elite. So powerful was this elite's perception of itself, it wasn't content merely to fulfill its prime directive, which was to kill. First, it had to annihilate the ego, the very soul of its victim, and this musicalized ritual, this dance of the doomed that waltzed the Aussen squads out of camp in the morning was one of the more theatrical, therefore enjoyable manifestations of that annihilation—visible proof of the completeness of the Nazi victory over the Jew.

Yet as low as this laid her, Roza had no choice but to abdicate self-respect and keep up with the others; to rebel would be suicide. As children, she and her siblings had been teased relentlessly because of their last name. That had stung, but now, with a hurt that burned fiercer than the fire in her feet, she had to endure the immeasurably greater shame of having been turned into a robot in more than name only.

But shame had never killed anyone. Nor its cousin, degradation; these were crosses that, though bitter, could be borne. What one had to worry about at Birkenau were those things that did kill. The morning of the blizzard, for example, as she and the rest quick-stepped it out of camp, Roza was focused less on the self-congratulatory Nazis and the brassy blare of their hated music than on the dark clouds churning to the north. Soon they would be here, shoving aside the sky, uncaringly disgorging their frozen tons.

Her squad hadn't been at its work site for an hour before a light flurry began to fall. In twenty minutes, the snow was blowing horizontally, the wind loud as a train.

All that the women cowering behind it could do was thank God for their half-crumbled corner of wall, and pray their guard was as grateful for his shelter. The teenager from Krakow was about to bring up the soup again, but only to ask how it would be managed in the storm—when a shout exploded from out the snow.

"Mein Gott! What is *this?"*

Their heads jerked up to the sight of the guard almost on top of them, gun leveled. So furious was the gale, they hadn't seen him coming. Four of them leapt up, scampering like rabbits for the concealing white. "Stop, you! *Halt!"* he commanded, but by then they'd disappeared. The one who remained, though she'd risen to her feet, clearly wasn't going anywhere. Her eyes weren't looking to either side for a way out, but straight into his.

It was Roza who stood her ground. Exactly why, she couldn't say. Out of stupidity? To retain some dignity? At this point, did it matter? All she knew was that her brain had ordered her legs to stay put; she could no more have run off than sprouted wings and flown away.

He was young, this *Oberschütze,* no older than she, but judging from his abusive manner earlier in the day, no less hardened than any Nazi. *"Was ist los, Jude?"* He crept toward her, rifle at the ready. "Why didn't you light out with your bitch friends?"

She didn't answer, kept her eyes glued to his. This in itself was a crime, not to come to attention, head bowed, when addressed by the SS. He was aware of her insubordination, too, of that she made sure.

"Well, what have we here?" he said, stopping ten feet from her. "A Jew with spirit, with a backbone? I didn't know there was such a thing."

Roza glared at him, not attempting to hide her hate.

"Still," he said, "there are rules here, and you appear to have broken two of them. The question becomes then, should I shoot you for daring to stare at me like that, or for sitting on your butt instead of working like you were told to?"

Having leaned on the shaft of her pick axe in getting to her feet, she found herself now clenching it in front of her. In that instant, with a fanfare only she could hear, it all came together for her: not only was this the chance she'd been waiting for but why she hadn't hightailed it out of there with the others. This was her moment, this German, this boy, the one she'd been seeking. The sacrifice to be offered on the altar of her vengeance.

Closer, she implored him under her breath, come a little closer, you dog, and I'll have you. If she rushed him now, he'd shoot her down before she could get to him, but any nearer, if she was quick, she could bury the axe in his chest. He'd shoot her still, but she didn't care. She was halfway to the grave already, and with Shoshonna dead, and her little brother, and her mama and papa and probably Godel, what did she have to live for? At least this way, one baby-killing piece of Nazi filth will have paid for his crimes.

But he didn't come closer. On the contrary, backed off a little, having seen something in the face of this evil-eyed Jewish skeleton that moved him to caution. He tightened his finger round the trigger of his gun.

"So, Jew, unafraid Jew, lazy pig of a Jew... before I do anything, I'm curious. What made you decide you could lay off working? Was it this storm, you damned gutter whore, or were you just using that as an excuse?"

At this, Roza lost it. Between her intended victim's invective, the fact he was now definitely out of reach, and the frustration and anger that had been mounting in her for years—she went berserk. Whirling on the ruin of wall at her back, she lit into it like a madwoman, hacking at it with the pick, screaming with each blow, tearing off chunks of masonry one after another.

The private let her have at it, the expression beneath the steel helmet unreadable. He watched in silence until she was done, until the wall was no more. In her frenzy, she'd obliterated it, then collapsed in the snow.

Only then did he react, taking a pad and pencil from his coat pocket. "What is your number? Let me see your tattoo number."

She rolled to her right so he could read it on her shirt. Bending over her, he wrote the number down.

"You are to present yourself to your Blockälteste tonight after the Appell. She will have been notified of this and be expecting you. I would suggest for your sake you don't fail to report."

Later, at camp and in their hut for the night, her friends were all over her. "You're lucky he didn't shoot you right there." "Now it's the 25 for you." "Or worse, the penal commando." "Or worse yet…" This last needed no finishing.

Roza was disconsolate, but only because she'd let her German get away. She'd missed a golden opportunity, nor was a better liable to come along. That she'd have been killed in the act was of little import, just as the punishment ahead of her didn't matter much, either.

"Enough of your bellyaching, please. I appreciate your concern, but whatever's going to be is going to be. There's nothing I can do about it now."

"Not now, no, but what the hell were you thinking then?"

"At such moments, you don't think, you do what fate tells you to. Not that I would change it if I could, not a single second of it. If nothing else, I got to hold my head up, look one of those scum in his mangy eye."

She didn't have to search out their *blockova*. The woman sent a Stubendienst to bring Roza to her room, where to the consternation of those watching, she remained. When finally she emerged, it was with a small bundle in her hands and a big grin on her face.

"What happened?" they cried as one. "Why on earth are you smiling?"

She had them follow her to a corner of the hut. "Did any of you know," she said, the smile spilling into that half-girlish, half-wicked giggle of hers, "that there's a commissary for prisoners in this rat turd of a place, and the kapos have leave to hand out coupons redeemable at that commissary?"

They could only stare at her blankly.

"I had no idea, either, but guess what I got for throwing my little tantrum today: not the penal squad, not a beating, not even a slap on the wrist, but a coupon worth the equivalent of one German mark. For doing good work. Exceptional work, the blockova said.

Maybe I should have gone hunting for a second wall to vent my spleen on."

Laughter wasn't a frequent visitor to *Frauenlager B1a* of Birkenau, but it rose now from half a dozen throats, partly from relief, partly at the wacky unpredictability of life.

"So show us," said one of them. "What is this coupon you're talking about?"

"I don't have it. I gave it back to her, as a gift. Which explains what I do have, here in this sack." She opened it to reveal a mess of boiled potatoes in their jackets. "And this," she said, producing a jar of orange marmalade from her shirt. "This she just handed me, on my way out. I didn't even have to ask for it."

Roza paused to gave them a few seconds to take in the wonderment of the potatoes.

"Was I right," she said, "or was I right? Sucking up to her, I mean. What was I going to buy with a single mark anyway? Definitely not something as valuable as the goodwill of a block elder. My Czech being what it is, I told her in German she could probably make better use of the coupon than I. She thanked me and smiled—yes, *smiled*, that foul-tempered brute of a Slovak—then asked me if there was anything I needed.

" 'Food, if that's permitted, *Frau Älteste*,' I said. 'A few potatoes would be nice.' So she goes and gives me some. As for the marmalade, who knows? My 'generosity' must have caught her off guard."

The women were in awe. "So what are you planning to do with all this, Roza?"

"Why, it's for us, silly, the seven of us. The SS may call us pigs, but that's no excuse to act like one." She unscrewed the lid on the little jar of jellied gold. "Anyone hasn't organized a spoon yet, help yourself to mine."

To organize was camp lingo for acquiring something of value, either by barter or theft. The Germans provided nothing, not even spoons for their prisoners' soup. A Stubendienst in Block 12 made them for sale on the black market, but she charged two rations of bread, a steep price. Roza had given her one ration and a spool of thread she'd stumbled upon, and considered it well worth it. Scarce were their masters who didn't delight in seeing them lap up their dinner like dogs.

The next morning after roll call, she was pulled from her work crew and ordered back to the hut. Not especially to her surprise, but most assuredly her unease, her benefactress from the night before stood at the door.

"I have a cousin assigned to the clothes-sorting warehouse," the woman said. "This morning, she told me they were in need of a couple more people. The work is light and indoors. Though you're not Czech, I thought of you, but you've got to hurry before the spots are filled. I must have an answer now."

Roza glanced at the sky, then her feet. "But what about my friends?" she said. "I can't just—"

"Yes, you can, don't be a fool. Many are the riches that pass through the *Bekleidungskammer*; the Jews like to hide their valuables by sewing them inside their clothing. You can help your friends best from there. All you can do here is watch each other die.

"I'm going to ask you once more, which is it to be: the warehouse, indoors, folding dresses, or the pick and shovel?"

*   *   *

Noah Zabludowicz's heart thumped like a triphammer as he waited in the snow. It had taken him a while to find out if Roza was alive, and a while after that to locate her. He'd had to bribe his share of individuals in the process, the final one the *Schütze* posted at the entrance to the sorting depot.

His joy at learning of her survival was matched only by his admiration at her having landed a job in the Bekleidungskammer. The position wasn't only out of the weather but potentially lucrative, and not easy to come by. The handling of clothes and other articles was incidental to the detail's real purpose, which was to hunt out the wealth the Jews had concealed in the linings of same. Up to a hundred women per shift inspected these, on the alert for suspicious bulges and such.

Half the items searched came from the undressing barracks in the woods, half from Jewish luggage. When valuables were discovered, the SS officer on duty entered them in a ledger and deposited them in a large, open box. But though guards circulated among them as well as watched from catwalks overhead, it wasn't impossible for a worker to pocket the occasional diamond and sneak it back to the barracks.

The commando was a part of what the prisoners called Canada, that multi-tentacled monster of a network that expropriated the goods brought in on the transports and redistributed them into German hands. At first, Noah hadn't understood the reason for the name, until informed it was known as Canada because of the riches associated with that country. Everything from furniture to pharmaceuticals was stored in warehouses within the camp until it could be packaged and shipped by train to Greater Germany. The same cattle cars that arrived spilling over with people sometimes left stacked to their roofs with the worldly goods of those from earlier transports.

Noah had been witness to it time and again: if anything could be said to rival the Nazi thirst for Jewish blood, it was the Nazi hunger for Jewish treasure. The SS were no less acquisitive than they were cutthroat.

Which wasn't to say they couldn't turn around and be generous after a fashion, too. Most of the booty was dispensed gratis to those on the home front to alleviate shortages and keep up morale. Of course, the more prized merchandise—the diamonds, the currency, the rarer stamp and coin collections, the gold—the government kept for itself, hundreds of pounds of it a month trucked from the coffers of Auschwitz-Birkenau to the *Reichsbank* in Berlin. Most was dental gold or came from the unloading ramp, but a good amount of it originated in the Bekleidungskammer, secreted until then in the seams of Jewish clothing.

If he hadn't known it was Roza he'd sent the guard to fetch, Noah wouldn't have recognized the woman who emerged from the building. She stepped into the morning sunlight and stood blinking on the landing, both her luxuriant head of hair and bountiful figure history. He was shocked at how wasted away she was. He knew she hadn't been on the job for long, less than a month from what her Blockälteste had told him, but he hadn't pictured her being so emaciated still.

She didn't recognize him at first, either, her eyes having yet to adjust to the sun. When they did, she let out a yelp and went bounding toward him.

"Fifteen minutes!" barked the guard. "And I'll be watching!"

She threw herself into Noah's arms, her own enclosing him as tightly as the shell its nut. Neither said a word, too overcome with emotion to speak. She was laughing and crying all at once, nor were his eyes exactly dry.

"Roza, you look lovely," he said at last, holding her at arm's length.

"Oh yes, lovely." She rolled her eyes. "A regular beauty queen, right? But a lot healthier than if you'd come calling a month ago, let me tell you."

"So how did you wind up here, in this commando? Not that I'm surprised, but..."

"Ah, so you're onto this place," she said, crooking her head toward the block at her rear. "How did I end up here? I got lucky, Noah, that's all, so very, ridiculously lucky. One day I was dying, then the next, saved. I'm still not sure why or even how it happened. When we have more time, should we, I'll tell you all about it.

"For now, though," she said with a smile, making a show of squeezing the muscles in his arms, "how have you stayed this nice and fat? Did you get lucky, too, or did you battle your way, you fighter, into those clean stripes?"

"You need luck here," he said, "I don't care who you are. Luck and an instinct for survival, an animal's instinct. Sometimes I think the best of us, the more civilized, died early. Welcomed death rather than live in such a place."

At this, her breeziness faded. The dark gray of the Bekleidungs warehouse rose mute and somber behind them. "Noah, there's something you should know. Your sister Deborah..."

"Yes, I heard. My brother Pinchas told me; he's here in Birkenau, too. The Hanukkah selection, that part of it from *B1a*, your lager— our Deborah, rest her soul, was taken with the two thousand. I still have Pinchas, though, and another brother. You remember Hanan; he's with me in the main camp. As for the rest of the family..." His silence was loud.

"But what of *your* peo—" He braked before finishing the word, but it was too late. *Idiot!* he spat at himself. *Moron!* How could you be so clumsy? Based on their ages, and her brother Israel's ill health, most of Roza's "people" wouldn't have made it past the first day. "Shoshonna, I mean," he added lamely. "How's that beautiful sister of yours?"

Roza's gaze fell. When it met his again, it was flint.

"Enough of the dead," she said. "What the hell good does it do to go down that road?" She squared her shoulders, forced a smile. "What I want, Noah, is to hear about you. You said you were living in the Stammlager. In Auschwitz. What—have you gone and joined the SS or something? Gallivanting from camp to camp as if you owned the place!"

In spite of his having put one of his size-twelves in his mouth, and what he'd just learned about poor Shoshonna, her remark eked a smile from him, too.

"No, Roza, not the SS... but I did join something. You're talking to an agent of Battle Group-Auschwitz, the camp underground. That's how I come to be here, and other than to feast my eyes on you again, *why* I'm here. Once long ago you gave me the chance to strike back at the Germans. Remember the day we met?"

She nodded eagerly, her own eyes two perfect circles of expectation. Was it possible Noah was about to ask her what she'd have sold her soul to hear? Though talk of the underground abounded, talk was one thing, proof another. Now all of a sudden... "The Yellow Rose. I remember, I remember."

"Well, I'm returning the favor now. The Resistance sent me to tell you we want you one of us."

She let out a gasp, took hold of his arm as if to steady herself. "No!" she shouted in disbelief. "Wow, I—I'm—wow!" Her next words tripped over each other in their rush to get out. "When can I start? I'm ready right now! You just tell me what to do and I'll do it, anything!"

"I figured that'd be your reaction. Would've been shocked if not. But I do have to warn you, before we go further—"

"Yes, I know," she broke in, "I know it'll be dangerous. But I don't give a flip, all I want is to help. Speak to me, Noah, how can I help?"

Never had he adored her more than he did at that moment. It was as plain as the nose flaring on her pretty face: she was panting for a fight, to get back into action.

"I'll tell you how," he said, "and you can bet it'll be dangerous. But what I was trying to say is it's got to be kept on the q.t. No revealing it to *anyone* but those directly involved. These you'll be recruiting from a specific class of prisoners. Do the words Weichsel-Union ring a bell?"

Roza's mission was to establish a cell among those women working in the gunpowder room of the Union factory with instructions to steal what quantities of the explosive they could. It would then be smuggled to her, she in turn passing it to the Sonderkommando. That she would see to when they showed up at the Bekleidungskammer with the clothes of the dead from the birch groves, or after they were operational, the new crematoria.

It would be arranged for her to be a member of the work party in receipt of this clothing. The cart carrying it would have a false compartment in which the contraband could be stowed. Some of it will have been diverted to Battle Group-Auschwitz, but all save that fraction was to find its way to the Sonder through her.

None of this, Noah cautioned, was going to be easy. The Pulverraum was actually two rooms, one in which six prisoners a shift worked the injector machines, and a smaller that served as the German Meister's office and housed the safe in which the powder was stored. The job of the Meister, a civilian, on top of supervising production, was to allocate and inventory this most precious material. He'd been given a female prisoner to assist him, also German and as diligent as he, which meant two pairs of eyes on the alert for any funny business. The women working for Roza would have to be more than careful.

But stealing it was just the beginning. A system was needed to funnel the gunpowder to her without arousing curiosity. Finesse would be required, too, when transferring it to the Special Squad; she should never assume the SS guarding the women unloading the clothing cart weren't watching her every move. Above all, again the strictest secrecy must be observed. Not only did the success of any attempt at a breakout depend on it, the underground itself could be endangered if the thievery was discovered.

"A breakout?" Roza said. "From the camp? Is that what this is about?"

"That," Noah replied, "and the destruction of the four coming crematoria. Thanks to Bru—thanks to one of my superiors, the two go hand in hand.

"I was given discretion on whether to tell you what the explosive was to be used for, though I would have even if it hadn't been given.

The Sonder will be spearheading the attack, but if this even makes sense, I guess you could say you'll be spearheading the Sonder. Without you, Roza, it isn't going to happen, not how we want it to. I thought you ought to know that. Would want to know."

She couldn't believe her ears. It was all too good to be true. Where before she'd dreamed of one day ridding the world of a single SS, now she'd been handed the opportunity of being instrumental in the killing—no, the justifiable execution—of who knew how many. And the dynamiting of their infernal death factories along with them.

From the Bekleidungskammer, she had an unobstructed view of one of the nearly completed crematoria, and it was an evil sight to behold, its heavy brick smokestack dwarfing the watchtowers behind it. A bank of concrete steps led below ground; soon thousands would be descending these and leaving through that smokestack. She could hardly think about it without wanting to cry.

But there was no need for tears now. Not anymore. Thanks to Noah, no longer would the sight of it sadden so much as motivate her, knowing she'd be working to destroy the vile thing.

"So what about it?" he said, this but a formality. "Are you with us, Roza?"

"To the end," she swore, her voice even deeper than normal, "and let the devil himself try to stop me."

"Time's almost up!" yelled the soldier from the landing. "Start saying your goodbyes."

Sliding back his sleeve, Noah glanced at his wristwatch, only to realize he'd done it again. Instead of the familiar white dial with its twelve Roman numerals, the number 73982 taunted him, tattooed on his forearm, tattooed on his soul. His watch was no more, but three months later he was still searching it out, not as frequently as before but as ugly a reminder when he did of the nameless piece of property he and every Jew here had become.

When he looked up, he did a double take, for looking back at him was a whole different Roza. The determined face had deflated as quickly as a balloon. With the guard's warning, she'd gone from struggling not to shout her excitement to the sun to acting as if she wanted to crawl into a hole and pull it in after her.

"What's the matter, Roza?" Even as he said it, he knew what was wrong, and it had nothing to do with the guard. He'd been dreading this moment, praying it wouldn't come. "Was it," he attempted, the words sticking in his mouth—"was it something I said? Something I—I didn't?"

"Yes, that." Her voice was tiny. "Something you didn't. But that's okay, because—well, to be honest, because I was afraid to hear what it might be. Have been since I saw it was you standing out here." Abruptly, she set her jaw, seeming to make up her mind. "But I do have to know, I must. There's no putting it off."

She stared him hard in the eye as if to will the desired response from him. "Is Godel... is he all right? Is he still alive?"

On the road back to Auschwitz, Noah chided himself for the cad, the selfish oaf he was. It wasn't that he intended on not telling her Godel Silver was alive, safely ensconced in the Ciechanow block of the Stammlager, he just wanted to see if she was going to ask about him herself. What a contemptible creature he was! Admit it, he told himself, you were hoping she wouldn't mention Godel at all, that maybe something had happened these last death-filled months to change her feelings for him. Or at least relegate them to an emotional back-burner.

Contemptible *and* blind! Made so by love, but blind all the same. Just who, he ranted on, do you think you are, Noah Zabludowicz? Not Roza's by any stretch, nor will you ever be. She belongs to Godel and he to her, which is the way it should be, to hell with your pathetic, delusional self. Would you in fact have brought his name up if she hadn't? It was a question that would haunt him for some time to come.

He'd conceded the wrongness, the absurdity of his conduct as soon as he saw her reaction at hearing him pronounce Godel well. Her eyes had lit up like a kid's at the circus, and he knew then not only the shabbiness of his sin but how, right now, he was going to atone for it.

"Oh, Noah, thank you," she'd said, hugging him, "for so many things. For giving me a mission. For giving me Godel. For—for bringing more good news than a body can stand. If I can ever—"

"Hush, Roza, hush, there's no call to thank me. Not for putting your mind at ease about Godel any more than for asking you to put yourself in harm's way. It's you who's doing us the favor by accepting this assignment. If you must show gratitude, show it for this: I'll be back in five days for a full report on what you've done, the progress you've made, only this time I'll be sure to have a certain Mr. Silver with me."

Her mouth had dropped open, and against his protestations she'd wrapped him in another hug. "Come back in five days, Noah, and I promise on my family's graves I'll have a good deal to report, a good deal and more. Until then, goodbye and God bless, my best and bravest friend."

Some friend, he thought, as he walked the limestone path back to Auschwitz, but he'd already sworn to never again let his love get the better of his loyalty. From now on, he'd comport himself as the man of principle he liked to believe he was.

He'd been wanting to tell Godel about the underground and invite him to join, which would now have to be effected posthaste if the lad was to accompany him to Birkenau in five days. What with events to come, it might be advisable as well to ask Bruno Baum about securing him a regular posting there; they'd soon be needing all the operatives they could get in that camp, and the boy's connection to Roza made him an obvious candidate.

For a moment, her face loomed before him, the same one she'd assumed upon learning the reason for his visit—the eyes as grimly black as obsidian, but as if to contradict their ferocity, that rascally grin of hers, like that of a schoolgirl planning a prank.

It was this face that from the beginning had drawn him to Roza as forcefully as any of her charms, and always would. He savored it as one might a lost love's, then banished it from his mind for the indeterminate future.

Spring

Marian Kaminski never tired of telling how a jar of pickled herring had saved his life. Upon coming across someone who hadn't heard the story, it wasn't often he didn't at least try to work it into the conversation. His fellow Sonderkommando, of course, were subjected to it *ad nauseam*, but never complained. Such was their fondness for their garrulous kapo, this was but one of the indulgences they allowed him.

Most had heard it so often, though, they could tell it as well as he. It was June 1942, and Kaminski just another new and disoriented internee. He'd arrived on a transport from the city of Białystok and was still in quarantine camp, fortunate to have made it that far. He'd come close to failing the selection at the unloading ramp; though not yet forty, half his hair was gray. He was, however, a thick-chested bull of a man who looked as if he'd have no problem lifting his weight. The SS doctor on the ramp had studied him for some seconds before waving him to the right and the privilege of working himself to death for the Reich.

One morning in Q-Camp, sent to return the coffee urns to the kitchen, on his way back he spied something shiny in the mud. Leaving the path, he picked it up—almost to drop it in shock. It was a small jar of preserved herring, its silver lid gleaming in the sun. How this treasure had got there and gone unnoticed until now he couldn't imagine, but to a man who'd been living on nettle soup and sawdust bread it was no less miraculous than the biblical manna from heaven.

Since the rags he'd been given to wear had no pockets, there was only one thing to do. Hurrying behind a corner of a hut, he wolfed the fish down, then buried the empty jar in the mud to hide the evidence.

For an hour, Kaminski felt almost human again as his body absorbed its bonanza of protein, until rebelling at the unexpected richness it struck back with a case of the runs. He held it in until he could hold it no more, leaving him no choice but to sneak off to the latrine. To be caught relieving oneself elsewhere was, as he'd witnessed twice, a capital offense.

He never made it to the latrine. Nor notice that his kapo had seen him slip away and was following at a distance. Suddenly, nature would no longer be denied; he sprinted from the path to as isolated a spot as he could find, dropped his pants, and squatted down.

His relief was short-lived. The last thing he remembered before the explosion in his brain was the thump of running feet coming up on him from behind.

He awoke on his back on a concrete floor, his right temple pounding. He touched it gently and drew back fingers wet with blood. He was covered in blood, his shirt, his pants, his feet, and bending over him an SS man in an officer's cap.

"How about that," the Nazi said through an interpreter, "looks like it's going to live after all. Enjoy your little nap? I hope so, because shortly you'll be needing all your strength.

"Your kapo told us what you did—what animals you Hebrews are! He was within his rights to kill you for your disgusting behavior, but instead brought you to us. Perhaps upon seeing what we have planned for you, you'll wish he had done you in. Now get on your feet."

He and another prisoner, also bloodied, were sped to one of the meadows in the forest where the Germans were burying bodies. These were arriving naked in trolleys being pushed by other prisoners. With a blow almost as felling as the one he'd taken earlier, from them he learned of the gas bunkers in the woods.

For the rest of the day, Kaminski and a few dozen others wrestled with the dead, dragging them from the trolleys down into the funeral pit. The afternoon was a scorching one and the SS in a rage, keeping them at a run with bullwhips and threats. By sundown, there wasn't a one of them not covered in a noisome paste of mud, blood, sweat, and powdered lime. On the truck taking him to his new quarters in Auschwitz, everyone was too exhausted to talk. Not, after what they'd spent the day doing, would any have had a clue what to talk about.

Thus did Kaminski, despite his age, come to join the predominantly younger ranks of the Special Squad. But for getting caught literally with his pants down, he'd probably have ended up in an Aussenkommando after Q-Camp and been history by now.

"I can't claim it the most satisfying shit I ever took," he liked to say, "but certainly the luckiest. We may be living in hell, boys, but for what it's worth, at least we're living."

To segregate the Sonderkommando from the other inmates, the Nazis in those days were quartering them in Block 11, the punishment block. Conditions were severe. Seven or eight men were made to share one of the ground-floor cells, with little sunlight, less ventilation, straw mattresses on a stone floor, their only toilet a metal bucket in a corner.

True, they were provided sufficient food to enable them to work. Decent shoes for the same reason. And regular showers and access to medicine so they wouldn't get sick; working in proximity to them every day, the Germans didn't want to risk catching a disease.

But the bunkers and the pit were the price they paid for these luxuries, and before long something that would prove as bad as either. One sweltering August morning, thirty of them, Kaminski included, instead of being trucked to the meadow were marched to the crematorium—not, as they feared, as fodder for the gas chamber, but to be taught how it worked, the techniques of mechanized mass extermination and incineration.

They'd been selected on the basis of their performance as the first of the hundreds of extra Sonder who'd be needed when the four death factories in Birkenau opened. Which involved not only learning how to operate and service the ovens but, for the burial and trolley men among them, how to deal with the living now as well: greeting the victims as they arrived, keeping them calm, keeping them moving... listening from the next room to their screams as they died.

It was Sonderkommando school, graduate or be killed yourself. Their professor, with the assistance of the few already proficient at the ovens, was the non-Jewish kapo of the crematorium, the Pole Mietek Morawa. Though only twenty-three, he'd long been feared for his cruelty and foul temper. Kaminski and his new kapo took an instant dislike to each other, but because of the prestige the elder had garnered in the meadow through the bigness of his character and the strength of his work ethic, Morawa was unable to squash as he had so many before.

Kaminski had tumbled from the start that not to comply in full with the orders of the SS was to court an early death. Never once working the burial pit had he shown hesitation or weakness, giving the impression that to him neither the gruesome nature of the labor nor its frenetic pace was anything more than routine. In fact, he'd made every effort to do the work of two men. Where the others had paired up in hauling a single corpse to the pit, he'd never failed to handle one by himself, two when at all possible, one slung over each shoulder.

As might be expected otherwise, his companions hadn't taken offense at his industriousness. Kaminski was a man of great charm, capable of winning almost anyone over. Perpetually florid-faced and raspy of voice, he wore his emotions for better or worse on his sleeve. He, too, had a temper and could be dangerous if provoked, but unlike Morawa had a good heart, was tolerant, even tender, toward those suffering or in need.

He also had a knack for defusing the tensest moments, for saying the right thing at the right time, imparting his own coolness under pressure to those around him. His self-confidence was contagious, if sometimes bordering on the arrogant. He appeared in control of himself and the situation no matter what.

In short, he was a born leader, commanding the affection and admiration of all. The Sonder knew from the way he spat on the Nazis behind their backs that he, too, despised them, recognizing the hustle he displayed on the job as less an expression of submission than defiance. There was no denying it bettered his chances of surviving, but it could also be said that by doing more than the Germans asked of him, he was *being* more, showing them that a Jew was as capable, therefore as human as anyone.

Nor did he slow down upon entering stoker training. It didn't take Kaminski long to know as much about mechanical incineration as his instructors, from how many bodies and what body types could best be burned in a load, to how and when to "clinker" (clean out) the ovens, replace the fire bricks in the chimney, whatever was needed.

As nightmarish as the work was, he shrank from none of it, passing himself off to the SS, as he had at the pit, as someone not only ready but eager for anything they could throw at him. He hopped to every order, he didn't care how horrendous, never hinting at the repulsion with which it filled him.

Some of those chosen for the squad couldn't, had trouble even believing what they were seeing, much less joining in. These were either shot on the spot or at the Black Wall. This rose to a height of ten feet at the rear of the courtyard between Blocks 11 and 10, the latter housing those women, those luckless, condemned to the bizarre vagaries of Nazi medical experimentation. (It was no accident the wall stood where it did, both buildings providing it with a steady succession of victims). Brick underneath, it was covered with a thick layer of black cork to receive the bullets of its firing squads, an expanse of sand at its base to sop up the blood.

The Black Wall had been a fixture of the camp from the beginning. Thousands had perished there, were perishing still.

Kaminski was the last person in any danger of such. His stock, as it were, continued to spiral upward, not least in the eyes of the Germans. Particularly beneficial was the high opinion in which *Hauptsturmführer* Hans Aumeier held him. Aumeier was in charge of the main camp, one step in the SS hierarchy below Höss, the overall commandant. The short, well-fed captain had acquired a grudging respect for the new stoker, who though much older than the other Sonder, twice as old as some, regularly left them in his dust at the workplace.

It was because of Aumeier that Kapo Morawa hesitated to do harm to this man the young, blond Pole had quickly sized up as a rival. Prevented from striking at him directly, therefore, Mietek went after those close to him, circumspectly at first, but with an escalating violence that threatened to turn lethal.

Upon discovering he had a patron of sorts in the *Hauptsturmführer*, Kaminski confronted his kapo and told him to back off. Not content simply to safeguard his friends, he applied himself from then on to countering Morawa's excesses against the rest of the squad, becoming a champion to them in the process. Accordingly, as his standing in the detachment grew, so did the other's jealousy-fueled hatred of him.

With 1943 shaping up to be the busiest year yet, and the 9th Sonderkommando still growing as a result, the Nazis decided an upgrade was in order. A home befitting what loomed the biggest squad ever was quickly readied for it in Birkenau's *B2d* lager. Block 13 was a barracks unlike any other. Enlarged to twice the normal size, a wooden wall eight feet high surrounded it, the only entrance a double-door guarded by a prisoner with a club whose function was to keep the inquisitive away.

Those Sonder accustomed to Block 11 felt as if they'd checked into a hotel. Each man was assigned his own bunk, complete with linen. They also had their own showers and real toilets, and within the confines of the wall unsupervised and glorious freedom of the yard and its night sky, its greening grass and fresh air.

Nor was it possible, even with a wall, to segregate the commando completely. Courtesy of the eminently bribable prisoner at the door, the more aggressive of the black marketeers were regular visitors. On top of what the SS already allowed these special slaves of theirs, this shadowy sales force brought food, cigarettes, alcohol, and other items in exchange for what gold the Sonder were able to retrieve from the dead. They'd succeeded in purchasing such before, but given the inaccessibility of the punishment cells on a hit-and-miss basis only.

But the grandness of their new residence wasn't the only surprise awaiting them. After settling in, they found themselves bunking with men who'd never seen Block 11, the largest single contingents those Sonder from Ciechanow culled from the unloading ramp in November, and Malkinia and Grodno in December. There was confusion on both sides.

"But the Nazis have been spoiling us since we got here," the newcomers said. "Now you say you've been living on lager food and sleeping on concrete?"

Kaminski thought he had an explanation. "Just another case of one hand not knowing what the other is doing. It's like that in any large outfit, be it the SS or the Red Cross. My guess is you people just lucked out, is all. The Germans may be pros at this, but that doesn't make them infallible. Witness our boy there on the other side of the wall with the big stick… and even bigger pockets," he added with a grin.

"You'd think the Krauts would want one of their own at that door to guarantee those in on their dirty little secret were in no danger of blabbing its particulars to whoever could pay the price of admission."

It so happened he was wrong. Beginning in November, the SS coddling of fledgling Sonder was a calculated shift in tactics designed to buffer the shock of their barbarous new lives by distracting them with alcohol and other comforts. It was a way of numbing them to the ghastly work they were doing, and more to the point, having them continue to do it rather than giving up and opting out for the Black Wall.

Why the men locked up in the punishment block weren't included was because they were inured to their harsh existence and producing just fine despite it. With no contact outside of work between the two sets of Sonder, and little even then, each remained ignorant of the other's situation.

Not that it mattered really if Kaminski was right or wrong, about this or anything. What with his irrepressible sangfroid and infectious good humor, and his being the oldest man in the squad, he'd become a magnet for the others' questions and concerns, especially the younger among them in aching need of a father, who'd seen their own trucked away never to return.

Even then, but for the change in their living arrangements, this might not have come about. Not to the extent and as naturally as it did. With the Sonder sleeping under one roof now, not only did Kaminski have their ear during the day but, as opposed to being shut in a cell at night with a mere few, could interact with them then in their entirety.

It was an opportunity both he and they took full advantage of. As the launching of the Birkenau crematoria drew near, the number of men in Block 13 swelled into the hundreds. With the elitist Morawa still billeting with his friends in Block 2, a prominents hut, Kaminski had these hundreds to himself, and quickly emerged as their de facto leader.

But the younger Pole, too, had his backers among the SS, notably the influential *Untersturmführer* Max Grabner, head of the camp's Political Department, home of the Gestapo. So a compromise was reached.

Both factions agreed that Morawa and Kaminski were the frosting on the Sonder cake, and their talents utilized best in Crematorium II, the largest and potentially most productive of the four. (Number Three had the same dimensions and layout as Number Two, but due to electrical and foundation problems was lagging in construction).

Instead of raising one man above the other, the Germans chose to make each a subkapo—Morawa in charge of cremation, Kaminski the undressing room and gas chamber—and bring in a third party as Chief Kapo, the German inmate August Brück, veteran of a long line of prisons and concentration camps. Brück's position was in essence a titular one. His assistants would be the ones running the operation.

The three were informed of this on March 10th, three days before Crematorium II was scheduled to open. Morawa was angry at what he perceived as more of a demotion than a promotion. He'd assumed he'd be appointed head of whichever *Krema* opened first, had been promised as much by the powerful Grabner. Then this usurper, this middle-aged old windbag of a Jew!

Not that there was any use fighting it, so he accepted it—but would never forget it. He made a show of welcoming Kaminski into the ranks of the kapos, but that was all it was, show. Secretly, he vowed to have his revenge one day, and was willing to be patient until that day should come.

Besides, beginning on the 13th, both had more urgent things to occupy them. Kaminski thought he'd seen it all, but the progress the Nazis had made in the science of mass annihilation was frightening. The new crematorium came with its quota of technological advances, but as eye-popping as these were, it was the *scale* at which the slaughter was to be conducted now that turned the blood to ice, made one see how a people might realistically suppose they could wipe an entire other from the face of the earth.

The night of March 13th, Crematorium II: the first transport to descend the steps into the underground jaws of this beast was from Krakow, and consisted of 1,492 men, women, and children selected from a shipment of 2,000. The women entered first. Kaminski watched as the lot of them stumbled out of the blackness above into the giant, rectangular undressing room, wave after wave of them blinking in the white light of the fluorescents.

"Sir, what is going to happen to us?" Their voices were strained. "Please, sir, where are we? What is this place?"

The Sonder were encouraging. What else could they be? These innocents from Krakow were as good as dead. Two squads of soldiers had followed them down the stairs, machine guns at the ready. For the Sonder to tell these living ghosts the fate in store for them would be to sign their own death warrants, and for what? So they might panic and be gunned down rather than gassed?

They did what they had to do, what they'd been trained to do, convince the nervous crowd it had nothing to worry about, a shower was all it was—"Everybody has to take one before entering the camp"—directing it all the while toward the line of benches running the length of each wall. Above these stretched two rows of numbered hooks.

A permanent sign affixed to the crematorium entrance had proclaimed in German, "To the baths and disinfecting rooms," a portable one below it announcing the same in Polish. Inside, plastered on the thick columns supporting the ceiling were other signs: "Cleanliness is life," "One louse can kill," and so forth. Some of the Sonder handed out pieces of soap.

Presently, an SS officer stood on a chair and made it official. *"Achtung! Achtung alles, bitte!*

"It is required you take a shower before proceeding further. This is not meant to inconvenience you, but to prevent the spread of disease. We did not bring you all this way only to have you carry typhus into the camp, or die of it yourselves. Everyone, therefore, must get undressed now. We regret any embarrassment this might cause, but it has to be done."

Those who could speak German gaped at him, as if told to do somersaults or stand on their heads. Again he gave the order to undress, and still no one budged.

"Ladies and gentlemen, please! The sooner you take your shower the sooner you will get to your new homes, where hot soup is waiting. If your shoes have laces, tie them together and hang them and your garments from the hooks on the walls. And remember your hook numbers. This will make it that much easier to reclaim your belongings later."

The Sonder wandered among them, translating. People stared dubiously at them and each other. Parents strip in front of their children, sisters in front of brothers? Are you sure that's what the young officer said?

The soldiers, their own nerves ragged, were done. "Undress, do you hear? *Alle Kleider!* Everything!"

Slowly, they began fumbling at their clothes, but not enough of them nor fast enough. Without warning, their guards attacked, wading into them with truncheons and the butts of their rifles. In minutes, all were naked and not a few of them bloodied, covering themselves with their hands as best they could.

With the SS on its heels, this stricken mob—the younger children hysterical, many of their parents close to it—was herded down a short corridor into a spacious anteroom. Through a curiously stout open door, they could see a long, electrically-lit chamber thirty meters deep and seven wide, the walls whitewashed from floor to ceiling. To their relief, a double row of flat, circular showerheads hung from that ceiling, though if more observant they'd have noticed no drains in the floor.

It was into this room that the phalanx of soldiers pressing from the rear drove them, and when all were inside, the thick, rubber-sealed door hastily secured with screw-in bolts. By then Kaminski and his team had gathered their equipment, hooked up their water hoses, and waited tensely in a storage room for the grisly task that lay ahead. Their job was to clear out the gas chamber once the deed had been done.

But this wasn't all that had them on edge. Ahead, too, lay the sound which went with the deed, that bloodcurdling farrago that as often as they'd heard it never failed to horrify. It was the worst sound in the world, the worst sound possible, every man pale in anticipation of it.

Above, jutting from the grass that covered the roof of the underground gas chamber were what resembled four miniature concrete chimneys. A pair of SS non-coms, the *Disinfektoren*, stood at two of these, gas masks in place, ears alert for the order. When shouted at last, each slid the heavy lid off the structure in front of him, opened one of the flat, round tins at his feet, and dumped its load of pellets down the shaft. After a second tin, they replaced the lids and moved to the remaining shafts.

Inside the chamber, the pellets rattled down induction columns anchored to the floor and protected by two layers of wire mesh. A metal cone pointing upward at the top of the column's core ensured their equal distribution. Later, this core would be taken out, and the little balls of spent poison discarded.

This was a safer and more efficient method of delivery than existed in either the main camp's crematorium or Bunkers 1 and 2. There, each Disinfektor had to balance on a ladder while opening his tin, then carefully pour the contents through a narrow, flap-covered vent in the wall. A pair of gas-masked Sonder stood nearby with buckets of water in case of spillage.

Zyklon-B, a hydrocyanic, was the German trade name for this gas, an acronym of its main ingredients: cyanide, chlorine, and nitrogen. The B stood for *blau*, from the brilliant blue color of the granules in which the poison was locked. Originally used to fumigate the lice-infested clothing of the prisoners, it was harmless until exposed to oxygen, and only achieved optimum utility at a temperature of 81° F. or higher. During the winter, a coal stove burned in each of two corners of the older gas chambers, but even with these and the body heat of the hundreds packed inside, it could take up to thirty minutes to reach the requisite warmth.

Crematorium II, however, came with a forced-draft ventilation system that channeled hot air from the oven room directly into the gassing one.

Zyklon-B killed by paralyzing the muscles of the lungs, causing its victims to smother to death. It was the devil's own brew in every sense of the phrase. Upon hitting the ground, the pellets would begin violently to hiss, like a thousand angry snakes. Or on this, the night of the 13th, more like two thousand, as the dosage had been doubled to deal with the larger payload.

The Sonder in the holding room stiffened, for they knew what was next, the horror they'd been dreading: the screams of those in the gas chamber after they understood what was happening. It was a noise few men had ever had to endure, a mix of shocked disbelief, bellowed outrage, and desperate pleading ripped all at once from fifteen hundred throats.

Of special hideousness were the high-pitched shrieks of the women and children. This was how their own mothers, wives, and babies had died, terrified, alone, feeling betrayed by not only the Germans but the men supposed to protect them, their sons, husbands, fathers. The very men listening now. Some of them covered their ears, knuckles white with the effort. Some wept softly, a few mumbled prayers. All kept their eyes riveted to the floor, unable to look one another in the face.

After what seemed like minutes but was only seconds, the cries gradually gave way to coughing and a convulsive gasping for air. Was this harder to bear, more devastating than the screaming? One might as well have asked oneself which was worse, dying of pneumonia or typhus.

As the gasping grew fainter, so did the banging on the death-room door. This hammering had been as furious as it was continuous; now only the sporadic weak thump challenged the massive door's impregnability. Then all was quiet, not ten minutes after the snakes of Zyklon-B had hissed their arrival, although the SS doctor in charge would wait ten more to be certain.

At which point, the mechanical de-aerator was switched on to rid the chamber of its fumes. The Sonder poised in the anteroom strapped on their gas masks, hoses ready, hearts pounding.

When the bolts to the door were unscrewed, it swung open by itself, propelled from behind by the crush of naked flesh spilling out. A wall of corpses always blocked this door, and the squad's first task was to untangle these and muscle them out of the way. With this done, the larger hose was brought up and the inside of the death room drenched. This was to negate any pockets of gas that might remain under its victims.

Kaminski, as usual, was the first into the stifling room. Though a kapo, he had no intention of sitting on his duff and simply dishing out orders. The dirtiest, sweatiest part of the whole business was tearing down the piles of bodies. The stench was unforgiving: blood, excrement, vomit, urine, the gamy smell of stale body odor, each intensified by the wet, clinging heat. Worst of all was the excrement; there was shit all over the place, on the dead, the floor, smeared on the walls. Gassing, like hanging, often produced a last evacuation of the bowels.

The Sonder carried an assortment of tools. Heavy iron rods were for prying the dead apart, in the process breaking bones, splintering ribs. Some wielded meat hooks, others picks, and all had leather thongs attached to their wrists they would loop over hands or feet to help them yank their owners free.

They never got used to how compact these stacks were, how intricately the dying had twined themselves together. In their madness to escape the gas rising from the floor, they'd trod each other underfoot, clawing and scratching their way to the ceiling. Thus those mounds of flesh as snarled as antiquity's Gordian knot, legs and arms interlaced as if crocheted together, hands clutching bone in frozen death-grips of steel.

As these were broken down, the dead were hauled into the anteroom, where a second team positioned them face-up in rows. The females' hair was shorn and stuffed into bags, and all spectacles, artificial limbs, and jewelry removed. An SS officer collected this last in an open briefcase. A third group of Sonder drug the plundered corpses to an elevator which sent them twenty-five at a time to the ovens on the ground floor. There, a tooth-pulling commando would inspect their mouths for gold.

Kaminski was forever preaching to his men the need for disassociating themselves from their work, to look at what they were trafficking in not as people but so much meat. This, of course, was easier said than done, especially when dealing with children. Smaller and lighter, these were less trouble to handle, but came with a psychological weight that made grappling with the corpse of an adult infinitely preferable. Even Kaminski's impassiveness was tested where children were involved, as happened that night, when at one point he stepped from the death chamber holding by their heels the bodies of three infants like so many plucked chickens.

The two Sonder who accepted this burden from him saw the tears staining his cheeks—by then he'd shed the cumbersome gas mask—but pretended not to, recognizing it as less the reaction of a hypocrite than a man.

It took two hours to empty the gas chamber, and another to sanitize it and dispatch the last of the bodies upstairs. The rest of the hoses were brought in, the blood and filth scrubbed off the walls, and the mess swept into the large grated drain in the anteroom. As a parting touch, the interior was slathered with a fresh coat of whitewash. As the Sonder waited to be led back to their barracks, they could hear the muffled roar of the furnaces overhead.

The crematorium was to be inactive for two days. This had been a test run, and any glitches were to be addressed then. Tomorrow, a Sonder detail would collect the clothes in the undressing room and take them by cart to the Bekleidungskammer. In the course of this, quick hands would knead the garments for valuables. The occasional pat-down the guards had conducted at Number One had all been on the perfunctory side, making it possible to conceal diamonds or even cash on one's person if one were careful.

The Sonder had no compunction against taking from the dead. The way they saw it, as Jews themselves they were the rightful heirs of that dead. They knew where any loot they might fail to preempt was headed, and better they should end up with some of it than have it all go to the Nazis. That the Germans should get hold of any was bad enough, as egregious an instance imaginable of adding insult to injury.

Back at Block 13, Kaminski couldn't sleep. As tired as he was, his brain wasn't cooperating. Giving up, he exited the barracks for the yard, which he was soon pacing deep in thought, thoughts as black and cold as the chilly March night. It wasn't as if this gassing had been his first. He'd been a party to plenty of them, seen things, done things no man was ever meant to. The gas chamber in the original crematorium held seven hundred. How many thousands had he helped connive into that room, or stuff into ovens and burn to ashes afterward?

This last 1,492, however, had been different. Gone were the haphazardness and improvisation characterizing operations before. The converted farmhouses in the woods, the fire pits, even the multi-purpose Crematorium I—all were the products of expedience, temporary solutions to the problem of how to rid Europe of its Jews.

Crematorium II on the other hand was the permanent answer to that problem, a mechanized, specialized, seamless assembly line of death designed from the outset, unlike its predecessor, as not merely a place to burn bodies but as an engine of pure destruction, as ravenous an eater of people as any *dybbuk* in Jewish mythology. The 1,492 were only the beginning. Three thousand could be crammed into this monster's gas chamber, then reduced to powder, come rain or shine, in a matter of hours.

And that was but the tip of the extermination iceberg. That Number Two would soon be joined by Numbers Three, Four, and Five was as big a reason as any he was having trouble sleeping.

But not the only one: the SS, it seemed, had been a bit off in their counting. It hadn't taken long for the pregnant girl to turn Kaminski's head in the undressing room. Though about as pregnant as a body could get, her belly impossibly distended, she was still a child, eighteen, nineteen at most. She was also as pretty as he could remember seeing, a true daughter of Israel, the strong yet graceful

Semitic nose, the large, limpid eyes of a desert antelope, skin the warm, golden color of aged olive oil.

It was neither her beauty nor her belly, however, that had captured the kapo's eye. No—somehow she wasn't fooled. He could see it in her face, in the way she watched him as he was explaining the necessity of a shower. She knew what lay ahead, maybe not its specifics, not that it was gas, but most definitely the end for her and her unborn child. How she knew, this random girl, this no more than a teenager, he had no idea, but there it was in her expression, the resignation, the reproach. The proud refusal to be suckered by yet another Nazi falsehood.

She held her chin up and glared him in the eye, hers not without fear but inflexible all the same in their condemnation of him. He could feel them even after he turned away from her, feel her disapproving gaze on his back, boring through his sham reassurances like a drill.

It didn't happen often, but he always hated it when they knew, when they could tell their minutes were numbered. To her credit, this one kept it to herself, no tears, no hysterics, probably to keep from alarming what family was with her. For that, Kaminski had to tip his hat to her courage.

It was no easy thing enduring that recriminatory stare, to be acknowledged by the victim of one's complicity for what one was, an accessory to murder. A helpless one, yes, hijacked into the job, but guilty all the same. Quickly, he slunk himself and his despicable spiel to the other side of the room, though even as he did was aware how futile this was. One way or another, alive or dead, odds were he hadn't seen the last of this girl.

And so he hadn't, coming across her an hour later in the gas chamber, not buried in one of the piles but among those corpses scattered on the floor. She was on her back, her spine arched, which made her stomach stick out even more when in fact it should have perceptibly shrunk. It should have shrunk because plain as day, its lifeless eyes staring into his, was the head of her fetus poking from between her open legs.

He'd encountered this before, but had never got used to it. There was something disturbingly unnatural, something not of this world about it, like the two-headed animals preserved in formaldehyde one paid half a zloty to gawk at back home when the carnival came to town. Never had this gas-chamber grotesquerie affected him, though, as it did with this brave and beautiful womanchild from Krakow. She deserved better than this, better than to be on display like some monstrosity in a sideshow, her and her baby stripped of not only life but all dignity.

Yes, the Germans to their everlasting ignominy had miscounted. It should have been one thousand, four hundred and ninety-*three* dead, not two, and the discrepancy wouldn't stop eating at Kaminski. Didn't this little one who'd lived for nine months in the womb—who'd never seen the sun nor ever would, but *had* lived—didn't he or she deserve to be judged a person, too?

As superficial an objection as he had to admit this was, he couldn't get past it, brooding over it, just knew it was going to haunt him for the rest of the evening. Together with the image of that unborn, bloody head.

Nor were the goblins of this evil night to disappear with the dawn. They would continue to torment him all through the next day, night finding him sleepless yet again in the yard of Block 13. Why should this one nineteen-year-old and her aborted baby, as awful a sight as they'd been, refuse to fade away, leave him be, as in his experience they should have at least started to by now? It was as if they were hanging around for a reason, waiting for something to happen, something they wanted to make sure he didn't miss.

Standing in the yard that second night, absorbed in the black stew of his thoughts, he'd been gazing at the stars without really seeing them. Not that there was any ignoring what greeted him upon his turning around. A full moon had snuck up on him, just now risen above the treetops, but such a moon as to cause his lips to part in amazement. In place of its usual pallor, it shone a startling, flamboyant scarlet, a red as richly velvet as the petals of a rose. He'd never seen anything so cosmologically lovely or out of the ordinary, as if Mother Nature had grown bored and decided to put on a show. He succeeded awhile in losing himself in its rare beauty, his dark mood forgotten—

When without warning it hit him, a shock of recognition like a fist to the stomach. With a grunt, he crumpled to his knees.

The moon was the dead baby's head all over again, an almost perfect facsimile, there could be no mistaking it. Not only was it as slightly off-round but as red, as if dipped in blood, the aghast, open-mouthed countenance of the proverbial man in it identical to that he'd beheld on the tiny face yesterday.

He was on his knees for a while, unable to move, the withering stare from the thing above pinning him like a bug to a board. Nor would he permit himself the relief of tearing his eyes from it, small punishment for his role in the tragedy it had chosen to mime. The more he did look at it, though, the more he began to wonder if maybe this charnel moon wasn't trying to punish him so much as get his attention. Tell him something. After that, it took him no time, and with a little gasp when he did, to realize just what that something was.

Not fully formed until then, the gist of it had been nibbling at him for a month, ever since a kapo from the main camp's Ka-Be had strode into this very yard to lay some extraordinary news on him. How Bruno Baum had managed to penetrate the Sonder compound Kaminski could only guess. The prisoner posted at the outer door may have been brazen in his cupidity, but did have his limits. Even the better-supplied of the black marketeers, able to offer the biggest bribes, had no choice but to conduct their business from outside the wall.

It was late in the day, the sun a blazing, orange ball of cold fire balanced atop the snowy tree line. The two of them had retired to a corner of the yard. Never had he seen a face as mournful as Baum's, a face so limned in pain, not even among the damaged men he worked with. Yet there wasn't a trace of surrender in it, nor despite a build as slight as a boy's in the dignified way he carried himself. Here was a man, Kaminski could tell, who hadn't stopped battling, a prisoner as at the mercy of the SS as any, but one it would take more than them to break.

"I come here, Herr Kaminski, with a proposal," Baum said, the voice a reassuring bass. "You have been recommended by reliable people as being reliable yourself, but more than that as a man capable of leading other men. We would like you to join us in making history, you and your comrades."

"Oh, we would, would we," said Kaminski. "And just who is this *we* you're talking about?"

"The Resistance, the camp underground. Battle Group-Auschwitz... you are aware, I presume, of its existence."

"I've heard tell of it, all right—Battle Group-Auschwitz, I like that—but can't say as I know a whole hell of a lot more. Since Q-Camp, I've been... excluded, you might put it, from much of what goes on around here."

"Understood," Baum said, "but believe me when I tell you we are a force in the camp, well-organized and determined. Our proposal is this: we are planning an insurrection that will take place in Birkenau, an escape of as many prisoners as it is possible to get out. And we want—no, *need* the Sonderkommando to be in the forefront of the attack. Do not ask why we deem a revolt advisable, but we do. The SS have plans for not only the Jews but others, none of which, as you might imagine, is born of the milk of human kindness."

Kaminski let out a slow, appreciative whistle. "An escape? From this place? You're pulling my leg."

"Trust me, good sir, I could not be more serious. We have a plan of our own, a battle plan. And you play a large part in it, you and your men."

"Awful nice of you to tell us." As flippant as this sounded, Kaminski was struggling to contain his excitement. "What I'd like to know, among a lot of things, is why us, why the Sonder? To lead this attack of yours." Then, unable to resist, "I mean what is it that makes us so—special?"

"Because you are in better—"

Baum caught himself, a shadow of a smile brushing his lips at the double entendre. The next second, it was gone.

"Because you are in better health, therefore stronger than the other prisoners, and have access to the wealth of the transports for the purchase of guns and ammunition. In this, I am afraid, you will have to rely on yourselves; the Home Army at present, engaged as it is at Wa—well, engaged as it is, needs every weapon it can get hold of. One of our operatives, however, will be supplying you with regular quantities of gunpowder, much of which you will be asked to set aside for a specific purpose."

A smile was all Kaminski had wanted. He found it difficult to trust a man as unrelievedly solemn as this one. "And what purpose might that be?"

"The dynamiting of the four soon-to-be completed crematoria." Baum paused for effect. "This is the main reason your men were picked to head the assault. The destruction of the four is integral to the operation and must be carried out simultaneously. It will be the signal to the rest of us that the fight has begun."

Again he paused, gave Kaminski the once-over. "So what do you think, kapo? Your first impression... and please, no holding back. I prefer you be honest."

"Honestly? I'm not sure. It's all pretty overwhelming. A hundred questions come to mind, the first being, I guess, when is this supposed to go down?"

"Questions may be difficult to answer at this point, everything being in the formative stages still. What I would like you to do is sleep on it for now. Give it some thought, hash it over with your comrades. Discuss it with them, those you can rely on to be discreet. When you are ready to talk again, I will be ready to listen, and hopefully have more to tell you."

"Fair enough. How do I get in touch with you?"

"You cannot, not directly. Nor will I be back." Another phantom smile. "My duties at Ka-Be don't warrant visits to Birkenau. These would only attract the wrong kind of attention.

"One of our top agents, though, will serve as liaison between you and us, a fellow named Zabludowicz, as dedicated a Jew as he is able a soldier. He will be our mouthpiece to you, and yours to us. When you need him, put a brick atop the wall on each side of that door over there. He is quartered in the Stammlager, but is in Birkenau almost daily."

"There is one question you can answer now, if you would." Kaminski pretended to examine his fingernails. "Are you, like me and this Zabludowicz, by any chance Jewish?"

Baum blinked in surprise. "Yes. Why do you ask?"

"Oh, nothing, just curious." He was quick to let it drop. "I must admit, sir, I'm intrigued to say the least. An armed revolt, you say? The gall of it alone... it's got this old tree's sap flowing, that much I do know. I'll do as you ask and talk it over with my men, see what they have to say about it."

He held out his hand. "Thanks, Herr Baum, and if there's nothing else, have a safe trip back."

Baum took the hand in both of his. "Actually, there is one more thing, and that would be the consequences of all this. Just so there is not any misunderstanding, there will be casualties, perhaps many. Perhaps no one will survive. The whole enterprise could turn out to be a disaster. The risks are as huge as the odds against it being an even partial success.

"But what should that matter to the men of the 9th Sonderkommando? Your fate has been ordained already; witness that which overtook the eight squads that came before you. What we are offering is the chance to save not only yourselves but others, or failing that, to go down fighting like men."

Baum let go of Kaminski's hand, but his eyes held the kapo's in their own grip.

"Again, there will be casualties, but not all of them ours. What would you not give to have a gun in your hand and a German in its sights? You might live awhile longer, if you want to call it living, by sitting on those hands and continuing to do nothing. But how much of that time would you be willing to sacrifice to take some SS with you, the murderers of your women, your children, your race?

"Tell that to your men when relaying our proposal. Ask them how they would feel avenging their families, taking the battle to those who have taken their loved ones from them."

Though Kaminski had been sincere in his enthusiasm—a revolt, guns, dynamite, *escape!*—the longer he ruminated on it, the more this began to dim. Baum, too, in his way, was enthusiastic, at the end even emotional, but Kaminski wasn't so unfamiliar with the underground not to be wary of any aggressive posturing on its part. The Resistance, from the little he knew of it, was by nature a defensive organization, set up to protect the inmates from the worst depredations of the Nazis. If anything, its mission was to keep the peace, not disturb it, to see that the applecart remained upright, not upset it. Out and out rebellion, by force of arms no less, wasn't something up its alley.

Plus, its members were almost exclusively Polish. The Poles had been at Auschwitz since its founding in 1940, their positions in the hospitals, the clerical offices, the kitchens long entrenched. And just as the power they enjoyed often approached that of the SS, so too did their anti-Semitism.

This he knew from experience, having been a target of it since boyhood. Why should this confederacy of Poles risk everything—their jobs, their privileges, their lives—to liberate Birkenau, the population of which grew more Jewish with every transport?

Those men of his he informed of Baum's visit echoed his concerns. The underground couldn't be trusted, was all talk and no action, one shouldn't count on the Poles sticking their necks out to try and save a bunch of Jews. Some, of course, not only argued otherwise but maintained the squad had an obligation to rebel against the slaughter, to stop aiding and abetting the kill-happy Germans. But at this early stage, they were in the minority. On the whole, skepticism ruled the day.

Something else, the kapo conjectured, was giving his people pause, not that any among them would have admitted to it. Many secretly harbored a desperate hope the war would end before long, or the Russians bomb the crematoria, or they'd be part of the lucky few to slip through the cracks, to be passed over when the day came to pay the pitiless SS piper.

In the Vernichtungslager, all was either ass-backward or a corruption of itself. The Ten Commandments were turned on their heads—thou *shalt* kill, thou *shalt* steal, thou *shalt* covet—the Golden Rule nonexistent. Here, the weak were at the mercy of the strong—the lame, sick, and feeble treated not with compassion but contempt. Here, nothing was less valuable than the life of a human being; a crust of bread, a pack of cigarettes, a needle and thread were worth more. Women with children and the elderly were the first to die, not the last. Here, the ailing were sent to the hospital to be killed, not cured.

So was it with hope. In the annihilation camp, hope was neither balm nor beacon, but an enemy. It was hope that led people unresisting from the undressing room to the gas chamber, that made men and women stand idly by while children were murdered. That prompted them to sink to any low for one more day of life, one small but essential step on the road to eventual liberation.

It was hope that helped make even the Sonder, men certain to die, men up to their waists all too often in the corpses of their own kind, unreceptive by and large to Baum's invitation. In that regard, their knees were as weak, their apathy as strong as they contended those of the men in the underground were. An observer of Block 13 would have been hard-pressed to ascertain where caution ended and hypocrisy began.

Kaminski was among those who remained undecided. Common sense told him that any notion of a mass breakout was folly. From

Noah Zabludowicz, he'd learned some of the details of Baum's battle plan, one of them that the underground had enlisted the Home Army's aid in providing firepower for the fight, along with help in escorting the escapees to safety.

Which was all fine and good, except the forces who'd be chasing them were hardly those of pharaoh's chariots in pursuit of the Chosen People fleeing Egypt. The Nazis had automatic weapons, artillery, even access to airplanes. What sort of safety, and where, did the partisans have in mind, especially should they find themselves responsible for who knew how many thousands?

Yet who could not applaud the opportunity to strike back, to give the killers a dose of their own medicine? Or as Baum had put it, if not by chance to live, then at least to die like a man, with a gun in one's hand.

The allure of this wasn't lost on Kaminski, but still he wavered. He knew full well what had befallen the 8th Sonderkommando, his second: two hundred of them had been tricked into an airtight room and gassed. What with the number of transports beginning to stream in, however, the 9th wouldn't have to worry for a while. Maybe a long while. How in good conscience could he be expected to rush men into risking what little life was left them by embarking on a project all but guaranteed to fail?

Though having taken an instant liking to him, he succeeded for weeks in stringing both Noah Zabludowicz and his organization along, telling him, not entirely untruthfully, that before he could commit them he needed more time to bring the Sonder to a consensus.

All that changed on the transformative night of March 14th, when on his knees in the dark of the Sonder yard, transfixed by the gory face of that accusing red moon, he saw what he hadn't before, with a clarity that shook him to his bones. Despite the emphasis Bruno Baum had put on escape, that wasn't what the uprising was about at all. And Baum knew it wasn't. Of much more importance, of paramount importance, was the razing of the crematoria, those four insatiable demon sisters poised even now to gobble up untold thousands.

That was Baum's real objective, the end to which any talk of forcing their way out of this place was merely the means. He'd been clever to dangle the twin incentives of escape and revenge so prominently while keeping references to the cremos to a minimum. Yet Kaminski knew that bottom line, Baum didn't care whether a single prisoner made it to freedom as long as those four devourers of men were put out of action.

Not that this would bring a halt to the slaughter. Nothing could do that; the SS were and always would be positively messianic in their bloodlust. But it would go far toward slowing that slaughter down, perhaps keeping it at a level that might see the war end before the Nazis achieved their dream of a Jew-free Europe. The transports were arriving from as far away as Greece and the Mediterranean now. It would have been folly to expect the two makeshift bunkers in the woods, even with Crematorium I, which was forever breaking down from overuse as it was, to dispose of what might wind up a quarter or even more of the continent's Jews.

The moon was trying to tell him something all right, and he would have been both a fool and a coward not to listen. In imitating the half-born baby, it was adding its entreaty to Baum's, one as tacit as the other but no less urgent for it. Somehow these mammoth new additions to the machinery of death had to be put out of commission; not only exigency but simple decency required it. Even the night sky was demanding an end to the butchery.

Kaminski wouldn't return to his bunk that night until late, even further from sleep than before. Two emotions had him on fire: a white-hot shame at having acted diffidently toward Baum's proposition, and a commensurate desire to make amends for that diffidence. What in the hell had he been thinking? The answer to that was he hadn't been, not for himself at any rate. He'd been listening in his nearsightedness to the blinkered, the timid, and to that selfsame little mouse that cowers somewhere inside every man, even the boldest.

Starting tomorrow, things would be different. Morning couldn't come fast enough for him. He knew of plenty in the squad eager to get at the Germans, men such as Zalman Leventhal, Zalman Gradowski, Leyb Langfus, and Yankel Handelsman to name but a few. These he would assemble at the first opportunity and discuss how best to proceed, beginning with how those either unsure of or opposed outright to fighting might be persuaded to change their mousy minds.

As Baum had foreseen, the word escape was the first requisite for attracting conspirators. Not even the most militant of the Sonder could be expected to agree to a suicide mission, to blowing themselves up along with the crematoria. But to make any talk of escape meaningful, Kaminski knew he'd have to persuade his men that the underground would have their back, if not as combatants then as providers of material and logistical support.

The latter meant mainly that there be partisans ready to assist the rebels in their war, while the former could be reduced to a single word: gunpowder. And lots of it. It was vital the Resistance follow through on its promise to supply the Sonder with gunpowder, not solely for the purpose of making dynamite with which to demolish the crematoria but to clear paths through the electric fence. It would also be needed to construct some kind of hand grenade for use in battle.

Until the day he held a pouch of the stuff in his hands, with the certainty of more coming, he would continue to set the bar of expectation high.

But he was convinced that day would arrive, if for no other reason than Baum had said it would. At their meeting, he'd asked his visitor if he was Jewish. His answer in the affirmative helped buttress Kaminski's suspicions that Baum was the driving force behind Auschwitz's decision to blow the cremos. That he occupied a lofty position in the underground had to be assumed, and it was difficult to see the Poles—many who'd no doubt viewed the smoke flooding from the crematorium's chimney with indifferent, even approving eyes—insisting on such a measure. A Jew on the other hand with the clout to push it through...

If this Baum, this Jew had anything to say about it, the Sonder would be getting all the gunpowder they'd need. Clear now was the why of the metal in the man's voice when he'd said the destruction of the gas chambers was "integral to the operation."

As the night of March 14th eased into the morning of the 15th, Kaminski still couldn't sleep. A key component of what he wanted to say to Leventhal and the others was eluding him. If the revolt were to appeal to those who'd be gambling their lives on it, it would have to have trappings as well as substance, a little window dressing. Like that of the underground, or so the nom de guerre Battle Group-

Auschwitz implied, Sonder activism could only benefit from a military touch: a rigid chain of command, a commitment to the giving and taking of orders, discipline, yes, and devotion to duty, but also that soldierly swagger, the camaraderie of men-at-arms.

But before it could acquire these, it needed an identity, something as basic yet unifying as a name. Battle Group-Sonderkommando? Not very original, he had to admit, but suggestive of affiliation with that other, older group. And it did accomplish what it was supposed to. The first step toward creating esprit de corps was establishing a definable corps.

Something else was needed, though, something he was overlooking. Something more… inspirational for lack of a better word. Or maybe that was the word. What, after all, was he searching for? A way to *inspire* the fence-sitters in the Sonder, as the moon had inspired him, to get off their butts and start behaving as if they had a pair. And where should a Jew seeking inspiration go? Why, to the Bible, naturally, and though he'd never been much of a one for religion, to the Bible he went.

As a child, he was taught all the old, familiar tales, and commenced in his mind to thumb through them now as if he had the Testament in front of him. He didn't have to go far. Upon arriving at the saga of the fall of Jericho, a smile began to play at the corners of his mouth and would grow, as slowly it dawned on him he might have found just what he was after.

Everyone knew the story of the battle of Jericho. The Israelite army, under its leader Joshua, successor to Moses, had encircled the heavily fortified city, its walls taller and thicker than any in the whole of Canaan. The defenders atop those walls, confident they couldn't be breached, hurled insults along with the odd projectile at their besiegers.

The Israelites, however, had a secret weapon, their God, Who directed Joshua to assemble a procession bearing the Ark of the Covenant which was to walk around the city once a day for six days, trumpets blaring. On the seventh day, it was to repeat this circuit seven times, the final sounding of the trumpets to be accompanied by a great shout from every man, woman, and child. Then would the walls of Jericho come crashing down.

And so according to legend did it happen. The city was taken and put to the sword.

Kaminski, being the realist he was, had never given much credence to this or any other biblical flight of the imagination, but whether he did or not was immaterial. What mattered was that he could use the hyperbole and very real audacity of the old battle to light a fire under the Sonder and win converts to the approaching new one. Just as the heroes of yesteryear had leveled the walls of the enemy with their trumpets, so would those of today reduce the walls of the crematoria to rubble with their dynamite. Except now not just the conquest of a city lay at stake, but quite possibly the future of the Jews as a people.

The trumpets of Jericho, the gunpowder of Birkenau—the two were one and the same. As it would be said for all time of the warriors who'd wielded both, unless this Special Squad proved itself unequal to the challenge and let history roll over it as all previous had.

Kaminski, the newly galvanized, the stick-at-nothing-now Kaminski, wasn't about to let that happen. He was as determined to set the wheels of rebellion in motion as he was to see the operation through to its end. Come dawn, he would put up the pair of bricks that summoned Noah Zabludowicz to learn what progress Auschwitz had made on its plan.

After that, he meant to get with the two Zalmans, Leventhal and Gradowski. He figured it might be best to test his persuasiveness on them: not only were both vocal about fighting back but had already put their money where their mouths were.

For some weeks, much to their peril, each had been writing down all he'd seen since the ghetto, plus what life was like in the commando of the living dead. Gradowski, at the kapo's request, had shown him something of his, and Kaminski had been both taken by its truth and surprised by its poetry. "The dark night is my friend," he'd read, "tears and screams are my songs, the fire of sacrifice my light, the atmosphere of death my perfume. Hell is my home…"

The pair intended to seal these and future compositions in moisture-proof jars and bury them in the yards of the different crematoria. If caught they'd be executed, and not quickly, with a bullet. Their masters had let the detachment know that any of them found divulging the secrets of *Sonderbehandlung*—special handling, the euphemism for mass murder—to either its selected victims or other prisoners, would be bound and thrown alive into one of the ovens.

Neither Zalman gave a damn. They were the bravest of the brave. They'd surmised that should the Germans lose their war, though the SS before then would have dynamited the death houses themselves, the area in and around what remained of them would be seen as fertile ground by historians and others seeking evidence of Nazi crimes. And they aimed to add to that evidence by leaving a record of the horrors. They weren't going to survive, but their testimonies would.

Though bigger and stronger and wiser to the ways of the world than either, Kaminski felt puny in their presence. Their valor dwarfed him.

Sleep would come slowly that night, but it did come. It was while honing his "trumpets of Jericho" peroration that he dropped off. When he awoke in the morning, to his relief he hadn't dreamed, or just as welcome, didn't remember any. This was always a plus. Experience had taught him that the dreams of a Sonder man weren't things one wanted to carry around with one all day.

*   *   *

It was a brisk, mid-April afternoon, the sky a bleached, bird's-egg blue, the sun so blinding white one didn't have to look directly at it for it to sting. Every shadow stood in sharp relief against last night's fall of snow, which had been unexpected but would also be the season's last.

But for the incandescent orange cherry of his cigarette, the man loitering in the shade of the crematorium was invisible. Even without shade, he might have been hard to distinguish from the dark brick he was leaning against, for his entire body was covered in a greasy black soot, his hair, his skin, his clothes. He could have passed for someone who'd been working in a coal mine all day instead of up to his knees in dead bodies.

Crematorium V had been in operation going on two weeks now, with Zalman Leventhal a part of its crew from the first. His station was the incineration room, where two Mogilev-style furnaces housed four ovens each, all fueled by coke, or refined coal, which explained his appearance. Why he should have been absent from work in the middle of a shift had its own explanation, part of which resided in the layout of the death house itself.

Unlike half of Crematorium II and the still uncompleted III, none of Number Five extended below ground. This was but one of the differences between them, all adopted (as they were in V's identical counterpart, Crematorium IV) with an eye to cutting costs. Each could claim only two-thirds the gassing capacity of Numbers Two and Three, and when it came to cremation were only half as productive. Leventhal knew this because he'd worked Two right after it had opened, not for long but sufficient for it to impress him with its size and sophistication.

In contrast, much of Crematorium V resembled less its modernized partner than it did the site of his first assignment in the Sonderkommando, Bunker 2 in the birch forest, where he and the rest of the hapless young conscripts from Ciechanow had received their first taste of the SS mania for destruction. As with that farmhouse turned slaughterhouse, Number Five had neither Two's forced-draft heating nor de-aerating capabilities; its gas chambers were warmed to the required 81° by large, pot-bellied stoves, its poison extracted by the natural draft that came from opening its gas-tight outer doors. The Zyklon-B pellets, too, were introduced in the same awkward fashion as in the bunkers, through vents in the walls covered with movable flaps.

Then there was its floor plan. Almost six times longer, seventy meters, than it was wide, a spacious undressing room in the center separated the gas chamber at one end and the crematory at the other. The corpses had to be hauled from the killing chamber back into this central room to have their hair cut, their jewelry and such collected, then dragged the rest of the length of the building to the ovens. When these already had more than they could handle, the only option was to leave the bodies stacked in the undressing room to wait their turn.

This tied up that area, pressuring the Sonder at the ovens to increase output. Resulting in the men, and more detrimentally, the machinery being taxed, this last exposing the principal flaw in the design of these smaller crematoria.

Originally commissioned for a proposed chain of low-budget facilities deep inside Russia to assist with the disposal of the millions being murdered there (but never built), the Mogilev set-up was at greater risk of breaking down, if cheaper to install, than the configuration existing in Crematoria II and III.

The problem was the overly centralized structure of the two furnaces that contained the eight muffles, or individual ovens. The four closest to the electric generators that ignited the coke and kept it burning tended to get hotter than the four farther away. This imbalance gave rise to distortions in the fire clay, which after a while began to buckle and split apart.

After only two weeks of admittedly heavy usage, both furnaces in Crematorium IV developed large cracks. These were filled in with rammed earth and cement, but eventually reappeared. And kept appearing, no matter what the Germans did.

To prevent the same from occurring in Number Five, they did manage—as they had in Four, if too late—to reposition the two generators and install protective ducts. This allayed the defect somewhat, but didn't dispense with it. Caution had to be taken from then on when using its ovens, while those of Number Four were rarely again at full service.

This was what had brought Leventhal out of the darkness of the furnace room into the bright light of day. Though the sun was still climbing, the Sonder were at work on their second transport, and had been warned there might be another. With the undressing room overflowing with corpses and the ovens backed up, his kapo had pulled him off the line.

The urgency in the man's voice was detectable even above the ovens and flues. "I need you to drop what you're doing and get your ass next door."

"Where, Number Four?"

"Goddammit, where else? Find out how they're doing, see if they can help us out. I need to know if—"

"Why not just call them on the phone?" chirped Leventhal, enjoying his boss's frustration.

"No one's answering the goddam phone! It's probably not working any better than anything else over there! Just do what I say and get going. I need to see if they can take some of these stiffs off our hands in case there's another transport."

Leventhal's SS escort was drunk. He didn't walk so much as weave his way to their destination. What with the prospect of another transport, he was more envious of the man than anything, a feeling fortified by what he discovered at Crematorium IV. Only five of its ovens were functioning, and one of those not fully; no way could its crew handle any more of the dead today. Indeed, it would take them until tomorrow to get rid of those they had.

Upon returning to his compound and shedding the guard, he was in no hurry to get back to work. For one thing, he wasn't looking forward to telling his kapo the bad news. For another, it was such a crisp, crystalline day, a heaven to the scorching hell in which he'd been slaving all morning. He decided to smoke a cigarette, hide out awhile. Seeking cover in the shadow of the house of the damned, he reached in his coat pocket for his pack and lit up.

Hardly had he done so than he heard them. Deportees on the march, large numbers of them, had their own sound. The footsore shuffle of their shoes on the road, the wailing of small children, the deeper flux of adult voices a tense, weary murmur—it was another transport all right. Leventhal shook his head half in disbelief, half in disgust.

They soon emerged from the greenbelt of trees hiding the crematorium, a long column of people flanked on both sides by soldiers. Like the two preceding it, it was a shipment of Greek Jews, this clear from the desperation in their faces.

Not that Leventhal thought Greeks inherently more prone to despair than Czechs, say, or the French. As he'd learned long ago, it was all about water, or rather the lack of it. The lengthier their journey, the greater the thirst of the new arrivals, and the greater this the more distracted they were. And the easier to control. The SS on the trains weren't denying their cargoes water just to be cruel, but as a ploy to reduce both their will and ability to resist. To so disorient and demoralize them that all other considerations paled before wetting their parched throats, their cracked lips.

It would take the Greeks a good week or more to make the trip to Poland, depending on what part of that islanded country they came from. By the time they got to Birkenau, they would have run off a cliff if the Germans told them there was water at the bottom of it.

He watched as the bolder among them would break ranks and snatch up fistfuls of the cleaner snow, only to be chased back into line by the SS. As they neared the barbed-wire perimeter of the yard, however, they forgot the demands of the flesh, and those in back craning their necks for a better view, turned their attention instead to the curious construction in front of them.

The Nazis had gone to great length to disguise the crematorium. Red brick trimmed in white held a gabled roof aloft, fake windows thick with drapery, their flower boxes full. Wrought-iron lampposts stood sentinel over a trimmed lawn patched with snow, a flagstone path winding through it, dodging stately pines. But for the ugliness of the wire through which the transport peered, the effect was of a well-to-do family's country home.

Except for two things: a low, plaster annex, windowless but for three slits cut in its side, and a pair of oversized brick chimneys, the Mogilevs requiring two smokestacks to Crematorium II's one. What the Greeks might have made of these anomalies, and the smoke pouring from the latter, Leventhal couldn't say, but for doubting that in their thirst they even questioned them.

What he wanted to see was what the SS were going to do now. With the dead piled like logs in the undressing room, how were those about to join them supposed to get ready for their "bath?"

He soon had his answer. After all had entered the compound and the gate was secured, the officer in charge gave the usual speech about the necessity of a shower, then ordered them to strip right there in the yard.

Leventhal would have expected some resistance to this, but there was none. Ignoring the nip in the air, and the lack of even the meager privacy afforded by four walls, after a moment's hesitation the Greeks began obediently to undress, with little sign of the reluctance the order so often inspired. The compulsion to modesty was no match for the prospect of water, even shower water, and the chance to douse the fire smoldering in their gullets.

With that, he was out of there. He feared what was coming and had no intention of sticking around. Nor was it because of the screaming and the rest that attended every gassing. As disturbing as that might be, something else in its own way loomed just as horrible. Number Five's gas chamber was divided in two, the bigger part large enough to hold the fifteen hundred people about to file into it. Twice before, mouth agape, he'd seen a chamber similarly packed seem to rock on its foundation from the upheaval inside. How much of this had been his imagination wasn't a riddle he was in any rush to solve now.

Blanking his mind, therefore, to the tragedy about to unfold, as only a Sonder could—as a Sonder had to if he wanted to stay sane—

Leventhal turned his back on the increasingly naked fifteen hundred and headed to work, toward the door that led to the flames and the smoke. A sign reading "Abandon all hope ye who enter here" would not have been out of place above that door, for like Dante forsaking the friendly sun for the inimical gloom of hell, he, too, was leaving the light and fresh air for the toxic black murk of the inferno that was the cremating room.

It took him a minute to adapt to the dark, but there was no getting used to the noise, the suffocating smoke. When the ovens were going without let-up, it was as if there was more smoke in the air than oxygen, the sweet-sour smoke of burning human flesh. In view of its importance, it wasn't an especially imposing room, twenty meters long and half as wide, made the more cramped by the two brick furnaces taking up its center. The walls, too, were brick and as permanently blackened as the low ceiling.

Two windows were cut into each side, but so soot-stained as to be opaque, the light that did leak through them a yellowish gray. A wide corridor separated this room from the undressing hall, while acting as a further buffer against the din and the heat was the *Kommandoführer's* office, a bathroom, a small storage area, and the coke bin.

The blanket of hot air blasting from the nearest of the two furnaces wrapped itself around Leventhal as soon as he walked in. His kapo was right behind it.

"Glad you could make it back. How was the movie?"

"Sir, it was the guard. He'd been drinking, and... well, wasn't in any hurry."

"Sorry lying rotter," the other said, but less angrily than he should have. Of more concern to him was what he'd sent his stoker to check on. "So what about Number Four? Can they help us?"

Leventhal had considered qualifying his report to maybe temper the kapo's wrath, but couldn't think how. He wasn't about to tell him, though, that a third transport had arrived. "Number Four, I'm afraid, could use some help themselves. Only half their ovens are working, and—"

"Blood and thunder! Did they say when they might—oh, never mind!"

The man glanced at the already grossly overloaded tooth-pulling station. "The fire pits full, Number Four next to worthless, and

Three still unfinished! Which leaves us on our own, us and Number Two. Which also—son of a *bitch!*—means express work. If the ovens can even take it. Let me find that prick of a *Kommandoführer* and see what his lordship wants to do."

He started off, then abruptly pivoted on his heel. "You, meanwhile, back on the job! And don't let me catch you loafing again!"

The first words to pop into Leventhal's head at sight of yet another transport had been "express work." But only after his kapo spoke them aloud did the reality of them hit home. Express work was used as a last resort only. The SS were no fonder of the tactic than their slaves, as it put a strain on the entire system—the ovens, the furnaces that held them, the generators, the chimneys—that none of those components was designed to withstand. For the Sonder, it called for not only more work and at a faster pace, but worse, the necessity of having to pay closer attention to the dead, to appraise and group them by age, sex, and physical condition.

Each oven had a manufacturer's recommended limit of two corpses per half hour, though seldom was this adhered to. The usual rate was three every twenty minutes, but with the gas chamber going full tilt and the flow of bodies a cataract, the figure was upped to five every twenty-five minutes. From the rows lined up at the dental station, the Sonder would mix and match, combining the different physiques in such a way as to enhance combustion.

Two children and a Muselmann might be thrown together with a well-nourished man and woman. Or two Muselmänner, a child, and two overweight women—every Sonder team had its own array of formulas, each predicated on the common denominator of fat. During express work especially, body fat was the oil that kept the engine of extinction running; the bonier the corpse, the more it needed another's fat to burn.

In that nature had endowed their sex with an extra layer of the stuff, the bodies of women were prized, above all those fresh off the trains. Where in happier, less hallucinatory days the men of the Sonder would have competed with each other for eligible females, now disputes often flared up among them over the rights to those same females' cadavers.

From his kapo's expression when he returned, Leventhal could tell what the *Kommandoführer's* verdict had been. Express work it was, there was no getting around it. Now they would be forced to get intimate with the deceased, to assess, to assort, to scrutinize their persons instead of trying not to look at them as they slung them about. He wasn't the only Sonder to pity the dental commando. It wasn't uncommon for one of them to close the eyes of his corpse before inserting the crowbar to prise open its jaws.

After the pliers had done their work, the dead were lugged toward the furnaces and arranged in the four apropos piles: adult males, adult females, children of both sexes, and from the camp the Muselmänner, always the Muselmänner, there was never any shortage of those to dispose of. From these piles, the oven-Sonder would select what they needed, and with the help of bearer-Sonder drag them to their stations.

There they were placed in accordance with the chosen formula into an open-ended metal trough atop a wheeled sled. With a loud rattling, the heavy iron door of the oven was cranked open not unlike a theater curtain rising, the fierce heat that gushed forth singeing what hair was left on the corpses' heads. When fully drawn to reveal the fire raging inside, two men lined up the sled and shoved the trough in. When extracting it, one held a long, iron fork against the bodies to keep them in place. The door was then lowered shut, but partially raised twice more to allow the stokers to "stir the stew" as Leventhal's kapo liked to say.

Air from the motor-powered Exhator ventilators, one to an oven, assisted the flames, which burned two wheelbarrows of coke per cremation. After every three or four of these, the ashes were removed from the bottom of the muffle along with any unconsumed bone. This was to prevent them from clogging the flues under the floor which channeled the bulk of the heat and smoke to the chimneys. The fiery tempest beneath one's feet not only caused the room to tremble (nor in this case could it be Leventhal's imagination) but compelled one to shout above its locomotive roar, the lawnmower racket of the Exhators.

It was Pandaemonium in its original, most fearsome sense, as the poet Milton had named his capitol city of hell. With their deafening noise, their fire and smoke, the mutilated bodies of the dead everywhere, Leventhal was sure that after the crematoria the real hell was going to hold few surprises for him.

That he was to be forever damned he had little doubt. As a cog in the SS machine, he expected nothing else from the afterlife, no matter that his only reason to go on living was to get the word on that machine out to the rest of the world. He'd made this promise to himself his first day on the job, that eye-opening day five months ago when he'd been marched to Bunker 2 in the woods and learned firsthand what the Nazis were up to, what those baffling columns of black smoke meant, that oily stench in the air.

Though he had no idea how he was going to make good on that promise, fortune would see fit to show him a way.

It came in the person of his friend and namesake Zalman Gradowski, whom he'd met in Block 13. Gradowski came from a small town in Poland near the Lithuanian border. The thing that first struck Leventhal about him was his methodical nature; even here, in the muddy slaughter pen that was Birkenau, he was a man of fastidious habits. His bunk area was never anything but military-neat, the nails of his childishly stubby fingers always trimmed and clean. A clerical worker by trade, he'd aspired to be an author and had had a few minor pieces published. But the German invasion forced him to set his ambitions aside.

The war ended up crushing another dream of his: an ardent Zionist, he'd been making ready to emigrate with his family to Palestine in the summer of 1940. Instead, it was the Wehrmacht, then the SS, and eventually the cattle car for them.

Physically, the two men couldn't have been more different. Where Leventhal, the redhead, was fair-complexioned and thin, Gradowski was broad in the beam and on the swarthy side, his coloring more typical of the desert Jew of the Bible. They differed in temperament, too. Leventhal was an introvert who'd never mixed well with people, a shy oyster of a man who until the ghetto made it impossible had spent his life avoiding them.

Gradowski by contrast loved a good party. He genuinely enjoyed the company of his fellow man, and when so moved could talk a blue streak. They also didn't see eye to eye on religion. The miseries of ghetto life had failed to impact the faith of either, but after Birkenau, Leventhal's had taken a serious beating. Argue as he felt impelled to as a friend to dissuade Gradowski from his and the enervating hope it fostered, he'd met with only limited success.

In spite of these disparities, the two had bonded from the start. This wasn't like the unsociable Leventhal, but upon discovering the other gifted with the same classical education as he, before long they were talking books, philosophy, history, and yes, religion.

Sadly, they had more than just this and their first names in common; both of their families lay in ruins. While Leventhal's parents, maternal grandparents, a younger brother, both sisters, and seven nieces and nephews had gone to the gas, Gradowski lost his wife, his parents, also two sisters, a brother-in-law, father-in-law, and three little nieces. Because of this, they also shared an unquenchable thirst for retribution, had sworn themselves to avenging the murders of their beloved.

But they also knew that vengeance, if attainable at all, would have to wait. The Nazis were too powerful, they too utterly helpless. Leventhal was content at first merely to observe, to remember, and on the chance he might survive the SS whirlwind bear witness one day. It was Gradowski who suggested the more audacious plan of keeping written accounts of what they'd seen and burying these in the crematoria yards.

His reasoning was twofold and hard to refute. Only a fool would bet on the Germans leaving a single Sonder alive, and with the news filtering in from the Russian front, the odds of the Third Reich winning its war were getting longer. If documents from eyewitnesses describing Nazi atrocities were to be unearthed afterward, it would make it difficult for the SS specifically, and the German nation in general, to deny responsibility for those atrocities. Or go so far as to maintain such outrages never happened.

Already, each had bottled one of these rough time capsules and planted it, Leventhal's a few meters to the rear of Crematorium V, Gradowski's at Number Two. To corroborate what they'd written, lest their intended audience find it incredible, they'd also strewn numerous teeth in both yards.

Gradowski worked Crematorium II's gas chamber under Kaminski. It was at his kapo's invitation that he'd buried his first effort there, an invitation that stood for however many more they might wish to put in the ground. But beyond that, he'd given the pair something for which they were even more grateful by informing them of the revolt, then asking them to be a part of it. Nor did he have to ask twice. If Leventhal was docketed for everlasting perdition, he wasn't about to pass on taking some SS with him.

He labored into the evening that day burning the Greeks, his kapo making him work overtime for his tardiness earlier. He was put to assisting the night shift as a bearer of both corpses and coke—each, what with express work in force, virtually without interruption.

When finally the night-kapo took mercy on him, it was all he could do to drag himself to Block 13, his body beat up, his clothes trailing coal dust.

Despite Gradowski having washed the gore of the day away and changed into a fresh outfit, he embraced his begrimed friend as was their habit. After he, too, had showered and sat down to eat, Gradowski joined him at the long communal table.

"The Greeks again?"

Leventhal nodded.

"Us, too, and more on the way tomorrow. Or that's the scuttlebutt. What's the word on Number Four?"

"Good news and bad." Leventhal looked up from his plate. "The bad is that only half its ovens are working. Which is, of course, also the good news. But judging from the smoke rising to the north all day, Sergeant Möll's fire pits are doing their best to pick up the slack. Who would have guessed there were so many Jews in Greece of all places?"

"The question is," Gradowski said, "how many are liable to be left a few months from now?"

Leventhal went back to his food. Neither spoke until Gradowski, clearing his throat, ventured to lighten the mood.

"Speaking of good news, there's an interesting fellow joined us a while back, works with me in Number Two. Tall, curly black hair, thick black glasses, around thirty—you run across him yet?"

"I don't believe so. What's his name?"

"Langfus. Leyb Langfus."

"Leyb *Longfoot?*" After the yeshiva school, Leventhal's Yiddish left little to be desired. "That's a peculiar name."

"He's a peculiar sort. Trust me, if you'd met him, you would remember. There's something, I don't know, a weird energy about him, a light in his eyes, as if he was looking past this world into a whole invisible other. If he was here, I'd point him out, but…"

Gradowski, half-rising from his seat, panned the room. "Anyway, he's quite devout, to the extent it's this, you could say, that defines him. Though like us he lost family to Birkenau, a wife and infant son, unlike us his faith hasn't dimmed, not a whit. But word has it he was *dayan* of the twin towns of Makov-Mazovietsk. And when the rabbi there absconded to Warsaw ahead of the Nazis, Langfus took over his duties."

Dayan, Hebrew for judge, was the title of a person versed in Talmudic law whose advice was regularly sought by rabbis among others. Leventhal was impressed. To have been a dayan before the age of thirty, then an acting rabbi, was unusual. But he was leery of that weird light in the man's eyes, or however Gradowski had put it; the phrase "religious hysteric" had grabbed hold of him and wasn't letting go. "Sounds…interesting, this Langfus of yours," he said disinterestedly.

"Wait, there's more," Gradowski said, "listen to this. Though assigned to Sonderkommando duty, he refuses to do the work. The most he'll concede is helping the sick and old in the undressing rooms. And janitorial work and such. He won't set foot near the gas chambers and ovens."

Leventhal's brow lifted in astonishment. "And the Germans haven't shot him? How can that be?"

"I don't know. No one does, it defies understanding. I asked Kapo Kaminski what was what, and he was as puzzled as anybody. He did say *Oberscharführer* Muhsfeld once approached him about it—Muhsfeld, that butcher, who kills as if he's swatting flies—and wanted to know what was going on. Kaminski lied and told him Langfus was recovering from pneumonia, and wondered if maybe the *Ober* had something useful but less than strenuous he could assign him to for now.

"Strangely, miraculously, Muhsfeld thought for a moment and said that he did; the next day, he put the dayan in charge of burning the incidentals left by the dead. You know, the passports, birth certificates, photographs, cheap kids' toys, all that the SS regard as rubbish.

"He tends his fires, reads from the Talmud and the Haggadah, recites the prayers for the dead all day, and the Nazis leave him alone. I've never seen anything like it. It's as if even the Krauts aren't sure what to make of him and his otherworldly ways. Did I mention he eats only bread and onions, the camp soup? He won't touch a thing that comes off the transports."

"Quite the individual," Leventhal said, "but I'm afraid I don't follow. What does all this have to do with the good news you said you had?"

"I'm just coming to that. This Langfus isn't one of those who wraps himself in a prayer shawl and rocks on his butt mumbling Scripture for hours on end. Turns out he's that rarest of Jews, both ultra-orthodox, and get this, a scrapper. I talked to someone from the same ghetto as he who said that prior to their deportation, he argued against boarding the cattle cars in favor of trying to sneak through the German cordon at night and making a dash for the forest. He may be as spiritual as they come, but unspirited he isn't."

"Go on."

"Yesterday," Gradowski said, lowering his voice, "he takes me aside and says we should be working together. I told him I thought we were, and he said no, not crematorium work, the work of the devil, but the holy work of keeping a record of Nazi crimes. I asked him how he knew about the jars we'd buried, and he said Kaminski told him. In fact, it was Kaminski who sent him to me.

"I asked the kapo about this later, and he assured me the dayan could be trusted, was one of his best men, as committed as anyone to making the revolt a reality. Who'd have pegged him for the type? I'd never have even considered recruiting him into the plot, and there he was, in on it all along.

"And now he wants to stick his neck out even farther and help you and I assemble our little narratives. I figured you'd be glad to hear we were three now instead of two."

Leventhal pushed his plate away. "Glad? Of course I'm glad. We could use more help. And in the end, a third diarist can only add credibility.

"But as far as news, I was hoping for something a little meatier. Have you any idea, say, what progress the Battle Group has made? In its hunt for weapons perhaps? I hear there've been some problems with that."

Gradowski's try at a smile wasn't encouraging. "Ammunition we're getting, from the military salvage yard outside the camp. It isn't coming easily, or cheap, but it is coming. So far no guns, though. Guns, I hate to say, don't promise well, not at present."

The smile brightened a touch. "Gun*powder*, however… One of the underground's operatives has been feeding it to us regularly, enough that our stash of dynamite, you ought to see it, is getting healthier by the week. I've heard it said this person is female, out of a Canada commando. Makes one proud to be a Jew, doesn't it? That we as a people can claim such women. May God continue to protect and watch over her."

"God?" Leventhal had a feeling this was coming, given all the fuss his tablemate was making over this Langfus character. "What, my man, are you backsliding on me already? When last we talked God—what, two weeks ago?—you said you were having more doubts about Him than ever."

"Yes, I was," the other sighed, "but now I'm beginning to doubt my doubts. It's the dayan: he can be most convincing when he's a mind to."

"I can only imagine."

There was no missing the derision in the voice, but Gradowski let it go. The last thing he wanted at this hour was to get into an argument about religion of all damned things. "Anyhow…" he said, overdramatizing a yawn as he rose from his chair. "I'm about done for the night, think I'll hit the sack. You should do the same, Zalman. You've *got* to be exhausted."

And so he was, but sleep wasn't in Leventhal's plans. Not just yet. He'd decided this morning to write another witness, and knew with what he was going to begin it. The incident had been tugging at him for days, demanding to be heard. He'd put it off, frankly, because he was loath to revisit the awful thing, but the hour had come to forget such selfishness.

It was something he'd seen in the morgue abutting Number Two's incineration room. This was where the newly gassed were temporarily stored when the ovens were backed up. When empty, it served as an execution site for groups too small to warrant the use of Zyklon-B. This often comprised those from outside the camp, usually Jews who'd fled their villages or towns for the forests. The Gestapo, frequently with the help of local Poles, hunted down these runaways, and after amassing a sufficient number trucked them to Birkenau.

A freestanding wall, open at both ends, divided the morgue lengthwise. Six or seven victims at a time would be driven inside, naked. Made to face the wall, each was held there by a Sonder as an SS officer went down the line with a pistol, shooting them in the base of the skull. Some required the Sonder position the head at the best angle for the kill. The bodies were then drug behind the wall and the next batch brought in. Once none were left, the gunman would step among the fallen, dispensing the coup de grace to those still breathing.

Short-lived as was his stay at Crematorium II, Leventhal wound up working two of these small-scale murder sessions. One of which, in its villainy, its heartbreak, stood out above the other. It was this, tired or no, he felt the need to set down while he could on the chance, the same chance every inmate ran, something happen to him tomorrow. It was urgent it be preserved for some future day, so those dwelling in that future might better judge the Nazi mind—see not only what the SOB's were capable of but that they knew, deep down they knew what they were doing was wrong.

He made for his bunk soon after Gradowski, lay there waiting for the dark. It was safer to hold off until lights-out before writing. As much a non sequitur as this sounded, there were always a few men who weren't done with their reading and would burn a candle or flashlight in bed. He himself would make a sort of tent of his blanket and scribble away under there. Not that he didn't trust his mates to keep his secret should they chance on it, but one couldn't be too careful. An innocent slip of the tongue could be as lethal as a snitch's knife in the back.

Leventhal shut his eyes, the better to relive that evil day. The Germans had herded about fifty people into the corridor outside the morgue, some still wearing the yellow Star of David decreed by the Nazis to identify them as Jews. Filthy, bedraggled, twigs and bits of leaves caught in their clothing, they were clearly from the forest. And as clearly aware their end had come. He watched a young mother, at the order to disrobe, slip out of her shoes and stockings before kneeling to undress her four-year-old.

"Mama," he heard the little boy say, "why are we taking off our clothes?"

"Because we have to, darling." There was a catch in her voice.

"Is this the doctor's?" he asked as she unbuttoned his shirt. "Is he going to make me not sick anymore?"

"Yes, my precious boy, soon you'll be all better." The mother was struggling to hold back her tears. "And we'll be with your daddy again, just like before, only happier."

Leventhal remembered not wanting to hear more and heading back into the morgue. The woman entered in the fifth batch, her babe in her arms. To his relief, it fell to another Sonder to lead her to the wall.

The shooter this day, the ill-tempered if normally adroit *Oberscharführer* Peter Voss—a lean man in his mid-thirties, with a sour, pinched look—started with her and immediately bungled it. Instead of doing away with the mother first, he sought to position himself for a shot at her son, to which she reacted by frantically twisting and turning in an effort to keep her body between the child and the pistol.

Refusing to admit his mistake, probably because he'd been drinking, Leventhal could smell it on him, Voss kept stubbornly after the little boy. "Hold her!" he snapped at the Sonder assigned her, but she wouldn't be held, nor cease her desperate maneuvering, until suddenly the gun exploded and the toddler let out a shriek.

What happened next stopped Leventhal in mid-breath. Red with the blood of her dying son, the woman wheeled and hurled the body straight at his killer's head, the startled Voss taking it literally on the chin. With an animal scream, she launched herself after it, but the pistol barked twice more and she fell at the sergeant's feet.

Voss's eyes threatened to burst from their sockets, but not until he reached up to wipe his cheek and drew back a hand wet with the boy's blood did he lose it altogether. He turned an instant white, let his gun clatter to the floor. For several long seconds, he stared slack-mouthed at the offending hand, then lurching for the door yelled at his SS assistant to take over, that he'd had it for the day.

The way Leventhal saw it, the encounter was remarkable for two reasons. Why the mother should have used her child as a projectile like that was beyond him. But who was to say what one would do with the light of one's life, the flesh of one's flesh dying in one's arms, his blood splashing one's feet? Was it temporary insanity or defiance that took hold of her—a cognitive breakdown at the horror of the moment, or a deliberate attempt even in the midst of that horror to distract Voss so she might get to him and exact some revenge with her fingernails?

Leventhal would never know, though had no doubt which scenario he would have liked to believe.

The meaning of the second act of the tragedy, however, was plain. Voss had self-destructed, but why? If the Jew was indeed a bloodsucking leech, the subhuman enemy of the German Volk, the only emotion elicited by his elimination should have been one of satisfaction at a job well done. Having a dead baby flung at him, admittedly, was neither routine nor something Voss was going to be forgetting. But Leventhal could tell this wasn't what had made him drop his gun and desert his post, not on its own.

His baptism in that baby's blood was what had done the trick. One look at the man's face after he'd felt it on his cheek affirmed that what had unhinged him was the crimson mark of Cain staining that face.

Which meant that at a gut level, beneath the veneer of ideology and blind loyalty to the Fatherland, lurked the recognition he'd just committed infanticide. Not disinfection, nor deverminization, nor the dutiful removal of a future hazard to the Aryan race, but the cold-blooded murder of a fellow human being, a child.

No wonder the SS drank. The privilege of playing God came with a price, an assault not on the ego so much as the superego, the conscience. As opposed to mitigating the offense, the occasional pang of remorse they showed only augmented the Germans' guilt, added to their crimes. They deserved to be doubly condemned, not only for the physical act of killing but for not heeding that inner voice that kept trying to tell them it wasn't necessary or laudable, but an atrocity.

As for the actual God, He Who wasn't playing at it, the God of their forefathers, the almighty Yahweh—Leventhal didn't know what to make of Him anymore. The question continued to vex others: what kind of God would allow a Birkenau to happen? Could it be the same God Who'd established a supposedly eternal covenant with the Jews, went so far in days past as to foster a speaking relationship with them, watched over and shepherded them down through the ages to the point where even the Gentile referred to them as His Chosen People?

It didn't make sense. Millennia of history had come to nothing. With Birkenau, the divine rug had been pulled from under them.

It wasn't as if he'd given up believing in God. One might as well doubt the existence of the mountains, the sky, the oceans. To say He didn't exist simply because Birkenau did wasn't only selling God short but letting Him off the hook.

Yet Leventhal did feel he could no longer trust Him, particularly after learning of the death of his family. With that had come the realization, sickening, abrupt, that most of the theology he'd been fed over the years, from earliest childhood to his studies at the yeshiva school, was pure pablum. God wasn't the loving father he'd been brought up to revere, the stern but fair father Who, though He could be demanding, was concerned above all with the welfare of His children.

He was the father Who abandoned His children, blithely left them to their fate without so much as a fare-thee-well.

God had either gone insane, or worse yet, lost interest. Why would He take the trouble to rescue the Jews from the Egyptians and slavery, keep them intact under the conquering Babylonians and Assyrians, keep them alive before both the fury of the ancient Rome of the Caesars and the New Rome of a Christian Europe, only to stand idly by now as they were ushered into extinction? What could have prompted this Yahweh to forsake His people, to change from God the protective, the nurturing, into God the aloof, the callous, the criminally indifferent?

Leventhal hadn't a clue, but this much he did know: whenever God entered his thoughts now, sorrow and betrayal weren't far behind. For this reason, he preferred not to think about Him at all, but there were times it couldn't be helped, days it was forced on him. Days like today. He had yet to meet this Leyb Langfus, but already didn't like him. Was he being hasty? Perhaps. Having never met him, he could hardly presume to speak ill of the man, especially given not just his offer to bury his own testimony with theirs but the courageous picture Gradowski had painted of him. From that alone, there wasn't a lot not to like about the Makover dayan.

But he couldn't help resenting that all this blather about him and his unshakeable faith, a faith he appeared to wear like some sclerotic suit of armor, had turned those thoughts of his toward his capricious God again. As would likely be the case whenever their paths crossed. Judging from Gradowski's precipitately improved attitude toward the deity, Langfus wasn't only a skillful proselytizer but an aggressive one.

He lay in his bunk staring at the wall next to it, rancor eating at his brain, loss at his heart. Everything he'd held dear had been stolen from him: his life in Ciechanow before the ghetto, the few friends he'd managed, his guiltless family, and with this last theft, his God. As both a child and a man, he couldn't have been more devout, nourishing a genuine affection for his father in heaven at the same time he leaned on Him for sustenance and support. Now this pillar of support, this last love was gone. God had fled the field and left the devil in charge.

"So be it," Leventhal said to the plaster wall in front of him, "let the devil have it then. Let him have the whole thing. Let the world be as bleak as this Birkenau that inhabits it. But in return, let the dayan keep his piety to himself or so help me I'll shut that damned mouth of his for him."

At that moment, as if holding back until he arrived at this conclusion, the overhead lights blinked off and on as a warning they'd soon be extinguished. He felt beneath his blanket for the sheaf of paper he'd snuck into bed. He had his flashlight ready, his pen and ink, and was anxious to start, to get his mind off what it had no business being on to begin with.

While he waited, he directed it back to that day in the morgue, recalling with a smile that wasn't a smile, with something more like the rictus on the face of a corpse, *Oberscharführer* Voss showing up the morning after his poor performance in a good, one could even say a jovial mood.

*   *   *

"Godel. Godel, sweetheart," Roza breathed in her lover's ear. "Are you awake, dearest? You awake?"

A low, luxurious moan told her he'd rather not be. She kissed him on the cheek and lay back in their makeshift bed. After a moment, she raised a hand to her nose and sniffed her fingers—it was the odor of sex, of animal rut, of wild, sweaty abandon. Of male and female, Godel and her, mixed all together. She lingered over them dreamily until there was no smell left, her fingers as leached of fragrance as if she'd licked them clean.

Though not much time remained them, Roza didn't begrudge her man his nap. She couldn't deny he'd earned it, having put him through quite a workout. That she was as energetic a lover as she was worldly a one wasn't a fact lost on her. Nor was this a source of either pride or shame, but simply who she was. It wouldn't have been easy to be more reserved, more "ladylike" (how that word made her gag!) even if she'd wanted to.

She stretched like a contented house cat, let her eyes wander their little love nest. It was dark but for some shafts of sunlight poking through a couple of small cracks in the wall. They were in a utility room in a seldom-visited corner of one of the Canada warehouses, locked inside by a friendly kapo. In thirty minutes, less, he would be back to let them out, having been paid as usual for his cooperation. The deal had been struck to assure the pair their privacy. They would never be discovered here, their accomplice told them, adding with a grin, "Provided you two don't make too much noise."

Motes of dust floated in the angled wedges of sun like lazy insects. A large, three-basin metal sink hogged much of the room, flanked on one side by an assortment of brooms and mops, on the other by rows of shelves lined with cleaning supplies. A squad of disconnected water heaters stood at white attention in the shadows; back of these was where she and Godel hid their mattress and blanket when not there.

It may not have been much to look at, this dreary room, this glorified closet, nor conducive to fostering romance. But to Roza it was as libidinous as any bridal suite. It happened every time: as soon as she set foot in it, before Godel even touched her, her heart would begin to race, her juices to percolate.

But there was a further allure to it other than as the setting for the couple's lovemaking. It was the only place in the camp she could be alone, or as alone as she wanted to be. Everywhere else, she was surrounded by people—all day in the Bekleidungskammer, twice a day at both the Appell and latrine, squeezed together with them at night in the noisy barracks.

The human organism has a need periodically to be apart from the crowd, removed from the hurly-burly. One would think this need might be met once one was in bed after lights-out. But even then, in the dark, on top of hearing, smelling, *feeling* the weight of humanity pressing in from all sides, from above and below, there were the bunkmates, always the bunkmates—those annoyances, those adversaries—with which one had to fight for space and a share of the blanket.

In the anthill that was the Vernichtungslager, scarce was the moment a prisoner could claim as her own. Solitude and its fair-haired child, uninterrupted thought, were luxuries. Yet another reason for Roza not to resent her Godel his nap.

She pulled the cover to her chin, cuddled her nakedness against his; not an especially cold day, neither was it warm. With a satisfied sigh, she let her mind drift. Much had happened the past two months. The mission with which she'd been entrusted had grown wings. After Noah re-entered her life that blessed day outside the Bekleidungs hut, bringing the double miracle of the underground and its gunpowder proposal with him, it hadn't taken her three weeks to get the operation up and running. Not that she'd accomplished this on her own, nor could she have so quickly. If it hadn't been for Marta, she might not have accomplished it at all.

Maybe that was putting it too strongly, she told herself. She would have got it done somehow. But it was no exaggeration to say that her friend and fellow Jew, Marta Bindiger, had sped things along.

She'd met the younger Czech at the Bekleidungskammer, where they worked the same table. Marta, who spoke a gifted Polish, had preceded her there by six months, and impressed by the new girl's disdain for their SS masters, had taken her under her wing. She taught Roza how to locate the jewels and cash hidden in the garments that passed before them, and more importantly, how to sneak some for oneself without the Germans noticing. The two women lived in different barracks, but saw each other daily at work, and before long were close.

Marta had one of those playful, puckish faces that made one like her at first sight. A smile that would fill it was never far away, the hazel eyes permanently crinkled at the corners from it. Her nose was gently flattened and the slightest bit crooked, as if broken long ago, but the imperfection only made her the more endearing. Adding to her elfin air, she was shorter than most, and had a habit of cocking her head to one side when asking a question.

She was more Shakespeare's Cordelia than his Puck, however, as forthright as she was upright, forgiving when virtue called for forgiveness, but adamantine in sticking to her ideals of right and wrong. She never spoke of the SS but with contempt, nor did her fellow captives get a free pass; as profligate as she was with her smile, she didn't bestow it indiscriminately. She could sniff out a liar or bully in a heartbeat, was quick to call them out when they offended. She was going to make a good mother someday, if she lived, indulgent as a rule, stern when she had to be.

At their soup break one noon, Roza asked her if she happened to know any prisoners attached to the Union munitions factory. To her surprise, prepared for a no—Marta said yes. "Two, in fact. Sisters, both from Warsaw by way of Maidanek. Why?"

Esther and Anna Wajcblum, one almost twenty, the other fifteen, hadn't stayed long at Maidanek, an extermination facility. But having failed the selection at its unloading ramp, their parents would remain there forever. After a month in the camp, the sisters were bundled back onto a train and shipped off to Birkenau, where they were housed in Block 8 of the *B1a* lager, the same barracks as Marta.

The three soon struck up an acquaintance, in large part because of Anna, whom out of a mixture of fondness and deference to her youth everyone knew as Hanka. Not only was she so very young but lived by her emotions, and with what she saw at Birkenau forcing her to admit at last that her father and mother were dead, she took it hard. Hard enough that her older sister, afraid she might put an end to her grief on the electrified fence, asked Marta to help her keep a watch on the child.

Marta only too happily agreed. Hanka reminded her of her best friend when she was growing up in Czechoslovakia, while in Esther she recognized a refusal to grovel before their captors on a par with her own. The elder of Block 8 was one Edith Weiss, a Sudetenland Jew, and providentially through marriage a distant relation of the Bindigers. It was she who'd got Marta a job in the clothes-sorting commando, and now the recipient of this favor sought another, though not for herself.

She asked the blockova if maybe there wasn't some indoor work somewhere for two women in need, if not the Bekleidungskammer, anywhere, it didn't matter. Within the week, Esther and Hanka, who'd been breaking their backs unloading truckloads of coal from the Fürstengrube subcamp, were transferred to the Union Metallwerke outside of Auschwitz. Excelling in first the stock room then quality control, Esther was promoted to the gunpowder detail, where she worked the day shift.

Roza almost dropped her bowl of soup. "You know someone who actually works in the Pulverraum?"

"Esther Wajcblum, yes. I talked with her just a few days ago."

"And how difficult is that?" Roza struggled to keep her voice casual. "Meeting with her, I mean."

"Not as easy as it used to be," Marta answered, "but not impossible. Not long after the two started at the Union, all the women workers were collected from the different barracks and isolated in Blocks 2 and 3. The men to somewhere in the main camp. Given the usual German concerns about theft—especially among the prisoners at a weapons factory, right?—the guards at these two huts are under strict orders barring visitors. But as you're aware," she added with a wink, "there are ways around strict orders."

Pausing, she frowned. "But not always. Sometimes their orders outweigh the soldiers' greed. Such is the story at the Union women's barracks, which remain off-limits to all male inmates. No matter what the guards are bribed. I remember Esther telling me about two men who tried for weeks to gain entrance, but no dice. I assumed it involved romance, but Esther said she'd asked around and failed to uncover any candidates."

"I've talked with those men," Roza said. "They work at the Union, too, but were never successful in getting anywhere near the Pulv—near the women."

"But why would they want to?" Marta cocked her head. Twice. "And what were you doing talking to them? You're up to something, you Polish fox, I can smell it. You might as well get it over with now and tell me what it is."

Roza thought for a moment, then proceeded to bare everything, from the underground's plan to steal the gunpowder to what it was being stolen for. She figured if she couldn't trust this one, whom could she?

Marta was enthralled, asked how she could help.

"I need to talk to this Esther," Roza said, "as in yesterday. If you could arrange *that*, I'd owe you big time."

They set out that night for Block 2, careful to keep to the shadows. Marta walked up to the *Schütze* at the door and handed him a pack of cigarettes. He took it, but didn't budge. "*Ein mehr*," he said. "One more, for your friend."

Roza's first impression of the barracks was how uncrowded it was, the same size as her own but without as many bodies. It smelled better, too; later, she would learn there were showers on the Union grounds. Civilian Meisters were needed to oversee the place, and it wouldn't do for them or the SS on duty to be exposed to the germs dirt can generate. They also ate better, this commando, lager soup and the hard, gray bread, but more of it. The Pulver women even received a glass of milk every day.

She worried as they made their way through the hut that she'd be spotted for a stranger, but no one seemed to notice, or acknowledge them at all. Presently, they pulled up at a set of kojen, like the others a three-tiered affair rising almost to the ceiling. On the bottom mattress, two prisoners sat holding hands.

"Esther, Hanka," said Marta, "I've brought a guest."

Even with their shorn scalps, Roza could see that one was disarmingly pretty, one no more than a child. Hanka's ears stood at right angles to her head, like those of a cartoon mouse, her sister boasting the button nose, bee-stung lips, and almond eyes of a film star. It was she who spoke first.

"Hello, I'm Esther. And you?"

"Roza. Roza Robota. Sorry if I'm intruding, but if you don't mind, Esther, I was wondering if you could spare a few minutes." She turned to Hanka and shook the girl's hand. "Hi, I'm Roza. Nice to meet you. I don't suppose you'd object, dear, to my chatting with your beautiful sister awhile?"

Marta stayed to keep Hanka company, Esther leading the way to an empty bunk. She walked with the grace of a movie star, too, or an athlete or dancer. No taller than Marta and delicately built, her step wasn't only smart, it had spine. She'd been through some things, this one, Roza could tell. Delicate or no, she'd have thought twice before mixing it up with her.

Their conversation was brief. In five minutes the deal was closed, sealed with Roza's promise that if Esther did choose to plant the seed of theft in the gunpowder room, the fruit of this seed might be a chance at escape all right, but also SS fatalities, the destruction of their crematoria. She took this tack because she saw in the other's face the same hate she'd been told burned in hers at mention of the Germans.

"But can what I'm asking even be done?" Roza had been sweating this since taking the assignment. "When you're working, isn't every move you make watched?"

Esther was dismissive. "There are at most two pairs of prying eyes in the Pulverraum at any given moment, the Meister's and those of his female assistant. They're watchful enough, I suppose, but not very bright, either of them. Nor are both always present. Can it be done? Yes. It won't be easy, but yes."

"And what of the other women on your shift? How many of them might be interested, and just as important, trusted?"

"One for certain, maybe more. I'm going to have to sound some people out. Then there's the night shift; I know of two there who would jump all over it."

"Let me come back in a couple of days then," Roza said, "and see what you've done. And be careful, Esther, please. If any of this were to reach the wrong ears…"

"Don't worry, I'm not approaching anyone I'm not absolutely sure of. You can rely on that, just as I'd like to feel I can rely on this: do you in all honesty, in your heart of hearts, believe there's any escaping this place? My little sister, she's all I have left. I don't know what I'd do if she were to die on me."

"She's not going to die. Nor are you and I. One day soon, we'll all be sitting around a partisan campfire. And then home."

As essential as it was getting her foot in the gunpowder room's door, this wasn't the only thing on Roza's to-do list. Critical, too, was establishing a network of smugglers, not only to deliver the powder to her but make its trail hard to follow. She, of course, was to be the terminus for every gram of it, except for that bit reserved for the main camp. But so it wouldn't be intercepted before it did reach her, its route would have to be as convoluted as those hoofing it were cautious.

Which meant a working knowledge of Union personnel and procedure, of which she knew nothing. An insider was needed, preferably someone with a little authority and mobility. Hanka was too young and wanting in credentials for the job, Esther too confined to the gunpowder section. Roza did know two male prisoners at the factory, Israel Gutman and Yehuda Laufer, the same men Marta had puzzled over earlier. As agents of Battle Group-Auschwitz, they'd been posted to the Union to try and infiltrate the Pulverraum. Failing that, they stayed on as intelligence plants.

But for briefing Roza on various particulars, their usefulness to her end of the operation stopped there. Since any gunpowder had to start out in the hands of women only, it could only be passed to women, for even on the factory floor the SS were strict about keeping their male and female slaves separated. There were times at the changing of the shifts or random restroom breaks when the paths of the sexes might cross, but the first was heavily monitored, the second sheer chance.

No, Roza was in need of a woman to help organize then oversee her ring of thieves, and unpromising at a glance as the search appeared, she had an idea who that woman might be. Marta wasn't the only contact she'd made at the Bekleidungs tables. She'd also befriended a Jewish prisoner in her mid-twenties from the town of Bedzin.

Ala Gertner possessed a beauty to rival Esther's. Though she towered a good head above the average for a female, like Esther she moved with that easy grace peculiar to the truly attractive; tall she may have been, but wasn't the least self-conscious about it. Her features were sharper, less rounded than Esther's, but glamorous all the same—hers was the fierce, aquiline beauty of the hawk, head proudly lifted, yellow-green eyes never still. Beneath the elegance with which she carried herself, and like the bird of prey she embodied, there was a restiveness to her that seemed subject to the laws of gravity only in so far as she wished it to be.

As with most of the inmates Roza was drawn to, Ala didn't hide her hatred of the Nazis. And she had reason to hate. One day at work, Roza asked her about the middle finger on her right hand, which was missing mid-knuckle. In fact, the wound wasn't quite healed. Ala told her this story.

At the unloading ramp her first day, she'd had her baby daughter Rochele ripped out of her arms and handed to an old woman, whom the SS doctor pointed to the left, Ala to the right. Not only did she refuse to go as directed, but howling like a hellcat, charged after her kidnapped child. It took three soldiers to restrain her, and not even they could stop her screaming, until one of them pulled a knife and cut off her finger. As if they knew the effect this would have, as if they'd done it before, her shrieks subsided to a whimper, and she was dragged to the right.

"From this hand, they tore my baby Rochele," she told Roza, holding the injured part up, "and for yelling so loudly cut off a finger. I fought for my daughter, but they were stronger and took her. And that's the last I saw of her, or ever will see.

"But I won't forget. Never will I forget, and someday, somehow, I'll have my revenge."

The week after this conversation, some Germans in white lab coats entered the Kleider depot and picked out the stronger-looking prisoners. These were reassigned to the Union works, Ala among them, nor did Roza find out where she'd been taken until Gutman and Laufer recommended her as someone who might be of use.

The night she met Esther in Block 2, Roza asked her if she knew Ala. She did, but as she hadn't seen her all evening, she was probably working the late shift. Esther promised, however, to have her there when Roza returned.

And kept her promise, though this wasn't what had her so excited that evening she couldn't sit still. Upon spying Roza, she ran to meet her, deciding at the last second, as a joke, to play it cute.

She put on a glum face. "Guess what happened."

Roza braced for bad news. "I don't even want to try."

"Answer me this then. How much is two plus two?"

A baffled Roza didn't know what to say. "Uh… four, last time I checked. Don't tell me that's what has you in such a funk."

"No," Esther said, beaming now, "but it is how many Pulver girls I've found eager to put a bad case of sticky fingers to good use. Isn't it wonderful? Can you believe it?"

"Why, you little faker, you!" Roza swept her up in a hug. "And yes, Estusia I can believe it, knew you wouldn't disappoint! I see you've brought someone with you, too. Hello, Ala, remember me?"

"Of course I do. And can't tell you how thrilled I am you remembered *me*."

"So I take it you know. Why I wanted to see you, that is."

"Esther told me everything, and I have just one question."

"Yes?"

"When do we start?"

Ala had performed so well at the Union she'd been promoted to assistant *Vorarbeiterin*, or forewoman, of quality control. This gave her access to all but a few restricted areas. Roza couldn't have asked for a better chief of operations, and during the meeting that night, much of the groundwork for the venture was laid.

Things unfolded quickly after this. In less time than she'd hoped, the business of relieving the Nazis of their gunpowder was running like clockwork. The only complaint that might be made lay in the quantity the conspirators were able to pillage. To keep from arousing the Meister's suspicion, only a little could be taken from the Pulverraum each shift.

Also hampering their efforts were the periodic searches by their guards. Though these tended to occur when the prisoners were returning to camp at the end of the workday, they could happen whenever and without warning, often leaving them no choice but to lose the day's take in the dirt. With the SS swarming their ranks this could be tricky, doubly so when it came not in powder form but tiny, pear-shaped disks, which had to be crushed by hand before being stomped in the mud.

As elated as Roza was at the success they'd enjoyed so far, she was also surprised no one had been caught yet. Gutman told her once of an incident that made her wince. With the freedom Ala had as forewoman to circulate among the Union workers of both sexes, she was soon slipping the odd packet of gunpowder to the German-born Gutman and his Czech friend Laufer, this that part of the dynamite consigned to Battle Group-Auschwitz.

One twilight, as the men of the factory were lining up in the yard before heading back to the Stammlager, the order rang out: "*Mutzen ab!* Caps off! Stand at attention and don't move!"

It was a search. Already their guards were moving among them, together with some officers who'd surfaced from out of nowhere. Laufer leaned toward Gutman and whispered that he had yet to transfer the gunpowder he was carrying to his shoe; it was still in the cigarette pack wedged between the waistband of his pants and his stomach.

Gutman went white. This was it, they were lost. It was too late for the Czech to try and secrete his stash; the Nazis even now were searching the prisoner in front of them. When the trembling

Gutman's turn came, one of the soldiers noticed his distress and patted him down extra thoroughly, inspecting his shoes, his cap, even his mouth. Finding nothing, he swore in disgust and waved him on, subjecting Laufer, who'd maintained his composure, to only a cursory examination.

It had been too close a call, made them rethink their strategy. They had a tinsmith friend create a food bowl with a double bottom, inside of which they would hide the gunpowder upon receiving it from Ala. Among the prisoners were those who would save a portion of their soup from the day and carry it back to their barracks to consume later. Gutman and Laufer were soon following their example, as their guards never did more than glance at these half-filled dishes.

Roza thought this most clever, asked them if they could get more such bowls. Other improvements to the thievery were devised, by far the most productive a ruse the daring Esther had hit upon. The elderly Meister of the Pulver department, one Paul von Ende, though in earnest about his duties could be absent-minded. And that was putting it mildly.

The main room of his little realm in the plant's southwest corner measured ten feet by twenty, its only furniture a long, metal worktable, some folding metal chairs. Atop this table, amid a clutter of large aluminum trays, miniature scales, various utensils, cups, and other odds and ends, stood six devices resembling small if elaborate kilns, each festooned with a panoply of gauges and dials. These were the machines that embedded the gunpowder in the *Verzögerungen*, or detonators.

Like the rest of the building, the two exterior paneled walls were windowless, the one facing the factory floor nothing *but* window, solid glass from top to bottom. The fourth adjoined an even more compact room that served as von Ende's office. This cubicle only had space for a cheap metal desk, a small sofa, and the imposing floor safe he kept his gunpowder in. From this, he would dispense it to his six workers, a precise half cupful per girl as needed. In this way, he knew how many Verzögerungen they were supposed to fill and could compare this to their actual output.

His position made von Ende a busy man. He was often called away to attend to some matter elsewhere, leaving his assistant Elsa in charge. It did happen, though, he'd have to go when she was off somewhere herself, on an errand or a break.

As if leaving his prisoners unsupervised wasn't asking for trouble enough, sometimes he'd rush off without locking his office, and even more astounding, forget to take his keys with him. Esther when she saw this wasn't shy about seizing both the moment and those keys, opening the safe, and pilfering the gunpowder at its source. With this circumventing the measuring process and its burden of accountability, she wouldn't be stingy about it, either.

Normally, however, the three day-shift *Pulverfrauen* in on the plot, Esther, Rose Greuenapfel, and Genia Frischler, had to practice their sleight of hand with two people watching them. (Their night-shift confederates, Mala Weinstein and Ilse Michel, had to contend with only one sleepy kapo). This was no easy task. The detonators were the size and shape of a small checkers piece, with a cavity in the middle a few centimeters in diameter. Each woman would fill half a dozen of these with a heaping quarter-teaspoon of black powder before loading them into her machine. Thirty seconds later, out they would come with the explosive compacted into a solid mass, all but for a scattering of residue. This leftover material, the *Abfall*, was so burnt as to be unusable.

The trick was to collect the worthless Abfall and substitute it for the real thing. When one of the conspirators noticed neither of her overseers paying attention, she would scoop the gunpowder she'd amassed into a pouch or matchbox and return it to its hiding place. When this would hold no more, at the striking of the hour she'd ask permission to use the bathroom, where Ala or one of her agents would be waiting.

The problem was that every fifty detonators or so, von Ende would test a few to check whether the batch was functional. From the metal trays like huge cookie sheets on which they were arrayed, he would select them at random. A couple of bad ones and he'd let it slide, but any more and he'd fly into a rage, beating the women and later withholding their rations. Of greater worry to them than missing a meal was that he begin to suspect something more than negligence, and either grow more vigilant or replace them with new workers.

Fortunately, the Meister, among his other idiosyncrasies, was a man of rigid habits, a foible the Jewish forewoman of the day shift, Regina Safirsztajn, would come to exploit. Deducing early on that her girls were up to something, and after worming it out of them, she insisted she be included.

One of her duties was to collect the Verzögerungen and arrange them on the trays for von Ende's inspection, and she'd noticed long ago that his selection of these wasn't random at all, but followed a pattern. In collusion with Esther, Rose, and Genia, she placed the defective pieces where he wouldn't pick them.

As he chose from the same rows time and again, it was all the four could do to keep from laughing.

Thus was the contraband obtained, teaspoon by teaspoon, and from the launching point of the bathroom started on its circuitous route to Roza. In the course of this, Ala having consolidated it into manageable bundles, these would travel from one set of hands to another before being taken by shank's mare at shift's end the two-odd miles to Birkenau.

There, Ala might reclaim a share—or Marta, Regina, Hanka, any number of women—before it made its way to Roza, the penultimate link in the chain. From her it would ride to the crematorium in the next Sonder clothing cart, and from there to the safety of Block 13.

After Gutman, Laufer, or a Greek in on the game got his quantity of it to the Stammlager, it was delivered to Battle Group-Auschwitz in a similar fashion. Roza suspected her Godel of being involved in this, and was almost positive Noah was, and feared for them both. She came close to asking each about it, but in the end elected not to. For her to know would be to put them in danger if she were ever caught and interrogated, though she couldn't imagine a torture so terrible to pry either name from her.

But it wasn't just Godel and Noah that troubled her. She worried for all the brave men and women who'd put their lives on the line to help arm the rebels. Happily, the risk was ameliorated by the utter stupidity of the Germans. Marta was right to harbor so low an opinion of the SS; why, for instance, the Pulver women weren't frisked whenever they left their machines instead of at the end of their shifts only was a mystery to Roza. One of many.

Then to everyone's surprise and even greater relief, it began to dawn on the conspirators that when the Nazis did conduct a search, they weren't on the watch for gunpowder at all. In their denseness, their pettiness, they were in pursuit of bulkier items: small tools, bars of soap, work gloves and such, anything that might fetch a price on the black market.

Once this was discovered, it made toting powder less slippery an exercise, as one could secure it in a place the soldiers weren't likely to investigate. More, as a result, began to get through instead of being tossed in panic on the ground.

Such were the thoughts, together with the blanket under which she snuggled and the heat of the man sleeping next to her, that kept Roza warm as she lay on the utility room floor, ticking off the triumphs of the past weeks. The double elixir of success and righteous vindication coursed through her like a drug, causing her eyes to shine at this bold and beautiful thing she and her fellow conspirators had wrought.

To be a soldier at last, finally fighting back! Engaged not in the token resistance of the ghetto, or that practiced in small, feckless doses in the lager, but in something much more rewarding, something decisive—something that would one day deprive the high and mighty SS of first, the crematoria, those factories of death and pain of which they were so proud, then hopefully their lives, a good number of them anyway.

Against odds too vast to calculate, too discouraging to contemplate, it was *Jews* who were rising up, *Jews* who were waging war on those gangsters, those preening goons who'd tricked them to this necropolis, this city of the dead and living dead, this graveyard that had already claimed their families and where they, too, were meant to lie.

For now the war was a secret one, but it wouldn't remain so forever. The time was coming when the quiet of Birkenau, that eerie, encompassing hush born of mud, disease, and slow death, would erupt in a confusion of shouts, gunfire, explosions, in roofless, burning buildings and barbed-wire trampled in the earth. Soon, those swallowed by the Nazi monster, buried alive in its monstrous gut, would no longer be entombed but dashing for the concealing forest and its army of partisans.

Roza lay on her back staring at the plaster ceiling, watching as if a movie this image of a mob of people, a cast of thousands, running for their lives, running to freedom, scared out of their wits but also exultant. And she and Godel are among them, fleeing hand in hand with Noah.

She sees the three of them reach the trees, disappear into the trees, then run a little longer until deep into the woods. Stopping to catch their breaths, they look at each other and all three break out in tears, laughter and tears interchangeably, overcome by the impossible thing that is happening. In the distance, the battle is still popping, but not as loud anymore, while ahead lies the forest, and beyond that the river—and beyond that, after the damned Germans lose their damned war, Eretz Israel, the Promised Land, the home of their fathers.

Suddenly a voice, his voice, snapped Roza from her reverie. "You know how beautiful you are when you smile?" Godel said.

Her gasp melted into a chuckle. "You spoil me, sir. Beautiful? With this hair, these skin and bones? If you need glasses, I could probably organize you a pair."

"No thanks," he said. "My vision is just fine. And you can say what you will: you're the most beautiful woman I've ever met, inside and out."

"So how long, you naughty boy, have you been watching me? Quiet as a mouse, too. Was I really smiling?"

"Not long. And you weren't only smiling, you were glowing, your eyes as lit up as by a Shomeir bonfire. What on earth, love, were you thinking about?"

Her sigh was wistful. "The future," she said, "our future, the near and not so near. In fact, I was just getting to the part where... Oh, please tell it to me again, Godel, how it's going to be. I love it when you tell me. You know how I love it."

He turned on his side and held her to him, his cheek pressed to hers. He enjoyed saying the words as much as she did hearing them. "Let's see, first it's to Palestine, probably by refugee ship. Nor will we lack for company; hundreds will have scampered to get aboard. After the war, after Hitler and the camps, who's going to argue with the Zionists then? I'm guessing it'll take us a week or more at sea. We'll get married before we leave port that week and make that our honeymoon."

She envisioned a ship, a big one, its deck buried beneath a crowd. Three, four, five hundred people, every face turned east, gazing east to the horizon. No one is looking at the sea in their wake. There would be no looking back, not then or ever.

"And when we're there, we'll get some land," he said. "Don't ask me how, but we'll get it. And farm it, grow things. Melons, lettuce—hell, rutabagas, who knows? Maybe even a vineyard. I might just fancy owning a vineyard."

Roza, having never seen a vineyard, tried to picture one.

"And while we're at it," he went on, "we'll grow babies, too, lots of babies. How many little Silvers did you say you wanted to have?"

"Four. I want four, two boys and two girls."

"Four it will be then. And we'll name them—I've been giving this some thought lately, Raizele, tell me what you think—we'll name them, each and every one of them, after the dead. I like that idea. See it doing both of us good. Maybe the dead won't be so dead with their names on our lips again."

This was news to her. This she hadn't heard before. Raising herself on an elbow, she cupped his chin in one hand, embraced him with her eyes. That he would wish to name their children thus brought a lump to her throat, a swelling in her heart. Not that it needed reinforcing, but such was the goodness, the grit of this man of hers. Should her life be gifted with two daughters one day, the names Faige and Shoshonna would live again.

She touched her lips lightly to his, lingered there a moment, then began walking them slowly down his body, kissing as she went. When she came to his right armpit, again she lingered.

With soap all but nonexistent, and the taps in the washrooms not always working—and even when they were, the liquid that leaked out a disconcerting brown—bathing as they'd once enjoyed it, with plenty of suds and hot water, was an extravagance unheard of for all but a very few prisoners. But though Roza would have been the last to deny either the necessity or pleasures of a good scrubbing now and then, she had to admit that life without a bathtub wasn't entirely to her unliking.

She'd felt the allure of the body's natural perfumes since adolescence, and on many an occasion during their more intimate moments in the ghetto had shared her taste for them with Godel. He for his part had loved it that, as opposed to some foolish and misguided girls, she didn't shave under her arms. Not only had the ostentatiously sexual fur that flourished there turned him on visually, he'd called the two black, bushy tufts she used to cultivate her little powder-puffs, in that they helped announce, as he'd been fond of telling her, "that mouth-watering scent of yours."

Now, sadly, they'd been reduced to ugly stubble, as had his and every prisoner's, casualties of the monthly denuding that was lice control.

Irrespective of when it had begun, it was here in Birkenau that Roza had come more than ever to relish the distinctive aroma of the not altogether unwashed but certainly undeodorized armpit, both Godel's and her own. Not only was there something thrillingly animal about it, carnal, something that fanned the flames of her unapologetically strong libido, it was also an old friend, a smell from a time before Birkenau, when the world, if not perfect, was at least not insane.

It was a spice, familiar yet exotic both, that triggered memories, brought back feelings of happier days, of growing up, growing fecund, discovering sex, becoming a woman. Though she much favored her lover's, his visits were infrequent. But again, even if only her own underarms, she was able to treat herself to the sweet stink of life when so inclined instead of the death-stench of burning flesh forever clotting the lager air.

Besides, it was only May, the sticky heat of deep summer still weeks distant. And with the underground having wangled Godel a job as a locksmith (an occupation propitious for her, too, in that it didn't restrict him to Auschwitz), he, like she, was freed from heavy physical labor. Consequently, they were able to keep themselves, even with the camps' woeful washrooms, if not civilian-fresh then clean enough for each other.

After getting her fill of his pungence up top, she resumed her leisurely descent down his body, dallying at his nipples, briefly tonguing his navel, before continuing to that part of him that was her ultimate destination. Where she did nothing at first but nuzzle into his manhood as she might into a pillow.

Her mouth was soon enthusiastically working its magic, but didn't stay at it for long. That was just to revive him, snap him back to attention. The next minute she was squirming impaled on top of him, riding him like a horse, riding him bareback, her bouncing loosing a desperate keening from her throat along with several rivulets of sweat down her back.

Time as the two knew it ceased to exist. For an eternity of a moment they lived for that moment alone, adrift in its deliciousness, lost in its splendor—until finally, simultaneously, they collapsed in a wet heap, shiny with perspiration, panting like dogs. They would lay there afterward without talking, too spent to move but for their hands feebly stroking the other, the occasional chaste kiss.

Godel ended up breaking the silence, and with it the spell.

"I'm not sure, and it pains me to say it, kitten, but I think our hour's about up. Shouldn't we be getting dressed?"

"Oh please, no, not just yet. Can't we lie here a little longer? You feel so good, and it's going to be a while, a long while I'm afraid, before we can do this again."

So there they remained, if longer than they should have, until their complicit kapo's footsteps sounded in the hall. Given the risk he was taking generally, and his exposure at that moment specifically, he would be angry if they weren't ready to leave on the instant. Hardly had they scrambled into their clothes than his key was in the lock, the door swinging open.

Summer

Kapo Kaminski had to have one last look at the three "potato mashers" to verify they were real. A hole in the drywall above the baseboard waited to receive them, after which it would be plastered over.

He opened the canvas sack and peered inside. The miraculous little bombs glinted dully back at him in the electric light from the overhead bulb, three Wehrmacht-issue beauties, combat grenades, their stems attached to heads the size and shape of tin cans. It was still hard to believe them the property of Battle Group-Sonderkommando. After an appreciative few seconds, he knotted the bag and placed it carefully in the wall.

Only through dumb luck had they fallen into Sonder hands. Kaminski wasn't there, but learned later how it happened. It had long been rumored that Crematorium I in the main camp was to be closed permanently. Since the increase in the transports starting the summer before, it was always having to be shut down for up to a week anyway; built in the camp's earlier, less populated days, it wasn't designed for heavy use.

The main problem was the smokestack. The firebricks composing its inner lining kept crumbling, not only blocking the flue but threatening the entire structure with collapse. Though regularly replaced by a new layer of brick, the problem persisted.

With the completion in June of Crematorium III—Kaminski not unexpectedly appointed its Chief Kapo—and all four of the death houses now on line, the Nazis deemed the original more trouble than it was worth. (The two gas bunkers in the birch woods had already been decommissioned, the smaller one demolished for its brick and timber). Number One's ovens and related equipment were dismantled, crated, and shipped west to the Dachau camp as adjuncts to the proposed construction of a gas chamber there.

Even before this dismantling, the eight Ukrainian soldiers that made up its guard—who sharing their countrymen's hatred of both Stalin and the Jews had volunteered for the SS after the German invasion of the Soviet Union—suspected that because of their nationality they, too, might be considered expendable. During an ill-conceived attempt to flee, they were overtaken, and in the skirmish that ensued all eight were killed. Their remains were trucked back to Crematorium I, where ironically theirs were the last bodies burned in its ovens.

The Sonder given the job, while undressing the Russians, discovered to their awe the three hidden grenades. Within the week, these had made it to Birkenau and Block 13.

Later that night, before lights-out, Yankel Handelsman pulled a chair up to Kaminski's bunk. "If those aren't a sight for sore eyes, kapo, then I've never seen one."

"What—the grenades?" Kaminski kept his gaze fixed on the bottom of the bunk above. "I suppose so, but a part of me wishes it a sight these sore eyes were spared."

"I... I'm afraid I don't—"

"Think about it, Yankel. This is our biggest haul since we began shopping for weapons, three lousy grenades! Don't get me wrong, I'm happy as hell to have them, but they also drive home how little progress we've made."

This was true. The search for arms had been a frustrating one. Aside from tonight's gift, all the rebels had to show for their efforts was a single pistol, that and assorted calibers of ammunition should they ever wind up with the guns to match. Both the pistol and bullets had come from the military salvage yard outside the Stammlager. It was there the Luftwaffe and Wehrmacht sent wrecked aircraft, trucks and other personnel carriers, even disabled tanks, to be cannibalized for parts.

The mechanics dismembering these, clad in the striped burlap of the camp, were no more immune than any caste of prisoner to the temptations of the black market. Most of what they smuggled out and sold were metal fasteners and fittings, electrical parts and the like, but had been known to chance upon small arms and ammo hidden in the wrecks.

"But what of our brother insurrectionists in the main camp?" Handelsman asked. "I still don't understand why they haven't been of more help."

"It would appear," Kaminski said, "we have two friends, and two alone, with any pull in Battle Group-Auschwitz: Bruno Baum, and his emissary Noah Zabludowicz. And neither seems to have had much success persuading the Poles in the Resistance to share what weapons they have with us Birkenau Jews. We can thank the stars for our *real* brothers, and sisters, at the Weichsel-Union, and all the brave souls helping them. A good amount of gunpowder, as you know, professor, continues to reach us. But as you more than most are also aware—"

Handelsman finished the sentence for him. "We have yet to come across with a serviceable hand grenade. Dynamite, yes, for blowing up the crematoria, but in the fight to follow we can't have too many grenades. Nor, I regret, do I have anything new to report on that front."

As one of Commander Kaminski's top aides in the Battle Group, Handelsman had been put in charge of developing a proper hand grenade, only to find the squad bereft of anyone with the least idea how to construct one. Just turned thirty, balding rapidly, his was a face shared by a good many Poles: high cheekbones, a large forehead, the lips pursed as if in disapproval or awaiting a kiss. The eyes took in the world shrewdly, yet had a gentleness to them. One could tell from his diction he'd had a first-rate education, the impression reinforced by a pair of round, wire-rimmed spectacles.

On top of committing the crime of being born a Jew, he was also political. A Communist labor organizer by occupation, in 1939 he'd escaped Poland for France, only to have the Nazis catch up with him a year later. Slow to anger, fast to forgive, he was liked and respected by all; everybody from Kaminski to the greenest kid in the detachment knew him affectionately as "the professor."

"If you ask me," his kapo said, "our best shot at help might lie *outside* the wire."

"You're referring, I suppose, to the partisans."

Kaminski nodded. "And the drop they made the other night, lacking as it was."

For weeks now, Soviet bombers had been making forays into the area under cover of darkness, their targets the factories at Monowitz.

Night raids being what they were, twice a string of 500-pounders had slammed into Birkenau by mistake, causing no real damage except to SS nerves. From then on, come the air-raid siren, many of the guards showed less interest in guarding than in staying close to cover.

Three mornings ago, in the wake of an especially lengthy blackout, a surprise greeted the Sonder in a secluded corner of one of the crematorium yards. Taking advantage of a moonless night and the Nazis' less than soldierly overcautiousness, a cadre of partisans had penetrated the camp's cordons all the way to Number Five's wire.

This, these fearless had cut, leaving a cache of gifts for the Sonder: a military-grade radio, a pair of field glasses, two compasses, some maps, and a well-intentioned if superfluous offering of food, clothing, and medicine.

"By 'lacking,' I assume you mean guns," Handelsman said. "Or weapons of any sort."

"But," said Kaminski, "if I can get Noah to petition his superior Baum to use his influence to convince the Home Army to leave something more substantial, we just might be in business. Anyway, it's worth a shot."

Alas, it was not to be. The Armia took its orders from Cyrankiewicz, not Baum, and the former was in no hurry to increase Sonder firepower. But its display of generosity at the crematorium wire had got Kaminski to thinking. His men had become adept at supplying themselves with more food than they could eat, nor did they want for clothes. And their pharmacy, thanks to the transports, was equal to that of the SS. The question begged itself: what then to do with the partisans' munificence?

On the other side of the road bounding the southern edge of Crematorium II spread the *B1c* lager of the huge tripartite women's camp. The Sonder were sometimes able to catch a distant glimpse of its occupants, and after the distribution of their bread at night, the breeze would occasionally carry the rise and fall of their bird-like chatter.

Many were new arrivals, these prisoners of C Camp, fresh from quarantine, still in shock at their surroundings, still in denial some of them that the Grim Reaper's scythe had cut a swath through their families. That they, too, would soon be dead of starvation and disease—of pulling plows and grading roads on eight hundred calories a day—they had yet to realize, though by the time they did they wouldn't much care. By then, they'd be well on their way to becoming Muselmänner, mindless, cringing caricatures of their former selves. By then, it would be too late for anyone short of God to help them.

But it wasn't too late now. If they tried, the Sonder could make a difference to some. Which was all Kaminski needed for him to take a stab at it. What was more, he knew exactly how he planned to go about it.

The hard part was gaining access to C Camp in the first place, no mean trick for a gang of men. Construction crews, however, continued to frequent its grounds, putting the finishing touches on what was the last female lager to be built. It shouldn't be that difficult, Kaminski reasoned, for a dozen Sonder to enter posing as one of those crews.

If a little bribery was called for, then bribery it would be. Nor would the sacks the interlopers be lugging contain tools, but rather the food and medicines the partisans had left them.

Once inside, they would smoke out the more lenient block elders and other functionaries—there were always a few who took pity on their charges—and arrange for the wealth to be distributed among the inmates, either by appealing to those elders' humanity or greasing some palms.

It worked, too, like a charm. Everyone from the *Rottenführer* in command of the *B1c* guard gate to the blockovas inside the camp had more or less cooperated. And were cooperating still, the Sonder having elected, with a little push from their kapo, to make the charity permanent by donating some of their own stores.

Not that they attempted the stunt every day, or even every week, but often enough not only to alleviate much misery but for attachments to form between the female prisoners and their Good Samaritans. In light of the biological imperatives that drive men and women, this was to be expected. But it wasn't just about sex. Of greater motivation to those of the squad seeking to ease the suffering in C Camp was the desire to have someone to care for again. Severed from their families forever, alone in the affectionless vacuum of the

Vernichtungslager, each needed a person to feel tenderly toward him and on whom he could lavish tenderness in return. Having failed to protect their own wives, mothers, sisters, it was important they again have someone to look after.

An operation such as this, of course, didn't come cheap, but Kaminski didn't care. He would have spent twice as much. Not that his motives were entirely humanitarian; there was a selfishness to them, too, an attempt at atonement. Engaged as he was in the obliteration of his people, he had a need to offset this by doing what he could for those of them still living. He might be reducing to ashes those they loved, but if he could contribute to even one of these women surviving, some of the debt bred of his complicity would be paid.

The Sonder assembled their formidable riches from a variety of sources. The dental commandos that worked the oven rooms swiped their share of gold teeth. Some of the squad sported penknives, with which, when their guards were busy, they would check out any unusual bulges in the garments of the dead. Sometimes these bulges and even pockets yielded a small treasure.

A far greater wellspring of Sonder wealth was a room on the ground floor of Crematorium III. One of the more restricted areas in the camp, a sign on its door prohibited entry to not only prisoners but all SS without legitimate cause to be there. This *Goldarb*, or gold foundry, had been moved from Auschwitz to Birkenau this summer to be nearer its source of supply. Manned by two Jewish goldsmiths from the Stammlager and one from its new home, the articles laid before the three consisted in the main of the bloody teeth of the slain.

These were soaked in tubs of hydrochloric acid to dissolve any flesh adhering to them. Using blowtorches, the smiths then melted the gold from them, collected it, and eventually cast it in either ingots of a kilogram in weight or round disks an inch thick and two across. These tipped the scales at one hundred and forty grams, or five ounces.

More objects than just teeth were mined for their metal. Everything from jewelry to timepieces to gold cigarette lighters were brought to the foundry in Number Three and melted down. With multiple transports arriving almost daily this summer, it wasn't uncommon for this workshop to crank out fifteen or more pounds of ingots and cylinders that day.

Kaminski knew this because one of the goldsmiths had told him as much. Though not even his status as head kapo of the crematorium allowed him into its Goldarb, it did make it easy to approach the three metallurgists after their day was done, in one of whom he detected a potential collaborator. An oddly named Frenchman, the Jewish Zysl Epstein had lost his young wife and baby daughter to Bunker 1. Short of revealing an armed uprising was in the planning stages, Kaminski promised him that any gold he might be able to sneak into the pockets of the Sonder would have dire, even lethal consequences for those who'd snuffed out his family.

This was all Epstein needed to hear. Soon his kapo was in regular receipt of a not inconsiderable number of the five-ounce gold cylinders. Both convenient and precise, this "coin" proved the perfect unit of exchange on the black market. The larger ingot was too pricey for most purchases, while the gold teeth from which both came, though long employed as currency, weren't only inexact but affronts to the eye.

Not that those in the Special Squad were the only ones engaged in relieving the Third Reich of its ill-gotten gains. The SS soldier could be just as larcenous. Kaminski had often seen them rifling the clothes in the undressing room, heard tales of them picking through the suitcases on the ramp. Zalman Leventhal could cite an even more damning example, witnessed when he was still working the gas bunkers in the birches.

"We were resting, my squad and I, at the edge of the trees behind the death house, waiting for the next group of naked. An officer we'd never seen before, a young *Untersturmführer*, was moving among the rows of dead. At first, we thought he was checking up on the tooth-pulling commando to see if it was doing its job, but in fact he had a pair of pliers and was wrenching the teeth out himself, dropping them in a coffee can."

Leventhal would smile dryly then. "Which kind of clued us in he'd taken on a second job. After a while, his progress brought him nearer us, whom he seemed to notice for the first time. With a grin somehow conspiratorial and contemptuous both, he held up the can and noisily rattled its contents. Then went back to his pliers, as if we weren't there."

Though outrageous, this was but one individual's avarice, as nothing to the collective greed exhibited by the Germans in their quest to profit from mass murder. As much as any blasphemy he'd observed or been a part of, Kaminski was shaken by the exploitation of Jewish corpses. The execution of the guiltless was sin enough, but to violate their persons afterward shouted a disturbing cynicism, underscoring the Nazi tenet of the Jew as less than human.

The harvesting of dental gold may have been the most lucrative of these efforts, but the SS didn't stop there. Those bones not completely incinerated were broken into fragments and mixed with crushed limestone with which to pave roads. The mountains of ash that were once people served an aggregate of uses: as insulation in construction, as fill in the reclaiming of bogs and other lowlands, even as fertilizer for the gardens and farms of the camp.

Of all the raw materials reaped from the bodies of the dead, however, none was utilized in as many different ways as hair. Sold by the ton to German industry, it was employed in the manufacture of felt, yarn and other threads, and certain fabrics. Mattresses were stuffed with it, as were pillows and quilts, and it helped strengthen rugs and carpets.

The military also coveted it. The heavy ropes used on ships consisted in part of hair, and since it expands and contracts uniformly in extremes of humidity, found its way, too, into the business ends of submarine torpedoes and delayed-ignition bombs. It wasn't all that fanciful to assume some of the U-boat crews firing those torpedoes were wearing socks into which the hair of dead Jewish females had been woven.

Though Kaminski could know none of this, he would have had to be blind not to take note of the diligence the SS showed in their pursuit of what they clearly considered a prized resource. Few were the corpses he'd burned or seen burn with hair longer than a few inches. He was reminded of this particular Nazi preoccupation one day when the *Kommandoführer* of Crematorium III, *SS-Oberscharführer* Erich Muhsfeld, ordered him to square away the attic of the building for its role as the site of what was to be a permanent operation.

"We'll call the men working it the *Reinkommando*," Muhsfeld said, "the cleaning squad."

As part of his strategy for survival, Kaminski had learned a middling German. "And what, Herr Sergeant, are they to clean?"

"Women's hair."

Kaminski stared at him, blinking. "Excuse me... did you say hair?"

"*Women's* hair, that taken from both the living and dead. This surprises you?"

"Now that I think about it, sir, no."

Muhsfeld made a clucking noise. With his perfect uniform, pencil-moustache, cropped pate, and trim build, he was the picture of the Prussian military man. He drank, and heavily, but was never sloppy about it, his tunic always buttoned, his posture board-rigid. He was dangerous in that he was unpredictable, could be almost sociable with a prisoner one minute, turn around and shoot him dead the next. Kaminski had seen him do it.

"You would do well, kapo, to hold onto that thought. There's a lot of money to be made from hair. Why else would we have had you people harvesting it?"

From Muhsfeld's tone, he decided it best to stay quiet. The SS man eyed him coolly before continuing.

"Anyway, the men of the Reinkommando are to wash, chemically treat, and dry the hair given them to prepare it for shipment by rail. You will be told the details later. Your job after you've got the attic in order is to assemble the squad, and in that you are free to choose anyone you wish. My only stipulation is no idlers or kids. Remember, you as kapo will be held responsible for the operation's success."

Though located in Crematorium III, every member of this new command but one wound up coming from outside the Sonder. Nor was this by chance. Over several days, Kaminski visited the unloading ramp bearing a pass signed by the *Oberscharführer* permitting him to select and take with him any deportee he desired. By week's end, he'd acquired a crop of older men only, most over seventy, all either rabbis or dayans.

As with the help he was extending the women of C Camp, his reasons for rescuing these aged holy men from the flames weren't solely altruistic. Not observant himself, he recognized the necessity of keeping the Jewish religious tradition alive, and saw in the Reinkommando, if in a small way, an opportunity to do so. The work itself would be neither arduous nor time-consuming, enabling his rabbis to devote themselves to the study and interpretation of Scripture, the recitation of prayers, and the perpetuation of Mosaic Law and belief in their ancient God.

Hadn't the prophets promoted the same agenda during the Babylonian exile, the Assyrian conquest? If Ezekiel and Isaiah had viewed the preservation of the Jewish faith as of the essence, who was he to disagree?

Muhsfeld, while initially disapproving of Kaminski's choices, soon found the whole thing humorous, and an excuse to have a little fun at his kapo's expense. "Graybeards in the Sonderkommando!" he would jeer. "What's next, Kaminski, women?" Or: "We build a crematorium and you try to turn it into a synagogue." Or: "I've finally figured out why you insisted on stocking your attic with senior citizens, kapo. So you wouldn't be the oldest man in the squad anymore."

Crematorium III now had two workplaces that existed nowhere else in either Auschwitz or Birkenau. But though the hair-drying room, unlike the gold foundry, was not a restricted area, it didn't get many visitors. Occupying one entire end of the spacious attic, it was a spooky place, ill-lit and claustrophobic. Most of its square footage was taken up by an impossible tangle of clotheslines, a crisscrossing skein of drooping cords from which hung knouts of hair in a collage of colors, from purest white to raven black. This maze was as difficult to look at as it was to navigate, inviting comparison to an image from the American Old West: strings of scalps adorning the teepee of a wild Indian war chief.

Even the floor was covered with hair, row after row of it laid out to dry in the heat rising from the ovens. Each stolen tuft told a different sad story, the grandmother's salt-and-pepper, the wife and mother's long, lush mane, the curly ringlets taken from a bouncing little girl. Kaminski never went upstairs any more than he had to, and invariably left this macabre loft with a heavier heart than when he'd entered.

The lone exception he'd made to the advanced ages and outsider status of this new detachment was a logical one, its only member to come from the Sonderkommando the dayan Leyb Langfus. That the man's faith was as unassailable as the most pious of the older rabbis there was no disputing. And by choosing Langfus, Kaminski was safeguarding one of his fieriest warriors. Having in a rare moment of benevolence given the dayan the job of burning the "trash" from the transports, the fickle Muhsfeld could just as easily rescind the offer and have him shot for refusing gas-chamber and crematory duty. But sequestered in Number Three's attic, he would for all practical purposes be out of the *Scharführer's* reach.

Langfus assumed quick leadership of the body of newly arrived rabbis, all of whom were in shock at the waking nightmare that was Birkenau. It wasn't just tenure, though, that gave him the advantage. He may have been younger than they, therefore lacking in the astuteness only the years can bestow, but did possess attributes that in the death camp were seldom seen in anyone, of any age. As evidenced by his renunciation of Sonder work and Sonder food, his moral fiber was without peer, his principles carved in granite. Yet when it came to offering what comfort he could to those around him, be it a deportee in the undressing room or one of his own in despond, his heart was softest soapstone.

Unimposing in appearance, if not downright comical—uncomfortably tall, gawky, he walked with a slight stoop, his thick, black glasses forever threatening to slide off his nose—he was blessed nevertheless with the gift of oratory, his deep voice made the more mellifluous by the power of its conviction. A natural speaker, he could be a passionate one, too, though his words generally had the effect of calming rather than exciting.

One might disagree with or tire of him, especially when he got on his religious high horse, but it would have taken a real *schmuck* not to concede the dayan his good points.

His value to Kaminski, however, resided in neither his heart nor his tongue, but his spleen. This Langfus may have been a man of God, but he was also a man of action, not at all the sort to hide behind his Bible, content to let that God do his fighting for him. He was as loud in calling for armed revolt as anyone in Battle Group-Sonderkommando, as Leventhal, Gradowski, Handelsman, Warszawski, and like them not only did everything his general asked of him to further that eventuality, never quit pestering him as to when it could be expected.

He'd done so just the other day. Having noticed him acting out of character of late, standoffish, if not out and out sullen, Kaminski asked what was wrong.

"You know as well as I do what's wrong, kapo," he said. "Is that mutiny we were promised still in our future, or was that a lot of talk? Our allies in the Stammlager may be mouthing all the right words, but aren't in any hurry to turn them into deeds."

"I hear you," Kaminski said. "The underground... it's maddening, I won't say it isn't. But you could also make the case it's still early. We've got what—a single pistol, three grenades, a little dynamite? How far are those going to get us? Not past that damned barbed wire, that's for damned sure."

Langfus spread his arms in exasperation. "But Auschwitz has yet to come up with a plan even! There has to be a plan, a strategy of attack. Something for us to familiarize ourselves with, prepare for. Have they told you *anything* about how they intend to pull this off?"

"Some, yes, but—"

"I saw something. Last week." The dayan let his arms fall. "I've seen a lot of things since I've been here, we all have. Terrible things. This, though..." He looked away. "This was unforgivable."

"What was? What'd you see?"

"Children, a couple hundred of them. Greek they were, had to be. Trucks full of little Greeks..." For a moment, his kapo thought the man was going to cry. "But—but I can't—

"With my own eyes I saw it, what the SS did to those children, but I still can't believe it. Still can't believe it."

Kaminski laid a hand on his shoulder. "Tell me, Leyb, what happened?" Not that he wanted to know. Was afraid of knowing, but... "Why keep it bottled up? Maybe it'll help to talk about it."

Langfus shook his head as if to clear it. "It won't help, and you know it won't. Nothing's going to help, nothing short of us putting a stop to the madness ourselves. We've got to put a stop to it, and we've got to do it soon. These were *young* children, kapo, none older than eight or nine. What's wrong with people that they could do such a thing to a child?"

Good question, a goddamned good one, Kaminski told himself. But a question without an answer. Or perhaps too many.

The dayan never did tell anyone what he saw. And not because by recounting it he'd be forced to relive it. Sealing his lips was a certain misgiving the incident had raised, a kernel of doubt that had taken root in him where none had before, not even when told of the murder of his wife and baby boy.

Though Langfus wouldn't have dreamed it possible, this doubt was directed at his God. Not that he challenged the Divinity's existence, or His dominion, but rather whether He possessed an acceptable quantum of mercy. Was He the loving God the dayan had been raised on, or an indifferent, even a cruel One? If either of those last, that would make Him no less divine, but less deserving of the adoration He demanded.

Langfus could abide, if he must, surrendering adults to an agonizing end—but children? The gas chambers, granted, claimed their portion of younger victims, as they'd claimed his precious son, but to watch them die as they had in front of him the other day, to watch them die like *that*, left him at a loss for words. Except for one: why?

He found himself in uncharted waters. A crack, the thinnest hairline but a crack nonetheless, had appeared in the foundation of the monolithic temple that was his faith. And if what he'd had the misfortune of witnessing that morning had caused him, the Makover dayan, the champion of his God, to dispute that God's infinite goodness, how might his repeating of the tale affect those less devout? The last thing he wanted was to further damage the already soured religious sentiments of his brother Sonder.

Which explained his keeping the episode to himself, counting it fortunate no one but him had seen it. Except for those from the squad dragooned into working the thing. And there was nothing to be done about them beyond not adding to the ugly story he was sure at the time they'd be bringing back to Block 13.

He needn't have fretted. From what he could gather, they'd kept their mouths shut about it. Curious, he took one aside, someone from his hometown, but the man not only refused to discuss it, he got angry almost to the point of blows that the dayan should have mentioned it. Clearly, the twenty present that awful day were either too traumatized or ashamed, or both, to admit their involvement.

It was understandable that so many of the Special Squad should have averted their faces from God. Made to escort an endless parade of the naked and defenseless into gas chambers, then burn them afterward like so many bags of garbage, they either had a hard go of it retaining their belief in a Supreme Being, or granting that, their continued respect for Him. The word guilt wasn't strong enough, nor despair, nor disgust; a new vocabulary was needed to describe the forces at work on the Sonder as the days and the bodies and the tears piled up, and still the crowds kept coming as if they would never slow.

But as unsettling as this erosion of their faith was, Langfus was careful never to be the one to bring religion up. Considering he was exempt from most of the obscenities heaped on them, he didn't see as he had a right to. He didn't shy, however, when they broached the subject themselves, from taking a position that argued on the side of the angels.

Not long after talking to Kaminski, and upon heading one morning to Crematorium III, he ran into the last of Sonder Squad 57B, the night shift, returning from work to their barracks. Even in the half-light of dawn, he could see the blood on their clothes.

"Well, what have we here?" said one of the dozen, a short, muscular boy named Menachem not yet out of his teens. Langfus recognized him from the block. "If it's not the prophet on his way to the mountaintop. How's the view from up there, holy man. Any windows in that attic?"

The rest snickered at the sarcasm, drawing a smile from Langfus, too. "Not the part of it I work in, Menachem. Which is a blessing, wouldn't you say?"

"Yes, I suppose it is. So how'd you sleep last night, rabbi? Pleasant dreams, I hope."

"No... no dreams, thank God."

"That's good. Is always good. Guess I don't have to tell you what we were up all night doing. More women and children than usual, or so it seemed, didn't it, boys?"

A few nodded, somber again.

"I'm so sorry, son," Langfus said, "but what choice did you have? God will forgive you."

Menachem leaned to his right and spat. "There's that name again," he said, wiping his mouth on his sleeve. "Refresh my memory, will you, rabbi? Who the hell is this *God* you keep bringing up?"

Langfus responded as to an honest question. "The one true God of our fathers. The God of Abraham and Moses."

"Oh… *Him.* Yes, I remember Him. He went away a while back, didn't he? For good, too, I'd have to say. But He did leave a message, want to read it? It's written right here."

Holding out his arm, he pulled his sleeve up to reveal the five-digit tattoo.

Langfus looked at it, then back to the unsmiling face above it. "I, too, bear the Gentile's unclean mark, but I'm afraid you're mistaken if you think God went away. We're hardly the first—"

"*Mistaken?*" Menachem flung the arm wide. "Take a look around, why don't you? Then tell me I'm mistaken!"

The dayan, feeling his pain, wished only to ease it. "We're hardly," he began again, "the first Jews in history God would appear to have abandoned. How often in the synagogue have I read aloud from the Book of Esther, which tells of the Persian Empire's attempt to annihilate its conquered Jews? And what of our three-hundred year bondage in Egypt, or the generations of Babylonian exile? On all three occasions, God, to whom the centuries are but seconds, delivered us from the oppressor."

Menachem half-turned toward the man next to him. "He'd best hurry this time," he said in a loud whisper, "or He's liable to find Himself with no one left to deliver."

Langfus waited for the laughter to die down. Then gazing at each in turn, "Tell me, don't you consider yourselves enemies of the Germans? Loathe the very ground they walk on?"

A murmur of affirmatives.

"Let us not talk then of God abandoning you, but of you abandoning Him. Can't you see what you're doing? Exactly what the SS want you to. Losing one's faith is a kind of death in itself. The Nazis would kill you twice, first your soul, then your body. Before stealing your breath, they must rob you of your heritage; that is how enamored of their power they are. They've slain your family, your friends—would you allow them the victory of murdering your God, too?"

There were a few smirks, but his query went unanswered.

"God has not deserted us. He has designs beyond our vision, beyond the scope of our understanding. Forget the three hundred years in Egypt—our people have been denied their homeland for almost *two thousand* years, scattered to the winds after the Roman legions destroyed Jerusalem and the Second Temple. Yet we have not been extinguished. God will not let us be extinguished. He has a plan for us still, a purpose, the particulars of which we're simply unaware."

Another boy spoke up, no older than the first. "Rubbish, Menachem is right. We're dying by the thousands every day, the tens of thousands every week. And that at this one camp alone. How is God supposed to work this plan of His if there's no one to work it for? If we're wiped out?"

"Which is why we won't be wiped out," Langfus said. "Again, God won't let us be. Throughout history, my brothers, there have been pharaohs who would exterminate us. As with God's benediction we've survived until now—praise be the Most Holy—so, too, will we this latest holocaust.

"Jewish suffering is not new. But for its brutish technology, Birkenau is not new. The Bible, if you'll recall your Ecclesiastes, is most precise on this point: 'What has been will be again, what has been done will be done again; there is nothing new under the sun.' One of the main lessons to be learned from this is that what happened to the fathers is often visited on the sons."

"What does that mean?" the boy sneered. "Because the Egyptians and Persians and who knows how many others have persecuted us, it's all right for the Nazis to?"

"That's not what I'm saying, son." Frustrated at having been misunderstood, the dayan was careful not to show it. "Just as our forefathers in their troubles kept the flame of their faith lit, their trust in God alive, so must we. And as in the end their descendants were rewarded for that trust, so will ours be.

"When our race is in peril, the Talmud commands each of us see himself not in contemporary terms but as a slave in pharaoh's Egypt. If that slave and his countrymen had angered God by despairing of Him, there would have been no Moses, no Exodus, no gift of the land of Canaan. Are we to risk by our short-sightedness denying our children whatever recompense for our torment God might have in store for them?"

"Children, you say?" This from a third Sonder, older than the previous. "Which children, rabbi? The ones I lost the first day here, my—my two little girls, or the dozen I carried out of the gas chamber last night?"

"My poor man," Langfus said. "I, too, lost a child, and his mother with him, but—"

"And why suffering? Why must we Jews always be suffering? We were doing just fine until the Germans came along. Is your God such a sadist He would make His people bleed before giving them back what He took from them?"

Langfus raised his face to the morning sky, as if searching there for an answer.

"Perhaps it is not God's intention," he said finally, "to restore the status quo, to make things as they were. Perhaps in His omniscience, His knowledge of the future, He's deemed our place in the world needful of change, radical change, so that in the end we may prosper as never before. Perhaps only by suffering to the degree we are now can this change come about. How can we know what the future holds? But God does, and maybe in light of it our present anguish is necessary.

"This, though, we *can* know, and take comfort in: after our ancestors fled Egypt, after proving their faith there and with a couple of lapses in the Sinai, God led them into Canaan, invited them to take the land of milk and honey as their own. Could something similar be ahead of us after the black night of Birkenau? Provided we remain steadfast and not renege on the covenant God forged with Abraham, might not our agony in the camps be our ticket to a new Canaan, perhaps even a return to Eretz Israel itself?"

Langfus expected this last to be met with jeers. But, except for the distant shouts of roll call from the Appellplatz, there was only silence.

Encouraged, he plunged ahead. "Who can presume to understand God's plan? Penetrate His all-knowingness? But if it should happen there is no plan, if He has forsaken us—if you are right and I am wrong—allow me now in all humility to beg your forgiveness. For then, God will have proved Himself a fraud, and I as His cat's-paw will have done you a great disservice. False hope, as you've observed it in those walking meekly into the crematoria, can be more destructive than no hope at all.

"It'd be foolish, however, to give up on Him now, at this the eleventh hour. One way or another, our fate is about to be decided, either at the bloody hands of the Gentile or by the saving hand of God. After two thousand years of oppression and exile, why chance displeasing Him at the last minute? Remember, while protective, He is also a vain God, and jealous of our devotion."

He turned to the last Sonder who'd spoken. "Yes, our children are no more. Nor is there any bringing them back. Yet some of us, maybe not those of us present, but some will be blessed with children again. There will be survivors; the SS can't kill us all.

"It would be a shame—no, a crime, would it not?—to deprive those children of their patrimony by incurring God's wrath with our rejection of Him. Just as it would if the dead were to end up dying for nothing."

Afterward, the dayan was philosophical. He hadn't convinced them, knew he hadn't, but that wasn't his intention. He wept for the men of the Sonder, especially those of them not yet men, those little-more-than boys made to wade in the gore of the death house. In deference to their lot, when obliged to bring religion to the fore he made it a point never to talk down to them. By approaching them not as a pontificator but an equal, a friend, he could be forceful yet still come off as someone who cared.

His words, while seldom changing their minds, did seem, by bringing their anger and pain into the open, to blunt the cutting edge of both, and that was all he ever really wanted. That and maybe to make them at least question their apostasy.

In the end, the six bid him a sincere good day, which in itself was a victory considering the antipathy with which they'd greeted him. He could tell from this that maybe they weren't only less sure of their position (for fear of sending a mixed message, he'd refrained from bringing up the revolt) but appreciated his attempt to buck up their spirits.

Not that they were the only ones to have gained from the exchange. Langfus, too, had benefited. Airing his convictions aloud had helped to clarify them in his mind, begin the process of restoring some peace to that mind. The *Sonderaktion*, or special action, taken against the Greek children, though appalling in its savagery, was made somewhat more explicable by the very arguments he'd advanced to the Sonder. That there was nothing new under the sun meant it wasn't the first time Jewish or any children had met so abominable an end.

Nor could God necessarily be blamed for its cruelty. Birkenau might not be novel in its bloodthirsty intent, but remained as pitiless a killing ground as the world had ever seen. Excesses were bound to happen, but one had to remember that at Birkenau it wasn't God in the details, but the devil. It was the nature of the place that it should spawn such barbarisms as the one weighing on him now. If occurring anywhere else, in any other day and age, it would have caused the rocks to weep, the heavens to blacken.

But here, if not commonplace, it wasn't that out of the ordinary. If God did have a new direction for His people requiring a good part of them be offered up for sacrifice, and if this and the other camps were the altars upon which that sacrifice was to be enacted, then such a fate as that which had overtaken those unlucky children was to be expected. God was no more responsible for it than the victims themselves. One could say He, too, was a victim in that this product of His love, this being He'd created, this Man, should be capable of such an enormity, such evil.

But while all of this may have gone a long way toward mending the dayan's fences with his God, to repairing that crack in the foundation of his faith, it did nothing to dispel the corrosive memory of the day in question. He could recall the Aktion in its every detail, and knew he'd be able to even if by some fluke he were to reach an old age.

It had rained for some days prior, a dense, nonstop rain, revealing several leaks in the crematorium roof. Not many, but any stray water in the hair-drying attic was too much. As the youngest by decades in the Reinkommando, Langfus had been drafted to scale the roof and patch it. With two of the oldsters steadying the ladder, he'd risen into the mid-morning sun with a bucket of tar and a brush.

He wasn't up there thirty minutes when something peculiar caught his attention, a convoy of open trucks lumbering from the direction of the unloading ramp toward a thick woods just west of the camp perimeter. This struck him as odd because there wasn't anything in those woods, not even a road leading to them; the five trucks were bumping across a grassy field. Four were heaped with corpses like so many broken dolls, two hundred of them if he were to guess, their heads flopping in unison with every jolt, eyes wide open and unblinking in the sun.

That all were fully clothed told him they came from the ramp, and given their numbers, were more than likely Greek. Those transports from distant climes, Greece in particular, often arrived with many of their passengers dead already from thirst and overcrowding. He'd heard of one from the island of Crete, after three unimaginable weeks en route, showing up with *nobody* left alive but a handful of the semi-comatose.

But why was this load of corpses being rushed to empty forest? The crematorium beneath him was still free, and the fire pits to the east just as convenient.

It was then he noticed the bodies were those of children only, very young children from the size of them. This was strangest of all. If fresh from the cattle cars, they should have been mixed all together, children with adults, young with old. Yet from what he could tell, there wasn't a one above the age of ten. Had they been brought to Auschwitz in a group, and if so, from where—some school, hospital, orphanage? Or perhaps the Nazis *had* culled them from the dead at the ramp, but why?

His curiosity getting the better of him, Langfus climbed to the top of the roof. From there he could see for miles. He watched the trucks enter the trees and disappear, then emerge after a hundred meters into a clearing. From his perch, they weren't only plainly visible but within earshot.

Also plain now was why they were there. A pair of small fire pits scarred the clearing, kindling in place, though never had he seen any like these. Instead of rectangular and deep, they were circular and fairly shallow, ten, maybe twelve meters in diameter. Why the Germans should have gone to the trouble of digging new holes was a mystery. Weren't the crematories at hand, both indoor and out, sufficient to dispose of these few remains?

Upon the convoy halting, from out of the covered fifth truck poured a squadron of SS and twenty Sonder. Instead of unloading the bodies and stacking them atop the pyres, the twenty immediately lit the latter and sat down to wait. This only deepened the mystery, departing as it did from the usual sequence. Their guards by then were drinking; Langfus could see the bottles, hear their voices louden as the liquor took effect. Later, he would learn that duty at a Sonderaktion, an operation outside the routine, typically entitled each volunteer to not only an extra ration of cigarettes but a half-liter of schnapps.

After ten minutes, both fires were blazing, though why he'd stuck around he had no idea. It wasn't as if he hadn't seen corpses burned before. Having months ago ended up on the labor detail sent to dismantle Bunker 1 and its undressing barracks, he'd passed close enough to the fire pits to observe bellies bursting open from the heat, arms and legs contorting as if those they belonged to were still alive. It was a sight he'd vowed then to avoid in the future, yet that morning he remained a rapt audience, as alert at his rooftop as a sailor in his crow's nest.

After the fires had subsided some, the wood starting to glow red at the tips, the order went out and the Sonder jumped to their feet. Working at a run, driven by the blackjacks and imprecations of the Nazis, they lowered the gates of the trucks and began hauling the bodies out, dragging them toward the flames. With the crazed soldiers at their heels, they didn't bother to undress them but heaved them still clothed into the pits.

The dayan sat awhile more before deciding he'd seen his fill after all, and was on his way back to where he'd left off tarring—when something froze him in his tracks, a sound to make the blood run cold, a broken wail more like a cry from deepest Abaddon than anything from a living throat.

As a young child, he'd come across some boys, thuggish, older boys, torturing a cat to death. He'd run from the scene horrified, but not before the unfortunate creature's yowl seared itself into his memory. A noise like it corkscrewed now from the clearing. He clambered back up top and shaded his eyes from the sun. Was that something moving? Yes, there in the farther pit, an animal must have blundered into the fire.

Except it wasn't an animal. It was a little boy, every time he tried to raise himself he would fall screeching down again. Nor was he alone. Other shapes were floundering in the flames, other voices now adding their shrieks to the original.

Langfus had to grab hold of the roof or he would have lost his balance. They weren't dead, these wretched children, not all of them. Some had been merely unconscious, survivors of who knew how many days in the stifling cattle cars. That they were from Greece there could now be no doubt. From his studies of the Septuagint, the

Greek translation of the Bible, he recognized the occasional word in their screams.

Most still alive when thrown into the fire were either too small or weak to do more than lie where they landed. Some of the older ones, however, succeeded in scrambling to the edges of the shallow pits from where they would attempt to hoist themselves out. But the SS, experienced hands at this, were ready for them. A soldier patrolled the circumference of each pyre, shooting these already badly burned children. A boy of about seven, clothing ablaze, did manage to get out and run howling from one conflagration only to lurch blindly for the second and tumble in headfirst.

How long the tears had been coursing down his cheeks, Langfus couldn't say. All he knew was that they hadn't sprung from grief alone. Rage had beget them, too. If this crime against the innocent failed to incite one to violence, to wanting to grab a gun and blast the drunken laughter off its perpetrators' faces, then one was made of stone, not flesh. The Nazis were smart to finish the job begun in the cattle cars where they did, out of sight in the woods; if in the meadow, there was no telling what it might have aroused among the main body of Sonder.

After what had to have been an hour, but in fact was only minutes, the cries from the clearing grew fainter, then ceased. The blackening stumps that had been toddlers sizzled mute and unmoving in the fires. With a parting round of toasts, the Germans wrapped up their drinking before loading their gear into the trucks.

The dayan saw a few Sonder bent double vomiting into the grass, but most stood heads bowed, keeping well away from each other. Even if some had been disposed for whatever reason to conversation, what could they have said? Words, any words, would have rung worse than false.

Langfus didn't remember finishing the job that had brought him to the roof, although he must have. It rained hard again two days later without further leaks. For one whole week, he wouldn't have anything to do with anyone, working alone, eating alone, ignoring every overture but for the one from Kaminski. He was both there and wasn't, like some will o' the wisp, some ghost flickering in and out of visibility. A dozen times a day he would stop what he was doing and just stand there, staring into space, as lost on the inside as he looked to those around him.

Behind this was his struggle to reconcile what he'd viewed from that roof with all he'd been taught to hold dear in life. Then came his dawn encounter with Menachem and the others, this helping more than anything to steer him back to his moorings. Once his old self again, or near to it, he spent half an afternoon scaring up some ink and paper.

Long before the Greek incident, he'd sat down with the Zalmans Leventhal and Gradowski, and they'd agreed to work together at holding the killers accountable. He'd found a large jar and in it had enclosed a log he'd been keeping since the ghetto, along with what he'd learned from a Sonder friend who'd been at Belzec. After burying it in the yard of Crematorium III, he'd felt more a man than he had in years. At last he was fighting back, inflicting real damage on those who'd been molesting him and his for so long. That this damage wouldn't be effected until the war was over and him dead didn't matter. Planting that jar in the defiled soil of the crematorium was like plunging a hundred daggers in the chests of as many SS.

He was hot to have another go at it. As spokesman now for the dead, saw it as an obligation. He also knew what his next effort would include. How better to illustrate the utter heartlessness of the executioners than by recounting what he'd had the evil fortune to witness that most evil of mornings?

Though from their first meeting Langfus had taken a liking to Gradowski, he couldn't explain his pal Leventhal. In the redhead, he'd run afoul of an animosity he'd done nothing to provoke. He'd debated confronting him over it, but in the end chose not to. As long as it didn't interfere with their new partnership, he was willing to ignore it.

Personally, he admired the man. Both men. Unlike some others, each had retained his humanity in spite of great loss, their actions since serving as proof that no one was more dedicated than they to waging war on those responsible for that loss.

Important, they told him, was that each man sign his depositions. The more traceable they were, the more believable their claims in what they hoped would one day be the court of world opinion. The dayan had given much thought to this signature. He wanted it not just to identify him but reflect his militancy. To that end, he hadn't used his Yiddish but his Hebrew name, Arye Yehuda Regel Arucha, the last two words translating to "long foot."

But a show of defiance wasn't all he was after. Partly out of whimsy, partly caution, he wanted the finders of his testaments to have to work a little in establishing their author—which, if they dug them up first, went for the SS also. He did this by making the acronym of his Hebrew name his signature, not only creating a smokescreen for himself but giving the historians of tomorrow a chance to play detective.

Less whimsical was the request he planned to include, starting with this one, asking those historians to piece together those entries signed with the letters A.Y.R.A. and publish them for the world, for all posterity to see.

He'd even come up with a title. His wish was such a collection be called "The Horrors of Murder."

*　　　*　　　*

As surprised as Noah Zabludowicz was to find his cousin Shlomo Kirschenbaum at Birkenau, he was even more taken aback to see him a member of the Sonderkommando.

Though they'd only met twice, and that when they were children, he recalled Shlomo well. He'd been a cheerful boy, big on cracking jokes, as quick to smile as he could make others do the same. He was also a scrawny kid, nor had the years beefed him up much; no way would Noah have figured him for Sonder duty. One of the first questions he'd asked him, as it couldn't have been his build, was what breach of the rules had landed him in the Special Squad.

"None," he'd replied, "I didn't have a chance to do anything. I looked up and there I was in a group the Germans had set aside on the unloading ramp, and the next thing I knew I was emptying carts piled with corpses."

The two grew up in different countries. Noah's Aunt Alicia had married a German-Jewish businessman at a young age and moved with him to Heidelberg. It was there Shlomo was born. Twice, the three made the trip to Ciechanow for a visit, once when he was seven, then again at twelve. After Hitler came to power, the family escaped to France, where eventually the Nazis and their war machine followed.

By then, Shlomo had a wife and child of his own, a baby boy. For two years they and his parents lived under the German occupation, the last few months of it in the transit camp at Drancy. One day he was picked out of a line, hustled onto a cattle car, and shipped east. Petrified at what lay ahead, lost without the family left behind, the only thing holding him together was knowing they were safe. And if there was a God, would remain so.

A different cousin than he remembered greeted Noah at the entrance to the Sonder compound. Kapo Kaminski had summoned him to Block 13 by placing the two bricks atop the wall, and with the kapo was Shlomo. Having got them together, Kaminski granted them their privacy and left.

"So," Noah said, "you seem to be doing all right."

In truth, he could tell something wasn't right at all. Shlomo struck him as more mannequin than man; the eyes were open but empty, the face human but not. Gone was all trace of the light-hearted child, in its place the pathetic wreck of an adult with not only a permanent frown but a voice bereft of life, a dry husk of a voice that instead of the emotion a reunion of long-lost relatives should have kindled possessed all the enthusiasm of someone reading from a grocery list.

"Doing all right?" If he hadn't forgotten how to smile, Shlomo would have here. "If you say so," he mumbled, the frown carved in marble.

Not that Noah adjudged his unapproachability odd. In the crucible that was Birkenau, one had to expect as much, especially from someone condemned to the commando of the living dead. It wasn't, however, exactly conducive to conversation. For a long, painfully long quarter of an hour, each in his way made an effort at this before having to admit defeat. But when they did part, they ended up embracing, though even Shlomo's hug lacked sincerity. It was as if he was going through the motions only, incapable anymore of showing real feeling.

Later, Noah was to discover why. By the bitterest of coincidences, his second week working the meadow Shlomo came across his wife and child among the corpses in one of the trolleys. Word was he'd carried them to the fire pits himself. That night, he tried to take his life by overdosing on sleeping pills, but the SS, informed of the attempt, had his stomach pumped. Upon his waking the next afternoon, the Germans told him they would determine when he was to die, not him.

Noah had trouble digesting so horrific a tale. No wonder his cousin was but a shade of his former self; something had died in him that day in the meadow, some flame been extinguished. He couldn't be sure how he'd have reacted in that situation—tried to imagine having to burn his parents and little Mendel—but didn't see himself able to smile afterward, either. Or in keeping with Shlomo's first impulse, if he'd even have allowed himself an afterward.

Despite their initial awkwardness, the two got together frequently after that, if not so much as surviving members of a decimated family—in the Vernichtungslager, one was careful never to bring up family—then as brother agents of the underground. True to his original mission for Battle Group-Auschwitz, Noah continued to collect data on the number of transports coming in, the amount of Jews in each, and how many of these went straight to the gas. Much of this information came from Kaminski, but the man couldn't be everywhere. With a trusted cousin in Number Four, Noah now had a reliable contact in each of the new crematoria.

Indeed, Shlomo had contributed by adding a whole new dimension to the count. Where the underground had overlooked the victims of selections inside the camp, he reminded Noah these could be considerable, and comprised mainly Jews. Normally running in the hundreds or less, during large-scale selections they could reach into the thousands. And with the transports this summer rolling in night and day, packing the barracks with their surplus, the stage was set for more of these ordeals.

Noah was all too acquainted with the in-camp selection. On a smaller scale they were ubiquitous, as much a part of camp life as the hunger, the mud, the fulsome stink of the chimneys. Most inmates underwent no less than two of them a day, when the camp orchestra blared them to work in the morning and at dusk when they got back. Those Nazis met at the gate to gloat over their slaves parading by were also there to weed out any who were hobbled or appeared otherwise unfit. These were forced onto trucks and never seen again.

It was the same in the medical blocks. Every prisoner knew to avoid the hospital if at all possible; death in the form of an SS doctor was a regular visitor there. Accompanied by an inmate-physician, he would "examine" each patient, this consisting of a quick glance at the person, then an index card on which was written the prisoner's ailment and whether he or she was Jewish. The cards ended up in three stacks, one for those healthy enough to return to their huts, one for those who were to remain in the hospital, and the last a pile of one-way tickets to the crematorium.

The mass selection was a different story. Noah would never forget his first. It came early December, part of the same Hanukkah purge that would take his sister at Birkenau.

In the main camp, the Polish word *Selekcja* was suddenly on everybody's lips, nor to the general angst was anyone surer of its coming than the more experienced prisoners. Noah didn't know what to make of any of it, but felt a tension in the air as thick as the smoke from the fire pits. These had been sending clouds of it skyward for days. *Something* was going on over at Birkenau, and it didn't bode well.

Rumors abounded, but later he was to learn this was always the case prior to a large selection. Someone said he heard his Blockälteste promise things would be different this time, that those picked were to be sent to a convalescent camp. A Czech younger than he, but an old Auschwitz hand, guaranteed—if refusing to divulge his sources—that this selection was to be overseen by the International Red Cross. Others said it was to be aimed at only the older among them, or that German Jews would be excluded. Or the low tattoo numbers, those who'd been at the camp the longest.

All Noah could tell was that everyone was as jumpy as a spooked cat, their nervousness making his more pronounced by the day.

Not that he was all that afraid for himself. That he could deal with; it was his brother Hanan who worried him. Trapped in the punishing Bauhof commando, lugging bags of cement around all day, starving to death, both men were in sorry shape, especially Hanan. Skinny to begin with, he was wasting away rapidly. His cheeks had started to sink, his eyes to hollow, nor was the diarrhea he'd developed showing any signs of dissipating.

He'd also injured himself on the job, breaking a big toe. The limp this caused was slight, but the day the Germans caught sight of it could be his last.

Even more treacherous was his state of mind. This above all had Noah alarmed. Each day brought Hanan closer to throwing in the towel, to quitting the struggle against what he'd begun to perceive was his inevitable death. Noah could tell he'd made up his mind to this from the way he was dragging himself around now, indifferent to his surroundings, to the hunger twisting his belly, the pain pounding in his foot. He no longer complained about either, had ceased to talk much at all. He didn't want to admit it, but neither could he deny it: his brother was turning into a Muselmänn right in front of him.

Noah had to do something. "You're not going to die on me," he told Hanan at their soup break one day, "because I'm not going to let you. What you are going to do is gut it up, lift that head of yours, get mad. I want you to get mad and stay mad, or I'm going to be mad at you."

"What are you talking about, Noah? Get mad at who?"

"Why, the Germans, who else? It's they who would suck the oxygen from your lungs, just as they did to mama, papa, and Mendel, and for all we know, Deborah and Pinchas by now. It makes it easier for them, Hanan, when they see you've given up. I won't let you make it easy for them. I won't let you give up."

"Just leave me be, big brother." Hanan went back to his soup. "Can't you see I'm trying to drink my—"

"Put the soup down!"

Some prisoners looked up before returning to their bowls. "The soup can wait, Hanan. This is important, this is about saving your life. They say there's a selection coming, and I believe them. One involving the whole camp. I've heard how these are run, and seeing as we're both skin and bones and you with a bad foot, it won't be easy to survive it.

"But it can be done. There are precautions we can take to help us get through it. Would you like me to share some of them with you? Tell me you would."

"Noah, I really don't want—"

"Good, let's go over them then. Stop me if you have any questions."

The veterans of the camp swore to the efficacy of managing a freshly shaven face on the day of a selection. It might cost half a ration of bread for the use of a razor, but all agreed this a price worth paying. Not only did it make the older prisoners look younger but everyone cleaner, therefore healthier to the SS doctors.

Another trick was to prick a finger and smear the blood on the cheeks to give them color. So many of the inmates, Noah and Hanan among them, wore the gray pallor of impending death. One should also remember, those in the know said, to keep one's muscles taut when parading naked in front of the doctors, head erect, chest thrust out in as military a bearing as one could muster. Above all, not to stumble, nor God forbid, fall. A steady step was as important as anything.

"And that's why I need you to get mad," Noah said. "Broken toe or no, you can't be limping before the selectors; it'll be the gas for you then for certain. You've got to walk normal, endure the pain as if there wasn't any. How? By becoming so angry the pain ends up as nothing to that anger, nothing to what you're holding against those forcing you to go through this humiliation. You following me so far?"

Hanan, sulking, studied the ground in front of him. Noah scooted closer.

"You're going to have to fill yourself, Hanan, fill yourself with rage, to the point there's no room for the pain or anything else. You have to despise that Nazi doctor like you've never despised anybody, at least for the few seconds you'll be marching past the bastard. It'll only be a few seconds. You can do it. I'll help you. Working together, we can beat this."

Hanan shook his head, "I can't get that mad, Noah, not anymore. Not after these last three years. I'm done, worn out, finished. Let the SS do their worst. I—I don't have it in me to keep on fighting them. I just don't."

"Oh, you don't, do you? I see." Noah's voice had gone cold. "To be honest, I'm not surprised. If you want the truth, I never thought you did. Have it in you, I mean."

"What are you trying to say?"

"I've always admired your smarts, Hanan; it was your backbone, your manhood I'm afraid I found suspect. You may be grown, have hair in all the grown-up places, but in a lot of ways you're a little boy still. A spoiled one at that."

Hanan glared at him. "Now you're just being spiteful. Why do you have to do that?"

"Spiteful? You want spiteful? Here, I'll show you spiteful." He reached across and cuffed his brother's chin, not hard but not playfully, either. Hanan's jaw dropped in shock.

"What was that for?" he said.

"Nothing. I did it because I could. Because I knew I could get away with it, knew you wouldn't hit back."

"Screw you."

"Oh, yeah? How about this then?" Noah slapped him on the cheek. "What do you think of that?"

"Stop it! I know what you're trying to do, but just stop it!"

"Make me." Noah slapped him again. And kept slapping him until they wound up grappling in the dirt like a pair of schoolboys. Their kapo wasn't present or it might have been the end for both of them. The prisoners nearest them clutched their dinner to their chests.

These would have been pressed to say which of the brothers gave in first, but seconds later their grunts and curses dissolved into laughter. Both laughed until the tears came, the struggle to pin the other having turned into an embrace.

"So you don't have any fight in you anymore," Noah said. "Sticking with that still?"

Hanan's smile turned shame-faced. "Alright already, older brother, you've proved your point. And I have to admit I love you for it. The question is, will it work? Is it possible to get pissed off enough to block out a broken toe?"

Sunday came. An *Arbeitssonntag*, which meant work. Every other Sunday, the prisoners were exempted from their normal labors, but the following one it was work as usual for half a day. After the Appell at noon, soup was dispensed, and the rest of the afternoon devoted to such tasks as sprucing up the huts and grounds, the blacking of their clogs with machine grease, the shearing of their heads and bodies, the search for lice.

This *Sonntag* would be different, beginning with the weather. It was a warm day for December, hardly balmy but far from freezing. Denied winter clothing, this was always a plus for the prisoners. The day's warmth was tempered, however, by another kind of chill: the certitude, inexplicable but no less strong for it, that what they'd been fearing was upon them. Everyone knew the selection would be today, as surely as if the Germans had announced it beforehand.

Noah and Hanan were prepared, and after eating had hurried to the washroom for an emergency shave. Between them the use of a razor had cost a full ration of bread, a crumb of soap half a helping of soup. Whether they'd wasted the purchase by using it on the wrong day remained to be seen.

Though not for long. At three o'clock the reveille bell exploded, which at that hour could mean only one thing: *Blocksperre*, immediate confinement of all prisoners to their barracks. It was a Selekcja, a major one.

Their block senior knew exactly what to do. First, he got everyone inside the barracks and counted, locked the doors, closed the shutters. A file box filled with index cards was produced on which were typed each prisoner's tattoo number, nationality, age, and occupation. Everyone was ordered to strip to the skin but for his shoes, and the cards handed out. After that, it became a matter of waiting for the SS to reach their hut.

The Blockälteste returned to his room, but every so often stuck his head out to see that all was as it should be. Most of his charges had made for their bunks and their blankets; the day may have been unseasonable, but was still cold. Others, oblivious to the temperature, stood about naked. Conversation was negligible, each man busy with his thoughts.

Noah was an exception. He held his mouth to Hanan's ear as one would a bellows to a fire, hoping to get the flames of his brother's ire going by leading him on a stroll down memory lane. Every insult, every injustice perpetrated against their family since the ghetto he recounted in relentless detail, leaving out nothing.

Hanan listened obediently, but showed no emotion. Noah couldn't tell what effect he was having if any, but kept at it. After twenty minutes, he'd barely got them off the train and into Auschwitz when a hail of shouts erupted at one end of the hut.

It was the Älteste and his helpers. With curses and blows, they drove the prisoners from their kojen and the whole apprehensive mass toward the quartermaster's office and storage area. This *Tagesraum* measured only nine meters by six and a half, but somehow all four hundred men were stuffed inside and the door squeezed shut. So full of flesh was the room that the boards in the walls creaked outward from the pressure.

By the time a *Schütze* started allowing them singly into the yard, Noah had resumed talking, reminding Hanan how their mama, papa, and baby brother had died in the pitch-black of the gas chamber, screams filling their ears, the stinging gas their throats.

"Picture," Noah said, "the terror of that room. Bodies crashing into bodies in the dark, people fighting, shoving, trampling each other. Imagine our mother holding Mendel in her arms as both choke to death, unable to catch their breaths."

Hanan listened without saying a word, but Noah could see the water brimming in his eyes. He didn't like what he was doing, didn't like it one bit, but if it worked his brother into the desired lather it was worth it.

Gradually, the pressure in the room eased as it emptied man by man, until it came Hanan's turn. When Noah was pulled outside a minute later, he stepped blinking into the late-afternoon sunlight to an SS doctor-major standing near the barracks' main door, on one side of him its elder, the other its quartermaster. He was told to walk to this trio, then back to the Tagesraum door and back again. He made every effort to emulate an infantryman on parade, step purposeful, head high, chest out, muscles clenched.

(Whenever coming upon such a performance later, with the selection limited to a hut or two and no Blocksperre in effect, the sight never failed to ruin his day. To see a living skeleton trying desperately to march like a soldier, naked, pale as a grub, the scrotum swollen with hunger edema swinging pendulously to and fro—there was something beyond obscene about it, a maneuver as debasing to those watching as those forced to execute it).

Upon completing the test, Noah handed his index card to the doctor and made for the barracks door. Before stepping inside, he turned and saw the SS man give it to the Blockälteste.

This detail would prove crucial. Each man's fate hinged on where his card ended up. There was a good side and a bad, the issue being which was which, whether the elder's or the quartermaster's was unclear at this point. But with it emerging that some of the more obvious candidates for the gas had watched the latter take theirs, those who'd noticed where their own had landed were spared the suspense of waiting to find out if they were going to live or die.

Most, though, wouldn't know for a couple of days. A worried Noah rushed straight to Hanan. "Well?" was all he said. To which his brother replied, "My foot feels as if its been hit with a hammer, but I'm guessing I did okay."

"Did you see where your card went?"

"No, but I think the *Sturmbannführer* might have been more focused on the daggers in my eyes than the limp in my step. It's a wonder he didn't shoot me right there for insubordination. At any rate, thanks, brother of mine, for looking after me. If it hadn't been for you…"

"Don't thank me until we're certain you're out of the woods. As for now, let's get dressed and see to that foot."

Two days later, the numbers of a hundred men were called, and as the rest of the barracks made for the Appellplatz and morning roll call, these were held back. Neither Hanan nor Noah were among them, were twice blessed in that not long afterward the cook Witek rescued them from the Bauhof as part of those chosen to be Stubendiensten to the Prominenz of Block 25.

As for the hundred, they were dispatched that morning to Birkenau, if not necessarily to their deaths. Not straightaway. For many of the selectees from the camp—depending on the influx of transports, or how long it took their guards to build their numbers up to warrant the expenditure of Zyklon-B—the route to the gas chamber might involve a layover of up to a few days at a restricted barracks known in lager parlance as the *Himmelblock*, or heaven block. It was called this because those sent to it were halfway to their reward already.

Making for A Camp one evening to see Roza, Noah took a wrong road and wound up at an out-of-the-way corner of the barbed wire. There, set apart from the others, was a noticeably larger hut with barred windows and a heavy door guarded by two *Schützen*.

It was the Himmelblock for women, Birkenau's Block 25. At each window, a flurry of arms floated from out the bars like the tentacles of some monstrous sea anemone. These belonged to those prisoners, who having spotted him began begging for water, while from behind them wafted an unbroken susurrus of female sobbing and moans. The reek of excrement was intolerable, the soldiers at the door having plugged their nostrils with cigarette butts.

The food given these doomed souls was freely plundered by the kapo in charge of them; it didn't take long for people sick and depleted to begin with to grow disturbingly worse. Shlomo Kirschenbaum, for the two weeks he was at Crematorium II, had twice worked the detail that received the condemned of the Himmelblocks. One shipment had been made up of women, the other men, an identical facility for them existing in the *B2f* lager. He described to Noah what the job entailed, using the former as an example. Even in the man's desiccated monotone, the other's heart wilted at what his ears were hearing.

"They entered the death-house grounds packed into open trucks, naked. Those not weeping loudly were in a state of shock, shivering despite a hot day, eyes big as saucers. We helped them to the pavement, then underground. Not a one resisted, knowing it would have been pointless. Twelve hundred women that afternoon descended their last stairs ever."

Shlomo had swallowed hard then, as if reluctant to continue.

"The final load, those unable to walk, arrived by dump truck. These were heaped one on top of the other as if they'd been thrown there. Upon pulling up to the crematorium, its bed began to rise at one end. Groaning, the women clawed at the sides and each other without success; with a cracking of heads and knees they spilled onto the pavement.

"A few ended up untangling themselves from this pile and staggered about as if drunk. The rest lay where they'd fallen. These we had to carry down the steps, careful not to slip in the shit and the blood."

The gassing of non-Jews had ceased in April on orders from Berlin. With the mounting crush at the unloading ramp, the SS high command decided wholesale purification was a luxury they could no longer afford. But as Shlomo reminded his cousin, while the quantity of selected from the camp paled before those from the trains, it could be significant and should be included in any tally. This moved Noah to refine his figures. If it was numbers Auschwitz wanted, he was going to give them all they could handle.

As dismaying as these numbers were, nothing drove the point of the slaughter home more than something he'd chanced upon one morning on the road to Birkenau. The dry arithmetic provided him by his Sonder contacts, though appalling, didn't pack half the wallop of what he saw that day. It was a sight as hard on the soul as it was improbable.

Intent on the limestone path at his feet, thoughts consumed by the unpleasant assignment he'd been sent on, he looked up to find a column of prisoners from Birkenau, men and women, quickly closing on him. Each was pushing a baby carriage of all contraptions, crazily suggestive of some ragged, underfed regiment of nannies. Except these carriages were empty, the weird procession simply a means of getting them from some Canada warehouse to the rail siding and the train taking them to Germany.

As might be expected, not a prisoner met Noah's gaze. What did surprise, and sicken him, was the sheer magnitude of the display. The strollers rattled past, a virtual river of them, every color and kind, from a dozen different countries. Nor could there be any doubt what had become of their erstwhile passengers. But for the segregated Gypsy and Czech Family Camps, there were no children at either Auschwitz or Birkenau under the age of fourteen.

Here was his people's future, or rather the lack of one, made visible. What could be more telling, more chilling than those lines of baby-less prams stretching to the horizon?

Noah had been witness to this proof of atrocity on his way to meet with the leadership of Battle Group-Sonderkommando. The mission Bruno Baum had laid on him was to relay to the Sonder at long last the plan of attack for the revolt, an announcement sure to fire their hopes, then dash those hopes by informing them the operation had been postponed.

The reason he was supposed to give for this was bogus, and he knew it. He'd been ordered to tell them the partisans, whose contribution to the uprising was intrinsic to its success, were in no position at present to help. Why? Since the world-shaking developments in the Warsaw ghetto this spring, Nazi military and police activity in all parts of the country had increased to the extent that the Home Army had its hands full providing for just itself now. There was no chance anytime soon of it diverting the manpower or coming up with the weapons and supplies it would take to support a mass escape from Birkenau.

But Battle Group-Auschwitz's reticence had nothing to do with the partisans. It was correct that beginning in May these had been pressed to the limit for a period, but SS anger at the humiliation it had suffered in Warsaw had abated much the last three months. Or so Noah gathered from what he'd been able to overhear in Baum's and Cyrankiewicz's offices. The Armia had replenished itself in those months to the point it again was capable of fighting alongside the rebels.

What was in fact moving the underground to caution was the electrifying news from the Russian front. Noah knew this because he'd been present when it had arrived via courier from Krakow: the Wehrmacht, having launched its third offensive in as many years against the Soviet Union, had been routed at the climactic battle of Kursk in southern Russia. The Germans were even now in retreat, leaving a hundred thousand troops dead or captured and the burning hulks of the better part of eleven armored divisions.

Kursk was primarily a tank battle, and for the Wehrmacht a disaster. The likelihood of it taking the initiative again in the east was all but nonexistent. From now on, it would be the Red Army on the offensive.

The significance of this wasn't lost on Auschwitz. Why chance a breakout from Birkenau with the Russians threatening one of their own? The Soviets could be in Poland before the year was out. Better for the underground and those it was responsible for to wait for liberation than try to force the issue by taking on the SS themselves.

Noah didn't like for one minute what he was being asked to do, hadn't since before even leaving Baum's office. The lone window had been open, letting in the flies and August heat alike.

"So why not tell the Sonder the truth, commander, instead of leading them on? What good does it do to try stalling them?"

"It does two things," Baum said, "both of them critical. It should be clear by now to the men of the Sonderkommando that whether the camp is liberated or not, they will not survive the war. The Nazis are not about to let the only eyewitnesses to their crime live. Now, if these walking dead begin to smell enthusiasm for the revolt waning, what do you think their reaction will be? What would yours be?

Having nothing to lose, they might attempt to make a go of it on their own, and succeed or not, endanger the whole camp by exposing it to SS reprisals.

"We do realize the Kommandos of the past have all gone unprotesting to their deaths, but these men are different. Months of inflammatory rhetoric and rising hopes have their blood up. But they cannot be allowed to act independently. The risk to the other tens of thousands of inmates is too great. That is why we are sending you to tell them we are still with them when… in actuality we are not. Not at present anyway."

Noah got the impression this wasn't Baum speaking, but came from others. He watched him shift uneasily in his chair, as if what he had to say next agreed even less with him.

"If on the other hand the situation on the battlefield should change, say the Wehrmacht regroups, and establishing a defensive line is able to hold off the Soviets indefinitely, then the Special Squad will be there to head the uprising as planned. Which is the second reason for leading them on as you so perceptively put it, to have them available should the Russian counteroffensives fail."

Noah struggled to keep the disapproval from his voice. "In the meantime, the crematoria continue to kill. I trust the Steering Committee is aware of what its new strategy is going to cost."

Baum rose from his desk and stood at the window, his back to Noah.

"Of course we are aware. It was not an easy decision to make. I personally opposed the call to stand down, and still feel we might live—or should I say die?—to regret it. Not only does it leave the death houses intact but should the Soviets indeed get close, I fear the Germans would do anything to prevent us, especially those of us Jewish, from falling into their hands."

Here he turned around. "However, I am also afraid the crematoria may have done their worst, that the time to destroy those diabolic mills is past. Despite every effort to err on the side of excess, it would appear we have underestimated their lethalness. Have you stopped to consider, with this bloodiest of summers not yet over, why the number of transports of late has been dwindling? You of all people, Comrade Zabludowicz, must have noticed, what with the figures you continue so admirably to collect."

"They have been tailing off, yes."

"I can assure you it is not because the SS have had a change of heart. Nor do we believe it an aberration, some kind of lull. With the exception of Lodz, and that because of its economic value to the Reich, the great ghettos of Poland have all been liquidated—Lublin, Krakow, Warsaw, Poznan, all drained of their humanity. Likewise Riga, Vilna, and others in the Baltics. And save for Hungary, the Balkans. The bigger transit camps in France and Holland are not what they used to be, either. As for the death the *Einsatzgruppen* are still sowing in the east..."

"Pardon me, sir." Noah hadn't heard the word before. "The... Einsatzgruppen?"

"Another, sad to say, in that long line of Nazi euphemisms—'rapid deployment units' will suffice as a translation."

Baum returned to his chair, looking older than when he'd left it. From the window, a gust of heated air ruffled the papers on his desk.

"In fact, they are SS murder brigades. Four of them continue to roam Russia behind the Wehrmacht lines, their task to round up and eliminate all Jews, political authorities, the intelligentsia, and others. Nor is their method as sophisticated, for lack of a better word, as gas. They use guns, machine guns for the most part, at least in their larger Aktionen.

"A pit is dug, or a ditch, and people lined up naked at the edge and mowed down. Families are often butchered together, parents and children, brothers and sisters, holding hands, their eyes meeting in— what, astonishment? Despair? It is as difficult a scene to comprehend as convey."

Baum's expression blackened. "The SS have been busy in Russia since the invasion of the country in '41. Outside the city of Kiev, thirty-three thousand Jews were shot in two days, with one hundred and fifty thousand to follow. This from Kiev alone! There are almost three million of us in the Soviet Union, Zabludowicz. Or rather, there used to be. Now..."

Noah dropped into the remaining chair. As if Birkenau and the other camps weren't enough, now this horror story from Russia. It made one wonder that such evil should occur outdoors, in the light of day, and the sun not hide its face in disgust. "But how—"

"I just told you how."

As much trouble as he was having processing Baum's Einsatzgruppen, that wasn't Noah's question.

"No, general, not how is it done, nor how can such a thing be, but how in blazes do you come to know all of this? And be so dead sure of it? If you ask me, it smacks of men who've let their imaginations get the better of them. Or have some sort of agenda to push. I won't presume to ask you your sources, but are you positive they can be trusted?"

"We have many sources," Baum said. "Rarely are we at the mercy of a mere one or two. The reach of the Armia Krajowa is long; little goes on in the occupied territories we do not see.

"But that is neither here nor there. The point I am trying to make is I fear the Jewish presence in this part of the world is history. Or just about. All of us able to be rounded up easily and unsuspectingly have been, leaving only those few in hiding or otherwise gone underground. It would not surprise me if there were as many who can be accounted for concentrated in the barracks of Auschwitz-Birkenau than in any country on the continent now except Hungary. And Hungary only because an ally of Nazi Germany, encouraged but not required to give up its Jews."

Baum's voice fell to a murmur, as if he was thinking out loud. "Which then is the better course of action, to sit idle until the Red Army shows and risk our fanatical keepers slaughtering us in our bunks? Or the even riskier tactic of attempting to liberate ourselves and imperiling those clinging to life here, one of the last remaining enclaves of Jews in all Europe."

He seemed to ponder this a moment, then in a normal voice, "Who can say? So I say this: I am going to obey the orders given me, Zabludowicz, as you are going to obey yours, which are to deliver the battle plan we've drawn up to the rebels of the Sonderkommando, then break the bad news it cannot be put into action just yet.

"Whatever you can add that might buffer their disappointment, lift their spirits a little, go for it—except, need I say, anything to do with the actual cause of the delay. Afterward, report back to me with their reaction."

"Yes, sir, as you wish."

Both rose, Baum catching and holding his agent's gaze. The tired, cynical eyes softened some. "It is a dirty business, but we depend on you, young man. Your people depend on you. Never forget it is to them you owe your first allegiance."

"Yes, sir, I won't. And will do my best, as always."

But it wasn't going to be easy. Noah wasn't a good liar. And he'd developed a real liking for some of the Sonder, the gruff yet big-hearted Kaminski in particular. To play so dishonest with men who'd come to be his friends, whom he'd laughed with, broken bread with, went against his grain.

Then en route to Birkenau and Block 13, he ran into that apocalyptic parade of baby carriages. Which didn't help his conscience any knowing that as a result of his mission, the four death factories responsible for that ghoulish display were to be given a new lease on life. He thought about trying to find his older brother and asking Pinchas whether he should return to the Stammlager and decline the assignment, but abandoned the idea as soon as it entered his head. Aside from revealing secrets no outsider, not even a brother, was entitled to, what in the end could that brother possibly have said to dissuade him from his duty?

Baum, of course, had been onto his misgivings, and with his closing words sought to offset them. And the more Noah went over them, the truer those words rang: however uncomfortable this latest job made him, vastly more was at stake here than his or any man's comfort.

The prisoner stationed outside the Sonder compound barely glanced at him. Kaminski and three of his top men were waiting in the hut. Two of them he knew, Yankel Handelsman and Yossel Warszawski, and after he was introduced to Zalman Gradowski the five adjourned to the empty Tagesraum.

He wasted no time presenting Auschwitz's plan. The two keys to its success were the element of surprise and a high degree of coordination among its participants. Timing was utmost. The wheels had to be set in motion by afternoon's end, no earlier, no later, so that when the escapees reached the woods, and not before, night would have fallen. They would need the light to recognize each other in the early stages of the fighting, then the dark to cloak them from the pursuing Germans.

The revolt was to commence at 5:30, a half hour before the change of shifts at the crematoria. The eight SS manning Numbers

Four and Five and the ten overseeing Two and Three were to be overpowered silently and their weapons seized. When their relief escorting the night shift arrived, they too would be killed and their arms taken. This would leave the insurgents with a fair number of guns and uniforms, these to be donned by those fluent in German.

After the pair of guards at the gate of each crematorium was disposed of, the men posing as SS would lead the day shift back to Block 13. On the way, they were to cut all telephone lines. After outfitting themselves with the supplies and munitions they'd stashed, the Sonder were to boil out of their barracks and spread across Birkenau, dealing death to any soldiers they met while herding what prisoners they could toward the crematoria.

The night crews at these, meanwhile, having rigged the four with explosives, were to blow them at the first sound of gunfire. That would be the signal for the partisans hiding in the woods to attack the western section of the outer guard cordon. This was a ring of watchtowers encircling the camp a kilometer and a half from its barbed wire perimeter.

Once past the outer cordon, the Armia was to move against the one at the edge of the camp. The Sonder who'd destroyed the crematoria would already have engaged this inner cordon preparatory to taking out the electrified fence.

By the time the first of the fleeing inmates reached the western perimeter, its watchtowers should have been knocked out, freeing those rebels with weapons to defend against any German reinforcements. The Sonder disguised in SS uniforms would have donned yellow armbands to identify themselves.

The aim at this stage would be to protect the prisoners pouring through the gaps in the fence. Only when the last of these had reached the forest were the Sonder to follow, serving with half the partisans as a rear guard while the other half quickly ushered smaller groups of the escapees away. This last was to confuse and scatter the Nazi forces. With their Polish rescuers as guides now, these groups were to converge via roundabout routes on the marshes surrounding the Sola River to the south, a Home Army stronghold since the war began.

That was the plan roughed out. It would be polished smooth later. "Any questions?" Noah asked.

Silence at first. Then, vintage Kaminski. "It's as good a damned way to die as any, I guess. Better than most, I'd have to say, in this puke of a place."

"I have one," said Warszawski, balancing his chair on its hind legs. He and Handelsman were tight, had been for years. Both active in the Communist Party, they'd escaped Poland for France together, been arrested there together, and were together still. But apart from the fact they were both just shy of thirty, and each committed body and soul to the revolt, they were two very different people. Where Handelsman was on the laid-back side, known for not wasting any more energy than was called for, rare was the moment some part of Warszawski wasn't in motion.

Little taller than five feet, packed into that small frame was the coiled vitality of two men. His face was all bone and sharp edges, and he would walk with it thrust forward as if it were in a race to outrun the rest of him. He talked fast, ate fast, even snored in double-time. Nervous tension radiated from him in all but visible tendrils. There was nothing subtle about him; as with Kaminski, one always knew where one stood with Warszawski.

Which, unless it was in favor of taking up arms and killing Germans, wasn't very high. One either showed oneself a man or not, there could be no in-between with him.

He let the front legs of the chair drop to the floor, on which his left foot was soon vibrating. "Answer me this. Those marshes you're talking about aren't exactly close by. I can see a few of us reaching them maybe, if we're lucky, but what makes your bosses, Zabludowicz, think the SS are going to let the thousands you say will be tagging along with us get anywhere near that far? That just strikes me as crazy, and suicide for those of us held back to protect them."

"Allow me please, Noah, to answer that," said Handelsman, "by suggesting we not overrate these Germans of ours. The deeper we get into the woods, the less of an advantage they have. Like us, they'll be on foot, unable to bring any vehicles or heavy guns with them. And keep in mind, the partisans have been living in these forests for four years now. They know the terrain and how to use it, where to lay ambushes, booby traps, the ravines and such to avoid. And what have our captors been doing these four years?"

"Enjoying the privileged life of garrison duty," Gradowski jumped in, "concentration-camp duty. Getting fat. Getting soft. Drunk half the day. I'm with the professor: should we make it into the woods, we'll stand a decent chance."

"Oh, we'll make it into the woods," Kaminski huffed, "and there will be battles there. But we're going to win those battles, just like we will have won the one to bust us out of this shitpile. We'll make it into the woods all right, I promise you, just as I can promise that a lot of those pig-eyed Krauts won't."

Noah nodded his approbation with the rest of them, then turned to Warszawski.

"The prisoners, remember, Yossel, won't be fleeing in one big mob, but fanning out in dozens of directions. That's one reason it's so important the partisans be involved; it's they who'll be responsible for shepherding all those little mobs to safety. Not that this is going to be easy in the dark, but neither will that dark be a friend to those chasing us."

"One thing I would like to know," asked Handelsman, "is how much support we can expect from the main camp. Does the underground have any intention of joining us in the fight?"

"Or at least do something," Gradowski said, "anything, to divert some of the SS from Birkenau."

At mention of the underground, Noah's heart dropped to his stomach. Up to then he'd almost forgot why he was here—now with a rush it came flooding back. His answer to Handelsman sounded memorized, mechanical.

"All I can tell you, Yankel, is what I've been told. If the breakout is successful, especially if the cremos are brought down, there'll likely be reprisals. The Resistance would rather these were confined to Birkenau. Should Battle Group-Auschwitz be implicated, not only would the population there be subject to German vengeance but the organization, to the detriment of all the inmates.

"It suffices, say my superiors, that they've stuck their necks out as far as they have by enlisting the troops of the Home Army. If the SS were to learn of that..."

Noah could have kicked himself for a fool. Clumsily, he'd got swept up in the excitement of the first part of his message, which in its instructions on how to conduct the revolt seemed to be saying that talk was about to turn into action. The time had come now to spill the rest of that message. He forced it from his mouth, his ears hot with the shame of it.

"This, I know, isn't what you were hoping to hear. But I bring even worse news. A lot worse." In his hurry to get it over with, he delivered it rapid-fire. "I've been instructed to inform you in light of recent events in the Warsaw ghetto that Nazi pressure has the partisans running for cover, hardly able to protect themselves much less lend a hand to others. Which for the moment—means the revolt has been put on hold."

Asked to define "for the moment," Noah hesitated before coming out with it, the words as bitter in his mouth as the berries of some inedible plant.

"A few *months?*" Kaminski snorted. "Have your generals lost their marbles? We might not have a few months, not a lot of us."

The others were just as floored. "Do you get what you're asking?" said Gradowski. "That we keep doing this—this work, living this nightmare, for who can say how much longer. Time, as our kapo said, many of us don't have."

Handelsman looked more saddened than angry, though he, too, bristled with accusation. "Your commanders have to know, Zabludowicz, that for every week they delay, more thousands of Jews will be reduced to so much dust. Gone, wiped from memory, as if they'd never existed. What kind of men are they that can live with such a decision?"

Forced to split his loyalty between his bosses in the movement and his friends in the Sonderkommando, Noah didn't know how to respond. "I'm not sure what kind, Yankel, but I'd guess they're no different than you and I, or any other mother's son trapped in this slaughterhouse: desperate, afraid, the grave a step away, their lives dependent on out-thinking, out-guessing the SS. What kind of men are they? I'd say that was for you to decide."

"Cowards," said Warszawski, "that's what they are. And liars to boot. Do any of you buy this claptrap about the Home Army being on the run, forced to lie low? Lie low from what? I'd say it wasn't the partisans stretched thin here, but the truth. Why don't you tell us what's really going on, Zabludowicz? The real reason your buddies at Auschwitz have come down with cold feet."

"That'll do!" warned Kaminski. "I'll have none of that. I'd be careful, too, if I were you, Yossel; from what I hear, Noah could whip the bunch of us single-handed. But we're not going to let it come to that, are we, boys? No, we're going to behave like the gentlemen we are and mind our goddam manners."

He'd stared coldly at each in turn as he spoke. Then, on a gentler note, "So the revolt is off for now." Kaminski didn't like what he'd heard any more than the next man, particularly as it related to what Handelsman had said. He wasn't the type, though, to let bad tidings get the better of him.

"There isn't a whole lot we can do about that, but then we're not ready to take on the SS anyhow, are we? Far from it, and now we have a plan to build on and prepare for. I say we put it behind us and move on to something more constructive. Or maybe *instructive* would be the better place to start."

He turned to their visitor. "And what I'm asking by that, Noah, is why do we keep hearing, to use your own words, about 'recent events in the Warsaw ghetto?' And now here you go telling us that's what has put the revolt on ice. Yossel has a point, and not just the one on his head. Why should the Germans choose this of all times to crack down on the Home Army?

"Enlighten us, sir, please. What the hell happened in Warsaw to get the Krauts' panties in such a wad?"

Noah's eyebrows shot up. "You mean you don't know? How can you not?"

"Again, we've heard talk, but nothing in detail," Kaminski said. "Something about some Jews resisting deportation. But then, we're a bit cut off over here; the SS don't like us hobnobbing with the general population. Most of the prisoners we do see are too busy getting ready to be murdered to stop and chat about what's going on in the war."

Like a gift dropped in his lap, here was a way for Noah to follow both his orders and his conscience. He recalled the license Baum had given him, once he'd deflated Sonder spirits, to try and assuage Sonder disappointment if he got the chance. And here that chance was, a means of softening the blow he'd just dealt them with as rousing a tale of Jewish heroics as any in all history.

"Then let me share what we've been told by those who were there, and prepare to be awed."

There could be no arguing it was a story for the ages. Beginning in July of last year, successive waves of deportations to the death camps, mainly Treblinka, had decimated the Jewish population of Warsaw. Starvation and disease also took their toll, so that from a high of half a million people, only sixty thousand remained in the ghetto come April. On the morning of the 19th, units of the SS, backed by the Gestapo, marched in to round up this last sixty thousand. The ghetto was to be liquidated.

Their would-be victims, however, were laying for them, hidden in prearranged battle stations. Having learned for a fact months ago that Treblinka wasn't a labor but an extermination camp, they'd agreed never to board another cattle car.

They used those months to prepare. Tunnels and bunkers were dug beneath the streets and provisioned, weapons smuggled in by bribing the Polish police guarding the ghetto walls—mostly pistols, ammunition, a few grenades, and gasoline, this last to make a small arsenal of Molotov cocktails. The rebels even got their hands on a heavy machine gun.

When the Nazis stomped in on the 19th at dawn all cocky and loud, singing their Nazi songs, they were confident the deserted streets meant the lily-livered Jews—the same Jews who by the hundreds of thousands the past year had been led like sheep to their deaths—were quaking under their beds waiting to be drug out by the scruffs of their necks.

And waiting they were, but nowhere near their beds. Nor did they have any intention of being dragged anywhere. No sooner had the Germans, four companies strong, filled the intersection of Mila and Zamenhofa Streets than a hail of bullets and explosives tore into them from three sides. Fifty soldiers fell in twenty minutes. As did the tank they'd called to provide cover for their retreat.

As unthinkable as it was a half-hour ago, the mighty SS had been repelled, slinking back the way they'd come. They hadn't expected the Jews to fight, hadn't thought the Jew *could* fight, but made now to confront this disquieting fact, returned that morning in force—at Muranowski Square, where a second tank was destroyed; at the enormous brush factory to the north a full city block long, where fifty more of the invaders fell; at the corner of Nalewski and Gesia

Streets, the soldiers attacking from all sides, but after a seven-hour battle failing to gain a foot of ground.

By late afternoon, not a German was left in the ghetto. All had withdrawn to the safety of the Aryan side of the wall.

The second day was the same, the Nazis repulsed wherever they tried, every other house, set of apartments, store front a fortress. By now the defenders' supply of weapons had grown, stolen from the hands of their dead enemies. Women fought alongside their men and with the same ferocity, even children jumping into the fray. Two weeks passed before the Nazis had their fill of trying to wrest the ghetto by storm and agreed on a less costly strategy: burning it to the ground building by building to flush the Jewish demons out of their holes.

The infantry set fires and the Luftwaffe dropped incendiaries, and after they were done not much of the ghetto remained. Those Jews who survived the flames were driven below ground, yet even then refused to give up. By day the SS used sound-detecting devices and police dogs to sniff out their bunkers, while at night furious skirmishes lit up the ruins. For ten days more, this war within the war raged, until, out of ammunition, the handful of guerrillas left alive escaped through the sewers into the city proper.

The four Sonder sat through Noah's account without saying a word. The disillusionment he'd planted in their faces was still there, but he could detect a gleam of pride alongside it now. It was the reaction he'd been hoping for, his amends for lying to them about the partisans. Feeding off that pride, and hoping to cement it, he sought to finish with a flourish.

"And so the ghetto fell," he said, his voice rising. "But though the battle had been lost, this was won: even with repeated German guarantees to grant the Jews safe conduct if they laid down their arms, most chose to die fighting. Or committed suicide rather than surrender. Having tasted freedom, if only briefly, they weren't about to eat at the trough of slavery again."

Later, on the road back to Auschwitz, Noah rehashed the meeting. It had, of course, left a bad taste in his mouth, but not as bad as it could have been. He'd salvaged a shred of self-respect after all by lightening the heavy load he'd originally laid on the four. He liked to believe, too, he'd done more than simply elevate their spirits, his words reminding them that despite their steel helmets, their firepower, their aura of invincibility, the SS were as vulnerable to hot lead as any mortal. Could be dished death as readily as they'd been dispensing it all these years.

It was a truism he hoped would resound when they shared the story with the rest of the squad. And in doing so, imbue them as well with a warrior tradition, a *Jewish* warrior tradition, a concept that had lain dormant for eighteen centuries until re-emerging just this spring from the smoldering wreck of the ghetto. No longer could the world disparage Jewish manhood, slander them as a race of effeminate weaklings. With Warsaw, the Jew as born coward had become a conceit of the past.

But this tradition, like many, came with a price; from now on, the Jew would be expected to fight. No more could he compliantly accept his fate, prostrate before the will of his God.

Not that Noah didn't feel this slur against his kind overblown, an opinion supported by what he'd come to know of the Vernichtungslager of all places, where Jewish servility looked to have outdone itself. But for almost four years, men and women had been dying at first Auschwitz then Birkenau, methodically slaughtered without rendering the least resistance. And not all of them had been Jews. Political and religious activists from a wide swath of countries, common criminals and other undesirables, the Polish intelligentsia and middle class, suspected partisans and other enemies of the Reich—all had been starved, shot, beaten, and gassed to death without lifting a finger in their defense. Even uncounted thousands of Russian prisoners of war, men trained to do battle, armed combat their profession, had in the early days of Auschwitz trudged quietly to their graves.

Under the right conditions, both physical and psychological, submissiveness to the point of walking obediently to one's death could hardly be called a flaw specific to the Jewish character, but rather a chink in the armor of the *human* character the SS had become adept at exploiting.

The martyrs of the Warsaw ghetto having led the way, now it was up to those in like straits to carry the fight forward. Nor could Noah imagine any more suited to the task than the Sonderkommando of Birkenau. His faith in this unfaltering, he'd sleep better tonight having made an effort to keep the flame of their rebelliousness lit in spite of the cold water he'd been ordered to splash on it. And if that flame, as he knew he shouldn't be thinking, ended up burning so fiercely as to ignite this detachment into acting counter to the designs of his superiors, then so be it. As Bruno Baum himself had confessed, who could be positive which was the right course to chart and which wasn't?

Despite his instructions, despite the Steering Committee, despite even Baum's closing admonition to him, Noah would have been fine with the men of Block 13 emulating their cousin insurrectionists two hundred miles to the north. And that without the consent of their tepid collaborators in the Stammlager.

Not that these, with the exception perhaps of Baum, wouldn't have had his hide for daring even to flirt with such a notion. By the same token, he didn't approve of some of the things they were doing, either. The duplicity of their explanation for the delay of the revolt aside, he'd neglected to tell the Sonder that some of the munitions smuggled to the fighters in Warsaw had come courtesy of the Home Army, the very people Auschwitz claimed had no weapons to spare the Special Squad. Which in truth they might not have back then, given what they were busy sneaking into the ghetto.

But that was back then, and besides, the partisans had supplied Warsaw with more than just guns. In addition to acting as a link to the outside world, some had gone so far as to join in the actual fighting. When on the third day, the rebels raised their flag atop their headquarters in Muranowski Square—a blue Star of David on a white field for the Germans, for all the city to see—next to it flew the red and white banner of the Armia Krajowa.

It wasn't that the leaders of the underground favored one group of Jews over another, nor as demonstrated by the support they'd volunteered Warsaw that they were opposed in principle to the idea of revolt. They merely questioned the advisability of launching one from the death camp. With the Red Army on the verge of rolling the Wehrmacht all the way back to Germany, any attempt at a breakout made less sense to them than ever.

When it came down to it, and in spite of his sympathy for the Sonder, Noah remained torn. It could be argued it was as rightful to praise the Battle Group as denounce it, that logic was on its side, all the more since its intelligence arm had discovered a week ago that newly promoted *Hauptscharführer* Otto Möll would soon be gone, transferred to another post. Not only did this reduce the chance of the dreaded Möll Plan being employed but, if in the opinion of his superiors the sergeant's more than estimable services were no longer needed at this biggest and most productive of SS killing centers, they, too, must have felt, as Baum had, that their war against the Jews was all but won. Making the moral imperative behind the revolt, the destruction of the crematoria, less of a must. Or less a one worth sacrificing who knew how many more thousands of lives for.

Noah shaded his eyes from the heavy summer sun. It had passed its zenith and begun its slow descent, an erratic breeze kicking up swirls of white dust from the road. In the distance, the reddish brick of the Stammlager danced in the heat. There was no sign of any baby carriages, nor the small army of prisoners who'd been pushing them. The latter were either still at the rail siding or already returned to camp.

He had the limestone road to himself, or so it would have seemed to someone watching. In reality, he was accompanied by two of his brothers. Not Pinchas, whom he'd tried his hardest to track down earlier but failed to, nor Hanan, to whom he couldn't get back fast enough.

It was the twins Ezra and Ehud who tramped at his side, and had since he'd left Block 13. Warsaw had only to come up in conversation for his thoughts to gravitate toward them. Though he couldn't be certain, the two were likely trapped in the ghetto from its onset. They'd moved to the big city when war had broken out to try to earn some money for the family, and no one had seen nor so much as heard from them after the ghetto wall had gone up.

Noah did his best at first to stay upbeat, but had since ceased holding out much hope for either of them. There were too many ways for a Jew in Warsaw to have died, if not from malnutrition, disease, or later SS bullets and flamethrowers, then Treblinka, always Treblinka. There were no selections at Treblinka. Everyone who got off the trains went directly to the gas.

But not everyone ended up at that terrible place. Maidanek got its share of the Warsaw transports, as less often did Birkenau. He'd kept a sharp lookout for the twins, but so far no luck.

He still had a soft spot in his heart for those two. As sweet-natured as they were inseparable, he remembered the grief that as children they'd caused their parents by taking in every animal in distress that crossed their paths, stray cats and dogs, injured birds, even—he had to smile every time he recalled it—a sick sewer rat once. Their decision to uproot themselves and brave Warsaw for the sake of the family had both surprised and impressed him, though he had a little trouble picturing them hurling Molotov cocktails at tanks.

In all probability they hadn't, not those gentle souls. As if it mattered a fig to him. Whatever they had or hadn't done, or wherever they were, or if they weren't anywhere at all anymore, he missed them and would continue to until he saw them again, be it in this world or the next.

Oh, his poor family, like a house burgled, a home ransacked. First Joseph, grabbed off some Ciechanow street by the Gestapo. Then his parents and little Mendel, Deborah not long after, Ezra and Ehud... Noah wept for them all. As soon as he reached Auschwitz and made his report to Bruno Baum, he raced his shadow back to Block 25 and Hanan, where to his brother's perplexity he didn't let him out of his sight for the rest of the day and night until forced to by the undisputable finality of lights-out.

Autumn

B ut for the mess of paperwork growing like a living thing atop his desk, SS-*Hauptscharführer* Otto Möll sat alone in his office. He dropped his pen onto the desk and rubbed his eyes with the heels of his hands. When he opened them again, the room was the same. Not that he'd expected it to change, of course, but a person could dream, couldn't he?

He saw the shabbiness of this office as but a reflection of the utter wretchedness of his new posting. The desk was a battered metal hand-me-down, its left bottom drawer stuck closed, a smudge of rust here, a dent there. An ancient radiator hugged one of the cheaply paneled walls, inadequate at a glance for the subzero months right around the corner. A bank of fluorescents flickered uncertainly above. He would have had new bulbs put in, except this he didn't mind so much; the last thing this place needed was efficient lighting. From the water stains on the ceiling to the cracked linoleum of the floor, nothing would have gained from more light.

The rest of the camp was no better. Fürstengrube, one of the smaller satellites in the Auschwitz cosmos, had with its coal helped build the huge I.G. Farben factory at Monowitz. It consisted back then of one weather-beaten prisoner barracks, a smaller one for the guards, a kitchen, a latrine, a tiny shack of an infirmary, and an administration hut built of the same unpainted, gray wood, all encircled by a loose wall of non-electrified barbed wire.

This past August, however, the overall commandant of Auschwitz, SS-*Obersturmbannführer* Höss, had brokered a deal with Farben Industries to dig a second mine that would raise Fürstengrube's inmate population from a hundred and sixty to seven hundred. As a reward for his services to the Reich at Birkenau, Möll was promoted to master sergeant and installed as commandant.

Not that he received so much as a pfennig to upgrade the place. But for the beehive of construction that was the new mine, and the addition of a second barracks to house the coming hundreds, it was the same decaying backwater of a subcamp it had always been.

Even shabbier than his new surroundings was how he'd been treated, promotion or no. He saw this last as but a sop to mollify him for removing him from the center of the action. The seven hundred prisoners soon to be his weren't much more than the number of *guards* he'd had at his disposal at Birkenau. Some promotion that! He would rather have been demoted if it would have allowed him to stay where he was.

Politics was the gremlin in back of it all, something he'd never been very good at. Diplomacy, compromise, tact were foreign concepts to him, weren't and never would be part of his vocabulary. This not an issue when it came to those prisoners so ill-fated as to be at his mercy, in his dealings with his fellow SS it worked decidedly against him. With his hair-trigger temper and lack of all patience, he tended to rub these the wrong way. But though recognizing this flaw in himself, he could no more have corrected it than start wearing a *yarmulke*, learn Yiddish.

On top of everything, there wasn't an officer out there not jealous of his success. The disinterment and cremation of the hundred thousand Jewish corpses a year ago, the performance of his fire pits since, the Kriegsverdienstkreuz—that the 5'7" ex-ditchdigger, a lowly sergeant no less, had triumphed where they had failed or been too timid to try, was too much for all those tall, dashing tin gods to bear, a slap in the collective face of the whole swagger-sticked bunch of them.

As for the reasons given him for his transfer—the discontinuing of the open-air incineration program now that all four crematoria were up and running, coupled with the decline in the number of transports—these were clearly an excuse by which to render him his comeuppance. It was far too premature to fill in the fire pits. Europe alone was still crawling with Jews yet to be dealt the just desserts their race's malfeasance had earned them. And once Hitler and the Wehrmacht were on the march again, back on the road to victory, there'd be countless more depending on how much of the world the *Führer* chose to add to the Reich.

Then there was Hungary, where a good million Jewish renegades continued to hide behind the skirts of its womanly government, some having fled from as far away as Greece and Russia. Though an ally of Germany, Hungary wasn't only blind to the Jewish cancer consuming it from within but deaf to all entreaties from Berlin to do something about it.

But Möll didn't see this lasting forever. Making it a point to keep up on such things, he knew that his Chancellery's Jewish Office, under the leadership of the indefatigable SS-*Obersturmbannführer* Adolf Eichmann, was increasing its pressure on Budapest to turn over its Hebrews. Given this, and the power and popularity of those anti-Semitic elements that had proliferated in Hungary since the alliance, it was only a matter of time before Admiral Horthy and the other leaders of the country would have little choice but to agree to the deportation of their Jews.

That was how Möll viewed it, and it worried him sick that he might end up missing out on the show to come.

On the other hand, if twenty thousand per day should begin showing up at Birkenau, he knew that though the gas chambers would be able to handle the load, the ovens didn't stand a chance. There simply weren't enough of them. Without him and his fire pits to pick up the slack, the bodies would be backed up for weeks, a less than pleasant prospect made incalculably worse should the thermometer read much above freezing.

This brightened his mood some, to the point of prying half a smile from his lips. To say he'd seen the last of Birkenau wasn't being realistic; just as their "magnificences" the SS brass had depended on him before, so would they again. Plus, it wasn't as if he'd been exiled to Lithuania or someplace. Fürstengrube was only nineteen miles from the crematoria.

At the moment, it felt more like nineteen hundred. He missed his old digs as much as he could remember missing any place. Birkenau had a majesty to it, a presence, this rat's nest of a camp couldn't touch; he'd seen interrogation rooms there better maintained than his headquarters here.

He could almost hear his desk groan beneath its stacks of papers. To the man of action Möll fancied himself, this was the ugliest part of not only his office but his job. He picked up a bundle of the confounded white sheets and leafed through them. Regulatory permits, construction invoices, invoices of every kind, guard schedules, guard payroll, purchase orders, requisition orders, you name them, they were there. From exterminating angel he'd been reduced to full-time bureaucrat; here it was midnight and he was still shuffling paper around, signing his name to this and that one, filling out forms.

To hell with it, he swore silently, tossing them back onto the pile. The blasted things could sit. He swung out of his chair and made for the room's one window, four curtainless squares of glass as black as if they'd been painted. Upon reaching it, in the distance he could see the lights illuminating the mine under construction, like a sprinkling of stars fallen to earth. Business was good, I.G. Farben hungry for coal. It had insisted its Fürstengrube project be worked on day and night.

Hopefully, this second mine would be an improvement on its predecessor. The original collected water, and its tunnels were always collapsing; the camp's mortality rate, by percentage, was as great as that at Birkenau. Not that this was in any danger of moving him to tears. As long as production quotas were met, Möll didn't care how many inmates were lost.

The human material sent here was of very poor quality. The various mines in the region, mostly coal and iron, were considered punishment duty; the prisoners handed over to them were from the bottom of the barrel, those unable or unwilling to adhere to concentration-camp discipline. They were the least palatable sort of Jew, lazy, slovenly, or worse, rebellious. So what if they dropped like flies; if there was one thing this part of Poland wasn't short on it was expendable bodies.

It hadn't taken long for the ex-*Kommandoführer* of Auschwitz's Block 11 to figure out that Fürstengrube wasn't as punitive as it could have been. The first thing he did was cut the prisoners' rations. The expense he saved there, and by abolishing the infirmary, went toward strengthening security. He requested and received more guards, had four watchtowers built, and was awaiting delivery on a pair of searchlights.

These precautions might have been deemed paranoid but for one thing. His first week there, two prisoners had escaped by cutting the wire. Not until then did he learn the camp had a reputation for being porous, three such attempts in the past six months alone. This fourth, he presumed, was the men's way of testing their new commandant, a test he had no intention of failing.

At the morning Appell subsequent to the escape, Möll strode to the front of those assembled, mounted a crate, and demanded to know where their missing comrades were headed. He didn't get an answer, but then he wasn't really after one. With their silence filling the yard, he stepped down from his perch and walked among the prisoners shooting them calmly and at random. He didn't stop until he'd left twenty of them splayed in the dirt before sending the rest off to work.

When they came back in the evening and as the night shift departed, both groups passed the corpses of the unlucky twenty laid out in neat rows on either side of the gate. There they would remain for three days, until the capture and return of the two fugitives, whom he ordered beat to a pulp before dispatching them to the gallows.

There would be no more escape attempts, the inmates from then on living in terror of their overseer. With no infirmary anymore, all the sick and wounded were diagnosed as incurable and shot, often by Möll himself. The list of transgressions now meriting a death sentence had lengthened, too. He was cracking the whip all right, and not just to tighten ship; having been railroaded into so humble a posting hadn't helped his disposition any.

But it wasn't only the place that was galling him. As trying as anything was being deprived of the chance to exercise his talents to the fullest, talents he wished nothing more than to put at the disposal of his country. He liked to think he'd been forged for one purpose, to act as a sword for his people, a blade to cut away the tentacles of the Yid monster strangling them. He hadn't been put on this earth to spend his days at a desk, but to wade hip-deep in the corpses of the enemies of his race, that most pernicious of enemies, that grinning jackal the Jew.

Yet here he was in an office where he'd been most of the day, not a spot of mud or drop of blood on uniform or boot. He spread his fingers in front of him and shook his head ruefully. They weren't smeared with red as they could have been, should have been, but with the blue from a leaking fountain pen.

Not that he wasn't grateful for the opportunities extended him up to now. In the event he were never to lay eyes on Birkenau again, he'd had a great run. Leaving the window, he regained his chair, leaned back in it, and stared at the ceiling. It had been a glorious summer. The success of the war on the Jews continued to exceed all expectations. Already much of the Reich was for all practical purposes *Judenrein*, Jew-free, including Germany and Austria, what used to be Poland and Czechoslovakia, all of the Baltics and much of the Balkans, with Italy, Greece, France, and the Low Countries not far behind. And much of this in less than a year and a half. But for the Einsatzgruppen in Russia, sanctioned hostilities targeting the Jews hadn't arisen until two springs ago.

The progress made since was almost too good to be true. Putting aside the iron will needed to see the thing through, the logistics for so vast an undertaking were hard to wrap one's mind around. From the sun-bleached islands of the Mediterranean to the farthest reaches of frozen Norway, those Jews under German authority, both urban and rural, had to be tallied, rounded up, then removed to embarkation points, either transit camps or ghettos. From those, it became a matter of transporting them to the killing centers in Poland, often many hundreds of miles away. The cost for this must have been staggering, never mind the technical complexities involved. Trains—in some cases even barges and ships—had to be procured, assigned routes and timetables, guards and engineers, then make their way through the bureaucratic jungles and rail systems of various countries until reaching their destinations.

All of this complicated by the necessity of adopting a cloak of deception designed to keep the deportees ignorant of their fate right up to the doors of the gas chambers. Which had been neither easy nor cheap in their own right to build. What was more, Germany had taken this task upon itself while fighting a world war for national existence against the mongrel Bolshevik hordes and their Jew-backed western allies.

No one was prouder of his country for assuming this burden than Möll. From an organizational point of view, it was a project surpassed by few if any in history. The larger pyramids of Egypt, the Great Wall of China, the towering cathedrals of medieval Europe, the colonization of the Americas—all had taken generations to realize, while in a span of little more than two years the Third Reich was poised to accomplish its goal of cleansing this critical corner of the world of its Jewish pestilence forever, an achievement as lasting and arguably of more benefit than the rest.

As for the killing itself, the method and equipment employed were paragons of modern German engineering. The apparatus of Birkenau wasn't much different in function from that of the Buna and Siemens factories operating day and night at Monowitz. One was as industrial in form and content as the other; the raw material going into the crematoria just happened to be people, the finished product coming out, death. Not simply death, either, but disposal, and in numbers never dreamt of. The Birkenau assembly line was capable of cranking out fifteen thousand "units" of untraceable ash a day, *every* day if required.

Little muss and less fuss, and no one the wiser. Not until the *Führer* should deem it expedient to let the rest of the world in on the good news.

That was the thing, Möll mused: ignoring what it might say publicly, there wasn't a country that gave so much as a snap of the fingers for the Jews. Before the war, the international community, while condemning the cruelty of the Nazi regime, had no desire to open its doors to any more of that conniving clan than its members possessed. Beginning in the 1930's, Hitler had tried to get somebody, anybody to take them off his hands, but had met with nothing but resistance.

Germany's initial proposal for the solution of its Jewish problem had been the deportation of that problem *en masse* to either the underpopulated African island of Madagascar or inland to the interior and Uganda. Why these of all places, the sergeant had no idea, but when they proved impractical a second solution was advanced, a more voluntary emigration. The Nuremberg Laws of 1935 were a body of precepts so draconian and degrading it was thought the Jews would have no choice but to pick up and flee. These laws ran the gamut from the serious to the symbolic, everything from denying them access to schools, hospitals, and banks to making it illegal to use the sidewalk or keep a pet.

Though it should have come as no surprise, they weren't as effective as hoped. For almost two thousand years, the Jews of the Diaspora, uprooted from their ancestral homeland and often ending up immigrants in countries resentful of their presence, had weathered many storms. They'd seen the Nuremberg Laws before, if under different names and in different languages, and harsh as they were they'd been nothing to the blood-drenched pogroms their host peoples had regularly visited upon them.

Through it all, however, they'd not only survived but grown prosperous. How? By hunkering down and holding fast, maintaining a low profile, bowing their heads and doing as the Gentile commanded, but never forgetting where their true loyalty lay, to each other and only there.

This had served them for centuries, nor was there any reason for them to think it wouldn't now. This storm, too, would pass. History as they knew it practically guaranteed it.

The flight of those few who saw what was coming, or were simply tired of being bullied and living in fear, didn't in most cases meet with a happy ending. Either for them or the Germans seeking to get rid of them. Ships full of the Chosen People (meaning those, as the joke went, who'd chosen to get the hell out of the country) steamed out of Hamburg and other ports with emigration papers and often the vessels themselves gladly provided by their evictors—only to return weeks later with their cargoes intact, their search for asylum having been rebuffed at every turn.

In every ideology, no matter how uncompromising, a crack sometimes emerged in the wall of belief, a whisper of doubt as to whether the end justified the means. Not even Otto Möll, the inveterate *Hauptscharführer*—the Cyclops, the Angel of Death, Mal'ach H'Mavet reincarnate—not even he was entirely immune from this doubt. Alone in his bed at night, slowly surrendering to sleep, his senses shutting off and defenses down, a question might creep up on him from out of the blackness: was all this bloodshed, this killing called for? Was what he was doing right? The logic of deverminization aside, it wasn't cockroaches or bedbugs he was helping to eliminate, but people. Or if not exactly people, a subspecies not far removed.

At such moments, his resolve was rendered implacable again by remembering those ships crammed full of German-Jewish émigrés returning still crammed to their original ports of call. Again, good luck finding a government that cared a whit for the Jews. He saw most as privately applauding the Germans for recognizing the Jewish menace and dealing with it.

Surely Churchill, Roosevelt, and Stalin knew what was going on in Poland and occupied Russia, if not the exact details then the substance of it. Their respective intelligence services were too sophisticated and far-flung, too infiltrated with double agents for them not to. It was one thing to keep the operations secret from civilians, both at home and abroad, quite another to hide them from the eyes and ears of enemy spies.

So what was the aforementioned triumvirate doing on behalf of the Jews? Continuing to bleat pietistic platitudes on the radio and in the newspapers about the evils of Nazi racial barbarism, when a few Soviet bombers could have leveled Birkenau's crematoria in five minutes. Clearly, here were men who in their hypocrisy were perfectly content to let Hitler do the dirty work of Judaicide for them. It made Möll want to vomit.

With the failure of its emigration program to make much of a dent in its Jewish population, a desperate Germany made one last push in that direction. On the night of November 9th, 1938, the country erupted in a spasm of violence, hate filling the streets of every city like lava from a volcano. The object of this hatred? The Jews, who else? Their homes, businesses, synagogues looted and burned, scores lynched on the spot wherever the enraged mobs found them, thousands more trundled off to concentration camps. This *Kristallnacht*, or Night of the Broken Glass, though touted as a spontaneous outpouring of popular ill will, was in fact a carefully organized, government-backed demonstration, a dance of death and destruction choreographed at the highest level in Berlin.

Möll couldn't be positive, but guessed the riots weren't intended so much to terrorize the Jews at home as shock those watching from afar into loosening their immigration quotas. If even a little sincere in their concern, this would have been the time for the nations of the world to act.

And so they did, notably Britain and the United States. In the months following Kristallnacht, England capped Jewish entry into Palestine at fifteen thousand a year, a significant reduction, while in America a piece of legislation known as the Child Refugee Bill was put to a vote in their Congress and roundly defeated. It would have allowed ten thousand German-Jewish children into the country every year.

Reclining in his chair, Möll had to smile, as he did whenever he recalled this last bit of American smarminess. Apparently, the invitation inscribed on that famous statue of theirs, "Give me your tired, your poor, your huddled masses yearning to breathe free," didn't extend to the Goldsteins and Greenburgs of the world. Nor their just as unwholesome children.

At any rate, Germany had run out of options. When three years later, the Semitic cabal that controlled America manipulated it into the war, Hitler's patience evaporated. He ordered that the third and Final Solution to the Jewish infestation commence, choosing Poland as the site for its enforcement. Möll trusted that when it was completed, and the time was right, the *Führer* would reveal his and his countrymen's gift to the world, and the world, sure to squawk in protest at first, would in the end be all gratitude.

The Jews, meanwhile, had only themselves to blame. In their greed for governance and lust for domination, they'd amassed a huge debt. Apart from ten centuries of behind-the-scenes scheming and machinations culminating in their ascension to the top rungs of power, not only had they engineered the mortifying German surrender of the last war but started the present one, as Hitler himself had so convincingly argued.

What they'd had the temerity to begin, however, the SS were intent on finishing. It had become their sacred mission to excise the Jewish tumor from the European body. Nor could anyone have predicted the success with which they'd meet.

The progress of the deverminization, though, wouldn't have been nearly as swift without the unfathomable cooperation of the vermin themselves. Möll just didn't understand it. Oh, he did, he supposed— if one wanted to, one could boil it down to simple arithmetic. For a thousand years, Europe's Jews had attached themselves like parasites to host populations outnumbering them hundreds to one. In such an environment, any attempt to assert themselves openly would have prompted serious retaliation, even a bloodbath. In their quest for sovereignty, therefore, they'd had to be sly, resorting to subversion of all types—bribery, racial defilement, collusion, fraud, and other trickery—all under the guise of cheery acquiescence.

As a consequence, both his culture long ago and the individual from childhood having forsworn overt aggression as a means of solving anything, the Jew was no longer capable of fighting his way out of a paper sack, not even to defend himself. In short, he had evolved into a natural coward. Physical resistance was as alien an abstraction to him as that generosity of heart and purse for which the

Christian was known. That brief set-to in the Warsaw ghetto these five months ago had been no more than an aberration, instigated and much of it carried through no doubt by outside agitators, namely that partisan rabble that called itself the Polish Home Army.

Still, it never ceased to amaze Möll how willingly, almost gladly the Jew went to his death. And not a heroic death, but a naked, shameful one. With few exceptions, they'd bent over backward to follow SS orders. When told to register in their native countries at the appointed place and date, they'd registered. When commanded to pack their belongings and relocate to the ghetto, they'd relocated. When driven out of the hovels they'd been jammed into there only to be stuffed into cattle cars literally lacking a pot to piss in, even then they hadn't resisted.

At the unloading ramp at journey's end, they continued to submit, climbing without incident onto the crematorium trucks, and later in the undressing room, having dutifully stripped to the buff, were easily herded to the "showers." Was it possible, with the smoke billowing from the enormous *Krema* chimney and the stink of roasting flesh stronger at this strange-looking building than anywhere, that they weren't suspicious of what awaited them inside? Yet for months in they'd walked by the hundreds of thousands with nary a whimper.

Möll had stayed in touch with several acquaintances from his days at SS training school, some of whom were sent east to work the Einsatz brigades. Together, two of these last had stopped to visit him in Birkenau while on leave and en route to Germany, and from them he'd learned much. The Russian Jews were no less gutless than their European kin. Not only did they let themselves be taken unresisting to the killing grounds, they dug their own graves, then lined up obligingly in front of them to be shot.

What happened then all too often was even less explicable. According to his friends, sometimes those women with children, after catching sight of the guns, would scramble to arrange their offspring in descending order, from tallest to shortest, as if posing them for a picture.

To a stupefied Möll, this was nothing less—what else could it be?—than a final, lunatic nod to decorum, one last show of propriety… at the very edge of the pit!

And in a way, so it was. As one of the soldiers explained, the other silent in agreement, the best anyone could figure was that these hell-begotten mother hens felt "if they could make us see them as a family, see how adorable their children were, we might have second thoughts about shooting them."

Who were these fantastical creatures the Jews? Were they indeed imps of Satan, spawned out of spite by the Father of Lies to vex and otherwise provoke that nobler creation of God, man?

That they weren't fully human was axiomatic. No one at death's door would have conducted himself as the Jew did. On and on they'd come at Birkenau this past year from early spring to the end of summer like waves of lemmings eager to launch themselves into the sea. Except, unlike the lemming, whose behavior was dictated by instinct, there was nothing natural about the Jewish fondness for self-obliteration. It wasn't normal for people to walk with such determination to the grave, yet how many times had Möll watched them muscle each other aside in their hurry to be the first into the gas chamber?

Granted, the SS took every pain to disguise the true purpose of the death houses. Nor after so long and dry a journey as most of the deportees had endured should the enticement of water, even lead-tasting shower water, be downplayed. This failed to explain the reaction of those Jews selected from inside the camp, individuals who couldn't have had the slightest doubt where they were headed. Yet never had he heard of any refusing to board the trucks taking them to the crematoria. All had done as instructed, if not without complaint then with the passive docility of brute animals.

Or maybe that docility wasn't so passive after all. Perhaps passive-aggressive would better describe it, a ploy on the part of the victim, whether calculated or not, to exact if only *post mortem* a modicum of revenge. If so, how cunning the Jew, how terrible his submission! By walking so lamblike to the slaughter, no dignity was to be got from his execution. The soldier responsible was reduced to nothing more than a hireling at a stockyard—his proud uniform to a rubber apron, his rifle to a cattle prod, his soldier's daring and dash to a menial's drab routine.

Leave it to a Jew to attempt to have the last laugh. And succeed. By making it too easy, depriving the warrior of the glory of the kill, he was in effect stealing not only that warrior's honor but his manhood, and by extension his humanity.

It was psychological murder, in its way as ruinous as the physical kind. Nor did one have to go far to see the damage it was inflicting on personnel. Of those two pals of his, for instance, who'd taken the trouble to come see him, one had the shakes from too much schnapps, while the other admitted to being on psychiatric leave.

The first, in addition to the tremor in his hand, never once during his stay was able meet Möll's gaze, his own darting about like that of an anxious dog. The second revealed an even more troubling symptom. His right arm hung in a sling, not as a result of some wound, but from a partial paralysis of that side caused by what he confessed, after some goading, had been a "nervous episode." He was quick to add that his doctors had assured him he'd be back to normal within weeks. Unlike his companion's, his eyes seldom strayed, but not to look *at* a person so much as through him, as at something behind him.

Möll had a good idea what that something was, too, or did after he heard this story from the poor man. "Our brigade, Einsatzgruppe B, was engaged in an operation outside the Ukrainian town of Janina. My duty that day was to man one of the machine guns. The boy was eight or nine, no different from the other boys I'd faced that morning, except for one thing. Just as I was about to pull the trigger, he—he did something strange. Something I'd never seen or thought I ever would."

The man sat staring, his mouth a puzzled frown. "What?" Möll said finally. "What did he do, the boy?"

"Waved goodbye! Yes, goodbye! Raised his hand, and with a little smile, waved... at me. Not the man on either side of me, or anyone else, but *me!* I could tell because his eyes were as locked onto mine as yours are now."

For the first time since his arrival, he was really looking at Möll, not past him but directly, imploringly at him. Then, in his next breath, was apologizing for bringing the incident up. Wasn't sure why he even had. He didn't come here, after all, to burden an old friend with his problems.

"I just can't get it out of my head, Otto," he said, "waking or sleeping. I still have dreams about that day, and they're not going away. Smiling, that miserable kid, as if I was his buddy or something. Can you imagine?"

Yes he could, yes indeed. Möll had seen the same leering smile at Gusen, Sachsenhausen, Birkenau, even here at Fürstengrube. It was a smile of triumph snatched from defeat, born of the knowledge that by giving up his life cheaply, without a struggle, the victim was taking a chunk of his killer's soul to the grave with him. That an eight-year-old should be in on the act, a child not old enough to be doing it on purpose, only demonstrated the depth to which this perverseness had entrenched itself in the Jewish psyche.

As for his visitor who'd owned up to drinking too much, he was far from alone in that. Möll could count on his hands the number of officers and men at Birkenau not driven by their work to consume inordinate amounts of alcohol.

Though as a brother SS he would have liked to forgive them their frailty, he couldn't bring himself to excuse either the reason or remedy for it. In his judgment, it stemmed from no less than a failure of ideology. One of the pillars of the Nazi world-view, its *Weltanschauung*, was its recognition of the Jewish threat to the survival of the German Volk, and its vow to expunge that threat. If the soldiers called to enforce this had to get drunk to do it, what did that say about their attitude toward that doctrine? It was, pure and simple, a repudiation of it, if not in so many words then on a subliminal level.

And these were the SS, the supposedly fanatical guardians of all that National Socialism stood for! He couldn't decide if such men should be pitied or shot. To him, their dipsomania smacked of betrayal. Despite their swagger and the fearsome uniform with the silver Death's-head on the collar, too many of them weren't cut out for the job. It was one thing to strut about and act the bully toward a bunch of weak-kneed ghetto Jews, quite another to send them by the thousands to the ovens, particularly women and children.

One had to remember, however, always remember, that these were no ordinary women and children, but the misleading human forms the subhuman Jews hid behind. Unless he accepted this, and without reservation, eventually it could get to a man, cause him to question whether he was purging the Reich of a thousand-year scourge or simply massacring defenseless civilians.

Möll had no such problem. He was unflagging in his belief, and credited this to the fact one was either a patriot or wasn't, loved one's country or didn't, trusted in the values and defining principles of that country or when confronted with a moral or similar dilemma destroyed oneself with doubt. Prior to joining the SS, he too had drunk his share and more, but even before he was sent to Gusen had sworn off such nonsense. From the day he'd pinned that grinning skull to his tunic, he'd found a purpose in life—more than that, had found *himself*—and as never before was at peace with both that self and the world.

Of course, it didn't hurt his abstemiousness that he took the utmost care to be on his guard. While many of his comrades concentrated on avoiding typhus, diphtheria, and the other diseases the Jews of the camp carried, he took care to insulate his person also from those illnesses originating in the corrupt Jewish heart, the deceitful Jewish tongue, the scheming Jewish brain. Seeing as how they were human in appearance only, when met with anything remotely human from them, a plea, a tear, a sigh, any emotion at all, he had to regard it as either a trick or an attack or both, and not only hardened his own heart against it but when necessary attacked back. One had to keep on one's toes around the Jew. Any contact, even conversation, could be dangerous.

God, how he despised this degenerate race, this woeful excuse for a people! After living for the past half-dozen years in proximity to them, what used to be strictly business had since turned personal, though the seeds of that odium sown at Gusen and Sachsenhausen didn't sprout until he'd reached Auschwitz and stewardship of its penal squad. And not until Birkenau had they begun to yield their harvest.

No matter, he reflected from the dubious comfort of his hard chair. Möll had his feet propped on the desk now, hands clasped behind his head. It might have taken a bit for his hatred to mature, but no one could say he hadn't made up for lost time. He closed his eyes in recollection of the recent past, the third smile of the night flitting across his face. As proud as he was of his fire pits and how they'd performed, as fulfilling were the weeks he'd spent at Bunkers 1 and 2. None of it had been easy, the stress, the long hours, the often messy work, but as compensation the rewards had been considerable, foremost among these the satisfaction of a job not only well but extraordinarily done.

He wasn't just trying to be noble here, either. Having once been motivated almost exclusively by ambition, he'd since turned selfless, dedicated without desire of recompense to securing his country's future by doing everything in his ken to exclude the Jew from it. He'd become one of that new breed of fighting man, the biological soldier, a role that while entrusting him with racial purification also bound him to refrain from both gratuitous violence and profiting from that task.

He'd be the first to admit, however, he was only good for the one. With the majority of his peers shameless in their greed, he would have none of it. But for the occasional cut of cured meat or other delicacy that would have been wasted on the Sonderkommando, he refused to take part in the plundering of the dead's possessions. On top of such banditry sullying their cause, it was something, if one thought about it, a Jew might have done.

As for the gratuitous violence… some rules were made to be broken, that it was advantageous to break. Or to put it another way, all work and no play made Otto a dull boy. Take, for example, his own little game of swim-frog, not only a welcome diversion from the humdrum but food for the soul. What could be more gratifying than to see the sons and daughters of rich Jewish bankers forced to mimic those amphibians that in the evolutionary scheme of things they weren't all that distant from?

Möll harbored a particular animosity toward the Jewish elite, the wealthy, the educated, the privileged of their kind. He had a knack for sniffing them out that rivaled his dog Hannibal's for flushing rats and other varmints. He would accost a group of prisoners, single out the most likely, and ask them their trades. Invariably, he would acquire a quick collection of lawyers, financiers and the like, then subject them to whatever appealed at the moment.

Another bit of fun he'd cooked up he called "brick-bashing." Dividing his victims into teams, he equipped each participant with a pair of heavy bricks. The object was to slam these together until they disintegrated, the winning team the one to accomplish this first. While its members escaped with no more than bruised and bleeding hands, the losers were ordered to scatter and run, whereupon he would grab a rifle from the nearest *Schütze* and pick them off one by one. He'd learned to shoot while hunting squirrels as a boy, acquiring a talent that bordered on the spooky. Whether his target was moving or stationary, rarely did he miss, and that without even seeming to aim.

"Walking the plank" was another game. A two-by-six was laid athwart a fire pit that had burned itself down to a bed of glowing coals. The prisoner would be blindfolded and made to cross the board to the other side. If he balked, he was thrown into the fire, or if his tormentors saw him so much as touch the blindfold when crossing, the board was tipped over. Should it look as if he might make it across, a gun was set off to startle him into stumbling. The reward for a successful attempt was a bullet to the head in place of the agony of burning alive.

Soon after they'd opened, Möll had taken to cruising the crematoria's undressing rooms for attractive young women. After culling out three or four, he'd have them brought naked to the incineration meadow and lined up before one of the more dissipated pits. There they'd stand trembling, staring into the mess of disintegrating corpses at their feet.

After soaking up his fill of this, he'd set to crooning that they were next, the only thing needed was his order and into the pit they would go. Even if they didn't speak German, the women got the message, and usually ended up bolting in panic. Waiting for just that, he'd sic Hannibal on them. The dog would leap after them, tearing at their legs and buttocks, until its owner tired of this and told their guards to round them up and drag them back.

By then, he would have worked himself into a frenzy. Shouting curses at his victims, hysterical themselves now and bleeding, he would line them up again in front of the fire, a growling Hannibal loping back and forth behind them.

"Go ahead," he would scream, "cry your pretty eyes out! It won't do you any good. In a few seconds, you're going to be frying with that lot down there!"

Sometimes he'd shoot them, sometimes he wouldn't, but after they'd either fallen or been pushed onto the coals, he'd always stay until they stopped thrashing about.

As head of the penal commando at Auschwitz, punishment had been Möll's job, but he didn't remember it ever taking so personal a turn. The change confounded him, until it occurred to him one day that these fire-pit frolics of his—nor were they the only occasion anymore at which he'd lose his composure—hadn't begun until he had a year of Birkenau under his belt.

Using this as a starting point, the more he thought about his quandary, the less a one it became. The build-up of tension as the act progressed, the fevered emotion and loss of control accompanying it, the abrupt sensation of release, of pressure relieved at its completion —all three responses were undeniably sexual, and all heightened, he noticed, when the victims were female. After toying with the young beauties he'd snagged in the undressing room, having had his way with them he'd often sneak off somewhere private, a shed or the like, to masturbate.

At first, Möll had supposed himself a closet sadist, and not in the loose but clinical meaning of the word: someone brought to actual physical arousal by the imposing of pain. Before long, though, he dismissed this as too simplistic an answer, if not false altogether. Apart from his having never known the least pull in that direction, incipient sadism was as common a misdiagnosis as a true case was rare. A more credible explanation suggested itself.

If little spoken of, it was widely known that among those SS detached to the Russian killing fields and the death camps of Poland there existed, in addition to the alcoholism, nightmares, and other infirmities deviling them, a curiously high rate of impotence. He'd first heard veiled complaints of this when stationed at the bunkers, but hadn't made the connection.

Now there was no missing it. The female body as sexual stimulus no longer served as such for the biological soldier. It had been transformed into something countervailing and ugly, a suppressant rather than a promoter of desire.

The rationale for the camp's existence, wholesale extermination, made this inevitable. The Jews spilling out of the cattle cars came with repetition to resemble nothing more than so much meat in transit, walking carcasses processed and consumed, most of them, the first day. To the SS at their posts, the danger inherent in this perception resided in the female form losing its power to titillate and turning cadaverous, into an object of repugnance, the impression reinforced by the sheer number of women that passed before one daily. Nudity only magnified the effect.

Those deportees who'd been interned for any length were even more unappetizing. Once the flower of youthful femininity—meticulous in grooming and dress, attentive to making the most of what beauty nature had meted them—they'd been reduced after a few months to gaunt, hollow-eyed mockeries of their former selves, their breasts empty pouches, legs swollen and streaked with excrement, heads shaven like convicts, faces pocked with open sores. The smell that washed from them stank of sea rot, of some brackish tidal backwater, a place of mud covered with a carpet of tiny, dead crustaceans that crackled underfoot.

If one defined the sex drive as a prerogative to good health, and the allure of the opposite sex as essential to that drive, then the loss of the latter could be as crippling as any wound received in combat. In its stead, new and different erotic incitements were needed. Doors that normal men in normal times were loath to open became expedient to walk through now or risk having their virility end up a fatality of war. How much say one had in which door to pick was anybody's guess, though Möll's appeared to have been chosen for him. As unprepared as he may have been for the shape it took, that didn't mean he wasn't glad to have it. To be left with nothing, to be less than a man, was not an alternative.

As for what was normal and what wasn't, who was to say anymore? Nothing he'd been engaged in for the last several years could be considered normal, and was only getting less so. With summer having boosted the exterminations to almost a million at Auschwitz alone, the orgy of death in which he was immersed had exposed him to phenomena unknown by any until now.

He'd marveled at the sights and sounds of a hundred thousand men and women held against their will while ten thousand of them went up in smoke every twenty-four hours.

He'd have sworn he heard, as if a faint, faraway wind, the haunting wail of a flock of newly disembodied souls as they fluttered skyward into eternity, calling to each other in their grief and confusion.

He'd seen nature herself turned on her head, the sky above the western, crematoria-end of the camp illuminated at night by a pulsing mantle of red, the sun blotted out by day with the smoke from his own fire pits.

That summer in Birkenau, and for miles around, it had rained more gray puffs of ash than it did water. Turnips from the camp fields reached the size of small children, tomatoes from its gardens that of cantaloupes.

Queerest of all perhaps, yet fascinating to behold, was the stubborn Jewish devotion to their schizophrenic God. Despite making it clear He'd washed His hands of them, they hadn't abandoned Him, even as they lined up to file into the gas chamber. Again, on they'd come all summer, naked as newborns: skinny, knob-kneed old men nervously stroking their long beards, menopausal women whose breasts rivaled their stout haunches in size, budding adolescents with eyes huge and skittish as a deer's. It never failed that more than a few were talking as they walked, not to each other but in a droning mumble to that unhearing God in Whom, even in the crematorium, they continued to confide.

Given the shabby way He'd treated them over the centuries, Möll found this intriguing. The Jew was positively gifted at making excuses for his divinity's disgraceful behavior; seldom was he taken aback by His wrath, nor discouraged by His thirst for the blood of His own children. Instead, he preferred to blame himself for his misfortunes, an arrangement, in view of his infatuation with self-guilt and his God's tyrannical self-righteousness, convenient for both parties.

All the *Hauptscharführer* could do was shake his head at such idiocy. Had their tradition of groveling before their sanctimonious Jehovah blinded the Jews to His brutishness? With the merest flick of a finger, He could have made a rubbish heap of Birkenau. And its five sister Vernichtungslagers with it. Yet for the past year and more the transports had continued to roll, the smokestacks to glow a dull red from overuse.

The Norse gods of his own culture's early days were as useless, a bunch of brawling, mead-swilling, overbearing clowns. Nor had the insipid, mooning double-talk of the Christianity that replaced them been much of an improvement. Except, and it was only fair to give it this, in its distinctly un-Christlike vilification of Jewry. He had yet to encounter a religion, in fact, that under even the flimsiest scrutiny it made sense to follow. To put one's faith in a god was tantamount to trusting in the rational benevolence of a four-year-old. A four-year-old intoxicated by his own power.

But for one, that is, though as the masses in their adulation had been wont to do these past years, to regard Adolf Hitler as divine was to do him a disservice. A messiah who'd led his people to unheard-of heights, yes. A giant, a titan, a superman among men, certainly. But a man all the same, born of woman like the rest, which made his attainments that much more impressive.

Now, *Hitler* made sense. One could count on him. He said what he meant and meant what he said, had laid out his intentions for all to see and carried through on them as no other figure, real or imagined, Möll was aware of. It was all there in his *Mein Kampf,* written twenty years ago, and which he'd had to read in SS training school. Since its publication, Hitler had made good on every promise he'd penned, none more ambitious and unabashed than two: the acquisition of *Lebensraum,* living space, for German settlers in the east, and the settlement of the Jewish issue once and for all.

Nor in pursuit of the second had the *Führer,* in his ineffable wisdom and foresight, hesitated when deciding to make the war holy. It was one thing to be an optimist and hope for the best, another to size up the map and try to be realistic. After Stalingrad and then Kursk, the Wehrmacht would be lucky to keep that part of Russia it still held. North Africa was gone, from where the Allies had quickly invaded Sicily, with presumably Italy next and Greece after that. Should the British and Americans cross the English Channel and establish a beachhead in France, this would leave the Axis to fight a three-front war, where at present it wasn't even holding its own against the Soviets.

Möll had no doubt that Germany would prevail. It was still fairly early in the game, and anything could happen. Meanwhile, half the railroads in Europe were funneling Jews into Poland, railroads that could be better used by the army to hamper the advance of the avenging Slavic legions and prepare for the coming of their Anglo-American allies.

Doubtless, a priority had been handed down. The needs of the Wehrmacht, the deployment by rail of troops and supplies, were to take a back seat to the annihilation of the Jews.

As commander-in-chief of the armed forces, this could only have come from Hitler, and though Möll failed in the beginning to grasp the thinking behind it, he'd come to bow to its genius. Rid forever of its deadliest enemy the Jew, Germany could weather defeat itself and in some future era, under the right circumstances—a favorable political landscape, a strong, new leader—gain the victory twice denied it before.

With a Jewish presence still part of the equation, however, there could be no victory, now or in the future, especially when the vindictiveness of any who might survive the racial cleansings was factored in. It was imperative, therefore, while Germany still ruled from the Atlantic Ocean to the Black Sea, that it dispose of those Jews beneath its heel, even at the expense of military necessity.

This was what was meant by the war having become holy, its thrust more purifying now than imperialist. One could add magnanimity to the list of Hitler's virtues: by putting the devastation of the Jews before success on the battlefield, he may have been courting defeat for himself, but facilitating triumph for coming generations of Germans. Not to mention doing the rest of mankind a favor in the process.

If one did allow that the war had been sanctified, then it must follow that Auschwitz-Birkenau be recognized as its spiritual center, its Mecca, its Rome, its Jerusalem if one would—a site consecrated by the advent of something unprecedented in history, a system of killing so audacious, so beyond anything that had come before or was likely to come after, as to approach the supernatural, the mystical, the sublime. That so many had met their end in so short a time on so small a plot of ground had made that ground sacred. From this, the slaughter could be seen as akin to a religious rite, and he, Otto Möll, an attendant priest at that rite.

Nor were they finished, the SS. Much was left to do. His superiors might not be aware of it yet, but Birkenau was a long way from having outlived its worth. What Möll didn't know was when it would be needed again, when *he* would be needed, but had a hunch it would be sooner than later.

When they did call him back, he would be ready. Was ready now. It wasn't as if he'd been sitting around these past months doing nothing.

Unpropping his feet, he opened the bottom-right drawer of his desk and drew out a scroll of thick paper bound in black ribbon. Tenderly, he untied it and spread it flat atop the clutter on the desk. It was a blueprint of that idea he'd lit upon a year ago during the cremation of the exhumed hundred thousand: the self-fueling fire pit, in which the liquid fat from the burning corpses could be collected and used in place of kerosene to keep the blaze going.

After his transfer to Fürstengrube—at first just to fill the nights, later as if there weren't nights enough—he'd kept at the project, and couldn't be prouder of what he'd ended up with. He often brought it out of hiding as now simply to admire it. Not only was it as professional a study as could be asked for, it seemed eminently workable. Two sloping cement troughs channeled the fat into a pair of collecting basins at opposite ends of the pit, from where it could be ladled over the fire.

He was hoping by now to have constructed a prototype to test it, but had yet to turn up a prisoner sufficiently skilled in cement to help him with that. Nor was he going to, not here. The misfits and rejects sent him from the other camps were fit only for burrowing in the earth like the animals they were.

But he was willing to be patient. With the cement experts of the Bauhof Kommando in Birkenau from which to draw, he could afford to be.

He had other ideas, too, for when he got back, plenty of them. As workmanlike as the system had shown itself, there remained room for improvement. How many of these he'd be allowed to put into practice he couldn't say, but if he were again in demand, his suggestions should be, too. Most were devoted, after all, to the refinement of that specialty which hadn't only made him renowned but at times indispensable: the disposal by fire, outdoors, without machinery, of ton upon ton of asphyxiated flesh.

Through no fault of his own, Möll had been denied a higher education. The hyperinflation of German currency brought about by Jewish speculators in the 1920's had bankrupted his parents and made any talk of college meaningless. He'd done well in his studies at the secondary level, however, and been blessed from birth with an inquiring mind. This led him down paths most others in his shoes would never have explored. Thus his interest in events, current and historical, that shone a complimentary light on National Socialism and its philosophy.

He was also good at figuring things out, for probing to the root of a problem and solving it. He had no doubt he'd have made a good engineer if he'd had the chance. If so, he'd probably be a major by now, building bridges somewhere, or air fields, or in armaments production. As it stood, even with this latest promotion, he was nothing more than a sergeant, had to end his sentences with a "sir" when addressing a lousy wet-behind-the-ears *Untersturmführer* fresh out of officer's school.

Which was why he never considered himself in full uniform until he'd hung the Kriegsverdienstkreuz from his neck. It helped in curbing the haughtiness of his putative superiors, some of who could hardly keep their eyes off the thing.

With the possibilities the war had laid at his feet, though, he'd be damned if he was going to let the absence of a diploma hold him back. He'd vowed while still at Birkenau that what he lacked in scholastics he would make up for with sweat and as much on-the-job training as his schedule would permit.

Möll was everywhere that spring and summer, observing, joining in: the unloading ramp, the undressing rooms, the anterooms to the gas chambers, the ovens, with the Disinfektoren emptying their blue pellets into the induction shafts. Not content with just the fire pits, he wanted to learn the ins and outs of every phase of operations, from how to handle the poison to handling the people. There wasn't a procedure at which he wasn't present at least once from prep to cleanup; he'd even driven one of the trucks that on occasion took the ashes of the dead to the Vistula and dumped them.

He was working eighteen hours a day and loving every minute of them, absorbing Birkenau like a sponge, a living sponge that feeds from the saltwater bathing it.

He'd made up his mind—he would be an engineer yet. Not a civil or a mechanical or an electrical one, but if not something qualitatively as worthy, then of greater service to the Fatherland. The title he'd relegated himself was *extermination* engineer, the first and quite possibly the last of his kind, a devotee of the art and science not of construction but destruction.

The *Vernichtungs Techniker* by definition created nothing. His output was entirely negative, success measured by how much he subtracted from the world, not added. The field was not for the faint, even less the unimaginative. It required man the builder to become man the destroyer, the antipode of what the traditional engineer aspired to.

A tall order, but Möll was gung-ho about filling it. In fact, when back where he belonged, in the happy confines of Birkenau, he'd have to insist the improvements he'd be suggesting be implemented. Precision was the name of the engineering game, anything less than perfection not to be tolerated. Nor was this the self-important puffery it sounded, a case of ego dragging both perspective and modesty in the dirt. Germany's future hung on winning the war, the one it was waging, of course, on that abomination the Jew.

With all that was riding on this, with generations to come affected by it, for anyone to give less than a hundred percent toward that effort—especially he who wore the uniform of the SS—wasn't only treason against his country but his race, his tribe, his Volk.

With a last loving look at the blueprint on his desk, he rolled it up in its ribbon and put it back in the drawer. In deference to his status and demanding itinerary, the commandant's office came with a small bathroom. Bending over its sink, its newest beneficiary splashed cold water on his face, then stood staring into the cheap, pitted mirror on the wall.

Returning a moment later to the window he'd left earlier, he again paused at his reflection before straining past it into the black of the Polish night. The lights of the unfinished mine still glittered in the distance, and would until the brighter light of day outshone them.

Not that they'd be given a respite even then, or at any hour. Nor, after it was producing, the man-made cave they lit: I.G. Farben would have its coal or know why.

Möll was determined to be as single-minded in committing his energies to the task fate had assigned him. The Jew was almost done for; all that remained was to finish the job. Unfortunately, this wasn't going to be as easy as those words suggested. Most of Abraham's unsavory seed left in Europe were in hiding, if not in the homes or on the farms of those outlaw Gentiles protecting them, then with the partisans in the forests.

The exception was Hungary, and a notable one it was. As long as its Jewish million continued to elude justice, whatever gains had been made against their brethren elsewhere were endangered. It was neither compulsory nor feasible that every Jew end up a statistic. Not even the SS were that thorough, or needed to be. What mattered was that enough were remanded to the hell whence they'd come to keep them from breeding themselves back into relevance. With this accomplished, the years and a negative birth rate would eventually render them extinct—unless a substantial bloc of them were left intact to spark their race's resurgence later on.

Möll saw Hungary as critical to both his own and his country's prospects. He couldn't envision Hitler leaving it untouched to fester like a canker in Europe's side, had high expectations it would one day prove the conveyance to rescue him from his exile and restore him to his beloved Birkenau.

He squinted as if to penetrate the blackness outside the window, and the even more concealing distance separating him from the instrument of his redemption. Beyond the lights of the new mine, in a more or less straight line three hundred miles to the south, lay the living bounty of the Hungarian plain, a million lives, if all went as it should, that would soon be intersecting with his.

He was dying to meet them. Planned on giving them a warm welcome, a very warm one indeed. His little joke touched off his fourth smile of the night, if but for an instant. The number troubled him; he doubted he'd cracked many more since his transfer. Was he not himself because the hour was late and he was tired, or was Fürstengrube starting to make him soft?

Wanting to think it the former, the paperwork staring him down from his desk, curse it, could wait until morning.

*   *   *

As soon as she saw him, she knew something was wrong. There was no reason for an officer to be anywhere near, especially one of his rank. Normally, all she and the Sonderkommando had to deal with during the exchange of the gunpowder were two or three *Schützen* bored out of their skulls, the occasional just as disinterested *Rottenführer*. That an SS captain no less should show at so ticklish a phase of the operation had Roza Robota in a sweat, the clammy sweat of fear.

The three Sonder saw him also and didn't know what to do. The boy Wrubel, Yankel Handelsman, and Zalman Leventhal stood uncertainly to the side of the cart they'd wheeled into the yard, half-buried as usual under its small mountain of dead people's clothes. To a man they'd gone nearly as pale as the corpses they were used to handling.

The source of their and Roza's discomfort, SS-*Hauptsturmführer* Franz Hössler, stood at an open door of the Bekleidungskammer not twenty meters away, arms folded across his chest, watching. If ever a man gave the impression he was onto something, it was he. By not showing himself until the cart came into view, as if waiting for it to arrive, he was in effect announcing why he was there—that it was no coincidence so august a personage should have materialized at so improbable a place.

Leave it to Hössler, she thought, to be the one to find them out. Of all the demons in gray presiding over the hell that was Birkenau, the prisoners regarded him as the most cunning. Gifted with a glib tongue, he had no qualms against using it to trick crowds to their demise. This was what had earned him his reputation, on both sides of the barbed wire. When those from a transport selected for death balked at taking the next step in their destruction, be it from the crematorium yard into the crematorium proper or from the undressing room to the gas chamber, Hössler would be called in, and with his placating manner and powers of persuasion invariably convince them to do as they'd been instructed.

So adept was he at allaying the suspicions of the doomed that the prisoners had given him the name Moshe Liar.

He was also as pompous and preening as a peacock, a dandy in both demeanor and dress. Six feet tall and darkly handsome, a full head of black hair combed straight back from a high, intelligent forehead, his uniform was always creased to a knife-edge. He didn't walk, he paraded, like a ship's captain on his quarterdeck, or someone posturing for a camera only he could see.

His vanity, moreover, was matched only by his cruelty; one had to be a fool to expect more mercy from the ostensibly amiable Hössler than from any other SS killer. Beneath the winning exterior beat a heart as hard and black as a lump of seasoned coal.

Such was the dangerous creature come to spy on them, who having left the doorway circled the cart like a shark checking out its prey.

It was a typical morning for early October, all silver and gray, the sun screened by a field of thin clouds. It was a farmer's field, furrowed, as if some cosmic plow had prepped it for planting. Though the thermometer proclaimed it by no means cold, a steady northerly breeze gave a different impression. As such, the day was a harbinger of the frigid months to come, less a morning to be treasured for its alabaster beauty than feared for the ice storms and arctic winds it presaged. Only the more resourceful of prisoners owned coats; the rest had to make do with a single layer of cloth as protection against the glacial claw of winter.

Still, it was as yet not unpleasant. The sun behind the clouds was more like the moon, a ghostly white ball one could stare at without harm. The pebbles dotting the ground glowed in its luminescent light like gemstones, as did the metal buttons and bars on Hössler's uniform.

How had the son of a bitch zeroed in on them, Roza wondered. Or had he? Maybe he just smelled a rat, had an inkling; it was possible he didn't know who or even what he was after. Was it his instincts that had led him here, his policeman's nose? In any case, this was no time to ask either how or why. The only question was *what*, as in what in the world was she going to do now?

Discreetly, she waved the Sonder off, and pulse racing, began to help her co-workers with the cart. That she had to ditch the powder she was holding was obvious, but with the packet tucked away in the crotch of her underwear and Hössler on the watch, this was easier said than done. As it was forbidden for the inmates to look directly at an SS man, she wasn't able to keep that close an eye on him, but the two times she did glance his way it was to discover the *Hauptsturmführer* staring straight at her.

So much for the bastard simply smelling a rat. He hadn't come on a guess, but to catch them in the act; no telling how long he'd been planning this, licking his chops in anticipation of it. She expected him at any moment to order the guards to seize her, and her three accomplices with her.

She couldn't let that happen, not when she was holding. No gunpowder meant no proof; she had to lose the stuff, and fast. Not to save her and her confederates' skins, but to prevent the dissolution of everything she and they had worked for, the end of their all-important, inviolable mission. The mission took precedence. The mission was everything. The flow of explosives to the crematoria mustn't dry up, should it cost a hundred lives.

She had to do something, but what? Her legs all of a sudden were as wobbly as a marionette's, the palms of her hands damp. It took all she had not to freeze in panic where she stood.

Instead, it was Hössler who froze, ceasing his circumambulations of the wagon and planting himself opposite its back end. Roza immediately sped round to the front, where she scooped up an armful of clothes before "accidentally" dropping them. This allowed her to squat down on the pretext of retrieving them. Hidden for the moment from the captain's sight, she reached in her pants, plucked the bundle from between her legs, ripped the thing open, and flung its contents on the ground.

What happened next stopped the blood in her veins. After stashing the empty sack into a pocket of some trousers, and before she had a chance to scuff the gunpowder into the dirt, she looked up to see Hössler bearing down on her almost at a run, his features lit with triumph.

"You there, stop!" he cried. "I said *you!* Stop right there!"

The crunch of his boots on the stony ground might have been death approaching, the Angel of Death come to wrap her in its wings. Roza's future flashed before her: the arrest, the torture chamber, the gallows, the end of all her dreams—of escape, of a life in Israel, dreams of the life she'd planned with Godel. She nearly got to her feet and raised her hands in surrender, though to run and be shot down would have been to suffer a fate kinder than the one awaiting her in Block 11.

Yet to her astonishment, Hössler barreled past her as if she wasn't there. Turning reluctantly, fully expecting to find him crouched in the dirt examining a handful of gunpowder, she instead saw him halt only upon reaching the far side of the cart. There, her terrified face peeping above the clothes she was carrying, stood the real target of his outburst, a Czech girl new to the commando.

While the youngster could have fainted with fright, Hössler was all smiles. "Don't be afraid, little Jew," Roza heard him say. "It's not you I'm after, but this."

Peeling a man's coat from atop the girl's load, he held it in front of him, admiring it, before slipping it on. "Just as I figured," he said, "a perfect fit!"

Then to the girl trembling before him, "That's all, you can go. Back to your work, get along with you.

"And thanks," he scoffed behind him as he wandered happily off with his prize, "for your generosity."

Roza had to admit it a magnificent coat, worthy of an officer of the SS. Black, supple leather from neck to ankle, buttons of polished ebony, a collar of gray fur—it was the coat of a rich man, a rich Jew Hössler had spotted wearing it, probably in the vicinity of one of the crematoria. No telling how long he'd bird-dogged it after that, but was doubtless hoping it would be on this morning's cart. He'd made his way to the Bekleidungs yard not because he smelled a rat but was one, a beady-eyed, greed-ridden rodent of a man.

"Jumping Jerusalem!" Roza said upon joining the others. "Was I the only one who thought we were done for?"

There was laughter, but it was labored.

"I was wishing I was somewhere else, that's for sure," Wrubel said. "What I'm *not* so sure of is what in the love of God just happened."

"It would appear," Handelsman said, "that our friend Hössler wasn't here in an official capacity, but to add to what I suspect is an already sizable wardrobe. That black-leather trench coat—you all saw the thing. We had the devil scared out of us because of a dead man's jacket."

Wrubel glared at the guards loafing about the yard, none of who was paying them any mind. "That's sort of what I figured, but didn't think even the SS could stoop that low. Is there nothing they won't do to bring shame on themselves?"

"And they call us Jews mercenary," Leventhal said. "It's they who seem determined to out-shylock Shylock."

Roza warmed at the reference. It was something her bookish Godel might have come up with.

"Just be glad," she said, "they're more interested in plunder than in keeping track of that gunpowder of theirs. Or those of us relieving them of it."

"The gunpowder!" cried Leventhal, smacking his forehead. "Shouldn't we, you know, be taking care of business?"

Roza sighed. "Nothing to take care of, not anymore. Convinced Hössler was about to bust us, I dumped it in the dirt, every gram of it. And was grateful for the chance. I couldn't look at him that he wasn't looking right back, I'd have sworn it. Sorry, but it would have been stupid to try and save it."

"You did the right thing," Handelsman assured her, "the only thing you could have done. Anything else would have been worse than stupid. Especially, given what that Zabludowicz told us, the lack of urgency now in stealing the gunpowder to begin with."

He slapped Wrubel on the back. "Better luck next time, huh, boys? Although I have to assume I'm not the only one feeling pretty damned lucky now."

In spite of having acted out of necessity, the loss of the gunpowder ate at Roza for the rest of the day. What a waste of something so riskily acquired! She would really have been upset if she, too, hadn't learned from Noah about the sorry state of the revolt, but even then found it discouraging to lose so large a shipment. It had been a good quarter-kilo if it was an ounce.

Most of it had come via Esther, directly from the safe in Meister von Ende's office. Lately, Roza had voiced some concern at the incautiousness of this, but Esther told her not to worry, she was on top of it. Which was all her friend needed to hear.

She'd fast become a big admirer of the Wajcblum girl, and not solely because of her boldness with the safe. Indoors it may have been, but work at the Metallwerke was no cakewalk. In response to Roza's inquiries, no one had anything but bad to say about conditions at the Union factory. Ala Gertner, as a forewoman, had been her main source, but she'd canvassed others, and the picture each had drawn of it was bleak.

For openers, a person had to travel a ways just to reach it. The plant was almost three miles from Birkenau, and this a twice-a-day hike, in all kinds of weather, in shoes that didn't fit, on blistered, swollen feet. And when it rained, it turned into more of a run than a walk; the guards didn't like to be out in the wet, and the whips they carried weren't for show.

The building itself hugged the ground like an enormous inverted baking pan, sprawling, metallic. Lacking a single window, wrapped in barbed wire, it exuded a forbidding air, a perception confirmed upon passing through its doors.

Another set of doors and you were in the main body of the factory, where all five senses were assaulted at once—your flesh by an embracing, damp blanket of heat, your ears by the roar and clank of machinery, your nose, eyes, and mouth by a thick yellow dust, as soon as you stepped inside you were choking on it.

Most of the interior walls were made of glass, giving the impression you could look anywhere and see everything, into every room, every corner. The first thing you did see were dozens of female workers seated at both sides of long tables, down the middle of which ran heaping piles of small yellow widgets. These *Einsatzstücken*, or insert pieces, were the casings for the detonators of various bombs, mortars, and artillery shells, and had to be measured by hand-held gauges to ensure they met spec.

They came from the *Pressen*, or stamping machines, hulking nearby. A ten-chambered mold was filled with yellow powder, the heavy mold slid into the machine, and after two minutes of heat and pressure out came ten solid pieces. The machines were air-hosed after each application to rid them of leftover powder. This was where the dust originated, but where it ended up was in your throat, your lungs, absorbed through the pores of your skin. After a week, you were coughing, feeling dizzy. The general assumption was that if the Germans didn't kill you, their toxic powder one day would.

Operating one of the waist-high Pressen was a torment, not unlike standing next to a hot oven all day. And those molds weren't just heavy, it was all a girl could do to lift one. The machine was the kind to sweat the life right out of you, squeeze you as dry as someone wringing out a dishrag. The body could take only so much of this before it gave out, before it sat down one day and had trouble getting back up.

Sabotage this was called, not surrendering to hunger or exhaustion, sickness or the heat, but daring to slow production on purpose. There were a hundred ways to commit this great crime. Going to the bathroom without permission, sabotage! Talking to one of the male workers, sabotage! Pausing to catch your breath, stretch your limbs, your aching back—sabotage report! Which if you weren't too worn down would land you in Block 11 for a while. Or if not so lucky, then it was off to the crematorium with you, goodbye and nice to have known you, *mein Liebe.*

Making things worse, you never knew who was watching you, or when. This was why the glass walls. The German Meisters, the kapos, the foremen and women, the SS *Blockführer* and his guard—hostile eyes were everywhere, able to spot sabotage from halfway across the floor. For twelve long hours, you were under the microscope of those eyes, like a germ on a slide, afraid to take a second to mop the sweat from your brow should it interrupt your work. This living in fear was hard on the nerves, in a way more of an affliction than the heat and the dust, the round-the-clock grind.

The more Roza learned about the Union, the greater her respect for Esther. That she'd not only survived but excelled in such an environment was a testament to both her stamina and pluck; a spot in the gunpowder room wasn't a position meted out lightly. Her sister Hanka, particularly in light of her youth, also deserved kudos. Compared to the Metallwerke, the Bekleidungskammer in which Roza had been fortunate to land was a stroll in the park.

What sold her more than anything on the two, however, was where they'd been living prior to their deportation. Both came from the Warsaw ghetto, and hadn't only witnessed the history-making uprising there but participated in it. Actually done battle with the SS!

Noah had shared with her what he knew of that glorious fight to the death, which because of his contacts in the underground was considerable. But it was Esther who'd put a human face on the affair. Roza could tell she didn't like to talk about it, but after the conversation turned one night to their lives before the camp, she started in on the ghetto and couldn't stop.

"Oh, Roza, we were so scared, Hanka and I. More scared than here, if you can imagine."

Before the war, their father owned a factory that manufactured wooden handicrafts. Months after the occupation, he was classified an essential worker, his job to make and engrave the crosses for those Wehrmacht from the Russian front who'd died of their wounds at the military hospitals in the city.

"Like most essential workers, he was relocated with our mother to the Aryan side of the wall, a mixed blessing for my sister and me. Though we knew life would be better for them, there we were, two teenagers all alone in the world, a world about to come crashing down on us."

Here, her tone brightened a bit.

"When the shooting and all the rest of it broke out, I don't know how many Germans I killed, if any. It must have been some, for I was one of those dropping Molotov cocktails from the rooftops. I can't tell you what that was like, fighting back. Fighting shoulder to shoulder with other Jews, with men and women fed up with being treated like lepers. Who come what may weren't going to take it anymore.

"Later, after the Nazis began bombing and setting fire to the ghetto, it was every person for herself. Hanka and I ended up hiding in a deserted apartment house on Mila Street. One day, the SS torched it, and we had to jump three stories to a courtyard, soldiers everywhere shooting at anything that moved.

"Somehow—it was a grass courtyard—Hanka and I escaped with no broken bones or bullet holes, and figured to try our luck in the sewers. Which was about all that was left of the ghetto by then. It took us two days up to our waists in the slime and sewage, dodging patrols, before we reached our parents and safety. But when the ghetto did finally fall, no Jew was safe anymore, not even essential workers. All four of us were put on the train to Maidanek. Where, we found out later, our mama and papa were gassed."

Esther ran a hand through the nap of her hair, the muscles in her jaw rippling.

"I may or may not have killed some Germans, but if I did it was too few. Which is why I can't get my hands on enough gunpowder, in the hope every ounce of it will go toward killing another. The way I see it, the fight in the ghetto isn't over. As long as there are Jews who continue to resist, the battle goes on. And will until there are either none of them or none of us left."

Roza had never seen her so lovely. Striking to begin with, sheared scalp or no, she was the kind of women anger made only prettier. Her big brown eyes seemed to get bigger, her nostrils to flare provocatively, the signature dimples at the corners of her mouth to deepen. Esther's face hateful was Esther's face idealized, its beauty exaggerated, as an artist might have painted her.

To Roza's undying awe, the girl's escapades in Warsaw made those midnight raids the Shomeir had conducted outside the Ciechanow ghetto look like what they were, glorified games of hide and seek. This Esther had fought the SS in armed combat and lived to tell the tale, with likely a fair number of German notches on her belt. That had been her own dream for going on four years now, ever since the invaders of her homeland had shown their true colors. It was only natural she should be in thrall to someone who'd actually lived that dream—and just as natural, given their similarities of age and disposition, that her adulation for this killer of Nazis should have blossomed into friendship.

To her delight, the attraction turned out to be mutual. Esther had taken to her as effortlessly as she had to Esther.

Roza had never lacked for companions growing up, even if most had been boys. A tomboy herself, she'd preferred the rough-and-tumble company of the male of the species. Her sister Shoshonna was the nearest she'd come to a serious girlfriend, this aspect of their relationship compromised by the very fact of their sisterhood. Neither had chosen but rather inherited the other, and no matter what were bound together for life.

Would they have bonded if they hadn't been sisters? Roza liked to think so, but in all honesty couldn't say. She'd loved Shoshonna with all the fierceness typical of her, but had to admit they were two different people.

Esther was in many ways her mirror image, and she was able to cut loose around her as she never had any female. Like the little more than adolescents they were, despite the grimness of their surroundings they spent a lot of time being silly together, gossiping, trading secrets, succumbing to prolonged bouts of giggling. Especially when the subject of boyfriends came up.

Esther had fallen for a young Pole named Tadek, a handsome fellow who also worked at the Union and was *Schreiber* of a block in the Stammlager. The position of scribe was a valued one. He or she was responsible for all a hut's paperwork: directives from the camp administration, occupancy and roll-call reports, sick lists, work assignments, special passes and such.

Esther was smitten. Not even Hanka could remember her being happier. Roza good-naturedly accused her of indulging in camp love with a capital L, and Esther had to agree.

"Funny that here of all places, in this stinking dung hill, this boneyard, I should have come across the person I was meant to have children with, a man whose heart is no less beautiful than that adorable face of his."

As might be expected of girls their age, the two shared a love of dancing. Esther had once dreamed of turning professional and knew all the steps. Soon she and Roza, upon the latter's bribe-fueled visits to her barracks, were to the glee of an audience doing the rhumba, the samba, the waltz, the tango, the American jitterbug even, this last closing with them falling into a laughing heap on the floor. The lack of music was no more an impediment than the absence of male partners; they either dah-dah-dah'd their accompaniment or were helped out by those watching.

On some nights, in that interval between bread and lights-out, the noise wafting from Birkenau's Block 2 was more characteristic of a children's summer camp than one built for mass murder.

Esther may have been the best friend Roza made at Birkenau, but was far from the only one. Marta Bindiger, Ala Gertner, Rose Greuenapfel, Mala Weinstein, Regina Safirsztajn—if she had kept a list, those names would have been at the top of it. All met the first requirement her affection demanded, namely the desire to do whatever it took to see the German beast vanquished, its victims appeased. Each was either pilfering or helping to move Union gunpowder.

Other than that, she was attracted to them for different reasons. Because of the coolness she brought to the tensest moments and a talent for letting nothing faze her, Marta played as big a role as she in holding this inner circle of conspirators together. She'd joined the underground not long after Roza and had risen as high in its ranks, if in duties unrelated, at least at first, to the plot. As the importance of her assignments grew, so did her freedom of movement. It wasn't long before she was showing up everywhere, and with impunity. A Camp, C Camp, the infirmaries, even the men's lagers—there was no limit to Marta's range, nor as a result the good she was able to leave behind her.

Her official status was as liaison between the Union women and the underground, but though not even those close to her knew how many pies she had her fingers in, she was never too busy for others, had a knack for being there when needed. People were always looking to Roza for strength, to reassure them of their mission. But when she was in want of reassurance and someone strong to lean on, it was to the imperturbable Marta she would turn.

Ala by contrast was a tinderbox of emotions, one never far from combusting. She could be the life of the party or the wettest of mops, depending on which side of the koje she crawled out of in the morning. As with her every sentiment, she didn't try to hide her hatred for the Nazis, and what a hatred it was. She'd have hurled herself off a mountain if it would help avenge her slain baby Rochele. Whenever the danger of what she was doing caught up with Roza and her own store of courage needed replenishing, she found Ala's bottomless well of it the perfect tonic.

Their indestructible *joie de vivre* was what drew her to Mala and Rose. Both worked in the pressure cooker that was the Pulverraum, Mala on the night shift, Rose during the day. Each had also lost family at Birkenau; Mala had watched all three of her sisters driven off in Himmelblock trucks. Yet she and Rose refused to give up, to abandon their lust for life, but rather made use of it to stave off despair.

The vehicle they chose was laughter. Roza would never forget the Sunday Mala gave herself a Hitler moustache with a dab of bootblacking and strutted around half the day without getting into trouble somehow. Nor could she keep from cracking up at Rose's gift for mimicry, particularly, she being German herself, when at the expense of Hössler and other of the SS.

But more than just a way of holding grief at arm's length, humor to the two women was a form of resistance, an attempt to inject a little normalcy into not only their own lives but those of their fellow captives, lives that had become as grotesque as they were ephemeral. In that respect, everyone profited from their daffiness, Roza among them, who when she could use a dose of comic relief knew where to go.

When her faith in the human race cried out for restoring, all she had to do was spend a few minutes with Regina. The Safirsztajn woman was a walking monument to kindness and understanding. Excluding the Nazis and those prisoners who'd sold out to them, she didn't have a bad word to say about anyone, insisted on giving them the benefit of the doubt. Regina was a short, moon-faced twenty-three, with in spite of her youth something of a matronly mien. This was heightened in that on a better diet, in a more tolerating era, one could picture her inclining to plumpness.

Just because she was a forgiving soul, though, didn't make her an easy mark. She hadn't been appointed forewoman of the gunpowder section because she was a pushover. She could be as hard as the situation called for; at any other time, she was everyone's big sister. When Roza sought Regina out, it was to feed off her sweetness, her generosity of spirit. In the bloody meat grinder that was Birkenau, which brought out the worst in so many, it was good to be reminded that people were made of more than clay, that they had something of the angels in them.

She counted others among her friends, too. As with most who'd crossed paths with the youngster, she'd taken a shine to Hanka Wajcblum, who exhibited the same disregard for danger as her older sister. Hanka was running as much gunpowder as anybody, and raring to do more. Beneath the pimples and the gawkiness, the teenaged self-consciousness, beat a heart the boldest man would have envied.

Then there were those Sonder to whom Roza was passing the dynamite, a couple from her hometown. She'd heard the SS had conscripted an unusually large number of men from the Ciechanow transport for duty in the Sonderkommando, many of them from the old Shomeir. But the only one she knew from then to make the trip to the Bekleidungskammer belonged to the young Wrubel, whose father had owned the neighborhood bakery.

Though just turned eighteen, Jukel Wrubel had gained the confidence of the Sonder leadership; few were those trusted with the job of picking up the gunpowder from Roza and carting it to the crematoria. Already a strapping six-footer broad in chest and shoulder, it was his mettle more than his muscles that had caught Kaminski's attention. The gas chamber had taken his family, a loss that instead of crushing him gave him reason to live. From the moment he heard of the revolt, he'd not only been on board but existed for nothing else, less for the chance at escape than to avenge his slaughtered kin. To see German blood spilled was all that mattered to him. Not your ordinary recruit, he was the kind of modern-day Zealot the Battle Group needed, happy to lay down his life if doing so deprived some Nazis of theirs.

Roza remembered him a cheerful boy, nor to her had the gruesome realities of his new life changed him. He was the same grinning kid who'd delivered her family's coffeecake. What she didn't know was how hard he worked to make it appear so. Or how often he was heard quietly crying himself to sleep at night.

The only other Sonder from Ciechanow to man the clothing cart was Zalman Leventhal, just recently assigned the duty. Unacquainted with him until now, she was always glad to see him one of the three. She suspected it was because he reminded her of Godel. Not only the same age, they shared the same boyish body, both skinny as flagpoles. They were alike, too, in their love of books; she could tell from his occasional casual reference to Shakespeare that Leventhal was well-read.

There the resemblance ended, the dour redhead being not half so personable. But the similarity was enough for her to regard him with fondness, which as far as he had it in him, he returned. Other than Gradowski and maybe Kaminski, no one did he feel more at ease around than Roza. Exactly why he couldn't say, unless it was her smile. All thumbs when it came to women, he wasn't used to smiles from them, yet here was one, and a pretty one, who served them up freely.

She also had friends she'd never met, men the likes of Leventhal's same Kaminski and the Steering Committee's Bruno Baum, both of whom applauded her yet avoided making contact. Aside from their having no business, as the SS saw it, to be within a hundred meters of her, what anxieties might it have caused her that two people she didn't really know were in on her secret?

Head and shoulders above the lot of them, of course, the new and the old, the known and unknown, stood the staunchest of all, her and Godel's best buddy, the formidable, the famous, the one-of-a-kind Noah Zabludowicz. For years, the three had been thick as thieves; not even Birkenau had succeeded in keeping them apart. In the ghetto, meanwhile, they'd been inseparable, together night and day, locked arm in arm most everywhere they went, sharing clothes, sharing food...

Sharing, some said, who knew what else. These whispered of impropriety, a *ménage à trois*, but they were in the minority, outsiders for the most part. Everyone familiar even in passing with their situation was aware that Roza and Godel were a number, with Noah no more than a platonic third wheel. That this was working for them without giving rise to complications was deemed deserving of praise for all.

She on the other hand knew better, having to her consternation come to realize long ago that Noah's affections were far from platonic. A girl would have had to be blind not to notice. That he'd never actually come forth and confessed as much meant nothing; love had a way of revealing itself that went beyond the verbal. There'd been too many instances when his guard was down for her not to have picked up on that look in his eyes, that plaintive, puppy-dog stare that *did* mean something.

Nor was there any mistaking the dead giveaway of his smile, which when directed at her was a shade brighter than it had a right to be. His whole persona changed when he was around her, going from assertive to something almost shy. He wasn't as exacting with her as he could be with others; Roza felt she could do or say just about anything and it would be fine by him.

Still, never had she held any of this against him. Or viewed his divergent passion as a betrayal of their friendship. Or for that matter, his and Godel's. That Noah hadn't come even close to acting on his feelings, that he'd had the discretion, the decency to keep them secret, was reason not to blame him for having them. Young as she was, she understood that like an untrained animal or undisciplined child, the heart didn't always behave as it should. Love tended to play by its own rules, and where these led, people were often powerless not to follow.

She'd once toyed with the idea of confronting him about it, if only to clear the air between them. That was how she usually dealt with a problem, not by running from it but facing it head-on.

Something told her back then, though, to let this one be, nor in the months and what became the years to come had she regretted the decision. Not only had his attraction remained harmlessly unspoken but time might have come to her rescue and solved the problem for her. Lately, without growing at all distant, Noah had been acting noticeably less spellbound. Indeed, she'd begun to question how much of it had been her imagination all along, until Marta having dropped by her barracks one early November evening, the subject of Godel came up.

They sat facing each other on the wooden edge of Roza's koje. "I hear your fiancé is starting to make a name for himself in the underground," Marta said. "The talk is he's been seen a lot at Birkenau. The Union plant, too."

Roza frowned. "Yes, and that worries me. That he's pulling too much exposure. I mean, you got wind of it, right?"

"I wouldn't if I were you. Worry, that is—I'm sure he knows what he's doing. Besides, his partner is as experienced as they come." Marta paused, suddenly interested in her shoes. "How's he, by the way? That pal of yours, Noah Zabludowicz."

Her casualness sounded too casual. "Okay, I guess. What makes you ask?"

"Oh, nothing. Nothing much anyway. I, you know, was just… you know."

"Are you all right, Marta?"

"I was about to ask you the same thing." She put a hand on Roza's knee. "I'm not the only one to notice you haven't been yourself lately, honey. That spark of yours, that fire we're used to feeding off of is gone. Is there anything you've been wanting to—to talk about maybe?"

"Talk about?"

"Yes. Involving Noah perhaps?"

Roza was really confused now. "Noah again. What's all this about Noah?"

Marta took a deep breath. "I don't know how to say this other than just to say it. It's no secret how the man looks at you, acts when he's around you. Is it something to do with you and him that's got you preoccupied?"

Realizing her mouth had dropped open, Roza clapped it shut. "I—I don't believe this."

"I don't claim to, either," Marta said, her expression pained, "but I had to ask. *Something's* been eating at you, that much is plain. I was just thinking if you needed someone to talk to, about anything…"

Roza could only stare at her, but as she did her indignation softened. She took Marta's hand in both of hers.

"I get what you're trying to do, and appreciate it, Marta. That's what friends are for. But understand, please, that Noah, too, is my friend—and nothing more. Godel is the one I love. Always has been and always will be. We plan, God and the Nazi devil willing, to get married one day, have babies, the whole *shmear*.

"Which isn't to say you aren't right about Noah," she admitted. "But those… emotions he unfortunately does have, he's been man enough to keep to himself. When we do see each other it's as friends, best friends, but again, nothing more. Do you really see me doing something that might risk my losing Godel? I've lost too many I love as it is."

"That isn't what I meant!" Marta cried. Then, "Heck, I'm not sure what I meant. But if it's not what in my clumsy way I was trying to get at, what *has* been bothering you, pet? As I told you, I'm not the only one who's noticed."

"I'm fine, Marta, really I am. Been under the weather a bit is all, no big deal."

"Under the weather? You've been moping around like a dying turtle for a month now."

"Trust me, I'm good." Roza's voice was convincing—not so her lack of eye contact. "Everything's good."

"Uh-huh." Marta leaned forward until their faces were almost touching. "The truth, Rozhka. Tell me what's wrong."

But she never did. All it would have done would be to bring Marta down, too.

Ironically, it *was* Noah who was to blame for her blues, though it had nothing to do with his misguided amour. After informing the Sonderkommando of Auschwitz's decision to delay the revolt, the next day he'd gone to her with it. He thought it only proper that as the brains, heart, and soul behind the gunpowder operation, she be kept in the loop about any such changes. He would have hated for something bad to happen with hurry for the present no longer a factor.

Roza was stunned at the news, then disgusted. Then despondent. She'd been expecting the signal for the revolt any day, at the very least sometime this year. Now even that was in jeopardy. Unconscionable as it was, 1944 could see the crematoria still standing, still gobbling up the trainloads of humanity filing into them.

When was it going to stop, all this talk and no action? What in the name of mercy was everyone waiting for? Was this what she and hers were putting their lives on the line for, so this precious powder, this gray gold they'd been ordered to gather could lie hidden away somewhere collecting cobwebs?

All Roza had were questions. She'd have given a lot for some answers. If she were to persevere on her people to continue risking their necks, she was going to have to find someone who could give her some answers.

1944

Winter

The liquidation of the 11th Sonderkommando followed the same pattern as the last few preceding it. One cold, cloudless February afternoon, the sun a shrunken circle of ineffectual fire, two SS officers and a platoon of *Schützen* stormed the yard of Block 13 and assembled the commando. As no transports were expected that day, all but a token crew assigned to Crematorium V were present. SS-*Obersturmführer* Schwarzhuber, a squat, sallow-faced man of thirty-five, approached them, a clutch of papers in hand.

Bursts of frost like cigarette smoke framed his words. "Men of the 11th Detachment!" he boomed. "Two hundred of you have been selected to help clear rubble in the aftermath of Soviet air raids on the city of Lublin. It will be hard work, but you'll be well-treated. You are to remain at the Maidanek lager in the likelihood of future raids. A train is at the ramp now to take you to your new home. You may bring what possessions you can fit in one bag."

It was a trick, of course, there wasn't a Sonder who spoke German that didn't see through it, the rest after these had translated for them. But what could they do? Unprepared, they were staring into the barrels of automatic weapons. Their only hope was that the Nazis were telling the truth. As slim a chance as this was, it did hold some water in that they'd been instructed to pack a bag for the trip.

Once Lieutenant Schwarzhuber began calling out the tattoo numbers on his list, those they belonged to stepped forward as commanded. Inside of an hour, belongings in tow, they were formed into a column and led out the compound.

Two days later, all too aware some of them were next, those left would learn to their relief the two hundred had been seen boarding a transport bound for Maidanek. Lublin appeared to have work after all, or so they kept telling each other. If a hoax, it was an elaborate one, and why should the SS here go to all that trouble when there were plenty of places in their backyard to commit mass murder on the sly?

Kapo Kaminski of Crematorium III harbored no such illusions. Those who had gone with the soldiers were dead, nor was it because their so-called four months were up. He'd come to find this theory of the four-month life span just that, a theory. And a half-baked one to boot, no matter the traction it had gained among the Sonder and others.

Though the Nazis were keen on regularly thinning the squads, it wasn't to silence them so as to keep Sonderbehandlung a secret. When one examined this, the air leaked right out of it. Aside from their practice of keeping a core group of veterans alive indefinitely, there wasn't a prisoner in the camp who didn't know what the Germans were up to, what those six fat chimneys and the smoke boiling from them signified.

The reality was that after a few months of living the Sonder nightmare, eventually it got to a man, all but the strongest or most stubborn of men, and when it did he wasn't good for anything. Least of all work, and to the SS nothing was more worthless than a Sonder who couldn't work. When a large enough number of these were singled out and led away never to return, it could appear a scheduled liquidation was in progress.

Not that this was the only reason for these purges, and how Kaminski knew this latest two hundred were dead: they simply weren't needed anymore. He'd seen a hint of this last September after the summer's carnage began to wane, but now there was no explaining it otherwise. The transports this winter had slowed almost to a standstill. There might be three a week, and none as big as before; the days of the forty-, fifty-car trains were over. And with them, those of the four-hundred-man Sonder.

Its kapo expected the 12th Squad, as soon as the Nazis were finished with the 11th, to end up numbering little more than a hundred.

Irrespective of the danger this posed them, even the veterans among them now, the increasing dearth of deportees made itself felt in other ways. So scarce was food becoming that the men of Block 13 had been forced to supplement their diet with lagersuppe. Same with the liquor that numbed them to their work; when available at all, it had quadrupled in price. And this with the twin rivers of wealth that had flowed into the crematoria from the transports and the Goldarb having been reduced to a dribble.

No one did this distress more than Kaminski. For one, it spelled the end of Sonder aid to the women of C Camp; his men could barely supply themselves anymore. Even more worrisome was how he was supposed to purchase the weapons those same men would be needing to shoot their way out of this hell. So far, they had the three hand grenades lifted from the dead Ukrainians, two large-caliber pistols, and double that of the small-bore pieces the SS used for executions, these being little more than popguns only effective at close range.

From the gunpowder smuggled them, they'd been able to fashion a growing store of crude dynamite sticks, but had yet to devise a grenade. Their reserve of bullets was nothing to brag about, either; this more than anything was gnawing at him. Say on the day of the attack they did manage to subdue their guards and take their guns. Would they have the ammunition, first, to take out the cordons, then hold off their pursuers as they fled?

They needed more cartridges, especially the 19 and 57mm sizes compatible with the German submachine guns and Mausers. These were difficult to come by even with gold. What, Kaminski asked, was he supposed to use now, his good looks?

Or to be more realistic, What the crap did it matter? For to entertain the probability still of staging even a semblance of the revolt as planned could no longer be called optimism, but wishful thinking. Obvious now was that when the leaders of the underground decided to postpone the uprising back in August, what they were really doing was cancelling it altogether. All he'd heard from them for six months was the word *wait*—for the partisans to be ready, for the weather to improve, for the Soviets to launch their spring offensive so the front would draw near enough to allow the escapees the protection of the Red Army.

What wasn't obvious was what had prompted their decision. Not, when Kaminski thought about it, that this mattered a crap, either. No Auschwitz meant no Home Army, and without it one could stick a fork in the revolt. Even if the Sonder were to break through the wire and reach the trees, there'd be two thousand soldiers from the camp right behind them, with a like amount from the surrounding subcamps, plus the local Gestapo and police, homing in on them from all sides. Nor, unable to protect them without the Armia's help, could they in good conscience attempt to free the thousands from the general population that by accompanying them would serve to spread the German forces thin.

The Sonder, thus hung out to dry, might as well draw targets on each others' backs. Their only chance lay in disbanding into groups of twenty or less and spreading their own selves thin, enabling a lucky few maybe to elude the Nazi net.

Dashed dreams and dead friends and the SS victorious again, Kaminski mused, the same old song and dance it had been since the ghetto.

But more than just escape was at stake. He wasn't forgetting his vow to that long-ago, bloody apparition of a moon that if the rebels wound up succeeding at nothing else, at least they'd have taken the four crematoria to the grave with them. The revolt, any revolt, was to kick off with the dynamiting of the death houses, but even if it should end there, that would be enough.

The tragedy was that even this might not matter. Not at this late date. Difficult as it was to conceive, was it possible the executioners were running out of victims? A year ago, Kaminski would have dismissed the question, but following the slaughter of last spring and summer, and with the transports tapering off, it didn't sound so crazy anymore.

But even if it were true, thousands could yet be saved. This, not the pipe-dream of escape, kept him from banishing a positive attitude entirely and saying to blazes with the whole thing. Just yesterday, he'd informed his Battle Group's lieutenants, out-gunned and now undermanned as it was, to start pumping the squad up mentally while preparing it physically for the fight and flight it would be his honor at last to lead.

He wasn't expecting much resistance from the ranks, either. Not with two hundred of them carted off just days ago. As ill-fated an effort as it promised to be, it beat sitting on their backsides doing nothing, waiting for the SS sickle to sweep through them again. And when it did, pretending it hadn't, that there really was work in Lublin. Or whatever fable their duplicitous masters foisted on them then.

Kaminski knew they'd have to hurry, though, if that sickle was to be avoided. He'd like to have them ready to go as early into March as he could. The significance of this date, when later it occurred to him, was as hard to believe as choke down. March would make it a full year of the "rebels" not having lived up to the name.

But with news that would sink his spirits further before making them soar, opportunity came knocking on the Special Squad's door with it still February. It was typical for the soldiers on crematoria duty to pick one Sonder from each shift to do odd jobs around the building, tidying the *Kommandoführer*'s office, polishing the Germans' boots, washing the dishes. The officer in charge of Crematorium V was *Oberscharführer* Voss, and his Sonder orderly-for-the-day happened to be in his office the afternoon an envelope arrived by motorcycle from the Political Department.

After reading its contents, a ruffled Voss tossed the note and with an expletive stomped out of the room. The Sonder man, left alone, darted to the sergeant's desk and scanned the letter lying there, then slower, to make sure he'd read it right. Addressed to Voss, it ordered him to prepare the crematorium for a major Aktion that was to commence in two days: the destruction by gas of the Czech Family Camp.

The *Familienlager*, designated *B2b*, Birkenau, had been established six months earlier with the deportation of five thousand Czechoslovakian Jews from the model ghetto of Theresienstadt. Two transports totaling five thousand more would come after. Unlike the other ghettos that dotted the map of Europe, Theresienstadt was a show-place concocted by the Nazis so that the world might judge the Third Reich's treatment of its Jews humane. The Red Cross had been allowed access to its streets from the outset, was even at one point invited to inspect B Camp.

No selections awaited the Theresienstadt Jews at the unloading ramp. Families were trucked intact to their new residence, nor were their possessions confiscated, their hair shorn, their forearms tattooed. None was subjected to forced labor. There was a school for the children, a small clinic, a smaller library. Pregnant women and babies received extra food, while everyone was permitted one parcel per month in the mail.

It was hard to imagine a Jew enjoying such privileges, but few were their kind outside *B2b* to begrudge the Czechs their good fortune. These had an emotional stake in the continued well-being of those lucky ten thousand, taking a vicarious satisfaction from knowing that some Jews, somewhere, were being treated as more human than animal.

Which was why it came as such a blow to learn that even these apples of the SS eye weren't immune from the exigencies of SS *realpolitik.* Having by now lost their propaganda value, and with the Soviets getting ready to continue their advance west, to the Nazis their pampered Czechs had become all liability and no asset.

After Voss returned to his office in an agitated state and with two equally flustered kapos in tow, the Sonder who'd bumbled onto the Gestapo order quietly left and hurried to let the Battle Group in on what he'd discovered. His story would gain weight the next morning when operations were suspended in Crematorium II and the shifts of it and Number Five ordered to begin a complete overhaul of both facilities. The Germans wanted everything not only in good working order but cleaned, painted, and polished by no later than tomorrow evening. Clearly, something over and above the normal was in the offing.

The night before, recognizing the gravity of events and the opening they presented, Kaminski had called a meeting of his lieutenants. He explained the situation and told them that though a massacre was imminent, it could possibly work to both the Sonders' and everyone's advantage.

"Lady Luck, lads, may be on our side for a change. There isn't a man here who doesn't realize that for us alone to try and break out of this place would be nothing short of suicide. We are two hundred, the enemy thousands. Our only hope is to be a part of thousands, too, which in the original plan meant those prisoners from the camp supposed to lam it out of here with us. The more of these the Nazis had their hands full with, the likelier it would be for some, us included, to slip through those hands."

Sensing something momentous, his audience of half a dozen was all ears.

"Without the partisan arm of Battle Group-Auschwitz to help us, however, help I'm afraid we can no longer count on, this isn't going to happen. Even if the time we'd not have anymore would permit our hunting them down and taking them with us, deprived of the Home Army's firepower and familiarity with the forest, any escapees that might make it to that forest would end up sitting ducks."

He didn't smile, but came close. "The Czechs of the Family Camp, though, are a whole other ball of wax. With death at their doorstep, they have nothing to lose. By refusing to just lie down and be killed and joining forces with us instead, they'd at least have a shot at surviving. A few of them anyway. Perhaps more than a few. Having lived in the shadow of the cremo chimneys for six months, they know all too well where that smoke they're spewing comes from.

"If convinced they were next to burn, I for one can't see them turning us down. Who could be more up to making a run for it than people certain that in a matter of hours they and their loved ones will have become smoke themselves?"

Kaminski was sure the time to strike was now, that they wouldn't be favored with a chance like this again. In anticipation of their agreement, he'd taken the liberty of formulating a plan.

"Before anything, we'll need to get the bad news to B Camp. Not that we can simply sashay past the sentries and announce it. Assuming the extermination order is true, not even bribery is going to get us through the Czech gate.

"But the maintenance commandos have the chops to go anywhere, and there's a plumbing crew that owes me big. I should send the Czech Müller along with them, Filip Müller from Number Two. He's got a head on him and speaks their lingo. He'll set the Slovaks straight.

"The *Familien* elders must be made to understand that the only out left them is escape. First, they'll have to set their barracks on fire, then with some insulated pliers I trust we can spare them, cut the barbed wire at the southern end of their lager. The Sonder on shift at the crematoria open that day—and I'll be the first to volunteer to sneak in and arm any that might not be—after overcoming their guards and taking their weapons, will dynamite the cremos and force the western perimeter. This is where I'll be, and probably a couple of you."

The hyper Warszawski started to say something, but the others shushed him. Kaminski was telling them what they wanted to hear, and they would hear it without interruption.

"With all of the pistols, our three grenades, and the rest of the TNT, those in Block 13 are to head out at the noise of the explosions, rendezvous with the Czechs, and punch a path through the eastern perimeter at the auxiliary gate nearest the main one. After that, in small groups, it's south to the Sola River; those of us who blew the death houses should already be on the way.

"Once we make it to the Sola and its marshes, the Krauts might not be so eager to follow. That swamp isn't only foul but alive, I've been told, with as many partisans as snakes."

The plan was as desperate as it was full of holes, but holes could be patched. And it had some points in its favor. With *B2b* and the crematoria on fire, and the inner cordon breached in two places, in the chaos it would take the SS a while to get organized. This should buy the rebels valuable minutes. Plus, thousands running in every direction wouldn't only add to the confusion but prevent the Germans from concentrating their forces.

Even more than what he'd proposed, Kaminski's air of calm confidence won his listeners over. Eschewing histrionics, without even raising his voice, he inspired them with the same enthusiasm and urgency of purpose that filled him. Which they in turn would that night pass on to the rest of the squad—who, mindful a lot of them might not have many more days left them than the Czechs, were in agreement with their kapo that a rare bit of luck had been dropped in their laps.

Come morning, Block 13 bustled with activity as the commando, spurred on by an adrenaline-driven mix of nervous fear and wild hope, began readying itself for both battle and the journey.

Their excitement was short-lived. When Müller got back from B Camp, he brought evil tidings. The Theresienstadt Jews refused to accept they were in danger. Why would the SS, they asked, bother assigning them their own camp, a model camp at that, if in a few months it was to be the gas for them? In its lack of logic, it was so very un-German.

The men of the Special Squad must be mistaken. Where had they heard this awful rumor? Or maybe it wasn't a rumor, but a deliberate lie to try and panic the peaceful folk of B Camp into joining some hare-brained Sonder escape attempt. Sorry, their elders said, but that was what it looked like to them. Show us some proof, they told Müller, and we'll talk.

There was no proof, so Kaminski had him return with the boy who'd been there when Sergeant Voss had received his orders.

"This didn't make a dent in them," Müller said, "this one old man in particular. 'So where is this paper you claim to have seen?' he asked the boy. 'The one authorizing our destruction—place it in front of me so I can read it myself.'

"He said something then that I'll carry with me forever." Müller's tone went from exasperated to sad. " 'You tell us to fight, and then what?' the poor man pleaded. 'Watch our wives and children, our elderly and ailing, cut to pieces in front of us, mowed down with machine guns? It would be better to die in each other's arms—in the gas chamber, yes, but locked in a last embrace, allowed the solace of touch. Of saying goodbye. And in the dark, we wouldn't have to see each other die.' "

Not, Müller would add, that he'd found a one of his countrymen who believed it would come to that. All had insisted his warning either a mistake or a lie, the most shameful of lies, and weren't about to concede otherwise unless confronted by hard evidence.

Their position was reinforced when the Aktion's two-day deadline came and went. Then another few days with life continuing as before, by which time even Kaminski was beginning to wonder if there hadn't been some kind of misunderstanding. Or maybe the undependable Germans had simply changed their minds.

Then on March 6th, the SS surprised the Familien leaders by informing them half the camp was to be sent to Heydebreck in Germany to work in war production. Apprehensive at first, they felt better after talking it over among themselves and agreeing that at this point in the war the Reich couldn't afford idle hands. The next day, five thousand of them made the short march to quarantine camp where they received rations and extra blankets for the train ride. A stop in Q-Camp was standard for most prisoners transferring out of Birkenau; before leaving, a delousing and change of clothing were mandatory.

It wasn't until the night of the 8th that the Nazi fog of deceit evaporated, and the first truckloads of Czechs rumbled into the yard of Crematorium II. (A second allotment was dispatched to Number Five). The SS were waiting for them, and not taking any chances. Floodlights reflected off a hundred steel helmets. Two machine guns on tripods covered every foot of ground. The angry barking of dogs came from everywhere, their breath jets of steam in the chill air. The Germans knew that for these people, steeped as they were in the ways of Birkenau, there could be no misconstruing where they were, and why.

Dropping all pretense, therefore, soldiers with nightsticks greeted each truck, beating those spilling out of it toward the bank of steps leading underground. The noise alone was enough to strike terror, the curses and shouts of the SS, the screams of their victims, the maniacal clamor of the Alsatians and Dobermans aroused by the smell of blood.

When the dust had cleared, three thousand cowered in the fluorescent glare of the undressing room. Many were bleeding, most weeping—some, in shock, staring silently at nothing. The air in the packed basement was thick with fear and betrayal. Even the children, even the smallest ones, could sense what was up. They hung onto their parents, eyes big, bodies trembling.

From the double line of soldiers blocking the stairwell came the order to undress. This galvanized the crowd. Cries of "What about Heydebreck?" and "We only want to work!" were soon cracking like pistol shots from out of the welter of moaning and sobs. A trio of officers showed their faces, not to investigate those shouts, but to celebrate the operation's success so far. They stood on the steps, all self-congratulation and smiles.

This was too much for those who'd spotted them. A handful rushed the stairs, whether to confront the Germans physically or verbally would never be known, for in an ear-splitting explosion of yellow muzzle blasts they were cut down.

Hardly had the echo of the shots ceased ringing than the SS surged forward, and with truncheons and dogs tore into the helpless crowd. So furious was this onslaught that several more were killed before their attackers backed off. Blood was everywhere now, the floor slippery with it. The doomed clung mutely to each other, the wild weeping of even the hysterical among them having subsided to a whimper.

Again the order to get undressed. But though most made an effort this time, the soldiers weren't impressed. Ignoring the fact it wasn't completely naked, they were soon pummeling the dazed mob into the narrow corridor leading to the gas chamber. In the claustrophobic semi-darkness of this hallway, bedlam reigned anew, people running over each other to escape the Nazis' clubs, the demon frenzy of the dogs, the shrieking of the driven even more bloodcurdling in this confined space.

Suddenly, impossibly, from out of this Babel of tears, pain, and SS fury climbed the soprano of a woman singing, a diva's voice, professional, powerful, as breathlessly out of place as a prize-winning orchid sprung from a patch of thistles. In the space of a few notes, this orchid announced itself the Czech national anthem, others taking it up until it swelled into a chorus.

At the open door of the death room, without missing a beat, it shifted into a less official anthem, that of European Jewry, the mournful, majestic *Ha Tikvah*, Hebrew for "The Hope." It was as if the men and women of this choir of the condemned were making a last statement, a farewell homage to their heritage. Loyal Czechoslovakians they were, and proud of it, but in the end bound less to country than race and religion, their Jewishness being the part of them they held the most dear.

By sunrise of the third day, the Family Camp was no more, its final five thousand having tracked the first into oblivion. The dirt streets were as bereft of life as the surface of the moon, the doors of its empty huts banging forlornly in the wind.

Not that it was to stay so. Though the Sonder couldn't know, twenty thousand Jews remained in the Theresienstadt ghetto, all marked for B Camp. As of now, however, it was a desolate place, inhabited by ghosts, the occasional child's toy in the mud a reminder of what had been.

Kaminski took the whole disheartening episode hard. Always quick with a grin and a slap on the back, or conversely a withering scowl and a rebuke, overnight he became withdrawn, apathetic. Despite making every effort to hide this from his men, so at odds was it with what they'd come to expect from him that none failed to see the change. When asked how they could help, he made light of his aloofness, but in truth felt as hollow a shell of a man as he had since arriving at the Vernichtungslager.

Noah Zabludowicz had no trouble noticing the difference in him, either. The underground had sent him to Block 13 to size up the situation. Having uncovered Birkenau's decision to move without them, Auschwitz wanted to make sure, with the Family Camp no more, that Sonder obstreperousness had cooled. They could have saved themselves the trouble: the Czech imbroglio had cured both the commando and its kapo of any desire at this point to take on the Germans.

From their first meeting, he and Kaminski had hit it off. They recognized a lot of themselves in each other, not least the soft spot beneath the hard, he-man exterior for those suffering or in need. It saddened Noah to find his normally exuberant friend a defeated shadow of his self, a sadness compounded by his having someone even dearer to him in similar straits. Roza Robota, too, wasn't herself these days, her usual bravado supplanted by a stubborn moodiness.

Though he knew what was troubling both—in Kaminski's case, of course, the Familienlager debacle, with Roza distraught over Auschwitz having lost its appetite for revolt—in neither instance did he have a clue what he could do to help.

Until from out of the blue one day, he came up with what he had to admit was the brilliant idea of getting the pair of them together. By arranging for them to meet, putting them in the same room, not only might Kaminski, as head of the Sonder, be able to answer those questions about the state of the uprising that were causing Roza grief, but if there was anyone whose words could restore the starch to a man, that person was she.

It was a sunny yet biting-cold March morning when Noah passed through *B1a*'s gate, the icy mud crackling like dry twigs beneath his boots. Kaminski had balked at going anywhere at first, but after told they'd be joining the operative who'd been feeding his men their gunpowder, he protested no more.

Roza was game from the start. She knew all about Kapo Kaminski from her Sonder contacts, and here was her chance to sit down with this founder and commanding general of Battle Group-Sonderkommando—and clarify a few things, was the way she'd put it to Noah. She swore she'd have no problem being there at the appointed place and time, as the blockova of her barracks owed her more favors than she had fingers. True to her word, but for a couple of Stubendiensten busy with their chores, he walked in on her sitting alone in the hut.

At sight of her, his heart began fluttering in his chest like a small, trapped bird; strict as he was about keeping his love for her under wraps, his body as usual wasn't playing along. She rose to greet him, and they exchanged hugs and how-are-you's, their breath like smoke. It was almost as cold inside the barracks as out, which like most of those in Birkenau was short on windows, shrouded even mid-morning in a permanent dusk.

"So where is this—Oh," she said, looking past Noah, "here he is now."

He turned to see Kaminski's barrel of a body silhouetted in the blazing white of the open door. Soon, the three of them were sitting well away from the Stubendiensten, Roza having got hold of three folding metal chairs. It was she who got the ball rolling.

"Finally I meet the legendary kapo of Crematorium III. You are aware, sir, that your reputation precedes you."

"What I'm aware of," Kaminski said, minus his usual bluster, "is that I have the honor at last of coming face to face with a person I've admired from afar for a while now."

"You know of me? Ah, yes... Wrubel, Leventhal, and the rest. I trust they haven't been too free with my name."

"Your name, dear lady, is known to a very few only. I've seen to that. Your bravery, however, has captured the imaginations of many. Whenever the courage of my men needs reviving, I like to remind them that the gunpowder, on which any success we might have is founded, comes to us thanks to the courage of a woman. Yes, a *woman*, I'm always careful to repeat, who would rather die than have the revolt do the same."

Roza fidgeted in her chair. She'd never been comfortable with compliments.

"So, when do we get on with this pow-wow of yours?" she demanded of Noah, but only, he knew, to hide her embarrassment. "I have to think we're not here, no disrespect to you, Mr. Kaminski, to be part of some half-assed, mutual-admiration society."

The men locked eyes for a second, then laughed.

"No, we're not," Noah said, quickly serious again. "For months now," he continued, indicating Roza, "this one has been after me about those I work for having put the uprising on hold. Whenever I see her, the first thing she asks is if Auschwitz has changed its mind, followed by when in the hell is it going to?"

"Can you blame me?" she said. "I'd hate for it to turn out me and the others had been schlepping that damned dynamite all this time for nothing. That the revolt should be over before it even started."

"Until just a few days ago, I kept telling her not to worry, that there was the Sonderkommando still. Which meant there was hope. The Sonder have no choice, I said: for them it's take up arms or die. And no squad knew this better than the 11th. She and I thought it impossible, aware as it was of what happened to the ten detachments before it, that this one would let itself be caught flat-footed and marched to its death without a fight. But... we were wrong. Couldn't have been wronger."

Now it was Noah's turn to look uncomfortable.

"What I have to say next is difficult, kapo. Difficult because of some things I myself did, at the expense of the Sonder no less, that weren't in the best interests of the revolt. Roza is right for getting on me about the people I work for, people no longer in support of the rebellion but against it. In their service, I confess to acting on orders I probably shouldn't have, orders if I had to carry out again, I wouldn't."

"But that was half a year ago, and as you might have picked up on yourself, I've been singing a different tune since. Which, if I may, sir, entitles me as I see it—me *and* Roza—to ask you this. Please don't think we're judging you, or for that matter anybody, but as someone I've always admired for his straight shooting, for telling it like it is, what do you figure are the odds of the next Sonder, the 12th, being the first not to let itself be trotted like a flock of sheep to the killing floor?"

For a long moment, the only sound was the swishing of the Stubendienst brooms on the dirt floor. Kaminski sat with his elbows on his knees, head lowered. A thin smile played at his lips, but that was it; for all the emotion he showed at what amounted to a challenge to Sonder manhood, this normally emotional man might have slept through the words.

When he did lift his head, the smile had fled the lips but lingered in the voice. "I like you, Noah Zabludowicz. Have from day one. No one has been more of a friend to the Sonder than you. But when it comes down to it, you're not one of us. And until you've seen through another's eyes, walked in his shoes, you can't begin to nail down who he is. What makes him tick.

"Every stripe of prisoner here is different, with different problems, different needs, and there are forces at work on the Special Squad you'll find nowhere else. Bear with me a few while I lay some on you. Maybe it'll give you a better grasp of where the Sonder are at—and where we're headed."

As if one person, the two inched forward in their chairs.

"True to what you were saying, Noah, no group of inmates would seem more open to revolt than the Sonder. Human nature being what it is, though, we could also be seen as the least likely to risk it. There's no getting around it: in an uprising the Sonder have something to lose. And by that I don't mean all those privileges we're allowed, that long table in Block 13 piled high with food and cigarettes, the civvy clothes and hot showers, the prescription and other medicines. Which among that last, I'd have to count the liquor at our disposal.

"All are spectacular to be sure, things a lot of us haven't enjoyed since before the ghetto. Some not even then. There are those of us, too, tied to the camp for other reasons, a wife or girlfriend in Lager C, a brother in Auschwitz.

"But again, this, none of it, is what I'm talking about. When I say the Sonder have something to lose, it has nothing to do with a full belly or some tug on the heart. We of the crematoria live under the axe, and who can predict when that axe is going to fall? Some claim it's every four months, but I'm not one of those; it depends on the situation, I say, not the calendar. But even if you were to hang a number on it, four months of life—four weeks, four days, four *hours*—is not something to be thrown away lightly. And to most Sonder that's what they'd be doing, throwing it away, for odds are the day of the revolt will be their last.

"So they wait and tell themselves they'll take it up tomorrow, get serious about it then. But they always wait too long, and time sneaks up on them like a thief in the night, until before they know it they're standing in formation in the crematorium yard and some *Unterführer* is calling out numbers from a list."

The smile returned, if thinner. "I'd be willing to bet, too, there's not a cremo man out there who doesn't believe that when that axe does fall, it's not going to land on him. Another man, yes, and more's the pity for that, but another's death isn't your own. Somehow, you tell yourself, that if there's any justice in the world you'll be one of the few to escape the SS head-chopper.

"People, none more than the young, have trouble coming to grips with the grave, and like a man falling from a tree will grab at any branch, no matter how flimsy. I've heard it a thousand times and might a thousand more: I've done everything they asked of me, jumped to every command. Why would the Germans want to do away with me?"

Caught up as he was in what he was saying, Kaminski rose from his chair and started pacing, head down.

"What can prepare a new Sonder, a young man, a boy, for his first shift at the ovens, the sights, the smells, the screams of the gas chamber? Many have never been around a dead person before, and here they are tripping over corpses. There are those who can't do it, not even for a day, those unable or unwilling to deal with the shock of the crematorium.

"These are taken somewhere and shot, or soon get hold of enough sleeping pills to keep from ever waking. Many, however, disturbing as it may seem, grow accustomed to the job. Or as accustomed as men can get to mass murder on a daily basis. Horrible as it is they adjust to it, learn to live with it, at least for a while. Some, a long while.

"To do this, though, they must learn how to see human beings as not people but objects, piles of dead bodies as nothing more than material to be sorted and processed. But that carries a price, for to master this trick of the mind is to become in the end less human themselves.

" 'Sonder sickness' I call it, and it can make men not men. Apathy sets in, indifference to not only where they are and what they're doing but what they *should* be doing to ease both their own anguish and the killing. You can tell it by how they move, stiff, mechanical, like machines. As if there in body only."

He continued pacing, utterly absorbed, not unlike a machine himself. Or better yet, a lawyer before a jury.

"It doesn't help that by then time has ceased to be what it was. Denied any prospect of a future, the past is also lost to them, as dead as those loved ones of theirs who inhabit it. Finding it too painful to ponder either, all they're left with is the present, the next hour, the next day, to think much further ahead is as depressing as dwelling on what was.

"All that matters then, all they come to care about, is making it from one shift to the next, counting out survival one day at a time. It's easier that way. Easier to give events their head as you might a horse, let them carry you where they will. Yet this isn't exactly an attitude conducive... conducive to..."

Almost as much to his surprise as theirs, Kaminski stuttered to a halt. He feared all of a sudden that words which a moment ago seemed to be hitting their mark were starting to sound like one long whine.

"Tell me," he begged Noah, "if I'm making a case." Then to Roza, "Or just making excuses."

Her response was quick. "If you have to ask that, maybe you ought to rethink your argument. Part of it anyway. But you make some good points, excellent points. I'm with Noah on this: we're not judging you, sir. No one has the right to judge you abandoned souls of the Special Squad. Yours is an unhappiness not seen this side of death.

"But I can't help wondering," she was as quick to add, "if there's something else at work here. That maybe Sonder misery isn't the only thing holding them back."

Kaminski did a double take, looked at her as if he hadn't really seen her until now. With an appreciative shake of his head, he returned to his chair.

"I don't fault you, Noah," he said, "for never telling me just how brave this young lady is. That goes without saying. And I already knew from some of my men not only how easy on the eyes she is but how inspiring she can be to the ear."

"Good God almighty." Roza's cheeks went crimson.

"You might have informed me, though, friend Noah, she's also as sharp as a brand-new pair of scissors. My compliments, missy, for those instincts of yours. There *is* something else, and I was just coming to that."

It took him a minute to figure how best to say it. And work up the nerve; confession didn't come naturally to Kaminski. But once he did get his mind right, he didn't pull any punches, wading into himself like a boxer on the attack.

Of all the negative influences working on the Sonder, none was more instrumental in curbing their aggression than the one he'd been saving for last. It was he who'd been keeping the more radical of his men on a leash, commanding they be patient until the underground was ready. How could he have been so stupid and stubborn in the same breath? For a year, he'd let Battle Group-Auschwitz lead him around by the nose, ignoring the calls to action from his own Battle Group.

Meanwhile, two squads had gone to the gas, and now part of a third, men he'd worked with, bonded with—boys, some of them, who'd adopted him as a father. He'd failed them all with his blind bull-headedness, might as well have marched them to the gas himself.

"My intentions were good. Nor am I saying this to try and wriggle out of anything. Guns were proving harder to get than expected. Ammunition, too. And without the underground and its partisans, both we and the thousands supposed to be escaping with us were as good as dead.

"So when Auschwitz told us those partisans weren't available yet and to wait, at my insistence we waited. And waited some more. Until one morning I woke up and blast my bones if it wasn't January. Only then did it start sinking into this thick skull of mine, Noah, that your bosses were playing us Sonder for suckers."

Noah could have crawled under his chair and stayed there. "I know, and I'm so sorry, so ashamed that I—"

"You can stow that. Right now. As you said earlier, you were only obeying orders. And who's to say you'd have made any difference? My own men had been after me for months to see how full of manure our allies in the Stammlager were. But I didn't listen. By then I'd even stopped listening to myself."

"What do you mean," Roza said, "you stopped listening to yourself?"

"You may be thinking," Kaminski said, "that I'm being overly tough on yours truly. That I was too trusting and let the months creep up on me, but only because I believed the success of any revolt depended on having the underground behind it."

He shrank in his seat. "But there's something you don't know, either of you, something that makes the betrayal of my brother Sonder pale in comparison. It's been a year almost to the day since Crematorium II opened. I was there that first gassing, I and 1,493 Jews from Krakow; never will I forget that night or that number.

"The following night—reliving it still in the empty yard of Block 13—I swore to the rising moon, a moon as red as the blood I'd washed from my hands hours before, that if it was the last thing I did, if I did nothing else with the life left me, I'd see that bitch of a crematorium and her three sisters destroyed.

"Don't ask me how I knocked to it, it's too long a story, but it was plain that's what the moon was demanding of me. That I serve as its agent in, if not stopping the killing, then slowing it down.

"*Escape?*" Kaminski spat the word. "The revolt was never about escape. Not ours in the crematoria or that of any prisoner. Its real aim was to put the death machinery out of action. And I *knew* this, practically from the beginning I knew it. But caught up as I became in the dream and drama of escape, in pandering to the underground, I let time get away from me. Assumed we had enough of it to spring both us and the tens of thousands of Jews here before too big a dent could be made in the hundreds of thousands out there.

"So I put it on hold, the oath I'd pledged to that bloody moon, shunted it away like a train onto a siding—which was what I meant by saying I stopped listening to myself. We should have blown the cremos as soon as we had the dynamite to do it, even if we'd had to blow ourselves up with them. But then who could have predicted they'd be so effective, drain half the continent of its Jews in a matter of months?"

He fixed his eyes on a point high up the wall, a faraway look in them. And a sorrow discernible even in the half-dark.

"Now it's too late. The hundreds of thousands are no more. The job I did on the Sonder was nothing to this. The day the bell tolls for me, when it's my turn to die, there'll be a special place for me in hell, a place for those who've not only forsaken their fellow man but, nearly as wicked, their own good intentions."

Neither Noah nor Roza knew what to say. Kaminski's pain had shackled their tongues to the same degree it had loosened his. Roza freed hers up first.

"There are two things, Mr. Kaminski, that need pointing out. One, you *are* being much too tough on yourself. You did what you felt you had to, what you thought best, which in a place such as Birkenau can be difficult to get right. It doesn't do us any good, though, to crucify ourselves when we're wrong. Blame the damnable SS for putting us in those positions to begin with.

"Second, you claim it too late to do something about the crematoria, that they've done their damage and there's no turning back the clock. I get what you're saying, but couldn't disagree more. To send those monsters back to the bottomless pit from which they came is a duty we owe to not only our own people, alive and dead, but to peoples everywhere, even those not yet born.

"It's been less than a year since history was made in the Warsaw ghetto, since our brothers and sisters walled inside it refused any longer to be led meekly to the cattle cars. What has Warsaw taught us, and will one day teach the world when the world hears the story?"

She paused for a second to shift into a higher gear. Noah could feel her do it.

"That the Jew can be as fearsome a warrior as the next person, true. But anyone with a brain could have told you that. The real lesson, the bigger one, is you can either submit to the tyrant, roll on your back and show your belly like a dog, or stand on your feet like a human being and hit back. No matter that you're a civilian, weak with hunger, disease, many of your weapons homemade, fighting with all but bare hands against tanks, artillery, and veteran troops. If you've got what it takes where it counts, if you've the brass, that can be half the battle.

"The heroes of Warsaw had it. For two months, the men, women, and even children of this ragtag excuse of an army took everything the Nazis could throw at them and didn't back down until too few were left alive, with too little ammo, to wage war on the student body of a rabbinical school.

"It was from Noah that I learned of these martyrs and their glorious fight to the death. He told me all he knew of it, though I wasn't going to let you go, was I, you poor man, till you did?"

An overdone stage-sigh was his yes.

"Of the many pictures he painted of that struggle, however, none moved me more than one. On the third day of the rebellion, the freedom fighters raised a flag above their stronghold, a big, in-your-face, blue-on-white Star of David. That flag said it all, its message to the SS loud and clear: 'We will be your slaves no longer. No more will we bow our heads to you. You may kill us, if you can, but never again will you own us.' "

Roza's gaze grabbed the kapo's and held it. "The rebels of Birkenau can send the same message. Leave the same legacy. If so, it will be said of the 12th Sonderkommando that here were men condemned to the ugliest job in the worst place on earth, men so degraded by guilt, so saturated with death that they hardly resembled men anymore, who broke free of their chains to do what none before them had dared.

"And will have done it right, their opening blow the tumbling of those crematoria in which they'd not only seen so much suffering but suffered themselves."

Noah had been watching Kaminski as she spoke, trying to size up his reaction. The man's expression revealed nothing. Roza on the other hand had edged forward in her chair, her eyes as boiling-black as hot tar.

"There are few better ways to hit the Nazis where it hurts than by making matchsticks of those four murder houses so dear to their hearts. And we must remember, after all they've done to us, everyone they've taken from us, that we can neither hurt nor hate the SS too much.

"Not many know this—Noah, a few others—but you could say I owe my life to, of all people, a young *Oberschütze*. Having stewed over it much since, I'd hesitate to call it an act of kindness on his part, but something born more of a grudging respect for my having stood up to him. Stood eyeball to eyeball with him, a carelessness that should have got me shot.

"I'll never forget what he said, or rather the way he said it. 'A Jew with backbone,' he called me, as if this surprised him, and instead of executing me on the spot or turning me in as insubordinate, gave me a favorable report. It was this report that touched off a series of events that in the end got me transferred out of an Aussenkommando and certain death.

"Though he couldn't have foreseen this, and would probably have desired it even less, that boy of a private did save my life. Should I be grateful and forgive him past atrocities he's committed—crimes that as a Death's-head SS he had to have committed—simply because he chose not to commit one against me?

"Does one show of human feeling, and a borderline one at that, make up for that skull he wears on his collar?"

Roza made a face that matched the venom in her voice. "I'd waste him in a heartbeat if I had the chance, shoot him down like the dog he is. They deserve no mercy from us, these murderers of children. All they rate is our ill will and the justice coming to them, and until that day does arrive, whatever resistance we can mount.

"Would my *Oberschütze's* death bring back those he's killed or helped kill? Of course not, just as the destruction of the crematoria won't restore a single one of the thousands deceived into entering them. For that, as you said, kapo, it *is* too late; our beloved dead are past saving.

"But there is still time for the Sonder to save themselves, if not their bodies then their souls. A few bundles of dynamite, and pardon my French, the balls to use them, and they'd be able to call themselves men again."

Kaminski sat silent until satisfied she was done. It had been a fine speech, beyond fine. But...

"Rest assured, my young spark-plug, that my men are in full possession of their, uh, equipment. Didn't they, and that in spite of all the things working against them, come within a hair of putting that dynamite to use? And would have, too, if the Czechs had only gone with the plan."

"Oh. Dear." Roza hadn't intended to offend. "I wasn't implying, sir, that your men... Or at least I didn't mean to."

"And you, my good Noah, *really*. What's all this about a 'flock of sheep' as you so unfortunately put it?"

Noah, in fact, had regretted this as soon as he'd said it. "My apologies, too, kapo. I spoke without thinking. Let me rephrase my question: with the squad as sick about the Familien affair as you are, what do you figure are the odds of a revolt happening anytime soon?"

"That's all that worries us," Roza said. "Whether it's still on."

Kaminski, having got the retractions he wanted, was good again. "Apologies accepted, thank you. As for the revolt, you can quit worrying, the both of you. The 12th Sonderkommando will be ready to fight. My lieutenants and I are already working on it, and we've been getting a good response. Encouragingly good. Recent… developments have arisen that are helping, but it's the men mainly, God love 'em. After coming so close, they're giving every sign of wanting to finish the thing."

"So when might…" Noah stopped himself, afraid of saying the wrong thing again. "I mean, if I could convince my superiors the Sonder had made up their minds to go it alone, without help, maybe they'd be shamed into offering some."

"When might it come about, is that what you're asking? Hard to tell yet. If I had this one at my side to scorch a few ears, it might be a lot sooner." His eyes found Roza's. "You've got quite a way with words, girl. Small wonder you have so many willing to put their heads on the block for you."

"Begging your pardon," she said, "but none of those relieving the Germans of their gunpowder could volunteer fast enough, no pep talk needed. How's that for brave? I don't know about you, kapo, but I'm tired of hearing how bad-ass the SS are. Maybe it's they who should be afraid of us."

Kaminski wasn't confident in setting a date for the revolt because he wasn't sure yet what to make of those developments he'd mentioned, all of which defied understanding. After the meeting was over and he'd returned to Block 13, he secluded himself in his bunk to puzzle over what the Nazis might be up to.

With the transports still scarce, the Sonder could have expected more men to be cut from their ranks by now. But after the February two hundred were packed off to Maidanek, there'd been no second attempt. Instead, the Germans had begun to build the detachment *back up*. Newcomers from the unloading ramp started flooding into Block 13, to the point where any further were going to necessitate a second barracks.

The 12th was closing fast on its predecessor in size, and with no need for such numbers. The SS were even bringing experienced hands in from other camps, nineteen of them last week from the double crematoria at Maidanek.

None of the commando could put a finger on it, though two of the rumors floating around did have possibilities. The first and most credible, and most frightening, was that the Nazis were readying

Auschwitz-Birkenau itself for annihilation. Those touting this cited the gassing of the Family Camp as but its opening phase, with more lagers to come.

This theory meshed nicely with what was common knowledge, the German military's mounting reversals on the eastern front. With hostilities to resume in full come warmer weather, in other words any day now, it wasn't a stretch to imagine the SS engaging in wholesale slaughter before the Red Army could liberate the camp.

A second rumor was less plausible, but did have its adherents. These saw a new wave of Jews rolling in, a last-minute multitude the Nazis had drummed up from somewhere. The problem was, from where? Some posited the Germans retreating from Russia driving its remaining Jews ahead of them. Others, the Gestapo making one final sweep of Europe, rooting out those who'd eluded them up to now. A few even suggested this might include the heretofore protected Jews of the neutral countries, Spain, Switzerland, and Sweden, though the Third Reich would have been hard-pressed to force this at its strongest.

Then there were the Jews of Hungary, so many they could have kept two Birkenaus busy. As an ally of the Reich, Hungary had been able to keep the SS at bay and its Jewish population intact. For the most part, their Gentile countrymen regarded the Hebrews within their borders as Hungarian first and Jewish second. Why now, at this late stage of the war, would Budapest give in to Nazi demands and send so many of its citizens off to be butchered?

Kaminski didn't know what to believe, if any of it. All he did know was what his nose was telling him, and it wasn't good. He'd seen no reason to bother Noah and the girl with it, but an indefinable uneasiness had begun to grow in him. He had no idea what was causing it, but neither was there any brushing it aside: some sort of calamity wasn't only knocking on the door but about to bust it in. Something as devilish as it was big, he could smell it.

Was it the revolt, now that it was again gaining support? He didn't think so. As suicidal an end as it promised, he dreamed of having a rifle in his hands and a German, as Bruno Baum had once sought to tempt him with, in its sights. Besides, his death no longer mattered much to him. He and death were old chums, and with him condemned to the Sonder for going on two years, the thought of becoming even better ones wasn't displeasing.

Just as inviting, he'd be dying happy having finally kept his word. Having seen that disapproving moon of last spring appeased in this one. Knowing a different kind of trumpet had brought down the walls of a different Jericho after all.

Ironically, the SS were playing a part in helping this along, having done themselves no favor by importing the nineteen Sonder from Maidanek. These weren't Jewish civilians but Soviet POWs, hard men hardened further by their violent captivity. They'd fallen immediately in with the conspirators.

Their leader, a Major Borodin, was an unprepossessing fellow on the surface, his granny glasses and weak chin making him resemble more a schoolteacher than a Red infantry officer. He had a talent, though, for commanding not only respect but affection from his men. If they weren't there already, Kaminski got the impression they'd have followed him into hell if he'd asked them to.

But Borodin's value to the cause extended beyond his knack for leadership. He'd been trained in explosives, that was his specialty; more than a demolitions expert, he was an artist. He demonstrated this when his new kapo approached him with the task of constructing a hand grenade using the gunpowder they'd accumulated and what materials were at hand.

That same day, he crafted a device out of an old tin can that he guaranteed would cause casualties, with luck even kill. Inside of a week, he'd assembled a dozen of these, and suddenly the Sonder didn't feel escape quite as remote a possibility.

The nineteen greased the wheels of revolt further with yet another contribution, if inadvertently. At their arrival, several were wearing the same navy-blue serge jackets and tan calfskin boots in which some of the two hundred yanked from the 11th Squad had departed for Maidanek. Questioned, the Russians told how after detraining, all two hundred had been gassed, but not before revealing where they were from.

Any faith the detachment might still have had in SS integrity was shattered forever. For the Germans to go to the length of masking their real purpose by shuttling those selected all the way to another camp meant they couldn't be trusted no matter how tricked-out a story they put forth. If they were to have any chance of surviving, the Sonder would have to stop sitting and start doing. Their fate, as it had and always would, lay in their own hands.

Kaminski would be in his bunk for the rest of the morning. He had a world of work ahead, many new bodies to try and win over to the Battle Group. But before occupying himself with anything, he wanted to etch into memory some of what that astonishing friend of Noah's had said.

Her last name might have sounded a funny note, but she was deadly serious. And feisty as a tomcat. He'd fully expected this Roza Robota to be a firebreather, just not so quotable a one. He saw her words having an effect on his men similar to Borodin's grenades, and like those grenades, the benefit in storing them away for use later.

The barracks that morning was awash in pale sunlight, and toasty warm from a pair of furnaces. Though not uncrowded, neither was it noisy. His wasn't the only bunk occupied, most of his fellow recumbents napping, a reader here and there. The conversation that did reach him was hushed.

Eventually, he, too, dropped off to sleep, lulled there by the caress of muffled voices. He dreamt he was on a train bound for where he couldn't remember. It was a coach, not a cattle car, with cushioned seats, curtained windows, a uniformed conductor. He could tell it was spring; the grassy countryside slipping by was a rainbow of flowers.

That he'd somehow forgot their destination nagged at him more with each mile. He turned his brain inside out, but to no avail—how absent-minded could a person be? Finally, he could stand it no longer and leaned toward the woman sitting next to him. Young, pretty, she was dressed to the nines; from beneath a black coquettish hat and a fishnet black veil peered eyes no less black, set in a strong but generous face.

"Excuse me, miss," Kaminski said in a low voice, not wishing to broadcast his ignorance, "but perhaps you could help me."

"I'll try." The smile was genuine. "What is it you need?"

"This may sound peculiar, but I'm drawing a blank where I shouldn't. Would you be so kind as to inform me... where this train is headed?"

Her expression clouded, going from hospitable to vaguely suspicious. "Why, Budapest, of course," she said, turning away. "Where else?"

*   *   *

The short, slender man in the dashing black uniform, having separated himself from the party, stood alone at the railing taking in the city below. Other guests milled about on the long, narrow balcony, but none had as yet to accost him. It was a typical March day for this part of the world, cold but not uncomfortably so. The sky was more white than blue in the early afternoon sun, a small, intense sun that burned with little heat.

A young SS subaltern in white serving jacket appeared at his side. "Champagne, sir?"

The tall, bubbly flutes glistened a watery yellow on their tray. "No thank you," the man said. If he was to drink now, he could forget about working later.

He would rather there weren't a party requiring his presence, but it would have been bad form not to show. Even without drinking, it was a waste of half a day, and much was left to do, their work barely begun. He might have declined to come anyway except that this gathering of SS and army brass was partly in his honor.

"Congratulations, Herr *Obersturmbannführer.*" He turned to see an SS officer, a captain, whose name he couldn't recall.

"You flatter me," said Adolf Eichmann with a slight bow. "The glory, however—or should I say the gratitude?—isn't mine alone. There are others who have worked as hard for this moment."

"Your modesty becomes you," the young officer said. "Permit me also to congratulate you for that."

Eichmann bowed again, then turned back to the railing. He wasn't trying to be rude, he just wasn't up for company. This was why he'd snuck out here, to get away from the press of bodies and innocuous patter inside. He wanted to be alone with his thoughts, and this view that never disappointed.

He'd fallen in love with Budapest upon first experiencing it two years ago. With its antique architecture, narrow streets, countless statues and parks, it possessed an Old-World charm Berlin couldn't touch.

The vista from the penthouse floor of the Majestic Hotel was a particularly good one. Visible was the winding, silver serpentine of the Danube, and three of the ornate Renaissance bridges that spanned it. Nestled against the river was the ancient Jewish Quarter, exotic in its timelessness. Oddly, it was one of his favorite neighborhoods; to walk its streets and bazaars was to enter a portal into the past.

Or maybe not so odd. Despite the route his life had taken, and though he would never have admitted it, he'd developed, if not an admiration for the Jews, then a respect for those isolated nuggets of worth and wisdom to be found in even the most degraded of peoples.

This, and so much more, would never have happened but for a career decision he'd made years ago. As a new enlistee in the *Sicherheitsdienst*, the SD, or Security Police, he'd been put to work keeping files on the Freemasons, as dead-end an assignment as might be imagined. Perceiving in the Jews an infinitely greater opportunity for advancement, he set out to become an expert on that peculiar race. Nor was it long before he was able to pass as such, having submerged himself in its history, culture, religion—in all things Judaic, down to mastering the basics of Yiddish.

After that, it became a question of catching the right men's attentions, notably *Reichsführer*-SS Heinrich Himmler and Himmler's deputy, SS-*Obergruppenführer* Reinhard Heydrich, commander of the SD. After several years as Heydrich's assistant, in 1939 Eichmann was appointed director of Gestapo Department IV-B4 of the RSHA, the Reich Main Security Office. As head of the Chancellery's Jewish Desk, he was responsible for the enforcement of Nazi policy toward the Jews in all occupied territories, making him one of the most powerful men in Europe.

Not bad, he allowed, as he let his eyes wander this scenic expanse of the Danube, for a man employed not all that long ago as a salesman in an oil-field equipment company.

Aside from his humble origins, his encounter with the captain had brought home what he'd always considered another drawback to his ambitions. No matter the pinnacles he'd reached, he'd felt a twinge of self-consciousness in this subordinate's presence. A full head taller than Eichmann, broad-shouldered, *blond...* this was one reason he'd turned his back on the man. His own appearance was a scandal to him in its resemblance to that of the archetypal Jew. Spindly of frame, balding, with a protruding, bony nose and a neck as scrawny as a chicken's, he suspected not even his SS uniform entirely made up for the Semitic-moneylender image.

Not that he could do a lot about it beyond continuing to make his achievements outweigh his looks. As much as he prized his official title, chief of IV-B4, he took equal pride in those less formal appellations his reputation had earned him. Foremost among these was a name the Jews themselves had given him, *der Bluthund*, the Bloodhound, for his success in tracking them down and handing them over to their fate.

His peers, meanwhile, lauded him as the wizard of transportation, the magician of trains, able to conjure rolling stock seemingly out of the air, fill it with Jews collected from the Norwegian Sea to the Mediterranean, then deliver those Jews relatively intact all the way to the gas chambers in Poland. And this with an increasingly hard-pressed military competing with him for access to both that stock and its rails.

The Wehrmacht had been busy in the Balkans recently, and with the direction the war was headed, about to get busier. The Red Army had targeted Hungary as the gateway to Austria, and once it finished reclaiming the Ukraine then sweeping south out of Romania, the land of the Magyars would turn into a racing ground for Russian tanks. Admiral Horthy, the Hungarian regent, had wired Hitler he was withdrawing his divisions from the eastern front the abler to defend his country. In truth, he was working in secret to negotiate an armistice with the Soviets.

Informed of this, the *Führer* flew into one of his patented rages and ordered his ally invaded. In little more than a week, Hungary's army was routed, its government toppled, Horthy under arrest—and its previously untouchable Jews there for the plucking.

Enter Eichmann and the well-oiled German engine of extinction. Actually, the *Obersturmbannführer* and his staff had made the Majestic their headquarters even before the invasion began. With its outcome in no doubt, he'd wanted to get a jump on mining the amazing bonanza of Jews fortune had seen fit to lay at his feet. At the rate the Reds were expected to advance, he wasn't counting on the calendar cutting him much slack.

Hungary had long been a boil on Eichmann's backside. Charged with making Europe permanently Judenrein, freed forever from the

Hebrew death grip, for two years he'd badgered, cajoled, threatened the authorities in Budapest into relinquishing their Chosen People, and hadn't so much as a single transport to show for it. Now, thanks to the bumbling cowardice of their government, the Hungarian Jews were his at last.

This was one reason for the party today, but not the only one. The SS had come, of course, to hail their and their colonel's victory, but the army was there to celebrate one, too. The Wehrmacht had taken Budapest without resistance the day before, and scheduled a ceremonial march of its troops down Nicola Boulevard for this afternoon.

He wondered if maybe he shouldn't be getting back inside—the babble of voices was insistent, the clinking of glasses, the laughter—but decided he wouldn't be missed a few minutes more. Going over it even briefly had put his mind on his mission, a subject admittedly never far away. Much had been accomplished, but a whole mountain of work remained.

The country, having been divided into six zones, was to be emptied of its Jews one zone at a time. Until this went into effect, arrests were ongoing, thousands of them, from leading anti-Nazi political, industrial, and religious figures down to Jews randomly snatched off the streets and from their homes.

A Central Jewish Council was formed. Consisting of that doomed people's leaders nationwide, its task was to compile lists of all Jews and their addresses. To avoid snags before they developed, every county and municipal administration, along with state and local police, were on their way to being Nazified. Without the help of sympathetic Hungarians, Eichmann knew not even German efficiency was going to outpace the Russians.

It would take the Council weeks to draw up its lists, and weeks more for the SS and its minions to round up those on them and herd them into ghettos. By mid-May, he hoped, the transports from Zone 1 should begin arriving at Birkenau. He estimated a travel period of two days, up to double that for the farther zones. Postulating a forty-car train on average, with a hundred deportees to a wagon (the Hungarian boxcar was somewhat smaller than the Polish), each transport would consist of four thousand units. How many of these could Birkenau absorb in a day? He reckoned three, maybe four, anything above that a bonus.

That it was to be Birkenau by itself couldn't be helped, with Maidanek, although its two crematoria were little more than sheds by comparison, taking on some of the load. The other four annihilation centers were long since shut down. The exigencies of last summer, they were built to be provisional, ill-equipped to handle such a deluge of flesh as was coming. Not only small by comparison, each employed the slow-acting carbon monoxide in its gas chambers, an all-around less efficient poison than Zyklon-B.

Prisoner disturbances had been the deciding factor in closing Treblinka and Sobibor, but by then, like their counterparts Chelmno and Belzec, both had outlived their usefulness.

Eichmann was fine, however, with it being Birkenau or nothing. Built to be permanent, it was a remarkable facility, and not the same camp it had been even a month ago. He'd been keeping tabs on what its hierarchy was doing to prepare for the Hungarians, and was impressed. The most dramatic of these was the building of a new rail spur. Hundreds of prisoners labored day and night laying lines right up to the steps of Crematoria II and III, a three-track system, complete with a concrete unloading platform even larger than the old one. This "Jewish ramp" would halve the time it took to get the payload from the trains into the gas chambers.

All roads running to the death houses were being resurfaced, and construction accelerated on the unfinished B3 lager. The work, again, knew no clock, the camp lit up at night by the phosphorus beams of anti-aircraft searchlights. The effects warehouses were being cleared of their contents to make room, and never had there been as large a Sonder or Canada commando.

Four transports a day, though, was the better part of twenty thousand subhumans. If four-fifths of these were selected for the crematoria straight off the ramp as projected, not even their forty-plus ovens would be able to cope.

Then again, Birkenau boasted an excellent fire-pit program. Open-air incineration had the potential to transform the very face of industrial-scale killing and disposal, its capacity dependent only on the availability of fuel. It was this more than anything that had put Eichmann's mind to rest about entrusting the operation to this one camp only. Say fifteen thousand bodies on average run through the machinery per diem, and this was lowballing it—at that volume, Hungary could be cleansed of its Jews before summer was over.

In contemplation of this, his heart went to beating faster, a glow like warm honey to spread from his stomach...

When a commotion to his rear snapped him out of his reverie. A rush of people was spilling from out the sliding-glass doors of the suite onto the balcony, its railing quickly two-deep in uniforms. It was what everyone had been waiting for, the column of soldiers supposed to parade down Nicola.

Within minutes, the first of it was passing below. The crowd that lined both curbs, mostly local Nazis, was making its crowd noises, farther back a scattering of silent, sullen citizens who for whatever reason had chosen to endure this indignity.

The soldiers marched without a band, but music wasn't needed. The boulevard resounded with the metronomic stomp of the goosestep—this was their music. At their head rode a lone horseman, a color sergeant in full battle dress, tall, stately, perched on the saddle as if born to it. With his ebony mount stepping as proudly as the formations behind it, upon drawing even with the Majestic the sergeant presented his sword in salute.

They were magnificent, these troops. The gray battalions tramped past in stiff, flawless precision, the sun bouncing off a solid river of helmets. Eichmann shaded his eyes to the west, but could see no end to the procession. Both awed and perplexed, he couldn't imagine legions as disciplined as these giving up a foot of ground to the Mongoloid rabble of the Russians. How this had happened, and was certain to happen again, could only be explained by the sheer force of numbers that rabble was able to muster. Such, he mused ruefully, was the power of vermin, its propensity for gaining the upper hand simply by breeding itself there.

All in all, though, it gladdened the soul to look upon such an army, on so reassuring a display of German might. Afterward, the party grew noticeably sprightlier. Eichmann, feeling more sociable now, too, was drawn back into it. At one point, he found himself in the company of three generals, all from the Wehrmacht—one of them the widely-known, curmudgeonly Steiner, a soldier's soldier of the old school. Who by this stage of the proceedings was well on his way to getting properly drunk.

"They tell me, colonel," he said, the condescension in the word "colonel" unmistakable, "this is a glorious day for you, too."

"It is a day of which any German can be proud," Eichmann said, ignoring the slight.

"Yes, but you've finally got your hands on those Jews you've been after. Is this not true?"

Eichmann nodded once, curtly.

Steiner turned to General Ehler on his right, and not entirely under his breath muttered, "Which makes it a bad day indeed to be one of those poor people."

While Ehler blanched, Eichmann stiffened. "Those poor people, as you put it, general, are the ones who started this war, a miscalculation they are rightly paying for now. Or are you not aware of the *Führer's* thoughts on the matter?"

"As the simplest of soldiers," the other replied with a smile, "I can only concern myself with those thoughts of the *Führer* that come in the form of orders issued me in the field. But on the subject of orders," he said, the smile falling, "I've a question, if you don't mind, that's been troubling me awhile now."

"Go ahead, shoot," Eichmann said. "As long as you don't take the invitation literally."

Steiner's companions laughed in relief at this attempt to break the tension. Only he remained grim.

"It's been my experience in the Balkans and elsewhere, Herr Eichmann, that without exception precedence has been given those RSHA transports of yours. And by that, I mean over supply and even armament and troop trains. Again and again, I've watched the military left hanging so the SS can use the rails to shuffle its cargoes of women and children around.

"My question is that in this desperate hour, this crucial stage of the war, can we expect the same insanity to prevail?"

Eichmann never ceased to marvel at the power of alcohol to loosen men's tongues. Could the fool not see he was flirting with treason?

"You mention orders," he told this Steiner. "Well, I'm only following mine. And in answer to your question, yes—the Hungarian transports will have priority over all other traffic."

"At the expense of success in battle? The lives of the brave men fighting the battle?"

"At the expense of Germany itself if necessary. There is more at stake here than you seem to realize, general."

"All I can say then is that you and your whole bunch of—"

"What—what the general would say, colonel," Ehler stammered, "is he wishes you and your men all the best in your mission." He then whispered at some length in Steiner's ear.

This had its effect; the man wasn't quite drunk enough to sign his own death warrant. With obvious effort, he composed himself. Not that he was done handing out the insults.

"You're right, Karl," he told Ehler. "I should probably shut up now. But first…"

Addressing Eichmann, he drew himself to his full height. "May your SS, sir, enjoy the same triumph over the noncombatants of this damned country that the Wehrmacht did against its armed forces. And you can take that for exactly how it sounds," he added with a scowl.

Though the taunt hardly escaped him, Eichmann took it in stride. He had more important things on his mind than this pathetic relic of the past. In fact, he sought to be gracious, sort of.

"Allow me, gentlemen, to propose a toast." A waiter was summoned, champagne passed around. "To our valiant troops!" he said, lifting his glass. "And the many victories over the Jew their conquests have brought us!"

He made a point to stare straight at Steiner as he spoke. Just so there wouldn't be any misunderstanding.

Spring

───────────────────────────────

SS-Master Sergeant Möll wasn't having the best of days. Here it was a long way from noon and already there were problems, beginning with the fifth straight morning of a drizzling rain that might let up for a while, then come back wet as ever. A featureless, gray ceiling so low it felt as if one could reach up and touch it had parked itself above Birkenau and had as yet to show the least sign of leaving.

It was purposeful, this rain, a living, malevolent thing come to torture him for the sheer pleasure of watching him squirm. Nor could its timing have been worse. Intermittent it may have been, but was playing havoc all the same with his efforts to get the camp ready for the Hungarians. Not undividedly, thank goodness, but in several critical areas, one of which, the fire pits, could prove calamitous if digging were to remain hampered.

As frustrating as this was, Möll had little cause to complain. That he was back where he belonged should have had him counting his blessings instead of his woes. Just ten days ago (ten days!) he'd been marooned at Fürstengrube still—until in the unpromising middle of a typically uneventful morning, a phone call had given him not only a second chance but what had all the trappings of the chance of a lifetime.

The founding commandant of Auschwitz, *Obersturmbannführer* Höss, had six months ago been transferred to the commission at Oranienburg that oversaw the entire concentration-camp system. Rumors were rife of personal gain and other improprieties Höss had committed on his watch, but the sergeant knew nothing of these, nor cared. All that mattered to him was that in response to the recent happy events in Hungary, the *Obersturmbannführer* had been recalled to Auschwitz on May 1st to supervise the elimination of that country's nest of Jews.

One of his first acts had been to telephone Möll and order him back to Birkenau, not merely to assist in the Hungarian action but to assume management of it. This meant command of all four crematoria, along with the other execution and disposal sites.

He, Otto Möll, in charge of the whole show! He'd fantasized such a thing often, during many a long, empty night in Fürstengrube, but though he would have bet at the time he hadn't seen the last of Birkenau, any thought of the crematoria being his to do with as he saw fit had remained just that, a fantasy.

But not an idle one. He'd filled it with as many practicalities as he could think of, imagining how he might improve operations were the power his. This ended up giving him a head start when the call to glory did come. Upon returning to his old posting, he'd hit the ground running.

His first order of business had been the shuffling of crematoria personnel. Having deemed him too soft for the job, he'd replaced the *Kommandoführer* of Number Two with First Sergeant Muhsfeld, already top dog at Number Three. The no-nonsense Muhsfeld wasn't only intelligent and an excellent organizer but a dedicated killer. Möll had seen him at work, and no one, himself included, was more devoted than the *Oberscharführer* to the holy task of rendering the Jewish bacterium extinct.

Still, two crematoria were a lot to ask of one man, so he appointed a brace of corporals to back Muhsfeld up. Number Four, which for some reason had been under the command of a lowly *Oberschütze*, he'd considered at first handing to the debonair Captain Hössler. But the man, as his superior in rank, would have been difficult to control, and too much the dandy to dirty his hands with Krema work.

Instead, he gave *Unterscharführer* Johann Gorges the job. The fortyish sergeant was a shameless blowhard and overly fond of his schnapps (his florid countenance had earned him the nickname Moshe Beetface among the Sonder), but could be counted on to obey orders, he didn't care what they were. Which was also why he chose to retain *Oberscharführer* Voss as chief of Number Five. He also drank to excess, and was far too lenient with his SS subordinates, but was a punctilious follower of orders, and as unshrinking a killer as Muhsfeld.

Just to be on the safe side, Möll assigned a trustworthy *Sturmmänn* to each, to aid them in their duties, of course, but also to keep tabs on them.

In what he had little doubt would be his best people move of all, he'd acquired the services of a young sergeant who gave every indication of having what it took to make his own job easier. Actually, *Unterscharführer* Karl Eckardt was older than he, but with his babyface good looks could have passed for twenty. Tall, athletic, with hair so blond it was almost white, he was every inch the Nordic nonpareil, which should have made the paunchy, freckled Möll dislike him at first sight. But so great was the respect Eckardt had shown him, deferring to him as demonstratively as he would a senior officer, his new boss took a shine to him, a view amplified when the man proved capable in the bargain.

He'd been seconded to the crematoria because of his fluency in Hungarian; born and raised in Budapest, it could have been his first language. That he also spoke a fair Polish was too good to be true. For now, he was keeping this Eckardt as his adjutant, and so in demand was he day and night, so laden with responsibility, he truly did need an assistant. Down the road, though, he had other plans for him, namely as *Kommandoführer* of what had been re-designated the Bunker 5 complex.

This was the larger of the two temporary gas bunkers decommissioned last year with the opening of the crematoria. The old farmhouse-turned-death-house was being revived for use again in special handling, in conjunction with three undressing barracks and four adjacent fire pits. Eckardt's linguistic acumen would be invaluable at this new site, and with Bunker 5 located in the woods, well away from its four cousins, Möll wanted someone over there he wouldn't have to babysit.

He'd had to make time this very morning to assess the damage done one of the complex's changing-barracks by last night's rain. A large tree had dislodged itself and crashed onto the roof. Repairs would be considerable, and a waste of man-hours. Apart from waking up to rain again, this would be the first thing to go wrong with his day, if far from the worst.

After he'd solidified his chain of command, he turned his attention to the excavation of the fire pits. No one was exactly sure when the Hungarians were due, but once they did come, the bodies would be spilling out of the gas chambers like grain from ruptured sacks. The ovens couldn't begin to keep up, which in the spring sun would create a mess repulsive beyond comprehension.

It was imperative the pits be ready. Why his superiors had filled in the originals and grassed them over he didn't know, but they were irretrievable now. Not even he could pinpoint where they'd been, nor was there a map to help him. The only thing to do was carve out new ones, and this was where the rain proved its most crippling. The dense, sticky clay soil only grew denser and stickier when wet; the Sonder digging in the stuff could have been shoveling into half-melted rubber. Nor were they able to get a decent footing in the ankle-deep mud. Möll had ordered five pits finished within the week, but despite a dozen tantrums, and as many dead Sonder to show for them, had to settle for two.

At least he had them, and to spec, each a rectangular forty meters by eight by two. He could take some satisfaction knowing these two pits alone would double the incineration capacity of Crematoria IV and V combined.

But something other than the Hungarians had him in a rush, something he'd been dreaming about since Fürstengrube. No, before then, since his revelation of a year and a half ago when disinterring the corpses of the 110,000. The self-fueling fire pit had the potential to revolutionize the field of mass disposal. By recycling the human fat that would otherwise be lost, one could dig as many pits as desired without fretting too much over kerosene. At twelve hundred corpses per pyre reduced to ashes every six hours, the only limit to the destruction became not how many Jews a day could be incinerated, but exterminated.

The gas chamber was now the weak link in the chain, if one could call, with the addition of Bunker 5, an easy seventeen, eighteen thousand deaths a day weak.

Möll had experimented with a few table-top models at Fürstengrube, but without an actual pit to try it out on his invention remained theoretical. Now he had that pit, and another if it came to that. All he needed to test theory against practice was for this insane rain to quit so he could lay some concrete—and as the morning wore on, it became apparent he was going to get his wish. Around nine o'clock, the one big cloud, as if afraid to try the Cyclops' patience any longer, started breaking up into smaller ones before tumbling out of sight to the east.

An ecstatic Möll, blueprint in hand, grabbed Eckardt and made on his motorcycle for the meadow abutting Crematorium V. After assembling a work gang, he picked the driest of the two pits, had it suctioned out, then he and his second, with a compass, tape measure, and a ball of string, staked out a strip ninety centimeters wide extending almost the length of it down the center. Helping them was the prisoner he'd recruited from the Bauhof to be his foreman. When satisfied with the placement of the string, his new boss called him over.

"I selected you for this job, one, because of your experience with cement, and two, because you are German. It doesn't pose that difficult a problem, but does demand a respect for detail. Are you with me so far?"

"Yes, Herr *Hauptscharführer*." He stood at attention, staring straight ahead.

Möll studied him as he spoke. "It's all there in that blueprint you're holding. I want two channels dug fifteen centimeters deep the width of the strings, each starting at the center of the pit and slanting downward at an angle of seven degrees. That's seven degrees precisely, no more, no less. How many degrees, kapo?"

"Seven, sir. Precisely."

"Each trench is to empty after twenty meters into a reservoir four meters long, two wide, and one deep. You said rebar would be required for these, but I want those grids put down quick. No reason to make them works of art. And you're positive the trenches when laid won't need reinforcing?"

"Not, sir, if we mix the cement with rock and bits of scrap metal. That should allow them to hold their shape."

The message in Möll's eyes was, You'd *better* be positive. "When done, the channels should catch their share of the liquid fat given up by the bodies and funnel it into the reservoirs. From where it can be ladled onto the fire. That, in short, is the mechanics of it—but do you remember me telling you what this is all about?"

Upon summoning him last week, Möll had explained everything from the how of his project to the why. The man had been startled, then sickened by what he'd heard. Not that, from a practical standpoint, it didn't make sense. This was what he'd found so dreadful about the thing, it made perfect sense.

"Yes, sir, I remember. Remember it... well."

"Excellent, for now I can add this. Not only is this job of yours, small as it may seem, significant to the future of Germany and its people, our people, kapo"—here he stood closer, facing him—"but to me personally. Do I make myself understood?"

The prisoner could only nod. A large bead of sweat trickled from out the stubble on his scalp.

"Let me spell it out for you anyway. I've been waiting a long time for this day. It means a lot to me. Do you envision anything cropping up, *anything*, that might spoil it for me?"

"Nothing, *mein Hauptscharführer*. All will be done as you say, down to the last detail."

"I do hope so," Möll said, walking away, "as should you, my dear kapo. Trust me, as should you."

Four steps up the small ladder to ground level, he paused. "Follow the blueprint, it's as simple as that. I'll be back in three hours. Don't let me find it unfinished."

He roared off on his motorcycle, Eckardt in the sidecar. It would take about that long for the cement to harden enough to do a trial run with water. In the interval, there was much to do at Bunker 5. He needed, among other things, to site and stake the four fire pits he intended to situate there. These would bring the total to nine, a number he was content with. It was hard to imagine needing more than nine.

When he reappeared a little early at 12:30, a grinning Hannibal was riding next to him. Unable in his excitement to put it off any longer, he'd left Eckardt at the bunker. He made for the pit at a trot, ignoring the ladder and leaping nimbly down. There it was, spread out in all its splendor in front of him—his vision brought to life, the dream made reality! Warily, he walked the length of one channel, inspecting it and its reservoir. Doing the same on the other side, again he seemed satisfied.

Returning to the center of the apparatus, he ordered two buckets of water lowered. Pouring the contents of one into the left-hand gutter, he watched eagerly. The water sloshed obediently along... until slowing to a stop short of where it was supposed to go. Managing to keep his calm, he emptied the second pail into the opposite side, only to see the liquid form a pool twelve meters from the basin at that end.

The half-dozen Sonder he'd had tail him into the pit looked on in terror. They knew what was coming, nor did it take long. Möll swooped up the first bucket, and wildly swinging both, launched himself at those nearest. Bashing a few heads wasn't enough for him, however. Flinging the buckets after the retreating men, he cornered the kapo he'd left in charge.

"You stupid shit!" he screamed, droplets of spittle jumping from his mouth like tiny, hopping insects. "I give you a simple enough job, and what do you do?" He whistled his dog over. The creature flew to him, ears vertical in anticipation. "Hannibal here could have done better, my dog! I ought to—"

For some seconds, he stared at the ground, gulping air, as if trying to get a grip on himself. But it was no use. "*Ought* to? The hell with that—I think I damn well *will!*"

He whipped out his Luger and aimed it at the man, who closing his eyes began a silent prayer. But two seconds turned into five, then ten, and to everyone's disbelief the gun went unfired. Möll let the outstretched arm slowly drop.

In spite of his bungling foreman's performance, he knew that to replace him would take more time than he could spare. On top of which, it was his own fault as much as anyone's. He, after all, was the engineer here, and should have led by example, this first go-around at any rate. He'd debated this earlier, but Bunker 5 had beckoned and he'd thought to save a few hours. Now he'd have to scramble to get back those he'd lost.

Jamming the pistol back in its holster, he called for a guard to fetch him a pair of overalls. And hurried another two off for more men and picks and shovels. In twenty minutes, he was hard at work with the angle board, a spirit-level, a reinforced crew, and a look that promised a bullet to any man who didn't snap to his orders.

As for the derelict kapo, he kept him glued to his side. His duties prevented him from installing the remaining eight of his contraptions himself, but he'd be damned if after today his protégé wouldn't be able to in his sleep.

The concrete was still wet enough to break up the defective parts of the channels without using jackhammers. In an hour they were gone, the downward angles re-dug where necessary, and new concrete in place. All that remained was for it to harden. Möll sent the crew to assist their comrades excavating Pit 3, and since his presence no doubt was needed elsewhere, somewhere, everywhere, decided to make a sweep of the entire area.

After this latest, most demoralizing one, he had to wonder what other mishaps the day held. At least the rain had ended. Released from its prison of clouds, the sun beat down as if to make up for its absence. He shed the overalls and slipped back into his tunic, but in the heat left it unbuttoned. With Hannibal next to him, he set off at a crawl on his motorcycle. He wanted to take it slow so as to satisfy himself everything was as it should be.

Not that he wouldn't have been tempted to dawdle regardless, the spectacle that swirled around him a fascinating study in contrasts. Dotting the lime-green, new grass of the meadow, its gaily-colored sprays of wildflowers, were greasy heaps of machinery and loose tools, everything from hand wrenches to pneumatic drills, spools of wire to electric generators. The 12th Sonderkommando was at five hundred men and growing; scores of them with wheelbarrows and carts crisscrossed the site at a run, dodging the big trucks lumbering in and out. These were busy provisioning the fuel dumps rising here and there—more like garbage dumps actually, this no exaggeration. Protected from the weather by tarps or ramshackle roofs on stilts, they sheltered dismembered trees, old railroad ties, broken timbers, pieces of planks and boards, barrels of methanol, kerosene, and waste oil, bundles of old rags for drenching in the latter and studding the pyres with.

It may have resembled so much trash, but stockpiled and covered it was going to come in handy, especially on rainy days. The fire pits would be as in demand in damp weather as dry.

Möll was in his element. What another might have decried as nature despoiled, the land scarred, he saw as a thing of beauty, the sum of careful planning and hard work. Winding his bike through the clutter, he marveled at its grimy pageantry, soaked up its music. The noise was without pause, men shouting, motors roaring, the woodpecker staccato of hammers. Blasting from the forest came the angry shriek of chainsaws.

Still in a huff over the delay at Pit 1, his anger was softened some by the sights and sounds of this mad, multidimensional hornet's nest he'd created. Whatever setbacks might arise, and these were to be expected in so vast an undertaking, it never ceased brightening the mood of its newest officiary to know that without him Birkenau wouldn't be close to reaching the level of destructive power it was approaching.

Take what greeted him on his way to Crematorium V. Here lay another of those ideas he'd hatched at Fürstengrube. No more now than naked rebar, a grid of interwoven steel rods hugging the ground, with the rain out of the picture it would soon become an enormous concrete slab for the crushing of material the fire pits left whole. One advantage the ovens had over their parallels outdoors was the thoroughness with which they consumed their human fodder. During express work, some of the larger bones might survive the flames, but as a rule all that remained were crumbly fragments, if that.

The fire pits, however, never failed to leave sizable chunks behind, entire femurs, skulls, pelvises, burnt to brittleness but intact. To the high-muck-a-mucks at Oranienburg this was unacceptable; they wanted as little physical evidence of the dead lying around as possible.

Möll had never understood this. He saw no reason to hide, as if ashamed of it, the selfless work they were doing, work he would have thought his superiors eager to take credit for. The world in its hypocrisy might holler some when informed of the fate of Europe's Jews, but in the end, having as much to gain from such a housecleaning as the Germans, could only be grateful.

Was grateful now. Both Russian and of late even American bombers droned regularly overhead, their targets on occasion the factories at Monowitz, but more often on a course elsewhere. There could be no question all three camps had been extensively photographed from the air, nor was it possible to mistake what the biggest of them was. Constant trains, the unloading platform, the lines of people filing into buildings with chimneys spewing smoke— even without their spies on the ground, the Allies knew all too well what was going on at Birkenau.

Yet continued to do nothing. A handful of planes could have disrupted the killings in minutes, maybe halted them indefinitely. So why in the name of all that was irrefutable hadn't they?

The answer was obvious. The adversaries in this great conflict that had come to be known as the Second World War may have disagreed on a lot, but on this clearly didn't: the Jew, their mutual enemy, had to go. If it were up to Möll, he'd have kept the foe informed of the body count as it progressed. Maybe then that foe wouldn't have been in such a hurry to beat a path to Berlin.

But it wasn't up to him. Or to paraphrase one of the few lines he knew from English or any poetry, His was not to reason why, his but to do and die. Good soldier that he was, therefore, and perfectionist to boot, he'd not only conceived of this site for the pulverizing of charred bone, and an identical one at Bunker 5, but would be equipping each with an array of sieves with which to sift the refuse. In error as they were, if his SS higher-ups insisted nothing remain of their victims, then nothing there would be. He had no intention of letting anything bigger than a fingernail get past him.

Not far from where the four hundred square-meters of this ash and bone slab were to be loomed Crematorium V. Möll noted with satisfaction that its chimneys were busy, a small transport from Belgrade. It was always a relief to see smoke coming from the Mogilevs, given what junk they'd turned out to be. He parked his motorcycle and with his dog went in search of Sergeant Voss.

The *Kommandoführer* was in the undressing area supervising the transfer of corpses to cremation. Voss's face, dripping sweat in the heat, fell at the sight of him before breaking into a fake smile. Möll was used to the reaction, enjoyed it.

"Sergeant," he said, parading toward him.

"Good afternoon, *Hauptscharführer*. What can I—You there!" he hollered at a group of Sonder. "Two at a time, you idiots! If you drag them by the wrists, you can take two at a time, Christ!"

Then to his visitor, with a conspiratorial roll of the eyes, "What can I do for you, sir?"

Was this little outburst meant to impress him? He was used to that, too. "I was passing by and wanted to see if that new paste was helping any." He'd come up with a different formula for filling the cracks in the furnaces, something hopefully more binding. "Have you noticed any improvement?"

"Some maybe, sir, it's hard to tell yet. So far so good, I guess. It—By the *wrists*, I said, goddammit!"

Möll observed to his chagrin no less than six hundred bodies cluttering the floor of the undressing room. How inefficient these smaller Kremas were, how poorly planned from entrance to exit. As troublesome a sight as this was in light of the multitudes coming, it was mitigated some when to his amusement he saw Hannibal sniffing tentatively at the private parts of a stack of females. One plus to keeping a dog, he reflected fondly, was its ability to distract its owner from his worries.

He indulged himself a moment before returning to Voss. "You do understand, I trust, sergeant, what even now is in your future. What's creeping up on you."

"My future?" Unsure just what the hard to predict Cyclops was getting at, he grew uneasy.

"Three, four transports a day. Some days more maybe, if that's even possible. In all honesty, do you see your Number Five being up to it? To dealing with such numbers?"

"Oh... that." Relieved to hear it only that, Voss gave his answer some thought. "In all honesty, sir, what would you have me say? We will do our very best, that is all I can promise."

Möll had hoped for more, but would settle for this. In appreciation of the other's candor, and what for him was no small concession, he dropped his distant tone for an almost comradely one.

"Which is all that can be asked of any of us, I suppose. You are doing a fine job, *Oberscharführer*. Keep up the good work."

His first day back in Birkenau, he'd discovered all four of the crematoria, in if not inoperable condition, on their way to it. And from little more than a lack of care. Among the many shortcomings of Höss's successor as commandant, the traitorously lax SS-*Obersturmbannführer* Artur Liebehenschel, was his failure to adequately provide for the death factories. Möll found himself the recipient of a long list of neglect. Most urgently, all six smokestacks were struggling, half of them near collapse. The firebricks lining their interiors had to be replaced—those that hadn't already fallen and were clogging the flues—those flues cleared, and the chimney walls strengthened with heavy iron bands.

Even more damning was the filth that had been allowed to accumulate. Not an oven looked as if it had been clinkered in days. He ordered them cleaned from the inside out, their cast-iron doors and facings re-blacked, the hinges and rollers oiled, even the brick furnaces enclosing them given a bath. He also had their electric generators overhauled, along with the motorized Exhators that fanned the coke. Each cremation room received so thorough a scrubbing, down to removing the soot many had assumed ineradicable, it shone as if it had yet to be used.

The undressing rooms were painted, the gas chambers soaped down, swabbed, and slathered with fresh plaster, all light bulbs changed, windows washed and fixtures polished, drains flushed, the floors refinished and disinfected. Nothing escaped him. Harking back to his original posting at the main camp as groundkeeper, he even had the crematoria compounds spruced up, the lawns re-sodded where needed, the flowerbeds replenished.

But there was more to it than merely giving the four a face-lift. In Crematoria II and III, it went beyond the cosmetic, the repairable even. Both were in sore want of new elevators, the old ones having shown themselves too light for the job. They'd been running in fits and starts awhile, and soon wouldn't be running at all.

At first, Commandant Höss had balked at the cost, but eventually acceded to his sergeant's logic: II and III with wonky elevators were like a horse with three good legs only, a car with no spare tire. Höss put in a rush order for replacements. Möll was also awaiting delivery of two forced-draft ventilation systems for the gas chambers of IV and V, the same as those in their better-appointed big sisters. Mechanical de-aeration wasn't only safer than the natural but quicker.

Though much of the work was done, much remained. He was on the go all day and half the night, hadn't slept worth speaking of since he got back. Not that he regretted losing one minute of that sleep, picturing himself sitting on his butt back in Fürstengrube still. Those minutes that would have been made empty by the semi-coma of slumber were packed full instead of the intriguing business of mass extinction. Or rather mobilizing for same, which had its own attractions.

The SS were breaking new ground, expanding old frontiers, entering territory unexplored in all of history. The world had never witnessed such a blood sacrifice as was coming, nor the consuming fires to follow, and there he stood stage center, the high priest, the anti-rabbi presiding at the pyre. It was as if his disadvantaged life, with its often deflating twists and turns, had been leading despite them to this exact point. Never had he believed more vehemently in the greatness ahead for him.

Nor was there any ignoring the fun of being boss, of strutting about like the cock of the roost, master of the regal pose, the theatrical entrance. Especially when that entrance set prisoners and guards alike to quaking in their shoes. To Möll, there could be no bigger praise.

Equally bracing, without him having anticipated the reaction, were the many obstacles thrown in front of him that instead of wearing him down only invigorated him. Despite the volcanic eruptions of temper they were apt to unleash, secretly he welcomed these roadblocks, the challenge they presented. Most of them, that is. There'd been nothing redeeming about the week's interminable rain, nor the setback today at Pit 1.

But not everything he'd inherited was a headache, the Jewish ramp coming foremost to mind. Collecting Hannibal, he set off for that inspired piece of engineering, bypassing Number Four and its hopeless ovens (it made him sick just thinking about them) and Three as well, which but for its elevator was functioning so smoothly there was no reason to stop in.

The Jewish ramp had been a pleasant surprise. Where the initiative for it had come from he couldn't say, except that it couldn't have sprung from the ineffectual Liebehenschel. More likely from Oranienberg, even Höss himself. Whatever its provenance, it was a stroke of genius. Such was its potential to hasten the Jews to the end they'd earned themselves, he relegated much of his time to helping superintend its completion.

Belying what he'd presumed upon beginning his little tour, his presence hadn't been needed anywhere after all—until he announced it at the ramp. Some snags had arisen involving supply and distribution, mainly the flow of tools and materials to the work site. Nothing too serious, these were resolved easily enough, but weren't the biggest problem. One of the tracks had veered off course due to a surveying error, but though the mistake had been caught before too much of the crooked rail was laid, it did take Möll and some others almost two hours to make the mess right.

Only when they were done did he happen to look at his watch, and let out a yelp. Jumping on his motorcycle, he dropped Hannibal at his kennel and raced to Bunker 5 to pick up Eckardt. Skidding to a stop minutes later at Pit 3, the pair rounded up their kapo together with his crew and bustled them back to where they'd botched it this morning.

The shadows were starting to lengthen, the sun to lose its teeth. The promise of evening and its cool hung in the air. The two soldiers he'd left on guard had turned into six while he was away, these leaning on their rifles in anticipation.

First into the pit was Möll, then Eckardt and the foreman, the latter looking as if he was bound for a funeral. Four buckets of water were ordered down. Möll grabbed one, a mischievous gleam in his good eye.

"I hope you know if this doesn't work, kapo, I'm going to blame you. For screwing it up in the first place, fair enough?"

"But—but this last try, sir, it was you who..." There was, of course, no arguing. "Yes, sir. Fair enough."

"I have a good feeling about it, though. Let's keep our fingers crossed. In your case, I would suggest the fingers of both hands."

Reaching the center of the pit in three strides, Möll emptied a pail into the channel on the left. The descending ripple of water promptly vanished from sight. Half expectantly, half reluctantly, he repeated the process on the right.

This water, too, disappeared. Glancing at Eckardt, he tried it twice more. The result was the same. Tossing the last bucket, he dashed to the collecting trough on the right, then for the one at the opposite end. A film of liquid puddled the floor of each. Lifting his face to the heavens, he held it there just long enough for those standing at the lip of the pit to see something none ever had, a smile untarnished by sadism's leer lighting up that face.

He didn't so much walk as saunter back to the center point. "Get your men down here," he told the kapo, his voice as with Voss uncharacteristically civil, "and let's wrap this up. I want that old concrete out of here, the reservoirs siphoned and covered, and the dirt packed down around the edges of the channels so it won't blow into them until they've hardened.

"And keep your head clear for tomorrow. I'll be expecting you to impress me at Pits 2 and 3."

Once back up top, Möll stood staring pensively at the ground. Calm as he was on the outside, within he was dancing. Gratitude, fulfillment, relief were all there, but of that whirl of emotions gamboling inside him, triumph leapt the tallest.

After years of working himself up from the bottom, from lower than the bottom—from digging ditches for godsakes!—not merely recognition but a measure of fame was in reach. Should he guide the Hungarian Aktion to a favorable conclusion, an end this brainchild of his could only further, his prospects were limitless. At the least, he could see a lieutenancy in his future.

SS-*Untersturmführer* Otto Möll... the sound of it in his head was enough for him to tick that head higher.

But he knew also any personal acclaim he might reap was as nothing to the big picture, to the discharging of that sacred oath he as a biological soldier had sworn. For his country to live, even should it lose the war, particularly then, the Jew must die when and wherever he was found. Who could quantify the revenge of any who might survive? It wasn't hard to imagine all of Germany made one gigantic concentration camp, with its people, the Volk, the master race on the wrong side of the barbed wire.

That was an insanity one must do everything in one's power to prevent, and to the extent this device sprawling at his feet like the fossil spine of some dinosaur contributed to that, therein lay its value and the only real justification for celebrating it.

But in the midst of celebration, even then doubt remained. As Möll reveled in the success of the afternoon's demonstration of his simple, yet precisely because of that, conspicuous feat of design, one question persisted, a final nagging uncertainty. He wasn't sure it even merited comment, but called Eckardt to his side. Below them in the pit and the full flush of his reprieve, the kapo was dutifully bullying his men to speed it up.

"What is it, sir?" his adjutant said. "Something is bothering you?"

Möll squinted into the distance. "I don't—That is, it's probably nothing, but... Fat is viscous, isn't it, Karl? Thicker than water, I mean."

"That is correct, sir. From my experience."

"What I'm wondering is if what we've built will work as well with fat as water. Do you see that making a difference, or am I overthinking it?"

Eckardt had to suppress a smile. So his boss had a jigger of humanity in him after all. "I wouldn't suppose it a problem, *Hauptscharführer*. Water, melted fat... the two aren't that dissimilar. I wouldn't trouble myself with it if I were you."

Möll felt better after this, but only some. The one way to banish any doubt wasn't with buckets of water, but corpses stacked atop each other in neat, sizzling rows giving up their fat for the Fatherland. He was proud of what he was doing to prepare Birkenau for those corpses, but to tell the truth was growing tired of it. As one might of hors d'oeuvres while awaiting the main course.

Enough, he thought with a mirthless chuckle, of cheese or salami or whatever on crackers. The time had come for a man-sized serving of Hungarian goulash.

*   *   *

The sirens submerged Birkenau in their mournful wail with the men of Sonder Squad 58B, the day shift, halfway back to Block 13 for the night. These assumed it an air raid. Only Kapo Kaminski recognized it for what it was.

"Don't worry," he assured those Sonder eyeing a darkening sky. "It's an escape, not a raid. Nothing to wet your britches over."

"And how do you know that?" came the translation from Hungarian.

"Because you've been here two weeks and I for two years, that's how. Any more stupid questions?"

Actually, Kaminski knew because he happened to be in on the thing, this the second time Battle Group-Sonderkommando had assisted the Stammlager in an escape. The first had been less than two months ago, and like the one tonight was meant to alert the Allies to not only the plight of the thousands already incarcerated in Birkenau but what was then the impending Hungarian slaughter. The help Auschwitz requested was information on the Goldarb and Reinkommando operations; a description, also in writing, of the extermination process, complete with detailed sketches of the crematoria and their equipment; and a label from one of the canisters of poison gas.

"Excuse me?" Upon hearing what the underground wanted, Kaminski had glowered at its agent. "Would you mind repeating that last one?"

"A label from one of the tins of Zyklon-B." The young Pole, an electrician by the name of Porebski, had done his best to sound matter-of-fact. If not as often as Noah Zabludowicz, he was a regular visitor to Block 13. This was all that had kept Kaminski from losing his temper.

"I don't know, my man, if your bosses realize it or not, but the Krauts are rather jealous of their Zyklon-B. They're not in the habit of sharing it or leaving it lying around, not even those used containers of it."

"Of course. But there must be a way to—"

"No there mustn't, not necessarily. And to get caught trying wouldn't only be fatal but something of a giveaway to what you're planning, don't you think?"

Porebski was apologetic. "Understood, kapo, sir. I'm just telling you what I was told. All we're asking is that you do what you can."

"Easy to ask, hard to do," Kamimski had said before dismissing him. "But what the hell isn't around here?"

Not that he hadn't seen the value in such a trophy. Come the next gassing, a shipment of Greeks, he'd informed his *Kommandoführer*, Sergeant Muhsfeld, that two new receptacles for the collecting of gold teeth were needed, as the old ones were rusting through. Muhsfeld, annoyed, wanted to know why his kapo was bothering him with such a triviality and told him to scrounge something up. Immediately, he made for the bogus Red Cross ambulance parked in the yard, telling its pair of Disinfektoren that the *Oberscharführer* had sent him for two empty cans of the poison.

Despite having participated in countless executions, he'd never seen a tin of the stuff up close. It hadn't felt quite real holding in his hands a pair of objects so ordinary they might have come from some kitchen cupboard that had nevertheless been instrumental in the killing of two thousand human beings. Later, as he struggled to peel the label off one of them without tearing it, the words on it, stark, chilling, had imparted the same eerie sensation.

Zyklon-B. Poison gas for pest control. Cyanogen compound. DANGER! POISON! To be opened by trained personnel only. Tesch and Stabenow International, GMBH

In three days, Porebski had everything he'd asked for, and on the night of April 7th it was discovered at the D Camp Appell that the Jews Alfred Wetzler and Rudolf Vrba were missing from formation. The sirens blared, a Blocksperre was ordered, and within minutes hundreds of soldiers thrown into the search. All night, the shouting of men and the baying of dogs could be heard as patrols scoured the vast forbidden zone between the inner and outer cordons.

The next day, the Germans started in on the camp itself, going through every hut, warehouse, workshop, latrine. They even combed the unfinished areas of the Mexico lager, where construction had resumed in anticipation of the Hungarians. Not a pile of lumber or mound of trash was left unexamined, but nothing turned up there, either. It was as if the earth had swallowed the two men.

And so it had. They'd been hiding in Mexico all along, having dug a hole not much bigger than a grave while members of a crew breaking ground for a future barracks. They'd situated this hole outside the barbed-wire perimeter of the lager; the fence had yet to be moved to enclose the newest build-out. Upon their dodging into it late on the scheduled day, those in league with them hastily covered it with a roof of light plywood and a layer of soil, sprinkling the area with turpentine and a dusting of tobacco to throw off any dogs.

For four days and three nights, Wetzler and Vrba crouched in this suffocating den, waiting for the SS to withdraw the outer cordon. This farthest ring of watchtowers, as a rule manned during daylight alone, wasn't only active at night if an escape was ongoing but fortified with boots on the ground. After three days, the routine would revert to normal even if the escapee remained at large.

On the fourth night, the two crept from their hiding place and sped for the woods. With the search in and around the camp called off, and all police and Gestapo for miles alerted, every farm was watched, every bus and rail terminal, the gendarmes at the border crossings warned to be on the lookout.

Equipped, though, with forged identity papers and work cards, the Wetzler-Vrba team made it—all the way to London, as Battle Group-Auschwitz was to find out three weeks later. Enthusiasm ran steep that the sixty pages they carried documenting Nazi crimes past and to come couldn't but persuade the Allies to bomb the crematoria ahead of the Hungarians, and in doing so free *all* the inmates from their threat. For two more weeks, men scanned the Birkenau skies day and night for planes.

But none ever showed. Something had gone wrong. Maybe Churchill and gang had had difficulty believing the story put in front of them, needed to see that story corroborated.

Auschwitz organized a second escape. On this, the evening of May 27th, the prisoners Mordowicz and Rosin failed to present themselves at their Appell, and again the sirens sang. Three days later, the gallows reserved for them remained unused, and Kaminski could only hope—dwindling hope that it was—his second Zyklon-B label would help stir the Allies to action.

Something had to happen, and fast. Even the Poles were shaking their heads at the rate the Hungarians were dying. Two transports a day now, every day, were disappearing into the flames, and this only the beginning. Soon the count would climb to three and more, numbers difficult to penetrate.

As for those Sonder whose job it was to burn those transports, most were no more receptive to the idea of revolt than any commando preceding them. Kaminski hadn't expected this, his optimism predicated on this 12th squad ending up mainly Hungarian. Which it had, six hundred men out of nine hundred now—and growing still—herding their own countrymen to the gas, feeding their own to the ovens. Their kapo would have thought this incentive enough to make them trip over each other exchanging their gas masks for dynamite.

The same forces, however, that had blunted the volition and bled the fight out of previous detachments cast their pall over this one, too. That they were being worked to the bone left them neither the hours nor energy even to ponder revolt, much less prepare for one. So torrential was the flow of deportees from the ramp, though all but a few were going directly to the chimneys, enough were surviving this first selection to strain the ability of the SS to house them. Hence the rush to expand Mexico.

But, as with last summer's squad, more than mere exhaustion was holding the 12th back. Such numbers, such a slaughter perpetrated so brutish an assault as to wear down not only the body but the soul, particularly that part of it the conscience called home. This led a person to obey without objection, without thinking, to react passively to the lunacy instead of acting counter to it. A month ago they'd been boys, young husbands, men with children some of them—still living in the neighborhoods they'd grown up in, safe in the bosom of friends and family, their surroundings as unthreatening as they were familiar.

Now those families were gone never to return, and they trapped in a nightmare, their days and nights so overrun with corpses it must have seemed half the world was being murdered.

Nor could Kaminski in all fairness find it in his heart to hold their uncooperativeness against them. He tried to put himself in their place, to remember his own first days in the commando of the living dead two summers ago, working the honeycomb of graves behind the old gas bunkers. He, too, had once felt he was drowning in a sea of dead bodies, had stopped using his brain and let his instincts take over. Not least the instinct of self-preservation, that compulsion to do whatever it took to stay alive—to follow every German order, do more than he was ordered, for another day of existence. One lousy day.

How could he fault then these men and boys, as dazed and terrified as he'd been, for responding the same way? For tuning him out when he got on his soapbox to preach revolt.

He and others in the Battle Group had won some over, Major Borodin and the Russian POWs being notable examples. The bulk of the Hungarians, though, were proving obstinate, stranding the conspirators shy of the quorum they felt necessary. Again, the more men they had, the better the prospects of some of them escaping by fleeing in so many directions as to make it difficult to chase them all down. Working to Kaminski's advantage, this 12th Kommando was by far the largest ever; to shake but half the new Sonder out of their lassitude would have sufficed.

But even that was looking less attainable by the day, leaving him with a decision to make. One he'd been avoiding: either continue butting his head against a Hungarian wall or gather round him those men of the same mind as he, take the four cremos along with Bunker 5, blow the accursed things to kingdom come, then see how far they could get before the SS caught up with them. This was suicide, and more than likely death to the hundreds of their brother Sonder who'd kept out of the fight. But in return, the crematoria in their farewell performance would be sending a different sort of smoke into the sky.

As extraordinary good fortune would have it, coupled antithetically with the Nazi lust to kill, it was a decision he would be spared. Something happened that changed everything, something jaw-dropping, as powerful and unforeseeable as a bolt of lightning.

One could have pushed him over backward with a finger when he heard about it.

It was the last hour of the last night of May, a night nearly as hot and humid as the day. From dawn to dusk, a wind had blown from the south, but instead of providing some relief had been nothing more than heat in motion. The sun was already acting the bully, indifferent to the discomfort of those at its mercy. A pitiless sun, a scorching wind, the sweat snaking down one's spine and it not yet nine in the morning—if this was May, one had to wonder what kind of summer lay ahead.

Kaminski stood in the open doorway of Block 13, a wedge of moon overhead. The barracks at his back was black save for the light from a smattering of candles. Around these, some men sat talking in low voices, the only other sounds from inside the odd cough, the buzz of snoring. But for the chirping of insects, the distant barking of a dog, it was quiet outside, too. Triumphant sleep held the field, having felled all but a stubborn few.

That he was one of these wasn't by choice. Tired as he was— two transports today, and a men's Himmelblock nastiness—his eyes wouldn't stay shut. Every time he laid down, minutes later he was up again. Something wasn't letting him sleep, but what?

He'd just turned to go back in and give it another try when to his surprise he heard the creak of the outside door, the crunch of shoes on gravel. What the—? A lone figure approached in the moonlight, its stride full of purpose.

Another dozen steps, and he untensed. "Noah? Noah Zabludowicz! *You* here at *this* hour... what gives, my friend?"

"Kapo? Is that you?" Then a curse, as Noah tripped and almost fell. "Boy, is this lucky! I was afraid I was going to have to wake half the block before I found you!"

The two embraced. Even in the dark, he could tell Noah wasn't Noah. A silly grin plastered his face; he looked giddy, as if he'd been drinking. "So, what *is* the occasion?" Kaminski said, still not sure if he should be worried. "I don't recollect, sir, having the pleasure, not at night."

"No, you haven't. But I've never had the pleasure of an assignment such as tonight's. I bring a message, from Auschwitz. From the Steering Committee. Bruno Baum."

Noah just stood there, still grinning. Kaminski looked at him as he might someone who'd lost it upstairs. "Well, you going to tell me or what?"

"Oh! The message!" Noah shook himself back to earth, came to attention. What followed, in its formality, was plainly rehearsed. "It is my honor to instruct you, kapo, to prepare your men for battle. The underground has determined an uprising advisable, with the Sonderkommando to lead the attack."

Now it was the other's turn to act stupid. "The—the—" was all he could get out.

"Yes, you heard me," Noah said, laughing, "the revolt! Hard to believe, isn't it? I just found out myself, from Commander Baum. He wanted me to tell you personally, and tonight, so here I am."

Kaminski had been about to ask him how in the world he was able to travel between the two camps after dark, but the thought had fled him as suddenly as his tongue.

"There is a downside," Noah said, filling in the silence. "It's slated, I'm afraid, to be a Birkenau operation only. If you want, I'll explain why later, and the explanation isn't without logic. For now, suffice it to say the Stammlager is serious. The date has been set for mid-June, two weeks from today."

Kaminski swallowed, tried again. "But—how? What made them change their minds?"

Noah had asked Baum the same, and the general, excited himself, had been all too happy to tell him. "There were three reasons. Is there a place out here we can sit down?"

Later that night, Kaminski lay awake in his bunk, sleep even more a lost cause than before. Was his restlessness earlier because he'd sensed the miracle about to walk into the yard? Whatever it was then, it was all he could do now not to roust the rest of the block from their beds and share the news. Instead, he contented himself with reliving the gift Noah had brought him. Nor did he have any difficulty reconstructing the man's words.

"The first of the three," he'd begun, "is that the madman Otto Möll, as if you weren't aware, has come back for an encore, recalled to the place he loves best to do what he does best. But it's neither the sergeant's talent nor enthusiasm for mass murder that has the Steering Committee worried. The Kraut scheme to keep its Jews out of Russian hands isn't, again as you know, called the Möll Plan for nothing."

"No, I didn't know." Kaminski was onto the Nazi intent to do away with their prisoners should the Soviets get near, but had never imagined an actual plan for it existed. Much less that it bore the *Hauptscharführer's* name. "The Möll Plan, you say?"

Noah quickly brought him up to snuff on the thing. "And in the opinion of those in fear of it," he'd concluded, "its architect having returned to Birkenau only heightens the threat. All the more when taken together with what we're pretty sure is going on a few hundred miles to the east. Which is the second reason urging Auschwitz to action."

Kaminski saw a cloud darker than the night pass across Noah. Who took a deep breath before continuing.

"The underground's intelligence network has uncovered what it suspects is just such a massacre taking place at the Maidanek camp. Even as we sit. We were alerted to this after discovering that while most of its transports were being diverted our way, its chimneys were smoking day and night.

"It wasn't any great trick for us to add to those suspicions, either. Unlike the other Vernichtungslagers, ours included, Maidanek isn't located in a remote area, safe from prying eyes. One of Lublin's busiest highways runs right by it; anyone with a pair of binoculars can see inside the camp.

"And what our agents did see, despite a deserted unloading ramp, was a steady stream of trucks hauling people to those chimneys and leaving empty. Could what's happening be any clearer?

"We think not. With the first stirrings of the Red Army in April having gobbled up large tracts of acreage, that army in German eyes is now positioned uncomfortably close to Maidanek. Vocal as they've been about not surrendering a single prisoner to liberation, the SS, from what we can make out, weren't just talking. And aren't taking any chances at Lublin of a Wehrmacht collapse or Soviet thrust catching them with their pants down."

Noah could tell from his expression that Kaminski had yet to pin down what he was driving at. But he wasn't finished.

"Neither is Maidanek the only river of blood spilling out of eastern Poland. Entire camps are being liquidated. At Poniatowa, thousands were shot. Machine guns were put in place in each corner of Trawniki, then the barracks clustered in the center set on fire. The Lublin area has been especially hard hit: Maidanek remains, for now, but the lagers Dorohucza, Budzyn, Krychnow, and Osawa are no more."

The kapo had in fact fallen short of grasping the implication. Poniatowa, Trawniki, Budzyn... tragedies all, but also all labor camps, and as such comparatively small and easy to dispose of. He could see how the Nazis might be tempted to make quick work of these. Maidanek, however, being huge, would take not only careful planning but a lot of work. Out of the hundreds of camps in Poland, it was second in size only to—

Kaminski's mouth went slack. "I'll be damned," he said. "Could I have been more of a goose? If at a place giant as Maidanek, why not here? I get it now."

"Especially," said Noah, "with that werewolf Möll skulking in the wings. Just itching, after he's done with the Hungarians, to wet his muzzle with more blood."

According to Baum, a third reason lay behind the underground's change of heart, though hardly had Noah brought it up than Kaminski was questioning it. Aware of the Ka-Be kapo's basic decency, he saw him projecting that decency onto others.

As Noah had it, Baum held that Battle Group-Auschwitz— meaning those Poles that made up its majority, and who'd been taught at their mothers' knees to hate and fear the Jews—was as repelled as everyone by this new and bottomless slaughter. Already it was closing in on the killing frenzy of last summer. The Hungarians flooding the camp were as many as the blades of grass in the meadows, the stars in a hundred skies. Birkenau itself resembled a small city ablaze. All day and into the night the Nazi cremation pyres roared, releasing airy cliffs of black smoke that blotted out the sun. From out of these clouds and the mouths of the chimneys rained flakes of ash the size of fifty-zloty pieces, powdering every surface with a gray moistureless snow. Like a synergy of noxious fumes released from the bowels of the earth, the lipid stench of burning flesh and kerosene drove every other smell away.

The entire western quarter of the camp teemed at all hours with long lines of deportees, lines moving, lines stationary, forming, disbanding, forming again, most disappearing into the gaping maws of the crematoria. The roads leading to these were so clogged with people that the trucks delivering the old and disabled often found them unnavigable.

The crowds weren't so much walking as dragging themselves along, weary, disoriented, wild-eyed with thirst, the shuffling of their feet raising a dense dust. When there was no wind and the heat hung in blankets, this dust would combine with the smoke to make the greenish air even murkier.

From out of this murk as from some choir of the damned drifted a cacophony of subdued weeping, children whining for water, wails of pain and bewilderment, the growls of the SS dogs and their masters. Out of sight in the rear of the crematoria or hidden by tall wattles, piles of grub-white corpses glistened in the sun, the overflow from the ovens awaiting their turn at the fire pits. The rats swarming them often had time to strip the smaller children to the bone. If there was a hell this was what it looked, smelled, sounded like, a spectacle that might well have moved the Auschwitz Poles to compassion.

That was what Baum asserted anyway. Kaminski had his doubts, forget the Stammlager's efforts in April and May to warn the West of the disaster unfolding in Hungary. That, as he was also aware, had been as much for the sake of those already interned as it was for the Hungarians.

Not when all was said and done that he gave a tinker's dam as to why. Whatever had sparked its reversal—the Hungarians, Maidanek, Otto Möll, the reading of tea leaves—what mattered was that the underground had seen the light of revolt at last.

In the morning, little sleep or no, he was up before the others. He wanted to catch Noah's cousin Shlomo Kirschenbaum when he walked in from the night shift. Both Zalmans, too, and from Block 10 that Major Borodin and the Wrubel boy. The quicker Langfus in the Reinkommando attic knew, the better. So much to do now, and not a lot of days to do it in.

As the next couple would show, though, he and his lieutenants wouldn't be forced to spend them struggling to convince the Hungarians the situation had changed for the miraculous. That overnight they'd been handed a realistic chance of escaping the bad dream their lives had become. With the Home Army and its guns, and the general population its numbers, the odds of surviving a breakout had grown exponentially.

Emboldened by this, virtually the whole commando cast in. Everyone was assigned a role to play in the hostilities to come, some specific, most generalized, but all vital to the plan; it was essential each man know where he was supposed to be and when. The plan itself would need honing and re-honing, tighter synchronizing, memorizing. Weapons and ammunition had to be distributed, and those firearms they'd be getting later from their dead guards earmarked for the men who knew how to use them. Supplies had to be stockpiled and carefully, so as not to attract attention. Each rebel was also to outfit a personal pack.

For the next two weeks, the respective Battle Groups maintained a continuous communication. Noah Zabludowicz was spending as much time at Block 13 as his own barracks, ferrying messages, being briefed, debriefed, offering suggestions. The Sonder, meanwhile, received four pistols and a submachine gun from the main camp, along with ammo. Kaminski drooled over this windfall for half a day before turning all but two pistols over to Borodin and his gun-savvy POW's.

Noah, though, wasn't the only one making Birkenau his second home. Porebski the electrician and Silver the locksmith—a stick of a kid who hadn't impressed Kaminski much until told he was the Robota girl's boyfriend—also became fixtures at Block 13, that while remaining the nerve center of Battle Group-Sonderkommando was but one of three barracks now housing the oversized 12th Squad.

Most of those dropping in, of course, were to make a single appearance only, theirs but a question to ask, an update to issue, a delivery to make. These the kapo would neither see again nor remember—except for one, and not just because the man had been in charge of the detail posing as a carpentry crew that had slipped the rebels their machine gun.

Mordecai Hilleli was the Schreiber of the main camp's Block 16, the Ciechanow hut. And an old running buddy of Noah and Roza, having partnered with them in those midnight raids the Shomeir had conducted outside the ghetto. The same age as Noah, he'd joined the underground the same time as well, and had risen high enough in his superiors' estimations to be entrusted with the job of smuggling weapons.

Hilleli was one of those prisoners little changed by the brutality around him. Though a large man, tall, big-boned, he sported the playful eyes and waggish smirk of a forest elf, and the mischief-loving sense of humor to match. If a laugh was to be had, one could rely on him to find it.

After entering the Sonder hut and handing over the gun, he marched up to Kaminski. "I've been told, kapo, you know the freedom fighter Roza Robota."

"I met her once, yes, and am hoping to again."

"I arranged to meet her today myself at the Canada warehouse where she works. We had to pass by there on our way here. If you've a moment, she asked me to give you a message."

Kaminski, intrigued, nodded his permission.

"She wanted me to wish you and the commando good luck in battle, and that your every bullet find an SS man. She also can't wait to hear the sweet crash of dynamite, then running across you later in the woods where the two of you can kill Nazis together."

"That's my girl. She say anything more?"

"In a manner of speaking, yes." Hilleli stepped closer. "She wanted me to give you this."

He took hold of Kaminski's shoulders and planted a kiss on each startled cheek. The Sonder watching guffawed their approval, their kapo blushing a color that would have done Beetface Gorges credit. With a crisp salute and as smartly military an about-face, Hilleli led his men outside where they hung around awhile pretending to do some carpentering.

Yes, he would remember this young Schreiber from Block 16. When he learned later from Noah what a cut-up the fellow was, it was clear from whom that last bit of encouragement had come. Just as there was no mistaking the author of the first part of the message. Or its intent. It was Roza reminding him and his men of their obligation to blow the crematoria back to that hell which had spawned them.

Not that their memories needed jogging. The rigging of the death factories for destruction played as big a part in the Sonders' makeready as any. Forty sticks of the dynamite were taped together into bundles of four each, all but two of these secreted under the crematoria's floorboards. The Germans kept two fifty-five-gallon drums of gasoline on hand in each building to fuel the generators that fired the coke and the ventilators that kept it burning. On the pretext of requiring more for the Hungarians, Kaminski was able to have this quantity doubled. A pack of explosive detonated anywhere near those barrels should result in a fireball sufficient to blow the roof off the place.

The demolition teams were to be composed of Borodin and his men. He'd be sure to have one of these working Bunker 5 that day, the remaining two bundles of dynamite and some gasoline having been buried behind it. If the kapo had his way, he wasn't going to leave the death houses with so much as a broom closet.

Though as the shock troops of the revolt they bore the brunt of gearing up for it, and had the transports to deal with besides, the Sonder weren't the only ones to have their hands full. Battle Group-Auschwitz had its own preparations to make, principal of these the mustering of the partisans. Its chief, Cyrankiewicz, had to have them in place and undetected by June 15th, the date chosen for the breakout.

The Home Army wasn't by any measure a unified body, but rather a rubric for a collection of disparate fighting units each operating under an autonomous leader. They may have called it one, but a true army it wasn't. A communications network that left a lot to be desired exacerbated the difficulty of aligning these independent outfits into a cohesive force. With radio transmissions considered too risky, Cyrankiewicz got his information and gave his orders almost entirely by courier. The Resistance had dozens of agents among those civilians employed inside the camp; it was they who relayed his directives to Krakow and his field generals, and brought anything pertinent back to the Stammlager.

It was neither the fastest nor most efficient of systems. But to coordinate and then launch the assault was as nothing to the problems facing Auschwitz immediately after, namely what to do with the thousands who will have liberated themselves. As dilatory as it may have struck the more radical of the Sonder, the logic attending the underground's insistence on postponing the rebellion until Soviet troops were in the area wasn't lost on Kaminski.

Behind Russian lines lay food and freedom, behind enemy lines a blood-filled shambles in the making. He wanted to know what steps its leaders were taking to prevent this shambles. And what the Sonder could do to help.

This had been a thorn in the paw of the Steering Committee since it proposed revolt a year ago. Say the partisans did succeed in ushering the escapees safely to the marshlands straddling the Sola—what then? As uncertain an outcome as even that promised to be, the provisioning of such a throng, as the sardonic joke making the rounds went, wasn't going to be any picnic, either. The Home Army could manage some food, possibly for an extended period, but it promised to be starvation rations until the Russians did enter the scene.

The only answer the Committee gave Kaminski on how the Sonder might help was for him to have his men load as many supplies as they could into however many carts they could handle in their dash for the river. This wasn't exactly the response he'd wished for, but not unexpected, either.

And so the days passed in a fever of death but also hope, days spent as usual with the Sonder moving heaps of dead flesh from one spot to another, eating meals that tasted of corpses, drinking themselves numb—but in the midst of it all, actually packing for an adventure so affirmative of life as to get the pulse galloping. The dichotomy was enough to make a surreal couple of weeks even stranger, so that between it and the lack of sleep and the affright of their work, by the evening of the 14th, Sonder nerves were all but shot.

Kaminski felt he ought to say something on the eve of their great escape, something over and above a last-minute finalizing of details. He called a meeting for midnight, by which hour a representative number of those he wished in attendance should be done with their work. (Their warden, the assiduous Möll, as if to accommodate him, had cut the second shift short this night only for general maintenance and cleaning). Leyb Langfus, living with the Reinkommando now in Number Three's attic, wouldn't be able to make it, nor whomever from the night shift the Nazis kept late. That was too bad, but couldn't be helped.

Come midnight, six of them and their kapo sat at one end of the long dining table that ran a quarter of the length of Block 13. Dirty dishes cluttered it, glasses purple to varying levels with a Hungarian wine. A single oil lamp cast a smoky yellow light. From the tall rows of bunks receding into the darkness came the deathbed gurgle of people snoring, as if gasping their last. Farther down the table, where the light struggled to reach, the few still awake had gathered to listen in, dim in the shadows. Kaminski, at the head of it, turned toward Yankel Handelsman.

"I was hoping Leventhal could be here, and that Russian major. And Leventhal's pal, Gradowski. Each fills such big shoes tomorrow—I mean, today —and has to be up on not only his own duties but those of the men under him.

"You're as familiar with the battle plan as anyone, professor, and there's so much I've yet to do. Perhaps you could see that those last two are up on their stuff. I'll catch Leventhal at work."

Handelsman agreed. "If you want, you know, I can take more than two off your hands."

"That'd probably be a good idea," Kaminski said. "You're in Number Four still, right? Go ahead then and touch base with the Greeks Baruch and Nadjary. And let's not forget Kirschenbaum. If all goes as it should later, Shlomo will be wearing a *Scharführer's* uniform."

"Anyone else?"

"That should do it. I can handle the rest, starting with Langfus in Number Three first thing in the morning. Which unless I get on with this meeting might find us still sitting here."

He rose from his chair. Conversation stopped, all heads turning his way. "I called you here tonight," he began, his grainy scratch of a voice low, "for a couple of reasons. First, it's important everyone at this table is clear on what will be expected of him in a few hours. It's you, after all, who'll be leading the assault, and nothing is more crucial to its success than the order in which it was designed to unfold. Is there anyone the least unsure of that order?"

The weary six eyed each other expectantly, but none spoke.

"I can see you've all about had it for the day, and God knows the sun will be up soon enough. But this won't take long, I promise. Think of it as humoring an old man, who would feel a lot better if we went over the plan of attack one more time."

Kaminski had indeed aged much the last year. Handelsman and Warszawski, also present, were almost as old as he but looked twenty years younger. The stubble covering his scalp and cheeks had gone from grizzled to a uniform white, and the lines in his face had deepened in tandem with the slouch of his shoulders. His eyes, though, were what sealed it, eyes that hadn't necessarily seen more than others but lost more in the process, more of that light which distinguished those holding onto life with both hands from those become tired of it.

Some of his lieutenants shifted in their chairs, but eager as they were for bed Handelsman spoke for them all. "You have but to wish it, general, for us to obey."

The revolt, if still scheduled to begin at 5:30 in the evening with the ambush of their guards, had been revamped some. This was necessitated by the squad's size, which now filled three huts; the original Block 13, and Blocks 10 and 11. Two clothes carts had been tucked out of sight behind each.

Upon returning from work under guard of Kirschenbaum and his "SS"—these quietly taking care of the sentry at D Camp's gate—the day-shift Sonder were to load the carts with the supplies they'd accumulated, break out their stash of weapons, and a dozen of them from Block 13, with Shlomo and company, hurry to the lager's Appellplatz where the evening roll call would have started. The freeing of these prisoners would be the first battle, and the signal for the night-shift Sonder to blow the crematoria. This would alert the partisans in the woods and the men working Bunker 5 to spring into action themselves.

The twelve at that point would chase their liberated prisoners back, pick up the rest of Block 13 and the carts, and the whole mass make on the double for Crematoria II and III. The men of Block 11 would already have left for the *B1* lagers, where they were to eliminate any sentries and free the inmates there, with Block 10 seeing to the same at the *B2* and Mexico lagers. The destination of both, when done, would be Crematoria IV and V.

Once the inner cordon was breached and people began reaching the woods, it would become mainly a Home Army show. After the mobs of escapees had been reduced to smaller groups and divvied up among the partisans, it was on to the Sola and its marshes, with those rebels who were armed and most of the Armia men providing a rear guard.

Kaminski grilled the half-dozen on not only their assignments but the details of the plan as a whole. When satisfied, he leaned forward on the table, his weight on his knuckles. If there were any questions, he said, now was the moment to ask them.

Silence, but for the snoring in the background. It was Warszawski who broke it. "Here's one," he said with a sly smile. "How long, Kapo K, before 5:30 rolls around?"

With talk of strategy out of the way, Kaminski could relax some. Gazing fondly around the table, he'd never felt closer to those gazing back at him. Instead of being united in the despicable work of the crematoria, they'd become brothers in an enterprise that wouldn't only be saving as opposed to ending Jewish lives but, one day, fill every race with pride that here were slaves who'd dared stand up to the slave driver, men willing to risk the little life left them for a chance, that was all, just the chance at freedom.

Men like Handelsman, their professor, whose wisdom and constancy had been both a crutch and a comfort to his kapo from the beginning. Or Handelsman's friend the impetuous Yossel Warszawski, who was still grinning at his wisecrack. But maybe he hadn't intended it to be funny, not entirely, for there he sat drumming his fingers on the table as if impatient with the clock. That was how he was, though, some part of him always moving, fingers drumming, foot tapping, that nervous tic he had of running a hand through his hair. One got the impression that if Warszawski ever did go completely still, like a shark that had stopped swimming it would be the end of him.

Or seated next to him, Isaac Kalniak, the same Kapo Kalniak who by taking Leventhal into his care his first day on the job at the old Bunker 2 had saved his life. He'd since shaved his beard, but cut as imposing a figure as ever, with the same bull-like body as Kaminski only taller. Also like Kaminski, he retained a genuine affection for his men, grieved for those both living and dead.

Not that he was a grieving man by nature. Had a laugh, in fact, as big and brawny as he was, a laugh not even the crematoria could kill. Kalniak claimed to have been the blacksmith of a shtetl outside of Lodz, a story backed by his peasant accent, a serious set of shoulders, and the dozens of tiny white burn scars dotting his huge hands and forearms.

Across from him sat Josef Deresinski, a fisherman from up north, the Pomeranian coast. Little taller than the barely five-foot Warszawski, he was as wiry and spry as a baboon; one could imagine him making it to the roof of a crematorium without a ladder. Deresinski walked like a true man of the sea, with an oddly rolling gait, as if still on the deck of his trawler. His hands were as weathered as Kalniak's, but unlike him he was a quiet sort, seldom spoke at all. To those who knew him, he didn't have to say much; his words, being scant, carried more weight.

But not enough, try as he had, as all of them had, to wake their kapo up to the stalling tactics of Battle Group-Auschwitz. Even now, mere hours from exonerating himself, Kaminski's blood burned with shame at not having been more aggressive. At allowing a year to go by without raising a finger against the SS. The mystery to him was that he should have been so damnably cautious yet surrounded himself with such devil-may-care officers. As if on an unconscious level he'd been trying to compensate for his own inertia.

But this was no time to be raking up the missteps of the past, though Jukel Wrubel sitting there wasn't helping at all. He couldn't look at the kid without his throat tightening. The precocious Wrubel may have been pushing six-feet, with a man's physique to match, but it was difficult not to see him as still a child. He had yet to lose the artlessness, that fundamental sweetness of the very young. The patchy beard he was struggling to grow only underscored his boyishness, a quality, like Kalniak's robust laugh, the crematoria had failed to burn out of him. How many such Sonder, men little more than children—men who'd trusted and obeyed him as they might a father—had he Kaminski condemned to an inglorious death by playing the patsy to the underground?

But again, this was neither the time nor place for regrets. It was enough that he'd betrayed not only others but himself without crying about it like some little girl. There was no resurrecting the dead. What was done was done. It wasn't a night for looking backward but ahead.

He stepped away from the table, and folding his arms, concentrated on the floor as if collecting his thoughts. But he wasn't so much attempting to collect as recollect another meeting not that long ago where a pretty young woman with stabbing black eyes had enthralled him with not only her hunger to see justice done but her rhetoric. Now would be the perfect moment to summon some of that rhetoric, some of the fire that had given her words muscle.

"As I said, lads"—he raised his voice to include those in the back—"I called you here for two reasons. Having shown you know *what* to do on this day of days satisfies the first. The second is so we can remind ourselves why we're doing it. The easy answer to that is to try and save our skins. It's safe to say there's no one at this table who doesn't understand that to sit back and do nothing, to trust in God or luck or German carelessness to spare him, is to be no less than an accomplice in his own execution.

"Some of us, of course, are going to die anyway. Such are the fortunes of war. But there are some who'll be leaving the mud, stench, and murder of Birkenau behind them forever—who will have fought their way out of here, and having made the forest, are going to stop, look around, and scarcely daring to believe it, realize what they've done.

"Call these the lucky if you want, the confounders of all odds, but they won't be the only ones to triumph today. Every man, live or die, who would brave the coming battle, defy the SS, will come out of it victorious. If not in body then spirit. For no longer the slave, the dumb animal the Nazis would make of him, he will have become a man again, reclaimed that humanity stripped from him.

"To save our skins? Yes, that's something worth fighting for. But as someone told me once—a slip of a girl, but twice the soldier I'll ever be—though Sonder flesh and bone might not survive a revolt, the effort would go far toward us saving our souls."

Kaminski's gaze swept the table, lighting on the man to the right of Deresinski. He'd undressed to his undershirt, revealing a trim, hairless body. One couldn't have ordered up a more Eastern European face: the nose as sharp and curving as an eagle's beak; high, aristocratic cheekbones; cruel yet sensual lips. Jewish he may have been, but bore the stamp, too, of the Magyar nobility of old.

After the German invasion of his country, the Hungarian Bela Lazar had refused to submit to the SS edict requiring all Jews to display the yellow star on their clothing and fled into the woods outside his village. Quickly captured by the Gestapo, he was put on one of the first transports to Poland. Selected on the ramp for the Special Squad, it hadn't taken him long to work his way into its inner circle. A ready smile and humble manner enabled him to make friends easily, but this wasn't what had led to his rise in the detachment.

A member of Squad 60B, the day shift, Lazar alternated between Crematorium IV and the fire pits northeast of Number Five. He thanked his stars every day that in the performance of these duties he had yet to come across anyone from home. Fear of this had turned him into a tiger for revolt. From his first day in the commando, even before he learned of the plot, he'd been loud about turning the tables on the Nazis, doing something to stop them. Within a week, he and Kaminski were talking.

Tonight, when the latter's eyes met his and didn't leave right away, Lazar had a hunch what the kapo was going to say next.

"For when it comes down to it, it's not about us at all, is it? There's more at stake here than simply saving ourselves, or the thousands we'll be busting out with us. More important, nothing is as important, are the hundreds of thousands to come, and not just the Hungarians. Who's to say how long it'll be before the Russians get here? And you can bet the Krauts won't be pulling the plug on this place until they're forced to.

"First, though, the Hungarians. The killing has got to end now. We all knew it was going to be terrible, but this? The cremos are running eighteen hours a day as it is! And the transports only starting to roll in. Noah Zabludowicz tells me there are close to a million Jews in Hungary. Are we supposed to sit on our keisters and do nothing while a million people go up in smoke, keep shoving them into the fire until it's our turn to bake?"

Kaminski had moved from the head of the table to Lazar's chair, stood gripping the back of it. "If it's all right with him, I'd like to toss Bela here a question. Have you ever wondered, young man, how the word Jericho came to be the code name for the revolt?"

Lazar had, but not enough to ask. Thrilled as a child by the battle of Jericho and other such biblical stories, he'd long ceased seeing them as anything more than tall tales to tickle children. Or in this case, a heroic name to rally around.

"Why is Jericho? I no able to tell you, please, sir." Having come to Birkenau without much Polish, he was adding more by the day. "But with you... wait for this night for tell me, I think is not... is not accident."

"So it isn't," Kaminski said. Nor was it solely for Lazar's benefit that he felt it worthwhile to chat the story up again. "When the crematoria began opening their doors over a year ago, we of what was then the 9th Sonderkommando saw that to leave them standing would amount to a crime almost as great as that of those who'd built them. We likened the obligation to destroy them to that felt by our forefathers to take and destroy the Canaanite city of Jericho. Just as, or so the legend has it, the trumpets of Joshua's Israelite army had tumbled those pagan walls, so would we with our dynamite the walls of the death factories.

"Then the days turned into weeks, weeks into months, until the month came when looking into the mirror, staring back at each of us was a face that had failed at that task. And by having failed, permitted those factories to succeed at theirs. The lifeblood of our race, the largest concentration of us anywhere—the millions of Jews who over the centuries had set down roots in Europe and Russia— were if not already done for then close to it. The transports slowed almost to a halt for a lack of bodies to fill them."

For a long quarter of a minute he was silent. "I blame myself for that failure. Myself alone. Somewhere along the path of firm purpose, I made a wrong turn, lost my bearings, then compounded the error by not listening to those of my men, to you at this very table, who would steer me right again.

"But now I've been given a second chance, the opportunity to redeem my undeserving self. Nor is this, as it was with the Czechs of the Family Camp, a false alarm. This time there's no keeping the wheel of history from turning. The trumpets of this latest Jericho will sound after all, the walls of our enemies dissolve into dust.

"Lastly, lest we forget, the devil take us if we forget, there are the dead. Our families, our friends, *all* who've perished within those walls... it is for them, too, that we dare this great thing. Our beloved may be gone, our dear ones past saving, but if there's any justice to be had, they're not past avenging."

Without turning around, Lazar reached over his shoulder and in what was either affirmation, affection, gratitude or all three, took Kaminski's hand in his. He started to say something, but Handelsman beat him to it.

"Nicely spoken, commander. Thank you for your eloquence, the power of your words... words all of us would do well to pass on to our men."

But Kaminski wasn't finished. Something else begged to be said, something he could see Roza Robota closing with. "It's not just for the present or the past that we fight, either, but the future—not only for ourselves, the Hungarians, the dead, but the living of the decades, maybe the centuries to come. For as long as the human story is soiled by the memory of Birkenau, so too will it soar with that of the 12th Sonderkommando.

"We rise up today to carve our names in stone, so that men will remember, will learn from what we did."

Stove in as he was, Kaminski would have trouble sleeping that night. His head a merry-go-round of all he had yet to do, he would doze off for a while then awake with a start, glance at the window behind him to see if it was turning gray. He wondered whether he was the only one who couldn't sleep, or if others lay tense and silent in the dark watching the same window he was.

Slow as the minutes were now, later they'd be growing even longer, and longer still the closer they got to 5:30. He pictured his men, those with wristwatches, checking them over and over, thumping them, shaking them, holding them to their ears, refusing to believe only five minutes had passed. Everyone's focus this June 15th would be on the clock and little else. Three transports or ten, SS or no, not a lot of work was going to get done today.

How he was supposed to hide this from the Germans he had no idea, but he'd come up with something. He always did.

Summer

Birkenau simmered in the July sun like some hideous brew, a witch's potion of blood, sweat, smoke, and excrement worthy of something the weird sisters might have cooked up in *Macbeth*.

No one could remember a summer as unmerciful as this one. It hadn't rained since May, and with no respite from the heat, it accumulated, grew denser, more concentrated each day, like sediment collecting at the bottom of a pond. People perspired the clock round, midnight, dawn, it didn't matter. The barracks were like dungeons, suffocating, airless. When the wind did blow, it was a burning, desert wind, or like the acetylene-hot gusts generated by a forest fire.

It was also the longest anyone could remember, or so it seemed to the men of the Sonderkommando. The veterans among them couldn't recall ever working this hard, not even the summer before, when three transports a day hadn't been unusual. Now it was four, sometimes five, though this last was pushing it; twenty-four hours simply weren't enough to dispose of that many dead.

As for the toll taken on the machinery, all eight of Crematorium IV's ovens had ceased to function, the two furnaces that housed them having cracked in half. Number Five's were hanging on, but sorely needed attention, as did not only its chimneys but those of Numbers Two and Three. Most Sonder held that if the current pace was maintained, the entire crematory system, that part of it indoors, would end up claiming itself as its final victim.

So bone-bruising were the last who-could-remember-how-many weeks, Zalman Gradowski didn't so much fall asleep anymore as pass out in his bed. Yet here he was after his shift on this stifling July night sitting on the edge of it, nor was he the only one up at this hour. Dotting the labyrinth of tiered bunks half-filling the attic of Crematorium II, a few candles flickered in the dark. Dwarfing their negligible little halos of light, four shafts of ghostly moonbeam slanted through the windows set in the slope of the roof, windows not built to be opened but for show only, part of the flummery intended to make the death house look ordinary.

Between the propeller-whoosh of four industrial-sized floor fans and the din from the ovens below, the attic wasn't only warm but noisy. Not that either was to blame for keeping Gradowski awake. July it may have been, but the wound of June 15th was far from healed; there wasn't a man who'd been one of the squad that day not still hemorrhaging defeat. To revisit it was to open the wound afresh, end up breaking the heart all over again.

But from the moment he'd crawled out of his bunk this morning, Gradowski had been able to think of little else. Today, after all, was *July* the 15th, a month to the day after the disaster. Fight as he had to fend off this reminder, to blank his mind each time it strayed in that direction, he was fighting a losing battle. With every load of corpses he fed into the ovens, the failure of June was driven home.

Now here it was nearing midnight and still he was reliving it, sleep as remote a prospect as a cool breeze.

The euphoria with which that Friday had begun made the recollection of it the more bitter. After a year of doing nothing but planning for revolt, talking about it, the time had come to turn talk into action. As the green ball of the sun behind its screen of smoke had climbed its molasses-slow way to its zenith, so, too, had both the angst and anticipation of the Sonder. All signals were go from their contacts in the Stammlager; the moment of either freedom or death was upon them. One could feel the electricity in the air, as before a violent thunderstorm. There was no denying the rebels their appointment with destiny.

At three o'clock, however, a three-man roofing crew, wheelbarrows loaded with shingles and tools, showed at the gate of Crematorium III. They were in reality agents of Battle Group-Auschwitz, sent to deliver this message to Kaminski: the revolt had been called off. Orders were to stand down. No reason was given, other than to proceed would make a grave situation worse.

Shattered, the Sonder argued over what to do. The issue was decided for them when not half an hour later, brakes squealing, trucks pulled up outside each crematorium and SS in battle gear poured into the compounds. Operation Jericho was done for. The dream had come to naught. The Germans had been tipped off, how and by whom a mystery.

Gradowski would learn the whole sickening story a few days later from Kaminski. On June 17th, Noah Zabludowicz showed up at Block 13 seeking its kapo. "How are your men taking it?" was the first thing out of his mouth.

"How do you think? Look at me, this face… that's how they're taking it."

Kaminski's expression did say it all. Never had Noah seen it so drained of emotion, not even after the Czech incident. The eyes were two stagnant, brown pools, the mouth a slit. The voice was just as dead, didn't have the life in it even to register disappointment.

"Not that it matters anymore, but what happened, Noah? Fill me in, what went wrong? I have to assume that's why you're here."

"What went wrong?" The disgust in Noah's face made up for the lack of it in Kaminski's. "What didn't. You're familiar with Battle Group-Auschwitz's preferred method of communication, with its forces in the field, that is."

"By courier you told me once. Radio being too dangerous."

"Well, that Friday, that afternoon no less, a courier from the Home Army command in Krakow was stopped by the Gestapo on the road to Auschwitz and arrested. Not just any courier, either. This one was carrying papers confirming—"

"Papers? *Papers?*"

"Unbelievable, right? Papers confirming partisan readiness for the attack, including their troop strength, firepower, escape routes. And the newest provisions made to deal with the thousands of runaways expected. The date of the uprising was listed, too, and requesting it be corroborated, the exact time."

"Good God."

"As quick as wheels could take them, the SS hauled their catch to Gestapo headquarters in the Stammlager. Not only were the Nazis relieved at their close call, they realized their good fortune needn't end there. If they could come up with the names of those in Krakow who'd sent the courier, and those in Auschwitz he was sent to, they stood a chance of decapitating both the Home Army outside the camp and the Resistance within.

"But he withstood their tortures, at least until we were able to sneak him some poison. The man died a hero, but though it could have ended up a lot worse, that doesn't make the revolt any less dead than he."

"So where does that leave us?" Kaminski asked, as if he didn't know.

"Back where we started. No—further back."

"How do you figure further?"

"The Germans know they've dodged a bullet, but do you honestly think they'll be content to congratulate themselves on their luck and leave it at that? Brace yourself, my friend—changes are coming. How severe these will be remains to be seen, but just because they've been fortunate in preventing a mutiny today doesn't mean the SS are going to let that be the end of it. Not until they've done everything they can to head off another in the future."

Noah's words were to become prophecy. A week after muddling onto the plot, the Nazis uprooted the Sonderkommando from its quarters in Blocks 10, 11, and 13 and billeted it in the attics of Crematorium II and III, IV's defunct oven room, and on cots in V's undressing hall. The idea was to cut the detachment off from any contact with the general population. There would be no recurrence of the underground assisting them in escape should either be tempted to have another go at it.

To further discourage such, the death-house guard was increased fourfold day and night, and the inner cordon to the west similarly reinforced. That part of the outer cordon was fortified, too, with soldiers on the ground. The Sonders' erstwhile barracks were searched, along with the crematoria, but nothing incriminating found. Their weapons lay safely hidden inside walls and beneath floors.

As the officer responsible for the squad, *Hauptscharführer* Möll played a major role in tightening things up. Having suspected for a while that its members were up to something, after June 15th he was to keep them under a microscope. It was his decision to move them into the crematoria, though if he could have, and he did give it some thought, he'd have extinguished the whole commando and drummed up a new one.

The Sonder had feared this very thing, but as the days passed, realized that for the SS to do away with them in the midst of the Hungarian campaign would be to risk wreaking havoc on it, if not doom it outright.

Möll was just as aware that the men of the Special Squad weren't the only ones who bore watching. He had his one eye as well on the soldiers whose province it was to guard them; from what he'd heard, some of these acted more like partners of the Sonder than their overseers. After he'd buried the 12th in its new lodgings, he had their every sentry reassigned, telling their replacements he personally would shoot anyone he caught abetting the Sonder in any illicit comings and goings.

This also went for whoever came calling on the squad, including maintenance crews—*no one* was to be allowed in or out of the Krema yards without a pass. The guards' days of looking the other way in exchange for bribes were over.

The most damaging change the SS implemented had nothing to do with the detachment. With the courier exposing the underground as in on the plot, and cognizant its core consisted of Poles, the Germans saw an opportunity to defang, if not that bandit bunch in Krakow, then this wing of the Home Army. Rounding up the Polish inmates of both camps by the thousands, they hustled them off by train to various lagers inside Germany. They hoped by catching enough meaningful fish in their net to leave those left behind a leaderless mob.

Nor were these abductions confined to the Poles. The Nazis targeted prisoners of every nationality, particularly those classified as political. Thus were Bruno Baum and others carted away, depriving the movement of some of its ablest. (Baum went on to survive the war and live in what became East Germany. He resumed a career in communist politics, wrote several books—one a memoir of his days at Auschwitz—and in 1971 died in his bed surrounded by family and admirers).

The upshot of all this was a Battle Group-Auschwitz left in tatters, not only its chain of command but countless cells fragmented, the labor of years erased within weeks. It wouldn't be the same again, and the specter of Maidanek notwithstanding, abandoned forever the notion of revolt.

It did make sure, however, with the Russians continuing to hammer westward, to alert London to the existence of the Möll Plan, forwarding the details of it via Krakow to the BBC. Attached, too, from its clerical operatives in the *Kommandantur*, the executive and communications center of the Auschwitz administration, were the names and SS identification numbers of the worst killers. These the BBC periodically broadcast in German with the warning that any

Nazis guilty of crimes against humanity would be held accountable for them after the war.

What impact this might end up having, for now appeared nil. Well after the Allies' threat should have given the Germans pause, the Hungarians continued to burn like so many dead leaves, the smoke over Birkenau to darken the sun.

It may have looked it, but not even their watchful sergeant was able to segregate the Sonder completely. Where before they'd had no need of the usual camp rations, now food carriers left the crematoria twice a day for the kitchen, and on top of concealed goods from the black market brought news and other information.

Then there were the men of the *Aschekommando*, the ash-processing squad, their job to empty the fire pits. After hosing down the whitish-gray surface left by the blaze, and once the clouds of hissing steam had quieted some, the prisoners of the ash team were lowered into the pit. Perched atop thick squares of wood sheathed in metal, they would shovel out the often still-shimmering coals. Though protected by heavy gloves, insulated boots, and goggles, burns to the arms and head were common, the windier the day the greater the casualties. The more severe of these ended up at a Dr. Pach's hospital ward in Birkenau's Ka-Be.

The doctor, a Belgian Jew long active in the underground, allowed them as many callers as asked to see them, people like Noah Zabludowicz, Porebski, Hilleli, Godel Silver, men whose visits were about more than simply wishing the injured a speedy recovery.

The young, handsome Jean Pach, as talented and loved a physician as he was fearless an operative, also began making regular house calls—and by that meaning to the death houses, less in a medical capacity than to do his part, too, in keeping the Battle Groups talking.

Which at this stage of the game, admittedly, seemed pointless. Auschwitz kept insisting that the abort of June 15th was merely a postponement until the partisans could be reassembled, and in light of the security changes the SS had made, a new battle plan drawn up. This, as even the good doctor had deduced, was a load of hooey. To the Resistance, what was left of it, armed rebellion had, again, become a bankrupt proposition. Their appeal to the Special Squad for patience was no more than a ploy to try and prevent it from going off half-cocked and acting independently. Its leaders would have said anything to keep Birkenau quiet.

They needn't have worried. There was as little probability now of the Sonder erupting in violence as there was of the Third Reich winning its war. Gradowski could see it in the droop of their shoulders, the slouch in their walk: this latest and cruelest of misadventures had bled all the rambunctiousness right out of them. The Germans could have torn down the barbed wire themselves and been at little risk of losing a single prisoner.

He was as beat down as the next man. To have been so close and come up empty at the last minute was too much, the final straw in a bulging bushel-bagful of them. The general opinion, unspoken but loud and clear, was that maybe it was time to back off, give things a rest for a while.

This, of course, meant leaving the Hungarians to the wolves. With a sigh, Gradowski fell backward on his bunk; the crematoria were no longer in danger and wouldn't be anytime soon, perhaps from now on. But there was more to his sigh than that. As he'd learned to his horrified incredulity last week, the Nazis if it came down to it would have been able to get along just fine without them. He'd heard crazy stories about what was going on at the fire pits, but believing these the irresponsible products of overheated imaginations, hadn't paid them much mind—until he had the misfortune of seeing them in action for himself.

The foulest crimes weren't necessarily occurring in the hidden rooms of the death mills. Worse, much worse, was happening out in the open, in the undeceiving light of day.

That he'd been given a glimpse of what to that point he'd refused to take seriously wasn't by any choice of his, but the result of another's spite. Without intending to, he'd managed to get on the wrong side of his boss Mietek Morawa, something about him not showing the young kapo the proper respect. This was the same Morawa who'd locked horns with Kaminski a year and a half ago, and who those days had been notorious for walking around with a permanent and sometimes murderous frown.

The man had mellowed some since, if not enough to avoid mixing it up with Gradowski. Words were exchanged, and the next morning he was assigned to duty on the Jewish ramp. It wasn't unusual, especially these last months, for the Sonder to be called from their posts to assist where help was needed, if seldom were the oven men and other specialists included. Morawa might not have been the tyrant he used to be, but didn't appear to have lost any of his vindictiveness.

Even with the sun still touching the horizon, when Gradowski and his fellow conscripts reached the ramp, it was to discover a fifty-car transport at the siding and a platform overrun with deportees. Not that they'd been commandeered to help with these. Bringing up the rear of the train were five open boxcars piled with old railroad ties, weathered timbers, and scrap wood in all sizes and shapes. A team was already hip-deep in the stuff, heaving it onto trucks, their shirtless bodies running with sweat, and soon Gradowski's group was sweating alongside them.

The work was punishing, most of the pieces heavy and bristling with splinters. When a truck could hold no more, off it would growl toward one of two massive columns of smoke, the farthest coming from the meadow next to Bunker 5, the other from that near the same-numbered crematorium. Three Sonder clung to the outside of each truck as it left, unloaded it at its destination, and returned in the empty bed. After two hours at the boxcars, Gradowski jumped at the chance to be one of those three, if only to catch a few minutes' breather there and back.

The truck he wound up on bounced along what was a road in name only until reaching the latter meadow. It stopped at a large fuel depot covered with a tin roof, where their SS driver grunted them to work. Thirty meters away a long trench leapt with flames, the rolling boil of its smoke obscuring half the sky.

He'd never been this near a fire pit. Puffs of ash floated everywhere like large, dirty snowflakes. So strong was the stink of burning fat, scorched hair, and kerosene, it stung the eyes, coated the inside of the mouth with a greasy film. Corpses the blue-white color of raw sausages littered the ground, provender for the next fire, while those in this one spluttered and sizzled, arms and legs writhing in slow-motion.

Eight Sonder worked the pit, each wielding a long steel pole, most with stoking forks at the end, some dangling buckets from which they poured what he'd been told to his revulsion a while back was liquid human fat over any trouble areas. Where the fat hit these dead spots, the fire would crackle noisily anew.

As he and the others wrestled with their truckload of wood, Gradowski couldn't keep his eyes off the pyre, fascinated by its surprising size and power. Suddenly, he heard pistol shots, but didn't pay them much mind; gunfire at Birkenau was nothing to get excited about. Instead of dissipating, though, they picked up until they were coming nonstop, accompanied now by a fearful shrieking. Both shrieks and shots seemed to be issuing from another pit seventy meters distant.

Their guard, having wandered off a way, was sitting in the grass with his back to them. After lugging one of the ties into the depot, Gradowski darted behind a stack of lumber, and hurrying to the far side of the shed clambered atop another. What he saw from there took some seconds to sink in, but when it did he had to hold onto the edge of the roof to keep from falling.

A line of SS stood bareheaded along one side of the far pit, tunics unbuttoned in the heat. It was an execution squad. A pair of Sonder holding a deportee by the arms would walk him or her, naked, up to one of the soldiers, who proceeded to shoot the person put before him in the back of the neck with a pistol. Dragging the victim by the heels, the Sonder would fling the limp body into the flames. That they were from the unloading ramp and not the camp was evidenced by the long hair of the females, and the children and aged among them.

Also evident was that most weren't actually dead from the guns, were being thrown into the fire alive. From the stingy pop the pistols were making, the Germans were using the same 6-mm's employed in similar Aktionen, and these tended not to kill right away. Screams so shocking as to make one envy the deaf filled the meadow.

Such was the abomination that had been tormenting Gradowski for a week now, its horror impelling him to a decision. It had been a while since he'd put pen to paper in his capacity as chronicler of Nazi crimes. He did have four jarfuls of damning testimony to his credit, but months had gone by since he'd buried the last. With the addition earlier in the year of the Greek Nadjary to their circle, the number of Sonder diarists had grown to six. For lack lately of anything necessitating a fifth jar, Gradowski had been content to pass the baton of accountability to them.

Now, as the only one of the six witness to this fiendish new component of the fire pits, he would take up his pen again and write about what he'd seen that awful day. Beyond what he'd seen. For having arrived at this decision, he'd sought out those Sonder forced to assist the SS in this latest obscenity of theirs—the same men he'd once accused of exaggeration—and from them learned more than he ever could have in person, the *modus operandi* of the crime in its every detail.

Those condemned to this worst of deaths were the surplus from the ramp, their fate settled because there was no room for them in the crematoria. Depending on how far they'd fallen behind, the Germans might dispatch a whole transport to the fire pits. At both sites, these unlucky ones trod a path in the forest until reaching an undressing barracks. A wall of smoke blackened the sky ahead, the air foul with a curious odor. Herded into the hut in increments of four hundred, they were made to strip naked, then run by tens through a rear door each into the grasp of a Sonder. These then sped them down a narrow trail lined on both sides by armed guards. Another ten would come seconds later.

So disoriented were these groups by thirst, the breakneck pace, and a burgeoning apprehension, they let themselves be led without resistance. At the end of the trail, each was handed off to a pair of Sonder this time, who grabbed their victim by the arms and rushed him or her to the row of SS assassins fronting one of the trenches. The crack of a pistol, a cry of pain and surprise, then into the fire the person went, followed by even more terrible cries. The men and older boys sometimes managed to break free and make a mad run for it, but were immediately gunned down.

Also shot on the spot were any Sonder who hesitated in their duty. While few made them as nervous as this one, every Sonderaktion put the Nazis on edge. Deviating as these did from the norm, outside the controlled environment of the crematorium, there was always the chance they wouldn't go as planned and deteriorate into untidiness, or worse.

With thousands of jittery people on tenterhooks in the woods— wondering where those preceding them had gone, what that smoke, that smell was—the soldiers couldn't see this particular affair to its conclusion too fast. Woe to the Sonder who gummed up the living chain extending from the undressing barracks to the pyres.

In his quest for information, Gradowski turned this up, too: of all the Germans involved in this newest display of murder, none had a bigger hand in it than the beast Otto Möll. To ease not only the congestion but the strain the Hungarians were putting on his stocks of Zyklon-B, it was his idea to enlist his infernal fires in double duty. He liked it, too, that it saved time, combining in one package the killing and disposal processes.

Those Sonder working outdoors had plenty to say about their fearsome sergeant. Resplendent in a spotless, dress-white SS tunic, the Kriegsverdienstkreuz prominent, he strutted about with the swagger of a general at his headquarters. Not that he commanded from some rear echelon at a comfortable remove from the fray. Möll was right down there in the mud and the blood, at all hours of the day and night, bouncing between the unloading ramp and the death houses, all nine of his treasured cremation pits. A big part of his duties was determining who of those selected for extermination went where from the ramp, meaning he had to be aware at all times of each killing site's status.

It also meant the newly detrained waiting in limbo for hours while a gas chamber or fire pit was cleared of its dead. Much of his day was spent dashing from one of these groups to another trying to smooth their harried nerves, deflect their demands for the water they'd been promised since the ramp. As empty a promise as it was, to have disregarded such desperate people entirely would have been to invite trouble. The last thing he wanted was a riot on his hands and the panic that might spread from its suppression.

But his days weren't all work. Busy as he was, he never failed to make room for the odd diversion, accomplished as always at mixing business with pleasure. He liked it when he saw a Jew putting up a struggle, or a tentative or otherwise underperforming Sonder; it gave him a chance to show off his marksmanship. Calling for a rifle, with a single shot he'd solve the problem. Could drop a man at a hundred meters, pick him right out of a crowd.

This was as nothing, however, to what came over him when his blood was up. When his day wasn't going right, or even when it was, Möll was known to work himself into a fury. According to those who'd seen it, he was no longer what could be called human then but a raging, profanity-spouting demon careening from one atrocity to the next.

If he wasn't setting his devil-dog Hannibal loose on whatever wretches he'd chosen for that bit of fun, he was stomping around with a wild look on him, preying on people at random, children and the elderly as a rule, the more pitiful his victim the better. He might ask an old woman if she enjoyed the smell of roses. Then take a whiff of this, he would say, putting the muzzle of his Luger to one of her nostrils and pulling the trigger. Or tearing a baby from its mother's arms, sling it into the fire or one of the reservoirs of boiling fat, laughing he'd just saved the Reich a bullet.

After shooting the screaming woman, he'd stand there hands on hips, expression defiant, as if daring anyone to object.

A more subdued moment might find him positioned where he could see the faces of the deportees when they first laid eyes on the fiery ditch roaring in front of them, soaking up the terror in those eyes as he welcomed them to his "little clambake." Like some kind of leech, some psychic parasite, he would feed off their fright, his own features glazing over with a voluptuary's bliss.

Whether manic or subdued, even his fellow SS were careful to keep their distance when Möll was around. Not only was there no telling what he might do—and when really off his nut to whom, not even they felt immune—there were things he did do that to no less than their hardened selves weren't easy to watch.

Scripture divided the Jewish hell into three realms: Abaddon, the bottomless pit; Sheol, the abode of shadows; and Gehenna, the lake of fire. Though there could be no question which the desecrated meadows of Birkenau resembled, it wasn't because of the pyres alone. From the tales told Gradowski, the sheer, inundating carnage of them was as evocative as the flames.

Not just bodies but body parts lay everywhere. Those fire pits still to be emptied of their coals invariably featured a macabre carpet of skulls. Smaller, subsidiary pits radiated outward from the ask-crushing slabs, their purpose to burn those odd gobbets of flesh not consumed by the bigger blazes. To see feet, heads, fingers all roasting together in a pile was in its way more unsettling than watching intact corpses burn.

From these same slabs came the music of this hell on earth, the monotonous chanting of those Sonder whose job was to pulverize and sift the flow of cinders from the pits. For some reason, these men were exclusively Greek. All day they walked the hot concrete tamping their tall, heavy mortars in front of them, turning baked bones into powder, boredom into song. More dirge in reality than song, these consisted of one deep-pitched requiem after another, refrains from the old country so mournful as to crush the spirit into its own semblance of ash.

With a long, melodramatic groan that would have done the Greeks proud, Gradowski hauled himself back into a sitting position. Sleep less likely a visitor than ever what with not only June 15th now but the excesses of the fire pits stuck in his head, tonight was as good a one as any, he figured, to begin a piece featuring both. One, after all, was as revealing as the other of the deadly madhouse that was Auschwitz.

He lit his candle and dug up a pen, some paper he had left over, a small bottle of ink. He thought about making the usual tent of his blanket, but it was too hot for that. Plus, his wasn't only an upper bunk but flush against a wall, and the few neighbors surrounding him down for the count.

It would take him a week to finish his testimony and bury it in the yard of Crematorium II. The demented Möll inhabited a good deal of it, but only as an extreme example of his kind. Those pages he'd devoted to the fire pits were intended to document the evils of the SS as an organization, not simply those of its individual members. If anything, Möll's debauches reflected as badly on the group as the man in that they demonstrated how an individual as sick in the head as the *Hauptscharführer* could not merely find refuge but thrive in the service of it.

Little did anyone know the murderous sergeant had arguably worse up his sleeve. If he'd delayed embarking on it another week, Gradowski could have topped off his account with a bombshell of an ending, a turn of events as undreamed of as it was devastating. The dog days of this hottest and bloodiest of summers would see Möll perpetrate, if not his blackest infamy, one that would rip the heart and soul right out of the Sonder.

If by some miracle he should live to be an old man, never would Gradowski forget that accursed August night. It was one of the saddest he'd ever suffered, and for a Sonder that was saying something.

*   *   *

By August, the Hungarian Jews were finished, or those the Germans had been able to get their hands on. In less than three months, half a million of them had disappeared in Birkenau's flames alone, and but for the religious leaders and more politically moderate of their countrymen, the even more heroic efforts of the Swedish envoy to Budapest Raoul Wallenberg, and the diplomatic pressure finally brought to bear by Great Britain, the United States, the Vatican and others, the toll would have been higher. Citing the groundswell of condemnation from both within and without, Miklós Horthy, who'd been freed from arrest to serve as head of the puppet government, stood up to the Nazis and halted the deportation of Jewish "workers" northward.

Unable to conclude the job they'd started without the cooperation of Budapest, and with the Red Army getting closer to the capitol by the week, *Obersturmbannführer* Eichmann and his staff were recalled to Berlin.

Transports from the south would continue to arrive at Birkenau, but grew significantly smaller and less frequent. Bunker 5 and its outbuildings were dismantled, its fire pits filled in, as were those in the meadow adjoining Crematorium V. This and other signs didn't bode at all well for the Sonderkommando. True, with the deportees again at a manageable level, the SS could concentrate on the badly needed repair and refurbishing of the crematoria. But how long could that last, a month? And then what?

Though none was so craven as to wish it, the only way the Sonder were going to feel safe was if the Germans at this point, with the arrival of the Soviets but a matter of time, should set their sights on those prisoners already in their clutches. To justify so large a commando, the number of selections carried out inside the wire would have to start rivaling that rung up at the ramp.

The liquidation of the Gypsy Camp in August appeared to foretell this very thing, especially when coupled with that of the Czechoslovakians prior to the Hungarian interruption. Like that of the Theresienstadt Jews, the gypsy *B2e* lager was a family camp, four thousand men, women, and children living in isolation, and but for scant rations, well-treated. They weren't required to work, wear the prison stripes or tattoo, nor have their heads shaved. That they weren't only Catholic but German had more than a few of their guards puzzled they were there at all.

In fact, they were a pet project of none other than *Reichsführer* Himmler, who'd had tens of thousands of them rounded up from all over the continent and sent to the camps. Fascinated by the myths and imagery, the archaeology of prehistoric Germany, Himmler fancied the mysterious gypsies as being a living offshoot of the proto-Nordic tribes of lore, the Stone-Age inhabitants of the primeval forests of northern Europe.

As far as Nazi ideology went, this was a stretch. The more orthodox of the Third Reich's racial apologists asserted the opposite, portraying the gypsies as not much different than the Jews in that they were non-Teutonic and parasitic, a culturally unassimilated infestation from abroad who prospered at the expense of their host populations. Himmler would not be denied, though, not entirely. Those gathered from the German countryside were sent to Birkenau, not for obliteration but observation, encouraged to continue their folk traditions and way of life as best they could.

What support this ended up furnishing the idiosyncratic *Reichsführer's* theory was never determined, but it did provide a break from their soldier's routine for the guards to whose care this flesh-and-blood diorama was entrusted. These were often audience to the gypsies at play, to the spirited music and dances for which this colorful people was noted. A few even struck up friendships among this exotic parallel of their race; the gypsies were Aryan, spoke German, had German loyalties, some soldiers themselves in the Kaiser's army of the previous war.

But with the present one going badly and his own future to worry about, Himmler lost interest in the project. Coming to view his Birkenau *Roma* as more of an encumbrance than anything, and potential witnesses against him post-war, he ordered them exterminated. Under the expert direction of *Hauptscharführer* Möll, this was completed in a matter of hours.

On the muggy night of August 2nd, twenty-five hundred of the disbelieving gypsies were trucked to Crematorium III, the rest to Number Five. What they couldn't understand was why their friends the guards should have turned on them. Like the just as confused Jews of the Czech camp, they argued, pleaded, wept, but to no avail—an hour before midnight, the pounding on Number Three's gas-chamber door weakened and then stopped. Thirty Sonder from Squad 57B, second shift, stood sweating in the steamy anteroom, hoses and meat hooks at the ready, waiting for the SS doctor in charge to order the door opened.

Before he could, the tramp of boots echoed from the corridor to their rear. All heads turned to see Sergeant Möll enter the room, a half-dozen helmeted soldiers at his heels. Fully armed, these fanned out in front of the men, Möll in the center. For several long seconds, he just stood there, glowering at them. But when he did speak, the voice was honey if the more sinister for it.

"Kapo Kaminski, front and center, please, sir. If you would be so kind."

Kaminski had been expecting this, having sensed Möll was onto him for his part in the stymied revolt. Many was the time he'd looked up to see the sergeant staring a hole in him, as if to let him know he hadn't got away with anything. His only surprise, now that it had happened, was that the bastard had taken so long to call him out.

"Upstairs with him," Möll ordered the soldiers. Then to the SS doctor, "Keep the gas chamber sealed until I get back."

The elevator door slid closed with Kaminski directing a wan smile and a thumbs-up at his men. Neither inspired much confidence. They knew this wasn't good, was worse than not good, but immediately fell to trying to convince each other it was nothing, that their kapo's expertise was merely needed elsewhere. The more they talked, the emptier their words, as devoid of substance as the flakes of ash soon to be whorling from the chimney.

Once at the ground floor, Möll left Kaminski under guard at the morgue while he checked to make sure all was as it should be in the oven room. Both men and equipment were in for a long night. This translated, too, into no sleep for him, but that was all right; the dicey part of the Aktion was over, the gypsies sent to gypsy heaven without incident. All that remained now was to clean up the mess.

The ovens were manned and ready. With a bounce to his step, he hurried back to the morgue, the happy task ahead of him a month and a half coming. From the first, he'd held Kaminski the driving force behind the attempted rebellion, and resented him for not only that but his fake loyalty. Now he had proof of the kapo's treachery, or all the proof he needed. Few things riled the sergeant more than hypocrisy; he'd been itching all day to wipe the phony affability from this Kaminski's face forever.

A single bulb burned in the morgue's ceiling, shadows growing in the corners like mold. Kaminski saw little point in feigning innocence.

"It was Mietek Morawa, wasn't it?" he said "The kapo from next door."

"Morawa?" Möll did play innocent. "What about him?"

"It was he who tipped you off. Ratted me out."

"Ratted you out? Pray tell, about what? I don't—"

"Lay off it, *Hauptscharführer*. You know perfectly well about what. I'd be glad to spell it out for you, if that's what you're waiting for."

"So you blame Morawa, do you?" Möll's laugh was cold. "I hate to disappoint, but you've got it all wrong. If you have to blame someone, my suggestion would be to dig up a mirror. There you'll find the man who put you in the fix you're in."

"And what fix is that?"

"Why, you're going to die, my dear fellow. And in a very few minutes. As much as I'd like to, we're not here to chat."

"Die?" It was Kaminski's turn to laugh, a long one. Too long. "I've died a thousand deaths in the past two years. I died every time I led a child into the gas chamber, then carried his little body out later and sent it up here to be burned. I died when I had to tell some terrified old grandmother to keep moving, it's only a shower, nothing to worry about, you'll be fine. I died when I heard the Zyklon pellets hit the floor and start hissing, at the screams that followed and never completely left my head.

"And when the tattoo numbers of my men were called—boys really, most of them—when their numbers were read from a list and they were marched away by you people, killed by you people, a part of me went with them and died as sure as they."

Möll clapped his hands in slow, exaggerated applause. "Touching, very touching. I do believe you missed your calling, Rabbi Kaminski. But just what is your point?"

"I should think it obvious: you can't kill a dead man. The dead are past harming. If anything, you'd be doing me a favor by shooting me."

"By all means then, let's get on with it. My aim, if you'll pardon the word, is to please." Möll loosened his holster strap, rested a hand atop the butt of his Luger.

"But first, this," he said, "Did you really think you and that degenerate trash you command would succeed in escaping? In getting the better of us?"

"What makes *you* think we won't yet? That we won't stop 'til we do?"

"Because the Jew is by nature a coward. And the SS invincible. Or haven't you, kapo, been keeping score?"

Kaminski lit the room with a smirk as big as the life he was about to leave. "We'll see how invincible you are, little man, when the Russians come knocking. When it's not defenseless women and children you're up against, but grown men with guns. Your days, I hope you realize, are numbered, Otto Möll. Yours and that pack of murdering dogs that—"

"So *you* say!"

"Yours and that pack of hyenas that wear the skulls on your collars. But then you already know, I can tell, what's in store for you and those like you."

"Shut your filthy kike mouth!" The German's color alternated between red and pale, one to the other and back again, as from some rare tropical fever.

"I can tell from what I see in that one real eye of yours that you know." Kaminski's smirk had a scornful chuckle to it now. "That you're more than just angry, you're—what? Scared? By God, that's it, isn't it? You're scared because it's plain even to you that someone somewhere in the not too distant future is going to have both the privilege and pleasure of slipping a noose around your neck."

"I said shut your mouth!" Möll jerked his pistol from its holster.

"And there's a good chance this someone, which I'd be willing to bet is what frightens you the most, will turn out to be, yes—nothing less than a Jew."

In the anteroom to the gas chamber, expecting exactly what they weren't sure, the Sonder heard the muffled bang of a gunshot overhead. Then another. Möll emerged shortly from the elevator. Having shed the restraint he'd shown earlier, he strode excitedly back and forth in front of them.

"Kapo Kaminski is dead! He has been found guilty and executed! His crime was to plot against the camp authorities. Against us, the SS!"

Though prepared for this, several of the Sonder almost collapsed where they stood.

"This is what you can expect if opposing the Third Reich! There is no future in such foolishness, you cannot win. You will only end up dying stupidly like your kapo. Do you understand? Are you following me?"

Many of them had the German to keep up with him, but kept silent.

"Say something, goddammit!"

"Yes, *Hauptscharführer*," came the uneven reply. "We understand."

Möll glared at them before ordering the door to the gas chamber opened. "See that you remember it then," he hurled behind him as he stormed out.

There were no secrets in the crematorium. As if by osmosis, the men in the oven room knew what was happening even as it happened, and were prepared. Two soldiers carried Kaminski in just as the first of the gypsies were coming up. He'd been shot in the neck and the left eye, this last leaving a gaping hole. But for this awfulness, his face was at peace, lips set in a serene smile.

Leventhal and Warszawski claimed the body and hastened it to a corner, where they spread a canvas tarp over it before returning to their stations. When the day shift showed at dawn, they were filled in. The plan was to assemble after the gypsies were taken care of and give their poor kapo as decent a funeral as possible.

At noon, word reached the attic the oven room was ready. Not everyone who wanted was allowed to attend, lest this arouse notice. Only those closest to Kaminski were invited, with the dayan Leyb Langfus to conduct the service.

The place was still wreathed in smoke when the mourners arrived. Möll, luckily, was long gone, having left two *Schützen* in charge. These sat at a table against the back wall deep into a game of cards. Muffle 15 at the far end was cleared to go, and while the day crew busied itself with the last of the night's corpses, a dozen men gathered in front of it.

The body was retrieved from its corner and laid on the metal stretcher. As it disappeared into the fire, some wept softly. Langfus faced the furnace and spread his arms. He'd chosen the *El Male Rachamim*, a ritual prayer for the dead not only shorter—he had no idea how long they'd have—but to him more personal than the formalistic *Kaddish*. He spoke just loud enough to be heard above the flames without attracting the attention of the guards.

"O, God full of mercy Who dwells in the heights, provide a rest upon the Divine Presence's wings—within the range of the holy, pure, and glorious, Whose shining resembles the sky's—to the soul of Marian Kaminski, for a charity was given to his memory.

"Therefore, the Master of Mercy will protect him forever, from behind the hiding of His wings, and will tie his soul with the rope of life. The Everlasting will be his heritage, and he shall rest peacefully upon his dying place."

The dayan turned to his congregation. "And let us now say…"

"Amen," they responded.

Brief it may have been, but tugged nonetheless at those heartstrings where grief and ceremony intersect. For a long moment, there was silence but for the clank and thrum of the ovens, all heads bowed as one. Until Langfus, raising his to find the two SS still hard at their game, realized he had time after all.

"The death of any person is a thing to be mourned, but none more than that of this man. Not only has our leader and inspiration been taken from us, but a dear friend. A friend to many. Hundreds of women survive today because of the food and medicines he ferried to C Camp. How many of *us* are alive that he talked out of suicide? And is there a man here who hasn't seen him sit down with a child, a frightened, motherless child on its way to the gas chamber, and comfort it into not being afraid anymore?

"He could be hard to deal with, this Kaminski, stubborn, egotistical, but never hard to like. Not for long. For all his faults, he was the best of us, nor shall we see his ilk again."

Scattered murmurs of agreement. The dayan was beginning to warm.

"What's important now is that we carry on without him, and by this I mean finish the work he started. It was Kaminski who planted then nurtured the seed of revolt, and though he later gave ear to the false counsel coming from the Stammlager and allowed that seed's bud to wither on the vine, in the end he made every effort to revive it, this probably costing him his life.

"Are we to let our kapo, our friend, die in vain and his dream with him? I would rather die myself than choose so cowardly a path. I haven't a doubt that he's watching us, waiting to see what we'll do in his absence. Would you betray him by doing nothing and letting the crematoria stand? Would you carry so damning a sin to your graves?"

His eyes were now blazing as hot as the oven at his back. "It is our duty to see Operation Jericho outlive its creator. We owe it not only to him and the thousands his vision might yet save but, if you'll recall what the man himself told us one June night, to ourselves."

Langfus couldn't say where these words of his came from. Unsure he'd have a chance to speak at all, he hadn't prepared anything. Yet so effortlessly had they rolled off his tongue, without him even having to think, it was as if they weren't his but dictated by another.

For all he cared, the devil himself could have spun them. For besides eulogizing his kapo to the extent he felt fitting, he was hoping they might, too, in their small way, keep the spark of armed rebellion alive.

This would soon prove of concern to their departed commander's lieutenants. Before his death, and as he had after the Familienlager letdown, Kaminski had put the disillusion of June behind him and begun psyching the Sonder up for another attempt at a breakout. This time on their own. Combination optimist and pragmatist that he was, he'd sought to turn a minus into a plus by arguing that freed from having to protect thousands of escapees from the camp, the rebels could move faster and disperse themselves more effectively once past the wire.

That the squad, too, was now quartered in the crematoria should make up for the lack of partisan assistance in the assault on this inner cordon. Critical also was his decision to reschedule Jericho for night. The commando's guards were to be overcome as before, but the main attack was to be delayed an hour and a half to take advantage of the darkness. Anything that might complicate the German pursuit was a help.

He'd also worked up a new battle plan. The weapons hidden in the old barracks would have been retrieved days before and smuggled into the death houses. The signal to launch would be the demolition of Crematorium III, followed by that of the others. As soon as each blew, its Sonder were to attack their section of the perimeter. The first through the wire would hurry to the aid of any still pinned down. This should have the squad out and making tracks for the Sola in minutes.

Propelled by this latest strategy's simplicity and the renewed prodding of its author, momentum was inching forward again, the pendulum of insurrection to swing the other way. Then came the game-changing night of August 2nd.

To the Hungarians, the revolt died with Kaminski. To them he *was* the revolt, its legs, its head, its heart; without him to lead them, they didn't want to hear it. Nor did those Sonder who'd replaced him at the helm of the Battle Group have yet to unstop any ears. Anything short of his ghost appearing to take charge again was going to leave the Hungarians unmoved.

The saddest part was, as if it could be any sadder, Kaminski needn't have become a ghost at all. Where he'd made his mistake—where he'd lost his head first figuratively then literally—was having trusted in Mietek Morawa. After learning of the foiled plot, and guessing his old rival had been in on it, Morawa went to him and asked why he hadn't been included. Still wary of the man, but willing to let bygones be bygones, Kaminski promised him a role in the upcoming attempt. Contributing to his decision was the potential he saw in the powerful young Pole to attract conspirators and hasten the revival of rebel morale.

Morawa, unfortunately, wasn't the type to forget a slight. He'd held a grudge against Kaminski since forced to share the kapoship of the new Crematorium II back in the spring of '43. His resentment had matured over the months like an expensive if nasty-smelling cheese, one he'd refrained from taking a bite of until it would do the most damage.

His patience paid off. Having got his nemesis where he wanted him at last, he rushed the minutes of their meeting to Otto Möll.

Though most suspected him of it, only later did the Sonder receive confirmation of the despicable kapo's betrayal. He got drunk one afternoon with his Polish buddies and began boasting loudly of his part in Kaminski's undoing. This indiscretion was soon the talk of the detachment, and while nothing could be done about it now, many in the Sonder also had long memories.

On hearing of his death, Noah Zabludowicz had headed straight for Roza Robota with the news. Who had difficulty believing then accepting it; in their one meeting, she'd taken an instant liking to the big, blustery kapo. But as cruel a blow as his murder dealt her personally, greater was her fear of how it might affect the revolt.

Fear became fact at her next rendezvous with her Sonder contacts in the Bekleidungs yard. With the packet of gunpowder safely in the clothing cart, she cornered Yankel Handelsman and asked him how the squad was handling its loss. He said it had in effect paralyzed the commando, draining the ambition right out of it. Kaminski, he explained, had been more than just their kapo; he was commanding officer, father figure, and friend all rolled into one. The hurt of his passing was too deep, the blow too heavy. Everyone, not just the Hungarians, was still reeling from it.

As frustrating as this was, Roza could sympathize. If she wanted to be honest, what with the kick in the teeth of June and now this, some of the stuffing had been knocked out of her, too. Not enough to dampen her enthusiasm for the revolt, but then she'd have likelier lost her enthusiasm for breathing.

She was, however, and almost as difficult to process, having second thoughts about her mission. One day she couldn't imagine living without it, with no longer sinking a big part of her energies, her time, *herself* into maintaining the flow of gunpowder to the crematoria. The next, she didn't see the profit in it anymore, not when balanced against the risks. If the Sonder didn't have a passable store of dynamite by now, when would they?

But with the summer winding down, the Nazis pulled a surprise that threatened to make up her mind for her. While the male prisoner-workers at the Union plant were housed in nearby Auschwitz, the females came from Birkenau, three kilometers distant. To increase their factory-hours, hence their productivity, the Germans decided to do away with this hike by relocating them to an area carved out of the main camp's Frauenlager.

This extension of the women's camp became a miniature lager unto itself, comprising three barracks only: one for those condemned to medical experimentation, one solely for the Union workers, and the third to be shared by the remainder of those and the much smaller group of *Shuhkommando* women, their job to recycle old shoes for their leather.

Hauptsturmführer Franz Hössler was appointed commandant of this encampment, and approached his new posting with a proprietary zeal. He was particularly proud of his Union girls, going to some length to elevate them above the common prisoner. Their new lodgings, Blocks 22 and 23, came with washrooms, wooden floors, better mattresses, and sufficient Stubendiensten to keep them clean. He even set aside an area in Block 23 to serve as a small cinema. Movies! What next, the women joked, popcorn?

They were issued clean stripes weekly, and flower-dotted white aprons complete with pockets. And allowed to grow their hair back, their bread ration upped. Above all, barring injury or illness, they were to be spared the ordeal of selections. Hössler, in justifying this, claimed munitions work too important to suffer from a revolving door of trainees. Wasn't it to make the women more productive that they'd been transferred in the first place?

So protective of them was he they took to calling him Papa Hössler, an appellation that never failed to make him smile. The SS captain couldn't have wished for an assignment better suited him. That vanity which kept him always impeccably groomed and attired found a perfect outlet in this corner of Auschwitz entrusted him. Little wonder he jumped at the chance to play the paterfamilias, even if only to a collection of scabby Jewesses.

Their new Stammlager address might have improved the lives of the Union women, but was a knife to the heart of Roza's operation. Two and a half miles now separated her from those she depended on for the gunpowder. Stealing it remained no problem, but how were Esther and Hanka, Ala, Rose, Regina and the rest supposed to get it to Birkenau?

Again, maybe they weren't. Maybe this was a sign, a warning from somewhere telling her to quit while the quitting was good. Whatever it was, from wherever it came, it hadn't left her much choice.

Until during their soup break at the Bekleidungskammer one day, her friend Marta sidled up to her. "So, Roza, what are you going to do now?"

"Do?" She looked tired. "About what?"

"Your Union girls. Now that they're in Auschwitz, how do you intend to keep things going?"

"Oh, the dynamite." A pause. "I don't," she said finally. "I mean, I don't know."

"Which is it," Marta said, "you don't or you don't know?"

"I don't know that, either." Roza had to laugh at her own absurdness. "A part of me is wanting to call the mission a success and be done with it. To stop while we're ahead. If even one of us were caught packing, so much for the revolt. We've been lucky so far, but how long can it last?"

"And that other part of you?"

"That's complicated. It's not easy giving up something you've eaten, slept, breathed, and otherwise obsessed on. That's figured so large in your life for so long. And if another ounce of gunpowder would see another Nazi dead, I wouldn't mind running the stuff until there wasn't any left to steal."

Marta took her by the hand and squeezed. "I'm with you there, love, and glad to hear you say it. For there may be a way yet to salvage the situation, and with next to no added risk."

"What—you have a plan?" Roza could have kissed her. "Don't tell me you've been losing sleep over this, too."

"Ever since I heard about it. And no, it's not a plan exactly, not yet. But I'm hoping."

"I should have taken it for granted you'd be ahead of me on this. Hope, you say?"

"We'll see. Let me work on it. I'll get back to you when I find something out, good or bad."

Marta knew someone who worked in the main camp's *Paketstelle*, or parcel room, where the packages from home for the non-Jewish inmates arrived and were distributed. Every Sunday, a truck loaded with these made the trip to Birkenau. Through her connections, she managed a pass for the Stelle, and the woman agreed to help.

She'd accept a bundle per week from one of the Union women, enclose it in a box disguised to look as if it had traveled the postal system, and send it with the others on the truck. It would be addressed to a different name each time, all fictitious, in care of Dr. Pach's infirmary. Marta would pick it up there and deliver it to Roza. She swore by this contact of hers, and indeed the first shipment came through without a hitch.

Roza never ceased to marvel at the resourcefulness of the women she'd surrounded herself with. In a way, she almost pitied the SS, whose parochial view of her sex had them always fighting with one hand tied behind their backs. A view, she liked to think, they would one day pay for in blood.

Satisfying as this latest victory was, it couldn't make up for the transplanting of her people. She hadn't just lost co-conspirators but friends, one above all. But for Noah, she'd never had a friend as close as Esther Wajcblum, wouldn't allow herself the thought she might never see her again. Before the move, as if touched by her sorrow, Dame Fortune wasn't so cruel as to deny Roza the chance to say goodbye. Upon catching word of it, she'd rushed that very evening to Block 2.

The Union's day shift having just finished its Appell, the barracks was as loud as one might expect with hundreds of women making up for the conversation denied them most of the day. Esther, however, lay alone in her koje. Her sister was working nights that week.

"Roza!" She jumped to her feet. "You came!"

They held each other in a hug longer than normal before sitting down. Roza got right to the point. "I heard today about the outfit's transfer to the Stammlager. When do you leave?"

Esther's smile wilted. "Day after tomorrow. Or that's what they're saying."

Not wholly convinced of it until now, Roza's own face fell. "Which is why I'm here, Esther. To say—well, I guess you know what I'm here to say."

"I do, and have been dreading it. I'm going to miss you, Roza Robota, more than you can imagine."

"What's hard for me to imagine is yourself up and running out on me like this. Who the hell am I supposed to dance the tango with now?"

Esther's laugh was hollow. "I used to live for those dances, you know, couldn't wait to see you walk through that door. It wasn't just the dancing, either, fun as that was. Hanka and the others singing, clapping us on, even the blockova joining in… everyone forgetting herself for a moment, her hunger, her heartache. Those were good times, weren't they?"

"The best. How about that night we…"

For a good half an hour, they blocked out why Roza was there, filling the minutes with memories instead. When they'd exhausted these, they simply sat, silent, basking in the warmth of them. Roza was the first to speak.

"I never told you this, Estusia, but from the week we met you've been like a sister to me. In some ways even more than my own dear dead sister. When Shoshonna died, a part of me went with her. I may have talked the same, acted the same, but something inside me was missing. Then you came along, and… It's as if I was meant to find you. And, I'd like to believe, you me."

Esther could feel the waterworks coming. Another few seconds and she'd be blubbering like a baby. She bit her lip. Harder. If she had to bite it half-off, she wasn't going to cry. The last thing this needed was tears.

"If that's true," she said, "and we *were* meant to meet, what's all this about goodbye? That doesn't do either of us any good, doesn't even follow; if it was meant to be, it was meant to last. I say we stop torturing ourselves with 'goodbye' and think of it as 'until we meet again.' "

Roza smiled her approval. "Better. Much. Until we meet again."

Not trusting her emotions, Esther hurried the conversation in a different direction. "There is something else been eating at me, though. What's to be done about the gunpowder, Roza? With you here in Birkenau and us in Auschwitz, how are we supposed to go about getting it to you?"

"I'm not sure, not yet anyway. It's not looking good, that much I do know."

"What about the underground? Can't they help?"

"The *underground*..." The word was as sour in Roza's mouth as if she'd bit into a lemon. "The SS would sooner come to our aid than those bums. The so-called Battle Group at Auschwitz, don't get me started, is doing everything it can to keep the lid on the crematoria, Sonder aggressiveness from boiling over. We'd be fools to expect any help from them."

Esther fell back on the mattress, lay there a moment staring at the wood slats above. Roza could see the wheels in her head turning. "Tell me," she said finally. "and be honest, Rozhka. What are the odds of it coming to pass?"

"As I said, they're not so great. But should I light on a way to keep us in business, you Pulverraum girls will be the first—"

"No, not that." Esther sat up again. "I wasn't talking about that. Ever since told we'd be leaving, I figured our smuggling days were done. And I'm okay with that. Not happy, but okay. By now the Special Squad should have all the gunpowder they need.

"What I want to know is if they're ever going to use it. If a revolt is still in the cards. Or if June 15th, that awful day, was the end of everything we worked for, risked our lives for. I'm not asking for myself, either, or my little sister, or Tadek. From what Marta's been saying, the Sonder would have their hands full just trying to save themselves now, forget about taking the rest of us with them.

"But I'd be good with that, too—as long as I lived to see *something* happen. Again, and be straight with me, Roza, what in your opinion are the chances of something happening?"

Painful a pill as it was to swallow, she, too, had come to have her doubts, but wasn't about to add to Esther's by sharing them. "An awful day if ever there was. Couldn't have been worse. But what about before it turned awful, before everything unraveled? Remember the excitement, the electricity of that morning?"

"My hands were shaking so, I could hardly do my job."

"Maybe we should be asking ourselves this then, and this is my point. Doesn't that morning promise well? The Sonder weren't only ready, they were raring to go, and would have made a warm show of it if the underground hadn't got careless. But just because things didn't come to a head then, isn't to say they won't ever. I wouldn't call June the end of anything, but a beginning. If the Sonder can rise to the occasion once, they can again, right?"

Esther nodded eagerly, as a child might. So ingenuous a response moved Roza to reassure her further.

"This Sonderkommando, the 12th, isn't like any that came before it. These men have no illusions about what the Germans have planned for them, and now, with the Hungarians a done deal, they know they're next. They'll fight before they submit, fight like cornered animals. Or that's what my buddy Noah says—I've told you about Noah—and no one is closer to the Sonder than he."

This wasn't altogether accurate. According to him, after the twin heartbreaks of first June then August, how receptive the Sonder would be to taking up the banner of revolt again was anybody's guess. Even more discouraging was the negative report Handelsman had given her, who being a Sonder himself ought to know. Roza, however, as a charity to Esther, had chosen to overstate the squad's toughness. With the desired result.

"I see what you're saying, and thank you, Raizele, for saying it. You have a knack for laying my silly fears to rest, a positive talent for making me feel better. What in the world am I going to do without you?"

"You're going to survive, that's what, you and your sister, until the Russians get here and the evil is over. A few more months and it'll be over. What's a few months? I'm going to come for you then, and I'd better find you, and by that I mean alive. I want you to swear, Estusia, you'll still be alive."

Before she could answer, the noisy barracks got suddenly noisier, a commotion breaking out in front of the quartermaster's office. It was the evening's bread distribution, chaos as usual, everyone stampeding that end of the hut.

Roza wondered if this wasn't a cue to start saying her farewells. She had to leave eventually, and conversation wasn't going to be easy in all this racket. If any conversation remained to be had—it seemed to her they'd said everything there was to.

Her question was answered when, momentarily distracted by the jostling crowd, she turned back to Esther. Who, having seen something in Roza's expression hinting at their visit drawing to a close, was unable to keep a tear from staining each cheek. Two tears, that was it, no weeping, no dramatics, but sufficient that Roza felt her own eyes misting.

And this wouldn't do. This was forbidden. The vow she'd sworn herself those two Novembers ago on the unloading ramp was binding still: any tears she might in a weak moment be tempted to shed would have to wait for the end of the war. Weak moments were luxuries she couldn't afford, not as long as she and hers remained in SS hands.

One last lingering hug, therefore, a whispered "Until we meet again," and she left before grief could get the better of her, pushing a path to the door without looking back.

She had a rotten few days after that. She'd wanted to see Ala off, too, and Rose, Mala, Regina. Given how it had gone with Esther, though, it was just as well she hadn't. One wrenching adieu had been plenty. Call it selfish, call it cowardly, call it what one would, she couldn't trust herself not to crumple into a wet, weepy heap if forced to go through another.

But the episode with Esther, then her guilt at flaking out on the others, weren't all that had her in the dumps. As impossible as she would have thought it a month ago, the revolt was as dead in the water as the harpooned carcass of some whale. With what might have been as little likelihood of resuscitation. Roza's spirits for those few days were at as low an ebb as they'd been since her Shoshonna had embraced the lethal fence.

But to her bafflement as much as relief, they didn't stay so. Faint at first but getting stronger by the day, a feeling crept up on her she was at a loss to explain. There was no accounting for it, but no ignoring it, either. It ran like a shiny, gold thread through the hanging black crepe of her despair: the unsupported yet rock-ribbed certainty everything was going to be just fine after all. Somehow she knew, regardless of how it may have looked, that the uprising was far from history, its arrival ordained, as unstoppable as the rise and fall of the sun, moon, and stars.

She was at a loss whether to be thrilled or disturbed by this. Was she the victim of wishful thinking, of self-delusion born of desperation, or was she tapping into something outside the pale of human understanding, being given a glimpse through a window not ordinarily open? Whatever it was, sixth sense or nonsense, it wasn't going away.

Which left her the choice of listening to her head or her gut, one the voice of rationality but fraught with misgiving, the other of irrationality and hope.

In the end, the choice was so obvious as to be none at all.

Autumn

The news broke the first week of September and swept through the crematoria like a cool wind: Otto Möll was gone, like as not for good, transferred to the subcamp of Gleiwitz as its new commandant.

Gleiwitz was one of the larger moons in the Auschwitz orbit, the *Hauptscharführer's* reward for a job well done at Birkenau. Where he was posted to or why, though, mattered little to the Sonderkommando, as long as it was far away. Death and the master sergeant were two sides of the same coin; where he went the other followed, as surely as tails followed heads. Given the impunity with which he'd had a hand in wiping out whole squads in the past, and his undisguised enmity toward the 12th as an incubator of revolt, his departure left its members breathing freer than they had since the spring.

But with Möll out of the picture, complacency entered it, adding to Sonder passiveness. Aggravating it was a rumor asserting the SS were putting an end to the liquidations that had eviscerated all previous detachments. It was no secret the Nazis feared these periodic vettings, should the day come those selected for "reassignment" resist the order. Many thought this why the Germans had yet even to hint at reducing the menacingly large 12th, and that with it going on seven months since its establishment. A year and beyond for the two hundred of them carried over from the 11th Kommando.

With their captors appearing content to let sleeping dogs lie, not only was this gaining the rumor converts but these strutting around as if they were leading charmed lives.

"Are they blind or just stupid?" Zalman Leventhal asked. "I don't get it."

"Neither," replied his fellow Zalman. "They're Hungarian is all, and I don't mean that an insult."

"Just what *are* you saying then?"

He and Gradowski shared a bench in the yard of Crematorium III, taking in the last of the sunset. The sun itself was sunk out of sight behind the trees, but above these floated a slurry of thin, horizontal clouds aflame in orange and pink. Gradowski had been sent from Number Two with tomorrow's schedule, an errand that should have taken him ten minutes instead of the thirty it had become. He could only imagine the hell he was going to catch from that prick Morawa.

"What am I saying?" Though he resented the innuendo, he let it pass. "With all the suicides and other fatalities among them from working the fire pits, a lot of the Hungarians aren't long from the transports themselves. New and without a clue, these lack the slightest concept of how it is here. We can tell them what's getting ready to happen, what happened to all past commandos, but we could be speaking Chinese for all the good it does."

Leventhal wasn't impressed. The argument was an old one. "That may be, but they can do arithmetic, can't they? Nine hundred-plus men on the squad and not enough work for a quarter that many, especially with the night shift having been scrapped. How can they not see the danger they're in?"

"By choosing not to look too hard, I guess. By hoping against hope things are different now. What puzzles me is why that should puzzle *you*. It isn't as if we haven't come across it before."

"Yes, but that was before, *eleven times* before, all told. Why on earth should it be different now? Except, of course, for this most ridiculous rumor ever, which by giving the fools false hope makes the—makes the prospects—"

Leventhal, in his frustration, couldn't get the words out.

Gradowski let his gaze drift back to the trees. He couldn't recall a lovelier setting sun. He'd always felt the more spectacular displays of nature, be they beautiful or destructive, God's way of showing He did in fact exist.

"Makes the prospects for revolt," Leventhal managed at last, "dimmer than they ever were. Hell, there *is* no revolt anymore! With Möll a memory and now this latest hogwash, those Hungarians of yours no more want to hear about crashing out of here than they do the Krauts cutting their numbers down to size."

"They will, you watch. They'll see the light, give them time."

"Time? While the gas chambers continue to kill, the chimneys to smoke? Despite this summer's slaughter, there are thousands yet that could be saved. Or are you forgetting what Kaminski was forever preaching, that the uprising was as much about the crematoria as it was escape?"

"Kaminski!" Gradowski pounced on the name. "Thanks for bringing him up; it reminds me of something. Not long before he died, he sat me down and asked if what he'd been hearing about the fire pits was true. He'd sought me out, he said, because of what you told him, that with my own eyes I'd seen them in action, seen the SS burning people alive.

"When I confirmed I had and proceeded to give him the details, he was quiet for a moment then thanked me. Was beginning to realize, he said, the urgency he'd attached to bringing down the crematoria was in part groundless. He went on to add that though nothing could come near to acquitting him of it, he didn't feel so guilty anymore at having listened to the underground and held the squad back. That the Nazis would have been just as homicidal even without their ovens and Zyklon-B."

"Okay, I'll give you that," Leventhal said. "That I can see. Skip the crematoria, let's get back to the Hungarians. And don't go telling me, I know you, the one has anything to do with the other."

"But that's exactly what I've been telling you. Or was trying to. Think, my unsympathetic friend. While we old hands were working the furnaces and such, the Hungarians fresh off the cattle cars, being unskilled, were outdoors getting up close and intimate with the fire pits. And reaching because of it the same conclusion Kaminski did. Meaning?"

Leventhal didn't have to think; he may have been short on sympathy, but not brains. He also knew when he was beat. "Meaning as we were telling them the shortest route to putting a stop to the killing was to take the death houses out, experience was educating them otherwise. Giving them one more reason, as if they needed another, not to rush into a revolt. Satisfied?"

Far from it actually. Gradowski was as worried as his benchmate about the future of the rebellion. But unlike him, refused to make it worse by surrendering to pessimism. He was convinced that something somehow, in some as yet undefined way, would end up jolting the Hungarians to their senses.

That it should take so divinable, so familiar a shape failed for some reason to cross his mind.

The 23rd of September fell on a Saturday, continuing a stretch of remarkable weather. Every day for a week had been a cloudless gem, this particular one having ripened into a dazzling autumn afternoon. The descending sun drenched the yard of Crematorium IV in a golden-red fire, recalling the biblical bush that burned yet was not consumed.

The changing of the seasons had come mercifully early this year, siphoning the meanness right out of summer. The air had cooled weeks ago, the shadows seeming to lengthen earlier by the day. This probably foretold a mad dog of a winter, but at the moment no one cared; the sun, for so long a brute, had turned benign.

Number Four was shut down the 23rd, hadn't been used much at all lately. Apart from the worthlessness of its ovens, with waves of deportees no longer jamming ramp and road there'd been little call for its gas chamber, either. Making it good for something, it served as a barracks now for the main body of Sonder.

At three o'clock it came alive. A string of trucks and a staff car roared to a stop at its gate, disgorging two platoons of *Schützen* and two officers. Most of its residents were outside enjoying the weather, some kicking a soccer ball around.

Everybody froze. Inside a minute, soldiers filled the compound, five of them beating a path for the crematorium to fetch those inside. All four hundred Sonder were soon standing in formation, most trying without success to appear unconcerned.

Scharführer Hermann Balthasar Buch was the officer in charge. The young sergeant, if not liked, was one of the less despised of the SS. As swept up as his peers in the philosophy and practice of murder, he lacked their coarseness. Seldom had he been heard to raise his voice in anger, generally went easy on the Sonder, could even be sociable. He gave the impression he believed the bloody business they were assisting in entitled them to a measure of equal footing.

He advanced to within a few meters of the squad, his chubby face made the rounder by a broad smile.

"Men of the 12th Sonderkommando! I bring you good news. A brand-new, modern camp is being built to the west, inside Germany. The security of the Reich requires it. What we require today is two hundred prisoners experienced in camp life to help man it as kapos, cooks, and other functionaries. These, as here, will be treated better while having to work less. All who wish to take advantage of this opportunity, step forward!"

A buzz arose from the Sonder, but it was only the sound of translation. Once it died down, not a cough disturbed the stillness, nor did a man move. Even the greenest of them recognized the *Scharführer's* spiel for the snow job it was.

Buch retreated to confer with his brother officer, the crematorium's *Kommandoführer*, Sergeant Gorges. That they'd anticipated such a response was evident from the conference's briefness. Soon they were moving among the assembled men, checking tattoo numbers. Those selected had theirs written down, then were directed toward the soldiers, who stood with weapons leveled. Only the men with high numbers were picked.

The two hundred had no choice but to do what the guns told them to, and before long were filing out the gate. They walked like men sentenced to death—slump-shouldered, heads down—but also like the dupes they knew themselves to be, victims of that false security which had kept their rebelliousness idle. Mortified that in their delusion they'd ignored every warning, they marched to their fate without so much as a backward glance. When the trucks began pulling away, there were a few halfhearted waves goodbye, but most in their humiliation never looked up.

The men watching them leave were no less ashamed. Nor the rest of the commando when it heard the news; few were those who didn't share the blame for letting it come to this. So visceral was their guilt, it was as if a part of themselves had gone on the trucks with their doomed comrades.

To any desperate enough to hold out hope the Nazis were telling the truth, what faith they had started to wobble that very evening, and come the next morning would collapse like a house of cards. The Sonder quartered in Crematorium II were shut in its attic for the night hours earlier than their usual lockdown. As if this didn't arouse suspicion, they were told its ovens would be tested later to see what adjustments and repairs might be needed. That, as every man who worked them knew, was twaddle: they themselves had overhauled Number Two's machinery less than two months before, leaving it in as good a shape as ever.

In the morning, they would discover what the Germans had been up to. In two of the middle furnace's five muffles lay the remains of corpses only partly incinerated, several identified as belonging to those abducted yesterday. Later, they were to learn the sequence of events that led to their grisly find. The two hundred were taken to the main camp and immediately gassed in an airtight room used to delouse clothing. After dark, the bodies were trucked back to Birkenau and Crematorium II, where for the first time in the history of the camp the SS would work the ovens.

Whether from incompetence or plain laziness, it would prove a poor effort. And as such a mystery. After all the care the Germans had exercised to be devious to that point, how could they have been so irresponsible as to leave such a smoking gun of a mess?

There could now be no misreading Nazi intentions. And yesterday only the beginning. Not a week later, the killers were back at it, except now they sought to be clever and deflect some of the incrimination from themselves.

Buch returned to Crematorium IV on Thursday to meet with Shlomo Kirschenbaum, the once-suicidal and withdrawn—but deriving from the revolt a reason for living—now enthusiastically insurrectionary kapo of Number Four. The city of Krakow's rail center, claimed the *Scharführer*, had been hard hit by Russian bombers, and the Wehrmacht had petitioned Auschwitz for three hundred strong prisoners to help with repairs and rebuilding. Buch wanted a list bearing the tattoo numbers of those not afraid of hard work, and he'd be back in two days to pick it up.

As soon as he left, Kirschenbaum hurried to pass the word, sending emissaries from Number Four to inform the leaders of Battle Group-Sonderkommando of the SS ultimatum. An emergency meeting was scheduled for 7:00 p.m. in Number Two. Handelsman, Leventhal, Langfus, Warszawski, Kirschenbaum, Gradowski—all were present, the Sonder having regained, among other privileges, the mobility they'd lost under the watchful eye of the Cyclops. With Möll away, the guards had reverted to their old habits and become as venal as ever.

The meeting took place in a corner of the death house's unlit undressing hall, a standing lamp having been procured. Handelsman opened the discussion. "We all know why we're here, so let's get to it. First, is everyone agreed the smart thing to do is comply with this latest demand from our keepers?"

Warszawski let loose a long, incredulous whistle. "Hold on just a sec! Have you gone nuts, professor? Allow me to rephrase that for you: does *anyone* agree that's what we ought to do?"

"Definitely not!" Leventhal almost rose from his seat. "I'd say it's obvious what the Krauts are up to."

"And that is?" Handelsman asked.

"Why, to shift the onus for their next massacre onto us!" Leventhal's face was threatening to turn redder than his hair. "To make it look it's we sending those on the list to their deaths. It's the old story of divide and conquer. The Germans have to be thinking if they can pit one half of the squad against the other, there goes any chance of us uniting to resist this latest purge of theirs."

"Is that what you want?" Warszawski said, "The Sonder, those left of us, at each other's throats?"

Handelsman answered quickly, before the others could. "No one wants that, Yossel. And I see where you're coming from, too, Zalman—but try this on for size. Say we did go ahead and give the Nazis their list. Those on it, rather than being caught unaware—standing in the cremo yard with their thumbs in their mouths, surrounded by machine guns, waiting for their numbers to be called—would instead have a chance to reflect on their predicament. And if you were one of them, if you knew in advance you'd been marked for death, wouldn't you jump at anything that offered you an out? Grab at any straw that might save you?

"Just such a straw, gentlemen, is there for the grabbing. It's called Operation Jericho, and who finding himself one of the three hundred wouldn't latch onto it with both hands if dangled in front of him?"

"Plus," Gradowski added, "after that sad show the other day at Number Four, it's not as if Jericho isn't on everyone's lips again. And that includes the Hungarians. Especially the Hungarians, given it was mainly their own put on those trucks last week."

"Meaning on top of the three hundred volunteers the list is likely to produce," Handelsman said, "we should have those remaining of their compatriots on our side, who have to figure they're next. As lonely a place as the unloading ramp has become, it would take a real *putz* to expect the Krauts to hang onto a detachment of five hundred of us."

Here he paused until in the murky light he found who he was looking for. "Bela, perhaps now would be the moment to share what you told me before."

The Hungarian Lazar, though still learning, knew enough Polish to have followed the conversation. "I talk with my people... more early. In afternoon. They say they not go with SS this time. This time they fight if they on the list."

Handelsman spread his hands. "There you have it, this time they fight. The Nazis' latest bit of shadiness may turn out a blessing in disguise. Providence has intervened with an assist from our clumsy masters to deliver us three hundred men, and that just for starters, whose only chance at survival is revolt. What more could we ask? I say we give the swine their list with a big fat thank-you scrawled at the bottom of it."

To the general surprise, the fisherman Deresinski went Leventhal one better and did rise from his seat, noisily clearing his throat. Rarely did he voice an opinion at such meetings, but left no doubt tonight where he stood.

"The professor is right as usual, and that should be the end of it. We give the SS what they want and get what we want; we don't and we might not. It's as simple as that."

That the tight-lipped Deresinski should have deemed it his duty to cast his ballot was a cue for the others. Gradowski was firm in siding with Handelsman, as was Kirschenbaum. Langfus, however, summed it up best.

"I can't help but ask how our much-missed dead kapo might have handled this latest threat. What would Kaminski do in this situation? And there isn't a question in my mind he wouldn't have passed up this chance to beat the Nazis at their own game, grinning like a fox even as he handed them their list."

With that it was settled. Whether he saw their old kapo doing as the dayan had said, Warszawski wasn't sure. But there was no dismissing the possibility, nor any minimizing the magic Kaminski's name wielded.

"Far be it from me to buck the majority," he said, running a hand through his hair. "But while I'd love to end up admitting you right and myself wrong, it still smells to me, for all your fancy arguments, you might be opting for the easier route of playing ball with the Germans. Zalman?"

Leventhal shook his head in disgust, but said nothing.

"That's it then," said Handelsman. "Now comes the hard part. Whose numbers are we going to put on the list?"

They would make a start on it that night, culling those individuals exempted from it. Buch had been adamant the more experienced Sonder be excluded. With transports still coming in, and the Theresienstadt ghetto among others yet to be liquidated, the SS were wary of doing without their skilled workers. Not even for the six weeks, according to the sergeant, the three hundred would be at Krakow.

This basically left them the Hungarians to choose from. The trick would be to pick those who could be relied on to resist if it came to that, who weren't merely talk; no one wanted it to end up an actual death list. Having set October 7th, a week away, as the date of the attack, the Battle Group's leaders had to know the men on it weren't going to cave in without a fight should the Kommandantur decide to lower the boom sooner. That such a preemption would force the rebels to extemporize, striking before they were ready and in daylight, would just have to be. The days of watching their Sonder brothers marched to their deaths were over.

As Bela Lazar would reveal the next day, his fellow lieutenants needn't have worried. They'd sent him that morning to identify the most militant of the over five hundred Hungarians remaining on the squad. After sounding a representative number of these out, he'd failed again to find any who didn't impress him as sincere in swearing to take on the Nazis with their bare hands if they had to rather than be herded onto trucks.

For the first time since coming to Birkenau, apart from the heady days leading up to June 15th, Lazar was proud to call himself Hungarian. Like all in the Battle Group who'd never stopped agitating for revolt, he'd despaired of his people ever recovering from that day, then the punch to the gut of August 2nd. Not to mention what those forced to man the fire pits had endured. What they'd seen and done while working those horrors would have sucked the living soul out of anyone.

But here it was October, and those who hadn't succumbed to suicide or been shot for refusing to continue at the hellish things— who'd succeeded in surviving them, blighted but not broken—were showing themselves the heroic men they were.

This wasn't all he was proud of. A great honor had come his way, bestowed as a gesture toward his butchered countrymen by none other than his comrades-in-arms. He would have begged for it if he'd had to, but he'd been granted it without even having to ask: leadership of the team given the job of blowing up Crematorium IV. As with the other death houses, this was to be done by dynamiting the reserve barrels of gasoline used to power the ovens' auxiliary machinery. Though Number Four's weren't operable anymore, luckily this fuel had yet to be removed.

In view of its limitations, of course, the demolition of this particular crematorium would serve little purpose beyond the symbolic. Which didn't make it any the less imperative to Lazar. Tens of thousands of Hungarian Jews and untold multitudes of others having suffered a vile death within its walls, to leave those walls standing would have been an offense in its own right, one only the timid or unfeeling would acquiesce to.

To him, but not only him, if the Sonder did nothing else—if they never made it past the wire—by destroying those demonic buildings that were the heart of the camp, they'd be sending this message: you Germans may have enslaved, corrupted, disgraced, and even killed us, but despite your best efforts you've failed to defeat us. Men we came to Birkenau, and alive or dead, men we leave. Either way we will have won, and as proof of our victory left your filthy death factories so many piles of smoking bricks.

More than the chance at escape it afforded, Lazar was among those who saw the revolt as a vehicle for sticking it to their tormentors. The weeks he himself had worked the fire pits had changed him. He'd never been an angry person, even less a vengeful one, but the SS had taught him how to hate and taught him well, and he was aching to pay them back for the education.

Fearing the Nazis would act on their list ahead of the Sonder timetable, Lazar's was one of several voices urging the men in charge of its planning to up the date of the revolt. Fortunately, these weren't forced to spend precious hours making a new order of battle; Kaminski's latest would serve just fine, with one exception. With no night shift anymore, the assault could begin no later than 6:00, the crematoria's new closing time. For a critical hour or more, the rebels would lose the advantage of darkness. And more damaging yet, what weapons they'd have gained from the changing of their guard. There was, however, no getting around either.

As for advancing the date, it quickly became apparent the opposite would be necessary. Having everything in place and ready to go by the 7th wasn't being realistic, not if the revolt was to have any shot at success. A couple of days could make all the difference. It was agreed, therefore, to aim for October 9th, a decision not as risky as it might have been a few days before.

From its friend Dr. Pach, the Battle Group learned of a shake-up in the Kommandantur. His Excellency *Obersturmbannführer* Höss had been transferred back to Oranienburg, nor was a replacement named. It would take the camp SS a while to adapt to their truncated new hierarchy , a period in which they weren't apt to be making any moves. And helped explain, too, though in their possession since the 1st, why they had yet to put their list to work. To everyone's relief, life had gone on as normal, one day piling on another as if there were no list.

Not that the tension emanating from the crematoria wasn't as thick as the smoke on a three-transport day. Sensing something was brewing, Auschwitz began sending people to investigate. It wouldn't take long for them to return with evidence suggesting the Sonder were poised for a breakout, prompting the Stammlager to issue Birkenau this warning: due to the peril it posed the inmates of both camps, an uprising was to be avoided at all cost. To what extent the Nazis might retaliate was unknown, but would surely be severe.

The rebels discussed at length how best to respond. In the end, they sent a message to the underground pretending to share its concern and promising to discourage any talk of a revolt "should it arise." Having lost all trust in their alleged allies, the Sonder wouldn't have put it past them to tip off the Germans if convinced trouble was in the offing. As painful as this was to admit, too much hung in the balance to ignore the possibility.

On the morning of the 6th, Noah Zabludowicz rushed from Crematorium II with urgent news for his commanders. If he, like the Sonder, had thought their loyalty suspect, he'd have kept this news to himself, orders be damned. In fact, he would have severed ties with them already. This had crossed his mind; with the exit of Bruno Baum from the scene, the Resistance had lost one of its more principled voices. As Noah saw it, perhaps its only.

His aim in gathering what intelligence he could from the crematoria was built on the hope that if revolt was inevitable, the Sonder intractable, his bosses might yet be persuaded to offer some assistance. His new superior was the Polish activist Ludwig Soswinski, like Baum a member of the Steering Committee. He showed up unannounced at Soswinski's workplace, Block 24, the main camp's registrar and primary records office.

The older Pole ushered him to a cubicle and had him sit, but wasn't pleased. "I told you never to contact me at the job," he said, his voice low. A fortyish, dapper non-Jew with his carefully trimmed moustache and odor of hair cream, unlike the mournful Baum he was the gregarious type, but in the studied, vaguely patronizing style of the politician. "Suppose an SS walked in and asked why you were here."

"I came to check out the lock on the front door. You people have been complaining about it sticking, am I right?"

Believable a cover as this was, it did nothing to lessen Soswinski's pique. "Since you're here, make it quick then. I assume it's something to do with those pals of yours in the Sonderkommando."

"I just talked with one of them, yes, and felt you ought to hear what he had to say. He's one of their top men, and to be trusted."

"So what is it so important it couldn't wait until later?"

"The revolt," Noah said. "It's on, and for certain. The Sonder are wise to the Nazis' latest attempt to thin the squad and determined to escape or die trying. They have weapons and intend to use them. I was told we could expect it three days from now, on the 9th. Sooner, if the Germans should force the rebels' hand."

"And you were told that by this... person you met with earlier. One of their 'top men,' as you put it."

"Yes." A disgusted yes, Noah could tell what was coming.

Soswinski rose from his seat, brushed imaginary dirt from a cuff of his jacket. "We appreciate the seriousness you attach to your orders, Zabludowicz. To all of your efforts, ill-considered as this one is. For just yesterday, Battle Group-Sonderkommando informed us, officially I might add, that no action against the SS was pending. Nor was this likely to change.

"So, as you can see, there is no cause for alarm. Not having been there, I hate to presume, but I'd say the person you were talking to was telling you something he thought you wanted to hear."

"And if he wasn't? Which, I know him, he wasn't—what then?"

"Then the Sonder, in addition to killing themselves, could end up, depending on the extent of Nazi anger, taking thousands of other inmates with them."

"I would think that'd be enough right there, general, for you to pass my report on."

"It would, my dear fellow, if I had any faith in it whatsoever."

"But—"

"That will be all, Zabludowicz. I don't know about you, but I've got work to do. If you wouldn't mind, at least make a show of fiddling with that lock on your way out."

There was no point in arguing, this Noah *could* see. The Poles on the Steering Committee, the fools, were the ones being told what they wanted to hear.

Besides, whom did he, Noah, think he was kidding? Considering the speed with which the Red Army was eating up the miles, to expect the underground to come to the aid of the mutineers was akin to looking for the heavens to part, and if a little belatedly, the hand of God Himself throw open the gates of Birkenau.

His energies, Noah decided, were better spent carrying through on his promise to Yankel Handelsman. In return for the information he'd just wasted on Soswinski, he'd given his word he'd do what he could to smuggle the insurgents some ammunition. It wouldn't be the first time he'd helped them like this, only back then the Sonder were living in barracks. Getting it into the death houses was going to be prickly.

The first step was tracking down the civilian workers he'd done business with before; in exchange for the gold the Sonder had provided him in the past and again today, these had been happy to bring Noah whatever he wanted. Except for guns. They wouldn't do guns. But ammunition, go figure, wasn't a problem.

Did he have time? That depended. He'd need to start the ball rolling this morning, and even then it would be tight—if he actually did have until the 9th. Handelsman had vouched nothing would happen until then, and Handelsman should know. But for all he or anyone did know, things could come hurtling to a climax tomorrow.

*   *   *

October 7th dawned cold. The dew had frozen, coating every surface in white; each crematorium's barbed wire resembled the symmetrical strands of some giant spider's web. But by mid-morning, the sun had imposed itself, the day shaping up to be a warm one. Jackets were shed, windows opened. What wind there was blew from the south, so that well before noon people were wiping the sweat from their foreheads.

While stuffy, Crematorium III's attic wasn't as uncomfortable as it could have been. No operations were anticipated this afternoon, which meant no heat rising from the ovens. With the revolt scheduled for the day after tomorrow, the building's hundred and sixty residents, not counting the hair-processing squad, were busy preparing for their departure. Some were sorting and packing, some sewing and repairing, some parceling food and supplies, others going over assignments and strategy.

The aged of the Reinkommando were busy, too, though they'd made up their minds months ago that should by some blessedness events reach this point, as much as they were in favor of the plot they were staying put. Armed rebellion was a job for the young, and they with their brittle bones and slow step would only have been a hindrance.

Also, as men of God, rabbis and scribes, it simply wasn't in them to be a party to violence, be it for the purpose of escape or any reason. They were content to sit by and let His will be done, justice be served in a manner He saw fit.

Neither was it because of their hated work that they weren't idle this Saturday. A transport, it was true, had pulled up earlier at Crematorium II. (Number Five was ready if another should arrive, but as of now was manned by a skeleton crew only). But the bags of hair soon to be coming, with the little still untreated from yesterday, could sit. For in addition to it being the Sabbath, the 7th was the climactic day of Sukkoth, the major Jewish holiday of the Tabernacles, or Booths.

Sukkoth was both a harvest festival and a commemoration of the end of the ancient Israelites' forty-year sojourn in the wilderness. A *sukkah* was a small wood-and-canvas structure roofed with pine branches the people of Moses had used as shelter upon first entering the land of Canaan, and later as temporary housing adjacent to their fields during harvest. Though evolving on the seventh day into a more solemn ceremony, dancing, singing, and other merriments characterized the week-long celebration, also called the Time of Our Joy.

This final day was a busy one for rabbis, including, never mind their lack of a congregation, those presiding at Birkenau's Crematorium III. Congregation or no, here the holiday's observance might be said to have assumed the most importance, an oasis of Jewish affirmation in a desert of Jewish negation and death.

Even as Leyb Langfus in the role of dayan was doing his part to keep the day holy by assisting the elders, during the lulls in these proceedings he was lending the rebels a hand on the other side of the room. Nor did he see a contradiction between the two. As respectful of the Divine Will as anybody, he also viewed it as inviting collaboration. Who was to say where God's intentions ended and the part men played in helping to advance them began?

Langfus was a firm believer that people, when necessary and in a just cause, should use every means at their disposal to further that cause. Which was why, unlike his brethren in the Reinkommando, he'd committed to following his other brothers down the path of revolt. And why he was doing his part to aid them in prepping for that journey.

Though his contribution was largely motivational, it wasn't limited to that. His tall, lanky frame went from man to man bearing words of encouragement, the random embrace or pat on the back, but where an extra pair of hands was needed the dayan was there with that, too.

While occupied thus, he happened to glance out a window and saw a line of trucks hurrying from the south. He thought little of it until passing by the same window a minute later. Pushing his glasses up on his nose, he watched all ten of them pull to a halt in front of Crematorium IV. Even then he failed to put two and two together—until as if someone had switched on a light, it hit him.

"Oh my God," he said half under his breath, attracting the attention of those near.

"What is it, Leyb?" said Zalman Leventhal, drawn to his gaze. "What's going on?"

Langfus didn't answer, didn't have to. Crematorium IV was half a mile away, but there was no mistaking what was in progress. One of the trucks was vomiting SS, the other nine, for now, empty.

"It isn't," Leventhal said.

"I'm afraid so." Langfus turned from the window. "The question," he added with a calmness he didn't feel, "is what do we do now?"

Yossel Warszawski was meeting with Shlomo Kirschenbaum in the undressing room of Number Four when he stopped in mid-sentence and cocked an ear upward. He'd been sent to see that the mobilization here was on schedule, and to deal with any problems the conspirators might be having. He caught Kirschenbaum's eye, his own uncertain. "You hear that?"

"Hear what?" The kapo tilted his head back, as if sniffing the air. "Wait... are those trucks?"

Hardly had the words left his mouth than a Sonder burst through the door from outside. "It's the Germans!" he cried. "They've come to—they've come for us!"

A squad of *Schützen* yelling like crazy men was soon bustling everyone out and into formation in the yard. The helmets of the soldiers glinted in the early-afternoon sun. As he'd been two weeks ago, *Scharführer* Buch was in charge, only he wasn't smiling this time as he stood before the assembled Sonder.

"The following prisoners," he shouted, "three hundred total, are to be transferred for reassignment. When I call your number, proceed to the holding area." He pointed toward the gate. "I will be starting with the higher ones and working my way down. If passed over, return at once to your quarters."

After allowing for translation, he bent to his clipboard and began reading aloud. As if not staggered enough, the Sonder were caught short by this curt new tack of the Nazis. There'd been no mention of clearing rubble or any kind of work. Or of easier conditions elsewhere, a better camp... nothing propitiatory at all.

They soon realized, too, that Buch's list wasn't the same one turned over to him Monday. As some of their own had warned, that had been a ruse to weaken their solidarity by turning Sonder against Sonder. The SS had made their own list, confining it to those prisoners bunking in Crematorium IV; to have to scour all four death houses hunting down those tattoo numbers the Sonder had compiled would have been both confusing and impractical. As well as multiplying by four the hazard of encountering resistance.

This wound up, though, not making a lot of difference. One list was as good, or rather as meaningless as the other, for while some of the Sonder were stepping forward when their numbers came up, others were ignoring the call and slinking back to the crematorium. Soon the quantity of men flouting Buch's order grew noticeable; from the dearth of them still standing before him, he could see he wasn't going to meet his goal of three hundred. With clipboard in hand and a squad of soldiers at his heels, he set out to find the shirkers and bring them back.

They hadn't gone but a few steps before an angry shout arose at their rear. When they wheeled, it was to meet a hail of stones and see those Sonder who'd been selected rushing their guards. Those yet to be called were right behind these. Wielding crowbars and other tools they'd pulled from their clothing, they actually made a fight of it for a few seconds. Their make-do clubs, however, were no match for submachine guns. The compound quickly turned into a killing ground.

The air hissed with bullets, the dirt jumped with them. The Sonder scattered, screaming, collapsing in bloody heaps, though almost all ended up reaching the safety of the crematorium. Greeting them as they flung themselves through the open double-doors of the undressing room was the figure of Warszawski standing tall with a machine gun. In fact the opposite of tall, he seemed a colossus with that gun at his hip.

Kirschenbaum entered shortly bearing the identical weapon, both having come at the expense of their guards. Two of these, overpowered at the first shots, were beaten to death. The other two—the Krema guard with Möll's departure having reverted to it's old strength of four—quickly fled their posts.

The sight of such firepower in the hands of their own instantly revived Sonder spirits, their panic in the yard forgotten. They scurried to break out the dynamite and Borodin's grenades from their hiding places. They were also in possession of two .45-caliber pistols, four of the 6-mm's, and the ammunition to go with their new machine guns.

These walls that since their raising had seen nothing but degradation and death now pulsed with the electricity of high purpose and hope. Men bustled about not at the command of vicious overseers, as accomplices to mass murder, but to put an end to their complicity in it forever. The Hungarian Lazar had already sped off with his demolition team to haul the drums of reserve fuel into the oven room and rig them with dynamite. Operation Jericho wasn't only talk anymore. It was about to elevate a lot more than just Sonder morale.

Warszawski, meanwhile, watched from the main doorway, Kirschenbaum from a window, holding their fire until Buch's men got nearer. Having broken ranks when chasing down the Sonder, these now descended in a ragged line on the crematorium. Unaware the squad was armed, their step was unhurried, discipline relaxed, some with rifles carelessly slung across shoulders.

When the two rebels opened up, the Germans were so close they could make out the astonishment on their faces. These dropped as if their feet had been yanked from under them, one never to rise again, three hollering they'd been hit. Coming as a further rude awakening were the three grenades that followed, forcing the attackers to fall back. Diving behind what cover they could find, they radioed for reinforcements.

Nor would these take long; they'd been dispatched without having to be called. Even as the Sonder, flush with victory, were yelling themselves hoarse, two convoys of trucks appeared at separate points on the horizon, one speeding in the direction of Crematoria II and III, the other straight for them. Both came from the area of the SS barracks, each leaving a ribbon of white dust in the air. As if announcing their approach, the camp siren commenced to wail, its apocalyptic howl ascending like a herald of doom.

"Soldiers! Six trucks of them!" Kirschenbaum had left his window for the door. "Not fifteen minutes since—"

"It was the two guards we let get away," Warszawski said. "They must have reached a telephone and given the alarm."

"So what should we do?" A shiver trembled at the edges of Kirschenbaum's voice. "Another minute and they'll be here. No way we can crack the inner cordon before then."

Warszawski had to think, and fast. *What should we do?* Good question, he told himself, repeatedly attacking his hair with a hand. If only he had a good answer.

He wasn't scared so much as mad. After all the planning, the months of doing nothing, the false starts, the dead, this was what the much-ballyhooed revolt had come to: an accidental, disorganized, desperation-driven mess. With as little chance of carrying the day as the damned Wehrmacht had of whipping the damned Russians. Here the rebels were, admittedly acting the part at last, but with the element of surprise gone, the sun high and siren blaring, the SS seconds away and they still sitting on their butts in a crematorium still standing.

And on top of it all, the very real possibility of them having to take on the Nazi garrison alone. The conspirators in the other death houses had to be wondering what was going on. They must have heard the gunshots, but Jericho wasn't scheduled for two days yet, and not in any case at so early an hour. Those Sonder sitting blind would have to figure out, first, what those shots meant, why they'd stopped twice now, then how, perhaps even whether they should respond to them. This would take time, something neither they nor Warszawski and his impromptu companions-in-arms had.

"Listen up, Shlomo," he said, "I've got an idea. You go on ahead with the men and start in on the guard towers, while I stay with maybe a dozen of them—we haven't the guns for more—and try to hold off the Krauts here, keep them pinned down. When we see you're through the wire, we'll disengage and follow."

"Leave us the pistols and some of the dynamite and grenades. Between those and this," he said, slapping his machine gun, "we should do okay. What do you think?"

"Good! Good enough anyway. It might just, if we're lucky, get us into the woods."

"In your assault on the cordon, short of guns as we are, there's no need to stray from the original plan. You'll want to take out the tower nearest you, blow that section of the fence, then keep the farther one occupied as the men make a run for it. Can you do all that with the one gun?"

"I don't know, Yossel, but this I do. Unless we get moving now, we won't be going anywhere."

As the squad made for its jumping-off points at the gas-chamber end of the building, Warszawski deployed his twelve. To the right of his station, he put one of the 6-mm's in the closest door; this person was to alert him when the inner cordon had fallen. He would then pass the order to withdraw to the three gunmen he'd placed at the windows studding the length of the undressing gallery, as would the farther one to the two in the oven room. Each of these shooters had a backup should he fall.

It was in this role and that room that Bela Lazar had set up his bomb, which he wasn't to ignite until the call to retreat. A single fuse connected two four-stick bundles of the dynamite, each taped to one of the six barrels of gasoline. These he'd clustered where they'd do the most damage, against that side of the inner furnace facing the interior wall.

No sooner had the men taken their posts than one truck after another came grinding to a halt at the crematorium gate. In rapid order, soldiers flooded the yard, and after conferring with those there to welcome them, began cautiously to advance. When the Sonder let loose, they again stopped the SS cold.

But Warszawski knew they wouldn't stay stopped. There were too many of them. The small-arms fire raking his part of the wall grew so intense he was forced to shoot without aiming, only his weapon

363

showing in the door. When a heavy machine gun took to tearing chunks out of the wall, even that was asking for it.

At this point, though, there was no holding him back. He fought like a man possessed, out of his mind, screaming unintelligibly with each pull of the trigger but so lost in the fury of the moment he didn't realize he was screaming. Despite the Nazi machine gun, the ground danced with his bullets. To the Germans hugging that ground, there might have been two guns working the door.

Yet even as the blood raged inside him and the battle around him, he managed to keep an ear on the one to his right. What he guessed to be Kirschenbaum's gun seemed to be holding its own. More hopeful yet when it came was the lightning crash of dynamite, three explosions in quick succession, the last joined by several bursts from Kirschenbaum.

Then, more than he'd *dared* hope, a different kind of noise—a roar of exultation from hundreds of throats, from men prisoners no more but spilling into the yard, past the wire, out the camp. He could tell they were out and running for the woods from their fast-receding hurrahs. For two years, Warszawski had been waiting for this sound, dreaming of it both asleep and awake. After that long, it felt like a dream still. Who'd have imagined the putrid air of Birkenau would ever ring with such a cry, its murder-soaked soil pound with the steps of men racing for freedom?

The backup he'd posted in the gas chamber tumbled into the room, the man's message redundant but thrilling all the same. "They've done it!" he shouted, eyes bulging in their sockets. "They're through the wire!"

"You two stay there!" Warszawski yelled above the racket. "I'll round up the others and—"

The next thing he knew he was sitting on the floor, as dazed as if just punched in the jaw. But for a high, electronic whine, he was also deaf. His first thought was an enemy grenade had landed near, but a check of his person turned up no wounds. It wasn't until he noticed the whole far end of the undressing room in flames, its wall no longer there, then through the door bits of debris raining from the sky, that he realized he'd been knocked off his feet by something much bigger than a grenade.

It had to have been the massed barrels of gasoline; either Lazar or a Nazi bullet had touched them off early. He picked himself up and cried out for survivors. Only three singed and shaken Sonder stumbled forward. With the just as shell-shocked SS having lowered their guns, the six took advantage of the lull to slip out of the burning building.

What Warszawski couldn't know was that prior to the explosion, the German attack had made some headway. Where the coke storeroom jutted from the crematoria it formed an ell, creating a blind spot, this allowing a dozen soldiers to work their way to the rear of the oven area. With the rest providing cover, two of them sprinted for the back windows, shot them out, and tossed a grenade apiece inside. The double concussion rocked the room, but protected by the massive bulk of the furnace they nestled against, the drums of fuel went untouched.

When Lazar came to, soldiers were stepping around and over him, the air still strong with burnt gunpowder. This told him he hadn't been out for long, but might have remained so except for the bony claw digging into his lower torso. His first impulse was to see where he was hit, but he didn't dare move. His partner lay motionless beside him, as did the pair beneath the far window.

The Nazis had obviously mistaken him, too, for dead. One had opened a door to the yard and was waving his *Kameraden* in. The other four were mustering outside the morgue from where they planned from the look of it to carry on their assault. The most troubling if also enticing sight of all, however, loomed eight meters away. In their rush to push forward, the soldiers had missed the bomb in their midst, and there it sat, beckoning, though setting it off might no longer be simple. Lazar had yet to determine how serious his injuries were, how far or even if he could drag himself across the floor.

Nudging a leg an imperceptible couple of inches, he had to stifle a cry. So much for that... his hip must be broken, or his pelvis. He'd be lucky to crawl three feet without passing out. He could forget reaching the dynamite, even should the SS in advancing leave him alone with it. As this sank in, what physical discomfort he was suffering became as nothing to the mental. Barring a miracle, the death factory would live to kill another day.

This was too much for him. He was sworn body and soul to wiping this heathen temple, this altar slick with his people's blood out of existence, both its brick and the obscene memory of it. Nothing else mattered. Escape, liberty, not life itself mattered, his or any other. Indeed, having failed at his mission, all he wanted was to die, and rather than endure another minute with so unendurable a failure, he wanted it right now. He was just opening his mouth to give himself up—

When he saw it. His miracle. Come from out of nowhere as if conjured from thin air. It lay under the body of the dead man splayed next to him, plainly, implausibly, breathtakingly—a pistol. It was one of the 6-mm's, its muzzle just poking from beneath the man's rib cage.

Puny a weapon as the thing was, to Lazar it looked a bazooka. The question was how many bullets were left in it. All he needed was one. Surely there had to be one.

Moving his eyes only, he scanned the room. The soldier who'd stayed to signal the others had gone outside, cursing at them to get a move on. Lazar heard the thud of running boots. Now was the moment, there wouldn't be another. Taking a deep breath to steel himself against the pain, he lunged for the pistol and yanked it free.

Hurriedly, he aimed at one of the bundles of dynamite, fired... and missed everything. Too hurriedly! That was dumb! Willing a second bullet into the chamber—he would not be denied—this time he *took* his time. Feeling someone dash into the room, he ignored it, his every nerve, his whole being focused on the piece of metal in his hands.

The world stopped. Motion froze. Slowly, he squeezed the trigger, so slow he couldn't tell if he was even moving it. Until with a bang the gun jumped, and the instant it did he knew it a bull's-eye.

The last thought to light up the young Hungarian's brain, a millisecond of a thought, was how right and proper that a gun used in executions, that had sent who knew how many Jews to the grave, should end up an instrument of Jewish revenge.

From the attic of Crematorium III, the explosion wasn't only visible but spectacular. Though a screen of trees hid all but Number Four's chimneys from sight, there was no obscuring the enormous column of fire climbing between them, toppling the inner one on the spot and leaving the other teetering at an impossible angle. What had been the roof rose in a volcanic eruption of supporting beams, boards, and shingles, the heavier pieces hovering briefly before crashing back down, the smaller drifting lazily to earth like confetti. The blast shook the ground for a mile, the windows of Number Three trembling in their frames.

The men watching from those windows greeted it with mixed emotions. There was awe in their faces all right, and no shortage of pride that this wellspring of so much misery and death should at long last have been dealt its own death blow, and by no less than the very slaves forced to work it. But where one might have expected cheers or some sort of celebration in order, the mood in the room was subdued.

This was because for these Sonder the fight was already over. It might have been different if they'd acted immediately, with the gunfire at Number Four having just started, but their reticence was understandable. The shooting hadn't lasted and was followed by an ominous stillness. That their comrades had resisted the soldiers come for them was clear, but from the sound of it the battle had been short-lived. With little doubt as to the victors. The camp siren had tripped, but any prisoner riot, whether suppressed or not, would have precipitated that.

For precious minutes, unsure what to do, the men of Crematorium III did nothing—until to their dismay the firing resumed, heavier now and punctuated by the dull whomp of grenades. But as they were to their even greater chagrin to discover, by then the window of opportunity had slammed shut on them.

In all fairness, it wasn't much of a window. Even if they had reacted sooner, like as not it would still have been too late. They did hustle to break out the few weapons they had—three handguns, a sack of grenades, another of dynamite—distribute them, and otherwise prepare to head downstairs. But no sooner had they set out than they were to encounter the obstacle that was to prove their undoing.

The only exit from the attic was a narrow outside staircase, a construct their four guards and *Kommandoführer* Muhsfeld had at the wail of the siren scrambled to secure. Upon the first of the rebels venturing onto its landing, a flurry of machine-gun fire drove them back inside. They tried again with the same result. Whether they should attempt it a third time became quickly academic, for within minutes SS reinforcements arrived by truck and a hundred guns were trained on the stairs. A mouse couldn't have made it down them alive, or at the other extreme an elephant.

The conspirators had no choice but to return their weapons to their hiding places, their adrenaline to the place it had come from. Where the electric energy of possibility had charged the room, now the air was heavy with the bitterness of a dream shattered. Aggravating it was guilt at what they saw as having flubbed it, at letting themselves be trapped in the prison of their own indecisiveness. Few were those able to meet another's gaze, while from Number Four the accusatory crack of the guns continued to taunt.

"We should have hit those stairs sooner"—this from one of the Maidanek POWs—"when we had the chance."

Langfus, no less devastated than anyone, saw no reason to beat themselves up over something he didn't feel they were to blame for. "What, in the first five minutes? If we had even that."

"He does have a point, Leyb," Leventhal said. "If we hadn't hesitated, we might—"

"Hesitated? Who wouldn't have?" The dayan showed a rare flash of impatience. "Especially after those first shots died down. Don't tell me you, both of you, didn't believe the jig at Four was up then."

When they said nothing, he looked past them, taking in the room. Not a man did he see that wasn't either sagging in defeat or laboring to hold back his tears.

"All I'm getting at," he said louder so everyone could hear, "is that the last thing we should be doing is hanging our heads. How long was it after we could hear the battle was still on before we were packed and ready to join it? A few minutes? I'd say that was pretty good, and then I'd say this."

He pointed in the direction of Crematorium II. "What do you hear coming from our brothers across the way? Nothing, not a whisper. It appears we're not the only ones the Germans were too fast for. If there's any comfort to be had in how things are turning out, I guess we can take some from that."

"So what now, rabbi?" came a boy's voice from the crowd. "There must be *something* we can do. Something..."

Langfus wanted to help, but what could he say? "My only advice, take it how you will, is to stop punishing yourselves with guilt and turn your energies instead to—"

He was about to tell them to pray for the brave men of Crematorium IV—when it blew up, rattling not only the windows but the dumbstruck men rushing for them. These ended up crowded together in shocked silence, transfixed by the fireball, the dayan and his words forgotten.

Not that, to arguably their even greater shock, they wouldn't soon be reminded of them. With the blast still reverberating, from behind them burst the distinctive jackhammer thump of automatic weapons. And the deeper, louder one of grenades, both coming from the direction of Crematoria II. Not only had Langfus been wrong about their "brothers across the way" but, in answer to what the boy had asked, there was something they could do now after all. Sadly, sickeningly, it was to stand there and watch in impotent disgrace as the crematoria on either side of them carried the torch of revolt.

Most were too ashamed to do even that. While at this newest outbreak of gunfire some raced to the windows on the other side of the attic, the rest stayed where they were, unwilling to subject their eyes to something painful enough on the ears.

What would have eased their pain some if it had occurred to them, the situation at Number Two differed markedly from theirs. It being the only death works in operation that day, half the men quartered in it were already downstairs when the shooting broke out at Number Four. This was to prove crucial in determining their response to what at first to them, too, were the mysterious goings-on to the north.

57B was the squad on duty. A transport from Theresienstadt had shown up in the morning, all twelve hundred Czechs having gone to the gas. Bombarded as they were by the roar from the furnaces and flues, the men sweating at the ovens wouldn't have heard a gun if fired directly outside.

Those Sonder left unsupervised to finish cleaning the gas chamber, however, below ground though they were, could hear the distant commotion no problem, and were soon bringing news of it up on the elevator. The question was, what did it mean? A question that would assume new urgency with the ululating wail of the camp siren.

Those at the ovens having dropped what they were doing, everyone melted into groups of three or four, their talk excited. Rifle fire at Number Four, and now the siren... could the revolt have started without them? How and why, if at all, was anybody's guess, nor did they have but seconds to try and thrash it out. A door slammed open and a fuming chief of the guard bolted in, demanding in fumbling Polish to know why they weren't working.

Kapo Kalniak, in charge of today's cremation, was among those who strongly suspected the gunfire for what it was. Where before he would have addressed the SS man in front of him with if not subservience then certainly deference, his tone now edged on the insolent.

"The stiffs can wait, *Rottenführer*," the burly Kalniak said, towering over the corporal. "It isn't as if they're going anywhere."

This drew a few snickers from the men who'd collected around him. The German even smiled, if coldly. Responding to their laughter more than the only half-understood Polish, he reverted to the familiarity of his native tongue.

"So I should give you boys a break in the middle of your shift to have a little chitchat, is that what you're saying? To plot who can tell what mischief. Or maybe"—here the soldier, his smile evaporating, pulled a nightstick from his belt—"maybe I should give you a taste of this instead."

Without warning, he cracked Kalniak a violent blow to the skull, sending him crashing to the floor like a tree felled. But the kapo, if a tree then as stout as an oak, didn't stay felled. After a few shakes of his head, slinging bright-red drops everywhere, he was back on his feet brandishing a short, thick knife. Which he promptly buried in the astonished Nazi's chest, who was dead before he hit the concrete.

The Sonder watching were horrified. "Great!" one of them said. "Now what? We'll pay for this for sure, all of us."

Yankel Handelsman, though, like Kalniak, wasn't at all sure. In fact, told the shooting from the north had flared anew, for those two that settled it. Today was to be a day unlike any other, a day where their world would be turned upside down, the past and its ground rules, its proprieties and prohibitions, as dead all of a sudden as the soldier at their feet.

At any rate, it was done. There was no turning back now. Whatever the story at Crematorium IV, here the die had been cast, SS blood shed.

"Quick," Handelsman ordered those nearest, "grab his gun and ammo, then into the fire with him. If we're to get the drop on his pals and make the crematorium ours, we can't be leaving dead bodies around. Not at first."

It took them a moment to comprehend. Make the crematorium ours? What was that supposed to mean? But no sooner did they think this, than to a man they broke into the same disbelieving grin and sprang to action. Within seconds, the entire shift awoke to what was up, so that even as some were loading the corporal into one of the ovens, others were busy in the coke store retrieving their hidden dynamite and grenades.

Cries of "It's on!" and "This is it!" hailed from a dozen mouths, a dozen more shouting their way outside and upstairs to alert the men in the attic.

"This is *what!*" a voice yelled, and in strode the imperial figure of their head kapo, Mietek Morawa, flaunting the thick mahogany cane he'd taken to carrying lately.

Since the death of Kaminski, the young Pole had been acting his old self more and more, arrogant, ill-tempered, and whenever he saw what struck him as the least bit disrespectful of his authority, lethally cruel. Just the other day, he'd beaten a teenaged Sonder so badly for "insubordination," the boy died the next morning. With his archrival and only constraint Kaminski removed, he'd again felt free to bully and brutalize.

"What in Christ are you numbskulls up to?" he shouted. "Who told you lazy scum you could leave your posts?"

Intimidating as he was with his booming voice and heavy cane, he didn't get very far. Another three steps and a gang of Sonder swarmed him and stuffed a cloth in his mouth. A rope was found and his arms trussed to his sides, and he was dragged struggling wildly toward Handelsman.

His captors were ecstatic. They'd dreamed of this moment, though none had foreseen it playing out so perfectly. Still grieving over the loss of Kaminski—and to the veterans among them, a lengthy and unforgiven list of others—at last they had the culprit responsible for these crimes in their power. Handelsman, occupied in sorting ammunition, glanced at Morawa and nodded.

Without a word, as if they'd planned it out beforehand, the Sonder roped the struggling kapo's ankles together, heaved him onto the metal stretcher attached to the open maw of Muffle 2, and slid him alive into the blazing oven.

It was an atrocious death, but the months had numbed the men of the detachment to atrocity. To them the gag-muted screams from the furnace were less an indictment of their own cruelty than the long overdue sound of justice being served. Many even stopped what they were doing the better to drink them in. If nothing else came of their mutiny, this one account would have been squared.

Then from the coke room, a shout. "Soldiers, at the gate! Thirty— No, sixty—No, a hundred of them!"

Even as they ran to the windows to see a company of SS pouring into the yard, a furious explosion set those windows to shaking. Some feared it a German mortar shell, until they saw a titanic spiral of smoke and flame rising out of the trees from what could only be Crematorium IV. There could be no doubting it now: the revolt may not have been on schedule but was unquestionably *on*. And looking healthy. Despite the soldiers outside, Sonder spirits soared as high as the fiery cloud still climbing.

Another of their guards blustered in only to be jumped and beaten to death. Counting the one Battle Group-Auschwitz had smuggled them in June, this gave the insurgents three machine guns, a few pistols. Zalman Gradowski and the men from upstairs showed shortly with a fourth, having made quick work of the guard sent to secure the attic.

As unaware as their counterparts at Krema IV that the Sonder were armed, the SS supposed to lock down this, its bigger sister, confidently approached to within twenty meters of its walls. Where they were met with an even greater fusillade of rebel steel than had poured from out of IV. The Germans reeled and fell back, tried again, and again were repulsed. They then attempted a flanking maneuver to the right in view of gaining the rear, but a hail of bullets from the *Kommandoführer's* office had them again diving for cover.

Thwarted everywhere, the Nazis loosed the guard dogs they'd brought with them, the idea being for these to infiltrate the building and maybe keep its defenders occupied as they moved in. But the dogs, normally so aggressive, wanted no part of bullets and grenades, and slunk back to their handlers.

By then, Handelsman, Major Borodin and their men had begun their assault on the barbed wire. Their target was the southwest corner of the compound, this providing an escape route bypassing all but one of the guard towers while starting them nearer the Sola River once they were out. What no one could have envisioned, what wouldn't have been a factor if the revolt had gone as planned, was the presence of a German machine-gun emplacement at that corner, the barrel jutting from between two mounds of earth fronting a hastily dug foxhole.

Put there to anchor the left side of the SS line, it prevented the Sonder from gaining the electrified fence to set their dynamite. They'd tried, and four men had died without coming near the wire. As long as this gun remained, the rebels were bottled in.

Someone would have to get close enough to lob a grenade. Handelsman felt a tapping on his shoulder and turned to see the Pomeranian fisherman Deresinski, one of Borodin's little bombs in each of his sea-calloused fists.

"Cover me, professor," was all he said, though Handelsman required neither clarification nor convincing.

"You're a brave man, Joseph. Hurry back to us, will you? We're going to need you today."

Deresinski took off at a run, hitting the grass after a few meters and worming forward. From his position at an outer door, Handelsman had a clear field of fire to the German gunners. His own machine gun, being of a lighter caliber, wasn't all that accurate at this range, but should enable him to keep the two helmeted heads down while their attacker closed in.

Which he did in short order, getting surprisingly close before the Nazis noticed. They'd been too busy whamming away at the crematorium, but upon spotting him swung the barrel to their left. Handelsman responded, if without the result he'd desired; his ammunition limited, he had no choice but to confine his fire to small bursts, after each of which the SS gun would chatter anew.

Not that this slowed Deresinski, who was able to advance nearer yet, ending up in a protected hollow ten meters from his objective. From where he hurled a first grenade. A decent toss it was, too, exploding just to the side of the foxhole, but as if to mock its ineffectiveness the machine gun let go another volley.

When a second toss proved as futile, Handelsman hung his head, not only at the other's failure but his own. He should have known the major's makeshift contraption would just about need to hit its target square-on to do any damage. Why hadn't he thought to suggest his man arm himself with dynamite instead? The Sonder were facing two enemies, the SS and the clock, yet here his incomprehensibly stupid self had squandered critical minutes.

The only way he saw to make amends for that stupidity was to follow in his gutsy fellow Pole's footsteps, and was just leaving to find some dynamite and someone to take over his gun when he heard his name shouted.

It was Deresinski, lying on his back against the far slope of the hollow. Handelsman's lips parted in wonder. He was holding a small bundle he must have drawn from his shirt, two sticks of the explosive bound with black electrical tape.

"Get ready, professor," he called, "and pour it on this time!" Then with a salute as of farewell, "God go with you all, and remember me to our people!"

At this he lit the fuse, jumped to his feet, and vaulted at a sprint toward the German position. Handelsman opened up and kept it up, prepared to spend his last bullet if need be. This took the machine gunners out of the equation, but Deresinski's grenades had attracted attention. As Handelsman watched aghast, a Nazi salvo from somewhere slammed into the man's stomach and sent him sprawling.

But though he'd gone down, he wasn't out. He'd made up his mind from the outset it would take more than a few little bullets to stop him. Like a corpse rising from the grave, he lurched to his knees, scrabbled the last several feet to the foxhole, and clutching the dynamite to his bloody middle threw himself in as it went off.

Handelsman wasn't the only Sonder to lose it. The same snarl of rage that welled out of him tore from a score of other throats. So savage was the fire now from that end of the building, the SS commander, his left flank now vulnerable and uncertain of the size of the force opposite him, couldn't discount a counterattack. He got on his field telephone, and soon two small, wheeled howitzers could be seen making their way from the east, bumping along behind a pair of jeeps.

The Sonder by then had flattened a section of the fence. The cry went out to the men in the crematorium, who were soon racing loudly through the gap in the barbed wire. The last of them supposed to quit the place, however, never did. Borodin had entrusted two of his Russians with the job of detonating the reserve fuel, but they'd waited too long in checking that every room was clear and lay where they'd fallen, victims of a Nazi grenade.

The revolt may have become a reality, but Kaminski's heart's desire of tumbling all sixteen walls of this latter-day Jericho wasn't to be: Crematorium V because, undermanned, its guard had been sufficient to secure it; III from its occupants ending up trapped in its attic; and now II, out of what could only be put down to bad luck.

The one death house, though, burned defiantly for all the camp to see, and no one did this stir more than Roza Robota. From the Bekleidungskammer, she could hear the gunfire popping on both sides of her, and through a window marveled at the fat pillar of smoke splitting the sky. The one was music to her ears, the other a treat for the eyes, and together glorious proof that her mission, with all its dangers, its sacrifices, had been worth every one.

Nor was she the only woman to have turned her back on the clothing tables, their work forgotten. Indeed, in their shock at the explosion and its fireball, the guards in charge of them were neglecting theirs, too. Even the warehouse's *Kommandoführer* was oblivious to his slaves, kept bouncing back and forth between the telephone and a window.

Roza could picture the camp's entire complement of SS in a similarly distraught state, and so intoxicating was the image of Nazis in fear of their lives for a change, she wasn't standing on the floor but floating above it.

Jews fighting back, and with guns! The ground red with *German* blood! She'd fantasized this for going on five years now, ever since her push for an insurrection in the Ciechanow ghetto had been overruled. How many of her race, her family, had perished in the interim? Her mama and papa, her sister Shoshonna, her poor sickly brother Isaac and even frailer Grandma Gemmy... their ghosts, and those of others, would haunt her forever.

But now when they came to her, in both her sleeping and day dreams, she would have this to tell them: their deaths, in so far as possible, had been avenged. The sword of justice—justice on *earth*, not some problematic heaven—had sought out the butchers and cut their own lives short. The guilty, some of them, not enough but some, had been brought to task in this world, not the next, made to answer for their crimes while they still had something tangible, something temporal to lose.

As enraptured as she was, the moment would have tasted even sweeter if Esther were there to share it with her. And Ala and Rose, Regina and Marta, Genia and Ilse—what could have been better than to celebrate the victorious conclusion of their mission with those of her fellow provocateurs most responsible for it? With all of the brave men and women who'd risked their lives helping to arm the rebels. She could only hope that wherever they were, the main camp or here, each was able to see the same mushrooming cloud of smoke as she, recognizing it for the triumphant thing it was.

What Roza couldn't know, and would have dampened her mood if she had, was that Crematorium IV would be the only one that day to go up in flames. Or that the revolt wasn't the robust animal its fury suggested.

It hadn't taken long for those Sonder fleeing Number Four in such elation to come back to earth. They'd made it to the woods, but now what? A quarter-mile into the trees, they paused in the sun-spangled shade, an uneasy mob heavy with sweat and an almost as material tension. The Germans would soon be hot on their scent if they weren't already, and though not that dense a woods, the undergrowth was matted, the ground uneven. This made for slower going than they'd predicted.

Nor did they have anywhere close to the guns they'd anticipated. So pitiful was their arsenal, they wouldn't have been much worse off with nothing. So as to divide their pursuers, they broke up into three units of a hundred each, one under the umbrella of Warszawski's machine gun, the second under Kirschenbaum's, and the third allotted what pistols were left. This last group set out west, the others to the north and northwest, all with the Vistula River their destination.

As they slogged forward, Warszawski's men cast nervous glances behind them. After twenty minutes, he held up a hand for them to stop and pulled out a map and compass he'd been keeping on him for days now. Both were from the supplies the partisans had left in the crematorium yard a year ago.

He leaned against a tree, absorbed in the tattered piece of paper. A handful of younger Sonder, all Hungarians, gathered near. One spoke a reasonable Polish. "Are we lost, please, sir?"

"No," said Warszawski, bent over the map. "Just getting my bearings."

"Your... bearings?"

"According to this, if we are where I think we are, there's a rail bridge that crosses the river two miles to the east, the line to Katowice."

"And this where we go?"

"This where we go. The forest on the other side is said to be full of partisans. If we can make it to that bridge..."

The Hungarian relayed this to his companions, who nodded eagerly. Then to Warszawski, "And we see bridge soon, sir?"

The Pole was already walking. "If we don't stand here jabbering all day," he said, but finding that bridge on the map had him saying it with a smile.

Twenty minutes more of battling the brush, however, and the fugitives to their growing puzzlement began to question how much of a need for hurry there was. Strangely, beyond strange, the SS didn't appear to be following them at all. Or at least they had yet to catch sight or sound of any.

As opposed to relaxing it, this only quickened their pace. Each step wasn't merely a step anymore but a tiny liberation unto itself, another foot closer to freedom. Could it be that escape was in their grasp? The general mood having flipped from frightened to almost frolicsome now, they might have been on some kind of romp instead of running for their lives.

Those in the front cried out before much longer that they could see the river through the trees, see it shining in the sun. "Come on!" they yelled. "We've done it, we're there!" These galloped impetuously ahead, as carried away as children—

Only to crumple to the ground amid a shattering roar before they'd gone twenty meters. What they'd seen was the sun reflecting off the helmets of a line of soldiers, who now emerged from their hiding places spraying bullets as they advanced.

"Back!" Warszawski screamed. "Fall back! It's the bleeding Krauts!"

For three long seconds everyone just stood there, mouths agape. Then the stampede was on. Lead filled the air, men dropping all around Warszawski. He saw a boy running by him catch it in the head, the top of it lifting off as neatly as that of an egg tapped with a spoon.

His machine gun was keeping the Nazis at a distance, but it was hopeless. The woods bristled with as many Germans it seemed as trees, not only in front of them now but to the right and left. From out of nowhere they came, as if sprouting from the forest floor like a goblin army from some dark fairy tale. He stood his ground for as long as he could, then with a final burst turned tail and ran with the others.

They didn't slow down until back at that part of the woods where they'd started, an upshot made the more farcical in that they weren't alone. There to meet what was left of them were the men they'd separated from earlier, themselves having toppled back in wild-eyed retreat. Evidently, they'd bumbled into the same sort of trap as Warszawski.

He wasn't the only one to feel like an idiot. With them crowing just minutes ago at its apparent success, their great escape had turned out to be a great big flop. Here they sat, the whole humbled, pathetic gaggle of them, gasping for breath in the shade of the same trees they'd set out from. Only this time, and shortly, they'd be having company.

Desperate, the two hundred of them took refuge in a small thicket rising out the middle of an adjacent clearing. When the SS did arrive, they proceeded at their leisure to take up positions in the woods along the periphery of this clearing. The Sonder soon faced an unbroken ring of steel.

Warszawski searched the thicket up and down for Kirschenbaum, but Shlomo hadn't made it. This was too bad; aside from his having taken a liking to the man these past months, they could have used his gun for what was coming. During his traverse of the place, he'd counted two heavy machine guns and six, seven hundred soldiers on the German tree line. He watched these now on his stomach from behind a rotting log.

The SS, silent, unmoving, watched back. "What's holding them up?" he asked himself, not realizing he was asking it out loud. "Why aren't they attacking?"

"What," came a voice—"you in a rush or something?"

Warszawski turned to the man lying next to him. It was one of the Maidanek Sonder, a Lieutenant Ustinov, Borodin's second in command. "Yes, I am," he shot back, unable to share the other's breeziness. "What good does it do to prolong it?"

"That I'm not sure, but speaking for myself, I'd just as soon our friends out there prolonged it indefinitely."

Warszawski could feel the iron band squeezing his skull relax a bit. Maybe this funnyman of a Russian had the right idea. "Your name is Ustinov, right?"

"That depends."

"On what?"

"To you I am First Lieutenant Georgi Ustinov, formerly of the 2nd Rifles of the People's Tenth Army. To them," he said of the Germans, drawing back his sleeve to bare the tattoo, "I am R-5212."

"So, R-5212, answer me this. How does a Soviet officer such as yourself come to speak Polish? And by that I mean better than some Poles I know."

"I was stationed in Białystok for two years, until the summer of '41. We all were, which was where all nineteen of us more or less picked up the language. And where we were captured when the Nazis got tired of sharing what was left of your country with us dirty

Bolsheviks. Then regret—how do you say it? Regrettably for them, made the mistake of marching into ours."

Warszawski had never got to know the Maidanek POWs. They'd been a clannish bunch, sticking mostly to themselves. This Ustinov was about the same age as he, and like him short and sinewy. Unlike him, he didn't appear the least perturbed by the spot they were in. The pale-blue eyes beneath the straw-colored hair were half-closed, the mouth a gentle smirk; he might have been sitting at a sidewalk bistro somewhere, sipping wine and ogling the girls going by, than here in this death trap of a woods about to breathe his last.

Admire this as he might, Warszawski wasn't built that way. Iron band or no, he'd quickly lapsed into frustration again. "What do you figure happened back there? It's as if the blinking Krauts read our blinking minds."

"And that surprises you?" The smirk deepened, but for a second only. "If you ask me, though, it wasn't our minds they were reading, but a map. They had to reckon we'd make a dash for the Vistula— given our exit point and lack of a head start, where else were we to go?

"So they humped it to get there first, and instead of chasing after us, sat and waited for us to come to them. After that, it was like tightening a net around a school of fish."

"Two steps ahead of us as usual," Warszawski said. "Oh well, nothing to be done about it now. Except prepare the men."

"Prepare them for what?" Ustinov said absently, intent on the Germans again.

"Why, to fight, what else? The bastard SS aren't going to sit there forever."

"Fight?" He turned back to Warszawski. "Fight with what? How many bullets you have left for that gun of yours?"

No answer.

"And it, unless you happened to find the missing Kirschenbaum, our only machine gun. As for pistols we have three." Ustinov held up a 6-mm. "This one as low on ammo as that thing you're holding. There might be a few grenades, a little dynamite maybe, but..." He didn't finish. Didn't have to.

"What are you saying? That we surrender, give up? You do realize, lieutenant, we're dead either way."

"We've already given up, or haven't you noticed? Good God, look around you! Look at your men!" With a sweep of his arm, the Russian took in the shadowy interior of the thicket.

Some of the Sonder were curled up crying softly to themselves. Others milled about as in a daze. Most just sat there, staring at nothing, that stare people wore when they didn't care anymore. When death was as acceptable a solution as any.

That they were cornered and virtually defenseless didn't help, but Warszawski felt that even if it were more of an equal fight, they'd still have lacked the will to break the grip of the defeat strangling them. To have caught a whiff of the heady perfume of freedom only to have it snatched away was asking too much of men, of boys, who'd suffered so deeply for so long.

He knew then all was over, and if any doubt lingered, it was squashed a moment later. "Over there," said Ustinov, pointing. "I guess that about settles it."

A team of soldiers was rolling two howitzers into place on the Nazi line. Redeployed from Crematorium II, where they hadn't been of use after all, they were capable of reducing the thicket to a heap of splinters. This was why the SS poised at the edge of the trees had sat tight; no sense incurring needless casualties when the rebels could be dispatched from a distance.

As much as Warszawski would have rather gone out in a blaze of glory, he questioned what glory was to be got from being pounded to pieces from afar. He did consider rallying around him those of a like mind as he and mounting a suicide charge against the Germans. Maybe even manage to take some of the muckers with them. But this would have condemned the men in the thicket to the mutilating terrors of the cannons, a worse death than the bullet to the head likely theirs if they surrendered.

Ustinov, though he hadn't come out and said it, was right. There was only one thing to do, and he, Warszawski, had to be the one to do it. He wouldn't have been comfortable asking somebody else.

Moments later, he stepped tentatively into the clearing, waving a stick with a white shirt attached. Prepared at any second to be gunned down, instead two squads of soldiers emerged from the woods with weapons pointed and ordered the Sonder to come out with their hands up.

After stripping them of what arms they had, the SS marched their prisoners back toward the camp. As these retraced the ground they'd crossed with such expectation earlier, to the south they could hear the faint, fragmented cadence of battle. If anything could milk the scantest jot of something resembling cheer from the black depths of their despair, it would be this, for it meant the revolt hadn't been confined to them alone. Somewhere out there were men who'd thrown off their chains and had yet to be subdued, who from the sound of it were giving the Nazis all they could handle.

The sound was deceptive. The rebels fleeing Crematorium II were having difficulties of their own.

Things at first had gone well. With the martyr Deresinski having allowed them to blow a path through the barbed wire, they ran— still within the confines of the camp as planned—down the road that bordered the female *B1b* lager. On impulse, Gradowski and Wrubel, as an invitation to the women to join them, dynamited a segment of this fence. It was a chivalrous gesture, but futile; most were away at work, those few hunkered in their huts too spooked by all the shooting and shouting to show their heads.

With only one watchtower to contend with at the part of the perimeter they'd set their sights on, the escapees were soon past it and in the woods, where they immediately went about parceling themselves into gangs of twenty. With these then departing by different routes, the race to the Sola and its marshes was on.

Before they could properly fan out, though, units from the subcamps of Budy and Rajsko closed on them from the front, and on their flanks troops from the Jawischowitz camp and the Stammlager. The Germans were better organized and had mobilized much faster than foreseen, and the Sonder soon found themselves surrounded.

Hammer at it as they might, they failed to break the Nazi encirclement. This slugfest in the forest ground on for an hour and a half, and wouldn't have lasted that long but for the weapons and ammunition the rebels were able to snag from their fallen enemy. In the end, exhausted, dehydrated, many of them wounded, the less than forty still alive limped up to an abandoned barn half-swallowed by the trees.

Even as they dragged themselves into it knowing they'd never leave it, this was fine by them; they couldn't have asked for a better place to make a last stand. Here, the Germans were going to have to come in and get them, and the Sonder still had enough fight left to make a lot of them wish they hadn't.

But even this was to be denied them. After tracking them there, and upon appraising the situation, the SS rejected the idea of an assault on the barn in favor of setting it on fire. A few swipes from a machine gun ignited the ancient thatch of the roof, the gray straw soon smoldering in three places.

Isaac Kalniak sat with his back against a wall, his rifle in his lap. There was no need to keep watch; once the high, vaulted ceiling began puffing smoke, he knew what the Germans were up to. Nor was he alone. Even in the half-light of the building's interior, he could see in the expressions of the men around him the struggle taking place in their heads: whether to flee and make the hated SS the gift of a turkey-shoot, or stay where they were and burn alive.

Next to him was the Russian major, he, too, cradling a submachine gun. He'd always admired this officer and his compatriots from Maidanek for not only their bravery but their bravado, the ability to laugh at whatever came their way. The kapo sought to emulate that same spirit now.

"I've heard of jumping from the frying pan into the fire, but this is ridiculous. I never thought I'd say such a thing, but I'm starting to wish I was back in dear old Birkenau."

Borodin managed a tired smile. "I must congratulate you, friend, on your offhandedness. Especially coming as it does from someone covered in blood." Kalniak was still clotted with the gore from his encounter with the Nazi corporal back in the crematorium. "Where were you shot, the side of the head there?"

"I wasn't shot, there or anywhere. But why I'm bloody is a whole other kettle of fish, and I've something more pressing we need to discuss."

"And not," Borodin added, frowning at the ceiling, "a lot of time to discuss it in."

"Exactly." Kalniak followed his gaze, could see not only smoke now but flames. "I'd say that roof has another twenty minutes in it tops. Which means every man here has a decision to make, and fast. I for one have no desire to be grilled like a lamb chop, but neither do I want to end up target practice for a bunch of damned German horse-apples. Or worse, be taken prisoner and tortured for information.

"On the other hand..." Here he hesitated. "There is a third option. Nor should a man smart as yourself need be told what it is."

Borodin didn't get it. Until helped by the insinuating rise of Kalniak's eyebrows. "Let me understand. What you're saying is we ought to... take matters into our own hands?"

"It's the only way. We're dead however you slice it, major. It's not a question of if anymore, but how. And apart from guaranteeing us as clean and quick an end as possible, the 'how' I'm suggesting would also send a message to those on the other side of this wall: we Sonder may have lost the battle, but by dying how and when we choose, not on your terms but ours—as men and not slaves—we win the war. Not by plucking victory but dignity from defeat. And if you SS supermen, you elite of the Third Reich don't like it—

"Tough shit. You can kiss our dead Jewish asses."

The Russian studied the gun in his hands, as if waiting for it to tell him what to do. When he did lift his eyes, there could be no mistaking what shone from behind his spectacles.

"Let me just say, kapo, it's as hard to fault your logic as it is your profanity."

"You with me on this then?"

"I'm with anybody who'd give me the opportunity to tell the Krauts, even if posthumously, to kiss my ass. Gentile though it be."

"Good." The big bear of a Pole drug himself to his feet. "Maybe you can help me find out who might be leaning the same direction, and see if we can't change the minds of those who aren't."

Their success would prove spotty. So obstinate were some of the Sonder in hanging onto life, they convinced themselves there was a good chance the Nazis would feel they couldn't get along without them. That after today's blood-letting, experienced crematorium workers would be in demand.

Upon these deluded souls, all appeals to common sense and self-respect were wasted. When the fire that by then had engulfed the ceiling began sending fingers of flame down the walls, and before that ceiling could collapse, ten of them ran out the barn door with their hands in the air, begging the soldiers not to shoot.

A heavy machine gun cut their entreaties short. But the longer the German gunners layed for the rest, the less they anticipated any. This received added credence when shots sounded inside the barn. These went on for some minutes, a pause between each—until only silence was heard, a silence that said it all, as loud in its implication as the blasting of artillery.

The SS faltered, unsure of their next move. Finally, the order came to machine-gun the Sonder redoubt from front to rear and back again. When this drew no response, a squad was sent at a run to investigate. Cringing before the heat, the soldiers cracked open the barn door to find what they were expecting. Vivid in the yellow-orange light of the fire, upward of thirty corpses littered the floor, each bleeding from a wound to the head.

To keep the blaze from consuming them, the camp's fire-control detail was radioed and told to step on it. The Kommandantur, as the men in the field correctly assumed, would require an accurate tattoo count to make certain none of its pigeons had flown the coop.

That some in fact had, their handlers weren't to discover until the day was almost done. In the running battle preceding the showdown at the barn, two of the Sonder bands fleeing south found their path blocked by the SS from Budy, leading them to make a right turn to the west and the Vistula. This, however, put them on a collision course with an even bigger force from the subcamp of Harmense to the north.

The firefight that ensued was brief. With Harmense in front of them and Budy on their flank, in addition to a company from Birkenau closing from behind, the rebels ended up a doomed pocket. But in the chaos, by dint of sheer luck, twelve of them happened upon a momentary gap in the German advance and blundered through it unnoticed without even realizing they had.

The farther they ran, the fainter the gunfire at their backs. But not until the trees thinned with still no soldiers in sight did they dare imagine they might have slipped the Nazi noose.

Handelsman was one of these charmed few, and Gradowski, and Wrubel. It was he, forging ahead on his eighteen-year-old legs, who upon cresting a small rise was the first to spot it. He let out an excited whoop.

"The Vistula! C'mon, hurry, I can see it!"

The river was wide at this point, but still low from the dry summer; here and there a white sandbar poked above the brown water like the back of some monster fish. The Sonder spilled down a steep bank to the muddy shore, threw off their backpacks and shoes, and tied the latter to their belts. The swim loomed a formidable one, but they figured if they took it in stages, one sandbar to the next, they could make it.

Once in the water, though, they discovered the current stronger than they'd thought. Instead of holding a straight line they were soon drifting harum-scarum downstream. The poorer swimmers among them kept bobbing under, but they hadn't come this far only to drown. With the help of the sandbars, if many a backpack was shucked, all twelve made it to the other side. With three guns.

But so spread out were they, it took a while to regroup. Which left them no time to catch their second wind. Instead, they were soon plowing a path through a scrub forest punishingly thicker than the previous, the branches of the stunted trees low to the ground and woven tight. Bleeding from these, sweating like mules, after an hour they were on their last legs.

Abruptly, as if by magic, for none had seen it coming through the impermeable wall of trees, they were standing in a plowed field stubbled with straw. The land to the horizon was an unbroken quilt of such fields, treeless but for the occasional copse resembling a cluster of broccoli. A mile away, they could see a silo and barn, a farmhouse with a ribbon of smoke coiling from its chimney.

"Should we?" said Gradowski. "It'll be dark before long, and it might be safer to travel by night."

"I'm with Zalman," said the paunchy Tevek, still breathing hard. "Rest up in their barn an hour or two, then push on."

"Night *would* be smarter," added another. And from a young Greek in crude Polish, "Food maybe have. Water…"

"I don't know." Handelsman didn't like it. "Who's to say they can be trusted? Whoever 'they' are."

"There is risk," said Gradowski, "but I'm about stove in. I can't guarantee how much longer I—"

All eyes followed his. A man had stepped from the house and stood gazing their way, a hand shading his face from the descending sun.

Handelsman shrugged. "That tears it, I guess." He started walking toward the house, the others falling in behind. "Let's just hope our farmer here dislikes Krauts more than he does kikes."

As the day hastened to wind down, the sun to lose strength, so too did the revolt. The unearthly caterwaul of the siren had long ago ceased, along with the noise of battle to the south. That eerie, suffocating silence a trademark of the death camp settled again over the kingdom of Auschwitz-Birkenau.

Not that the infuriated SS were done. To the rear of the smoking ruin that was Crematorium IV, in that section of the yard bare of grass, the two hundred Sonder who'd surrendered in the thicket lay chin down in the dirt, bleeding. After being forced back to the scene of their earlier triumph and ordered onto their stomachs, their guards had gone to work on them with the butts of their rifles. Unable to contain their anger, they'd waded into the prostrate rows. This went on until there wasn't a rebel who escaped their wrath, nor a soldier who didn't feel better at having vented it.

Joining them on the ground was an assortment of prisoners from Crematorium II. These consisted of those who hadn't fled the yard, some from a last-minute failure of nerve (this including a smattering from IV); some who'd left too late and got captured; and a few not part of the revolt who'd stayed at their posts. These last, mainly the squad's chief physician and his assistants, were exonerated after a quick investigation and released.

Then came the rifle butts, the SS begging them afterward to utter a word or even raise their heads so as to give them the excuse to blow those heads off.

While there wasn't a Sonder who didn't see what was coming, as the minutes dragged into an hour some began to question themselves. What they couldn't know was the Nazis were merely waiting to find out if more prisoners were on the way, namely any that might have been taken captive in the fighting to the south.

When confirmed there weren't, the SS at Number Four were free to take their anger to the next level. To those of the doomed desperately thinking reprieve, this evaporated at the clap of the first pistol shot. Even with their heads flat to the ground, many could make out the executioners moving among them, administering the fatal bullet Sonder by Sonder.

Warszawski lay at the extreme northern end of one of the farther rows. To his right was the perimeter wire and the woods beyond, on his left a boy whom he recognized as the Hungarian Svoboda of all people. Since a nasty dustup between them months ago, each had made it a point to stay far from the other, or as far as space and the Germans would permit. Yet here they were these two enemies, in the last minutes of life left them, so close they were practically touching each other.

Far from startling him, the bang of the guns barely registered with Warszawski. Not only had he resigned himself to their inevitability the moment he was ordered to his belly, when at last they did appear his attention was elsewhere. Focused on things both ordinary yet strangely unfamiliar.

Never had the trees shone so green, the sky so boisterous a blue. He could hardly tear his eyes from the creamy, billowing beauty of the late-afternoon clouds. The birdsong trilling from the woods was as intricate and loud as a symphony, the buzzing of some bees in a patch of clover the violin section.

With death footsteps away, his time on this earth running down like the sand in an hourglass, his senses donned wings, and as if to make the most of that time flew him to heights unvisited until now. The soil against which his cheek pressed wasn't just dirt anymore but a little universe unto itself of glittering, silica solar systems and cosmic dust. The breeze on his flesh was as cool, as intimate as a lover's touch. He even fancied he could hear the electricity humming in the barbed wire—or perhaps it wasn't that at all, but the subsonic hum and throb that since the beginning of creation had pulsed through every living cell of every plant and animal, that indefinable energy which hadn't only sparked life but continued each second of every day to sustain it.

As goofball as he would have labeled such observations a day ago, now they weren't only real but a refuge. His hyperkinetic ways hiding it from him before—those senses of his shuttered his whole life by him blurring through it without ever slowing to smell its flowers— he saw now with the suddenness and clarity of, well, a gunshot, that he and the birds and the trees and the dirt, even the clouds and the sky with its stars not yet shining, were all part of the same fabric, the same warp and woof of existence, the essential substance of one indistinguishable from the other.

That he was about to return to this oneness from which he'd come, from which everything came, filled Warszawski with a peace greater than any he could remember. He heard the pistols all right, but didn't. Knew what they meant, but could not have cared less.

It helped that another person was nearby. This end-of-life epiphany of his was all well and good, but it would have been harder to die without someone to say goodbye to. That this had turned out to be Svoboda only figured, not that he was complaining. When it came down to it, did it really matter who it was?

József Svoboda had entered the commando late, shortly after the bollixed June attempt at revolt. He'd kept mostly to himself, shying from conversation, except when the talk turned to having another go at rebellion. Then he was all over it, eager to hear about what might be in the pipeline, loud in encouraging any who would listen into taking up arms again.

Warszawski became convinced the newcomer was a plant, put there by *Hauptscharführer* Möll to report any further subversiveness. Nor did he try to hide his suspicions. Upon these reaching Svoboda, a confrontation ensued, ending childishly in a schoolyard-like scuffle. When later determined the Hungarian wasn't a spy after all, simply one of the more enthusiastic Nazi-haters among them, Warszawski tried to make amends, but his antagonist would have none of it. The insult had been too great. This only aroused the Pole's resentment, and stiff-necked as both were, they'd kept the feud alive.

He stared to his right until Svoboda's eyes found his, large, elliptical brown eyes that winced at each crack of the guns. Other than this, his demeanor revealed nothing, the dark, gypsy-flavored features unreadable. From out the curly mop of black hair, a thread of bright red eased down his forehead. Warszawski, too, had been bloodied, could taste it in his mouth.

"You're not frightened, son?" he was fortunate to be able to ask in his native tongue. Everybody who knew Svoboda knew also that his father, half Polish, had bequeathed him the language.

The young Hungarian studied him suspiciously before answering. Then, "I'd be lying if I said I wasn't, but not as afraid as I thought I'd be."

Warszawski had a feeling most of the rest in the yard were of the same mind. Not that the air was in want of weeping, but it was as subdued as it was scattered. There was a manliness to this, a nobility that almost brought a tear to *his* cheek, not one of pity for but pride in the mettle of those around him. The kid beside him. A sudden tenderness toward this Svoboda took hold of him, and with it the urge to reach out, to try and blunt the sharp edges of the fear he knew, despite appearances, had to be working on the boy.

If that boy would let him. "When I was a few years younger than you," Warszawski hazarded, "maybe fourteen, I found my grandfather, who was living with us, dead in his room. He wasn't that old but had a weak heart, so weak he ended up confined to his bed.

"It was morning, and I'd been sent upstairs with his breakfast. He was sitting propped up by his pillows with a book in his lap, but I could tell he was dead from halfway across the room. He stared past me, unblinking, his body as stiff-looking as the headboard against which it rested. My instinct was to bolt for the stairs and raise the alarm, but as panicked as I was, I didn't. You know why?"

Svoboda shook his head.

"The expression on his face. Stopped me right in my tracks. And not, as you might be imagining, because it was horrible. A regular soup of emotions was bubbling inside me, emotions to be expected of a child in that situation—fear, confusion, disgust, and not least of all grief, for I'd loved my grandpa and here I'd lost him. But trumping them all, and what kept me rooted to the floor, was the look that had frozen itself on that face.

"I set the breakfast tray down and walked up to the bed. That the end had been quick was clear; neither fright nor suffering had had a chance to leave their mark. Instead, the lips were parted in a little smile, the eyes brimming over with... I don't know, call it wonder. Or more like longing maybe. I can't describe it still, but never will I forget it."

Warszawski spat some dirt from his mouth. "Not that I knew what to make of it. Not at fourteen. What was it he'd seen in his last moments, perhaps *the* last moment, to leave him smiling? How could death be anything but awful?

"Only later did I come to suspect what he was telling me, his last if unintentional gift to his grandson. That death isn't something to be feared or even mourned. That it isn't the end of anything, but a beginning. Not a door being shut so much as one opening."

Svoboda continued to betray no emotion, his own face as blank a slate as before. Warszawski started to think he might be wasting his breath—when he noticed the boy no longer flinching at the bark of the guns.

"I never did really grieve for my grandfather. It would have been selfish to be anything but glad for him. Not only was he now rid of that illness which had made an invalid of him, he'd gone to that place, that uncharted country he'd glimpsed through death's curtain, to enjoy whatever had shown itself to him. The same country we're about to enter ourselves."

As if to underscore this last, a pistol went off louder than any previous; the German gunmen had arrived at the row of prisoners directly back of them. This seemed to jolt Svoboda into speaking, though when he did he wasn't looking at Warszawski but beyond him, as at something in the distance.

"So tell me, what awaits us in this... country of yours?"

"I'm not sure. Who still in this world can say for certain? It's not, however, as if I haven't given it a lot of thought over the years. Was thinking about it, sort of, just minutes ago."

"And? What did those years tell you?"

"The same thing that awaited my grandfather. What awaits everyone who travels there."

"Which is?"

"What you've lost in this life that's dearest to you. Either that or something you never had to begin with, but should have. What, if you could only have or have back again, you wouldn't want for anything more."

When Svoboda's eyes returned to his, they weren't the same. No longer inscrutable, they'd become two revealing wells of sorrow, openings into a soul in which pain had taken up permanent residence. Warszawski had but to glance at them to understand. How many pairs of eyes like this had he had the misfortune to peer into?

"You didn't come to Birkenau alone, did you, son? Your whole family was with you."

Svoboda could only nod, his lower lip trembling.

Warszawski smiled, held out his hand. The boy took it, and biting his lip until it trembled no more, responded with a pallid smile of his own. When it came their turn and the SS stood over them, they were still holding hands. One of the soldiers nudged the other.

"Look... another two," he sniffed as he reloaded his gun.

After finishing the last of the rebels off, the Germans didn't send them to the ovens right away. It was imperative first they take an official tally of this vagabond 12th Squad; it wouldn't do to leave a single bearer of their secret unaccounted for. They began by matching personnel lists against both the dead they had on hand and the living who'd sat out the revolt. As this was in progress, having already taken care of their own dead and wounded, they had the forests scoured for Sonder corpses, with these to be trucked to Crematorium IV for identification.

Assigned this task was the crew from Number Five, along with thirty prisoners hastily conscripted from the general population. They and the roundabout two hundred survivors of the 12th Kommando were to fill the ranks of the new, reduced 13th.

Once all four hundred-plus bodies were collected and identified, the Nazis discovered to their alarm twenty men still missing. Though what was left of Crematorium IV had been picked through earlier, a more exacting examination yielded the remains of four more Sonder in the debris. This left a by no means acceptable discrepancy of sixteen. Despite the sun sinking rapidly, the Kommandantur decided to launch a search. All SS and Gestapo within a radius of fifteen miles were to join in.

It didn't take them long to meet with success. Darkness had yet to descend on the Polish countryside when a farmer in a horse-drawn cart flagged down a patrol out of Birkenau. The soldiers followed him to a barn and the twelve Sonder who hours before had eluded them and crossed the Vistula. They lay asleep in the hay, having opted with the farmer's blessing to rest here awhile before pushing on under cover of night.

In the vanishing gray of late twilight, the Germans prodded them awake with the muzzles of their rifles. When the twelve learned they'd been betrayed, they weren't so much angry as sick at heart. To have come this far, this close to pulling off the impossible only to wind up back in the clutches of the Nazi devil! As the SS frisked them, most avoided each other's gaze.

Gradowski leaned toward Handelsman. "Think they'll shoot us now or march us back and do it then?"

"Hard to tell," Handelsman said. "Maybe neither."

"What do you mean?"

"I'm thinking they've something else in store for us."

"Like what?"

"Like Block 35. The interrogation cell. Torture. It's what I'd do if I were them, try to wring us for information."

"Torture," Gradowski said, and shuddered. "My God, I don't know if I—"

"You won't have to. There's no reason to. Not if we choose not to." Handelsman showed his teeth. "I say we die standing up instead of strapped down, go out like men and not so many bloody pieces of meat. I'm for rushing the sonsabitches, ending it right here. Hell, who knows? There are twelve of us and not all that many more of them. If we can get the jump on them..."

Gradowski smiled grimly now himself. "I'd settle for buying just a lousy few seconds. Long enough to get my hands around one of their Kraut necks."

"Count me in!" hissed Tevek.

"And me!" said another.

"Good." Handelsman paused until a soldier walking by was out of earshot. "Pass the word. And see that the Hungarians get what's going on. Everyone needs to watch me, be ready to move the second I do."

As it turned out, he was right. The Nazis had no intention of shooting anyone; their orders were to return unharmed any escapees they might come across. The Kommandantur, beyond irate at its soldiers for executing those Sonder taken captive earlier, wasn't going to see the mistake repeated. The SS refused to accept that Birkenau could have acted alone, without help, and as they had in June with the captured courier, saw an opportunity in their incessant war against it to gain some ground on Battle Group-Auschwitz. If they played their cards right in the torture chamber, possibly wipe it out altogether.

By now the day had given way to night but for a smudge of gray to the west. Their escort led the prisoners out the barn and toward a bridge two miles distant, an electric torch in front and one bringing up the rear. They hadn't gone far when Handelsman darted for the guard nearest him.

With an animal roar the others jumped in after, and instantly all was madness. Wild shouts and the thunder of guns ripped the night apart. The beams of the torches swung crazily about, illuminating a swirl of men running, falling, wrestling, tearing at each other with their bare hands.

Jukel Wrubel grappled his German's machine gun away and blew half the man's head off. Still on his knees, he stitched another up the middle and yet another in the legs before being blasted from the front and behind. Even then, on his back, coughing his life's blood out, he didn't stop squeezing the trigger until they let him have it twice more.

Gradowski, his wish granted, strangled his man unconscious before being knocked out himself. Handelsman, too, and another were only clobbered, not killed. As determined as the twelve were to die fighting, the Nazis, mindful of their orders, did their best to show restraint. In addition to the three Sonder merely bashed senseless, one more survived, felled by a shot to the knees.

These were bound hand and foot, and a runner sent to fetch a truck. By nine o'clock, two of the captured sat shackled to chairs in separate interrogation rooms. Ignoring the care taken to get them there, their Gestapo inquisitors, half out of anger, half clumsiness, came down too hard on the four and bungled the job. Five hours later, all but Gradowski were dead. And he, with a fractured skull, slipping in and out of consciousness.

With him of little more use to it now than his murdered accomplices, the Political Department looked to salvage something from its ineptness. Few affairs satisfied the SS and shipwrecked inmate morale more than a good hanging done right. A physician was assigned Gradowski to see he made it through the night, lights set up in the yard of Crematorium IV, and carpenters put to work erecting a shiny-new, five-stepped, one-man gallows.

The 13th Kommando was led there after morning roll call. The weather had cooperated to fit the occasion, a claustrophobic fog obscuring everything outside the wire. The visible world was reduced to the gutted carcass of the death house, the expanse of the yard itself, and the pastel-yellow pine of the scaffold.

Parading slowly atop this in full-dress black uniform was the patrician figure of *Hauptsturmführer* Franz Hössler. A mix of triumph and disdain pulsed from his face, seeming to darken the air around it. A deathly stillness enveloped the scene, made the more acute by the fog. No calls for quiet were necessary from the guards ringing the assembled men; no one dared even whisper. The only sound was the hollow thump of the captain's boots on the pine.

Breaking the silence, a Red Cross ambulance rolled up and coughed to a stop next to the platform. Two *Schützen* slid a stretcher bearing a body out the back and ran it up the steps. When they stood it on end, there hung Gradowski, eyes shut, head lolling to one side and swathed in a red-stained bandage. The rest of him was tied down so he wouldn't fall out. From the crossbeam above him dangled a crude noose.

Hössler flung a dramatic arm wide. "Behold the price of disloyalty!" he shouted. "Here is what awaits the dog who would turn on his master!"

Again silence, the Nazi's icy stare sweeping the rows of men at his feet.

"Can you be so blind," he said finally, "as to think you could best the SS? Are you that foolish? There is no prevailing against us, especially by such as you. It runs counter to all that is reasonable and right in this world, the natural order of things. Even if the tables were turned, if we Germans were the prisoners and you the guards, it would not stay so for long. No longer than it would take a lion to get the better of a pack of jackals."

Hössler resumed his pacing.

"And where has this treachery, this mindless stubbornness got you? You are still here, and will remain here at our pleasure, but hundreds of your brothers are among us no more. Their lives have been thrown away, and for what? For nothing, sacrificed in pursuit of something that was never there in the first place.

"You could have prevented this, too, you who stayed put yesterday. You could have persuaded your comrades of the error of their ways. But I doubt you even tried. You were as rebellious as they, I'm sure, in word if not deed.

"You should be ashamed of yourselves! You are as responsible as anyone for this treason—and its punishment, which is what you're here to witness."

Most of those present had no idea what he was saying; the little German they did know they'd picked up in the camp. There was no misapprehending the man's poisonous tone, though, nor the gloating expression twisting his features. They didn't have to understand the words to catch the drift of them.

An exception was Shlomo Kirschenbaum, born and raised in the city of Heidelberg. That he was there to hear the bombastic Hössler at all was by chance, the slimmest of chances. Where in the battle the day before, Warszawski had presumed him dead when he couldn't find him among those run to ground in the thicket, here Kirschenbaum stood very much alive, his only wound a large knot on the back of his head.

In the forest, his group, too, had crashed into the SS in its flight to the Vistula, and were sent careening back. It was during this retreat that a German grenade almost ended up his undoing. He'd stopped running and had turned to fire a covering burst from his machine gun when a terrific explosion lifted him from his feet. The last thing he remembered was flying through the air, then a blow to the head. Then blackness.

He awoke on his back to someone dragging him by the ankles. Two men actually, both clad in the civilian garb of the Sonder. He cried out, and letting go his legs they bent over him. Soon he was staring up at others, and even without his brain fully working yet, could see they weren't part of the troupe he'd been leading.

They were, in fact, from Squad 60B, pulled out of Crematorium V to help search the woods for Sonder bodies. Nor was he the only one they'd found still alive, but the soldiers, they said, who were everywhere, were shooting those they did. If he wanted to *stay* alive, he'd better try to stand up.

Which with some assistance he did, if it took him a minute before he could walk on his own; his head felt so large and unconnected to the rest of him he could have been balancing a pumpkin on his shoulders. During that minute, his rescuers checked him for wounds, but except for an ugly bump on the skull he was unhurt. The shrapnel from the grenade hadn't even nicked him.

Later, he would learn three others from Crematorium IV had escaped death, one by hiding in the flues beneath the floor of the destroyed oven room, two in the belt of trees separating it from Number Five. By tomorrow's Appell, all had snuck back into the commando, Shlomo never did ask how. With the Sonder head count now correct, the Nazis weren't in any rush to investigate the matter, either, figuring that in Saturday's confusion, with bodies coming in from all over, they'd simply overlooked some.

German may have been Kirschenbaum's first language, but Hössler's megalomania was being lost on him nonetheless; he'd ceased listening to this Moshe Liar soon after he'd started spewing his venom. It wasn't as if he hadn't heard such before, could probably have finished the *Hauptsturmführer's* speech for him.

Instead, he busied himself scanning the men around him. What he was searching for were old faces, if without much success. He did spot Zalman Leventhal, the redhead to his surprise visibly crying. He knew he and Gradowski were friends, but hadn't thought the mumpish Leventhal capable of tears.

The beanpole figure of Leyb Langfus was easy to pick out, and he, too, was emotional, if in a different way. He glared openly at the still-blathering Hössler, making no attempt to hide his loathing for the man, his malignant words, the barbarity he was about to conduct. Kirschenbaum could relate: hanging an unconscious man for God's sake! There was an excessiveness to it that communicated pure malice, as if less to deter the Sonder from repeating the folly of rebellion than to rub their noses in the one they'd already tried.

He recognized a few others he'd come to know over the months. Filip Müller, the young Sudeten Czech who'd been a Sonder as long as anybody—now twenty, he was seventeen when sentenced to the crematorium. He could have passed for seventeen still but for the centuries-old eyes that stared back at one. Some of the Greeks were fixtures, too, and the Frenchman Maurice what's-his-name, a handful of Italians. Far fewer remained, however, than not; almost five hundred of the detachment were missing that had been there this hour yesterday.

Kirschenbaum wondered, facetiously, if he wouldn't have been better off joining them. Among his myriad foibles, some of which, to the uninitiated, were often mistaken for charm, the SS captain regaling them was a born ham. He loved being center stage, regardless if called upon to play the likable guy, the good Nazi, or more to his taste, the bad. On this occasion, it being the latter, and the offense at issue so dastardly, he could have raked those guilty of it over the coals indefinitely. Indeed, with him displaying no sign of shutting up, that looked to be his intent.

Until a sympathetic sky, as if tiring of it, too, chose to end his rant. What had been a negligible wind began abruptly to gust, whisking the fog away to reveal ominous clouds closing fast. Hössler swung his nose into the breeze and smelled rain, figured he'd better get on with it.

He stood legs apart at the front of the platform, arms crossed. "I would advise you of the 13th Squad to listen to what I have to say in conclusion, and listen well. Should you be tempted again to imagine you can win freedom with a gun, know you won't be the only ones to die. There will be others, thousands of others. We'll take out the whole camp and not give it a thought. We have a plan for just that, all we've been waiting for is the justification to use it.

"Do not give us that justification! I warn you, don't push us! Or the blood of your people will be on your hands, not ours."

With that, he spun on his heel and made for Gradowski, still vertical in his stretcher. He pinched him on the cheek. Again, and when that didn't rouse him, slapped him across the face. A groan arose from the Sonder, half protest, half plea.

"Shut your traps!" shouted Sergeant Gorges, this morning's second in command. As the ex-*Kommandoführer* of Crematorium IV, he'd been granted this privilege. "One more sound and you will regret it!"

Another slap, and Gradowski's eyes fluttered open. He didn't know where he was at first, cast about him in bewilderment. Only when the noose was looped around his neck and made snug did he understand, looking more sad than afraid. Kirschenbaum saw him lean forward, and as with the last of his strength, say something only the men in the front could hear.

Hössler saw it, too, and wasn't the type to share this or any podium. Quickly, he gave the order and the rope was pulled taut, lifting Gradowski into the air, stretcher and all. Half-dead as he was, the end didn't take long; a few feeble twitches, a ragged gasp, and it was over. At that exact moment, it began raining heavy, bullet-sized drops, a timing some, to cushion their grief, saw as the heavens weeping in commiseration.

The day begun so badly wasn't to get any better. Though no transports would show, hundreds of bodies needed burning, bodies with recognizable features and names, the bodies of friends. With Crematorium II under emergency repair after the fighting there, Number Three took most of this sorrowful load, the rest going to Number Five.

Yet come evening—in spite of yesterday, in spite of this morning, what followed the morning, in spite of everything—the mood in the undressing room of Crematorium V wasn't as bleak as it could have been. None of the fifty Sonder huddled among their cots was exactly smiling, but the heavy cloud that lowered over them was lightened some by what Gradowski had spoken before he died. Inaudible then to most, now everyone knew it.

"I am the last," he'd said, a statement interpreted by the majority of those grappling with it tonight to mean there would be no more interrogations. That the Nazis had elected to terminate their investigation. To those who feared they might be next for the torture chamber, this was all the interpretation they needed.

Consoling them further was the news, broken by Battle Group-Auschwitz just prior to the rebellion, that the Red Army was as close as a hundred miles. With its arrival a possible matter of weeks, it was agreed the SS were bound to have more pressing considerations than ferreting out those who might know something about an affair that hadn't only come and gone but resolved itself in their favor.

Or as Kirschenbaum heard one of them say, "Why would the Krauts persist in crying over the spilled milk that was the revolt with the Bolsheviks on the verge of overrunning the whole dairy?"

The man could have been right, but he wasn't buying it. For one, he'd ceased long ago to trust Auschwitz, and smelled a rat now, too. It would have been just like the Steering Committee to try and defuse the Sonder powder keg by implying the Russians and liberation were near. Funny they'd release so seductive a morsel even as they were begging Birkenau to be patient.

But even if true, wasn't everybody forgetting something? Shouldn't he with his head wound and poor Gradowski with his be the only two permitted the excuse of amnesia? What in the world would lead the rest to forget their jailers weren't about to let a single one of them live and spill his tale to the Reds?

Plus, a hundred miles was a hundred miles. Which unless certain conditions prevailed could just as easily be a thousand. What, for example, was the extent of German forces in the area, how imposing the Wehrmacht's defenses? Were the Soviets on the offensive or was the front static? What position did Poland occupy in their strategy at this juncture—were there more pressing objectives in the Baltics to the north, the Balkans to the south? A dozen variables had to be weighed, each of which might find the Russians still a hundred miles away three months from now.

The thing fretting Kirschenbam about those purported miles the most, however, was the behavior of the SS. But for the *Sturm und Drang* of Saturday, it was business as usual at Birkenau. The Nazis were their usual arrogant, and unless provoked, indifferent selves, not a trace of anxiety in their faces or speech.

All that appeared to concern them was the only thing he'd seen them really care about since he'd been here: that the machinery of extermination be kept oiled and running, the assembly line moving, the requisite *ordnungsgëssemer Ablauf*, that orderly procedure so compelling a part of the German makeup, maintained as before. They revealed nothing to show they knew the Red Army existed, much less stood poised scant miles distant to descend upon the camp in numbers to rival a plague of locusts.

As for Gradowski's *I am the last...* A touching, one could even say charitable farewell, but to Kirschenbaum impossibly enigmatic. The last of the conspirators to be held accountable? Or the last with the spunk to rise against the Nazis. Or if on the off chance directed at the SS, an attempt to try and deter them from making any more arrests. One couldn't tell, which made for less than solid ground on which to tether one's hopes. Yet here he was in a room with forty-nine men doing just that.

It was time to call it a night. He could have stayed up half of it playing devil's advocate to his bunking mates, but aside from having had it with this shamefulness of a day, a lot of good it would have done. They were clearly uninterested in hearing anything that might contradict their consensus.

Besides, what would it accomplish if he were to burst their bubble? Kinder to let them live in denial while they could. It'd come to them soon enough that instead of being over, the Nazi inquiry into the events of Saturday had, from where he was sitting, yet to begin. Anyone familiar with the SS had to figure as much. As long as Soviet guns remained too distant to hear, the men with the silver skull on their uniforms and the black of night in their hearts weren't likely to rest until all who'd had the gall to defy them had been flushed out and extinguished.

He slid his cot a little away from the others, where they couldn't disturb him with their naiveté, he them with his skepticism. Not that he had any intention of falling right to sleep. As he'd done last night, and could envision himself doing for many more to come, he lay awake on his rickety bed in delicious contemplation of the two Germans he'd killed in battle. How many others he'd wounded who might have died, he didn't know. But these two were confirmed fatalities, of that there could be no doubt: the one in the watchtower who'd got it in the head, and the other in the forest he'd shot through both lungs.

Kirschenbaum was not by disposition a bloodthirsty man. Until Birkenau and the Sonderkommando, the sight of blood had made him queasy. But without the prospect of an uprising to cheer him anymore, if he could be said to have one pleasure left it was replaying in his mind the taking of those SS lives. Nor was it because of what he'd seen and suffered in the crematoria at the hands of their insidious fraternity. Or the by far more inexpiable misery the Nazis had inflicted on his race, the torture and murder of what had to be millions by now—

But rather the murder of two. That was all, just two, his beautiful wife and baby boy, both whom he'd picked out of a pile of corpses a hundred years ago and carried in his own arms to the fire pits in the meadow. It was because of them that he grew warm all over whenever he recalled his pair of soldiers, because of them that he lay there tonight killing them all over again. And would until sleep did draw its cloak over him.

Two for two, what could be fairer? If that wasn't justice, what was? An eye for an eye, straight out of the Bible no less, a verse so famous the Gentiles had co-opted it, and with as telling a gesture as any of Gentile respect, given it a Latin name. The *lex talionis*, the law of retaliation... there it was for all to read, in the damn Bible. To use another Latinism, how much more of an imprimatur did a person need?

In fact, if Shlomo Kirschenbaum had still believed in God, which after eighteen months working first the meadows then the death houses he most definitely did not, he'd have thought the elegant symmetry of two for two a sign from above.

*   *   *

Coincidental to the Sonderkommando revolt having run its course, the main thrust of the gargantuan Soviet summer offensive was also grinding to a halt, if of its own impetus. The final phase of this offensive, named for the fiery Russian prince who'd died fighting Napolean a century and a quarter earlier, Operation Bagration had torn the eastern front wide open and permanently broken the back of the Wehrmacht. Five German armies were destroyed with a loss of half a million men, along with two thousand tanks and heavy artillery pieces, hundreds of aircraft.

Not only had Bagration reclaimed the Ukraine and Byelorussia in their entireties, and much of Poland, but, save for a few isolated pockets, the Baltic republics. For the first time since the Nazi invasion of 1941, the war in the east would be fought on foreign and not Russian soil.

But none of this had been easily won. The Red Army's losses rivaled the Wehrmacht's, the difference being that while the Soviets possessed the men and matériel to replace them, the Germans did not. All the same, come October the Russian giant was exhausted. Except for limited fighting in the Balkans, it would remain quiet for the rest of the year, refitting for the big push to Berlin. Though its forces, true to the Stammlager's claim weeks ago, had driven to a line not far from Auschwitz, there they would stay until on the move again in January.

The camp SS were hardly oblivious to the menace at their doorstep, but what distress this caused them they were careful to hide. When the subject came up, here and in the rest of Hitler's dwindling Third Reich, it was invariably accompanied by the stated if not always heartfelt conviction that their *Führer* would yet save the day, either by means of his legendary cunning, the introduction of a game-changing secret weapon, or some other miracle. With the result that Nazi hauteur was little altered from what it had been two years ago, when both the Russians and the possibility of defeat seemed a million miles away.

Where the proximity of the avenging Bolsheviks did discernibly affect them was in the negative attitude most displayed toward an investigation into the revolt of the Sonderkommando. As many of the squad's members had predicted, the Germans had more on their minds than getting to the bottom of a plot it had taken them but hours and a minimum of effort to crush. Not that there was any slighting the casualties they'd incurred that bloody Saturday, but the resentment this bred had been sated some by those they'd levied on the Sonder in the field and afterward.

Notwithstanding, therefore, the faith they continued at least publicly to show in Hitler, his SS myrmidons at Auschwitz weren't as troubled by the past as about that uncertain future threatening to roll over them.

Berlin was of a different mind. Appalled that a mutiny on such a scale as to blow up one crematorium and deface another should have occurred at his prize Vernichtungslager, and by a rabble of Jews no less, *Reichsführer*-SS Heinrich Himmler ordered an immediate inquiry, woe betide any who didn't give it the highest priority.

He wanted the names of the rebels responsible, how they had done it, and why it had been allowed to happen at all. Not only to punish the guilty and prevent a recurrence but to soothe his wounded pride. To the vainglorious Himmler, this latest embarrassment was the exclamation point to the insult that had been the Warsaw ghetto uprising, that contretemps of a year and a half ago that until now had constituted the lone blemish on an otherwise sterling career. He would have those who'd made the Sonder insurrection possible, on both sides of the wire if it came to that.

One didn't argue with the *Reichsführer*, one simply obeyed, leaving the camp Kommandantur no choice but to get after it. As a first step, a dozen survivors from the old 12th Squad were selected at random and taken piecemeal to Block 35. Exempted were the stokers and other specialists, there being too few of these to spare after the carnage of the 7th.

The arrests were to prove an exercise in futility. Of primary interest to the Gestapo was where the conspirators had got their explosives. But once the torture began to loosen their captives' tongues, the most any of them relinquished was having heard it a *woman* who'd armed the insurgents. Asked the name of this alleged female, or how she'd pulled off such a feat, they of course had no idea.

A woman indeed! What were these Sonder trying to pull? The Gestapo had neither the patience nor time for such silliness, and wasted no more of it dispatching the worthless twelve to the Black Wall. A decision was made to change strategy, abandoning interrogation for the present in favor of a hunt for physical evidence that might be of help. Had the dynamite and grenades been smuggled to the Sonder intact, or in the form of raw gunpowder they'd used to assemble the things themselves?

Either way, where had the material originated, the partisans outside the wire or the underground within?

The Political Department undertook a search of its own, starting with Crematorium II. Those conducted by the regular soldiery before them had all been on the cursory side, the goal anything incriminating left lying around. The Gestapo expanded on this by probing under floors and behind walls, and barely had they begun than they hit pay dirt.

It came in the shape of a wooden box the size of a large suitcase beneath the floorboards in Number Two's no longer inhabited attic. Inside it was a miniature workshop, all the tools and supplies someone manufacturing homemade grenades might have needed. Included were two small jars of gunpowder, the contents of one the consistency of ground coffee, the other with it in the form of flat, pear-shaped pieces. These were unique to one place, the Pulverraum of the Weichsel-Union factory.

More of the tiny disks were subsequently retrieved from the rubble of Crematorium IV. The SS were stunned. Suddenly, those prisoners who worked the plant's gunpowder room were the prime suspects in providing the Sonder that substance from which, as was apparent now, they'd constructed their crude bombs. Females may have played a part in the revolt after all, a major one. To the ideologues of the Gestapo, this only offered further proof of the depths to which the degraded Rassenfiend had descended: even their womenfolk were capable of foul play.

In that it aligned with their chauvinism, another explanation soon surfaced that the Germans jumped on as not only likelier but more palatable. From the moment the dictum from Berlin had arrived, the Gestapo had been a presence day and night at the Union Metallwerke. Where before, his whole shift might pass without a prisoner coming across a single SS—the civilian Meisters were who ran the show—the factory floor now swarmed with uniformed men in implacable pursuit of clues, poking their noses into every closet, every corner.

During a search of the workers one night, they turned up the evidence they'd been seeking. It was a key to the powder pavilion in the possession of someone it most definitely shouldn't have been, a kapo named Schulz.

That he should be the culprit was almost as startling as blaming a woman for the crime, Schulz being among the Nazis' more loyal servants. Typical of his office, he was one of those men who in the outside world was destined for prison or the gallows, but at Auschwitz had found a home in which his sociopathic tendencies weren't condemned but extolled. A mixed-Croatian Jew, he arrived on a transport from Yugoslavia in mid-1942, and despite his Jewishness was quickly recognized as prime kapo material. Thus began a long roster of murder, rape, extortion, and other brutalities, his reward for them a coveted posting to the Union.

He even fit the part of the brute physically: arms too long for his stubby barrel of a body, a protruding jaw and sloping forehead, combined to give him a distinctly simian mien. Those at his mercy lived in utter terror and abhorrence of him. How a Jew could so wantonly prey on other Jews was difficult to comprehend. One didn't see the Germans, or for that matter the Czechs or Poles as a rule, turning on their own.

No matter the faithful dog he'd shown himself, the SS were confident they had their man and hurried the bewildered Schulz to Block 35. They didn't tell him why until he was sitting in a room across a table from two officers, blinking in the white glare of the light in his face.

"Gunpowder?" he grunted. Then in ungrammatical German, "I don't know nothin' about no missin' gunpowder."

"Oh, but we think you do," said one of the Gestapo. "In fact, we believe you know everything about it."

"And what, I gotta ask, sirs, makes you believe that?"

"This," said the other officer. He reached in a pocket and plunked a heavy key on the table. "Look familiar, kapo?"

"It's—it's the key to the boss's office." He flushed a guilty crimson, "So—what of it?"

"What of it, he says!" Both Gestapo men laughed. "This is what: the company's gunpowder is stored in that room." The first officer leaned forward. "Just *what*, my good man, was the key to it doing on your person?"

"If your honors don't mind, I—I'd rather not say."

"I'm sure you wouldn't. But I'm afraid we must insist. Why, pray tell, would you have such a key?"

Schulz squirmed in his chair, eyes darting left and right.

"We can do this the easy or the hard way, kapo, it's up to you." The German nodded toward the shadows in the back of the room. "For the last time, what were you doing with this key?"

Their prisoner raised his head to see three large men standing over him, uniforms unbuttoned. "Aw right," he said, "aw right. I guess you got the goods on me. But not for what you say. I had the key made because… well, because I was needin' my privacy."

"Your *privacy?*" the two Nazis blurted as one. "What are you talking about? Privacy for what?"

Aware of the danger he was in, Schulz held nothing back. Since the termination of the Pulverraum night shift months ago, he'd been using the Meister's office for his own purposes. And these had nothing to do with the stealing of gunpowder. His only theft, he swore, "if you sirs wanta call it such," was that of the virtue of the occasional female prisoner he would coerce there to have his way with her without fear of interruption. If he was guilty of anything, and why he'd been hedging, it was of neglecting his duties on the plant floor to slake his appetites on von Ende's leather sofa.

Though underneath the doubtful expressions this elicited from his interrogators there lurked the sinking feeling he was telling the truth, they detained him overnight in Block 11 until they could check out his story. Come morning, they rounded up seven of the girls and women from the names he'd given them, and every one, several in tears, confirmed what he'd said.

This Kapo Schulz of theirs, the SS lamented, may have been an unscrupulous pig, but a smuggler of gunpowder he wasn't, leaving them no recourse but to release him.

Which left the Gestapo back where they'd started. Uncomfortable as it made them, they had no choice but to reject their antediluvian approach to gender, swallow their prejudices, and instead of groping about for offenders that fit their preconceptions, follow what evidence they had to its logical source: those females employed at the Union Pulverkammer.

The question was where, or rather with whom to begin? The Kommandantur was already pressuring the Political Department for results; it wouldn't do to come up empty a third time.

The only obvious candidate for arrest was the Jewish forewoman of the crew, Regina Safirsztajn. As Vorarbeiterin, no plot could have proceeded without her knowing of it. A second choice wasn't so easily come by. The Nazis figured their best shot lay in picking a woman who by having transgressed elsewhere had demonstrated a disrespect for the rules; such a person might by nature be more inclined toward the criminal. The problem was none of the Pulver girls fit the profile. Each had risen to so trusted a position on the basis of an exemplary record.

But with a timing that couldn't have been more opportune, fortune smiled on the Gestapo. It came in the person of a Russian Jewess who worked at the Union named Klara—"Black Klara" as the prisoners called her. Her dark good looks, though, weren't what had earned her this nickname. As the long-standing paramour of none other than the odious Kapo Schulz, she enjoyed a prestige she elected regularly to abuse. This extended to her putting on the airs of a kapo herself, where she could be as pitiless toward the powerless as her philandering lover.

To the SS, however, she was just another number, so when caught with an unauthorized loaf of bread, no light offense, she was sentenced to the penal commando. To escape this, she offered to turn in a sister worker she'd seen consorting with a man, which for a Union female was a far greater infraction than hers.

To the delight of the Germans, it was no less than one of von Ende's girls, Esther Wajcblum. Black Klara had spotted her months ago sneaking into one of the Union washrooms with her lover Tadek, and filed the incident away should it come in handy one day. In verifying her story, the SS ransacked Esther's bunk and found a pencil sketch of Tadek hidden inside the mattress. She and Regina were promptly arrested and taken to Block 35.

The mid-October morning was a frosty one, the first real cold front of the season. A long central hallway ran the length of Gestapo headquarters, with offices on one side, interrogation rooms on the other. The largest of these offices was the *Standesamt*, an adjunct of the main camp's registry, staffed by German-speaking female prisoners. For some days, they'd been busy with the death certificates of an abnormally large number of escapees, this seeming to corroborate the rumors floating around of a sizable breakout attempt from Birkenau.

One of them, all excitement, burst in from the hall. "There's a young Jewish girl standing with her face to the wall next to Broch's door, another opposite the restroom. And a soldier watching over them with a machine gun."

Every typewriter fell silent, the women at them turning quizzical faces to each other. "What can it mean?" several asked. Then to her who'd seen them, "Have they been arrested?"

Their curiosity was more reactive than reasoned; the presence of the two outside that door was self-explanatory. SS-*Unterscharführer* Karl Broch was one of the camp Gestapo's top interrogators. A man nearing forty, round-shouldered, pudgy, with the tired, cynical if harmless air of the overworked and under-appreciated bureaucratic drudge, few were those nonetheless who didn't give his office a wide berth.

"Of course they've been arrested," said their discoverer, "use your heads. But arrested for what? One is just a girl, the other not much older. What could they have done to wind up here?"

Though several suspected it had something to do with whatever had happened at Birkenau, none was so sure as to air her suspicion. Except for one.

"Wally, what do you say? You have any idea what's going on?"

The prisoner they called Wally wasn't just the oldest among them but interned the longest. She had a reputation for knowing things ahead of anybody, a talent she had fun attributing to her most distinguishing feature, a long, curving nose that gave her the look of a Grimm brother's witch. She laid an index finger against it for emphasis.

"Wally has a tracking nose, children, created this way to sniff out news. And it's telling me that pair out there are from the Union."

"The ammunition factory? What makes you say that?"

"Wally's nose," she grinned slyly, "isn't one to reveal its magic." At which she shed the grin. "Suffice it to say this is connected to the noise coming from Birkenau the other day. Those two brave girls in the hall aren't the last we'll be seeing."

Pressed to elaborate, she went back to her typing. The tension in the room was palpable, but as nothing to that later when dreadful screams could be heard coming from the direction of Broch's office. Not that the women hadn't heard the like before, just never in the childlike soprano of a girl barely out of her teens. Woven among them was the deep, brassbound bellow of the sergeant's voice.

Not long after these stopped, Broch's secretary, the Polish prisoner Raya Kagan, entered the Standesamt and asked for attention. An attractive younger woman with a pleasant smile and a quiet way about her, not given to dramatics or easily rattled, today her voice sounded as strained as her face was haggard.

"The *Unterscharführer* has sent me to inform you to stay out of the hall unless absolutely necessary. If in need of the restroom, you're to have nothing to do with any prisoners you see. What contact you might attempt will be dealt with severely. He further commands that you say nothing of any of this. If caught having done so, again you'll be sorry."

She hastened to add, "This isn't me speaking, you understand, but he who sent me."

Her audience seized on this disclaimer as an opening. "Can you tell us whether the two now are from the Union commando?"

Raya turned and made for the door.

"Or if any of this has something to do with what we've been hearing about Birkenau?"

Halfway into the hall, she paused. "I'm sorry, but I'm forbidden to say anything. At the risk of my own neck. But what's the rush? Be patient. You'll have the whole story before long."

And so they would. The arrest of the girls wasn't the type of thing that could be kept secret. Roza Robota would learn of it when Marta Bindiger, on a parcel run from the Paketstelle, showed up at the *B1a* lager that Sunday night. Marta had arranged herself a transfer from Birkenau to Auschwitz and a job in its mailroom, where she'd been for a month now. Her contact there had fallen victim to a heart attack, and to maintain the flow of gunpowder, she'd called in some favors and succeeded in replacing her. Though no more, naturally, did her trips include the explosive.

With Marta in the Stammlager, it had been two weeks since they'd seen each other, and Roza looked harried. Noah had filled her in on the unfortunate details of the revolt and its failed escape, but was it true about the SS investigation, that it had turned up some loose gunpowder and traced it back to the Union?

"I'm afraid so," Marta said. "And while the fools couldn't bring themselves to admit the obvious even then, eventually the Gestapo took two of the Pulver women into custody."

Roza grabbed her by the arm. "Who?" she said, bracing herself.

"Esther and Regina. Came in and plucked them right off the factory floor. They're back now, however; the Germans only held them two days. They're in bad shape, I won't say they're not, but both are up and walking again."

Roza flew from the edge of the koje they were sitting on. "Esther! My beautiful Estusia... and poor sweet Regina! But—" Her brow puckered in confusion. "They were tortured, I take it?"

Marta nodded.

"Why for two days only? What made the Krauts let them go? Not that I give a good damn what happens to me, but did they—did they talk?"

"Oh, no!" Marta was vehement. "Gracious, no! Not a word out of either. How gutsy is that? We're all in total awe of them."

Roza let out a long breath. "Good. Very good. And gutsy as all hell, except... You swear they're all right? *Everyone's* all right?"

"Here, dear," Marta said, patting the mattress, "why don't you sit back down and let me catch you up on what happened? From the beginning this time. You'll want to hear it from the beginning; it'll make you proud. If you'd like me to spare you some of the—you know."

"No!" Roza said, plopping herself down. "I don't just want to, I need to hear it, every bit of it. Don't you dare hold back a thing, I don't care how awful."

Esther and Regina, if hesitant to relive it at first, ended up after their release recounting their ordeal in full. Marta began with them standing in the hallway of Block 35.

Esther was the first to see Broch. He ordered her, his secretary interpreting, to sign a deposition stating she was guilty of stealing gunpowder. Proclaiming her innocence, she refused. He then said a verbal confession would do, but again she pled guiltless. Finally, if not her, he needed the names of those who had stolen the powder. She told him she knew nothing, had no idea what he was even talking about.

She was then taken to a room followed by the sergeant and two soldiers stripped to their undershirts and wearing thin leather gloves. But for a metal desk and a couple of chairs, the room, too, was stripped down, the only illumination an oversized light bulb hanging by a cord from the ceiling. She was bound to a chair directly beneath it, and Broch took up his questioning anew. Upon her remaining uncooperative, he sent his secretary from the room, and at a sign from him one of the soldiers sauntered up to her and hit her square on the nose with his fist.

Soon both were taking turns at her until they'd battered her unconscious. She was revived with a bucket of water to the face. Broch, impatient, began shouting at her to confess, but though she could tell her nose was broken and probably her jaw, either despite or because of this, she wasn't sure which, she was more determined than ever.

Again the fists ripped into her—face, ribs, breasts, stomach—the *Unterscharführer* haranguing her between punches. After a while, Esther could hear a woman screaming from another room. Even in the grip of her own pain, her heart went out to Regina. Only later did she realize the screams were her own.

That evening, the SS carried both of them, fading in and out of consciousness—Regina, too, had been worked over, also without success—to the basement of Block 11 and separate cells. In the morning, they were brought back and the interrogation resumed. When further beatings produced no results, Broch upped the ante. They were strung up by their wrists, naked, and flogged with leather whips, some blows so savage as to knock the wind out of them. But even this, save for the shrieking and the begging for mercy it wrung, didn't loosen their lips.

Finally, the Nazis, in what bore a whiff of desperation, drug them back to Block 11 and stood them against the Black Wall. The last thing they saw as hoods were pulled over their heads was a six-man firing squad lining up in front of them. The Germans told them it was now or never, that they had half a minute to surrender either some names or their lives.

Seconds later, a shouted "*Feuer!*" and the rifles thundered, but the soldiers sent their volley harmlessly into the air. Her hood removed, Esther assumed her companion shot dead, but Regina had only fainted. When kicked awake, she started to laugh and couldn't quit. That afternoon they were whipped again, but again to no effect.

"Filthy bastards," Roza muttered.

"Yes, but guess what happened then."

From Marta's expression, she didn't have to. "The sorry mothers let them go."

"The next morning! We couldn't believe it! There wasn't a one of us thought we'd ever see them again. They were more dead than alive, but they were back.

"Oh, Roza, you can't imagine! You'd have wept to see what the Germans did to them. Not only were their eyes swollen shut, their faces were puffed out to half again their normal size. Their clothes had to be scissored off them, and carefully; where the whip cut the skin, the blood had glued itself to the fabric. They couldn't talk, much less walk, and we were worried we might lose them yet.

"As I said, though, they're better now. Another week maybe and they'll be able to work again. In the meantime, we're taking as good care of them as we can. Medicine, bandages, extra rations… whatever our courageous Esterke and Gina need. Funny thing is, every bit of it is by order of Commandant Hössler."

"What's so strange about that?" Roza said. "I heard he was partial to his Union girls."

"Oh, he was. He practically doted on them—until the authorities began linking them to the plot. Since then, it's as if he's been trying to out-Gestapo the Gestapo. They say his spite has no limit anymore. As he sees it, as I see *him*, for the commando to have repaid the kindnesses he heaped on it with so glaring an act of treason wasn't merely a crime against the camp and its administration but an affront to him personally.

"And he's reacted as a man with his ego might be expected to. Gone is the Papa Hössler who always had a smile and a wink, a cheerful '*Guten Tag!*' for his charges, in his place a snarling devil of a Hössler who stalks about with a club at his side now. And isn't shy about using it."

"I don't get it then," Roza said. "If he's so stopped up with hate, why would he encourage a speedy recovery for the two women he ought to be angriest at?"

"That's just it," Marta said, "it doesn't make sense. Just as it doesn't the Nazis would release the two after only a couple of days. But with a little help from an unexpected source, we've pieced together a sort of explanation for this last."

"Oh, really?" Roza lifted an eyebrow. "And what is that?"

"A couple of things actually. One by way of an incident I haven't mentioned yet. With Esther and Regina still captive, the SS arrested two more women, Rose Greuenapfel from the Pulverraum and Esther's sister, Hanka. Not so much to accuse them of any wrongdoing—they were only held a few hours—but in an attempt to dig up evidence on the other two. So tight are Rose and Regina, as you know, they might as well be related."

"Some think they are."

"But instead of reinforcing the Gestapo's case, their testimonies might just have undermined it. Half out of her head as Hanka was at what had befallen her sister—what is the child, fifteen, and Esther all the family she has left?—she had the snap to see through what the SS were trying to put over on her. Not only see through it, but use it to her advantage.

"When the Nazis informed her that her sister had admitted to stealing the gunpowder, and all they wanted from her was what she might have said about it, if anything, Hanka flat-out told them they were lying, because not in a million years would Esther have. That she in fact hated lies and the liars who spread them. Hated them like the plague. How then could she have confessed to a crime she hadn't committed? Unless she was being tortured, in which case a person was liable to say anything."

"The little girl said that? To the Gestapo?"

"She did!" Marta's face beamed with a mother's pride. "But here's the kicker. Rose during her interview basically told them the same thing, that if Esther had confessed to something untrue, which knowing her she hadn't, it could only be because they'd bloodied her into doing so.

"Not entirely convinced as I wager the idiots were up to then that women could have played a role in arming the Sonderkommando, here they were with two continuing to plead innocent under torture that would have broken most men, and two more failing to betray any evidence to prove different. If that wouldn't add to SS suspicions they might be shinnying up the wrong tree..."

"And that's why you're saying Esther and Regina were let go?" Roza thought this rather lame, but let it slide for now.

"That's part of it, yes, but hear me out. That help I said we got? From an unexpected source? Israel Gutman, one of our contacts in the underground—you and Gutman are chummy, aren't you? Or once told me you were."

"He *and* his buddy, Laufer. But I haven't run into them in, gosh, I forget how long."

"So Gutman," said Marta, "walks up to Ala, our Ala, the other day—he works at the Union, too, as foreman of some machine shop—and tells her he came across something she might find interesting. Seems the underground got wind of the latest audit the Nazis conducted comparing the quantity of gunpowder they should have against that which they did, and get this: the figures matched! No powder was missing after all.

"We were as thrown for a loop as the Germans must have been. Until we presented the Pulver team with the mystery. According to them, it's all about what's called the Abfall, the residue left over after the dynamite is compressed into the detonators. Made worthless during the process, instead of discarding it as they were supposed to, the women would save it on the sly and substitute it for the fresh. Clever, huh?"

"Inspired," Roza said, "but sticky."

"Isn't *that* the truth. It always struck me as incredible what our sisters whose job it was to pinch the stuff were able to get away with, especially with a pair, two pairs of eyes looking over their shoulders. Thank goodness Esther, though, God bless her, backed off from plundering the Meister's safe when she did. I'm guessing you remember what happened last spring to bring that to a halt."

Roza still blanched inside when reminded. "If that Kraut assistant of von Ende's had returned to the section a minute earlier that day, she'd have caught Esther with her hand in the cookie jar. What a mess that would have been."

"Worse than a mess. But close a call as it was, it couldn't have turned out better."

"Sorry, I don't follow."

"Sure you do. No amount of Abfall, Roza, could have covered up for what would have been missing from that safe if Esther had kept at it. And it was the morning after Gutman said the SS audit took place that she and Regina were released.

"A coincidence? Some say not. There are those, in fact, who claim the danger is passed, that in view of the findings to come out of their inventory, the Nazis can't still hold that the Sonder gunpowder came from the Union. And have turned their sights back on the underground and the partisans. Or even, as some have it, suspended the investigation altogether. I can see how easy it would be to think along those lines."

"And what does the one named Marta Bindiger think?"

Marta let her eyes wander, as if engrossed in the chaotic ebb and flow of a barracks trying to wrap up the night's business before lights-out.

"Given their track record," she said finally, "it would be tempting to assume the Germans as dim-witted as ever, and that the audit, coupled with Rose's and Hanka's contributions, were enough for them to set their two Pulver prisoners free.

"But I for one doubt it. It would be a mistake, something tells me, to underrate those stumblebums in gray. Not this time around. I can't help feeling the SS are onto some trick, a slicker, faster way to get what they're after. What this trick might be, I haven't a clue—except for something both girls have been saying since they got back."

"Which would be?"

"They keep telling us, the poor dears, to stay away from them, that the Gestapo are probably watching to see who's tending to them. Or just as damning if not more, those prisoners who come calling. Can the Nazis be using them to lure more flies into their web? I don't see the point. Wouldn't their time be better spent preying on the ones they have?"

Roza frowned. "I'm not positive," she said, "but of this I am: you can't trust those two-legged spiders of yours, not as far as you can throw them. They're up to something, and anyone who imagines different is kidding herself."

A new face had appeared among the male contingent of the Union. His name was Eugen Koch, a full-blooded Czechoslovakian, but as he was quick to make clear, only half-Jewish. He wore the striped uniform of a prisoner, but clean and cut to fit; a blue armband declared him a subkapo. Though second-in-command of the revolver machines section, in which various metal parts were honed to spec, he was frequently nowhere to be found, sometimes for hours at a stretch.

To be regularly absent from one's workstation was a serious offense for a kapo, a rule that for some reason didn't apply to this Koch. It was whispered he had powerful connections, was perhaps even an agent of Battle Group-Auschwitz.

Two things about the new man stood out. For one, he was good-looking, extraordinarily so. In his mid-twenties, his body trim beneath its starched burlap, he stood a shade over six feet, a thick growth of barbered black hair crowning a set of features a movie star would have envied. His eyes were a startling cornflower-blue, the nose gently flared, the lips full and with just the right proportion of pout to them.

But the pearly smile they were wont to flash hid a second defining characteristic of his, a mean streak that would reveal itself at the expense of the weak and defenseless only. While his behavior toward the stronger prisoners bordered on the servile, to those he could push around he showed little restraint.

A perfect example of both involved Israel Gutman, foreman of Revolver Machines. On his shift one day, he saw Koch knock a worker to the ground and begin kicking him, a boy who'd attached the wrong grinder onto a rotor. The error was easily rectified, but the Czech screamed he was going to report him to the Germans and have him removed from the commando.

"Hold on there!" Gutman said, pulling him off the frightened teenager. "Get hold of yourself, man!"

Koch tore from his grasp.

"Who the hell do you think you are?" he spluttered at Gutman. "How dare you interfere! This little shit was committing sabotage, right in front of me!"

The Vorarbeiter had learned Czech from Laufer. "Sabotage? More like inexperience if you ask me. The boy is new to the job, give him a break."

"I'll break his skull, is what I'll do," Koch said, strutting up to his challenger, "and yours if you're not careful."

Gutman laughed. "That I'd like to see."

"Oh yeah? Then maybe I'll report the kid and you both, him for sabotage, you for putting your hands on a kapo. What do you think of that, tough guy?"

"That you're a slimy little worm with more mouth than brains. And I suggest you back off if you know what's good for you."

Instead, Koch took another step, fists clenched. Gutman drew back his right and let him have one on the chin. That was enough for his opponent, who after picking himself up from the floor and cradling his jaw in one hand, left the room, mumbling.

Appalled at his rashness, Gutman spent the rest of the day and all night expecting to be arrested, but to his surprise woke in the morning still a free man. First to meet him at the factory was Koch, with outstretched hand and an apology. And thereafter carried on as if he wanted to be the other's pal. He took, when he was present, to hanging around his foreman's machine, prating away about nothing in particular.

The German contributed little to these sessions, never mind the importuning of some of his comrades in the underground. These, after noticing Koch's efforts to establish a rapport with him, suggested he sound the man out about joining up. Foremost among them was Laufer, ever eager to welcome a countryman to the cause.

Gutman was leery. Not only had Koch shown himself a bully and a coward, even more disturbing was his attitude toward their overseers. Where the other prisoners would fall silent at the approach of a guard, their expressions hardening, the young Czech went out of his way to glad-hand every soldier who came within reach. More worrying yet, Gutman would spot him on occasion deep in conversation with the odd SS officer, and just as bad, the despicable Kapo Schulz.

This, of course, could be nothing. Koch was, after all, a kapo himself, and as such answerable to his fascist bosses. Still, something didn't smell right to Gutman, and he not only dropped any notion of opening up to the newcomer but warned Laufer and the others to keep a wary eye on him.

It would prove advice well heeded, for as he was ultimately to make plain, Eugen Koch was a man who'd sold his soul to the devil. And at bargain-basement prices. In return for elevation to subkapo and other perquisites, he'd agreed to be an informer for the Nazis. His instructions were to gain the affections of one of several women the Gestapo had targeted, then sweet-talk her into disclosing what she knew of the pilfering of the Union gunpowder. This accounted for the many hours he'd gone missing from his post; he'd spent them making his pretty face visible in those parts of the factory staffed by female workers.

The women chosen were those buzzing around Esther and Regina the most, making it a good chance they weren't only friends but co-conspirators. Excluded were any who worked the Pulverraum; for a male to have access to them could only arouse suspicion. The recuperating girls' blockova was under orders from Hössler to allow them whatever succor they required, but to report back to him who was administering it. Koch was briefed on whom to look for, then sent out to snare the best prospect he could.

When eventually he did, prized indeed was his catch, none other than the pivotal if also vulnerable Ala Gertner.

The Czech couldn't have picked a victim riper for seduction. Never having recovered completely from the theft of her baby Rochele, she'd been acting moodier of late than usual. Not that she was alone. With some of their confinements having swelled into two years or more, many of the women, together with their other deprivations, were feeling the effects of prolonged lack of contact with the opposite sex.

Ala, high-strung as she was and with a libido to match, was hurting more than most—until the day she began to have trouble ridding her mouth of its smile. Vanished overnight was any trace of her recent glumness. She went around now humming bits of song to herself, her step as tripping as a schoolgirl's.

When asked what had got into her, she'd smile a little bigger but say nothing, though it didn't take much to hypothesize a man behind her happiness. This was confirmed when she and the new kapo were seen keeping company, sparingly at first, but before long it was daily, twice a day, nor did they even try to pretend it anything other than a romance. Koch regularly plied her with gifts: food, cigarettes, chocolate, even a gold chain those who witnessed the giving of it saw him fasten around her neck himself.

Ala for her part was equally obvious. One could see the longing in her eyes when she looked at him, how she blushed when he was near. Quick, surreptitious kisses, ill-concealed caresses, it was all they could do to keep their hands off each other. Most were delighted for her, even envious in an unbegrudging way. The two made such a glamorous couple and were so sweetly in love.

Then there were those who weren't delighted at all, who'd glimpsed a side to this Czech that was anything but sweet. One of these was Mala Weinstein, whose talent for seeing beneath the surface remained as sharp as her subversive sense of humor. If not

Ala's closest friend, she was in the running for that distinction; they may have made deprecating fun of the fact, but the similarity of their names pleased them no end.

Until its abolition, Mala had worked the Pulver night shift, during which she and Ilse Michel had snuck out their share of gunpowder. Afterward, she was transferred to the *Spritzraum*, where some of the Werke's finished products were hosed off and dried before being packed for shipping. A gullible Meister, though, and a fictitious bladder problem enabled her to take as many bathroom breaks as she wished, permitting her to stay an active link in the smuggling chain.

When first she saw Ala cavorting with the unctuous Koch, she couldn't believe it. The irreproachable Ala of all women fallen for someone of such shady repute! Aside from the stories she'd heard about the man, beneath the handsome exterior she scented something ugly, and would have warned the girl already if it would have done any good. Others had tried before her, and not only had she refused to listen but accused them of sticking their nose in something none of their business.

She'd been denied the attentions of a man for too long, even before Birkenau, and in the heaven-sent person of her beautiful Eugen felt she'd stumbled on the answer to a question she wasn't even aware she'd been asking. She'd found against all odds, in the most loveless place imaginable, the love of her life, and wasn't about to let anyone talk her out of him.

No one, Mala included, realized at first what the kapo was about. What worried them was their Ala ending up with a broken heart, victim of an irresponsible cad. Only when the rumors flying around him took a more sinister turn did Mala go from merely protective to frightened.

Fear became panic when working the late shift one night, she rounded a corner on her way back to the Spritzraum with a load of dustcloths only to spy Koch and the factory's *Kommandoführer* off to the side in the shadows, deep in conversation. So animated was the kapo, his hands working as hard as his mouth, neither man noticed her. Though she couldn't catch a word they were saying above the clatter of the machinery, one was clearly as pleased as the other, the Nazi grinning like a Jack-o'-lantern. Upon passing them, she turned to see him ruffle Koch's hair with the same playful approval he would a dog's.

Her skin went immediately cold. What she'd happened on might have been innocuous; for all she knew, the two were celebrating an increase in the revolver machines' output. But a voice inside her screamed otherwise, and where before she'd kept quiet out of respect for Ala's privacy, she now couldn't alert her fast enough to the peril she was in.

With the Spritzraum short-handed—poor Yoli had crushed her foot beneath a full pallet and gone to the gas yesterday, while another in Ka-Be probably wasn't far behind her—Mala volunteered to work straight through the day. Certain that after what she'd seen she wouldn't be able to sleep, this would allow her to snag Ala first thing in the morning. But it wasn't until noon that was she able to follow her into a lavatory, and knew as soon as she saw her it was too late.

The girl was leaning on her hands over one of the sinks. With a start she looked up, her mouth twitching at the corners.

"*Ich hab so moira*, Mala," she said in Yiddish for some reason, quickly rephrasing it in Polish. "I'm so afraid."

Mala could have cried at the sight if her. She wasn't the same person anymore, the same Ala. A tall woman, she'd shriveled into someone three times her age. She stood bent over, shoulders hunched, as if beneath some heavy load. The skin of her face was pulled as tight as a scrap of dried hide over bone, a bright rash splotching her forehead and cheeks. Underneath it, the flesh was as colorless as a corpse's, the mouth a grimace of unrelieved terror.

"It's that boyfriend of yours, isn't it? That Koch."

Ala's eyes were a red-rimmed mire of fear and self-reproach. They told the whole story, she didn't have to say a word.

Mala put a hand on the wall to keep from sagging against it. So the frightful thing she'd begun to suspect last night was true: the man was a Gestapo plant, and he'd got to their Ala as sure as the cockroach he was.

"What—what exactly does he know? You didn't say anything about the gunpowder, did you? Talk to me, Alina. What happened for heaven's sake?"

At this, the words came pouring out of her, but dubiously, as if she had trouble believing them herself. "Eugen let me know a while back that he, too, was a member of the underground, and had just heard what I'd done. That Israel Gutman told him. He was proud of me for being so brave; my little soldier he called me. All he wanted to know was how I'd pulled it off, been so smart as to get all that gunpowder past all those Nazis.

"I didn't have to tell him if I didn't want to, he said. He was just curious was all, but also didn't think we should be keeping secrets from each other. That if I wanted to show how much I loved him, and more than that, trusted him, I'd tell him. So... I did."

"Oh, Ala. Oh God."

"But not everything! I never mentioned any names. At least, thank goodness, I didn't do that. But mine they do have, and soon they'll be coming for me. Why they haven't yet is beyond me. All this happened two days ago, and I—"

"Wait a minute—two days ago? Hold it right there. Maybe it's not as bad as you're making it out to be." It was a straw, a thin one, but in her desperation Mala latched onto it. "Two days and you're still here. They haven't arrested you. What has you convinced this Koch is the scoundrel you think he is?"

"Because he's disappeared, that's what! I haven't seen him since I spilled my stupid guts to him! *Nobody* has. Besides, I went to Gutman just this morning and asked him if he'd told Eugen about my role in the plot. Or anything about me at all."

Ala paused, looking as if she might burst into tears. "And?" said Mala dully, the question rhetorical.

"Of course not. He was horrified I'd even ask him such a thing. Oh, Mala, Mala... what have I done? How could I have been so blind, such a meshugga?"

Here the tears did come, in great heaving sobs, prompting Mala to scoop her up in a hug. Not that she had the slightest idea what to say. On the one hand she was wanting to scold her for, yes, being a fool, for compromising not only her own but dozens of other lives by falling under the spell of so transparent a blackguard.

On the other, who was she to blame anyone for being no more than human, for succumbing to the allure, the illogic of love? She continued to hold the poor shattered thing tight, until slowly the sobs ceased and Ala stepped from her embrace.

"You don't have a cigarette, do you?" she sniffled.

Mala lit one for each of them. Her hand trembling, Ala took a couple of deep drags. She glanced at the ceiling, then back.

"They're going to torture me, aren't they? Of course they are, and I'm not a strong person."

"Don't talk like that, Ala. You're as strong a person as I know, as I've ever known. You've got yourself in a fix, there's no arguing that, but you don't want to pull others in with you. You've got to promise me something."

"Promise you what?"

"Should the worst come, should you be arrested, you've got to take yourself back to that first day on the unloading ramp, the day the SS stole your Rochele from you. You'll need to live it over and over again when in the interrogation room, never letting yourself forget that the men who'll—who'll be in that room with you are wearing the same uniform as those who murdered your innocent babe. Killed her, then threw her away like so much trash.

"Remember then how they tore her from your arms, and how it felt once they did. Let that feeling be your strength. Let hate bolt your lips when they start asking for names.

"You mustn't forget, too, who you are, Alina, and will always be, a hero and an inspiration to your people."

Mala didn't see this being much help, until noticing Ala's hand no longer shook as she smoked. The girl was silent for some seconds, staring into space. Then, crushing out her cigarette, took Mala by the shoulders and kissed her on each cheek.

"My good friend," she said, and without another word walked out the door. She seemed taller as she left, her back a little straighter, more like the Ala beloved by all.

Alone now, Mala saw no reason anymore to hold it in. Sliding to the floor, she buried her face in her hands and wept it all out, all the grief that comes from watching someone you care for walk away knowing you're never going to see her again. Unlike most, it didn't surprise her when she heard later some soldiers showed up and took Ala with them.

They whisked her to Block 35, where Sergeant Broch began that very afternoon to pry what his superiors wanted from her. Which, as opposed to Esther and Regina, was simplified to the names of her partners in treason, her own guilt having been established by the artifices of her counterfeit lover. As with her predecessors, the abuse was confined at first to a series of beatings.

Gestapo techniques were as varied as they were savage, but as a rule began with an attack by fists, feet, and assorted blunt instruments. The object wasn't so much to inflict pain as to daze and disorient the victim, a gambit designed to knock him or her off balance. It became tougher for a prisoner to put up a defense with nose and ears leaking blood, eyes swelling shut, lips smashed, the front teeth floating in their sockets.

As ruinous as the physical were the psychological effects of torture. Arguably the worst of these was the alienation it imposed, a feeling of utter and isolating ostracism at the hands of one's fellow human beings. Bravery became that much harder to muster when facing such antipathy alone—and when coupled with the remorseless application of pain, few places were capable of generating an aloneness as corrosive as the torture chamber. Cut off from all support and goodwill, not a sympathetic ear to turn to, an encouraging word to be heard, a person could quickly begin to doubt both himself and his resolve.

Nor was this doubt trained inward only; one's faith in humanity tended not to last long under torture. Was fractured, in fact, by the first slap to the face, then demolished entirely by whatever indignities followed. With the result its recipient wound up alienated even further, repudiating the fellowship of his kind even as he felt repudiated by them.

To such was Ala now subjected, not only the brutalization of the flesh but the psyche. Yet she held her own against it, even after things escalated, which in her case was much faster than with the two women before her. Again, unlike them, the SS had her dead to rights; she represented their first real break in the investigation, and they couldn't exploit it too soon.

Early the next morning, they started in on her fingernails. This required four participants: Ala herself, bound to a chair clamped to the wall; *Unterscharführer* Broch; and two subalterns. One of these, a specialist, sat facing Ala across a table upon which a forearm and hand of hers were pinioned. The second was a soldier conversant in Polish, needed because the sergeant was careful to send his secretary from the room before things turned bloody. He'd had too many of them in the past get emotional, even faint on him. Broch would make his demands through this interpreter, and when Ala refused to answer, nod to the specialist.

The man was good at what he did, having from experience devised a system. He would open with a lesser finger and work his way around to the thumb, not ripping the nail out but extracting it slowly, a fraction of an inch with each tug. Occasionally, he'd jiggle it from side to side, or bend it up and down with his pliers, both taking the hurt to another level. Yet again, the shrill screams of a woman traveled the halls of Block 35.

Holler as she did, Ala didn't buckle, not even when they strapped an ankle to a bench and performed the same obscenity on her toes. When this to his annoyance didn't work, after lunch Broch had a washtub sloshing over with water carried in and her head held submerged in it until she began to go limp. She was then revived, water bubbling from her mouth as from a fountain, and again pressed for names.

Another unfruitful dunking, and the *Unterscharführer* was ready to make it easier on the both of them. "Ala, listen. *Ala!* Are you with me?"

Slowly, she raised her head, still coughing water. Her eyes struggled to focus first on the interpreter, then Broch. "I'm not guilty," she panted, her voice barely audible. "I was just trying to impress my boyfriend. How many times do I have to—"

"All right," Broch said, "you're not guilty. I believe you. But I also think you can point out who is, which means I could use your help. And to get it, I'd be willing to make a deal."

"You believe me?"

"I believe you."

"What kind of deal?"

She was sitting down, a soldier at each arm. Broch knelt beside her. "It would be more a sign of good faith on your part than anything. All you have to do is verify what we already know, that it was Esther and Regina who stole the gunpowder. That, and the name of one of the persons responsible for delivering it to the Sonderkommando. That's not so much to ask, is it? Just one name, and after it I promise I'll never bother you for another."

When the interpreter finished, Ala worked up a sort of smile. "And if I agree?"

"You do those two things, show me you're trying to cooperate, then you have my word as an officer I won't trouble you again. You'll go free today, back to your barracks."

She thought on this a moment, then setting her jaw, came to a decision. "It's a deal," she said, "but on one condition."

Broch's heart was pounding so, he could feel it in his wrists. "What's that?" he said, trying not to sound eager.

"Before I tell you anything, you give me back my baby."

"Your *baby?* What baby?"

"The one you people took from me on the unloading ramp over a year ago. You give me back my little girl and you'll have more names than you can count."

Frowning, Broch rose to his feet. "But you know that's impossible."

"Yes," Ala said, her head sinking back down, "I know."

Two more simulated drownings found her as unforthcoming as before. Worse, at risk of slipping away for good; her tormentors almost weren't able to bring her to after the second one. Afraid of pushing it, they chose to call it quits for the day. Hauling her back to Block 11, they left her in her cell to recoup.

Probing for a weakness, for the thing she couldn't endure, the next day Broch tried substituting fire for water. He went through half of the morning and two fat cigars applying their glowing heads to this and that part of her, only to end up again having to admit defeat.

With minimal experience interrogating females, if not at his wit's end he was on the path to it. Here was this prisoner, this woman, this *girl*—young, pretty, and if Eugen Koch was any indication, of a demonstrably susceptible and frivolous nature—managing all the same, with the gristle of two men, to withstand every hurt he was laying on her. This didn't only frustrate but was starting to infuriate him. Still smarting at how she'd toyed with him yesterday, Broch decided to turn up the heat, literally.

He had Ala moved from a wooden to a metal chair, and an electric generator wheeled into the room. A single thick wire coiled from the machine, a large alligator clip sprouting from the end of it.

"What—what are you going to do?" she said. "What is that thing?"

"This," the sergeant said cheerily, "is the gift of electricity, the answer to both our problems. By loosening your tongue, it'll provide me what I want and relieve *you* of further suffering. Unless you have something you'd like to tell me first."

Ala groaned and looked away. Broch shrugged, affixed the clip to a leg of the chair, ordered her doused with a pail of water, and turned on the juice.

Her body arced outward as if to burst the bonds holding it, muscle and tendon visible in sharp relief beneath the skin. It didn't take Broch but a second to realize he'd forgot something. So violent were her screams in the enclosed, windowless room, he had to unhook her until he could stuff a rag in her mouth.

He stopped repeatedly to remove this gag, but beyond blubbering for mercy, the words eerily liquid as if she was speaking underwater, Ala had nothing to say. Not even to his request for just the initials to a name, any name.

This last so enraged him that though he knew better, knew he was messing up even as he did it, when next he switched on the device, he left it on. Her reaction after fifteen unbroken seconds of current was to drop her chin to her chest as if poleaxed, her body as shut-down as the generator Broch hastened to disengage.

She came to in Block 11, curled up on the icy floor of her cell. She could tell where she was by both the tininess and unsparing emptiness of the room, its only "furnishings" the waste bucket in a corner and the single caged light bulb in the ceiling. What she didn't understand was how she'd got there. Or presuming she was carried there unconscious, how long she'd been out, what hour or even day it was.

She tried to sit up, but couldn't, the damage not confined as before to specific areas. While true the tips of four of her fingers and toes were on fire, pulpy cavities seeping fluid where once were nails, and the burns left by the cigars no less alive and throbbing, the electricity had made one big wound of her whole body. Every joint, every muscle, every bone felt bruised, as if each had been singled out and mangled in due order. She would have thought her freezing cell a help, but instead of numbing her nerve endings, the cold only made them rawer.

These thorns the Nazis had planted in her flesh weren't her only source of discomfort. A formless disquiet prowled the dusty, back rooms of her mind, not anything she could pin down but there all the same, like a tune with no name she couldn't get out of her head. Only this tune wasn't fading as those things do, but growing louder. Worse, her unease didn't stem from something to come, but of events already come and gone, past undoing.

As the hours piled up and turned into a day, then two—she knew this because she was fed once daily—and with the Germans unaccountably leaving her alone, this anxiety began to take on a disturbing shape. Her bout with the electric generator had played havoc with her memory. Her recollection of this part of the torture was sketchy. The pain she remembered—how could she not?—but of the rest there was almost nothing.

This led Ala to ask herself a question. Could the machine have broken her and she'd given the *Scharführer* what he wanted? Again, there was no forgetting the agony it had inflicted. When the electricity slammed into her, it was as if gigantic hands were trying to rip her in half, wrench her inside out, pulling her skeleton, her ligaments and tendons, in opposite directions—tearing apart not only her body as a whole but each piece of it individually. This in addition to every square inch of skin burning with the same fire one felt when touching a hot skillet.

Try as she might, though, to recall what had passed between her and Broch, it remained a question without an answer. The only other thing from the session that stuck was thinking she wouldn't be able to stand much more of this. That if the Gestapo kept at it, she could no longer guarantee the stronger side of her holding the weaker in check.

Which in a way *was* the answer. Broch, in a mixed gesture of sympathy marred by gloating, to ease her perturbation would explain it to her later. The blank spots in her memory weren't so much a case of it failing her as she not having been in her right mind to begin with.

With him losing his cool that day and almost killing her, it had taken a good ten minutes to restore her to consciousness, and even that only partial. Groggy, unsure of where she was, unable to string two thoughts together, she'd entered what in psychiatry was defined as a fugue state, a waking dream in which she was responsive, but as a layman might put it, not all there. The sergeant, who'd encountered this phenomenon before, saw an opportunity to turn near-disaster into triumph and pounced on the defenseless, discombobulated Ala. Another grilling, but coaxing this time, crooning, in the lulling singsong of the hypnotist, and like a sneak thief he soon had what he was after.

What he didn't explain later was that as a salve to his conscience, it acquitted him also of having to release her as promised in that she hadn't voluntarily given him the name he'd been demanding. Not that he would necessarily have done so, despite his word, but now he would sleep sounder telling himself he might have.

Soldiers came and snatched Esther and Regina that evening from Block 22, and any hope the SS inquest had run its course, sapped by Ala's arrest, now vanished completely. Fear again stalked the Union factory floor, as pervasive a presence as the ubiquitous yellow dust, the heat and the noise.

This was as nothing to the news that broke the next day. Roza, too, had been taken into custody, sped by car that morning from her job at the Bekleidungskammer straight to the main camp's Block 35. Roza Robota in the hands of the Gestapo! It tried the imagination to conceive of a greater catastrophe.

It wasn't just that she knew most of the women at the Metallwerke involved in the theft and smuggling of its gunpowder. And those men still alive who'd helped make the revolt possible. What loomed even more calamitous were the ties she had with several key members of Battle Group-Auschwitz. Four in particular stood out: Marta Bindiger, the underground's liaison with the Weichsel-Union women, and three of Roza's Ciechanow connections, Noah Zabludowicz, Mordecai Hilleli, and of course, Godel Silver. While highly placed in the Battle Group, they weren't critical so much for who they were as whom they knew. In Noah's case, and probably Marta's, this likely extended to the top levels of the movement's leadership.

If Roza were to crack, the damage done the organization might transcend the incalculable and enter the realm of the fatal. With a cost in life equally as grim.

Fear no longer inhabited the Union alone, but spread like a heavy, ground-hugging fog throughout Auschwitz and Birkenau. The men and women of both prepared for the worst, cringed at the approach of every soldier, made up stories and alibis to tell under interrogation, contemplated suicide. To the bravest, the prospect of death wasn't what had them unstrung, but torture, and not just the unimaginable pain of it. They worried that unable to stand it, they would betray their friends, the cause, the Jewish people.

And all that stood between them and the horror, the disgrace of the torture chamber were four young and manifestly destructible women—one, or so the talk went, who'd earlier knuckled under to the Gestapo and sold out the others.

Everyone could only hold his breath and wait to see how the four were going to fare. Roza especially. None who'd crossed paths with her had failed to notice her fire. Yet how long could she or anyone be expected to bear up when forced without respite to drink from the cup of agony?

Though it was the new prisoner's first time in Broch's office, Raya Kagan knew who Roza was and why she was there. What caught her short was the girl's attitude—she didn't seem the least intimidated. If anything, she regarded the sergeant and other uniforms present with open contempt. The young secretary, who'd watched countless ushered trembling into this room, couldn't recall a one who'd swaggered in.

But to her further surprise, when the Gestapo confession was shoved in front of her, Roza didn't hesitate to sign it. The deposition stated that not only was she a conduit through whom the stolen gunpowder reached the insurgents but knew the purpose for which they intended to use it. When Broch, too, appeared startled at the ease in obtaining her signature, she was quick to tell him why.

"Don't get your hopes up, *Unterscharführer*," she said, infusing his SS title with ridicule. "That piece of paper I put my name to is the only accommodation you're going to get from me. And I give it freely because more than just willing to admit my role in the revolt, I'm goddamned proud of it. I'd rate it the finest thing I've ever done, and if I had it to do over again, would in a heartbeat.

"Even if I knew beforehand I'd end up having to answer"—here she leaned to her right and spat on the floor—"to the likes of you."

Raya couldn't believe what she was hearing, and her translation showed it. The words came reluctantly, as if by repeating them she, too, might be said to share in their insubordination. Not that she didn't feel a shiver of pride at their fearlessness.

As for Broch, he broke out in applause. "Bravo! Well said, my little spitfire! Refreshing, too, I might add, in contrast to the whining I'm accustomed to. I can tell we're going to get along splendidly, you and I. Except we will, need I say, have to work on your—what was the word you used?"

Roza glared at him, silent.

"Accommodation, I believe it was, yes. But if it's convenient for you, we can start on that right now. Frau Kagan, if you please," he said with a nod toward the door. "We'll call when we're ready."

Despite a temperature in the forties, and windy, Raya chose to wait outside the building, where she ended up smoking her last two cigarettes. She wasn't about to subject herself to any more of the screaming to come than she had to. Not this time. Not from this person. Not from someone who dared talk to the SS the way she had.

But while Broch's bellicose roar reached her even out here, not a single cry of pain accompanied it. Nor would she hear one upon ducking back inside; other than the sergeant, the only sound was the muted clacking of the Standesamt typewriters. Who *was* this girl to endure torture without so much as a peep?

Summoned to an interrogation room an hour later, she wasn't prepared for what she saw. Roza was as she expected to find her, conscious but only just, her face broken and bloody. Broch, sitting at the desk looking like the cat that ate the canary, was what threw her off. Holding a sheet of paper above him, he waved her impatiently over. He wanted this typed up immediately, he said, so the prisoner could sign it.

Back in his office, no sooner had she sat down than the reason for his poorly concealed glee became clear. In front of her was another, more detailed confession, this one with names. Roza had conceded passing gunpowder to the Sonderkommando by way of four men: a Jukel Wrubel, a Yankel Handelsman, one Zalman Gradowski, and a Yossel Warszawski. Each transfer had taken place in the yard of the Bekleidungs depot, under the cover of accepting the clothing of the dead from a crematorium.

Raya had never seen her boss so puffed up. Having anticipated in Roza a tough nut to crack, with little effort he'd succeeded in wresting multiple names from her. That they weren't the kind of names he was ultimately after made no difference. One had to start somewhere, and once a suspect began yielding even incidental information, it became that much simpler to prod more meaningful from him later.

Raya was as blind-sided as her employer by Roza's rapid capitulation. Her attitude earlier pointed to her being made of sterner stuff. This, though, she had to remind herself, was easy for her to say. The Nazis had had a whole hour to work the poor thing over; the face she'd take out of the room wouldn't be the one she'd walked in with. Such was her condition that after the statement was put in front of her, she had to have help holding the pen when signing it.

It wouldn't take long for both the *Scharführer* and his secretary, to the ill-humor of one and silent apology of the other, to discover their error in assuming Roza a pushover. Two days weren't to go by before her "confession" would prove of less value than the paper it was printed on. For when Broch went in search of the Sonder she'd fingered, he found each listed among those who'd perished in the revolt.

At first, he cursed his bad luck, then himself when it hit home he'd been made a royal fool of. She'd tossed him the names of four dead men on purpose, was probably having a good laugh about it still.

He would not underestimate this prisoner of his again. On the contrary, in acknowledgment of the exceptional individual she was, he'd singled Roza out for special attention. Because she was already shaping up to be the sole portal through which every ounce of the illicit gunpowder had entered the crematoria, it was probable she'd organized the smuggling ring herself. This wasn't only revealing of the vital part she'd played in the rebellion but the status she enjoyed in the underground. Making it a better than good bet she had a working relationship with both the actual perpetrators of the uprising and those in Battle Group-Auschwitz who'd backed them.

These last, even more than the criminals in the Union and the Sonderkommando, were who had the Gestapo salivating, and Roza just the acquisition who could deliver them. Now that he had them in his clutches, Broch had no intention of going light on any of his captives; he was confident each would contribute in her own way to the investigation. There could be no question, however, on whom he'd be concentrating his energies.

Thus did the ordeal of the four begin in earnest, nor despite her head start was the half-crippled Ala cut any slack. Every few days at dawn, a squad of *Schützen* walked them the length of the Stammlager from Block 11 in the northeast corner to Block 35 in the southwest, keeping them apart to prevent any contact. Once there, they remained separated, each alone in a cell with just her thoughts and another's screams in her ears—

Until the footfall of heavy boots coming down the hall got louder and louder before stopping at her door.

By the middle to late afternoon, their day's nightmare was done but for the trek back. Rarely in any shape to walk it unassisted, they were held upright by soldiers, their bare, bloody feet often dragging in the dirt. Or when unconscious, laid out on stretchers like the victims of some terrible accident.

Not an interrogation passed without a scattering of prisoners lining the return route of this Via Dolorosa. Some came out of curiosity, most to provide what moral support they could. Aware that to give voice to this support would result in their own arrests, their hope was to make eye contact with the women and flash them a thumbs-up, a smile, anything to tell them they weren't alone. That they hadn't been forgotten. That people were thinking about them, praying for them, suffering along with them.

The effort was well-intended, but wasted. The ravaged four were in no condition to acknowledge anyone. If sensible at all of their surroundings, it was of the path directly in front of them. Glassy-eyed, heads hanging, they either shambled forward or were carried, immersed to the exclusion of all else in their pain.

"Here they come," Noah said in the burnished light of the sinking sun. "Brace yourself, Godel."

The two stood alone just off the edge of the limestone path. As dreadful as the vigil was, they'd maintained it without let-up since Roza's confinement.

Godel as usual teared up when he saw her. "God," he said. "My God, *look* at her…"

"You can't let that get to you," Noah said. "Remember why we're here."

The boy's shoulders began gently heaving. "I—I'm not sure why, not anymore. If I could only get her attention, just once…"

"All we can do is keep trying. I don't know what else we—"

"Well I *do!*" Godel wheeled on him, the tears suddenly angry. "I know exactly what we can do! Me anyway. But then that's why when we're out here—I'm onto you, don't think I'm not—you never stray more than a foot away. To keep me from running up to her and throwing my arms around her."

"Like you tried to three days ago? It's a good thing I *was* there. They'd have shot you down before you got even close to her. Or hotfooted you off to Block 35 yourself."

"I don't care, let them. It'd be worth it. All I want is to hold her one more time, tell her—tell her how much I love her."

Godel, actually, wasn't as "onto" him as he took credit for. Noah had indeed taken it upon himself to stay near him, and not only at this excruciating part of the day. Alarmed that the boy was showing signs of deteriorating emotionally the more Roza did physically, he'd become Godel's shadow when that was possible, and when not, had others maintaining the suicide-watch. Roza he couldn't do anything about. Her boyfriend, and a double tragedy, he could.

The two didn't have any luck that evening, either. The guards who bundled a grimacing Roza past them could have been propping up a side of beef. Afterward, Godel tried to explain himself.

"I appreciate you worrying about me, Noah, I really do. And how terribly you must be hurting, too. But mine is a different hurt, an even deeper one. Roza may be a good friend, your best friend, but to me she's no less than my other half, the light of my world, my lady and wife in everything but name only.

"Not to downplay what you're going through, but awful as it is, it's just not the same. Just not the same."

But, in fact, it was. Precisely the same—there was nothing Godel was feeling that he wasn't. Never had Noah hated the Germans more than when he saw what they were doing to his Roza, not even upon learning of the death of his parents, sister, baby brother.

His instinct to combat injustice with blows, suppressed out of necessity since entering the Vernichtungslager, was undergoing its most rigorous test yet. To have to stand helplessly by as the love of his life was run through the Gestapo wringer, forced to watch her body and beauty reduced to ruin, bordered on the unendurable. If there was a chance, though, the slightest chance she might look up one day and see him there, neither God nor the devil was going to keep him away.

But punishing as the experience was, one positive could be gleaned from it, if nothing remotely capable of compensating Noah for his grief then a lifeline a man drowning in it could hold onto. With the calendar creeping forward and the days succeeding the arrests turning into weeks, he and those keeping track of them were witness to something incredible happening.

Or rather, not happening. Since those arrests, not a soul had followed after them. In spite of the violence they were piling on the women, their torturers hadn't managed to gouge a single name from them.

How this was possible no one could fathom. Strong men, rugged, raised to be tough, couldn't imagine withstanding what these mere girls were. That they were in desperate condition was evident. Their trips to Block 35 were becoming less frequent by the week, presumably because they were taking longer to recover between sessions. Even then the journey, both there and back, was entirely by way of the stretchers.

Yet to the reverential amazement of all, they continued to hold out, their lips to stay sealed, nor did anyone find this more boggling than the SS. A confounded Broch was at a loss where to turn. Not even his faithful workhorse the electric generator was getting results, even with its alligator clip attached directly to toes, nipples, genitalia. Despite realizing he'd be lucky to repeat the success he'd blundered into with Ala, in his frustration one day he left Roza to cook longer than he should have. But it not only didn't work, he almost lost her, too.

Since assigned to the Political Department a year ago, the sergeant had participated in innumerable interrogations, if not all of them conclusive, then certainly unexceptional. As admittedly limited as his experience with female subjects was, he'd found them, as was to be expected, more pliable than the average male.

Granted, the Gertner Jewess hadn't broken easily. But Broch had considered this more a fluke than a portent, and anticipated little of the same from the three women she'd given up. But now even she had closed tighter than a clam again, and opposed to what practice and his upbringing had taught him, her accomplices from what was commonly accepted as the weaker sex were shut as tight.

Unable to account for this, in Ala's case he might have guessed. In her anguish at learning from Broch that in the semi-delirium touched off by her overexposure to the electricity she'd betrayed the three, she'd have killed herself out of shame if she'd had the means. Lacking these, she instead made an unshakeable promise to herself that it was going to take more than the Nazis had in their depraved repertoire to extract another name from her.

Nor did she see this as insurmountable, if for no reason than she'd also made up her mind to accept what lay ahead as penance for having got both herself and the others in this spot in the first place. What began with Eugen Koch and ended up in the torture room was her fault and hers alone. To compound it now by implicating any more of her erstwhile comrades was a sin she was prepared to suffer all the pangs of hell before committing.

As for Regina Safirsztajn, despite the heroism she'd shown in the course of her first detention, few trusted her to outlast the Gestapo's more diabolic torments. Opinion had it she was too gentle-hearted, too soft psychologically to overcome the concerted animus of prolonged abuse.

But it was just this, paradoxically, helping stiffen her to it. Hers was an empathy for those under the Nazi boot not even torture could erode. The matronly persona she'd adopted as a forewoman ran deeper than the office; if no older than most, she felt the same affection for the women of the gunpowder room, of the Union in general, as a mother for her children. She'd sooner have signed her soul over to Satan than the death warrants the SS were in effect demanding of her.

Esther was even harder to read, not that it had taken Broch long to figure out the Wajcblum prisoner wasn't going to be the straightforward proposition he'd hoped. Beneath her dimpled, deceptively melt-your-heart beauty something inimical lurked, malignant, he could see it in her eyes, a mortal hatred of him and his uniform that burned below the surface like a fire in a coal mine. He'd got a taste of this when he had her a while back, but unless he was imagining it, this enmity and the contrariness it fueled had grown more pronounced.

Which wasn't to say she was impervious to pain. When lashed to the chair or the bench, she screamed louder, wheedled for mercy more than anyone. But whenever she appeared on the verge of breaking, she would draw upon some inner reserve and pull herself together.

What Broch couldn't know was this had less to do with her spite for his kind, or even fealty to her own, than it did with the love she had for her little sister. What she'd done was evolve a tactic that guaranteed she'd stay her tongue, and it was working. Through pounding it without end into her head, Esther had persuaded herself that should she be driven to spilling names, the first to leave her lips would be that of Hanka. If she was going to betray anyone, or so she'd conditioned herself to believe, it would have to start with Hanka.

And that wasn't possible. That wasn't going to happen. All the demons under heaven couldn't have pried that name from her. With this or silence the only choices open to her, nothing the Germans could do would make her talk.

Of the sergeant's four catches, however, none both depressed and *imp*ressed him more than the one named Robota. He couldn't recall encountering a prisoner quite like her, male or female. Not only did she plead guilty to everything she was accused of but boasted about it. She took a scornful delight, for example, in informing her captors that for nearly two years she'd passed gunpowder to the Sonder right under SS noses, gunpowder she knew would take SS lives.

"My only regret," she would taunt, "is not having smuggled more. How does that grab you? A twenty-two-year-old girl, a Jewish girl no less, getting the better for so long of so many Nazi *Übermenschen*. Doesn't it make you wonder, the thought cross your minds, that maybe you're not so damned *über* after all?"

Roza paid handsomely for her words. To the Gestapo strongmen, Broch included, taken as he was with her pluck, what would have been just another day on the job became something more when she was brought into the room. Then it was game on as each strove to outdo the others in being the one to wipe the smirk from her. Not that they'd found this easy. For after they'd done their worst, or sometimes even as they were doing it, she might gasp something to the effect that if it allowed her the privilege of telling them to their faces the low opinion she had of them, however hard they leaned on her was welcome.

But again, she would have rated the extra attention even if she hadn't been so smart-mouthed. Her three companions, though far from having no value, meant less to Broch together than Roza did alone. With everything, everybody, every secret she harbored, she was too enticing a plum to be left unpeeled.

Yet in spite of all his efforts to bare the fruit beneath, this plum's skin remained intact. In her unbendingness, the *Unterscharführer* could scarcely squeeze a cry out of her, much less a viable name. Those she had doled him belonged predominately to the dead, a couple to men long transferred to other camps. Running out of both options and time, his mood was glum. The outcome of the investigation and doubtless his reputation, maybe even his career, were at stake. The Kommandantur had been breathing down his neck for a month now, increasingly livid that he had only the four women still to show for his troubles.

A solution did present itself, if not a pleasant one. It came in the person of SS-*Sturmbannführer* Wilhelm Boger, also of the Gestapo, and his eponymous invention, the notorious "Boger swing." Not that Broch had any objection to using the major's device, which could be most effective. It was the man who gave him pause.

Boger was one of those individuals whose appearance perfectly fit his occupation. He might have been born to play the part of the professional torturer. To the eye, he wasn't quite human-looking, could have passed for one of hell's minor fiends made flesh. No taller than a fifteen-year-old and built close to the bone, not an ounce of fat on him, his ears stuck almost straight out from his head, his nostrils two flat holes, like a pig's snout. His lips when they opened revealed a pair of overlarge front teeth, making it hard to say which he resembled more, swine or rodent.

But it wasn't his off-putting looks keeping Broch at a distance, reluctant even in this emergency to seek his assistance. A rivalry had long existed between the two, precipitated by the major's jealousy at the success of his junior officer. The latter's adroitness in the interrogation room, unpromoted as he yet was, propelled him swiftly upward in the Political Department's operational hierarchy. A ranking member of same, this didn't sit well with Boger, especially with his subordinate of late appointed to lead the more prestigious cases.

He was loud in labeling the sergeant not only an upstart but soft, jumping at every opportunity to cite him publicly for lacking the harshness, the heavy hand the job called for.

In point of fact, working against the *Sturmbannführer* was this very heavy-handedness. Too many of those prisoners assigned him had died under questioning before they could be fully exploited. Rare was the mentality that was needed for filling the role each of them had chosen, spending his days occupied in the methodical demolition of his fellow man. As rare was balancing the ruthlessness this required with knowing, sometimes literally, when to loosen the screws.

Broch, who had his issues, a quick temper being one, at least made an effort to control it. Boger, though, to his undoing was an undisguised sadist, whose relish for dispensing pain often got the better of his prudence. That he relied largely on his namesake swing for results did him no favors; such were its mechanics that it lent itself to fatalities.

It was the simplest of concepts. From a stout metal bar a meter long, a thick chain welded to each end was looped over a reinforced hook in the ceiling. The resulting contraption hung five feet above the floor, resembling a crude trapeze. The victim was handcuffed wrist to ankle and suspended naked from the bar, either facing outward, his spine bent back on itself, or inward, in profile like a giant teardrop. Both positions, especially the former, were painful enough, but as nothing to what was to follow.

With his prisoner dangling defenseless, every part exposed—face, genitals, buttocks, spine, depending on how he was displayed—Boger, brandishing a heavy club in both fists, would rear back and with a fearful yell let him have it. Flat-sided clubs functioned the best, maximizing the damage without delivering a knockout blow. So vicious was the attack, so violent the impact, often the swing would go flying in a tight, twisting arc. Or even more horrid, the wretch shackled to it do a complete three-sixty around the bar.

His "talking machine" Boger called it, and not without justification. Unless he got carried away, and the person he was working on never talked again. Those who did survive the thing were unrecognizable afterward. What had been a face was so much strawberry jam, a human voice a frog's croaking. The skin of the thighs, buttocks, and back was frequently split open, that of the ankles and wrists scraped off by the handcuffs.

It took Broch two nights of little sleep and a lot of back-and-forth with himself to decide he had no choice but to hand Roza over to his adversary. He wasn't getting anywhere with her, and losing confidence he ever would. If he had to swallow his pride to advance the inquiry so be it, even should his stature take a hit. He was too dedicated the Nazi, patriotic the German to put his own interests before those of his Fatherland.

Besides, who was to say how even Boger and his toy were going to fare against this Jewish she-devil? Broch had seen her spit, actually spit in the faces of his men even as they were torturing her. A part of him was relieved to be dumping the bitch on someone else. Let the big-talking major break his teeth on her awhile, see how he liked it.

Some days later, Noah Zabludowicz answered a summons from his new boss Soswinski, who informed him of something as promising as it was unprecedented coming out of Block 11.

"You've no doubt heard of the infamous kapo of the punishment block," Soswinski said, "the Jew Kozelczik. His position has earned him the ill will of all, particularly your people, who regard him a traitor."

"I've heard tell of him, yes," Noah said, "but never had the misfortune to run across him."

"He does, though, fortunately for us, have one friend in the camp. None other than Erich Kulka, Bruno Baum's former lieutenant and one of our top agents."

"Him I have met, often."

"Anyway, this Kozelczik contacts Kulka this morning with what could end up good news. A woman in one of his cells, tortured half to death, in her stupor keeps mumbling the same thing over and over. 'Bring me Noah,' is all she says. 'I have to see Noah.' "

Soswinski watched his agent's eyes grow as round and white as eggshells. "According to the kapo," he said, "it's the prisoner Roza Robota. And it appears you're the Noah she's referring to. Is that correct?"

Noah could only nod, too flabbergasted to speak.

"Your mission, should you take it, would be to go to this woman and find out what she wants. I won't say there's not an element of danger to it, but neither can I overstate its importance. What do you think? Are you up for it, Zabludowicz?"

He managed to choke out a hoarse, "Yes—yes, of course I am, sir."

"Good. You're to be in front of Block 11 by nine tonight. Kozelczik will be there to let you in."

From Ala's arrest onward, Battle Group-Auschwitz was intent on communicating with the imprisoned women, Roza foremost. Its leaders were eager to offer what help they could, but also to get a handle on how each was holding up. Much, perhaps everything, depended on this. It was vital the underground have time to prepare, as an organization and individually, should further arrests be in the offing.

No one, however, had got remotely near them. Not even Kulka, as tight as he was with their jailer.

Now here was one of their agents being issued an all but engraved invitation. As tantalizing as this was, it also aroused apprehension. Were the SS setting some sort of trap? But if they did suspect Noah of affiliation with the underground, why the ruse? The Germans could have picked him up whenever they wanted, unless their aim was to trace him back to those who'd sent him.

In the end, it was agreed to proceed with the mission. What cemented the decision was the trusted Kulka swearing to the integrity of his most unusual friend.

Jakob Kozelczik was an Auschwitz institution. The only kapo the Stammlager's punishment block had ever known, he also served as both camps' official hangman. He'd earned these jobs by virtue of his uncanny strength. A tall man, he weighed over three hundred pounds, most of it as solid as the human mountain he resembled.

At the request of the SS, he'd sometimes put on a show by bending heavy iron bars with his bare hands, and other such circus feats. In a more practical vein, no prisoner being led to the gallows or the Black Wall, no matter how much he might resist, could wriggle free of his bone-crushing grip. If need be, he could lug two simultaneously to the execution site, one in each hand. He was as adept at subduing the violent or panicked, and when necessary extricating these from their cells.

The Jewish inmates called him *Shimshon Ayzern*, the Iron Samson, and their dislike of him was as intense as their fear. In their eyes, he was a disgrace to his race; that one of their own should collaborate to that extreme with the Nazis made him no better than their vile masters.

Of the handful who thought differently, who knew otherwise, most had concluded as much from time they themselves had served in Block 11. There they'd seen firsthand that Kozelczik was anything but a monster, often sticking his own neck out to provide the prisoners in his care some relief from their suffering.

He might slip a victim of the starvation cells a draught of poison so he could die a quick rather than this slowest of deaths. Or distribute extra water when in the summer the bunker was like an oven. When administering the "25" as he was called on every so often to do, he was skilled at making a convincing show of it while delivering a lesser blow. He even on occasion, through one form of trickery or another, was able to save those marked for execution.

He also refused to preside at the hanging of children, regardless of the pressure put on him. This he left the Germans to work out for themselves. Kapo Jakob was one of those prisoners, like Kaminski and Leyb Langfus, whom the SS for various reasons tended to show a certain permissiveness.

He would test this to its fullest come the end of the year in a situation involving the four most celebrated residents of his block, though for now wanted only to satisfy the wishes of the one.

Before dismissing him, Soswinski briefed Noah on what the Steering Committee sought to learn from his meeting with Roza. But he only half-listened. Already his heart was racing, the adrenaline pumping, the one thing on his mind that somehow, tonight—O blessed, blessed night—he'd be hearing her voice, looking into her eyes, taking hold of a hand he never in a hundred years would have dreamed he'd be given the chance to hold again.

It was no less than a prayer answered, and though he wasn't a praying man, it had him hard-pressed not to wonder if maybe something, some power beyond his understanding, had taken pity on him in his sorrow and favored him with this kindness.

By 9:00 p.m., straining at the bit though he was, Noah stood a cautious twenty meters across from Block 11. The building wasn't much different from its neighbors, a two-story affair of pink brick with a roof of dun-red tiles. The only discrepancies lay in the windows, which were barred, and a door of unpainted steel instead of wood. An electric lamp above this door kept the dark at bay. He'd worried there might be a guard; a cold knife of a wind may have explained why there wasn't.

Right on the minute, the door creaked wide in metallic protest to the unmistakable bulk of the kapo framed in yellow light. Picking Noah out of the blackness, he motioned for him to hurry. In the *Kommandoführer's* office, a soldier leaned back in one of three folding metal chairs, feet propped on a table.

"Herr *Sturmmänn*," Kozelczik said in German, "this is the cousin I was telling you about." Then to Noah in their native tongue, "The corporal doesn't speak a word of Polish. Feel free to say what you please."

The kapo left the room and returned with a liter-bottle and three glasses. "Sit," he told his visitor. "This shouldn't take long. Have you ever had egg liquor? It's like drinking liquid fire."

Soon the glasses were clinking, the *Prosits* and *Heil Hitlers* flying. Their host suggested Noah down his first shot—"You look as if you could use one"—then dump all that followed under the table. He made sure to pour the guard doubles, who long before they reached the end of the bottle passed clean out. After depositing the limp *Sturmmänn* on a sofa, Kozelczik took a ring of keys from its peg on the wall.

"Ready?" he asked. "Careful on the stairs, there's no railing."

At the end of a short corridor was another steel door. As if waiting for it to unlock, an evil stench leapt out at them: excrement and soured urine at first blast, which was awful enough, but underneath it something else, the moldy odor of prolonged neglect, a subterranean rot of rancid fungus and decomposing soil. Of air so long immured it tasted as if even it had begun to decay.

A dozen stone steps descended to a second corridor, longer if poorer lit. A row of narrow doors stretched the length of it on either side. As the two walked between them, from behind some came an urgent imploring in a medley of languages. Noah was able to recognize those in Polish and German as begging Kozelczik for a blanket, for water, or simply to know what day it was.

Turning down another passageway, the kapo pulled up at door #18, unbolted it, and swung it open. Nodding Noah inside, without a word he locked it after him, his footsteps swiftly fading.

The tiny cell was even dimmer than the hallway, the only light a weak bulb in the ceiling. Bunched in a corner was the broken carcass of some animal. Drawing nearer, however, Noah could make out human hands and feet, a naked female torso. He knelt beside her, his lower jaw dropping in disbelief. It was Roza all right, but...

From her scalp, streaks of dried blood ran down a face that wasn't a face, more like a photograph torn apart and pasted sloppily back together. He laid a hand on her shoulder, but got no response. Gently, he shook it, then more forcefully. She at last let out a long, deep-throated moan.

"Roza, it's Noah. Can you hear me, dearest? I said it's Noah. You sent for me and I've come. Nod if you can hear."

Her head moved tentatively up and down, though it took a moment for her eyes to blink open. "Noah? What—what's happening? How did you—where am I?"

"You're in your cell, my brave girl. It's okay, you're safe, it's just you and I."

With his help, she was able to rise on one arm. "Is it really you, Noah? I don't understand. How—how'd you get in here? Past the guard, the locked doors? *Why* are you here?"

He started with her calling out his name from her cell, and with that it began coming back to her. He went on to spell out the part Kapo Jakob had played, and that without him they wouldn't be sitting across from each other now.

Roza wasn't surprised. "This Kozelczik," she said, her eyes already clearer, her voice steadier, "isn't the vulture everyone thinks. He has a lousy job, but so do a lot of good people in this plague of a place. He's been sneaking me extra food, when I can eat it, and I would imagine the other girls, too. He even brought me a blanket the other night, but the Germans came and took it."

Noah whipped off his jacket and draped it around her. As he did, he took a closer look at her injuries. He'd seen a lot of ugly sights in his days at Auschwitz, bodies in every stage of ruin, but never anything quite like this. A shocking patchwork of devastation covered her from head to foot: green-yellow bruises the size of dinner plates; large, inflamed gashes where the skin had either been cut or burst open as from some savage blow; uncounted lesser lesions and abrasions that glistened blackly in the murky light like so many smudges of used motor oil. Worst of all was what had become of her face, her poor face... He could only hope he was hiding the revulsion in his.

She couldn't help, though, but pick up on it. "It's a good thing beauty," she said, smiling crookedly, "is more than skin-deep."

"You're more beautiful to me than you ever were!" he protested, disgusted at himself for the disgust he'd let show. "How could I or anybody be less than in awe of those wounds, those badges of honor you're wearing? Besides, it's not forever. You'll have healed in nothing flat. Soon you'll be your old self again, pretty as ever."

"Healed?" She'd have laughed if it didn't hurt so much. "Come on, Noah, we both know the Krauts aren't about to let me live long enough to heal. And that goes for Esther, Ala, and Gina. We've each of us a foot and some toes in the grave already."

He wanted to insist this wasn't true, but though he'd spent the last weeks swatting the thought away, knew in his heart she was right. And that persisting in the charade would have made it the more awkward. Instead, he scurried to change the subject, to something that had been nagging at him since leaving Soswinski.

"So tell me, Roza, and don't take this wrong, but... why me? I mean, how come you've been moaning for *my* useless self? If anybody, I'd have figured you'd want Godel sitting here. It seems only natural you'd have asked for him."

Though a full two feet separated them, he could feel her body wilt. That brash grittiness so a part of her, which despite her condition had started asserting itself, fled like smoke in the wind. Noah was afraid she was going to crumple back into a heap.

"Why not Godel?" She hung her head. "Because I didn't want him to see me like this. Because I knew it'd be too much for him, that he'd take one look at me and fall to pieces. As much as I love him, am aching for him—pray I somehow get to tell him goodbye—I can't have him or anyone falling apart on me. Not now. I need someone strong, someone I can lean on instead of the other way around.

"I need *you*, Noah," she said, looking up, her voice not unlike those behind the cell doors he'd passed earlier. "My—my what? The

441

center of me, the part that makes me *me*, is as shattered as this sad body of mine. Where before it was all so simple, my path uncluttered, now it's as if I'm wading in mud. If you could peer inside me, take an X-ray of not what but who I am, you'd find me as much a wreck as on the outside."

He was struck dumb. In all the years since they'd met, regardless of how bleak things were, never had he seen her so low, not even last winter with the uprising on shaky ground. Of course, that was before she'd been run through the Gestapo torture mill, a gruesomeness to snuff out the spark in anyone.

"Roza, I'm so sorry," was the best he could come up with, and felt like the world's biggest lamebrain for it.

But, her mind elsewhere, his words hadn't registered. "All we worked for, sacrificed for, risked our lives the past two years for… now that all is said and done, was it worth it? Worth the lives risked, those lost?

"I won't say the revolt wasn't noble in the attempt, or that it lacked glory, but neither was it what we were led to believe it was going to be. Between the cowardice of Battle Group-Auschwitz and the bad luck of the Sonderkommando, the effort was doomed to fall short. Of those who did rebel, not a one survived, much less escaped, while three of the four death houses continue to stand, to suck the living into them and spit out bone and ash."

What left her mouth next would normally have had some ginger to it; instead it came couched in a sigh. "Operation Jericho? Operation Fiasco would be more like it. As genuinely as I wish he was still with us, a part of me is grateful friend Kaminski didn't survive to see the hash made of his dream."

Noah tried to say something, but she shushed him. "Answer me this. Have there been any more arrests?"

"Since you, none. Your courage, all four of yours, is the talk of both camps."

She manufactured a weak smile. "I'm glad my three sisters in pain are holding up their end. But…"

The smile was short-lived. "But when it comes down to it, again, is it worth it? Those we would save with our silence are just marking time, theirs as unpreventable a death as ours. The SS aren't about to let a single Jew from the camps live, and not simply to get rid of us as witnesses. Being German, they won't rest until they've carried out their orders, until we on the wrong end of those orders are no more.

"Is this why we've been offering up our bodies in the torture chamber, to try and spare those already as good as dead?"

Her voice breathed defeat. "But never mind them, or the thousands yet to follow them. Or, as if it can compare, our expendable four selves. What of the countless gone before us, the millions from every corner of Europe who've disappeared from among us like— like beads of dew in the sun? Unburied, unmourned, as if they'd never existed."

Noah couldn't recall a voice as lifeless since reuniting with his cousin Shlomo two summers ago, then Kaminski's after the failed revolt of June. "Roza, listen. You've got to try and stay pos—"

"But I have tried, Noah, and there is no staying positive. Not anymore. After five years of ghettos, of deportations, extermination, how many Jews can be left? How many will there be a year from now? My heart wants to say enough for our race to survive, but my head isn't so hopeful. My brain begs to differ.

"Once, in the ghetto, long before Birkenau, I overheard an SS man boasting to another that one day the only Jews to be found this side of the Atlantic would be those made of plaster on display in museums. Back then, I didn't know what to make of that, or him. What kind of fool would suppose there were enough ships in the world to ferry all the Jews in Europe to whatever countries would have them?

"Now I get where he was coming from, and can't help suspecting that day of his is near. That the Nazis may have lost to the Russians and Americans, but won their war against us. That all our hardships, and even crueler, our resistance was for naught."

That Roza had hit bottom emotionally was clear, a depth neither she experiencing it nor he observing it knew how to deal with. Yet plumb his brain as he might to scrape up something to comfort her, buoy her spirits, he was drawing a blank.

Until, from out of nowhere, as with a clash of cymbals, the memories of a decade ago came tumbling to his rescue. Having remained buried for all those years, that they were retrievable at all was cause for wonder. Echoing the words of a God he'd long ceased talking to made them even more improbable.

"I can identify, Roza, with what you're feeling. From where we stand, with what we've seen—with what we haven't seen but has happened wherever the SS have set foot—to speak of a future for the

Jewish people is to risk sounding naïve. If not downright nuts. After five years, as you said, of murder, it's no easy thing to stay positive.

"But there's an argument to be made for optimism, too, guarded though it be. And it begins with something I've got to believe still strikes a chord with you. Tell me, how much of your Ezekiel do you remember?"

Conscious she was no more religious than he, that wasn't the angle Noah was pitching. There weren't a lot of scouts from the old H'Shomeir H'Tzair, religious or not, who couldn't recite from the biblical book of Ezekiel. An important part of the Shomeir's curriculum was the study of this book, as its message existed in direct complement to that of the Zionists.

The prophet Ezekiel had stood tall as his nation's champion during the Babylonian exile. Though preaching that the defeat by Babylon was God's punishment—the Israelites, among other sins, having turned their backs on Him by resuming the worship of idols—he also foretold God's forgiveness and their eventual return to the Holy Land.

If the Shomeir, and by extension Zionism, could be said to have a patron saint, it was Ezekiel.

His question had caught Roza unawares. "How much do I remember? I—I don't know." She quickly collected herself, though, and took a stab at it, the words halting at first.

"Thus—thus sayeth the... Lord God. Behold, I—I will take the children of Israel from... the midst of the nations where they are gone; and will gather—will gather them on every side, and bring them back to their own land. And I will make them one nation in the land on... the mountains of Israel."

Even this early into her attempt, Noah was surprised by her powers of recollection. But his surprise, like those powers, had only begun.

"Nor shall they—nor shall they be defiled anymore with their idols, nor with their abominations, their iniquities; and I will save them out of all the places in—in which they have gone. And I will cleanse them, and they shall be My people, and I their God."

She was on a roll now, surer of herself, the dead voice growing more alive with each sentence. "See, I will instill breath into you, and you will live. I will restore you, put flesh upon you, cover you with skin, and—and put breath into you, and you will come alive. See, I open your graves and will raise you from them, My people, and bring you to the land of Israel, to the land that is restored from the ravages of the sword, where people are gathered out of many nations."

When she stopped, Noah saw beneath even their disfigurement that her features had brightened with the warm glow of nostalgia, of happier days, days before death replaced life as the norm. In the course of those few revivifying lines from Ezekiel, she'd become a teenager again, back in the empowering arms of the Shomeir.

Marvel as he did that she'd retained so much after so long, even more did he at the abruptness of this change in her. As at the touch of a wand, flown was the morbidness that had got hold of her, in its place the Roza he looked up to and loved.

"Perfect, my beauty," he said. "You couldn't have picked a better passage. What planted hope in the Jewish breast twenty-five hundred years ago can do so today."

"As," she said, "brief as it was, it's just planted in mine, try as the Gestapo men have to beat it out of me.

"But their unkind hands are no match for the prophet's vision. Like the Babylonians, like all in our long history who've done their worst to get rid of us, the Nazis—as Ezekiel, as *you* have reminded me—will not succeed. And when the Third Reich is no more, a casualty of its own wickedness, Eretz Israel will beckon as never before.

"Funny, how in the end we'll have a Hitler and his insane hordes to thank for waking us up, shocking us into leaving where we were never wanted for the only place we ever really belonged."

Godel, of course, had often shared these same thoughts with her, and might have shared them again if given the chance. But far from surefire was how he'd react when he saw the state she was in, and hard a choice as this had forced, she couldn't take that chance.

What she could take was credit for having the instincts to turn in her desolation to someone she could rely on not to break down on her. "Believe me, Noah, when I say I owe you more than words *can* say. That you really came through for me. I had a feeling you would, that you'd know just what I needed."

"Roza, you would have worked it out for—"

"Because of you," she cut in, not at all convinced she'd have worked it out herself, "I can die in peace, content the battle won't have been for nothing. With you and Ezekiel making the argument you do that the Jew will have a tomorrow after all, who am I, one of your two's biggest admirers, to say different? Thank you, Noah, for not only that but everything. For being... well, Noah."

"You thanking *me?*" This was too much for him. "That's like a doctor thanking his patient for getting better. It's I who owe you, and always have. Besides, what did I do that any friend wouldn't have?"

"Oh, you've been more than a friend, trust me. But never more than tonight. I can only—"

"Wait, more than a friend?" Noah's eyes grew as round as a couple of marbles. "I don't think you get, Roza, just how true those four words are."

It was the way he said it, almost with regret, more than what he said. "What do you mean, Noah? I—I don't..."

He didn't answer right away, nor look at her when he did. "There's something I have to share with you I couldn't before. Something I've been keeping inside me forever. But I don't see the harm in letting it out now, as I'm hoping you won't. The situation being what it is"—his gaze sought hers again—"the real harm would be in leaving it unspoken."

At this, she woke up to what he was aiming at, and felt her heart stop. She may have been bloodied, but wasn't blind; it was all there in that beseeching stare of his.

She'd been living for years in dread of what he was about to say, stressing over how she was going to deflect it without tromping on his feelings. But as fast as it took her heart to resume beating, it occurred to her that she had to admit things were different now. There had been a time when it would have been in poor taste for him to come out with it, even destructive, but with her fate sealed, her future in ruins, those days were as dead and gone as the promise they'd once held.

"What is it you're wanting to tell me, Noah?" She chose to play dumb, let him do the talking.

Having labored for so long to bury his passion, ever on the watch that in a weak moment he blurt it out, now that it was about to be secret no more, he wavered. How to begin? Should he ease into it? Deciding not to tiptoe around it, he dove in.

"When you say I'm more than a friend, Roza, little do you appreciate how much more. I—I've loved you heart and soul from the day I first met you. From the first thirty minutes. That morning at the Yellow Rose Café, remember? Hardly had the waitress brought our order than my life was no longer my own."

To his befuddlement, she took his confession in stride. Acted as if she hadn't even heard it. "The Yellow Rose, certainly I remember. It'd been spitting rain all morning. The three of us were drinking coffee. You smelled of aftershave and were much handsomer than Godel said you'd be."

"I don't know about that last," he said, "but as with Ezekiel, there's no faulting your memory. In fact, as for that day at the Yellow Rose, it's sharper than I expected. And I'm not sure what to make of that. Or why you didn't so much as flinch a second ago when I told you... what I told you."

Roza did her best to be gentle. "Don't be upset, Noah, but—I've known for a while."

"What, that I was in love with you?"

"I'm afraid so. I never let on because what good would have come of it? That was a can of worms begging not to be opened, for no telling what might have slithered out. Not anything very pretty. I'm only thankful you saw it the same. Had the good sense, the graciousness to keep it to yourself."

He was silent as his brain struggled to process what his ears were telling it. When he did speak, she had to strain to hear him. "You knew all along? I was that obvious?"

Bad as she felt for him, she couldn't suppress a smile. "I don't mean to condescend or anything, my poor Noah, but you had a habit of mooning after me like a baby calf its mother. You couldn't have been more obvious if you'd tried."

With her putting it like that, he almost smiled himself. "That may have been, I won't say it wasn't. I've heard I wear my emotions like a sign around my neck. But never was it intentional, something to put ideas in your head; I hid it the best I could. I'd rather have cut off an arm, Roza, than come between you and Godel."

"Didn't I say how grateful I was? Thought the more of you for it as both a friend *and* a man."

She shifted beneath his coat the better to face him, wincing at the effort. "But—that's all water under the bridge now. My days are done, and that changes everything. Not least whatever secrets you and I were keeping from each other. You've bared yours, and with no danger anymore of it messing with Godel and me, were in your rights to do so. But I've a secret, too, one I bet you never came close to suspecting."

She pondered how best to confess what all of a sudden she felt compelled to. "Life," she said at last, "can get complicated, especially when one muddies it with what might have been. But this can also be a comfort in that events, be they big or little, good or bad, can hinge on nothing more than—what's the word? Happenstance.

"I was drawn to you, Noah Zabludowicz, even after I'd committed myself to Godel. Not that I considered ever leaving him for you—this I couldn't do, not if my soul depended on it—but drawn nonetheless, deny it as I might. To be truthful, as I found myself sometimes *having* to deny it. We're too much alike, you and I, not to feel that tug of one kindred spirit for another. It's like the coin to the magnet, lightning to the rod; the attraction is built-in, an edict of nature."

She took one of his hands in both of hers. "What I'm trying to get at is that but for an accident of timing, a roll of the dice, I can imagine myself, Noah, having fallen in love with you as opposed to Godel. That if fortune had brought you into my life first, who can say... what might have been."

She let out a long breath. "There, I've gone and said it. And am the lighter for it, for telling you what I've often wanted to, but couldn't. What needed to be told."

She squeezed his hand before letting go. "I'd hate to have left this world without doing that. Without you ever knowing. That would have been not only cowardly of me but unfair."

Roza was right in saying he hadn't suspected this, though that wasn't doing the shock of it justice. Words failing him, in their stead he reached for her face and began gently stroking it with the backs of his fingers.

As he did, it ceased being the one the Gestapo had given her. The swelling and the cuts, the blackened, bloodshot eyes, the flattened nose, the fractured cheeks—all either melted away or reconstructed themselves, so that what ended up gazing back at him was the vibrant, young face that had grabbed him in the ghetto, as pristine as when he'd first seen it that morning it came waltzing into the Yellow Rose.

It was the same face that had swept him off his feet then and still did, a mix of seriousness and mischief, severity and warmth, that even as it warned you not to get in its way invited you along for the ride of your life. Noah couldn't have resisted it if he'd wanted, nor would any barbarity the SS inflicted on it ever blind him to its enchantment.

Upon getting his tongue back, the first thing he did was thank her for her generosity in opening up to him when she didn't have to. When she could have kept it her secret. He did have trouble persuading himself she meant everything she'd said, but whether she did or not didn't much matter. That she cared enough about him to say it at all made up for more than a little of what he'd suffered all these years longing for her from afar.

There would be no more talk of love. Apart from the disrespect it would have shown Godel, having come out and declared it, or in Roza's case the potential for it, what was left to add? Elaborating on it would only have brought them grief. With neither the present nor the future offering much solace in that or any regard, their conversation retreated into the safety of the past. To those days in Ciechanow before their families, their townsfolk, and their own belief in the inherent decency of mankind disappeared forever in the fires of Birkenau.

They spoke until midnight of years gone by, of life both before the ghetto but mostly during, when things seemed abysmal but in retrospect weren't so bad. When if little else they still had their loved ones and a modicum of freedom—when they and Godel, inseparable, would inhabit the streets by day, and at night dare to venture beyond them in dangerous if exhilarating pursuit of contraband.

They'd have continued reminiscing, too, but for the sound of steps, the clank of a bolt, the door swinging outward to reveal to their relief, but also sorrow, the unsurpassed heft of Kapo Jakob filling it.

"It's time," he announced. "That idiot *Sturmmann* is starting to show signs of life. We'll all be sorry," he told Noah, "if he should stumble down here and find you."

Roza smiled through her disappointment. "Allow me to thank you, kapo, for bringing Noah to me. For being the good man you are. If one day I'm remembered for what I've done, you won't be forgotten, either. Would it be too much to ask that good man for one more favor?"

"Not if it's quick, child."

"A pencil and a piece of paper, and I promise to be fast. Just a few words for Noah to take back to my comrades."

A desk stood at the foot of the stairs in which the bunker's daily logs and other papers were kept. It took less than a minute for the kapo to return with her request, and another two of her scribbling away before handing Noah a sheet of paper folded in half.

"If you could get this to the right persons," she said, "it would make what lies ahead of me easier."

"Consider it done. And what else?"

"What else?"

"There must be something more I can do for you, Roza. Or if not me, another. There's no shortage of people willing to risk anything to help you through this."

"No, nothing else. Not beyond, as you'll see when you read it, what I've set down in that paper you have. Unless... Wait, there might be something after all."

She motioned him closer. "I don't wish to pester this Jakob any more than I have," she whispered, "should he come to think me a nuisance. But, what I said earlier, about Godel—maybe you could approach the kapo about trying to smuggle him down here, too. Not in the condition I'm in now, but after the Krauts are done with me and I'm maybe more... more presentable.

"Would that be too much to ask of him, you suppose? I can't imagine not telling my Godel goodbye."

"No, Roza, I doubt it'd be too much at all. He's obviously a decent fellow, never mind his reputation. I'll ask him before I—"

There was a rumbling from the doorway as their benefactor, his back to them, made a show of clearing his throat.

"I'll ask him tonight," Noah promised, "don't worry. But speaking of goodbyes, the time, it appears, has come for us to say ours."

At that, despite having hardened herself against them, Noah appeared to her through a blur of tears.

"Trouble is," he said, "I don't know how. Or if I even can. How do you tell someone dearer to you than life itself goodbye?"

"Simple," she said, wiping her eyes. "You get up off the floor, kiss her on the forehead, then march your ass out that door without turning around. No words. No tears. Just go and don't look back. It may not feel like it, Noah, but it's best that way. Please."

He would stay up all that night, what remained of it. The electric explosion of the 4:30 reveille bell would be wasted on him. Indeed, many was the night to come when sleep stubbornly declined to, when he would lie in bed replaying every minute in Cell #18. Some would always be a treasure to revisit, but others would haunt him for as long as he lived.

Among these was his departure. He'd done as Roza had begged and left without a word, but it didn't sit right with him. As soon as he had, in fact, he stopped, and would have darted back inside—to say what he wasn't sure, he hadn't planned that far—but for Bunker Jakob emerging from her cell to block him. As if that weren't disgruntling enough, to his disbelief the man was clutching the gray canvas jacket Noah had given her as protection against the cold.

Before he could blow his top, the kapo hastened to explain he had no choice. The Germans had made it clear, after discovering the women with blankets one morning, that they, not him, would pay for any such trespass in the future.

"Besides," Kozelczik added, "if the *Sturmmänn* were to identify this coat as belonging to my 'cousin'..."

There could be no arguing this. Noah would just have to live with it. But as he lay later in the comparative comfort of his koje, the image of Roza naked on the concrete floor of that freezing cell so filled him with guilt that he tossed and turned like a man in the throes of delirium. How this failed to wake his brother Hanan, or the other two occupants of their mattress, he didn't know.

Not that it took long before the thought of the coat warming himself instead of her got the better of him, and jumping from under their blanket to the edge of the bed, he ripped the thing off as if it were on fire.

He'd acquired it that summer, trading some tire rubber he found on the road and three rations of bread for it. Tattered and thin, heavily frayed at the cuffs and with holes at both elbows, it was better than nothing at all. It had no lining, but a makeshift pocket had been sewn on the inside. It was while tearing it off that a piece of paper fell from this pocket and glided to the floor.

The note Roza had given him... how could he have forgot that? He lit one of the candle stubs they kept under their mattress, unfolded the paper, and held it up to the light. The words rang in his head as if she were speaking them.

"Friends and fellow soldiers, I send you my final regards. It is not an easy thing to exit this life, but I go to my death without regret, convinced our fight was a just one.

"As for yourselves, you have nothing to fear. There will be no more arrests. In spite of every cruelty the SS have thrown at us, I and the three brave women imprisoned with me have refused to cooperate. And will continue to refuse.

"In return for our silence, we ask only three things: that you remember our names, not quit resisting until the battle is won, and most important, never forget your obligation to the dead. They call to you from the grave—your parents, brothers and sisters, husbands and wives, your children—call for the righting of an unforgivable wrong.

"The Nazis are finished. Their end as our masters is near, but we can't just leave it at that. The dead demand vengeance, that justice be done. Those of us who survive must see that they get it."

Roza closed as Noah would have expected her to, with the Shomeir's traditional farewell: *Chazak ve Amatz*, the Hebrew for "Be strong and of good heart." He would pore over these words of hers several times that night, for though there was no denying the heartbreak they evoked, he had to smile at their characteristic spleen. And the impression they gave that she was right there, sitting next to him.

This would become the more tangible when he happened to notice blood on the discarded jacket, a spot here, a smear there, not red but more like chocolate in the yellow light of the candle. Somehow he'd missed these before, but now, with the same urgency he'd taken the coat off, he wriggled back into it and sat there rocking gently, hugging it close to him.

Winter

By the final weeks of November, the long, golden afternoons and invigorating briskness of autumn had given way to the gelid embrace of its sister season at her harshest. Winter arrived with all its teeth showing, the first snowstorm a violent one that raged for days. The guard towers, barely visible, hovered like phantoms in the swirling white.

After the storm blew itself out, Auschwitz-Birkenau lay half-buried under immense, rolling drifts, as if hit by an avalanche. In parts of Birkenau, with its single-story barracks, the wind had piled these to the roofs. The smothering silence of deep snow ruled the land.

But there was more behind the silence than snow. For months, the usual clamor from the Jewish ramp had been in decline, the wheeze and chug of the trains, the barking of the Germans and their dogs, the growls of the trucks carrying the old and infirm to the crematoria. Now, with the Lodz and Theresienstadt ghettos no more, the transports had dwindled to less than one a day. Sometimes much less, with two or even three days between them. The number of cars in each had also shrunk.

While this hadn't passed unnoticed by the general population, no group was more dialed into it than the Sonderkommando. To the men of the Special Squad, it came down to the difference between life and death; the fewer the transports, the less call for their services. Two hundred remained, with work now for maybe fifty, each awakening every morning to the very real possibility of it being his last.

This was as nothing, though, to the blow dealt the detachment before the month was out. Hard as it was to believe, word began circulating that Berlin had ordered the exterminations to a halt. When this was supposed to go into effect no one could say, but all of Birkenau was on fire with the news. When it reached the dayan

Leyb Langfus, he assumed it no more valid than most of the rumors he'd encountered, all giddy conjecture and no substance. And would have dismissed it as such but for it having been a week since the unloading ramp had yielded *any* victims.

That, and the behavior of the SS of late. Overnight, they'd become shadows of their former selves. Fled was the arrogance they'd worn like a second uniform, in its place a groping confusion, as if they weren't sure how to act anymore. Though still abusive, their belligerence lacked the nastiness it once held, seemed at times almost perfunctory.

Some had even taken it a step further, making an effort at altering their attitudes entirely. So subtle was the change Langfus couldn't be positive, but every so often thought he could detect something like familiarity from these: the trace of a smile, the wink of an eye, an order given civilly that in the past would have been snarled.

But something else was flitting at the fringes of the SS face these days, and there was nothing subtle about it. Fear had sunk its hooks in them, the same cold pinch of fear they themselves had inspired for so long. Moreover, it declared itself by virtue of deed as well as demeanor, Birkenau having become a veritable ant bed of Nazi paranoia. The Sonder found themselves burning more paperwork than the dead Muselmänner still trickling in, whole truckfuls of it. True to their reputation for thoroughness, the Germans had kept a meticulous record of what they'd been up to: hundreds of thousands of falsified death certificates, half as many police dossiers from the Political Department, four years of hospital diagnoses and the like, a rough accounting of those transportees who'd gone straight from the ramp to the gas and fire pits.

These all had to be made smoke, nor did the killers' paranoia stop at paper. Hundreds of prisoners were put to work emptying the warehouses of Canada, packing what was judged valuable for shipment west, the rest made into bonfires. Others were employed in disinterring what human ashes had been buried and shoveling these onto trucks bound for the Vistula. All baffles were torn down, along with any fuel and other supply depots. Bunker 5's gas chamber and undressing barracks having been dismantled months ago, for good measure its grounds were planted with saplings culled from the woods.

Clearly, the Red Army was on the move or expected to be soon, and in anticipation of its arrival, the SS were determined to erase their bloody footprints. If, however, the gassings had ceased, why would they take such pains to obliterate so much other evidence yet ignore the most damning of all, the crematoria? But for Bunker 5 and the useless shell of Crematorium IV, Birkenau's murder machinery remained available in its totality if required. Perhaps this newest rumor was as baseless as it sounded, the Nazi thirst for blood unslaked.

Langfus decided to investigate for himself. It wasn't as if there weren't any trains at all, the Sonder could hear them. Could they possibly be arriving empty, their purpose to carry off the plunder of Canada? The more one examined this, the less sense it made. After a week of no deportees anywhere near the death houses, the dayan, Zalman Leventhal, and the ex-kapo Shlomo Kirschenbaum resolved to set out at the next whistle of a locomotive to see what they could discover.

The morning that whistle sounded was sunny if cold, the snow piled high and white except where it met the grime of the street. A short walk from Crematorium III led to a small rise from where the three had an unobstructed view of the unloading platform. The transport that had lured them consisted of only half a dozen cars from which the last of five hundred people were descending. All were male and adult, wore the yellow star on their clothing.

They were also either ill or extremely weak; many, unable to stand, lay on the icy concrete. A pair of officers sat in a staff car passing a flask between them, a handful of *Schützen* cozying up to the flames licking from the mouths of two steel barrels.

"What do you make of it?" Langfus said. "Why no selection?"

"I wouldn't think they'd need one, not this bunch." Kirschenbaum made a grunting noise. "Look at the poor devils, they can barely walk."

"Shlomo is right," said Leventhal. "It's the gas for these, the lot of them. The Krauts are merely waiting for the cremo trucks."

Seconds later, as if on cue, these began rolling up. As each filled, it rumbled off in the direction of Crematorium V and its subdivided gas chamber. But as the incredulous Sonder watched, one after the other took a right turn into *B2d* and its housing barracks.

The three could only stare at each other—D Camp, not death! Not for the moment anyway. Should it prove some sort of aberration, one never knew with the SS, they elected to keep what they'd seen to themselves. At least until the next transport. To jump the gun on something so incendiary would have been as irresponsible as it was hasty.

They only had to wait another day. The train the following morning was larger than yesterday's and composed of a different crowd completely. Twelve hundred climbed clumsily down from the cattle cars to stand blinking in the white winter sun, mainly women and children, the only men a few elderly. They, too, wore the star, but again there was no selection. All twelve hundred were steered away from the death factories and down the path leading to B Camp, their guards showing unusual patience with the slower pace of the aged.

The three witnesses to this observed it in silence, until Kirschenbaum gave voice to what the others were thinking,

"That's it then. We're as good as done for, even us old hands. We'll be lucky, I get the feeling, to see December through."

That Thursday brought with it a freak break in the weather. The temperature managed to straggle into the forties, and come the next day the camp was swampy with melting snow.

At a little past one o'clock, both inhabited crematoria, III and V, erupted in shouts of "*Antreten! Alles antreten!*" as the soldiers storming them hurried from room to room flushing the Sonder out. Coming in the middle of the day, this augured no good. The men formed into rows in their respective courtyards, trying their best not to but fearing the worst.

Abating this fear some, the Germans unexpectedly led both groups out their gates and onto the road. Up to then, it had shown every sign of being a selection, but this was something different, and anything different at this point was welcome. Maybe, the men whispered as they marched, they were merely needed for a special job somewhere.

Both whispers and hope died, however, upon their crossing the empty train tracks and pulling into the yard of Crematorium II. Fifty SS were there to greet them, guns at the ready. Five officers were also present, two from the Gestapo and each *Kommandoführer* of the crematoria, Sergeant Gorges having taken over the duties at Number Three. A couple of these were bent over a list of what could only be tattoo numbers. It was a selection all right, except today the Nazis had taken precautions. There would be no repeat of October 7th.

Not that the Sonder were in any way up for one themselves. They'd spent the last several days girding for this, though despite the report their three workmates had brought back from the ramp, it had yet to sink in all the way that—after eight months of living on borrowed time, quadruple that much some of them—their final hour was at hand, death come for them at last.

Remaining in formation, they awaited the inevitable. An unshaven Gorges, giving every indication he was drunk, stepped forward and ordered those men whose tattoo numbers he read to break ranks and collect at the gate for escort back to their posts. This was a reverse of all previous selections, with those on the list the fortunate this time.

First to be called were the squad's half-dozen medical personnel. Next, its newest additions, the thirty prisoners tagged as replacements in the aftermath of the revolt. Finally, Gorges shouted the numbers of twenty individuals, a reserve to assist, if and when the day came, in the disassembly and demolition of the crematoria. Among these was the preternaturally lucky Kirschenbaum, who'd not only survived the 7th but succeeded afterward in slipping under the SS radar.

This left a hundred and fifty doomed souls already contemplating the manner of death in store for them. Would it be by gas, bullet, or something new? Again, one could never tell what might come crawling out of the Nazi brain.

Soldiers quickly herded these into Number Two's cremation room and locked its doors. A few of the condemned wondered if this was it, despite it hardly being the place for an execution. There was conversation, but it was brief, each withdrawing into the privacy of his own thoughts. The only sounds then were the muted sobbing and random whimper of protestation one might expect of those about to meet their end.

Until the main door burst open and in strode *Kommandoführer* Muhsfeld, a squad of soldiers in tow. Try as he did to project a casual air, his expression was tense, his voice as stiff as his Prussian spine.

"Men of the 13th Sonderkommando! You are about to begin a new life. Today you will embark for the concentration camp at Grossrosen, where you will be put to work in an underground armaments factory. The work is essential to the war effort, which means you'll be well-treated. Trucks will soon be arriving to—"

"Herr *Oberscharführer, bitte!* Please!" Separating himself from the others, the dayan Leyb Langfus halted a few meters from Muhsfeld, his German more than adequate. "We are not children," he told the sergeant, "we know what lies ahead for us. There is no need to insult us with talk of Grossrosen. With your permission, I would make your job easier and speak to the men myself. It will be to everyone's benefit—including, judging from your obvious discomfort, your own."

Taken aback as he was, Muhsfeld didn't show it. It was an outlandish request, even criminal in its impertinence, but his years in the camps had taught him to keep a leash on his emotions. Not that in all those years he could bring to mind a prisoner so bold as to have addressed him in such a fashion.

But as the Jew had intuited, he wasn't entirely averse to the idea of that Jew filling in for him. He was too proud the soldier to embarrass himself with a ruse so transparent even the dullest Sonder had no problem seeing through it. His only reason for taking it on in the first place was that as the Krema's *Kommandoführer* the chore had fallen to him. Fifty words into his patently phony spiel and those words had felt as unclean in his mouth as he'd anticipated.

After looking the dayan up and down, to the surprise of everyone the Nazi nodded his assent.

Langfus turned to face the hundred and fifty. "Brothers!" he cried, spreading his arms." Fellow Jews! It is God's inscrutable will that we now lay down our lives. It has been our cruel fate to have participated in the extermination of our own, and now we ourselves are to be reduced to ashes.

"Many of you ask why, and not alone with self in mind. You ask why the heavens never sent rains strong enough to drown the funeral pyres, bolts of lightning to blast the crematoria. How could God, you ask, have turned His back on His chosen? Permitted the Gentile to lay waste His children?

"It is not for us, however, to challenge God's decisions. As His children, as sons of Israel, we can only trust in and accept them, taking solace that in His omniscience He knows what is best. That in the long term somehow, somewhere, someday, even Birkenau will have worked to our people's advantage."

Most had heard similar from him before, but sensing something new in his voice, listened expectantly.

"Rather than question God, therefore, we should put one to ourselves. What do we, the accursed of the Sonderkommando, have to fear of death? After what we've seen, what we've been forced to do, we ought to take the leaving of this world as a mercy.

"Even if by some miracle we were to be saved, what happiness would that bring us? Our families are dead; in vain would we search for them. Our homes are no more, too, stolen by our neighbors if they continue to stand at all. We would return to our towns and villages only to find ourselves unwelcome, alone, remnants of the men we were, as much like ghosts as those of our loved ones destined to haunt us for what did remain of our lives. For us, the uprooted, there would be neither rest nor peace. We would roam the earth broken men, wishing we were dead."

Langfus seemed to grow gaunter, the eyes behind the black glasses to burn with an invisible fire. He could have passed for a fevered prophet resurrected from the pages of the Bible, sprung from the world beyond to lead his flock back with him. What he said next filled the room with all the power of a call to arms.

"So why not end it here, right now, today? What sense does it make to pile grief upon grief, one mountain of suffering on top of another? Instead of weeping, I say we lift our heads and go forth to meet this Death whom we have come to know so well, this companion who has trod in our footsteps for so long. Let us confront it not as an enemy but a friend, and show the damned Germans how a Jew can die!"

Muhsfeld, because he knew little Polish, had harbored reservations about giving the dayan the floor, until he started noticing the effect his words were having. But for the patter of translation into Hungarian, the place was soon as still as a crypt, not a sob or muttered protest to be heard. Instead of what he'd found upon entering the crematorium—men on the brink of losing it, pale with fright, dangerous with resentment—a calm had fallen over them born of acceptance, as if they'd surrendered to a reality that before they'd resisted.

Still, when a second prisoner rose to say something, he almost didn't allow it. But went ahead and let him, figuring he'd sit him down fast if he saw the mood in the room reverting.

It was Zalman Leventhal, his voice low but head high. "Heed well, you Sonder, what the rabbi would tell you. He is a holy man, and speaks with the wisdom of the Lord.

"His words have moved me to add my small part, to remind you of that October day not two months ago when we should have gone to our deaths with dignity but didn't. We have been living in shame since, but that's not to say we need die in it.

"Look at today, therefore, as not a tragedy but an opportunity: the revolt saw us timid—let this hour witness our bravery. Let us be the soldiers now we should have been then."

To his surprise as much as that of Langfus, when finished Leventhal walked up to him and wrapped him in a hug. He'd once had his doubts about this eccentric emissary of God, the same God that back then he himself had renounced for abandoning His people. But true to what the poor dead Gradowski had tried to tell him, his misgivings about the man had proved unfounded. He wasn't at all the insipid sniveler of religious platitudes, the aggressive proselytizer Leventhal had labeled him. If anything, he avoided the subject of religion. Quirky, yes, and head-strong as a mule to boot, but a parroter of Scripture and advocate of blind submission to God's will he most definitely was not.

What was more, he'd refused to judge or act superior to any but the SS, was as humble, as plain *decent* a human being as Zalman had crossed paths with in this dog-eat-dog place. After getting to know him, he actually came to enjoy the dayan's company, and from there it was but a small step to giving shrift to what he had to say on those occasions when the talk did turn to religion.

Which to his annoyance at first, reluctant as he'd been to admit it, bore more than a little truth. Who was puny man to try and outguess his God, to presume to penetrate the mind, the motives of his Maker? Before long, Leventhal was questioning his own motives, wound up seeing not only the short-sightedness but the petulance behind them. Ultimately, it would be this newfound honesty with himself that led to the recovery of that faith which had played so big a part in his life.

Back was the loving Father he'd relied on since childhood, nor would this have happened without Langfus.

But while it may have made these final months the more bearable, not until now, his final day, did he reap the full benefit of this spiritual renascence of his. With him about to meet his God at last, it wouldn't have done for it to be on less than amicable terms.

He'd been meaning to share this with Langfus man to man, but wasn't good at such things. To make up for not having done so earlier, he not only hugged him now but held it.

"What was that for?" the dayan asked when Leventhal finally let go.

"I guess you could say for opening my eyes. Unclogging my ears. Getting rid of the rubbish that was clouding my brain. But mostly just for ending up a pal, however unexpected."

If not sure what he meant, Langfus nodded as if he was. By then Muhsfeld and his escort had returned whence they'd come. The room would remain quiet as the Sonder again retreated into themselves, not to bemoan their fate anymore but to prepare for it like men. As the two who'd stepped forward to speak headed back to join them, the dayan stopped, as if remembering something.

"Zalman," he said, "tomorrow is a Saturday, you know."

Leventhal looked at him, puzzled. "Yes, Leyb?"

"Are you as excited about celebrating the Sabbath with your family again as I am?"

The next morning, a detail of Sonder boarded one of four trucks and was driven into the woods to the west. In a clearing, they came upon dozens of corpses, which their guards ordered them to load onto the trucks. They quickly recognized some of their comrades from whom they'd been separated yesterday, still in their clothes and all horribly burned.

On the ride back to the crematorium, they were at a loss to explain it. Only later, after the ovens had finished the job so mysteriously started, did they learn what had happened. The night before, the Germans had marched this remainder from the 12th Squad into the forest. There they turned flamethrowers on them, burning them alive. According to one of the detachment's doctors, who heard it from Muhsfeld, this was SS revenge for those casualties they'd suffered the day of the revolt.

Not that this was going to satisfy them. The Nazis had plans for a certain and very special group of others they deemed just as responsible for that day.

With the passing of November, the Political Department had halted the interrogation of the four girls in its custody. To the Gestapo's exasperation, their every effort to extract the desired information from even one of them had come to nothing, and they saw little point in persisting. To do so, in fact, might have resulted in the last thing they wanted; if the four were to die under torture, it would deprive their captors of trotting them out in front of the other prisoners and hanging them.

This the Kommandantur had established early on as the only suitable finale to the affair, for two reasons: to appease a still irate

Berlin, which was expecting as much; and because the punishing of a crime not only so brazen but potentially catastrophic merited a spectacle. To have the guilty perish without fanfare, out of sight in some underground room, would only diminish the seriousness of their offense.

Not only were the sessions in Block 35 terminated but the women transferred from the bunker of Block 11 to cells on the ground floor. These were airier, more spacious, even furnished with cots, and though solitary confinement remained in effect, a small barred window high up in each gave access to the sky. They also received adequate food here, warmer clothing, shoes.

The aim was to allow them to mend some from their ordeal, or enough so they could walk unassisted to the gallows. The less sympathy they inspired among the inmates who'd be watching, the better; the whole point of such a demonstration was to showcase the execution of vicious, self-serving criminals, not pitiable invalids.

This change in their quarters did have its downside, for the prisoner Robota a double one. Their new cells came with a 24-hour guard, these under instructions to keep a close eye on the four, checking on them periodically through a slot in the door to prevent them from escaping the noose by way of suicide. They were also there to put an end to Kapo Kozelczik's surreptitious mothering of this favored quartet of his, which the SS had begun to suspect extended beyond the occasional blanket.

Captivated by the valor of these little more than girls, he'd taken it upon himself to ease their lot when he could. He was even awaiting word from Roza to smuggle her boyfriend into the bunker. Gone now was any chance of that, a realization that not only cut her to the heart but, Noah having unwisely told him what the kapo was planning, might have resulted in Godel's undoing if his protector hadn't been there to see he didn't harm himself.

Nor was he the only relation to the imprisoned women who had people worried. Following the second and final arrest of her sister, the now sixteen-year-old Hanka was inconsolable. She'd lost interest in eating, become dangerously apathetic, was practically sleepwalking through her shifts at the Union factory. She had to be prodded out of bed in the morning and retired to it early, well before light's-out. When she spoke it was in monosyllables or words bled of all emotion. Those close to her noticed with alarm the attention she began paying the electrified fence, sometimes coming upon her just standing there staring at it.

One of these was Marta Bindiger, who didn't like at all what she was seeing from Hanka. Marta had ties with an inmate-physician assigned to the Stammlager's Ka-Be, a Polish Jew named Dora Klein, née Slawka. Having left Poland to study medicine in Prague, where she'd earned her degree, many mistook her for Czech.

A petite woman in her mid-thirties, with a sweet, childlike grin and the youthful face to match, her appearance belied the life of adventure she'd led. In 1936, after joining the Communist Party in Prague, she made for Spain during that country's civil war to practice her profession in the International Brigade. With the victory of the fascists, she fled to Paris. When the city fell to the Nazis, she served in the French Underground until arrested and deported to Auschwitz—where as a member of the main camp's Battle Group, she continued to oppose the enemies of both her race and leftist ideology.

Marta had no trouble persuading her to admit Hanka into the hospital barracks, in which she would at least be under supervision. As it happened, she received more than just that. With the Czech having filled her in on the sad story unfolding, Dr. Klein's heart bled for the teenager, and she took it upon herself to look after her personally. Not only did she see that the child was watched, she kept her close whenever possible, to the extent of including her in her daily rounds as a sort of helper. This also served to divert the girl's mind from her sister.

Hanka proved a surprisingly able assistant, making up in enthusiasm what she lacked in training. She exhibited an innate curiosity for all matters medical. Often, after the day was done, her mentor would invite her into her cubicle of a room where they would drink tea while she regaled her with tales of her own experiences in medicine and the promise the science of it held for the future.

This was but one avenue for insinuating herself as something of a surrogate older sister, and not without success. There were still days when Hanka refused to leave her bed, but others, especially when at the doctor's side, she was almost her old self.

Marta became a regular visitor to Ka-Be, partly to try and cheer the youngster with treasures unclaimed in the Paketstelle, but also to stay abreast of her mental state. Then came the afternoon she showed up with a very special gift, not anything one could eat or wear or even see, but that surpassed any previous.

A nurse led her to Hanka's bed. She was lying on her side, wrapped in the bathrobe Marta had brought her last week. Her eyes were open but glassed over, gave no hint they knew anyone was there.

"Hanka, Haneczka—look at me, beautiful. Can you hear me? It's Marta. I've come with good news."

This had its effect. Slowly, she rolled onto her back. Her expression, however, seemed to say, *How good could it be?*

Marta came right out with it. "There's talk of a pardon!" she cried. "You heard me—a pardon! It's far from certain yet, but there is talk."

Hanka shot out of bed as if yanked out. "A pardon? For my Estusia? When? Who said so?"

"Remember me telling you that Kapo Jakob was on our side? That he wasn't only doing what he could to bolster the morale of the girls but remained on the alert for other ways he might help? Well, just this morning he told me, what with all the other changes the Germans have been up to, they're giving serious consideration to a pardon. How he knows he didn't say, but he sounded pretty confident."

Hanka was beside herself. Unable to stay still, she'd sit then spring up again. "I—I'm—I'm not sure what I am," she bubbled "except thrilled! Beyond thrilled!" She pressed Marta's hand in hers. "Has anybody said when they might be released?"

"That's hard to tell. It could be a while yet. All we can do is be patient, not give up. You have something to look forward to now, Hanka, to live for. I don't want you moping around anymore."

Later, Marta would feel guilty for lying. She would have liked to tell her the truth, but feared that would only have made things worse. She wouldn't have said anything at all if the situation didn't appear to be coming to a head. But to keep Hanka completely in the dark might have backfired, particularly if she were to learn what was really going on from someone else. This way, if that happened, she would have the lie to use as a defense against it.

There was no pardon. She'd made it up. But there was news, and not all of it bad. As the days passed and winter solidified its grip on the land, Kapo Kozelczik's compassion for his most prominent charges likewise strengthened. He made it a point to check on each of them regularly, both to see if they were in want of something it might be in his power to sneak them—which, guards or no, he was able to now and then—and to keep them up on the as yet indeterminate status of their cases.

Not that it took long for these to turn out as expected. Ten days into December, the SS bade him prepare for a quadruple hanging to be staged on the grounds of the main camp's new Frauenlager adjunct. As dismaying as this was, Kozelczik had prepared himself for it. No one, including the four principals themselves, had need of a fortuneteller to show them what lay in their future.

By the time the verdict came down, though, the kapo had hit upon a possible end-run around it. Nothing foolproof by any stretch, but possible. His years as hangman had been quite the education, teaching him not only the techniques of his dark trade but its due process, its legalities. Nor from what he knew of these were the Germans adhering to them.

For a crime of the magnitude of which the women were accused, the crime of treason against the state, the SS of the camps weren't authorized to pass sentence. This had to come from the courts in Berlin, and in writing. Until he had said document in his hands, technically those hands were tied by law. Upon the Kommandantur's order reaching him, therefore, he submitted a statement respectfully declining to take part in any execution unless handled through the proper channels. And further advised all concerned that should they be tempted to proceed anyway, he in his official capacity would be obliged to file a formal protest.

What did end up catching Kozelczik by surprise, aside from his not being shot for his effrontery, was the readiness with which the Nazis acceded to his ultimatum. He'd thought it at best a throw of the dice, more bluff than threat, never dreaming they'd comply, and without so much as an argument. But true to their slavish devotion to the principle of ordnungsgessemer Ablauf, the SS declared the hangings postponed until the requisite clearance from Berlin.

The kapo entertained no illusions as to its coming, but that wasn't what his scheme was about. His hope, aware of the legal and bureaucratic slowness in the acquiring of such a writ, all the more so at this late stage of a war all but lost, was that the Russian Army would reach Auschwitz before it did. This loomed a distinct possibility, too, given that the Soviets weren't that far over the horizon, with some predicting liberation before the year was out.

Marta by now was in regular contact with Kozelczik. He'd filled her in on the German capitulation promptly after sharing it with its four beneficiaries, but though applauding it and him, and dying to pass it on to Hanka, she couldn't without also disclosing the death sentence decreed her sister.

This had led her to make up the story about a pardon. She felt rotten about doing so, but should Esther and the others end up escaping the gallows, what difference would it make how? Or what she had or hadn't told Hanka? With the way the lost little girl had come alive when she'd heard it, it had been a lie worth the telling.

Marta didn't know what to make of the fantastically fat hangman, except for seeing he wasn't the devil everyone thought. Behind the brutish façade, the villainous reputation—the stories to chill the blood—was a man, if this woeful business was any example, with a heart as extravagantly large as the rest of him. To her, in fact, he was no less than an angel come to their rescue. It was Esther who'd engineered the link between the two. In response to his inquiring one day whether she needed anything, she'd made two requests: pencil and paper with which to write a letter to her sister, and his help in getting it to her. To that end, she recommended he deliver the letter to Marta.

The first of several such missives from Esther, their intent was to assure Hanka she was well and in good spirits. And so they did—until the day one came that left the girl in tears. After Marta succeeded in stanching these some, she read it and saw why.

"Dearest Hanka, I have missed you so much, my darling, but never more than today. It hasn't been easy, but I have tried to keep my letters to you positive, not to burden you with my troubles.

"On this longest and somehow loneliest of days, however, I am finding it more difficult than normal. The sunny words just won't come. I sit here listening to the footsteps of the prisoners returning from work, the tramp of thousands of tired feet making for the Plätze. Through the bars of my tiny window, the gray light of dusk filters in. Twilight, if you remember, was always the saddest part of the day for me.

"The sounds of the camp at this hour—the tramping of those feet, the yelling of the kapos, the endless counting and recounting of roll call—all those noises once so hated are now precious. If soon, I'm afraid, to be no more. Not for my ears anyway. Those outside the walls of my prison still have hope for a future, but all I can realistically see in mine is a rope. The companionship of the barracks, the glow of your smile, the joyful cry of "Liberation!" one day?

"I can't help thinking that for me all that is gone, and I want so to live. Oh, Hanka, I cannot tell you how much I want to live!"

The last part of the letter, a little brighter, attempted to offset the first but failed. Marta, after finishing it, felt the urge to weep herself. Not to mention cringe at the damage it might have done her story about a pardon.

It also got her to worrying about the other three; if Esther's state of mind was any indication, there was reason to worry. What questions she had along those lines, though, would have to wait. Kozelczik was wary of making his trips to the Paketstelle too frequent, and neither had arrived at an excuse for Marta to show herself at Block 11.

Days passed before he was back with another letter, this one from Roza. She, too, had entrusted it to Marta, in her case for delivery to Godel. As discouraged as she was upon learning she wouldn't be saying goodbye to him in person, Roza had to thank her stars and the goodwill of her jailer for the chance to do so in writing.

As usual, two *Schützen* accompanied Marta's angel in starched stripes, whether as prisoner guards or bodyguards she never asked. Like before, these planted themselves at the coal-burning stove, this giving the other pair their privacy.

Marta skipped the small talk. "So tell me, kapo, our girls know what's going on, right?"

"Of course. I thought I told you."

"You did. I'm just curious how they are with it now. How they're holding up."

He thought a moment before answering. "They're doing all right, I suppose. For the most part."

"For the most part? What does that mean?"

"A couple of things actually. They know what's going on, but sadly aren't buying into it. Not from what I can tell. Then again, why should they? This stunt of mine you flatter by calling a plan is nothing if not desperate. More wishful thinking, I'm afraid, than a plan. It's been over two weeks; I was hoping maybe we'd have heard from the Russians by now. Their artillery at any rate."

Marta, too, was sweating the Russians, but what he'd just said had her in a more immediate sweat. "You mentioned there were a couple of things. What else should I be alarmed about?"

"I'm not sure alarmed is the word, not yet. However—" Again Kozelczik paused. "It's like this. Two of your friends are handling themselves as well as can be expected, which after what they've been through is no small potatoes. The one named Regina is as solid as they come. Has yet to even ask anything of me. When I am able to supply her some small comfort, she won't go near it until I've promised the same to the other three.

"I've met with her type of selflessness and quiet strength before. Though when I told her of it, she showed little faith my trick would save her —I could see it in her face—she pretended to be all grateful. Is pretending still.

"Same with the other strong one, this Roza with the funny last name. She, too, said she appreciated me trying, but I can tell she isn't optimistic. She's a tiger, she is, that one. Though from the shape she's in the Gestapo put more hurt on her than the others, I get the feeling they could have pounded on her forever and still come up empty. I've been watching her for two months now and can honestly say she's as full of vinegar as when they first brought her in.

"She did go through a rough patch when a visit from her boyfriend fell through, but has since put that behind her. If you ask me, as much as I'm touched by that courage of hers, the SS were smart to put her in a cage. You should see the razor blades she stares at them when they show."

What Marta found as difficult to reconcile as the kapo's big heart was his articulate tongue. To look at him, one wouldn't have guessed him possessed of either. "And the other two?" she asked.

He shook his head. "That, it pains me to report, is another story. The tall one, Ala, is a nervous wreck. She spends a good part of the day pacing her cell. Isn't quiet about it, either; when she's not bawling her eyes out, she's talking to herself. Mostly about herself. And what she's saying isn't exactly complimentary.

"From what I can tell, she's eat up with guilt, takes the blame for not only her own suffering but that of the others. For something else also: did she lose a child when she got here? At the unloading ramp maybe?"

"Yes, a little girl. Rochele was her name."

"That's it, Rochele. She carries on about her, too, something about not putting up as fierce a fight as she could to keep her."

Marta bridled, reflexively making two fists. Whenever she recalled Ala and her stolen child, the hate rose inside her like bile filling a beaker. How many Rocheles in this godless place had been torn from their mother's arms? How many children made to confront the horrors of the gas chamber alone?

"Anyway," he continued, "that's where Ala is. What she could have done to be punishing herself so, I can't imagine. When I sat her down and told her the executions had been halted pending word from the courts, she thanked me for my past kindnesses and trying to help again, but said I needn't paint a rosy picture for her. That she wasn't only unafraid of death but welcomed it."

It was just this that had Marta scared, the threat posed by suicide. As long as the Red Army stood a chance of beating Berlin to the punch, for even one of the girls to give in to despair and end life on her terms, by her own hand, would be inexcusable. Criminal. A kick to the face.

Ala sounded ripe for it, and she feared for Esther, too. It was true that her last letter to Hanka, or at least those sentences about wanting so to live, would rule out her harming herself. But how certain of this could one be? To be ambushed by death, to have it pounce, was one thing—another to sit alone in a jail cell day after day anticipating it, obsessing on it, the suspense and pressure building, until waiting to die becomes harder than the thought of death itself.

"Now the last one," Kozelczik said, "the youngest, that Esther— she's just the opposite. A wreck to be sure, but far from a nervous one. She wasn't that bad off at first, either. Of them all, she seemed the most upbeat at having escaped the awfulness of the bunker.

"But that didn't last. With every day another day closer to the gallows, she began to withdraw from the world, brick herself off from reality, so that now it's as if... as if she's not there. Not all of her anyhow. When I brought her the news of the postponement, I had to repeat it twice more before she responded, and then with so cookie-cutter a smile I'm still not sure she understood. Or was even listening."

He tried but fell short of a smile of his own. "Then again, what with the spot she's in, I'm thinking maybe her disconnect is a blessing."

"A blessing?" Marta's voice mimed the doubt etching her features. "You're not worried that like Ala she's in danger of hurting herself?"

"Hurting herself?"

"Getting tired of it all, the waiting, the strain of it. Giving up and, you know—putting an end to it."

"You don't mean suicide, do you?"

"What else would I mean?"

Here he did manage a smile, if an indulgent one. "What makes you believe Ala is in danger of that?"

"From what you said, how could I not?"

"Let me tell you how, and you can take this to the bank. For if there's one thing I've come to know more about than anything, it's death. I've seen it in all its guises, reflected in a lot of different faces, and experience shows me Ala no more inclined to suicide than you or I. I've looked into her eyes, and it just isn't there. Whatever's chewing up her insides, she's venting it with talk. That's all it is, talk.

"Few her age, trust me, are comfortable with dying, no matter what they might say. Or how heavy their guilt. She'll change her tune, you watch. Probably, should it end up coming to that, the nearer her days get to being her last one.

"As for Esther," he said, returning to her question, "I definitely wouldn't fret myself about her. Suicide is the last thing on that young one's mind."

Marta wasn't going for it. "Not to sound glib, Jakob, my new friend, but if it walks like a duck, quacks like a duck, then it must be a duck. It's pretty clear to me that retreating from reality as you say our Esther has, she's lost any hope she might have had of surviving it. And having lost that, I suspect she——"

"Hope maybe, yes, but not the will, the instinct to survive. I've seen that plenty often, too, men on the scaffold twisting their heads to avoid the noose, or when lashed to a post at the Black Wall struggling to break free. There's something in people which moves them to cling to life when it no longer makes sense to, when even that last shred of hope has been snatched away.

"So it is with Esther. I noticed that more often than not when I dropped in on her, it'd be to find her staring at the window up near the ceiling in her cell. And with such an expression of wonder, it got me to wondering. The other day, unable to resist, I knelt beside her cot. 'What on earth do you see up there, little one?' I asked.

"No reply, so I followed her gaze. Visible through the bars of the window were the upper branches of a tall pine tree, one of a small stand inside the perimeter. 'Is it that tree out there?' I said, not expecting an answer. But she nodded, adding, 'It's amazing, isn't it?' 'It's... it's a pine tree,' I said. She ignored what I suppose, if questioned, she'd have called my cynicism. 'It keeps me company, that tree,' she said, 'in my loneliness, at my lowest.' 'And how does it do that?' I asked. 'It speaks to me. Not in words, but just by being there.' 'Oh, it speaks to you, I see.' Though I didn't, not yet. 'So what does it say, this tree?'

"She'd been looking at me, but now turned back to the window. Her face seemed to give off—how can I put it?—a kind of cloudy light, like the sun shining underwater. These were her exact words: '*I am here*, it says, *I am alive—I am life itself, life eternal*. It tells me not to be frightened, that death is no more than life interrupted.' "

The way Kozelczik interpreted it, and sought to explain it to Marta, was that with death so near she could feel its bony fingers on her shoulder, smell its carrion breath, so enthralled was Esther with life, any life—even that of a tree—there was little chance of her being profligate with her own.

"Besides," he would add "if according to how she sees it death is but a part of life, the one flowing naturally into the other, why try to force it?"

Thanks to the efforts of its SS, Christmas this year was in the air as never before at Auschwitz. Rising conspicuously in a corner of the main Appellplatz was a large and impeccably proportioned forest fir, complete with a silver garland cut from metal foil. At night a searchlight lit it up in defiance of Allied bombers.

Other decorations surfaced here and there, most affixed but not confined to official buildings and soldiers' barracks. Such display was unprecedented, but understandable: against the godless Bolshevik armies again on the offensive, the comforting accoutrements of this most Christian of holidays offered both a welcome antidote and distraction. Plus, with the approach of the Soviets, the Germans were drinking more, this contributing as much to their observance of the season as anything.

With a timeliness some saw as rewarding their embrace of the yuletide, on Christmas morning the camp's top brass received a present that couldn't have delighted them more. Battle Group-Auschwitz, through its agents in the Kommandantur, was the first to hear the bad news. Shortly before noon, a military courier motorcycled in bearing something prodigious in his pouch, the order from the high court in Berlin sanctioning the execution of the Gestapo's four "traitorous" prisoners.

The Nazis promptly set a date for the hangings. Estimating the Russians a month away at the earliest, and to allow themselves time to dress up the proceedings, they picked January 5th as the big day.

Word of the courier and his delivery spread. When Marta heard about it, she dropped what she was doing and rushed to Ka-Be. Thankfully, the news hadn't reached Hanka yet. Dora Klein promised to keep the child's contact with the other prisoners to a minimum, but there was no isolating her entirely.

After the hospital, Marta started working on getting a message to Kapo Jakob, always a delicate process. She needed to know how the victims of it were reacting to this new and horrible development. Two days later, he and his SS shadows were tracking snow into the mailroom. He'd got her summons, he said, but was also there at Esther's behest.

"She wanted me to give you this." He produced a slip of paper from his coat. She took it, but leaving it unread, cut to the chase.

"Level with me, kapo. The four... how are they taking it?"

"The news from Berlin? Better than a lot I've seen in the same straits." Though a spark of pride flared at this last, he wasn't the same Kozelczik she was used to. Vanished was the cautious optimism he'd projected just days ago, in its place a voice as funereal as the look on his face. "They're more resigned than upset, which I guess is only natural. It's not, after all, as if they weren't expecting it."

"Ala, too, and Esther? They're—they're okay?"

"Ala has settled down considerably, as I told you she would. And Esther, after learning of the courier, is mostly back with us again. Read that message of hers and you'll see what I mean."

It was indeed written by someone with both feet on the ground, its tone all-business. "Dear Marta, I know what is in store for me and go readily to the gallows. I only ask that you take care of my baby sister Hanka. Please tell me you'll watch over her after I'm gone, that I may die the more easily."

"She asked that you make it official," Kozelczik said, handing her a pencil. Caught short by not only the note's request but its finality, she, too, was brief. "Esther, I promise," she jotted on the piece of paper, "that I will never abandon Hanka." She underlined "never."

As grieved as the note left her, Marta felt, too, for the man who'd brought it. He stood slumped before her, the soul of dejection.

"Hard as it may be, Jakob, try not to let what's happened get the best of you. We both feared there was a better than good chance of it coming to this; you can, if nothing else, console yourself knowing you did everything you could to prevent it. In fact, you've done more than a body could reasonably be—"

He raised a hand to quiet her. "I don't doubt you intend well, dear, but you're mistaken. As disappointed as I am, it's not what I've tried and failed at that has me upset so much as what I'm going to find myself doing ten days from now. Already the thought of it sickens me. Come January, my duties will require me to loop ropes around the necks of four heroic young women whom it would be no exaggeration to say I risked my own neck to save.

"The gallows will have produced five corpses that day, the fifth being that fragment of what is left of the man I once was."

After locking up the Paketstelle for the night, Marta went to see about Hanka and found her asleep. But not the healthy sleep of the physically spent—so upset was she earlier, said Dr. Klein, she'd had to give her a shot to knock her out. Somehow, she'd heard of the warrant from Berlin, and there was no calming her. The girl went out of her head, would later confess to remembering nothing of the next days.

In the course of them, her maniacal wailing and tortured sobs were to become a fixture of lager life. They weren't continuous, but neither were they confined to Ka-Be, often reaching half the camp. This had its predictable effect on the inmates. Less a cry of this world than one of pure anguish from hell, it was a sound to lay bare the nerves, raise the hairs on one's arms. It haunted the prisoners by day and woke them at night, but thanks to Dora Klein's diligence and ample stock of tranquilizers, its frequency wasn't what it might have been. Not that she could be expected to keep her patient doped up twenty-four hours a day.

There was one prisoner, of course, it affected more than any. Kapo Kozelczik noticed the change in Esther right away: like Ala before her, she grew agitated, restless, the serenity she'd enjoyed earlier gone. During Hanka's outbursts, she, too, would get vocal, weeping noisily in shared pain. More worrisome yet, even with her sister quiet she'd taken to walking her cell, mumbling to herself, falling to her knees and clasping her hands together as in prayer.

With the days tumbling rapidly on their way to January 5th, whether this was out of concern for Hanka or fear for herself was difficult to say. All Kozelczik knew was that as hangman he had a potential problem on his hands, Esther giving every sign of having become unhinged. To have to drag her hysterical to the gallows was a scenario neither he nor the SS would find acceptable.

Marta, meanwhile, at the hospital daily now, was having as little luck as Dr. Klein at getting through to Hanka. The child had fled deeper than ever into that cocoon she'd spun for herself before Marta had rekindled hope in her with her white lie about the pardon. Now there was no rousing her from her lethargy. Refusing to acknowledge anyone, she lay in her bunk staring silently at the ceiling, until the next fit took hold of her and she'd commence to screeching for her sister, for someone to save her sister. At the more violent of these, it taking two people to restrain her, she'd have to be sedated.

She didn't know if it was because they sprang from someone she'd grown to love, but Marta had never heard anything so disturbing as the howls ripped from Hanka when in one of her frenzies. Contained in each was all the pathos and pain of Auschwitz, the very essence of the place, a distillate of every vileness perpetrated here in the five years of its vile existence. It was as if through this tormented teenaged girl, all the victims living and dead that had passed through its gates beneath the mocking *Arbeit Macht Frei* had been given a single voice with which to express their agony, their outrage.

Awakened by the crazed Hanka in the middle of the night, Marta would lie in her koje listening with a combination of pity and foreboding, sad for the wretched creature behind the screaming, but also tense with premonition. For there was a balefulness to these episodes beyond mere lament, especially coming when they did in the night's stillness. As the disembodied, ghostly weepiness of them splintered the quiet, rose and fell on the black air, they seemed to be announcing what everyone knew was just a matter of time, heralds of an offense few could bring themselves to admit was near.

Or as Marta lying sleepless in the crowded solitude of her barracks read it, the selections at the ramp may have stopped, evidence of the slaughter been whitewashed over, the SS lost some of their appetite for murder, but the Vernichtungslager wasn't done with them yet. It had at least one more gauntlet to run its captives through, one more atrocity to enact.

It was only fitting it be foretold, if not by one of its upcoming victims, then someone bound to same by ties of family and blood.

1945

Winter

As different as the two processes were, the destruction of the crematoria had several points in common with their construction.

The difficulty, for one, involved in tearing them down was in direct proportion to the labor and time needed to build them. It had taken half of December to finish the job, and that with it confined to Crematoria II and III; Number Five was left intact to deal with the dead continuing to arrive from the barracks.

Additionally, just as it had been Jews forced to assemble these houses of murder, so were Jews given the tasking of dismantling the things. Teams of Sonder, on a rotating basis, were each split into two crews of twenty men, one per crematorium.

The final bond connecting the razing of them to their conception almost three years ago was a study in contrasts, reflective of the sea change the course of the war had taken. In 1942, with Nazi military might and ambitions at their highest, the blueprints for Birkenau's death factories were drawn up with their architects confident these were but the first of more such installations to come, to be used in turn, when the Jews were disposed of, against the Russians and other subjugated peoples.

Now with those same Russians approaching Birkenau not in cattle cars but tanks, the Germans were bent on making it appear there never were any crematoria.

To the few prisoners outside the Sonder who knew what was up, the analogy that emerged was hard to miss: the deconstruction of those unholy temples to Nazi terror was but a portent of the Third Reich's as a whole. Once invincible, unstoppable, victory all but assured, the Wehrmacht and the SS were in irreversible retreat on all fronts, their war and extermination machines grinding to a halt. Just as the walls of his and his henchmen's death mills were destined for collapse, so one day soon would the entire rotten edifice of Hitler's evil empire come crashing down.

In keeping with their fabled thoroughness, the Germans weren't content simply to blow up II and III and be done with it. First, they had to remove everything that even remotely smacked of what they'd been up to; this was what had stretched the demolition into weeks. The ovens had to be taken apart, their components cleaned and oiled, then packed for shipment. The generators that had sparked the fires were detached and also packed, along with the ventilating Exhators. The disemboweled brick furnaces that remained would later receive a bundle of dynamite each, the coke rooms doused with gasoline the better to burn. The fans that had powered the forced-daft systems in the gas chambers were ripped out of the walls, and the induction shafts by which the pellets of Zyklon-B had entered those chambers disconnected and trashed. The fake showerheads were unscrewed and discarded, too.

The elevators to the oven rooms took almost as long to disassemble as they had to install, and with the rest of it were crated and marked for delivery to the Grossrosen and Mauthausen camps. Retrieved, too, were the crucibles and other equipment in Crematorium III's gold forge. Even the wooden benches and wall hooks in the undressing rooms were gathered and burned.

Nor did the Nazis overlook the blackened hulk of Crematorium IV. It also was cannibalized of impugnable parts, and only then it and the other two rigged with dynamite. The explosions shook both Birkenau and the Stammlager. Most inmates, unaware of what they signified, argued, hoped, prayed it was Russian artillery. The truth, when they learned it, was almost as cheering.

While the Germans were busy ridding Birkenau of its homicidal past, at Auschwitz they weren't in the business of demolishing but building. A small project to be sure, yet one close to the SS heart: a brand-new gallows on the grounds of the lager housing the Union women. At its completion on January 2nd, it occupied a prominent place center-rear of the Appellplatz; too prominent, indeed, by half, being that much larger than needed. Rising above the barbed-wire fence at its back, a flight of a dozen steps rose to a spacious platform from which two tall, heavy hanging trees grew, united at the top by a long crossbeam.

Those prisoners mystified by it were promptly set straight by the others; like their comrades awaiting execution in Block 11, they, too, had been found guilty, their sentence to be party to that execution. The death warrant from Berlin had become the talk of the Union, and all too familiar lately with the enraged state of their *Blockführer*, the women suspected Hössler of locating the gallows where it was. How better to punish not just the four but his entire disloyal commando?

Nor judging from the dimensions of this pinewood monstrosity planted in their midst was it to be a simple hanging. If they knew their commandant, and provided as was likely he was to play a major role in the proceedings, they knew also he wasn't about to shy from making as sensational a show of these as he could.

From her hospital bed, Esther's sister Hanka could hear it going up, the angry whine of the electric saws, the pounding of hammers. But though she knew what it was, it didn't affect her as one might have thought. Instead of launching into her usual wild allegro of woe, she covered her ears, screwed her eyes shut, and afraid to open either, retreated deeper into that safe, hermetic part of herself where the world couldn't follow. There she would remain, more insensible to her surroundings than ever, no matter what her two nursemaids did to try and coax her out of it.

"This is worse," Marta said, "than when she used to wake half the camp at night. Is she responsive at all?"

Dr. Klein didn't try to hide her frown. "Off and on, but mostly the former. If I badger her long enough, I can sometimes get her to look at me, but that's about it. She isn't exactly catatonic, but not far from it. And only getting worse."

"Does she eat? Is she eating?"

"If somebody feeds her, and not always then. She's already lost weight, can you tell?"

Marta felt powerless. Never far from her mind was her promise to Esther that she see Hanka taken care of. "So what would you suggest, Dora? There must be something we can do."

"Nothing I can think of—except not to give up on her. I've a hunch time is the cure for what's ailing our girl, and after this sadness with her sister is over, with help she'll be able to put it behind her and move on."

Marta prayed they'd all be able to put it behind themselves, and soon. The strain of living with what was coming wasn't getting any easier. She could only guess what Roza and the others in Block 11 were going through, what maggots the noises of the hammers and saws had set to squirming in their brains.

She'd have given much to intercede in their anguish, to offer what solace she could, and in person. To picture them pining alone in their cells, without a shoulder to cry on, an ear to confide in—women, who over the months and in perilous pursuit of a common cause she'd become more than just friends with, had trusted her life to—drove Marta to the same despair that until recently Hanka had howled. For all the good it would do to dream of visiting them in their jail, though, she might as well have fantasized about busting them out of it.

In the meantime, that enemy the calendar inched forward, the days unreeling in slow motion. Not that prisoner nerves were the only ones wound tight. A certain German was suffering, too, none other than the spiteful Hössler, the source of his particular torment the weather.

The suspicions of the Union women proving correct, he'd been granted the honor of superintending the executions, but barely was the gallows up than a storm to rival any this winter blew in. And had yet to slow down. The snow had piled in places twice as tall as a person, the only part of the scaffold visible its two hanging posts and their crossbeam. The event would have to be pushed back, the only question being how far back.

Having waited months to avenge what he saw as his betrayal by those cossetted Union girls of his, the SS captain's patience was gone. He'd practically begged the Kommandantur for the privilege of organizing then presiding at the hangings, and was slavering at the mouth to get on with them. As if his temper weren't foul before, he now raged like a captured jungle cat in its cage—at the excessiveness of this latest storm, the Polish winter in general, his ungrateful commando, the gutter race that could birth such trash.

"If it were up to me," Hössler let it be known loudly and often, "I'd start with those four then hang every bitch in the Union. Then every Jew I could until the Russians rolled up."

What worried him was that the storm wouldn't permit him time to gild the lily, to make of the executions the grand ceremony he'd envisioned. Should it drag on much longer he might have to settle for something quick, a blah mediocrity of a hanging no more memorable than any other. But in the very early morning of January 5th, he stepped outside to a glorious sight. What had been an impenetrable ceiling of clouds was now exposing patches of sky, these broadening rapidly to unleash a blinding-orange dawn upon the world.

The *Hauptsturmführer* would pause long enough to drink this in and thank the gods, then with a vengeance set to work.

Before the sun had risen the width of a hand above the horizon, a dozen prisoners were shoveling the gallows free of its snow, a bulldozer clearing the Appellplatz. Two anti-aircraft searchlights were wheeled to the corners of the yard farthest from the scaffold, the boulder-sized eye of each leveled unblinking at it. This all that could be done for now at the site, Hössler had plenty to attend to elsewhere. Leaving a *Sturmmänn* in charge, he hurried off with three privates in tow.

Vanished was his foul mood; no one had seen him this smiley in months. In spite of realizing he hadn't a chance of reaping his revenge on schedule, today, he was happy having to postpone it only twenty-four hours. About all that could have dampened his spirits was another round of clouds, but though he must have glanced aloft half a hundred times that day, he didn't spot a one.

The sunrise of the 6th was as gaudy an orange, the sky as unblemished a blue. Hössler was all over the place, frantic to make sure everything would be ready and all the players in the drama to come, save the convicted, were properly rehearsed. He motorcycled a constant loop that morning and afternoon between the Frauenlager, the SS storehouses and barracks, Blocks 35 and 11, his own rooms. A spinning top of orders and advice, his energy infected not only the soldiers under his command but those prisoners drummed into the effort. Even they worked as if imbued with his urgency of purpose, so that once the sun was on its way down, he could congratulate himself on a job nearly done.

At 2:45 that afternoon, their Blockälteste and her assistants rousted the Union night shift from its bunks. After rushing the women through coffee, these ran them in and out of the latrine with even more speed than usual. Both the haste and irregular hour boded ill, as did the presence of a platoon of SS. That their routine was staying more or less intact, however, did ease their concern some, if not sufficient to dispel the feeling that something wicked was in the works.

What this was revealed itself when they entered the Platz for roll call. The gallows at its rear was an alarmingly different one from yesterday's. A collective moan escaped five hundred throats, as many pairs of legs stumbling to a stop. It took every threat their guards could hurl at them to get them moving again, and even then few could bring themselves to look at the thing.

Hössler had draped it in bright scarlet cloth, creating an enormous splash of red against the white of the snow. Broad swatches of it hung from the handrail attached to the stairs, and from the platform to the ground, all pinned in place to prevent them from flapping in the wind. Even the vertical beams of the hanging posts were swathed in scarlet. As if this weren't enough, two huge bolts of the same cloth covered the fifteen meters of electrified barbed wire that ran behind the scaffold, its juice turned off for the occasion.

The message delivered by so overdone a display was twofold. First, of course, it announced to the women cowering before it that the hour they'd been living in dread of was here. They'd been pried prematurely from bed and barracks to witness the killing of the four heroines.

The second part of the message was a symbolic one, and there wasn't a prisoner who didn't read it loud and clear. Though it was to be a hanging and no blood would be spilled, Hössler's choice of red as a motif was his way of saying that this production of his, make no mistake, would not lack for violence.

Soldiers surrounded the grounds, some holding back dogs whose mad barking added its note of terror. A dozen female SS roamed the ranks of women, demanding those with lowered heads raise them. By now the sun was skimming the rooftops to either side, the lengthening shadows portending twilight. Opening the *Hauptsturmführer's* passion play, two *Sturmmänn* ascended the gallows steps and marched stiffly to opposite ends of the platform. Resplendent in black tunics adorned with silver braid, their ceremonial chrome helmets polished to a mirror sheen, they brandished snare drums also trimmed in silver. Soon each was beating a roll in ten-second intervals, rapid yet soft, the sinister metric of the classic military execution.

To this dirge-like cadence, a squad of soldiers advanced slowly down a central aisle. At their head was the bony figure of the feared *Scharführer* Anton Taube, in their midst two of the condemned, Ala and Regina. Both were coatless in the cold, clad in identical gray smocks. They walked without faltering, staring straight ahead. Flanked by the SS in their helmets and jackboots, they looked shockingly frail, not unlike a couple of children.

Trailing them and their escort up the steps to the platform was the hangman Kozelczik. The guards, after dropping the two off beneath the nooses suspended from the crossbeam, faded into the background where they remained at attention. Kozelczik tied the girls' wrists behind them before he, too, backed away, his expression impassive next to the glowering Taube's.

Many couldn't watch, not even at this early stage. The uniformed harpies dashed among the rows shouting, "Eyes front! Pay attention! Look to the front!" Sticking the butts of their whips under the women's chins to force them up, they beat any who resisted.

Ala and Regina, aloof to the commotion, stared with a sad longing at something in the distance. To those who'd worked with them, bunked with them, shared food and swapped stories with them—who'd dreamed aloud with them during the hours before lights-out of the day the Russians would come, the day of liberation—what held the two's attention and the reason for their sorrow was plain. They were absorbed in that unfenced world beyond the barracks and barbed wire where not only freedom but the future lay, a future they'd once hoped had a place in it for them.

This was too much for the crowd. What had been a few muffled sobs swelled into a chorus sodden with grief. But also bristling with anger. The SS ringing the Platz gripped their rifles tighter, their female counterparts glancing uncertainly about.

Staff Sergeant Taube strode to the front, his face skeletal. "Enough!" he bellowed. "Stop your sniveling! For every tear, I promise twenty-five lashes!"

At this he smiled, a repulsive gash of a smile, like a wound that had reopened. "And as you should know by now, Taube is a man who keeps his promises."

His audience, unable to stifle it entirely, did choke back its pain, just enough of it enduring to enhance the graveside solemnity of the snare drums. The rays of the dying sun, meanwhile, falling full now upon the platform, bathed each person inhabiting it in a garish gold. It was no accident the stage-managing Hössler chose then to make his entrance.

He didn't climb the stairs, he levitated up them, the effect derived from the black woolen cape that hid his legs. A silver chain clasped it at the neck. From beneath it peeked a black uniform with every button and bar gleaming, knee-high boots polished to a shine, and as a final touch fur-lined gloves of black leather. His silver-embossed officer's cap might have passed for a crown.

He motioned to the drummers to sheathe their sticks, then facing the yard, swept his cape back with a flourish. Drawing a scroll of heavy paper from his tunic, he unrolled it and began to read. It was the death writ from the court in Berlin, the words stabbing in the frigid air.

"By unanimous decision of this highest and most honorable tribunal, it is decreed that the following occupants of SS *Konzentrationslager* Auschwitz-Birkenau, for endangering the security of the Reich with their actions, be put to death for their crimes:

the Jew Ala Gertner
the Jew Regina Safirsztajn
the Jew Roza Robota
the Jew Esther Wajcblum

"We leave it to the discretion of the camp authorities to determine the appropriate time and place for this order to be carried out. In the name of the German people and their *Führer*, let justice be done. Heil Hitler!

"Signed: Judge Roland Freisler, President, People's Court
Countersigned: Dr. Otto Georg Thierack, Reich Minister of Justice."

Hössler lowered the paper and glared at the women below, his gaze as malevolent as if he'd penned the words himself. In fact, he had edited a good many of them out, omitting the legalese and other trappings that for his purposes he felt diminished the document's impact. Now, having read it with what he trusted was sufficient vitriol, he was ready to get on with the theatrics.

He retreated to one side, relinquishing the stage to his hangman. Kozelczik went rapidly to work. He took hold of one of the nooses and slipped it over Ala's head, clinching it tight around her neck. Then Regina. The touch of the rope jolted each back to the here and now, eyes darting confusedly about. When Ala's landed on Hössler, she didn't speak the words, she flung them.

"Today you hang me, you piece of Nazi filth, but your hour will come! Remember me, this face, when they put the rope around *your* neck!"

She was about to say more, but at his boss's angry signal, Kozelczik grabbed that end of the rope draped across the overhead beam and started pulling hand over hand. She rose in three jerks, legs kicking, after which he secured the line to a hook in the floor.

Regina was groping for some sort of last words herself, but her heart wasn't in it. Whether cowed by the noises of her friend strangling to death next to her, or even now too mild-tempered to give in to the adversarial, all she could come up with was, "I pray that every one of you winds up getting her liberty."

Then she, too, was hauled into the air. Death didn't come easily for either. They lacked the weight that would have made the end quicker; despite the recent increase in their rations, the bunker had left them more bone than flesh. For an eternity of a minute, they wriggled on high like two freshly caught fish, mouths gulping hungrily for the breath that wasn't there. Their clogs having gone flying, it took another minute for their bare feet to surrender the last convulsive shudder and go limp.

Throughout, the SS demons in skirts were back at it, shrieking at their charges to keep their heads up. Hössler had made it clear he wanted this pig commando of his tuned in to this part as to no other. What no one noticed, prisoner and Nazi alike, distracted as each was by the death struggle, was the hangman's reaction to his handiwork. In violation of what was expected of him as executioner, Kozelczik had turned his back on the scene. He may have had to hang them, but he wasn't going to watch them die, let the Germans try to make him if they were feeling up to it.

As this last act of the tragedy played itself out, an uncontainable keening went up from the Union, a sound of utter helplessness and heartache. Many ignored the blows from their guards and refused to look. Some who did were so sickened, they vomited. A few fainted. At the very least, scarce was the woman who wasn't weeping, if not openly for fear of Taube then on the inside, her invisible tears no less the scalding.

Towering above them all was the magisterial person of the *Hauptsturmführer*, his eyes contented slits as he soaked up the misery from below like an insect nectar from a flower.

Eventually, he backed toward the two corpses and stood between them, laying a hand on each. To the prisoners, his black gloves suggested a pair of carrion birds. His features, too, were transformed, having made the leap from the blissful to an exaggerated concern; he could have passed for someone on the brink of tears himself. Instead of crying, however, he let out a long, emoting sigh.

"My dear children, I both feel sorry for you and don't. Here you have two friends whose loss has clearly devastated you, two wonderful girls, I'm sure, their untimely deaths having left a hole in your lives. It's always a shame when those too young to have lived long are taken from us. Even more so when there is no good reason for it."

With an affectionate pat to each, Hössler slid from between the swaying bodies and returned to the fore of the platform. "This absence of a reason," he continued, an edge to his voice now, "the senselessness behind these deaths, is what tells me to pity you not. For here one must ask, Just who is responsible for them?

"It is not we SS, who had no choice in the matter. Laws were broken, and we as instruments of the law were duty-bound to see the transgressors brought to justice. No, you and only you are to blame for the deaths of these two beautiful young people, you who aided and encouraged them in their folly."

Here he affected amazement. "Do you think I and my Gestapo associates are stupid? We know more of you were involved in the theft of the gunpowder than the four arrested for it. And even more, who while not playing an active role, saw what was going on yet did nothing to stop it. Now look what has happened, and all because of your complicity. I can only imagine the guilt working on you. Did you not realize, are *you* so stupid, that any plot directed against us, your rightful masters, was doomed to fail?"

Most of the women understood little of what he was saying, but from what German they recognized, they figured out this Moshe Liar of theirs was trying to blame them for the two corpses swinging above. Outrageous as this was, it was also to be expected. One of the oldest of Nazi tricks consisted of transferring the onus for their crimes onto their victims. Or in this instance, those who identified with same. This both shifted culpability, and in keeping with that sadism they so delighted in, rubbed salt into whatever injury they'd inflicted.

Given the great wrong he saw the commando having done him, Hössler was all about this last. His aim in soft-soaping it at the outset was just that, to soften it up, sucker it with kindness. That had been the carrot—now came the stick.

"*Doomed, I repeat, to fail!*" he roared, his mouth a lipless scowl. "Any who would be so rash as to test us"—he pointed to the carnage behind him—"will end up like these, that I guarantee!"

Strutting stiff-legged back and forth, he dared those below to meet his stare. "Do not make the mistake of supposing the war over!

It is not, nor will it be until Germany says it is. The Third Reich is too powerful to be defeated outright. It will still be here long after you are no more.

"It knows also who its enemies are, from the barbarians advancing on its borders to they who would undermine it from within. Now that you've shown what you're made of, where your loyalties lie, be warned that we're watching you as never before. Should you be so foolish as to allow treason once more to tempt you, you would do well to keep this in mind."

Like the chameleon he was, he again changed tack and confessed in his best wounded voice how deeply his audience had hurt him, he who'd bent over backward to be more of a father to the commando than a warden. At the same time, he cautioned them not to misinterpret his leniency for weakness.

"As much as I care for each and every one of you, am willing to start afresh, to forgive and forget, I promise no mercy—*none*, do you hear?—to any who would stray from the straight and narrow."

To demonstrate how much he did care, and as a token of his good faith (but in reality, to settle the women down some prior to their heading off to work), Hössler announced a *Zulage*, or extra ration, was waiting for them at their barracks. With that, wrapping himself in his cape, he floated down the stairs.

Of even greater welcome than the slab of bread and sliver of horse meat sausage handed each woman before the hike to the Union was not having to undergo a second round of hangings. According to their Blockälteste, the execution of the criminals Wajcblum and Robota was a privilege reserved for the day shift.

To the relief of these, who'd learned from a kapo what had been scheduled them, an air-raid warning was in progress upon their return to camp. Instead of the Appellplatz, they were ushered to their barracks, where regulations required they remain until the all clear. Which to their further relief had yet to sound by lights-out. They assured each other it was too late by then to go anywhere.

They weren't in their kojen ten minutes, though, before the siren went off, with the blockova and her crew hard on the heels of it in full shouting fury. Driven outside into the arms of a detachment of SS-Frauen, they were bundled into a column. The mercury hadn't registered above freezing all day, and was dropping; hands and feet went quickly numb, but cruelly the heart continued to feel. All too aware where they were headed, at the command to move forward—what else could they do?—they moved forward.

Upon their reaching the Platz, the gallows anchored their gaze as with a steel bolt. They were no more able to avert their eyes from it than prevent what it was there for. With the searchlights zeroing in on it, the cloth festooning this instrument of death didn't just show red, it glowed red, as if emitting a radiance of its own. It hovered in the air before them, a blazing, crimson islet adrift in a sea of black.

Half-prodded toward it by their guards, half-drawn to it entranced, like the mouse to the snake, the five hundred approached the scaffold with wary steps.

Unlike that afternoon, the Union wasn't the only group in attendance. But for the human guinea pigs from the medical-experimentation block too crippled to walk, the entire Frauenlager stood at attention in the snow. Along with them was a collection of prisoners, all female, from throughout the camp, anyone Hössler could think of who might have had contact with the girls. His revenge only partially slaked, he was bent on jamming as many as he could into the yard for this encore performance.

He had his Union bunch, of course, crowded up front; like the night shift preceding them, he wanted them to hear their two friends' every strangled gurgle, their last dying gasps. Since he couldn't hang the lot of them as he would have liked, they'd at least get a taste of what it was to perish at the end of a rope.

Other than the numbers he'd amassed and the inspired touch of the searchlights, he saw no reason to deviate from the day's presentation. What hadn't crossed his mind, but couldn't have pleased him more, was the excitement the dark of night was bringing to the occasion. The pageantry, the tension, the terror—all were elevated by night's witchy feel to a pinnacle unmatched in the earlier hanging. No way would the scene have been as mesmerizing, true, if missing the arc-lamp power of the searchlights, but without those other spells the hands of the clock were weaving, it wouldn't have been the same. Hössler made a note to self should the future call him to execution duty again: when it came to putting on a show, no noon could compete with midnight for sheer effect.

If pleased with this afternoon's success, tonight he was walking on air. Under a sky full of stars instead of sun, his preparations weren't just meeting, they were exceeding expectations. The only problem was, with everything going so right, he couldn't shake the feeling something was bound to go wrong.

Which, since he was after no less than perfection, something did. As their SS escort led the final pair of condemned down the aisle toward the gallows, neither was playing her part as he'd have liked. Esther shuffled along on unsteady legs, arms outstretched precariously at her side as if for balance. One second her expression appeared glassy, troubled, the next carefree and lucid. Once, she stumbled and almost fell, just managing to stay afoot.

She'd obviously been drugged, which while not a calamity, was enough of a wrench in the captain's works to make him nervous. There was no predicting what she might do under the influence, and if there was anything he desired less at this point, it was unpredictability intruding on his carefully programmed script.

Everybody assumed it the Germans who'd doped her, but in fact it was her hangman. A quick check on her an hour before convinced Kozelczik that Esther wasn't going to make it through this without help. The weeks of torture, then of waiting in isolation for this awful day—along with her sister's cries having done their number on her—had in the end proved too much. With the ticking time bomb that was the death watch winding down, she lay in a tearful heap on the floor of her cell, begging for her life, rubber-legged with fear.

Such behavior was hardly new to the kapo, nor had he ever seen it turn out anything but ugly. Rather than have the Nazis get rough with her when the hour struck—or the task fall to him—he decided to take action. Somehow he got a cup of tea down her in which he'd dissolved a couple of tranquilizers. When *Scharführer* Taube came to fetch her, she went without a whimper.

Accompanying her on this last, short journey of her life was her old dance partner and girlish confidante Roza, but so out of it was Esther she didn't seem to notice. Not that it mattered much, for as they had with the other two, the SS kept them separated. There would be no show of solidarity, no handholding on the death walk.

Like Esther's, only worse, Roza's face still bore the marks of the beatings lavished on it. There was no swelling anymore, but neither the cuts nor even all the bruising had faded, while the most severe of it—her new nose, the broken teeth, the rearranged jaw—were permanent. The shapeless gray shift she wore concealed the rest of the damage, with the exception of a pronounced limp.

But as if to trivialize these wounds, and the manhood of the Germans whose every effort had failed to break her, she made an effort herself to hide her condition. Her back broomstick-straight, chin up, she walked despite the limp with as military a bearing as the *Männer* on either side of her. Eschewing the disengagement Ala and Regina had seized on, she refused to insulate herself from the grim goings-on. If anything, she gave every sign of glorying in them. Her ravaged features were as contemptuous and proud as her step—pride in the crimes for which she'd been sentenced, contempt for those about to carry it out. This rankled Hössler to the same degree as Esther's sorry state.

Not that he was to stay rankled, courtesy of a sudden incredible embellishment to his playbook that he couldn't have written into it even if it had occurred to him. It declared itself upon the doomed two reaching the stairs to the gallows. Esther would need a soldier to assist her up the steps, and no sooner had she taken the first one than a long, shrill scream knifed out of the blackness.

So loud was it that it drowned out the roll of the Nazi snare drums, continuing afterward to echo in the night air. Following it was an only too familiar sobbing that had each person in the yard asking herself how on God's earth the poor thing could have known. Was it coincidence or something more that had led Hanka, confined in Ka-Be, well out of sight of the Frauenlager, to vocalize her despair at the very instant her sister set foot on the scaffold?

The child couldn't have timed her *cri de coeur* better if she'd been there, and with foreseeable effect on those who were. A chill distinct from the January cold snaked down every spine, the assembled women gaping at each other with wide, frightened eyes. As if their nerves weren't shot already at the tragedy unfolding in front of them, now they had the supernatural to contend with. Fear slipped into the Appellplatz on swift, padded feet, circling the prisoners like a pack of hungry wolves.

Hössler grinned like a wolf himself at his luck. Just because he hadn't scripted it, didn't mean he wasn't going to mine so serendipitous a gift for all he could get out of it. He held back until the deranged sister's unsettling serenade had dwindled to nothing before gliding up the steps and onto the platform.

It was different this time all right. The air crackled with an electricity that hadn't been there this afternoon. The *Hauptsturmführer* discovered an extra bounce to his swagger, a mordant glee to his voice missing when he'd first read the warrant from Berlin. Was it the night, the searchlights, the bigger crowd? Did it matter? The input of the leather-lunged banshee Jew surely hadn't hurt. After finishing the court's edict and tucking the scroll away, he nodded to Taube, who clicked his heels smartly and advanced to the edge of the pine.

"*Pulverraum, vortreten!*" the sergeant blared. "Powder room, step forward! *Nach vorne!* To the front!"

No one moved. Testily, he repeated the order, whereupon Rose Greuenapfel, Ilse Michel, Inge Kutzvor, Genia Frischler, and the two replacement members of the crew collected tentatively in the main aisle. A group of SS women pushed them forward until they formed a row directly beneath the gallows. Hössler looked on, beaming. With the Union night shift no longer carrying a Pulver detail, he'd been denied this pleasure earlier.

Upon arriving at her noose, Esther had broken out in song of all things, a soft, almost inaudible ditty she'd often crooned to her sister when Hanka was a toddler. A remembering smile on her lips, she sang it to her again as if back at their home in Warsaw, singing it as if the last dozen years hadn't happened.

As someone bound her hands and slid her own noose over her head, Roza fought not to listen. Her friend's refrain had brought the water to her eyes, and the last thing she needed in the minutes left her were tears. That wasn't how she was meant to exit this world. After battling her whole life, she mustn't let herself melt into a puddle at the end. She had something to say still, a duty to say it, something these women brought here to partake of yet another Nazi atrocity had a duty to hear. She couldn't let her emotions interfere with that, not the sadness she was feeling for Esther, or even more dangerous, for herself.

For while all rock-hardness and chutzpah on the outside, within she was anything but. Suppress it on the surface as she had, there was no exorcizing the loss, the regret eating at her insides. How wasteful to die at twenty-three! To have one's dreams, so many of one's years stolen. All she could do was try to block the regret out, gut it up and block it out, banish it along with Esther's song from her head. One battle was left to fight, one last appeal to the living on behalf of the dead.

"Remember this night!" she shouted, her voice a sword. "And the faces of the SS you see here! The day is coming soon when they will be the prisoners, you the free. You must survive to that day, use your freedom to help bring them and the rest of the murderers to justice. Only you can speak for the dead, only—"

She felt movement to her right as a groan went up from the women, turned to see Esther rising in the air. But though tearing her eyes away, she was too late. The rest of what she'd wanted to say froze in her throat.

The next thing she knew, unseen hands tugged the rope tight around her neck, its bristles pricking her skin. Then footsteps receding rapidly, and she realized only seconds remained her.

"*Nakam!*" yelled Roza Robota, head lifted high. "Revenge!" she thundered with all the fierceness at her command. Like Hanka's scream earlier, the word echoed off the sky, seeming to sound on even after she herself was no more.

Hössler's routine after was a repeat of the day's, the same preening imperiousness, the same speech, first the carrot then the stick before signing off somewhere in-between. But unknown to him, both the retaliation he sought against the commando and the submissiveness he would restore to it were mitigated—if only some, but mitigated regardless —by the louder-than-life Hebrew valediction *nakam*. The word grabbed the women and wasn't letting go; it reverberated in their skulls, saw them through not only the Nazi's subsequent harangue but was something they could take back to their huts with them.

Lying in their bunks that night in the dark, it wasn't toward Hössler's spite and petty *Schadenfreude* that the women's thoughts gravitated, or the wantonness of the hangings themselves and the sting they'd inflicted—but rather the courage of a frail-looking and defenseless young girl, who even as the noose was about to squeeze the life out of her, had the temerity to spit her final breath at her executioners.

A courage that in the morning, when yanked from their beds by the reveille bell, was still with them, keeping their spirits as up as could be expected. Then again, strangely, it would be a day for raised spirits, this in spite of what greeted them at roll call. The Germans had left the bodies hanging and would for three days. There they dangled, twisting gently, dusted with snow, like broken puppets drooping from their strings.

But as the five hundred huddled in the freezing pre-dawn grayness, dully answering "*hier*" as their tattoo numbers were called, a rumbling reached them from the east. Visible through the gaps between the barracks, a bank of angry clouds darkened the skyline. Too far away yet to say just how serious, it was a storm and a bad one, the thunder an uninterrupted roll. Groaning, they prepared for a misery of a morning, for they still had the Appell to get through, then the jog to the factory and work. All they could hope for was that it be a snowstorm; drenched to the skin by wet needles of sleet wasn't the best way to begin the day.

As it happened, it would develop into the finest start to a day any could remember. For in the midst of their Appell, most picked up on something that didn't make sense. The clouds hadn't only failed to grow larger, they were gone, but the thunder continued unexplainably to growl. How could there be thunder without clouds?

By the time the Frauenlager was behind them, and they leaving the limestone path to file through the Metallwerke gate, there wasn't a woman who didn't know the answer. And wasn't struggling to hide her excitement from the guards.

It wasn't thunder at all, but the rolling cannonade of battle, of artillery, the Russians. It was the Red Army on the move, slugging its way west, who knew how many miles off but close enough now that you could hear its big guns. Just, but you could hear them. Upon the column entering the factory, these were silenced by the racket of the machinery, and later at shift's end, as they headed back to camp, to everyone's disappointment the evening was a peaceful one.

But wasn't to stay so. That night in the barracks, after lights-out, the grumbling from the east began anew. The dark came alive in a ferment of whispers, until the door to the Blockälteste's room flew open and without her saying a word, the hut fell quiet. Some time would pass, however, before the usual snoring. To a woman, its occupants lay awake warmed by the noise of the guns, then gradually, deliciously, allowed it to soothe them to sleep, like children borne away by a mother's lullaby.

*   *   *

Marta Bindiger was having as much trouble making her mind up as anybody. In the wake of the hangings, the Russian artillery continued to pound. At first this was encouraging, morale high, but soon the prisoners were asking questions. Since proclaiming themselves days ago, the guns were still no more than a distant booming. Why weren't they getting closer? Had the Soviet advance stalled? Was the Wehrmacht holding its own, or worse, winning the battle raging beyond the horizon?

The fear was that this man-made thunder might return whence it had come. Having fought their way this far, there was no guarantee the Reds would be able to stay, much less keep pushing forward.

By the 13th, however, the dawn sun wouldn't only set the sky on fire but bring a surprise to ignite the soul. With its burning head just poking into view, what before one had to strain to hear now packed a startling punch. To the silent hallelujahs of the thousands standing at roll call in Auschwitz-Birkenau, Monowitz, and their surrounding subcamps, the artillery had got briskly louder. If the Russians had been bottled up, they weren't anymore.

To everyone's greater thrill, as the day progressed so did that loudness; the front was drawing nearer even as they listened. Come mid-morning the guns went mute, but would resume that night, accompanied by huge, circular bursts of luminescence like giant flashbulbs popping the length of the eastern sky.

Jn the morning, all three camps were abuzz with a rumor so shocking it outdid the arrival of the war at their doorsteps. Every conversation opened with it: the entire complex was to be emptied by forced march to the west. Two more days, and by virtue of repetition and a transparently frantic SS, the rumor had solidified into a *fait accompli.*

Few were the prisoners by then who hadn't resigned themselves to it, leaving them a decision to make. Would it be better to obey orders and embark on this exodus into the unknown, or try to avoid it and stay put? To go, in January, with the temperature routinely dipping below zero—sparsely provisioned if at all, and in their weakened condition—would be to risk a trip a good many had little chance of surviving. Not to mention their having to abandon any thought of liberation, no telling for how long. Maybe forever.

Then again, what awaited those who opted to sit tight? Who attempted to hide when the call came, or played too sick to answer it? If an evacuation could be said to have a point at all, it would be that no witnesses were left behind to document Nazi crimes. The Germans no doubt had plans to shoot or otherwise dispose of any who were either genuinely ill or simply malingering. If one *were* able to hide, though, if only until the coast was clear…

This was the predicament facing Marta, aggravated by her having Hanka to look out for. In the end, this was what settled the issue, when on the morning of the 17th she went to check on her in Ka-Be and see what Dora Klein might have to say.

The news wasn't good. "Hanka," said the doctor, "has yet to show the slightest improvement. If anything, she's worse. Hasn't got out of bed since the death of her sister, sleeps the day through now. I don't know what to do."

Marta tried to keep it positive. "As you said once before, doc, for Hanka to be Hanka again isn't going to happen overnight. I see patience as still the best medicine for her. Unfortunately, the SS may have something to say about that.

"If there should be an evacuation, if the rumor is true, in your opinion is she up to it? I've been leaning toward taking off myself, but I'm not about to leave without her."

"Oh, there will be an evacuation. That I learned for a fact yesterday. An officer was here and said so, came to inform me the sick in Ka-Be wouldn't be going anywhere. That and... something else," she said, suddenly hesitant. "Something you ought to know."

"What, Dora? Go on, spill it."

"He ordered me to draw up a list of the Jewish patients. The Jewish patients only. He's supposed to be coming by today to pick it up."

Marta knew what that meant and reached a decision then and there. Indeed, there was no longer a decision to be made. When the time came, she and Hanka were quitting Auschwitz if she had to hoist the child on her back and carry her out.

Before returning to her hut, she asked Dr. Klein what she planned on doing.

"Why, I'm staying. I've no choice. What kind of physician would I be if I didn't?"

Marta began preparing for the journey that day, gathering what food and extra clothes she could. Nor was she a moment too early. By the following night she was ready—and so were the Germans. At nine o'clock, the Stammlager exploded in a tumult of shouts and running feet, soldiers descending on the barracks and herding their inhabitants toward the gates. Even if they were hoping to, most of the inmates weren't given the opportunity to hide.

Marta was lucky in that, bag of provisions in tow, she was able to sneak off before it came her block's turn, and by avoiding the camp streets reach the hospital undetected. Hurriedly she dressed Hanka in multiple layers of clothing, but while the teenager went along with this, she balked at anything further. It took Marta several tries before she could get her up and out the door.

With her continuing to resist, she thought about trying to find a hiding place after all, but the machine-gun fire ripping the night made her think again. What could it be but SS murder squads at work? At an auxiliary gate, a bottleneck of mainly female prisoners had formed. Nazis with flashlights were conducting a selection, turning back any deemed too frail for the trek ahead. Those who qualified, Marta and Hanka among them, were handed half a loaf of bread and shoved out the gate.

It had stopped snowing hours ago, but a vicious wind cut through their ranks, the women fearing if they didn't get a move on, get the blood flowing, they might freeze where they stood. Most didn't have even a blanket for protection, much less a coat. Some wore rags wrapped around their feet instead of shoes.

The Germans waited until the column was four thousand strong before shouting it forward. The snowy ground shone a neon-white beneath the moon, the night almost as bright as day. Still, it was slow going, the wind pushing people back a step for every three they took. Hanka fought Marta every one of those steps; she wasn't walking so much as letting herself be alternately pushed and pulled.

The longer they marched, the deeper seemed the drifts. Its guards began cursing at the floundering column to pick up the pace. "Faster, you dogs! You lazy Jew bitches, faster!"

Soon after that the first shots rang out.

Marta figured these merely goads to keep the momentum up, until she came across a woman face-down just off the trail, the blood pooled beneath her black in the moonlight. More corpses appeared. The SS weren't only shooting those who could go no farther but those lagging. This last was scary, for with Hanka still uncooperative, the two were slipping steadily to the rear. Marta had to double her efforts—death walked with those bringing up the rear.

Their objective was the camp at Grossrosen, but not only was it a hundred and fifty miles away, the soldiers had only a vague idea how to get there. The plan was to plod west until they hit a railroad track and follow it to a station. Which was how two days later they arrived at the town of Wodzislaw and its switching yard. The bigger part of the three thousand prisoners left alive were marked for a transport to the huge Ravensbrück concentration camp for women, with the rest to continue, also by rail, on to Grossrosen.

By then the bread issued them at Auschwitz was gone, as were but a few crumbs of what Marta had been able to scrounge beforehand. Nor were there any rations at Wodzislaw. Word of a train, though, lifted their spirits. The prospect of giving those blistered, frostbit feet of theirs a respite compensated them some for their empty bellies.

But this was only to prove a different kind of torment. The women weren't loaded into boxcars but open wagons, wedged in so tightly there was no room to sit or even fall down. Later, they wouldn't only sleep but die standing up.

For two days and a night they rode the rails deep into Germany, the snow melting when it hit their heads and shoulders then icing up again, coating them in white. They could no longer feel their feet, but it hardly mattered, propped up as they were by the press of bodies. With no choice but to answer the call of nature on the spot, what excreta they were still capable of without food and water froze their shoes at night to the floor. The dead remained vertical, eyes open in accusation, as if to demand of the living how they could have let such a thing as this happen.

Marta and Hanka never made it to Ravensbrück. They were among the six hundred detrained at Neustadt-Glewe, one of its satellite camps. Here they received a shower and delousing, a fresh set of stripes, and most miraculous of all, a bowl of hot soup. Neustadt-Glewe was a labor camp devoted to one industry, an underground factory for the manufacture of airplane parts. It was overcrowded and muddy and alive with lice, but there was no crematorium or other evidence of murder. From the stories told them later of the ghastly inferno that was Ravensbrück, the new arrivals counted themselves fortunate.

That the two weren't assigned labor right off was a good thing, even with the starvation rations allotted idle prisoners. In her state, Hanka wouldn't have been able to work anyway, a situation that if she were to survive needed to change. Marta plunged into the task with her usual energy, caring for her as she might a sick toddler. She fed, washed, held and cuddled her, sang her to sleep at night, but also got tough with her when toughness was called for.

Until with as satisfying a sense of accomplishment as she could recall, Hanka began to come around. Slowly at first, almost shyly, a word here, a smile there... but with her and Marta finally put to work in February, the girl, if not herself yet, was getting there.

Marta manipulated it so they would be on the same shift. From six in the evening to six in the morning, they riveted metal plates onto airplane wings. The plates were heavy, the nights long, and it felt as if they had more lice on their skin than food in their stomachs. But each day brought them closer to The Day, and this kept them going. This and the increasingly balmy weather of approaching spring, that as it did every year, but never more than this one, not only warmed people's bodies but brought hope to their hearts.

Yet the nightmare wasn't over, death ever near. Not long into April, the factory was shut down in the middle of the day and the camp put under Blocksperre, all inmates confined to quarters. It was still in effect the next morning, with no word from their keepers why it had been called. The prisoners paced behind locked doors in a wallow of fear, sweating over what the Germans might be up to.

The artillery that had been a low rumble for a week was now loud. Were the Nazis readying a massacre to prevent their Jews from falling into Allied hands? It would have been easy to set the huts on fire, an outcome that would have surprised no one.

Then on day three, through the cracks in the wood, a peculiar sight greeted those watching from the blocks fronting the main gate. Some of their guards had shed their uniforms in favor of civilian mufti, and with suitcases in hand were making for a truck. Inconsistent with the barbed wire, the mud, the monochrome gray of the place, the two SS females among them sported brightly colored dresses.

It was a scene replayed throughout the day, until by sunset there wasn't a soldier to be seen, the gate wide open.

A few of the bolder prisoners decided to investigate. Breaking out of their barracks, they came back moments later with the electrifying news that every German was gone. Soon the kitchen block and various storage areas were crawling with people. Their jailers hadn't left much, but what they did dazzled: a roomful of old bread, another of turnips and some potatoes, an enormous cache of dried vegetable shavings that had formed the basis of the inmates' soup.

After eating their fill, and afraid the Nazis might change their minds, some elected to brave the black night beyond the gate. Too depleted even to consider this, the majority were content to sit and see what tomorrow might bring.

Marta and Hanka awoke in the morning to a ruckus of motors, men shouting. The youngster pulled the other to her, rigid with fear. "It's the Germans!" she groaned. "They—they've come back!"

Marta wasn't so sure. "Let's find out. Or better yet, you stay here. I'll be back in two shakes."

When she returned, all she said was, "It's not the Germans." And smiled. Hanka let out a whoop, and together they joined the others running toward the men in the unfamiliar brown uniforms and bowl-shaped combat helmets. A mud-spattered tank and three half-tracks sat idling at the camp entrance, prominent on each a painted red star.

It was May 2nd, 1945, and just like that they and the mob of ragged, malodorous scarecrows gawking at their Russian liberators were no longer human garbage, but human beings again.

After a week, the Soviets relinquished control of the camp to the Americans. With death no longer dogging them and on the road to recovery, the question for the saved became, What to do now? Or more immediate, Where to go? For those whose families were no more, who had nothing to go home to, the decision was at once made simpler and more complicated. Hanka was one of these, convinced that for her Poland held only sorrow.

But if not Poland, where? She remembered a prisoner who'd worked the same table as she at the Union, a Belgian always bragging about how special her country was. Belgium seemed as good a place as any to try, and she went to Marta with it.

As Hanka with Poland, she had scant faith that anything but emptiness awaited her in Czechoslovakia. She, too, took to the idea of Belgium, especially after learning of a rest camp for survivors set in the Ardennes forest. The Americans had requisitioned buses to take the ex-prisoners wherever they wanted, and in a matter of days the two found themselves in the majestic, wooded hills of the Ardennes.

Marta was to stay in Flander's fields for the rest of her life. After falling in love with a young Brussels man, she was made Mrs. Marta Cigé. Hanka's destiny as well was to take an unexpected turn there. While at the rest camp, Marta had enlisted the aid of the Red Cross in tracking down any of the Bindiger and Wajcblum families who might have made it. As she'd feared, with regard to hers the search yielded nothing, but to Hanka's shock her eldest sister turned up in Palestine.

In late 1939, Sabina Wajcblum with her boyfriend Mietek had fled Warsaw and the SS for Soviet-occupied eastern Poland, never to be heard from again. Everyone had presumed her dead, but over the phone in the Red Cross office Sabina explained how she and Mietek had escaped across the Baltic Sea to neutral Sweden, and from there over time to Palestine—and suggested, since they were the only blood each had left, that her baby sister make aliyah herself.

The girl was reluctant to part company with Marta, who'd become as much sister as savior. But strong as the cord binding them was, with Marta's marriage the time had come to cut it. In the spring of 1946, Hanka arrived by ship in Tel Aviv and reunited with her long lost "Saba." Some years later she was married herself, her husband's business ultimately taking them to Canada.

But despite the distances that ended up separating her and Marta, be it the length of continental Europe then the width of the Atlantic Ocean, never in all the decades that ensued did she come close to losing contact with her lifesaver and best friend.

Others outlasted the camps, some against even longer odds. In the week leading up to the evacuation of Birkenau on January 18th, Shlomo Kirschenbaum and the rest of the Sonderkommando expected the SS hammer to drop any day. By then the Russian artillery had crept so near, one couldn't only hear it but feel it through the soles of one's shoes. Kirschenbaum watched the Germans like a hawk that last week, trying to scent their intentions, read what was in their faces, but so wracked were those faces with anxiety, lack of sleep, and alcohol, there was no deciphering them.

What he did have no problem seeing was the total breakdown in discipline among his fellow Sonder. In what would have been inconceivable just a month ago, orders were obeyed sluggishly if at all, maintenance and cleaning of the remaining death house spotty at best. Bodies were allowed to stack up for days, and not even the SS acted as if they cared. The camp as the onetime kapo knew it was coming apart in front of him.

At 3:00 in the afternoon of the 18th, the commando's last hour looked to have arrived. The writing on the wall had appeared days before when its sixty members were put to work dismantling Crematorium V and loading the imputable pieces onto trucks. Due to its unsophisticated layout and the number of men involved, this hadn't taken long. After wrapping the job up at 3:00, the sixty were escorted out its gate for what had to be the final time, heads bent, shoulders stooped, feet dragging, the walking dead.

But instead of being led to their extinction, they were brought to the *B2d* lager... and dismissed. Simply dropped off and forgotten. Glancing at each other in disbelief, they quickly dispersed, disappearing into the faceless masses of D Camp. So preoccupied were the Nazis by this point, so fixated on distancing not only their captives but themselves from the Russians, they allowed the most damning witnesses to their crimes to get lost in the shuffle.

That night, still puzzling over the gift of anonymity bestowed them, the misplaced Sonder followed the herd out of Birkenau into the subzero semi-darkness of a full moon. Behind them, they could hear the explosions leveling the last of the crematoria they'd somehow outlived.

Not that all of them cheated death. The mortality that marked the death march, its killing pace, the killing cold, the itchy trigger fingers of the guards, took the same toll on the Sonder as it did the other prisoners. Shlomo Kirschenbaum, however, wasn't among these. He and the rest of those in his caravan still hanging onto life surfaced via open freezer-train at Mauthausen.

The large Mauthausen concentration camp in Austria acted as a magnet for the mass of prisoners streaming west before the Soviets. Consequently, it had little space and even less food to offer, though as yet no shortage of either order or discipline. Kirschenbaum hadn't been there but days when during one of the incessant roll calls, an officer roared up on a motorcycle, stood before the assembly.

"All prisoners of the Birkenau Sonderkommando," he shouted, "step forward!"

Kirschenbaum all but jumped out of his skin. Heart pounding, he stole a quick peek to either side. Earlier, he'd spotted several familiar faces in the crowd, all cremo men, but from what he could see none were budging. The officer repeated the command, and still no response. After a third, he strutted up and down the rows of men peering hard into eyes, trying to intimidate those he was after into exposing themselves. Kirschenbaum was trembling as much out of fear as from the cold, but luckily the death-dealing motorcyclist gave up before reaching him.

None of the Sonder would sleep easy thereafter. What with the incriminatory numbers inked on their forearms, the fake names they'd assumed were flimsy comfort. Impossible to gauge how deep the Germans would dig to make up for their oversight of January 18th, few were those who believed they'd heard the last of it. Again luckily for Kirschenbaum, or so he thought, some days after the incident he was one of two thousand prisoners selected for transport to the subcamp at Ebensee. The farther removed he was from the inquisitive atmosphere of Mauthausen, the safer he felt.

He would soon see his error. The sole purpose of Ebensee was to furnish slave labor for the excavation of vast tunnels in the surrounding hills in which to house various armaments to protect them from Allied aircraft. In twelve-hour shifts night and day, the shoeless inmates hacked at the frozen earth, their daily sustenance a cold "tea" made of leaves and tree bark for breakfast, at noon three-quarters of a liter of hot water infused with a few dehydrated vegetable bits, and at night five ounces of a crumbly something supposed to be bread. Each hut, built to hold a hundred men (there were no women at Ebensee), contained seven hundred or more, the lice so thick they swept in visible waves across the floor.

By the time Kirschenbaum arrived, corpses lay everywhere, the camp enveloped in an unspeakable miasma of death and human feces.

Though work on the tunnels was halted not long after, people continued dying by the hundreds. As an ex-Sonder in better shape than most to begin with, Kirschenbaum held on. When American forces at long last entered the camp on May 6th, he was one of those able to welcome them standing up.

After weeks of convalescence, he grew strong enough to strike out on his own. With his parents, wife, and little boy dead, nothing remained for him in his hometown of Heidelberg, even if he could see himself returning to live in Germany. He did have an aunt and uncle in America, however, willing to help him start a new life there.

In July, financed by Jewish charities, he departed London on a ship bound for New York City. During the voyage, as he had since before leaving Austria, he hoarded bits of food and hid them—under his mattress, in drawers and closets, behind the grates of air vents, in his clothing. To the amused sympathy of those in his adopted land, a month later he was still at it, but eventually came to recognize his obsession for what it was and that would be the end of it. From then on, he led as normal a life as his memories would permit.

Some nine thousand of the evacuees from Auschwitz-Birkenau wound up at Mauthausen. Many would breathe their last before the

Allied armies could get to them, but not all died at the hands of the SS, or from cold, hunger, and disease. Winter saw a mixed bag of prisoners pour into the western camps, including the ex-kapos and collaborators now shorn of the protection they'd enjoyed under the Nazis. Eager to take advantage of this were their surviving victims, or the friends of those who hadn't.

High on the list of a lot of these was the rapacious Kapo Schulz of Auschwitz infamy. Unlike his almost as revolting girlfriend Black Klara, who died en route to Ravensbrück, he made it alive through the ice and bloody snow, but was not to last a single day at Mauthausen.

Officially, he was never admitted. The camp sat on the crest of a hill overlooking the town of the same name. A steep road wound to a bathhouse through which each new inmate had to pass for a shower and delousing prior to entering the main grounds. Schulz's exhausted, starving column reached this hill after sundown. Three thousand strong, it would take a while to process, enabling those who'd singled him out to exact a justice long overdue.

All through the march, its guards had shielded Schulz, but at the bathhouse were replaced. His executioners quickly cornered him and beat him to death. Already dozens of others, too far gone even to attempt the hill, had lain down in the snow and were shot. How much notice could another body attract?

The prisoner Eugen Koch would also meet his end at Mauthausen. He was found in one of the latrines with his trousers pulled down and his throat cut. The two instruments he'd used to seduce Ala Gertner were resting atop his chest—his tongue and his penis. Schulz and Koch had fended the Grim Reaper off during the long, lethal flight from Auschwitz, only to perish for past crimes once they'd reached their destination. They might have saved themselves if they'd simply stayed put, but who was to say the sword of Jewish revenge wouldn't have caught up with them even then?

With some exceptions, the inmates who did decide to risk avoiding evacuation made the better choice. Reprisals weren't lacking against those who refused to fall out, but these were isolated incidents; shootings did occur, in all three camps, but not as a part of some grand SS strategy. The bombast of the old Möll Plan was revealed to be the baseless threat it had probably always been.

The morning after the fateful night of the 18th, Dora Klein ventured out of the Stammlager's Ka-Be to reconnoiter the situation.

With nothing having come yet of the roster of Jewish patients the Gestapo had demanded, she wanted to see how many soldiers might be left. To her relief she spotted few, and the next day not a one. The watchtowers, the main gate, the guard stations all were empty.

That the Nazis had fled was reason to rejoice, and not. Before leaving, they'd turned off the power permanently, and no electricity meant no lights or heaters. They'd wrecked most of the plumbing, too. Klein and another doctor quickly organized foraging parties from among the nurses they still had and the stronger patients. Their targets were first the kitchen, then the Prominenz blocks, the SS barracks and hospital, and any warehouses the Germans might not have picked clean.

They set out equipped with laundry bags and the carts that had been used to ferry rations. The initial haul was encouraging, among it a pair of cast-iron stoves, a hefty supply of wood and coal, some medicines, three hundred pounds of turnips and potatoes, and several multi-gallon containers of water frozen solid.

But such bounty wasn't to last; on a subsequent attempt, the carts returned with next to nothing. By then hundreds of the hollow-eyed half-dead roamed the camp, shambling skeletons in rags, searching for anything that might prove of use. Those who could no longer walk crawled on their bellies like so many giant worms, fouling the snow behind them with blood and their own waste. Corpses lay everywhere, both indoors and out. Even if the living could have mustered the energy, the icy ground was too hard for the digging of graves.

In Ka-Be, men and women were dying at a rate Dr. Klein had never experienced, nor was there much she could do about it. After four days and despite the strictest rationing, the medicine and potatoes were gone, the turnips almost. The stoves were a help but there were only three of them, one per each barracks still housing patients; even during the day these failed to raise the temperature above freezing. The only water now came from heating the snow, and it swimming with particles of dirt.

Diphtheria and pneumonia stalked the halls, invisible killers, but worst of all were the dysentery wards. The filth there was indescribable. Few were the sick with the strength to leave their beds, the excrement frozen an inch thick on the floors.

On each person's mind, when he wasn't asking it aloud, was a question that grew daily more urgent: where in the name of all that was merciful were the Russians? For three days following the dash from the camp, the crash of the artillery was louder than it had ever been, punctuated off and on by the faint burp of small-arms fire. The German Army in retreat packed the roads outside the wire. Wave after wave trundled past day and night, tanks, armored cars, horse-drawn 88's—soldiers in trucks, on motorcycles, but mostly on foot. They trod in silence, tired, dirty, the picture of defeat, until one day they were gone and would stay so. The noise of the guns trailed after this parade of the vanquished, was soon as it had been weeks ago, a morose grumbling in the distance.

To those waiting to be rescued—what else could they do but wait?—the war had passed them by, much as the world had for years ignored them in their torment. They kept telling each other the Russians would be there any day, but in their hearts few could bring themselves to believe it. Too often had the lunatic monster that was the Vernichtungslager made a mockery of their expectations, of rationality itself, distorting what should have been into something improbable, perverse.

The only visitors to show up were those birds of ill omen, the raven. Nor with the unattended-to bodies piling up was it any mystery why.

For once, the prisoners' cynicism was to betray them. In the early morning of January 27th, the sun not yet free of the horizon, a reconnaissance patrol in white parkas from the 1st Ukrainian Front Division scaled a small hill to behold a sight they weren't sure what to make of. Three miles away on the snow-covered plain below them stretched row after row of low, rectangular buildings enclosed in a perimeter of barbed wire. The Russians studied it through field glasses but could detect no activity. An hour and a half later, larger patrols descended on what they were to learn was the concentration camp Birkenau, named after the preponderance of birch trees in the area.

What had confused them was the immensity of the place. Since crossing the Polish border they'd come across their share of such facilities, but never one so gigantic. And just down the road yet another, smaller if no less hideous. At both sites the troops were swarmed by mobs of weakly cheering, living cadavers, gray wraithlike figures with hairless scalps and huge eyes, so impossibly thin none looked capable of standing. They didn't resemble human beings so much as inhabitants of another world, a planet of insect-men all long, bony appendages and bulging eyes.

Hands reached out to touch the Russians as if to confirm they were real. Others waved scraps of red cloth in the air. The men had seen this before, but many wept all the same, partly out of pity, partly from the shared joy of the moment. It was something one could experience a hundred times and never get used to.

Among the throng to greet them at the Stammlager was Dora Klein. Three months later, with the Wehrmacht disbanded and Allied victory in Europe formally declared, she would go back to practicing medicine in that place on the map she missed most, her beloved city of Prague. But her idyll wasn't to be a permanent one. In 1951, her egalitarian spirit undiminished, she was put on trial by the repressive, Soviet-sponsored regime of Czechoslovakia for speaking against the state, and imprisoned for three years. Upon her release, she returned to the country of her birth and set up shop as a physician in Warsaw.

Rose Greuenapfel and Mala Weinstein, who'd also evaded the march, were to find basically the same destinies as each other though departing Poland in opposite directions. After liberation, upon learning her entire family had been wiped out, the one would emigrate to America and in lower Manhattan become Mrs. Rose Meth, starting a family of her own. In answer to the genocidal mania of Hitler and his Nazis, she would give each of her three sons the middle name Dafka, Hebrew for "despite."

Mala by contrast headed east, arriving by illegal ship in Palestine. There she joined a *kibbutz* and like Rose fell in love, but upon marriage and with the support of her husband chose to retain her maiden name. Her kin, too, had been destroyed in the camps, and with a defiance similar to her friend's would preserve their memory as a Mrs. Weinstein. Mala also had children, and the source of her greatest pride was their being born *sabras*, native Israelis.

Jakob Kozelczik would also remain in Auschwitz. The SS emptied Block 11's cells, but to his surprise, considering all he'd seen, left its kapo behind. Afraid that vengeful prisoners might come after him, he barricaded both doors to the building and hid out for the ten days it took the Red Army to show. Not that one soul, even with the Gestapo gone, so much as came near that erstwhile house of pain.

Allegations against him were quick to arise, though, and the Russians arrested him. Amid the cries for his blood, however, enough ex-inmates came forward in his defense to move the conflicted officer in charge to place him in protective custody. There he would sit for a month, after which, under the auspices of the Red Cross, he was sent with a shipment of prisoners to a displaced-persons camp inside Germany. From there, he would wangle passage on a freighter to Palestine, but the ship was intercepted by the British, and its three hundred illegal immigrants interned for two years on the island of Cyprus.

When at last he did set foot on the ancestral soil, Kozelczik's notoriety followed him. He settled in the town of Holon, got married, and fathered a son. To earn a living, he formed a traveling act that featured feats of strength and other circus razzle-dazzle. He was soon a popular draw, often playing to packed houses. Whatever the Germans had taken from him, the shows he'd put on for their amusement in Auschwitz had given him a taste and flair for the limelight.

Then during Hanukkah, 1949, an article appeared in the newspaper *Haaretz* accusing him of war crimes and collaborating with the Nazis. The Polish and Czech governments clamored for his extradition. Yet again, eyewitnesses flocked to his defense, this time with hundreds of letters citing not only his many deeds of kindness in the camp but the lives he'd saved at risk to his own.

The Israeli government denied extradition, with *Haaretz* printing a retraction. But the damage was done, the stain on his name there to stay. The public stopped coming to his performances, would even accost him in the street, spit on him. He couldn't get a job and started drinking. His wife left him, took their son.

Forced to go on the dole, Kozelczik rented a room in Holon, rarely leaving it. In 1953, he was discovered dead in that room of a heart attack at the age of fifty-three. Or that's how his obituary read. In fact, to those who knew him for the man he was, that big heart of his hadn't given out, it had broken in two.

As for the person he'd served so well if unwillingly as hangman, Franz Hössler ended up stuffing a steamer trunk full and exiting Auschwitz in a covered truck with other SS. Their destination was the Dora-Mittelbau camp in Germany. Come March, with the American Army closing in on it, he supervised the evacuation of prisoners out of Dora to the smaller Bergen-Belsen. Except Bergen-Belsen was no longer small. Built to house seven thousand, by then its population had soared to in excess of seventy thousand. Without the food and shelter to accommodate them, people were dying faster than they could be buried.

When British forces entered the camp on April 15th, there to welcome them were fourteen thousand naked corpses rotting in the spring sun. Fourteen thousand more were to die in the next week, too far gone to save.

They also came upon *Hauptsturmführer* Hössler dressed in muddy stripes, if compromisingly well-fed, trying to blend in with the survivors. Appointed deputy commander of this den of horrors on his arrival, he'd since bathed his manicured hands repeatedly in blood. Irrespective of his crimes at Auschwitz, he and forty-four other SS were brought before a British military court in what was dubbed the Bergen-Belsen trial. Convicted in November, he was executed a month later.

As opposed to his sneering prolixity at those hangings he'd conducted, when it came his turn at the gallows he didn't have a word to say.

Another who'd figured conspicuously in the martyrdom of the four young Jewish heroines did manage to elude the rope, but whether he escaped justice altogether was never determined. *Unterscharführer* Broch of the main camp's Block 35 was last seen in mid-April leaving the Sachsenhausen subcamp of Hennigsdorf by motorcycle, headed southeast to Berlin and his family. By then the Soviets had entered the city's eastern suburbs prior to encircling it and commencing the climactic Battle of Berlin. Whether he was killed in transit, died in the battle, or lived to acquire a new identity would never be known. No body ever revealed itself, nor the name Karl Friedrich Broch appear on paper again.

An old antagonist and fellow Gestapo officer of his did sidestep justice, or at least that which he had coming to him. Arrested on three different occasions after the war, *Sturmbannführer* Wilhelm Boger escaped the first one and went into hiding for several years, then was released a second time for lack of evidence and on the basis of his "sound and irreproachable character" as the West German court put it. Finally, in 1965, twenty years after the fact, he was named a defendant in the second Auschwitz trial held in Frankfurt. Convicted of multiple counts of murder, accessory to murder, and torture, with West Germany having no death penalty he avoided execution and was sentenced to life in prison.

Where he died in bed, unrepentant, at age seventy-two. He maintained to the end that as a military man in wartime he was honor-bound to do as his superiors dictated—that as he was fond of reciting with more of a smirk, it was said, the older he got, "*Eine Befehl ist eine Befehl.* An order is an order..."

This became the all but universal rationale, whether public or private, for those Germans charged with war crimes, from the highest ministers of the Nazi state to the humblest *Schützen* on lager duty. The opportunistic *Oberscharführer* Erich Muhsfeld, who in the Schutzstaffel had sought the power and prestige denied him as a lowly baker's helper in civilian life, would put up one of the more aggressive of these defenses at his 1946 trial in Krakow.

But the Polish judges would have none of it, nor for a public court waste any time avenging the sergeant's many victims. Condemned to hang by the neck until dead, the sentence was carried out ten days later.

Yet as common a defense as it was, to anyone familiar with the violent fanaticism of his anti-Jewish ideology and proven commitment to the extirpation of the hated *Rassenfiend* root and branch, it would have come as a surprise to see the pathological Otto Möll trying to squirm out of responsibility for his past. Yet that was what the arch-exterminator of Birkenau would do, so much for his self-congratulatory denunciation of hypocrisy.

With the Soviet hammer-and-sickle bearing down on his Gleiwitz domain, and after dispatching its population westward with an underling at the helm, Möll would bounce through a succession of camps before assuming command of the Dachau *Unterlager* of Kaufering. When that, too, was menaced by an American push to the south, he led its inhabitants on a frantic forced march to the mother camp, leaving the snow red behind him.

On May 1st, Dachau itself was liberated and Moll taken into custody. Nor did his captors have to probe very deep before realizing they had a true fiend in their possession. Not until November, though, in front of a United States military tribunal, did he take his place in the dock with the rest of the defendants in the Dachau trial. Where instead of standing up for the beliefs he'd lived by, incriminating as they'd have been, he not only insisted he'd acted under orders and against his will at Birkenau but denied ever killing anybody. The only involvement he would admit to was conducting the transportees to the gas chamber, then cremating them after.

Never had he personally, he said, either by issuing the command or with his own hands, taken a Jewish or any life.

But the Americans knew all about both his official duties and individual excesses, and had the witnesses to prove them. They even put Auschwitz's ex-commandant Rudolf Höss on the stand.

Prosecution: "Do you know the man sitting at the far right end of the dock?"
Höss: "Yes, his name is Otto Möll."
Prosecution: "Where do you know him from?"
Höss: "First at Sachsenhausen, then later at Auschwitz."
Prosecution: "What did this Otto Möll do at Sachsenhausen and later at Auschwitz?"
Höss: "In Sachsenhausen he was a gardener, and at Auschwitz, supervisor of a punishment commando. Then at Birkenau he participated in the various actions."
Prosecution: "You mean the actions wherein people were executed and then cremated?"
Höss: "Yes."
Prosecution: "You've already told us about an assignment of his in 1942, when certain Polish farm buildings were converted into places of execution. Will you restate what you said about that?"
Höss: "After working the farmhouses that became Bunkers 1 and 2, extermination plants, he oversaw the disinterment of old burial sites and the burning of their corpses."
Prosecution: "And later?"
Höss: "Much later, in 1944, during the Hungarian Action, he was in charge of all five of the extermination plants."
Prosecution: "Just what operations was he responsible for then?"
Höss: "In the final analysis, everything. The operations as a whole, including the killing sites outdoors. In the end, of course, as commandant mine was the ultimate responsibility."

Möll contested Höss's and every assertion made against him, blaming those testifying for either failing to remember correctly, confusing him with someone else, or lying outright on behalf of those who for whatever reason had it in for him.

The court was unreceptive. At the close of the trial some months later, he was one of those pronounced guilty and sentenced to death. On the appointed day, his step was steady all the way to the gallows. He slowed only once, pausing at the foot of the scaffold to look up at the noose. Those present would say later that his expression seemed puzzled, as if to question how such an apparition could possibly be meant for him.

Noah Zabludowicz, too, had known Dachau. From Auschwitz he, Godel Silver, and his brother Hanan endured the slog by foot to Wodzislaw, the freezing ride by rail to Grossrosen, from there to Dachau for a month, and somehow still together ended up at its rotting subcamp of Mühldorf, where they were to suffer for another month on little to no food.

Then one sunny day in mid-April, they were loaded onto a train and sent nowhere in particular just to keep them ahead of the Americans. Come night, with it stopped at a deserted station, the three slithered through a small hole in the floor of their car and made a run for it. Walking skeletons by then, too weak to get very far, they were quickly caught and prodded back at gunpoint. Why their guards didn't shoot them was something none could answer, then or ever.

At dawn, still in the station, the train was overrun by an American patrol. Over the next weeks, its hundreds of occupants were nursed back to health at a military hospital set up nearby.

Having survived by the skin of his teeth, the sun of inexplicable good fortune continued to shine on Noah. Toward the end of his recuperation, he received a letter from Italy. It was from his two brothers who'd made aliyah years before, Judah the firstborn and Aron, soldiers now in the Jewish Brigade stationed in Bologna. The Brigade was a gesture by the Allies, when what was unfolding in Poland began to surface, offering that persecuted people a chance to play a role in the war. A force of resident Israelis trained by the British, it would go on to distinguish itself in the Italian theater of operations.

His brothers had tracked him and Hanan down, as they would Pinchas later, first through the International then the American Red Cross. That they had accomplished this while still with their unit in the field made it, in his eyes, something of a miracle.

What with the knowledge gleaned from their own emigration, they added to the miracle by helping the three find a ship to Palestine. By August, Noah stood at the rail on the open deck of the *Eva Louise*, an old rust bucket of a freighter out of Marseilles. Despite her age, she was making good time; already much of the Mediterranean lay in her wake. The day was summer-perfect, clouds as fluffy and white against the cerulean sky as huge, floating balls of cotton. The deeper blue of the ocean was as calm as a lake, the wind a warm, salt-flavored breeze. It was late enough in the morning that the sun was beginning to flex its muscles, if not to the point yet of him having to shed his coat.

He turned to find Hanan standing beside him. After two days of rain and rolling seas, few were those not taking advantage of the sunny day, but so large was the ship and its deck that privacy was no problem. "How is our poor Pinchas doing?" Noah asked.

"About the same, I'm afraid. Tell me, how is it that two out of three brothers should be relatively immune to seasickness, the other half-dead from it?"

"You don't know? Why, it's a medical fact: the handsomer the man, the stronger the stomach."

"I figured," said Hanan with a straight face "it must be something like that."

They were content afterward to bask silently in the splendor of the morning. As with quite a few survivors of the camps, from the moment of liberation the world had appeared different to them, its colors more vivid, its smells and sounds noticeably sharper. Freedom had thrown wide more than the confines of their prisons. Until it ceased to define their existence, they hadn't understood how smothering barbed wire could be.

Each soaked up the sea awhile, breathing the salt air like a hungry person the aromas from a kitchen. "So how long, do you think?" said Hanan. "Before we get there, I mean."

"A week. Ten days maybe." Noah spoke this to the beautiful blue water gliding by.

Hanan turned to face him. "And what about this blockade everyone's talking about? You know, by the British... you given any thought to it?"

Noah's gaze grabbed his brother's. "What, you a mind-reader? I was just opening my mouth to ask the same question."

"You're asking the right person then," Hanan said, "for I have been giving it some thought. You are aware, I presume, it's been in effect for some years now. Even before the war."

"The blockade? Really."

"Oh, yes, since the '30's... '36, I believe. And for the same reason now as then: oil, it's all about oil. The British would do anything, short of letting go their Mandate, to appease their petroleum-rich friends, the Arabs, which in this instance translates to putting the clamps on Jewish immigration to Palestine. But where before that immigration was a trickle, thanks to Hitler it's now a flood. Or getting ready to be."

There it was, that professor's robe his egghead brother was prone to wrapping himself in. Noah found it as endearing this time as ever, if not exactly reassuring. "Which means what? Are you telling me we should be worried?"

Hanan smiled. "Just the opposite. A trickle is one thing, a flood another. It's going to take the British time to ramp up operations. The logistics, the ships, coordinating it all, the politics... I'd say another month at least, probably two."

"In other words," Noah said, "we've a better than good chance of reaching the Promised Land. Unless this tub decides to sink."

"Or the Mediterranean," Hanan added, "dry up in the next week to ten days."

Never one for the hyperbolic language that tended to accompany religion, Noah was somewhat startled by his use of the phrase "the Promised Land." But as revealed to him once before—that night with Roza and Ezekiel's ghost in the basement of Block 11—there were occasions when religion would not be thumbed at.

This voyage being one of them. There was a mystique to engaging in aliyah, to turning one's back on the centuries of exile in Europe and one's face toward the land of one's ancestors, which lent it an unmistakably biblical feel. He wouldn't be poring over the Torah anytime soon, or counting the days until the Sabbath, but something of what dwelt in the lives of the devout had infiltrated his, if only for the time being.

Then again, there'd been more chipping away at his jealously guarded agnosticism lately than the imminence of Eretz Israel on the horizon. That not only he but his two shipboard brothers, and Godel with them, continued to occupy the land of the living was so implausible as to suggest a supra-worldly intervention. For going on three long years, each had defied death in the Vernichtungslager, when as Noah suspected and was later to learn for a fact, the mortality rate for those who'd trod its unloading ramps was almost ninety percent.

At those odds not a one of them, much less all four, had any business being above ground.

That his other brothers should have materialized out of thin air when they did, managing to unearth both Pinchas and a ship, was also cause to give one pause. None of it, however, astounded him more than discovering those brothers part of an army. Not a Russian, or a British, or an American, or a Free French—but impossible as it sounded—a *Jewish* army, thousands of men, three battalions of them, the first organized, officially recognized Hebrew combat unit since the fall of Judea to the Roman legions eighteen hundred years ago. They weren't parade-ground troops, either, no token soldiers these. This Jewish Brigade had bloodied the Wehrmacht in numerous encounters.

Noah was as envious of the two as he was proud of them. They'd told him in one of their letters of the flag they'd followed into battle, the same blue Star of David on a white field that had flown above Warsaw's doomed ghetto. Painted, too, on the Brigade's vehicles, stitched onto its uniforms, was the yellow version of that *Mogen David*, until recently a symbol of subjugation and shame—but in this new and unapologetic incarnation, a sight, he imagined, to get the heart to thumping.

Perched on the sun-drenched deck of the *Eva Louise*, he closed his eyes the better to picture what the faces of the Nazis must have looked like as they watched this bizarre flag approach their lines. Were they more incredulous or uneasy at this banner of revenge advancing toward them? He wanted to believe it the latter, and something to unnerve them even more perhaps: the realization, the shock they might have been wrong all these years.

That to their soldier's way of thinking, with a rifle in his hands and a uniform on his back, the Jew was as much a man, a human being, as any of them.

But the emotions that flag roused in him were bittersweet. Linked as it would forever be with Warsaw, he couldn't visualize it without also summoning the twins Ezra and Ehud, who'd died there. Or so it was assumed they'd died, as neither the Red Cross nor any survivor's agency was able to turn up a trace of them. In the final tally, Noah hadn't been so blessed after all: four brothers and a sister slain, both parents, untold aunts, uncles, cousins… when one sat down and examined it, the list was a long one. Nor was this taking into account she who perhaps was the cruelest loss of all.

He could add Godel to the list of the missing, too. With a sudden pang, it hit him how big a void his friend's absence had left in his life. As if in fact a mind-reader, Hanan chose that moment to confess the same void.

"I don't know about you," he said, "but I can't get Godel out of my head. Stop wishing he were here. I miss the skinny runt even more than I thought I would."

"Look who's calling who skinny. But I'm of the same mind as you. Exciting as it is to be heading where we are, it would be that much better if he was with us."

"To tell the truth, I'm still not sure why he isn't. He lost as much family as we did, more if you count—"

Hanan could have kicked himself. He'd learned months ago not to blacken his brother's mood by bringing her up.

"If you count Roza, you mean?" Funny, it struck Noah, how painful that name on his lips still was. "But as I've told you before, and this from what he told me, it was because of her, what happened to her, that Godel could no longer bring himself even to say the word Palestine.

"They'd dreamed, the pair of them, of making aliyah together and raising a family there. Not a whole lot meant more to them. You saw how pumped he got when talking about it."

Hanan agreed. "It sometimes seemed that's all he did talk about. I always felt that as much as anything it's what kept him going."

"It should be obvious then," Noah said, "why the last thing he'd want would be to make the trip without her. For Godel, the so-called land of milk and honey would have ended up a land of ghosts and regret, a constant reminder of both the woman and the dream that had been stolen from him. Come on, little brother, you're smart enough to—"

"All right. Forget it. Forget I ever opened my mouth."

They didn't speak for a minute. "Tell me this then," Hanan asked. "Did he say if Canada was still in his plans? Ottawa, wasn't it?"

"I guess," Noah said, again to the blue water. "He has family there, cousins or something. He didn't sound all that sold on it, though. Who the hell knows? Or for that matter, cares."

His brother's abruptness neither surprised nor offended Hanan. It happened whenever Roza's name came up. The kindest thing then was to give the poor man his space, allow him to work through the grief still hobbling him. As much as he was lapping up the sun and fresh air, he said he'd better return below and check on Pinchas.

Noah made for the prow of the ship, his favorite spot. Gazing at the sea and sky ahead reinforced the sensation of leaving the past behind. The sun was high enough now to urge him out of his coat, which he wouldn't have been wearing to begin with if it hadn't been *the* coat. There'd been some pilferage on board, nothing major but worrisome, and though it would have taken a petty thief indeed to give so shabby an article of clothing a second glance, he wasn't taking any chances. When settled in his new country, he would keep it in mothballs, but until then wasn't about to leave it to the mercy of strangers.

He'd kept the coat on or near his person ever since the night Kapo Jakob had handed it back to him outside of Roza's cell. Never more than half-rag, it bore the grubbiness now of a year's unlaundered use; able to sponge-wash it some following his captivity, to have it done right and dry-cleaned would have removed the bloodstains as well as the dirt. And those were one of the only two *memento mori* he had of his murdered Roza, the other being the farewell letter she'd left in his care that same November night. This, too, he'd kept close, secreted all these months in the inside pocket of the coat.

He drug it out now for what felt like the thousandth time and began to read, not for its content, which he could recite now by rote, but to let his eyes wander the loops and whorls of a handwriting that couldn't have been more of a treasure if penned in gold. It served the same end as her blood on his jacket, both so singular, so personal a part of her as to make him feel she was there beside him, as real as if resurrected from the grave. Many were the moments, in fact, occupied with one or the other, he'd look up from it fully expecting to see her at his elbow, smiling at him with that smart-alecky grin of hers.

He could tell, too, in his heart, his bones, that she would never be far away, no matter what the future brought. Though he had yet to concede it much thought, a wife undoubtedly loomed in that future, and hopefully children—if the bogeymen in the gray uniforms hadn't come along when they did, there was little disputing that his life would have taken this direction already.

Which was by no means to say that when he did meet the woman he wanted to spend the rest of his years with, should he live to be a hundred and father a dozen little Zabludowiczes, there wouldn't continue to exist a place in some corner of his soul for the woman once known as Roza Robota.

With a frown he remembered the day the word Auschwitz first defiled his ears, he and his family one of many out of a frightened mass of people crushed together in a suffocating cattle car. He remembered the foreboding born of the mysterious stench in the air that would turn out to be the work of the ogre Otto Möll. And the uncertainty that accompanied it as the train slowed and left the main track, a nebulous dread that wrung a hundred questions from as many throats, but no answers. He recalled wishing in his anxiety that Roza was there next to him, having lost her and Godel as he did in the chaos at the Ciechanow station. Grown man though he was, and no stranger to courage, he would have welcomed some of hers in those terror-ridden minutes.

Instead, he'd tried to pretend the girl squeezed against him was Roza, but that hadn't worked at all—she was shaking with a fear even greater than his. By the time the train jerked to a halt, it was all he could do to keep from trembling himself.

But no more would there be cause for either trembling or pretending. Not should Noah, if such was possible, again face something as scary. Roza would always be with him, as concrete a presence as that conjured now by the letter he was holding. Together, arm in arm, they leaned against the railing at the frontmost edge of the ship, scanning the open ocean stretching limitless ahead… and would be standing in the same spot a week and a day later, Hanan and Pinchas alongside them, watching the sliver of dusky land wavering on the horizon grow bigger, more solid before their eyes.

Addendum to

The Trumpets of Jericho: A Novel

I. the **Author**

Meet J. Michael

A Conversation With J. Michael Dolan

II. the **Novel**

Acknowledgments

A Word About Awards

Bibliography

III. the **Reader**

Write a Review!

Book Club Questions

Recommended Reading / Viewing

I. Meet J. Michael ———————

Fascinated from an early age by the Holocaust, J. Michael Dolan has used his talents as a published novelist and historian to bring the heroic if little-known story he sets forth in Trumpets to life.

A traveler in his youth, he has lived in many places, preferring the tropical, but recently moved outside of Austin, Texas to be near his family and because it is a magnet of a city for the freethinking young. Or in his case, he says, the young at heart.

Taking a break from the horrors of the Holocaust but not the fertile ground of Jewish history, he is working on a novel set in the Roman-occupied Palestine of the 1st century. Though heavy on iconoclasm (Dolan's literary idol is Gore Vidal), and not lacking in the glorification of the flesh, he claims it at heart a religious book, if not religion as most are taught it. The narrator/main character, he adds, might surprise you, too—

And no, it isn't who you may be thinking it is.

Visit him at www.jmichaeldolan.net

A Conversation with J. Michael Dolan ———

The following interview was conducted by
Amy Lignor of Feathered Quill Book Reviews, 2018

When it comes to a book as large as this one, readers are always interested in knowing how you did the incredible amount of research to bring it to fruition? Can you tell us a bit about the process of gathering the information?
If you're asking me how difficult a time I had, it wasn't as hard, say, as committing ritual *seppuku*. But, if not quite as bloody, it did put a hurt on me.

Fortunately, I had a head start, as you could say I've been researching the Holocaust my whole life. Even as a child I was reading adult books about it, I'm not sure why. I suspect it's something like passing a horrendous wreck on the highway; don't tell me the temptation to look isn't overpowering.

In creating my own wreck for readers to rubberneck, I spent many an hour in the formidable library of the Holocaust Museum Houston, filling notebooks by day from works in the reference section, taking home what books I was allowed to, and buying others online. 80% of my material came from these, the rest from the internet and even a few movies (no, nothing from *Schindler's List*). At the museum, when whole pages were called for, I had some success schmoozing employees into letting me scan them on the HMH copy machine. As if all that wasn't laborious enough, I had to organize what amounted to a mini-Everest of data so I could find what I needed when I needed it.

What first brought about your fascination with the subject of your book?
I was in the HMH eight years ago strolling the exhibits when I came upon a temporary one honoring the young Jewish freedom fighter Roza Robota. That was my introduction to both her and the heroic 1944 uprising at Auschwitz she played so big a part in. Intrigued, I was soon investigating the revolt, only to discover to my surprise, and with a smile that got bigger each day, it was a story without a book. Before the grass could grow beneath my feet, I decided to put an end to that woeful state of affairs.

After reading your novel, I must say I'm amazed the name Roza Robota is not more well known. Do you have any idea why that is? Have you come across any other books that even touched on her or the revolt?

Touched on them, yes, but little more than that. A few years ago, a book-length nonfiction account of it came out in German (he says, still smiling), but *Trumpets* remains the first novel devoted to the Auschwitz uprising in its entirety.

As for Roza and the general public's unfamiliarity with her, I believe it but a reflection of not only that surrounding the Holocaust but history in general. It's a phenomenon, I'm afraid, emblematic of the times: readers of serious writing are becoming as rare as uncorrupted politicians, none more than those with an interest in history. Save for Spielberg and their DVD players, how many people would know Oskar Schindler from Oscar Madison in *The Odd Couple*?

Sad, very sad. Dangerous, too. The written word is and always has been a bulwark against tyranny. Ask Orwell.

Of all the amazing characters in The Trumpets of Jericho, *do you have a favorite, a man or woman you most admire?*

Roza and her best friend Noah Zabludowicz rank at the top of my list, but I must admit to having a soft spot for Kapo Kaminski, one of the architects of the rebellion and de facto leader of the Sonderkommando who launched it. These were the mainly Jewish wretches forced at gunpoint to do the messy work of the crematoria. As every survivor who knew him has attested to, beneath the man's rough, bulldog exterior beat a heart as big as all outdoors.

No prisoner did more to ease the suffering around him, and given his high place in the inmate pecking order, with no little success. How much am I drawn to this Kaminski? His granddaughter in Israel told me his name came up 247 times in my novel. *Quod erat demonstrandum.*

Writing the roles of the evil characters in the book must certainly have taken a toll on you. Was there a way you were able to "step away" from the project when need be? How did you handle all the scenes of darkness you had to put on paper?

You're right: one of the hardest things about writing *Trumpets* was putting myself inside the heads of those ("evil characters" is way too good for them) cold-blooded bastards you mention—thinking as they thought, seeing the world through their eyes, in essence *becoming* the sons of bitches to make them realer for the reader. There were long stretches where I had to say some loathsome things, "perform" loathsome deeds. Crawling inside the skin of a baby-killing mass murderer? Sometimes I felt as if I needed a shower afterward.

Then again, the vast majority of my characters are sympathetic to the extreme, and I always had them and their nobility to offset the barbarity of those others. I can only imagine the weirdness Brett Easton Ellis must have gone through while writing *American Psycho.* I'm pretty sure back then I wouldn't have wanted to be within a hundred yards of the guy. How did I handle "all the scenes of darkness" as you put it? An hour or two afterward of some "I Love Lucy" and "Arrested Development."

Apart from the Holocaust, are there any other periods/locations/historical events that might interest you enough to be grist for a future novel? What can your readers look forward to down the road?

I'm researching a novel that has nothing to do with the Holocaust, yet remains rooted in the fertile ground of Jewish history. It's set in the Roman-occupied Palestine of the first century, and is a book I've wanted to write for a long time. Beyond that, though, other than telling you I'm looking forward to it provoking no end of controversy (call it a blend of Vidal at his most contrarian, Theroux at his most peripatetic, and Kathy Acker at her lewdest), I'd rather keep its narrator and plot secret for the present. As much as I respect them, I don't trust my brother authors as far as I can throw them. And no, that narrator isn't who you might be thinking it is—but close.

The world, unfortunately, seems to be in a constant state of turmoil these days. After taking on a subject that is, for lack of a more fitting term, nightmarish, do you see a way in which the writer can maybe help to change things: open minds somehow and at least lessen the negativity that's out there?

All kidding aside, I think Holocaust books, fiction and nonfiction, are particularly valuable in this respect, the more nightmarish the better. Based as they are on an event that actually happened—as opposed, say, to some dystopian invention—gives the agenda underlying them that much more credibility. And to me, what with the ultra-nationalism and hatespeak that seems to be finding renewed vigor in not only this country but others, that agenda should be this: to show people how easily the tiniest flame of prejudice can grow into a forest fire of deadly malevolence and persecution.

Do you believe your book, focusing as it does on this particular event, might be therapeutic to people, make them more tolerant, understanding?
See my answer to your preceding question. I will add that works like *Trumpets* aren't going to change the perceptions of any die-hard racists, fascists, flat-earthers, or Republicans, but might very well help prevent the ordinary citizen from going off the nativist deep end.

Readers love to know what "A Writing Day in the Life of _____" is all about. Do you have a certain time set aside to write, a certain way of writing, in a certain location? Are you one who needs complete silence or perhaps prefers music, etc., in the background? What does a J. Michael Dolan writing day consist of?
I honestly don't see it interesting anyone other than maybe my mother, but here goes.
An injection of coffee in the morning to wake up, breakfast, my anti-cancer regimen (I've been in remission for over five years now, *ta-da*), then retiring to my writer cave where, yes, I require SILENCE. I start by editing what I wrote the day before to get into the flow of things, end up working the day through only breaking for meals.
After dinner I'll review what I bled onto paper earlier, then try to forget the damn thing. All too often unsuccessfully. With a first draft under my belt, I can tack on another six months to a year for polishing. All of which translates to me having no life when in the Vulcan death grip of the Muse. And probably accounts, too, at least I like to think it does, for why I'm no longer married.
Ah, well…. "*C'est la vie, c'est la guerre,*" said the Frenchman to the judge at his divorce hearing.

Is there a way, in your eyes, to make sure a new Holocaust doesn't occur? Do you think we'll ever be free of the possibility of another?
Again, there's no humor to be mined here. Another Holocaust? Unlikely, not to the extent the Nazis perpetrated it. Theirs was a program of genocide unprecedented in history, a meticulously planned, rigorously systematic, *industrialized* form of mass murder with the full power of a modern European state behind it. It would take a very special and extreme set

of circumstances for anything approaching it to be repeated. On the other hand, variations of it can all too readily crop up, have, in fact, both before and after the Third Reich: the Turks' slaughter of their Armenian minority in the 1920's, that against the Ibo peoples of Nigeria during the Biafran tragedy of the 1960's, and more recently the wholesale massacres in Rwanda, Bosnia, and Darfur, to name only the biggest.

Something of a lesser sort even happened right here in America, the internment camps in WWII California and Arizona, in which U.S. citizens of Japanese origin—men, women, and children—were incarcerated for years in frightful conditions. These weren't death camps, but *were* harsh and racially motivated.

So—in answer to your question, how can we make sure another genocide doesn't occur? We can't. Too much of the human race isn't far enough removed from the caves to have stopped preying on itself; the horror of ethnic cleansing will be with us for some time to come. What we can do is keep our eyes open. Speak out against it when we see it happening. Don't read it in the morning papers then blot it out on our way to work.

Write or share a post about it on Facebook. Make sure your congressmen are aware of it. Make sure your children are, if they're old enough, and the rest of your family, your friends. Should the situation arise, do just one of these things, trust me, and you're going to feel pretty good about yourself.

II. Acknowledgments

I cannot thank the following people too much:

James Graham and his wife **Kristen**, founders and CEO, CFO respectively of Austin Texas Print, Inc. I can truly say *Trumpets* wouldn't be the book it is without them. James especially was a part of the process every step of the way, from formatting to layout to cover designs to editorial help to conversion and more. ATP, Inc. is a big company, and I a small client compared to Facebook®, Samsung®, and Ebay®, among others, but both bent over backward never to make me feel small. I'm only grateful I get this chance to show them in writing how much I appreciate them.

Rebecca Hoag, educator, author. Besides introducing me to the only Holocaust survivor I know, her friend the indomitable **Rose Sherman Williams**—whom I, too, now count as a friend—Becky has done more to promote *Trumpets* than anyone. It was she, for instance, who helped establish me at The Twig. In collaboration with its subject, Becky is the author of *Letters to Rose* (store.bookbaby.com/book/letters-to-rose1), Mrs. William's stunning memoir. I recommend it as a first-hand account of true heroism, unimaginable suffering, and in the end, redemption.

The staff of **The Twig Book Shop**, San Antonio, Texas. They've always taken pains to display *Trumpets* in a prominent place on their shelves, face out. As a result, it has sold more here than in any other store. An upscale shop, a great selection, community-oriented, run by women... check it out online to see what a bookstore should be.

Rick Cantrell, my friend of 35 years. Unwavering in his encouragement and support of the book from Day One, he's been a patient sounding-board, too—what author, after all, doesn't love to talk a blue streak about you-know-what? Though he probably didn't know it until now, that accommodating ear of his helped inspire me to put my money where my mouth was as it were.

Kathy Kramer Hill, a schoolteacher's schoolteacher. And also a good friend. In addition to doing her share of promotion, she contributed something even more memorable: an invitation to speak in front of her 7th grade class. Less about my book, a work hardly suitable for thirteen-year old's, than about Holocaust (lite) in general. I'll never forget some of those sweet faces looking up at me, all wide eyes and open mouths—and afterwards, get this: the best Q & A I've ever had!

Last but far from least, **Susan Raja-Rao**, wife of the world-famous Indian writer/philosopher. She welcomed *Trumpets* into her heart with something of the same zeal she did her husband's books. My biggest fan? That's a tough call, but she'd certainly qualify. The book, as she liked to remind me, was my *dharma*, what I was put here to do, and even with its unavoidable bleakness and violence, took every opportunity to praise it as "beautiful." Like me, she saw it as more hopeful than bleak, and for that and many other things is why she's here.

A Word About Awards

Though I put the First Edition of *Trumpets* on the market too soon, without benefit of professional editing, along with other shortcomings, it did manage to earn some acclaim. The 2017 Independent Publisher Book Awards, or "Ippy's," recognized it with a **Silver Medal** in their Military/ Wartime fiction category. The 2017 Foreword INDIES Book Awards also gave it a **Silver Medal** in War & Military fiction. Blue Ink Reviews (see front cover) honored it as one of its 2017 **Notable Books of the Year**. Again in 2017, it came heartbreakingly close, in spite of its flaws, to winning a **Bronze Medal** in the Independent Book Publishers Association's prestigious Benjamin Franklin Awards.

In the Second Edition you've just read, however, I've righted the ship, making *Trumpets* the novel it was meant to be, fully deserving of the remarkable, true-life story it chronicles. I mention this because should you wish to recommend it to others, please cite the Second Edition as the much wiser choice. Indeed, in my book, if you'll forgive the expression, the only one.

Bibliography

*Lore Shelley (editor), *The Union Kommando in Auschwitz, Vol. XIII* from *Studies in the Shoah* (University Press of America, 1996)

*Filip Mueller, *Eyewitness Auschwitz: Three Years in the Gas Chamber* (Stein and Day, 1984)

*Primo Levi, *Survival in Auschwitz* (Touchstone, 1996)

*Primo Levi, *The Drowned and the Saved* (Vintage Intl., 1989)

*Ysrael Gutman and Michael Berenbaum (editors), *Anatomy of the Auschwitz Death Camp* (Indiana University Press, 1994)

*Victor E. Frankl, *Man's Search for Meaning* (Pocket Books, 1984)

*Dalton Trumbo, *Night of the Aurochs* (Viking, 1979)

*John Toland, *Adolf Hitler* (Doubleday, 1976)

*Robert Jay Lifton, *The Nazi Doctors* (Basic Books, 1986)

*Tadeusz Borowski, *This Way for the Gas, Ladies and Gentlemen* (Viking Penguin, 1967)

*Anna Heilman, *Never Far Away* (University of Calgary Press, 2001)

*Otto Friedrich, *The Kingdom of Auschwitz* (Harper Perennial, 1982)

*Miklos Nyiszli, *Auschwitz: A Doctor's Eyewitness Account* (Arcade Publishing, 1993)

*Rebecca Fromer, Steven Bowman, *The Holocaust Odyssey of Daniel Bennahmias* (University of Alabama Press, 1993)

*Marco Nahon, *Birkenau, the Camp of Death* (University of Alabama Press, 2002)

*Olga Lengyel, *Five Chimneys* (Chicago Review Press, 2005)

*Albert Speer, *Inside the Third Reich* (MacMillan, 1970)

*Howard Blum, *The Brigade* (Perennial, 2002)

III. Write a Review! ———————————————

Dear Reader,

Need I say how pleased, encouraged, excited I am that you not only read my book but enjoyed it enough to be reading it still? That you've come as far as this page speaks for itself, is as much an affirmation as any review.

Trumpets was not an easy book to write. 500+ pages rarely if ever is. (Actually, pre-edit, it topped 700). There were times I wondered if I'd ever reach the end; the more I worked on it, the more it seemed there was to say. Then came the editing. The editing hurt my body. All told, I could tack two years of edits onto the five it took to write those 700 pages.

But that isn't the half of it. Try this on for strange. Though the novel wound up everything I hoped it would be, I can't take full credit for that. It took me a while to figure it out, but I had help. Every scene, character, page that was giving me fits, every corner I'd written myself into and couldn't get out of no matter how hard I tried, each not only resolved itself but turned from the blackest of galactic holes into the yellowest, friendliest of suns. Went from base lead to pure gold, didn't just improve but IMPROVED—and, trust me, I know I'm not that good a writer. Something else was at work here. It was as if someone was looking over my shoulder to make sure I got the story right.

And so someone was. Or rather, more than one, the dead Jewish heroes I was writing about. They were why I decided to embark on *Trumpets* in the first place, to resurrect forgotten bravehearts, names few had ever heard of, people swept into the proverbial dustbin of history despite a courage so extraordinary as to quicken the heart.

It was the unremembered dead standing at my shoulder, putting the words, the right words, into my head when I couldn't find them. The words they wanted to be memorialized by.

Don't believe me? I don't blame you. Only part of *me* believes me. But whether I had help then or not, I could use some now. That's where you come in. That word "review" in the first paragraph? Why not write one of your own? And guess what, I happen to know the perfect book for it.

Aside from aiding your fellow readers in determining if *Trumpets* is as good as its back cover says it is, the more reviews it gets on Amazon, the better it will rank. The better it ranks, the bigger the chance people have of seeing it. Which is the whole point behind not only mine but every Holocaust offering—to be seen, to survive, to stick out like a red flag. To keep sticking out so the lessons that dark period of history has to teach our sometimes slow-on-the-uptake species can continue doing so.

Heck yes, write a review! Let that critic inside you *out*! Or at least think about it. It can be a few paragraphs or a few lines, but whatever it ends up, it *will* be an experience. Very likely a fun one, too, or so I've discovered. Having written many a review myself, to tell the truth I've come to find them addictive. Clicking on that SUBMIT button isn't exactly going to flood you with endorphins, but it can be empowering.

Again, just think about it. Sleep on it. Or if you've already made up your mind—if you've decided *Trumpets* did move you enough that you'd like to do your bit in keeping it and the memory of the Holocaust alive—find the **Second Edition** on Amazon when it suits you and scroll down the page until you come to **Write a customer review**. Make sure it's the new and improved Second Edition you're reviewing (it will appear on the cover) and not one of those early efforts fated, I'm afraid, to haunt me forever.

Who knows? Maybe a few endorphins will float your way.

JMD

Book Club Questions ─────────────────

1. As you saw in *Trumpets* from the earliest pages on, the violence the SS heaped on defenseless Jewish men, women, and even children was horrendous. Nor was the hatred behind the violence restricted to the SS—it was abundant in every stratum of German society. Indeed, existed to varying degrees wherever the European Jew had laid down roots. Why were they so despised?

2. Back to the violence: *Trumpets* is rife with atrocity. I didn't invent a one of them, true—all turned up in my research—but why did I find it necessary to lay them on so thick? To justify the single most powerful, if normally negative emotion driving Roza and the bulk of the heroes in my book. Can you name it? It begins with an "R."

3. History has painted the Jews of the Holocaust as being so passive in their destruction as to be virtually complicit in it. What are your thoughts on this? Given the dynamic of genocide as Nazi Germany waged it, discuss the obstacles facing those Jews who would resist.

4. Almost two years passed from the 1944 revolt's conception to its completion. If its noblest aim was to destroy the crematoria and their gas chambers, some might question this gap. But as you who have read my book know, the call to arms was a complicated one. Discuss some of the baggage keeping the Sonder from rebelling, including that resulting from the Czech Family Camp setback in March of '44, and the fiasco of June 15th. Should the Sonder, *could* the Sonder have overcome all this and acted sooner?

5. I started out by writing *Trumpets* as nonfiction, but quickly changed course. Provided the novelist is scrupulous about adhering to fact, what advantages does fiction bring in making both history and the people who created it more accessible?

6. How did seemingly ordinary men, Möll and Hössler as extreme examples—men who in all likelihood would have lived ordinary lives but for Hitlerism—how could they have perpetrated the horrors they did? Are there monsters lurking somewhere in us all?

7. Who among my characters was your favorite? Not necessarily the one you admired most but could identify with personally? As I said in my FQ interview, mine was Kaminski.

8. Noah's secret love for Roza is undocumented, but in light of human nature, I thought it not improbable. Do you agree, or did I overstep? What of her just as hidden feelings for him?

9. As with the great Elie Wiesel's, the flames of Birkenau burned away many a religious faith, though there were exceptions aplenty. Notable among these was the *dayan* Leyb Langfus, who served in both my book and real life as a counterpoint to that loss of faith. Weigh his arguments in support of God against those of Zalman Leventhal, who (at least at first) angrily renounced Him. Imagine yourself in a death camp, your loved ones murdered, slowly dying yourself—who would you have sided with, and why?

10. I not only described the hell that was Auschwitz-Birkenau in some detail but the mechanics of Nazi genocide from ghetto to crematoria. I also referenced more than a little Holocaust history. Despite this adding to an already prodigious word count, I felt an obligation to. Why would I feel this?

11. Though again there is no documentation corroborating it, I postulate Roza's life inadvertently saved by something akin to decency on the part of an SS man. What am I saying by this?

12. At several points in *Trumpets*, I touch on the Nazi condescension toward women as members of the "weaker," less capable sex. I demonstrate the fallacy behind this, first, by showing the major role women played in making the revolt a reality, then the inability of the Gestapo afterward, in spite of the severest tortures, to pry any names from even one of the four female conspirators they've arrested, Roza, Ala, Regina, and Esther. What are your thoughts on the subject of male/female parity?

13. In the way it approaches tolerance and goodwill toward people of all races and religions, our species has made little progress in the three-quarters of a century since the Holocaust. Indeed, it sometimes seems we've learned nothing. How are *Trumpets* and books like it more relevant than ever in these increasingly divisive, nationalistic times? This may be the most important question you address tonight.

Recommended Reading/Viewing

The Drowned and the Saved, Primo Levi

Levi's last work before his tragic suicide in 1987, *The Drowned* is commonly regarded as a summation of this immortal author's stunning *oeuvre*. It is a part expository, part philosophical treatise on Nazi violence against the Jews as practiced in the death camps, primarily Auschwitz. Levi was a prisoner there for eight months (see also his seminal *Survival in Auschwitz*). If one book could be said to put the incomprehensibility of the camps into comprehensible form, *The Drowned* would be it. As with *Survival*, the man's decency, his humanity shine through the bleakness; reading him, you feel here is someone you wish you'd known in real life.

The Very Rich Hours of Count von Stauffenberg, Paul West

Of all the men and moments that might have altered history, Count von Stauffenberg and his selfless attempt to assassinate Adolf Hitler is in its heartbreaking failure perhaps the most agonizing. In a brilliant weave of fact and imagination, West uses his protagonist's voice to give a bold new dimension to historical fiction. In the words of one critic, "Nobody else writes like Paul West. He'll stay in your brain until the day you die." As you'll see when you read this groundbreaking work, from the small boy's heroic, grandiose dreams to the immeasurably more ambitious actions of he and the band of conspirators he assembled, Stauffenberg's hours were rich indeed.

This Way for the Gas, Ladies and Gentlemen, Tadeusz Borowski

Borowski's novel is a cry, if disarmingly subdued, torn from the throat, the heart, the soul. If it even is, in fact, a novel. Many see it as a memoir once-removed, its author, like Levi, having survived Auschwitz. At least for a while— in 1951, he, too, was driven to suicide. To me, *This Way* is less a memoir or novel than a fever dream, but one ranted in measured tones, as if hallucinated by a person under hypnosis. Though beautifully written, it is a cruel book, the border between kindness and atrocity, good and evil a porous one. This makes for an unsettling, even surrealistic read, but we don't go to a Holocaust book in search of the normal, do we?

The Plot Against America, Philip Roth

No Recommended list would be complete without an entry from Roth. *The Plot* is alternative history set in an America that has lost its way. The famed aviator Charles Lindbergh—head of the America First political party, virulent anti-Semite, an admirer of Hitler and his Nazi Germany—has just defeated FDR in the 1940 presidential election. With him having repeatedly attacked them throughout his campaign, dread grips the Jews of America, who fear what lies ahead. Insert the word immigrant (or half a dozen others) for Jew, and it all sounds too familiar, doesn't it? Once again, Roth plays the seer; though copyrighted in 2004, his novel could have been written today as a cautionary tale. Every American should read it as such—unless by the time he or she happens to read this, hopefully the political scene, if you get my drift, will have changed.

My Life on the Road, Gloria Steinem

Now for a counterpoint to these outpourings of woe. *My Life* was more autobiographical than I expected, until learning that much of Steinem's life, from early childhood, was indeed spent on the road. It traces the arc of her activism from its tentative beginnings to the unstoppable force it became. The author is a master—mistress?—of the anecdote, making this as entertaining a read as you'll find. Even better, her positivism, sense of justice, and just plain compassion lard its every page, whether in the cause of women, blacks, Hispanics, native Americans, the LGBTQ community, the sexually abused, the poor, and yes, even men. This is a book, once you're done with it, you should pass on to your older children—your sons certainly, your daughters especially. They just might thank you for it when grown.

Viewing

---Defiance, 2008

---American History X

---Schindler's List

---1984, 1984

---The Wannsee Conference, 1984 (W. Germany)

---Judgment at Nuremberg, 1961

---The Grey Zone

---Selma

---Trumbo

---All The President's Men, 1976